2231

MARS AGAINST EMPIRE

KENNETH TAM

2231

MARS AGAINST EMPIRE

Martian War - Omnibus 1

KENNETH TAM

ICEBERG

Published in Canada by Iceberg Publishing, Waterloo

Library and Archives Canada Cataloguing in Publication
Tam, Kenneth, 1984-
    2231 : Mars against empire / Kenneth Tam.
(Martian War ; omnibus 1)
Contents: The rogue comodore -- The almost coup -- The Hawke
    mission -- The independent squadron.
ISBN 978-0-9784902-9-4
    I. Title. II. Series: Tam, Kenneth, 1984- . Martian War ; omnibus 1.
PS8589.A7676T84 2010   C813'.6   C2010-900091-9

Iceberg Publishing
55 Northfield Drive East, Suite 171
Waterloo ON N2K 3T6
contact@icebergpublishing.com
www.icebergpublishing.com

Cover Image: Wesley Prewer
Cover Design: Kenneth Tam

DEDICATIONS

THE ROGUE COMMODORE
For Richard Joseph Barron, my grandfather.
I hope Ken Barron lives up to your standards.
Rest Well.

THE ALMOST COUP
For John, Greg and Marlene.
Thanks for the support all the way along.
Now go save the Empire!

THE HAWKE MISSION
For my friends Peter and Wes.
Gentlemen, thanks for the continued support.

THE INDEPENDENT SQUADRON
For the many armed forces personnel who've
faced the real crises upon which I based Egesta.
Your heroism is truly humbling.

THE
ROGUE
COMMODORE

THE AUTOBIOGRAPHICAL REMINISCENCES OF
ADMIRAL THE LORD KEN BARRON FOR 2231

THE MARTIAN WAR - 1

KENNETH TAM

FROM THE AUTHOR

Welcome to a new series!

Well, actually, in some regards this is an old series — the *first* one I ever worked on, in fact. I started recounting the adventures of DCNS (then DCSC) *Wolf* back in 1995, in a set of 20-page stories called *Star Defenders*. I was 11 at the time, so the main character (perhaps unsurprisingly) was Admiral Kenneth Tam (that's me!). In 1996, I began expanding the story of the first *Star Defenders* novel into *Defense Command: Guardians of Earth, Book 1: The Fleet Clash*. That was my first manuscript, and it shares virtually none of the plot and only some of the characters with *The Rogue Commodore*. It was shelved in favor of the *Bonaventure* series in 1998. Now both those have been locked away in my personal archive — never to be seen in their original forms by outsiders — and I've poached the best elements of each and melded them with many new ideas to bring you the new *Defense Command*.

So again… welcome!

Now, the logical question you might ask: is Ken Barron in fact a thinly disguised, escapist version of Kenneth Tam? The answer: sort of. When bringing forward many original *Star Defenders* characters, I realized their chemistry with the old 'me' main character had been good — and I shouldn't really give it up out of hand. With that in mind I created Ken Barron as a replacement for myself… and if that doesn't sound bizarre, I don't know what does… because obviously I'm not a fleet officer living 250 years in the future. But I did give Ken his sense of humor (let me apologize for that from the beginning) and his tendency for using obscure historical allusion.

One tradition with the original *Star Defenders* stories was to base characters in the books on friends at the time. None of those original friend-based characters came forward to this new *Defense Command* series, but I have kept the tradition alive. As such, some of the characters in this series are closely based on real-world friends of mine, though I won't tell you who they are because I'll never kill those characters (come on, give me a chance at building suspense!).

I do have people to thank, though. First of all, my good friends Peter Caron and Wes Prewer, who from the first have been supportive about this series and its unusual style. Wes' rendering work for the covers has been a major asset, and both gentlemen have offered great perspective and advice whenever I've needed it.

My thanks too to everyone who allowed me to steal their personalities (and to some extent their names) to create my characters — I hope the *Defense Command* versions live up to your standards. Many of you were also instrumental in supporting the development of this series, or the previous books upon which it was based, so thanks for the support!

Finally, the biggest thanks have to go to my family — Peter, Jacqui and Atlas. Iceberg is a family company, and as ever, I wouldn't be doing this without you!

– Kenneth Tam

PREFACE

Alright, so you're probably asking why I'd start the story of my Defense Command career in the middle. Why skip past the defeat of the countless pirate factions and the Syndicate, past the espionage and the exciting days of DCNS *Friendly* and the early days of DCNS *Wolf* and all that? Well, to be honest, I wanted to start these books at the very beginning, with my academy days, but I have a tyrant for a publisher.

See, he said that my memoirs about the academy days and even the battles with various pirates and the Syndicate wouldn't sell as well as my account of the beginning of the Martian War. I guess it's sort of like Naval historians skipping Nelson's victories at the Nile and Copenhagen to get right to Trafalgar... not that I think I'm as great as Nelson or anything, just... well, you get what I mean.

That's why we're starting in the middle.

That and the fact that this book is being released to coincide with the twentieth anniversary of the beginning of that war, so it'll sell well when it hits the market. The bottom line *does* count.

We're starting in the middle of my career. You're probably already somewhat familiar with this bit —at this point, the media was already paying attention to me, Karen, Wes and everybody, so you may have seen clips of us talking and pointing in documentaries and whatnot. This book is my take on those days.

Well, here's the inside scoop on what happened, all dramatized with my usual flair for the narrative. Enjoy!

Actually, I know you were just expecting to turn the page, figuratively speaking, and see Chapter One (and cheer or applaud or something delightful) but on the second draft of this manuscript, I was indelicately told by my publisher that I needed to "seamlessly insert some historical background" to these days —because apparently most of the readers who pick this up might not be familiar with what happened twenty years ago.

So here I am, following orders. How's this for "seamless"?

Anyway, let's talk history (admittedly one of my favorite subjects): what you're about to read takes place in the summer (Imperial Standard Calendar) of 2231, less than a year after the Syndicate had been put down (we thought once and for all) by Admiral Greg Noyce, at the Battle of Deep Black. That battle had featured our Belt Squadron, including me, Karen, Wes and a lot of other names you'll be reading about in this book, against the cream of Grant Merger's pirate mercenary fleet. We sent him running, the Syndicate collapsed, and Admiral Noyce was promoted to command the Heavy Squadron of the Home Fleet.

That's where we are, so let's get started.

◆◆◆

Or not. This is a new add-on from the *third* revision. Because apparently that last seamless addition didn't satiate the publisher. If you already know the history I'm about to write, please feel free to skip it...

So what else should I explain? The Earth Empire was founded in 2055. We colonized Mars just before that in 2046, then they rebelled in 2088. Hope you're keeping up. We had nothing to do with the Martians for the next 143 years; we started setting up the Venusian colonies in 2103, and then the Belt colonies (in the asteroid belt!) in 2156. Our ridiculously foolhardy attempt at colonizing Jupiter's moons (with the help of our arms manufacturing friends at EM Weapons Limited) was begun in 2186, and that operation was a money pit from the first day. That's why there's no more EM Weapons Limited.

While we were colonizing, the Martians were consolidating into an Imperium, and then they colonized Mercury in 2160 and their 'Asteroid colonies', next door to our Belt colonies, in 2188. Ironic, since they'd rebelled against an 'evil empire'.

I work for Defense Command — that's the Earth Empire's *defense command* — that sees to Imperial *defense*. I'm an officer in the Naval section of the Command — the senior service. Other branches include DCSF (Security Forces) and DCI (Intelligence) as well as Communications, R&D... you name it, we dabble in it.

Defense Command fights a lot of pirates, including the very well organized pirate Syndicate, under Grant Merger. That was our main job right up until 2231 — we fought the pirates, protecting our trade and colonies (the backbone of Imperial prosperity) from looting and terror.

And that about covers the history lesson. You may find a lot of this repeated in the book... sorry about the duplication. Now here's hoping I won't be back a fourth time to add to this...

Here we go... first chapter... I hope...

CHAPTER ONE

A COMMODORE'S JOB DESCRIPTION

"Commodores aren't supposed to get themselves into trouble, you know. That's why they made you one," Karen McMaster's words came with their usual smooth elegance, and I smiled and glanced at her as she spoke.

Of course she was right — Commodores were supposed to stay out of the messy bits of Naval duty, and instead take care of squadron command and paperwork. My particular job description probably had 'stay out of trouble' written right into it.

But since when had a job description actually described what any Defense Command officer *really* did?

Seriously, I don't mean that in an arrogant way… for me it's just a question of my style when it comes to dealing with the Belt frontier. Generally, my approach with that rough side of space didn't fit the template of the academy playbooks. That's why I got my job done.

But thinking about such things at that moment was irrelevant, and besides, Karen was smiling at me. One of her trademark smiles. If you don't know what I mean by that… well, you will soon enough.

Containing a contented sigh, I managed to grin in response to her words, "You know, they really should know better than to think an extra rank bar's going to keep me from being stupid."

"Those were my very words to Admiral Noyce. He wasn't holding out much hope," her eyebrows rose playfully as she said it, and I chuckled.

"Yeah, so I'll take that as de facto authorization for this then."

Karen's smile stretched wider still, and I stared at it for a second as she looked down at her mag and slapped a fresh power cell into the pistol.

The way she could make anything look elegant never fails to amaze me. Even loading a pistol —how can that be elegant and still serious? Karen. That's how.

Sorry, I got distracted then; I get distracted now just thinking about it.

Oh and in case you're wondering, this was still early days of us being together all the time on the same ship. She'd only transferred over from *Lion* a week or two before this, I do believe. So cut me some slack for allowing my mind to wander.

Prying my eyes slowly away from Karen's smile, I slid my electromagnetic disrupter (mag) pistol from its holster on my hip, then tabbed the power cell release and quickly examined the conduit heads to make sure they were clean and free to send energy into the blast emitter. Satisfied, I pushed the cell back into the pistol and tabbed it online, then set its output to moderate.

The goal here was to take Jones alive, after all. Hopefully he'd go along with that plan…

"Matt's going to kill us both when we get back to the ship," Karen looked back up, satisfied with her own gun's state of readiness.

My eyebrows went up and I met her eyes, my grin remaining, "A Commodore and his Flag Captain are about to storm a notorious pirate's hideout with only sidearms and no immediate backup... and you think *he's* going to kill us? Our dear friend Matt is the least of my worries."

Somehow, Karen's smile brightened a little more. Let me tell you, she needed an overload switch on that thing. I was always sure that one day I'd just be staring and get hit by a bus or something.

Anyway, moving on.

She was referring of course to Commander Matt Baxter, First Officer (but until his promotion the previous week, head of security) of DCNS *Wolf*, my... well, now *our* frigate. He never liked it when we did stupid stuff. He actually called it 'stupid *stuff*' to our faces.

It was remarkable he hadn't given up on us already...

"Alright, ready?" Karen purposefully took the smile off her face. Her heart rate was still up, and so was mine. This was the exciting part — the moment that promised action and maybe even a shoot out, but which came before the mind-numbing terror of being caught in a crossfire. It only goes downhill from here.

"Yep," I raised my mag and settled my upper body into a good firing posture.

Karen did the same, turning her torso to get a good sightline down the barrel of her pistol, holding that weapon in both hands and shifting her balance to make sure she could move steadily.

She did that *really* well — with that elegance I keep blubbering about. She sells that gracefulness magnificently. Like a praying mantis; beautiful and so very lethal. Not that I'm saying Karen's like a bug... guess I should have thought that one through a bit better...

Sorry. Keep getting sidetracked.

"Here we go..." Karen's smile was gone entirely and her leg suddenly flashed forward in a blurred kick. Jones' old front door flew off its hinges and thudded into the room inside.

A stale, hot stench hit us both as Karen led the way in with quick, even steps, "Defense Command officers, everybody on the ground!" Her words go from smooth to steel in a flash.

I covered left and she covered right. The room was dark — there'd clearly been no lights on inside, and now we had to wait just a moment for our vision to adjust from the simulated daylight outside to the blackness of–

"Down!" I threw myself to the ground before I actually realized what I was doing; I'd seen the shape of a man taking aim with a shoulder-laser and just reacted.

Karen threw herself to the ground on the other side of the room, and just in time, too, as the frame of the front door and the wall surrounding it were disintegrated by a geyser of red energy.

That's right, Jones was defending his *house* with an *anti-tank weapon*. Hey, I guess it never hurts to think big.

Rolling across the floor away from the hot beam, I waited until an alloy table got between me and the line of sight of the shooter, then came to a stop and rolled up on one knee, leveling my hands with firing-range style and a good line of–

"Yikes!" I dove flat as the red geyser swung right for my head and evaporated the front of this old dump of a house. At this rate that shooter was going to bring the house right down on top of us… that's what Jones would get for thinking big, then.

"Will you stop that you *idiot*, you're going to collapse the house on all of us!" I bellowed. Of course he shouldn't answer…

"Says you Defcom!"

I covered the back of my head with my free hand and tried to keep my face off the filthy floor as chips of plaster from the ceiling dropped on me. Karen would be getting ready to drop him in just a few seconds, so I needed to distract him again. Swinging my hands under me, I pushed myself into a sideways roll, extended my mag and squeezed the trigger twice as I rocked up onto one knee.

The shots were close but not quite on target, and he turned a bit further towards me, the red geyser still spewing.

Then the energy abruptly stopped, the shoulder-wielded laser dropping to the filthy floor with a thud. The shooter was on the ground with his hands meekly up, and in fine form, Karen's boot was on his chest and her mag leveled at his face.

Smiling with no small measure of relief, I pushed myself to my feet and let my mag hand fall to my side as I crossed the floor, "That's better. What took you so long?"

Karen looked up and flashed her smile, "Dunno. Went shopping. New shoes."

I laughed — Karen wasn't a shopper. Because you clearly needed to know that fact in order to get the joke.

"Oh God, it's McMaster and Barron, right? Why don't you two just get a friggin' room already…" the shooter, still on his back, suddenly seemed to get a surge of guts.

"Chatty one," I frowned. Karen nodded and put on a 'scolding parent' expression, looking back to him and pulling the trigger.

He 'eeped' as the bolt of electromagnetic energy split the floorboards next to his head, singing his hair in the process, "Quiet now, that's hardly polite talk."

The shooter lost his nerve — and command of his voice — and I nodded approvingly, then looked him over once. If this was Jones, he sure didn't look like his picture.

Fair skin, blond hair, freckles… yeah, the pictures of Jones I'd seen didn't quite match that. For one thing, Jones was black. In the academy, they teach us to look for such details.

"So where is he?" my question was friendly-sounding enough… I let Karen's boot on his chest do the menacing.

The shooter opened his mouth, then closed it and shook his head.

"Great," my tone shifted to slightly disappointed, and I dialed the setting on my mag down to low. "Well, I guess you're going to be loyal."

Karen pulled her boot away and the shooter tried to lunge upward for one of us, but I shot him square in the chest. On the low setting, my mag overloaded his nervous system and sent him into a hell of a coma.

"Upstairs maybe?" Karen shrugged and pulled her ponytail over her left shoulder, playing with it as she thought things over.

The house made a crunching sound — the sort of sound a house makes when it's starting to collapse on you. Ridiculous as it might seem, I'd heard that particular sound a number of times in my career... and so had Karen.

"Guess we get out of here," she said, looking at the ceiling and pursing her lips.

"Yeah," I sighed, dragging my eyes from her to the shooter. "Guess I should drag him out too..."

Karen started to nod, and then the ceiling over the front door... or more precisely, over the gap in the wall where the front door had been... collapsed.

And then with a rather distinguished screech, Jones dropped through the collapsing ceiling and landed with a satisfying thud on the ground next to the door.

He looked pretty stunned by his abrupt fall, but I'd seen that before. Yes, I'd had people I needed to capture drop through ceilings into my presence in the old days...

Anyway, he'd stand up and start running any second. So I shot him before he realized I was ten feet away.

"Okay, you get him and I'll get the shooter," Karen's tone was casual, and she holstered her mag and bent down to grab the shooter by his boot.

Stepping over falling bits of ceiling, I grabbed Jones by one arm and dragged him out the front door. Karen was right behind me, and so as the building folded in on itself, we stood outside over the comatose bodies of two notorious pirates and dusted ourselves off.

"Well that should be enough noise to get us some backup," Karen finished straightening her uniform and stood with her hands on her hips, staring at the pile of rubble.

My uniform jacket was sticky from being face down on the floor, so I'd be washing it... er... getting my *steward* to wash it, when I got back to the ship. But ignoring that fact, I nodded at Karen's words and smiled, "We do tend to have this effect on buildings, don't we?"

"Pirate ones, anyway," Karen nodded and then folded her arms.

We stood there for about a minute, just thinking about what we'd done. This was our pirate-beating style — over-the-top and absurdly dangerous. Many officers I've talked to later in life can barely believe we were actually this... well... irresponsible, and I don't blame them. All I can tell you is we got a lot more serious during the war... hell, by the end of this book you'll see our attitudes changing.

You'll think I'm nuts to say it, but during the war I'd sometimes wish for this kind of work against the pirates. Enjoy it while it lasts...

But anyway, after that minute of standing, we heard the telltale drone of a hovervan approaching.

"Ten bucks says it's the media."

Karen blinked and looked at me, "I thought it was my turn to bet first."

Shaking my head, I grinned, "You called it at the promotion ceremony, remember."

"Oh right. Yeah, I'll say it's Matt because you took my bet," she frowned thoughtfully.

The news van pulled up a minute later, and while the camera crew threw itself out of the floating vehicle we waved and continued our inane conversation.

Defense Command Security Forces and Special Branch turned up two minutes later to take the pirates into custody.

Then we went to get some burgers.

+++

"Mmm, Gold-Arch Burger never fails to deliver…" I managed to get the words out before biting into the bacon-and-cheese 'Belt Burger' that I'd just ordered.

I felt very Commodorial (I know it's not a word, thanks) as I chewed. We'd done what we were famous for: taken down a building, then sauntered into the nearest fast-food joint looking filthy and disreputable, and demanding cheap, relatively unhealthy food.

Now we sat at a small, sticky table in a busy burger joint, with just about everybody gaping at us.

"Yeah, but it was more fun when everybody didn't know who we were," Karen spoke between chews, her eyes scanning all the other diners who sat and stared.

One guy was literally sitting there frozen, staring at us with his mouth clearly open to bite his burger, and the thing right there in biting range. As I met his eyes he looked away hurriedly. I bobbed my eyebrows and kept chewing. Again, this was how we got things done in the Belt — look and act larger than life, subtlety and old-school professionalism out there just doesn't work. You want information, you want cooperation, you have to have presence. And you don't get it just because of the uniform.

Proving that point, the six vidscreens in the restaurant all stopped their regular broadcasts and flashed up the 'Breaking News' graphic.

A news lady appeared on the screen, "This just in: the east end of Belt Nine Dome Six today saw an exciting shoot out between the infamous pirate Danfield Jones and Commodore Ken Barron and Captain Karen McMaster. With more, let's join Trisha Phi in the field. Trisha?"

I tuned it out after that, eating curly fries instead.

You know, curly fries are a very traditional food — they've lasted the centuries quite well. Most people never realize they pre-date the Empire… but now *you* know they do.

I heard my own voice on the vidscreen and looked up. Karen and I had done the required, friendly, after-action interview, with all the self-effacing grace and humor we could muster… which was a lot.

Then the reporter asked Karen *who* she was wearing, and who'd done her hair.

I chewed and shook my head, wondering how I'd kept a straight face as Karen had explained that there aren't actually *designer* uniforms, and that she did her hair herself. With a regulation hair clip and a brush.

"I think we're disappointments as celebrities," Karen said before sipping some of her soda through a straw.

I shrugged, "Yeah, well, at least it's not in the job description."

Karen frowned — and the way she frowns really doesn't have the unappealing look a frown should —then waved at me with her cup of soda, "Didn't we say something back there about not really following job descriptions."

I frowned in reply — and my frown is a real unpleasant frown, I'm sure — and thoughtfully chewed a couple of fries, "Guess you need to order some designer uniforms, then. I can't wait!"

Karen smiled. And you know what that's like.

CHAPTER TWO

AND THEN THERE WERE COMPLICATIONS...

At this point you might be thinking, "Hey, I bought a book about the war... what do I care about Ken and Karen shooting up a pirate house and capturing Danfield Jones?"

Patience! We're getting to the war part.

Some people scoff at the F-194 Starlight fighter. They say it looks too much like an air jet fighter from the late twentieth century, that its wings make no sense for space combat, and that its elegant long fuselage is a liability.

Some people are also very dumb.

For the record, thanks to variable-direction thruster pods on those wings, and the low profile cut by that 'liability' of a fuselage, the F-194 was the most maneuverable and most deadly fighter Defense Command had put into space at that point. Period. And it could outperform just about every atmospheric craft you could find.

That all said, it was relatively new in 2231, and it still had a few bugs.

"So how long?"

Karen had her arms folded and she was tapping her foot on the deck of the servicing bay, looking decidedly unimpressed — something that she did exceedingly well when she needed to.

The technician who'd just crawled out from under her fighter shrugged and wiped some grease off his hands with a rag, "Well, ma'am, looks to me like I'm going to need to swap the entire motor assembly. So... say an hour?"

Karen's left eyebrow slowly climbed, "A whole hour?"

Shrugging, the scrawny man nodded again, "Yup."

Her eyebrow settled and her brow creased, "*Yup?*"

"Er... yes ma'am."

Karen released a short sigh and then nodded, "Get to it then."

The technician turned and hustled away from her, yelling at someone else in the distance and demanding help with the project. Karen turned away from her plane and shrugged at me, letting her arms drop to her sides.

"Better safe than sorry, my grandmother always says," I smiled, and Karen matched my expression with a thin smile of her own.

"Yes, well I'm eager to get cleaned up, and Matt's going to kill us at this rate."

I grinned. We were rather overdue — just about two hours overdue in fact. We'd come down to Belt Nine, Dome Six, ostensibly to check in with the asteroid's Governor and to ask about pirate activity. Then we'd gotten the tip about Danfield Jones when we'd run into an informant, so we'd gone off on that little escapade.

But now we couldn't get back to our ship. The landing foot on Karen's fighter wasn't coming up when she lifted off, and odds of it getting torn off by the acceleration as we broke orbit were too great to justify a hasty departure.

Well, such were the pesky details of flying fighters on the Belt frontier. Things tended to go wrong out here now and then.

"Matt can wait," I finally thought to answer. "I mean, unless you want to ride back in my lap. But that'd just be a bit scandalous now wouldn't it?"

Karen flashed a grin and then walked past me, "Just a bit."

I smiled and turned to follow her.

There really wasn't anything left for us to do in Dome Six, so Karen and I elected to just walk through the streets and enjoy the simulated evening. We left the Defense Command spaceport and hung a right, wandering our way towards one of the older residential sectors of town and ignoring everyone who gaped at us as we walked.

"You know, we could check in and see where Carlos is. Just for kicks…" Karen let her head loll towards me as she said it, barely hiding her ambivalence.

Carlos O'Sullivan was one of our informants — one of the guys in the Belt we turned to when we wanted to hear the latest about the pirates' movements. He'd usually send us a message when one of our ships pulled into orbit, but he hadn't this time.

"Well, he could have kept quiet when we showed up because he's in trouble," it was one of those half-hearted 'well we shouldn't' sort of answers you give before eating the whole cake.

Karen managed a slow nod, "Yeah, or he could be tied up in his basement being tortured for our secret communication codes by a couple of pirates."

Frowning, I slowed to a stop, "Um. Nice logical jump there."

With a smile, Karen turned and shrugged, "Well I don't want to get the guy killed, but there's nothing else to do right now. Let's just go see if his house looks normal. If he's under surveillance we'll walk by as if we don't know him."

What a horribly irresponsible idea. Seriously, the last thing a deep cover informant needed was to have two Defense Command officers showing up at his door to sit down for a glass of lemonade and to catch up. But remember, irresponsible sells in the Belt. Sells like hot cakes… I'm sorry, I'll never use that cliché in print again.

Anyway, too bad for Carlos. I raised my arm to hail a cab.

The hover taxi deposited us in one of the seediest parts of the dome town. Since urbanization had taken hold of Earth centuries before, slums had developed some characteristics that just stuck. Literally *stuck*, in fact, because a lot of the trash littering the streets around here was sticky and covered in waste.

I don't know what kind of waste, and by God I had no interest in finding out.

We watched the cab speed away as fast as its hover engine could carry it, the driver keeping his hand on the pistol on the seat next to him as he hurtled up and away. Rough neighborhood.

Karen gingerly stretched her arms out and then bobbed her head in the direction of Carlos' house, just down the street from the corner we'd been deposited on. With a nod and a smile, I waved for her to lead on and we set off down the sidewalk.

Street gangs did own this territory, the reports said. Indeed, a branch of the Belt Widows — that gang whose membership was, paradoxically enough given the name, more than half male — ran this section of town, and they usually only gave passes to pirates.

So this was, in retrospect, a very irresponsible idea. True to our idiom, then.

Pleasantly enough, we only passed a couple of tough-looking people before we reached Carlos' house. His front door was at the top of a flight of concrete stairs... and it was open.

I frowned at that, "Isn't Carlos paranoid about leaving the door open?"

Karen looked up the steps to the door, slowly nodding and letting her eyes narrow, "Last time I stopped in I left the door open. I swear he was going to have a conniption."

"Mmm. Know what that means?" my hand settled on my mag, and Karen nodded.

Twice in one day. I wish I could say that was some kind of record... but it was only half way to equaling our record for number of gun-toting house entries in one day.

"Alright, I go left... again," I pulled my pistol loose of its holster, and Karen nodded again, drawing hers.

Smoothly, we climbed the stairs, and I went in first, sweeping my mag left while Karen covered right. The stench was immediately obvious — and not just the usual stench that our informants tended to surround themselves with. This was the sickly smell of a rotting corpse.

"Well I could have done without the smell after the burgers," Karen crinkled her nose but didn't lower her mag.

"You're not kidding. My bet's his office, so follow me in," I bobbed my head at the office door on my side of the room, then slowly crossed through the 'living room' — now looted and empty, though never really 'livable' by my standards to begin with — and stopped at his office door.

Yep, face down on the desk, with his portable comps long gone and his papers scattered all over the floor.

Karen stepped up beside me, lowering her mag slightly but still not inclined to holster the weapon, "So we go through the papers on the floor and call the emergency services, I suppose."

Shaking my head slowly, I sighed, then tried to somehow not smell as I breathed in. I wasn't altogether shocked or miffed by finding Carlos dead — this guy was scum of a low order, and I'd lost many a better woman and man under my command over the years. He was selling out his comrades to us, after all; we appreciated the information he provided, but didn't think all that highly of him in the end.

Satisfied with my justification for what was somewhat callous coldness at the sight of a corpse, I turned away from the room and shrugged, "Or we start with the recorder."

Karen nodded, "Or that."

We made our way to the kitchen where, a few years back when we'd first seriously cultivated Carlos O'Sullivan, we'd covertly installed a roaming cambug recorder in the ceiling. It was a fabulous piece of kit we'd acquired from Special Branch — it basically followed the occupants of the house with camera bugs that were so small they were virtually invisible amidst the filth and grime.

Any rudimentary anti-bug scans would have caught them, of course, but this really wasn't the part of town that saw many high-end bugs, or scans that would detect them.

Well, not *electronic* bugs, I should say…

Hopefully Carlos hadn't found ours — we hadn't needed to check on it to confirm the authenticity of his information since he'd joined our cast of snitches.

Tugging her comm out of its pouch on her belt, Karen tapped the correct frequency to activate the recorder's transmitter, then sent out a ping. The bug answered instantly, still happily occupying the ceiling with its nanocams, and it immediately beamed a stream of data to Karen's comm.

"I've got everything here from when we installed the thing," Karen turned back to me. "My guess from the smell is we're looking for two days ago… give or take."

I shrugged and bobbed my eyebrows, "In this place, I'm amazed he wouldn't be consumed entirely by that time. I think I can feel the bacteria building a town on my forehead."

Karen smiled and nodded towards the living room. A vidscreen dominated one wall in that sty — looters had clearly tried to rip it out of the wall, but Carlos had anchored it well. Even with most of the wall missing, it still held onto the alloy beams of his house.

Tapping a frequency change into her comm, Karen beamed the recorder's feed into the vidscreen's buffer, and detecting the input it glowed to life, the picture grainy from the abuse it'd suffered, but watchable enough.

"So who killed Carlos?" I advanced towards the screen and slid my mag into its holster, then frowned and crossed my arms. "I don't believe the Widows would have taken him out, unless they made him for one of our snitches."

Karen was only half-listening as she scrolled through the vid files the recorder had provided, then she stopped at one and pressed play.

"Right the first time, as usual," I looked back over my shoulder and smiled at her, pretending not to notice the seven Widows' tough guys standing in the door ten feet behind her.

I don't know if they saw me seeing them, and again, success in these situations was all about the appearance of being cavalier, so I didn't care.

Karen stepped forward a couple of paces, clearly having heard them come in but ignoring them as well. Instead we both stared at the screen as the nanocam looked straight down on Carlos working at his desk.

Right on cue — Karen had managed, it seemed, to hit just the right time frame — a man walked in, raised an energy gun, pressed it against the back of Carlos' head, and pulled the trigger.

I stopped myself from wincing at the image. I'd seen worse. Unfortunately. And in person. And involving better people. It's the sort of thing you pretend to get used to… maybe you do get used to it. I don't know. I've done one or the other.

Blinking once to clear my head, I focused as best I could on the image of the shooter. He looked familiar. *Very* familiar.

"It's… Roy. Isn't it?" Karen took two more steps towards the screen and leaned in to get a look at the man with the gun.

"Yup," I nodded slowly. "So we better go ask him why he didn't mention killing our top informant when he told us where to find Jones. Rather rude of him, wouldn't you guys agree?"

Karen smiled and didn't answer. She knew this game, we used it a lot.

I counted to five, keeping my arms folded and my posture steady. Then, at five, I turned around and smiled at the seven Belt Widows who'd entered the room, "I said, people, wouldn't you agree? Come on, feedback please."

That genuinely surprised them — it always did. They wanted their moment of menace, and I... well, I'd seen and heard it all before. And these thugs weren't particularly intimidating. One of them had a piece of metal that he'd sharpened into a machete, another had a knife.

"What, no guns and no tongues either?" Karen was holstering her comm again and re-drawing her mag quite casually.

I nodded, still leaving my arms crossed, "Seems they wanted to come get our autographs or something."

Karen grinned at that, and finally the lead Widow huffed and stepped forward, "Oy, who da hell da'ya think yar?"

I raised both eyebrows, "We escape our celebrity at all the wrong times... yeesh."

With a laugh, Karen started shooting. By the time my mag came out there was only one left standing, and he was making for the door — Karen's a great shot, I have to say. And a mag is a fast-firing weapon, especially when set on light like hers was.

They'd all wake up in a couple of hours. That's part of the success pattern too — you leave them alive to tell their friends, and your myth as a benevolent but invincible Defense Command officer grows... But in the meantime, we had an informant to find. We had to know why Roy Ugessi — the very fellow who'd tipped us off about Jones' whereabouts — had killed a fellow informant.

But finding Roy might not be easy. He'd surprised us on the sidewalk outside Governor's House after our meeting there (a meeting that I didn't describe at the start of this book for the sake of pacing), and then told us about Jones. At the time it had seemed a little too helpful, but we figured he was just getting ready to ask us to look the other way on some smuggling ring or the other.

In retrospect, he'd probably come to us so that we wouldn't know where to find him, and to make sure we did find out Jones was in the dome before we left.

But why would Roy want us to take Danfield Jones... and not want Carlos to talk to us? Was he stealing Carlos' info so he could get the credit? Seemed a bit pathetic.

There were plenty of questions, so we had to find Roy. But if he wanted to get lost in the city, he very easily could. We needed a different way to get him.

So we sauntered up to the reception desk in Defense Command HQ, smiled at the Ensign working there, and when the young man's eyes widened a little in recognition, Karen flashed a top-notch smile, leaned on the counter, and asked him to call every media outlet in town.

The press conference started about ten minutes later.

CHAPTER THREE
CASUAL INTERROGATION

"Another comm call from your ship, sir. Commander Baxter requesting to speak with you again."

I looked up and locked eyes with the Ensign bringing the message, "Sorry Taylor, tell him we're too busy to be disturbed."

Remaining credibly unmoved by my response, the Ensign turned and left the break room, and I yawned and crossed my legs at the ankles as I propped my boots up on the coffee table.

"I think *I'm* one of the answers in this crossword!" Karen glanced up from her folded newspaper with some disbelief, then looked down quickly to read it to me, "Eight letters. Fleet Captain. *Sexy belt protector, Karen.*"

I grinned and then started laughing, "They actually said '*sexy*'. Nice paper, it's the local rag?"

Karen raised a ladylike eyebrow and nodded, "The *Belt Nine Informer*. About as shameless as the vid news."

"Ah, the price of fame... desperate to get back to the ship, yet?" I let my head fall back against the couch and Karen nodded as she tossed the paper onto the coffee table.

"About ready to jump out of my skin. Where do you think he is?"

Letting my eyes narrow, I glanced at the clock on the wall. We'd wrapped up the press conference about an hour earlier... so ten minutes for the Widows to get a mob together, another forty for him to get out of the seedy section of town on foot, and another ten for him to stumble in...

"Sir, he's here!" Ensign Taylor stuck his head into the break room, and I smiled.

"Show him in."

Roy Ugessi instantly burst into the room, his burly pale-skinned figure a mess of filth and a little blood, his chest heaving. He made a line right for me, hands out in front of him as though he wanted to strangle me.

Not that I could really blame him, we had rather sold him out.

Karen stuck her foot out in front of him and he wound up face-first on the floor at my boots.

"Roy, good to see you again," I didn't budge from my seat, just nodded my head at Taylor to get the young officer to stand outside with the SF guards.

"You told *everyone* you fucker!" he spat as he tried to get his hands under him to push himself up off the floor, but Karen's boot landed between his shoulder blades.

"No swearing, please. And yes we did," she said in a pleasant voice. "But *you* killed Carlos O'Sullivan. Care to explain why you did that?"

Roy grunted, "I got no clue what you're talking about bitch..."

Karen leaned into his back a bit more and he let out an abridged cry.

"Language, Roy, please. And we've got you on vid," her tone didn't change.

"Bullshit—" he grunted again as Karen's heel compressed his spine even more.

He stopped talking, wisely, and as he looked up at me with murderous eyes, I smiled and pointed at the vidscreen in the wall. Rolling his head around with some difficulty, he caught the end of the latest repeat cycle of the press conference we'd just held. During that widely-broadcast vid-extravaganza, we'd thanked Roy Ugessi for tipping us off as to the location of the evil Danfield Jones. And as Roy's picture flashed up on the screen and the news anchor started reciting the home address to which good citizens could send thank-you gift baskets for Roy — a part I loved, I must say — Karen overrode the feed with her comm, and played back the last moment of Carlos' life.

"So, why'd you need him out of the way, Roy?" I asked as he watched, and he gritted his teeth and tried to shake his head.

I frowned for a moment and looked up at Karen, "I guess he's not going to tell us. I'll tell Taylor to get him a ride home."

"You can't do that! You can't kill me!" he snarled into the carpet.

Smiling again, I leaned forward, "Well first of all, under the articles of Empire that's not quite true, I can *kill* you if you pose an immediate threat to the safety of Imperial citizens. And since we just watched you kill a valued informant I'm pretty sure you qualify. So the only thing keeping me from executing you right now is the fact that I don't, as a rule, do that. But turning you over to the Widows, well then I wouldn't even be executing you. Surely your gang friends would give you a fair trial for selling them out."

His face twisted, but there was nothing he could do but sputter a few inappropriate words before closing his eyes and letting out a petulant huff.

"Alright, I was told to shut Carlos up. So I did, to protect my cover, 'cause if I didn't they'd know I was an informant. Now you fucked all that—"

Karen ground her boot in again at the language, which drew another four-letter word from him, and thus got the heel driven even deeper.

"Spinal regen therapy takes months, Roy, so I'd suggest you stop the language," I leaned back again. "But anyway, you're not selling that story too well. Why come to us and break protocol to make sure we know about Jones if you're feeling the heat?"

He grunted again, "I was feeling the heat for coming to talk to you, that's why I killed him."

"Oh for God's sake, read the time stamp on that vid, man. You shot him a day before we got here."

Closing his eyes and cursing again, Roy ground his teeth together and Karen shrugged at me.

"Well," she said after a moment, "you could be telling the truth. But I get the feeling you're not... why did Jones need to be taken out of the way?"

That question brought another spell of silence, and I cocked an eyebrow and nodded to Karen with a smile, "Way to cut through the fiction!"

Her smile matched mine again, "You know me."

Then she stepped down on Roy *hard*, and he let out a sharp scream, "You can't torture me!"

"I'm restraining an assailant who tried to attack a Commodore," Karen said innocently, and I grinned. "So answer my question."

"Look, all I know is Jones wasn't playing ball with Yat Sen and Cooper. He was in town to meet Cooper but Cooper wasn't coming 'cause he knew you'd be here."

"And how'd he know that we'd be here, Roy. Did you tell him?" I let my eyes narrow again.

"Maybe," Roy released another grunt, and my lips thinned considerably.

Things were coming together in my head…

"*Maybe*. So you needed to get rid of Jones without implicating Cooper. And Carlos found out why Jones was in town and was going to tell us so you were told to take him out."

Roy's dagger-shooting eyes tried to ravage me, so I made sure my gaze was as cool as possible as I stared back at them.

"You telling the story or am I?" he hissed.

Shrugging, I finally pulled my boots off the table and put them on the floor next to his head, "Stop me when I'm wrong. But here's the question: why tell *us* that Jones is in town? You know I don't like killing, and he's the sort of prisoner I'd definitely want alive."

"You're a fucking idiot, Barron…" Roy gritted his teeth as Karen's boot actually made something crack. "I figured you're a Commodore now, you'd send SF to get the bastard. But *no*, you had to go yourself, be stupid and nearly get your ass shot off. Catch him by surprise, he doesn't get the chance to get himself killed…"

"And besides," Karen looked up at me, "he couldn't kill Jones himself without getting the Widows on him, because I bet they wouldn't be bright enough to see how killing one of their best might help the cause. So he had to let us evil Defcoms do the dirty work so he could stay in everybody's good graces."

Nodding, I slowly came to my feet, "Yeah, that sounds about right. So let's have Jones moved up to *Wolf* so we can be sure he's in our hands, and then let's go talk to Matt before he sends a rescue party after us."

"Gladly," Karen's boot came off Roy's back and he let out a very notable sigh of relief before managing to roll himself over. We were already at the break room door when he called after us.

"What about me?"

I didn't look back, but as the door swung open and Taylor stepped forward and nodded, I bobbed my head back towards Roy, "Get him booked for murder, make it a closed court and tell the prosecutor that if he isn't in isolation he might not live through the trial. Snitches aren't popular."

The Ensign contained most of his smile and nodded, "Very good, sir."

And with that, Karen and I went to find our fighters.

CHAPTER FOUR

WE ALWAYS CAUSE A STIR

"Uh oh."

I was looking down at the buttons in my Starlight's cockpit when Karen's voice sounded in my ear. My headset was still on even though I'd taken off my flight helmet, so we could still chat while we ran the post-flight shut down sequence on our planes.

Her comment, of course, drew my eyes upward, and through the canopy I saw what was concerning her.

We were *so* dead.

Commander Matt Baxter stood on the deck between our two fighters, his arms crossed and his foot tapping impatiently. The way his jaw was set, there was no question what he was thinking.

"Daddy's about to give us a scolding," I tried to hide my smile as I glanced to the left, and Karen chuckled before keying open her canopy.

I keyed open my own canopy and stood up as it cleared my head. Tugging my headset off, I dropped it onto the fighter console and then swung my leg out over the side and began to climb down the ladder the deck crew had kindly wheeled over to me.

As I got to the deck I turned to Matt, wondering if his expression would change at all.

Who was I kidding? It wasn't going to change.

"Matt, hey…" Karen smiled and walked towards him first. "Listen… we were going to call… but we got tied up…"

"Bloody well *storming two houses with known criminals in them with no backup and without so much as telling me!*" The tall black man's strong British accent tossed the words out over the din of the landing deck, and Karen stopped and shrugged meekly.

"Yeah… I guess…"

Shaking his head and then literally throwing his hands up in the air, Matt turned away from the two of us to collect himself. By the time I got to Karen's side he'd turned back, slightly more composed… and then he went off again.

"And *you*, Ken! A Commodore and still? What do I have to do, put SF on you both around the bloody clock?"

I shrugged, "We'd shake 'em. You know us."

Poor Matt sighed and shook his head, his hands dramatically gripping his scalp.

Yes, this was Matt Baxter, our famed First Officer, and long-time compatriot and friend with both Karen and I out on the Belt frontier. He still had a lot of the security chief blood running through him — he'd only lately been moved up to his executive officer's post.

Matt, you see, understood that the cavalier, irresponsible approach was key to getting things done in the Belt. He understood that reality, but he hated it. And so he was always the voice of reason that kept me from… well… dying. Pushing it too far and getting myself killed. Since I'm able to write this twenty years later, he obviously did a good job.

"You and your stupid bloody *stuff*. Dammit…"

"We promise to be good for a while," Karen smiled.

His eyes narrowed and settled on her, "Don't humor me, I'll find a way to make you both responsible yet. You know it's my ass on the block if you get yourselves killed, what?"

I smiled and reached out, patting him on the shoulder, "So that's how you know we'll always come back fine, Matt. We'd never put your backside on any line at all!"

That earned me a glare.

Wincing, I glanced at Karen with a shrug, "Well I tried."

"Ship's alright, I take it?" Karen looked back to Matt and his expression exploded.

"Of *course* it's bloody well alright! And there's a message from Admiral Noyce sitting in your mailbox, Ken. Otherwise I'm making the arrangements for that pirate you two nabbed in that irresponsible escapade to come aboard. Anything else?"

I raised my eyebrows and looked to Karen again, "That about covers it, I think."

She nodded and with a smile stepped past her First Officer. I followed, patting him on the shoulder again, "Now you should get to the rec deck or something, Matt. You seem to be a bit stressed."

I walked away in case steam actually started shooting out his ears. It was fun to push his buttons… or more precisely, to mash one's palm into his keyboard. He didn't like it when we were irresponsible.

A wonder he liked us at all, actually.

Karen and I left the flight deck.

"You know, if anyone outside the squadron saw that he'd probably be court martialed for talking to us like that," Karen said quietly as we waited for the lift to take us to the deck of officer's cabins.

Wolf was a big enough frigate for the trip in the lift to take some time — we had to move from the bottom of the forward battle pod through the ship's neck and into the crew section.

Cocking my eyebrow at her concerned comment, I looked her way, "Let them try. Anybody goes after him and I'll use my new rank to tear them to pieces."

Karen smiled, "Might as well do something productive with the extra bar."

Her concern was, of course, valid; a Commander chewing out his Captain and his Commodore, complete with raised voice, fist-pumping, and in full sight of everyone on the flight deck… that wasn't exactly in the manual.

But clearly Karen and I didn't pay that much attention to the rules — this was the Belt Squadron, after all. Besides, Matt was not only one of the finest officers ever to serve, his fire-and-brimstone pseudo-parenting had saved our lives often enough for us to rather appreciate it.

"So, Jones is due aboard in an hour. You want to have the first crack at him?" Karen leaned back against the wall of the lift, sliding her hands into her pockets.

Frowning, I tilted sideways against the wall, "You know, after that I think I'd rather put him in a room with Matt. We'll know what he was up to in ten minutes or less."

Karen's smile grew, "Hell hath no fury like a First Officer with us for seniors, eh?"

"I don't know, I hear you 'women' are still worse," I grinned.

Karen crossed the lift to elbow me but the door opened in time to allow my escape.

Stuffing my grimy uniform into a laundry bag, I grabbed the vidscreen remote off my bed and activated my wall unit. The usual screen came up: 'Welcome to *Wolf*Net, Captain Barron' (IT hadn't yet fixed my rank on the header).

"You have one external message waiting," the computer's mechanical voice followed immediately.

After tying up the laundry bag and stuffing it in the wall hatch that sent it to the cleaners, I turned back to the screen and sat down on the edge of my bed. In reality I probably had about sixty new messages — Commodores got an obscene amount of paperwork — but most of that was automatically diverted to the two aides I'd been given when I hit flag rank.

I'd thumbprint various things later when they brought them in. For now all I wanted was a message from an old friend, so I fumbled with the remote and finally scrolled to the 'View Message' button. The screen went black for a moment as the message buffered, and then Admiral Greg Noyce appeared.

It hardly needs to be repeated that Noyce's career had been long and distinguished… but, I want to repeat it, so too bad for you. When I'd joined the frigate *Alberta* as a Lieutenant many years earlier, it had been his ship, and the Belt Squadron had been his. He'd moved up from Commodore to Admiral through successful pirate campaigns, and over that time I'd moved on to command *Friendly*, then *Wolf*. After his stunning victory at Deep Black, he'd been recalled to command the First Division of the Home Fleet, leaving me to be promoted and to take charge out here.

He was smiling as he appeared on the screen, and he nodded in greeting, "Good morning Ken. I expect Matt's already set you straight for being so incredibly impetuous this morning, I just wanted to let you know that you've caused a stir here in Earth space. Half the Admiralty is ready to court martial you, the other half is laughing at them. First Lord Fiora sends his greetings and says he'll smooth things over for you, but he, Rear Admiral Stoll and I just wanted to remind you not to get into too much trouble out there."

I chuckled. Of course being all over the press would make it impossible for me to hide my antics, but I had good friends in high places to make sure that didn't cause me too much grief. First Lord John Fiora had been Commandant of the Academy when Karen and I had gone through, and I'd served out my time as an Ensign and my first year as a Lieutenant on his bridge aboard *Warrior*. Rear Admiral Stoll was on leave from Venus Station, getting her flagship serviced and doing some extensive planning with the Admiralty, and as a fellow pirate fighter (hers were the Venusian pirates, a strange and lethal bunch) she was a high-ranking member of our group.

Between them, these Admirals could contain any hissy-fits thrown by old-fashioned desk Admirals who didn't like to see the fleet represented as anything but stoic and austere on vidscreens.

"Anyway," Noyce continued after a pause, "I'm heading out to go golfing with the kids. Let us know what you find out from Jones. It sounds like these meetings might be the precursor to a new Syndicate formation. Alright, I'll look forward to hearing from you. Give my best to Karen and Matt!"

The screen went black again and then returned to my home screen.

I have to say, I was just a bit pleased with myself — we'd made a big stir, and that's not just fun, it adds to the mythos floating around your name. When every channel shows me and Karen bringing in one of the biggest pirates still out there, it sends a nice message to deviants everywhere: don't mess with Defense Command, especially if *Wolf* is nearby.

But now I was hungry. The burger at lunch had been good, but it was time for some home cooking. Er… some ship-home cooking. Which I counted as almost as good.

I got up and wandered into the kitchen.

Chapter Five
Torture

"So you're here to meet Cooper but you don't want to tell us why, is that it?"

Jones stared impassively at Matt Baxter, and our fine Commander smiled back.

"That's alright. We're allowed to torture known pirates like yourself, though I'm sure you knew that already?"

Jones didn't blink.

Standing behind the one-way glass that peered into *Wolf's* interrogation room, I frowned at the scene, "He still stunned or something?"

Karen crossed her arms and shook her head, "Matt said the doctors stimmed him right up. He probably has enough drugs in his system to let him break his chains and go psycho on us."

I grinned, "With Matt in there, I'd *love* to see that."

"He'd last ten seconds, maybe twelve," Karen smiled.

"Nah, five. Matt's angry today remember," I glanced at her.

"Right, right," Karen's smile grew, and then we watched as Matt left the interrogation room. Seconds later he was standing beside us.

"Well, I'm either going to actually have to torture him or you two are going to have to have a go at him," he said sternly enough.

"We'll see what we can do," Karen looked past me at her XO. "Do we even have torture equipment aboard?"

Matt frowned, "Aside from your senses of humor, damned if I know. I'll go see if I can find out, and see if anybody aboard has any idea how the damned stuff would work if we do. I could always start punching him, I suppose..."

The Commander started to walk away in mid-speech so we didn't get to counter-attack with some doubtlessly brilliant repartee. He walked right out of the brig room, leaving us to our own devices.

"So under the Articles of Empire, we can go in there and tell jokes until he cracks?" I let my eyes settle on Jones, and Karen chuckled.

"Some day they're actually going to have to rewrite those things. When's the last time you heard of one of us *torturing* somebody?" she let her arms drop to her sides and started walking towards the interrogation room door.

"I thought that was the nature of our relationship!" I called after her as I followed.

My chin slumped into the palm of my left hand while the fingers of my right hand drummed the table in front of me. According to the clock we'd been at this for... almost half an hour. It didn't sound like a particularly long time to be questioning a pirate, but, well, I'd had a long day.

I looked from Jones to my fingers drumming the table top up to Karen standing behind him and back. This was going nowhere.

"So… we've got the 'fiery mutilator of doom and excruciating pain' coming in ten minutes. You might want to talk before it gets here."

I actually said that, and with a straight face too. Karen stopped in her tracks and looked at me with an open-mouthed 'what the hell?' expression.

Jones raised his eyebrows — not in fear but more in disbelief that I'd said something so incredibly ridiculous, "You really are as much of a clown as they say."

I frowned at that, my posture instantly correcting and my hands coming to rest on the table in front of me, "Excuse me. *Clown?*"

"Yeah *clown*. Idiot and clown. Biggest conspiracy in Belt history is going down and you're sitting on your ass making jokes."

That sent my eyebrows up, "Biggest conspiracy, is it? Sounds like you're fluffing your own importance just a tad. What do you have in your little pirate fleet, two converted haulers and an up-gunned *yacht?*"

I didn't expect him to actually bite at that question, but to my credit, I really had managed to sound petty and juvenile, as though I was a kid insulting another kid's toys.

"Three haulers and a purpose-built *raider*, and that's just what you should know about. I'm a big player now…" Jones bit off the reply, realizing he'd been baited.

"Hmm, now those sound like targets that'll get us some coverage when we take them, eh Ken?" Karen began pacing again, but quickly elected to stop and prop herself on the edge of the table to my left, pulling her ponytail over her left shoulder and toying with its end. "I think I'll look good on the raider's bridge. We should make sure they send cameras."

Jones' face twitched but he wasn't going to be baited a second time.

"That's a plan. But Danfield… *Danny*… tell me, if you're such a big player, why were you in that rotting old dump of a house with one guard — a guard who was a *very* bad shot, I might add?" I leaned back in my chair, letting my eyes narrow. "You tell us, I might get charitable all of a sudden."

Jones' eyes narrowed too, his mind clearly turning over his options. The fact that he thought he actually *had* options was interesting.

"I tell you and you cut me loose. No charges, no nothing, I disappear."

My eyebrows climbed again. Yes my eyebrows move a lot — it's one of my delightful quirks. Hey, at least I don't let my jaw drop.

Karen hopped off the table and crossed behind me, staring him down with one of her icy gazes, "That's not likely to happen."

"This time it is. What's going down is big, bigger than you two even, and if you want what I know you're going to make it worth my while," Jones was starting to sound a little smug.

I let my brow settle into a frown, "Done. What's going down?"

Jones' eyes flashed from Karen to me, "What?"

"Done. I'm a Commodore, I can do whatever I like. You get a pardon if you tell us what you know."

"You're shitting me."

Karen frowned, "Can you *please* watch your language? This isn't a pirate ship, thank you."

A grin twisted onto Jones' face, "Yeah no kidding. You wouldn't be dressed so conservative on a pirate ship, honey."

I smiled and shook my head, looking down as the back of Karen's hand smacked into Jones' nose, "That's *Captain*, Danny boy."

He yelped — actually *yelped* — and did the typically pirate thing: released a string of curses. Karen crossed behind him and we waited for him to stop swearing before I leaned forward again.

"So tell me what you've got, then we can get you cleaned up and out of here."

Jones frowned at me, "No, we do this my way. You let me go and I send you the—"

"Not happening," I shook my head with a thin smile. "Tell me now. You're just going to have to believe me."

Closing his mouth, Jones studied me with narrowed eyes.

I guess he was sizing me up to see how much of a deceptive pirate-sort I was. Or how staunchly honorable I was... something like that.

"Cooper and Yat Sen are forming a new Syndicate, and the Martians are supporting it. Latest I heard they were working out of Asteroid Theta with a Martian front company. They're getting all sorts of weapons."

That actually stopped my thinking for a second. What the hell were the *Martians* doing getting mixed up in this? I looked up at Karen with a frown, and she raised an eyebrow, "You expect us to believe that?"

Jones shrugged, "You think I'd make up something that stupid? If I was trying to trap you I'd get you looking for my base or Cooper's or something, and lead you into an ambush. Asteroid Theta's too public, honey... er... Cap'n."

Karen tilted her head and looked down at me. That was a surprisingly good point to come from a pirate.

"So you're not in on this new Syndicate, that's why they set you up for us to take. Gave you a stupid guard with a weapon so big they figured we'd have to use deadly force."

Jones' mouth twitched towards a snarl but he stopped himself, "Yeah that sounds like that shit Cooper. I don't work for nobody, Martians or otherwise. But if Cooper starts getting their guns he'll be able to wipe me out. So you guys go stop him for me, will ya?"

I smiled, "Of course we will... but we won't do it for you."

Standing slowly, I scratched my head and looked at Karen, "Let's get the senior staff together to talk this through. Thanks Danny."

I nodded to the pirate and then Karen and I headed for the door.

"So you're cutting me loose?" Jones turned in his seat.

I stopped at the door and looked back with a smile, "Legally, I could be using the 'fiery mutilator of doom and excruciating pain' on you right now. I think you got off light with a white lie."

Jones' eyes widened and he tried to jump to his feet. Evidently the doc hadn't woken him up with *that* many stims, because the chains holding him to the chair didn't break. He collapsed into his seat with a grunt and started cursing again.

Karen and I smiled as we left.

CHAPTER SIX

A LONG, BORING BRIEFING THROUGH WHICH YOU MUST SIT

Briefings sometimes bored me. You can probably sympathize; they're ultimately a bunch of people hanging around a table and talking about things they already know, some of them taking notes... others doodling.

I have very impressive doodling skills. I use them often. My editors wouldn't allow me to put my favorite doodles in an appendix to this volume because they thought it'd make it seem like I don't care about my job... er... didn't care about my job. But anyway, I did doodle a lot.

But today's meeting wasn't going to be a good one for doodling. This whole 'Mars' connection had me intrigued. Granted, it could be a story spun to mislead us, but as Jones himself had pointed out, it was a story that could be confirmed relatively safely and easily.

Before getting into the particulars of this meeting, though, I better pause to remind you of the stellar situation in these days — things looked rather different than they do today. Hopefully the publisher will put down the cash for some maps at the front of this volume to help make things clear, but in case not, let's do this properly.

At the beginning of 2231, the Earth Empire included sixty-seven worlds and stations, not counting the lunar facilities and Earth itself. Moving from sun-side to deep-side, the major bases were at Venus, Earth (obviously), in the Belt sector, and in Jupiter orbital space. Now, the Belt was clearly the richest of these areas, with its mineral mining pouring plenty of money into the Imperial economy. Indeed, Belt mining profits had been making up just about sixty percent of the Empire's revenue since about 2190.

I give you that detail so you can sound really smart at dinner parties, in case you're wondering. Anyway...

By the time I was made Commodore of the Belt Station, there were thirty-one Belt colonies, each of them creatively named along the 'Belt Number' method — like 'Belt Nine' that *Wolf* was floating over for this briefing.

Beyond them, Jupiter was ringed by orbital facilities and domes on its moons which were sustained by the water under the surface of several of them. Basically it was a secret R&D station with very little civilian presence, and it was damned expensive to run.

Aside from Earth, the Martians were building their Imperium with all irresponsible speed. They'd seeded over fifty 'Asteroid' bases, like 'Theta' where Jones said Cooper and Yat Sen were getting armed. They also had a base at Mercury, and rumors said they were checking out real estate around Saturn, though everyone in Earth's government was sure the Martian economy could never afford to maintain a deep-range base like ours over Jupiter.

There was plenty of tension between Mars and Earth, especially in the Belt, because of the vast resources in the area. We'd gotten out there first and taken a particularly rich sector of asteroids. Their set of bases was sprawled over a much less manageable area of space — they had nearly twice the number of bases we did, and they were spread over *four times* as much space.

And it goes without saying that between both our colonizing ventures, we hadn't even come close to exploring a third of the Belt. We charted one area and stuck to it because it was defensible; the pirates and independent colonies owned the rest... or sporadic parts of it. That autonomy had allowed the pirates to collect themselves into the well-organized Syndicate under Grant Merger, the notorious pirate and once-classmate of mine (don't ask).

But Admiral Noyce and the Belt Squadron had sent them running back into the depths of the Belt at the Battle of Deep Black, so we'd been in a nice lull for the better part of a year when this matter with Jones fired up. I mean, of course there were tons of little independent pirates, but dealing with them is a lot different than dealing with an organized squadron of ships that mostly outgun yours. Anyway, that'll all be covered in an earlier (but yet-to-be-written) volume. Actually, if you're reading many decades after I'm writing this and reading my other, yet-to-be written books in chronological order, you might already have heard about it. That was a confusing sentence. Sorry.

And if you are indeed reading these chronologically from a book I haven't written yet, sorry for repeating all this.

Back to the narrative: I was sitting in *Wolf's* briefing room, drumming my fingers on the table and watching as my senior staff settled into their seats. I didn't have my own full staff like many Commodores did — I really couldn't justify wasting the space in *Wolf's* compartments with the secondary Command and Control they'd want to set up — so I just trusted the bridge crew that had been out here on the Belt Station with me for ages. All of these officers were veterans of Belt service, whether they'd all been with me through my own misadventures or not.

Karen was sitting at my right hand, and Matt at my left. Matt had been with me for years, and Karen and I had been out here for the same amount of time. I'd only passed her in rank with my latest promotion to Commodore — up until the piece of luck (good or bad, I don't know) that had me promoted over her, we'd been neck-and-neck in advancement.

The rest of *Wolf's* crew was like a who's-who of the Belt's elite officers: Lieutenant Commander Andrew Jenson was Chief Engineer and a remarkable cobbling expert on the side. He could build just about anything, and quickly. Lieutenant Kyle Stranks was the new head of ship security, now that Matt had been promoted, and he'd been one of the SF guys to help Matt bail me out of a bunch of scrapes. The department head for Sensors and Communications — two sciences that went together because the pulse transmitters and receivers were pretty similar for both — was Lieutenant Commander Jim Hannigan, and the Navigation and Helm Officer was Lieutenant Commander Erica Martin.

Because *Wolf* was a full frigate, we also had two more senior officers: the squadron leader for our wing of twenty-four F-194s was Lieutenant Commander Adrienne Thompson, and she sat at the table across from the other very redoubtable officer (one you might have expected to show up before now, given the house-storming Karen and I had done).

Of course I'm talking about Major Charlie Peters, the head of *Wolf's* unit of Special Branch troops. Charlie had started in *Alberta* with Greg and me, and then he'd been transferred over to *Friendly* with me when I took command. Without him, my cavalier antics would have doubtless led to many painful deaths. Being a Special Brancher, he has a way of making death not happen… to me at least. Nope, can't think of a better way to phrase that, sorry.

That 'Special Brancher' title should be clarified, I suppose: Defense Command has never had 'marines' like the Martians do. Ground fighting was the job of the Earth Imperial Army (a force that admittedly sounded much grander than Defense Command). For special personal combat roles, then, Special Branch had eventually been created as an adjunct to Defense Command Security Forces, and its men and women were elite combatants trained in boarding and ground strike ops.

You know how the Imperial Army has its [flashy and self-important] Gamma Force Commandos? That's what Special Branch was to the regular SF. And because *Wolf* was big and relatively new, our twelve-officer Special Branch team had all the new kit, including MAG-90s (which I'll doubtless rave about later).

Put all that under the careful command of Charlie Peters, and, well, I almost wanted to find a pirate bar on an asteroid and stir it up — just to watch the fireworks as he cleaned up the mess.

Anyway, that's a whole lot of exposition, some of it not terribly relevant. Hope I didn't lose you there.

"So… the Martians?" Charlie Peters was the first one to toss out a question as he settled into his chair. Charlie was always good for leading out discussions — some people think that, because he's a Special Brancher, he's all brawn and no brain. Farthest thing from it — to be a successful Special Brancher you have to be smart. Very smart indeed. So Charlie was probably smarter than me, and he could almost certainly break me in half. Good thing he was my friend.

"That's what Jones said, and I don't think he was lying. Ken had him going pretty good with the whole 'we'll let you go' line," Karen nodded, shifting in her seat and playing with the end of her ponytail as it sat on her left shoulder.

There were confused, perhaps uncertain frowns on the faces of everyone at the table except for Karen and me, and rightly so. The Martians didn't do much in those days, besides occasionally blockading an asteroid that belonged to us and saying it was theirs.

Since I'd gotten out to the Belt frontier, ships from our squadron had traded shots with the Martians exactly four times, and each time it had been written off as a minor incident, the home governments having no interest in starting some sort of Imperial war over a couple of rocks. We were all reasonable humans, surely…

Right.

"Why would they be arming *pirates*? Seems a bit counterproductive," Hannigan looked from me to his fellows at the table as he asked the question.

"Presumably, they'd be making an agreement with Cooper and Yat Sen," Martin suggested in quick reply. "You know, the 'we give you guns, you don't attack us any more' deal."

"Yeah but that kind of thinking doesn't work with pirates," Charlie piped in knowingly.

"Give them an inch and they'll take your long intestines. So unless the pirates were being scared straight by something the Martians were threatening, there'd be no reason for them not to turn around and hit Martian targets with their new weapons."

Mmm, yes, that was exactly the problem with this picture. Trying to wheel and deal with pirates was like trying to spoon feed sharks while swimming with them. Not a good plan, by all accounts. Surely the Martians weren't so naïve as to try it.

"The Martians aren't renowned for being politically astute," Adrienne Thompson said her first words of the meeting, and she got quite a few sympathetic nods — including one from me.

Indeed, the last news out of Mars Colony… er, the Martian Homeworld as they liked to call their home planet (still trying to shrug off that century-and-a-half old colonial legacy that we liked to keep up)… was that indentured service terms had been re-extended from three years to six, in order to accelerate the growth of the fledgling Asteroid colonies.

Since indentured service was pretty much self-imposed slavery, the Earth government scoffed at the change, but could do little more than declare the Martians to be backward and foolish.

That indentured service issue had sparked riots on a dozen Asteroid bases, according to rumors we'd picked up, and there'd nearly been a coup against the Imperium government. That had been… oh… two years back? Since then things had been quiet on the Mars front. Traders carried rumors and miscellaneous newsbytes and papers, but the Martians refused to openly broadcast official signal traffic, and they even tried to encrypt their public vidcasts so we couldn't see them.

It worked; after two months decoding a high-priority-seeming feed that turned out to be daytime talk shows and soaps, Defense Command Intelligence had given up on monitoring the regular traffic. Who could blame them, when the pirates were the real threat to the Earth economy.

Anyway, that's all to demonstrate that the Martians were a pretty… unimpressive Empire… er, *Imperium* — they picked 'Imperium' for their name to sound different, but failed to actually read the definition. No matter, they were quite clearly dim enough to attempt things like buying off mad pirates with *weapons*.

"Soooo," I finally opened my mouth and had words come out, "they might be arming pirates. And if they are, we can't really let that slide because it makes Cooper and Yat Sen a bigger threat to our colonies. Think we should pay a visit to Asteroid Theta?"

Karen flipped the end of her ponytail back over her shoulder and propped her elbow on the arm of her chair, then settled her chin in her hand, "We could do a formal visit, show the flag."

"Yes, but if Cooper and Yat Sen have a fleet of pirate ships there getting stocked up on all sorts of nasty bits of kit, what do we do if we show up on our own?" Matt's usual responsible outlook drew several frowns, but nods followed.

"Yeah, the Martians theoretically would be obliged to stop the pirates killing us — if a famous ship like *Wolf* was blown to pieces by pirates over a Martian rock, the press backlash and Admiralty outrage would probably lead to a declaration of war," Charlie, ever there with the apt observations, continued the line of thought. "So any Martians with any common sense would stop such a thing happening… but I can't say I'd bet on any of them having common sense, assuming they've got any ships in the area at all."

Very good point, the Martian Asteroid Squadron was surprisingly *smaller* than ours, or at least that was what our informants were telling us these days. Keeping ships at the Belt wasn't cheap, and no matter how much they puffed up and what rhetoric they hid behind, the Martians didn't have the economy for it.

Maybe paying off Cooper and Yat Sen was a really desperate move to try to secure their weak borders. Admiral Noyce might have scared the pirates off attacking the Belt colonies, thus shifting the attention to the Martian asteroids...

Sorry, got sidetracked again.

"So we don't go to Theta by ourselves," Andrew Jenson spoke for the first time. "How many ships come with us?"

That question was more or less pointed directly at me: it was my squadron, I had to divide it up. First thing to think about, then, was how many ships we actually had: precisely nine, including four frigates (three new and one older) and five corvettes (two new and three older). Three of the ships were held as a standing reserve at Belt Two, the central Defense Command HQ for the Belt Station, and the rest were traveling alone or in pairs on their patrols around the Belt colonies, stopping piracy if they found it, checking with informants otherwise.

To take too many on a mission like this — one that could be a wild goose chase in the long run — would be irresponsible (in a bad way). But too few and Matt's prediction might come true.

Compromise was thus in order.

"Alright, let's send a signal to Belt Two and get *Lion* and *Honesty* to meet us at a point just short of Theta... let's schedule the rendezvous for four days from now. Send that for me, Jim?"

Hannigan nodded, "Yes sir."

"Erica, you plot our course and pick the rendezvous point, then pass it on to Jim," I continued my orders and Martin nodded, locking eyes with Hannigan for a moment to confirm before looking back to me.

My eyebrows went up and I realized — with no minor sense of relief — that the briefing was pretty much done, "Now let's get out of this room."

People smiled and pushed themselves out of their chairs.

Chapter Seven

Shortly After The Briefing, At Belt Two

Let me just start this chapter by explaining why I'm using the third person and describing things I wasn't witness to. My tyrannical publisher says this is confusing, I think you and me are both smart enough to figure out that I'm telling you what happened in places other than *Wolf* because I talked to people who were there. Historians do it all the time!

Belt Two was the biggest of the Belt bases, not least because Defense Command had invested trillions there on a yearly basis to build up and maintain the biggest Naval installation aside from Luna Prime. Its fixed defenses were *epic*, and we thought entirely impervious to all raiding activity.

Keeping a small force of ships at the base was pretty much just a formality — mainly, ships like *Lion*, *Honesty* and the recently-returned *Sackville* stayed there because it was a central point from which they could cruise to any threatened sector of the Belt colonies in a relatively short time. They were rapid response, so to speak.

For her part, Captain Kris Jacobs — that ever-popular (and fiery) Australian — was appreciating being that responder, because it was giving her the chance to get used to the job of ship command. She'd been my executive officer aboard *Wolf* when I'd been Captain, and she'd moved to *Lion* when Karen had come over from that ship to take up the role of my Flag Captain.

Now it might sound like bad policy for ships to be swapping officers like that — a long-time Captain leaving one ship and joining another, just to be replaced by a lately-Commander — but it wasn't. *Wolf* and *Lion* had fought alongside each other many times since they'd reached the Belt three years earlier, and their ships' companies were by this time pretty much extended family. Kris was welcomed happily by her friends on *Lion*.

Still, the responsibilities she had as a Captain were rather different than those she'd had as an XO. She was the one calling all the shots, making the big decisions, determining the fate of her ship.

"So ma'am, what do you say?"

Frowning, Kris folded her arms and let out a long breath. It was a tough call, this one...

"Let's go with... the teal. The blue's just a bit too drab, I think."

The Lieutenant nodded, "Very good ma'am, I'll get maintenance in immediately."

"Leave the samples on my desk," Kris nodded. "And thank you, Omar."

Her Security Chief smiled, "You're welcome ma'am. I know you'll like it."

He turned on his heel as soon as he deposited the carpet samples on the desk of Kris' day cabin — the room next to the bridge that was reserved as her office. It was currently carpeted with rather modest burgundies from when Karen had set the decor, but Kris was more a teal sort of woman.

So that was big decision number one. Hopefully they'd keep being this incredibly *pointless.*

Well, that wasn't fair, it just seemed a little strange that she was spending her time as skipper of one of the best frigates in the Defense Command Fleet choosing carpet.

At just about the moment where the absurdity of that was spinning through her brain, her *Lion*Net screen made a 'ping' sound, denoting the arrival of a priority message in her inbox. She got plenty of junk mail as a Captain — even Defense Command comm grids were vulnerable, amazingly enough, to junk mail. If Kris ever wanted a good deal on a mortgage, a university diploma at cost, or to improve her... um... intimate abilities, she'd be set.

But when the computer detected a message coming in from someone on the 'priority' list it pinged to let her know she had something worth viewing. With that in mind, she turned her chair towards the vidscreen in the wall and grabbed the remote off her desk, tapping through to the message screen.

She saw my 'Official Orders' message come up at the top of her inbox, selected it, then waited for a few seconds as the computer buffered the vid stream.

Then I appeared (she probably cringed at my horrible visage, but she was too nice to tell me she did).

"Hi Kris... you've probably seen the news about me and Karen getting Jones. Turns out Cooper and Yat Sen are putting a new Syndicate together... and the Martians are seemingly paying their tab. We have *no* idea why they'd do that, and the story itself needs confirming... it's what Jones told us under interrogation, so I'm going to take *Wolf* down to Asteroid Theta, because that's where Jones says Cooper was going to be. Means we might tick off our red planet friends, and it could also be a huge trap. With those lovely possibilities in mind, I want you to bring *Lion* out to the coordinates embedded in this signal, and get *Honesty* to come with you. We'll meet you there and then go for some Martian cooking on Theta. Signal Wes and tell him to bring *Cheetah* and *Friendly* in to take over for you on home station — I don't want Belt Two left lightly guarded."

Kris stared at my picture on the vid as I basically delivered an inelegant soliloquy of orders, her eyebrows climbing a little more every time I added a new element to her task.

"Wow," she said to herself quietly.

She has never told me what exactly she *meant* by 'wow'.

About four hours after the orders got to her, Kris Jacobs had *Lion* and the new corvette *Honesty* boosted out of Belt Two, both ships making 196 kps as they accelerated away from their base. That speed was remarkable — before its refit, veteran old *Alberta*, the fourth frigate on the line out at Belt Station, had only been able to pull 186 kps. These new ships with the higher cruising speeds, though, could make the in season trip from Earth to the Belt Station in just about ten days. Out of season, of course, it was twice that, but that was why we tried to avoid out-of-season travel.

And that's the signal for me to explain the space 'seasons', in case you're not familiar. Unlike the Earth seasons most people have experienced or at least read about, these seasons are much more fluid. Basically, there's an 'in season' travel period when the orbit of one planet brings it closer to another. Because everything's orbiting the sun at a different pace, relative distances between planets change all the time, and sometimes the sun gets in the way of direct shipping. At the height of the in season, two planets are as close together as their orbital patterns will ever allow them to be.

Anyway, that's what seasons mean. For travel between asteroids in the Belt it didn't much matter, because things out here were relatively consistent — rocks didn't move too much in relation to each other. That actually is a very important fact... but probably for another time. More to the point right now: *Lion* and *Honesty* were making good time as they sped out of Belt Two.

As they left, the laser comms at that base sent a reply through our network of relay ships and relay posts to Belt Six, and to Belt Eleven, the next port of call for Captain Wes Pellew's DCNS *Cheetah* and the home port of DCNS *Friendly*, my old corvette.

They'd head to Belt Two to cover the gap in the main reserve, and Belt Eleven and *Cheetah's* patrol route could do without those ships... for now.

Things were in motion.

CHAPTER EIGHT

MEANINGLESS WAITING

Passing time in transit is something you get good at when you join the Defense Command Navy. There's never that much to do, and while some Captains with green crews run endless drills, Karen and I both knew that *Wolf's* company was more than up to snuff. We'd be doing them a disservice if we wasted their time with endless drills on this trip.

So instead there was much free time and relaxation. *Wolf* had a pretty damned good rec deck for that sort of thing — everything from a little dance hall to a gym and pool to a small cinema. All of these spaces were easily converted to emergency cargo or personnel holders, but for normal days they provided a necessary diversion for a crew far from home.

Me, I wasn't really in the mood for any of them. Usually I could be caught going for a swim, but for some reason the idea of being submerged in water didn't work for me today.

Perhaps I thought I was in well over my head already... Ha. My brain is funny.

Right.

So instead of swimming I was shooting in *Wolf's* target range. I'd remembered missing that goon back at Jones' house, and I was a little bit miffed at myself for not dropping him on my own. Why I was bothered that I had missed and Karen had swooped in is beyond me, because more often than not that was the way it went.

But I suppose I thought I needed to improve my shooting with my idiot-proof mag sidearm before I got into any more trouble.

"So, you really need to start bringing me back in on these ops of yours."

I leaned back and looked around the divider between my booth and the next one over. Charlie Peters smiled and waved.

"Hey..." I nodded to him, realizing in some mild terror that my brain didn't seem to be coming up with anything to say. Yes, terror might seem an overly strong reaction to something as simple as not having coherent words available, but I prided myself on always having the right word in brain.

Er. In *mind*.

"Well... um. Yeah. Look, it wasn't really an *op*, just an impromptu apprehension of a suspect..." I leaned forward again, putting the divider between myself and Charlie as I slapped a new power cell into my pistol.

"I don't care what you call it, you and Karen aren't going to be able to keep getting away with this sort of thing. At the rate you're going, you'll get yourselves killed. Unless you let me — *just* me, even — look after you both."

I smiled, "Yeah that's probably true..."

Letting the sentence die, I swung my mag forward and settled into a good firing position, then started squeezing off shots. The light pistol hummed softly with every burst, sending the yellow-blue bolts down range at a target projected onto an absorption screen.

My shooting was... well, let's say it wasn't *great*. Part of the media-spun mythos is and was that I've always been a great shot, putting every bolt through someone's eye or some other impossible-to-hit-spot. That's not quite fair... really I was *serviceable*, just not Commodore Sharpshooter...

Charlie opened up with his mag assault rifle from the next booth and I stopped to watch. Every shot left a mark in the 'head of the target', and he was firing twice as fast as me.

"You damned Special Branchers, always showing off," I grinned.

Over the hums of his rifle, I heard Charlie chuckle, "Karen might be glad to finally have a good shot to back her up."

I laughed, "I won't even try to deny it. Alright, I promise, we'll try not to get carried away too much anymore."

Charlie's chuckle grew into a laugh, but despite that, every shot was going between the eyes of the target.

At sixty meter range.

"Did I mention I hate you?" I voiced my mock disdain.

There was a wounded pause, then Charlie's rifle started chopping up the face of my target from his lane. With a sigh I keyed off my mag, holstered it, and slipped out the back.

Leaving the range, I secured my sidearm in its holster and sauntered around rather aimlessly. It was warm on the deck — despite the climate control, it tended to get stuffy when most of the crew was cycling through here during the day. I was glad I was in ship dress — the blue shirt and pants without the tunic.

Then again, that was probably why there was 'ship dress' — because someone had realized (possibly with divine assistance, because this is quite a revelation) that it could get stuffy in a metal box crammed with 600 people.

I nodded as each crew member passed me. Technically, Defense Command protocol required everyone to salute, but nobody was foolish enough to do so, thank goodness — every stop and start as we crisply saluted and exchanged useless words would have made the saunter rather brutal.

Naval tradition was wonderful... it was just a bit too cumbersome sometimes.

Eventually I passed the gym. The big room had everything from weight machines to a punching bag, but no free weights — those could become a problem if grav panels took a surge.

I never used it, really. I'd had a private exercise facility next to my cabin in *Wolf* since I'd been promoted to Captain, so I didn't have to compare my weight-lifting ability to some of those SF muscleheads who spent every spare minute on the bench.

Then as now, I was in decent shape — but I've never been a bodybuilder.

That said, my job description didn't include physically restraining pirates and whatnot, whereas some others' did...

Right now that was all irrelevant, because I'd seen someone in that gym through the window. Well, why be coy? Karen was in there.

With my eyebrows up, I keyed the door and stepped into the busy fitness room, then ambled up behind my Flag Captain. She was facing away from me but the mirrored walls on all sides of the gym betrayed my approach.

If you're thinking 'mirrored walls? Ooooooh' you're right — these *Predator*-class frigates were premium ships with all the trimmings. I sure didn't mind.

Karen, who I'd thought was on duty, was wearing a pair of sweats, a well-fitting t-shirt, and fight gloves, and she was enthusiastically hammering one of the 80-pound bags.

She threw a flurry of punches as I stopped behind her, "I thought you had watch."

Slamming the bag a bit more, she shook her head, "Only until 1800."

My eyes twitched up to the clock and read 1830. Aha, well then.

"Hmm, alright. Well. How much longer you going to be?"

Karen stopped swinging and the bag swayed as she bounced around and smiled, "I don't know, how long are you sticking around?"

Her ponytail bounced up over her left shoulder, and she kept hopping from foot to foot the way boxers do. I smiled and then stopped, looking out at the rest of the gym. Everybody was staring. Men, mainly. Uncouth bastards, the lot of them.

I cleared my throat loudly enough for most of them to hear it and they got back to their business.

Restoring my smile I looked back to Karen and shrugged, "Dunno, how long you going to stay here trying to convince everyone you're... Athena?"

It had taken effort, but I'd come up with a sophisticated, subtle way of saying she looked fantastic. Come on, Athena's a good reference for that!

Her smile broadened slightly, "I won't even touch that one. I'll be a while... You want to get into the ring? A bit of sparring would do you good."

I grinned, then reached down and tapped my mag, "Yeah sure, I've got my gun..."

Karen chuckled and raised her hands in a boxer's style. I almost took a step back but realized she was turning back to the bag.

"At some point you'll have to fess up to the fact that you actually did get hand-to-hand training like the rest of us," she teased.

"But it's messy, I like shooting much better. See you at dinner?"

Karen started throwing punches again, "Yes indeed, say around 1930."

"Good enough. Have fun, don't hurt anyone."

Karen laughed and I slipped out the back.

Standing in the lift, I tapped my foot on the deck and leaned against the wall. Waiting during travel was a royal pain. No offense to His Majesty intended.

We'd be at Theta soon, but in the meantime we were just going to have meaningless days like this... and for all my years in the service, I never (not even to this day — as I'm writing) got used to the waiting. Never...

Then Karen's smile flashed through my mind. She did have great fighting technique.

So I suppose in some shallow ways these weren't wholly meaningless days.

But I don't think like that.

Wolf flew on through space, two days from Asteroid Theta.

CHAPTER NINE

EARTH POLITICS

Slipping out of *Wolf* again, let me just explain what was happening back at Earth...

Admiral Greg Noyce was sitting in the briefing room aboard the fleet flagship *Ark Royal*, waiting for a meeting with some of the other Defense Command Admirals. He had arrived early because his own flagship, the battleship *Warspite*, was just a few hundred kilometers from *Ark Royal*.

Waiting didn't really much bother Greg Noyce, he was a renowned Naval officer, and one of his great qualities — one that I didn't possess in such quantities as he did — was patience. Case in point was his victory at the Battle of Deep Black. He'd chased those pirates relentlessly, and his unwavering determination had let him catch them at their rendezvous.

But I'm not going to spoil that story. If I play my cards right, I'll be writing about it some day...

So back to Greg, sitting on *Ark Royal;* he was scrolling through a number of reports on his pad as he waited. He commanded one of the two divisions of the Home Fleet now, and he was just getting oriented. A combined force of seven battleships, three frigates and two corvettes was a bit of a step up from the old Belt Squadron, and he was still deciding how he wanted to handle the force.

Just for the record, his was the 'Heavy' Squadron of the Home Fleet — its battleships were powerful but slow, its frigates (under Commodore Rachel Hunter) were top notch, and its corvettes were brand new. Ultimately, then, it was a great defensive unit, but in formation it'd take twenty percent longer than, say, *Wolf*, to reach the Belt Station.

By comparison, the other 'Light' Squadron — with its supercarrier and three carriers, two battlecruisers, four frigates and six corvettes — could move just as fast as *Wolf*, but lacked the power and protection to survive a firefight. That was what the Heavy Squadron was designed for.

You might ask yourself why the Home Fleet was so disposed; in retrospect it looks almost like a careless disposition of ships, and not a very logical one. What was basically happening, though, was a doctrine fight in the Admiralty — some wanted to go light and fast with carriers and battlecruisers (battlecruisers were battleships minus most of their armor plating, decreasing their mass, and making them faster and more brittle) while others, like Greg and First Lord Fiora, were in favor of building a new generation of battleships.

The argument of the carrier crowd, headed up by Second Lord Dave Caldecott (and his Caldecott Circle) was basically that the faster and lighter armed ships were better for finding the pirates. Admiral Noyce, First Lord Fiora, Rear Admiral Stoll, myself, and a few others liked to point out that finding the pirates was only half the battle — or more precisely, it wasn't even the battle. And carriers and battlecruisers, while they looked great in the theory, just weren't up to slugging matches with some of the brutes the Syndicate had hit us with out on the frontier.

We wanted armor and lots of guns for insurance, and often we got labeled as backward and paranoid for that.

Anyway. How did I get sidetracked... Right, Admiral Noyce was waiting for a meeting. Wow, I should be the poster-man for going off on tangents. Not that I can imagine anyone needing a poster for tangents...

First Lord John Fiora was the next to enter the room, and Greg stood as he entered, nodding to the nominal head of the Defense Command Navy. John Fiora was an easygoing man of Italian background, with a trademark mustache that set him apart from most of the fleet. He shook Greg's hand now and waved him back into a chair before sitting as well.

"Marlene's supposed to be coming too — last meeting before she boosts for Venus again," John said as he seated himself, and Greg nodded.

"It'll be good to see her off," he turned his chair towards the First Lord. "So, why are we meeting here — aboard *Ark Royal?*"

John smiled, "Optics. It'd look too much like a conspiracy if I went up to your ship and brought Marlene over. Technically as First Lord I have to conduct all meetings from the fleet flagship or from Admiralty House, unless I'm on tour."

Greg frowned, "You sound as though someone's keeping tabs on you."

"Someone may well be. I don't want to get into it too much before Marlene gets here, but I'm hearing rumblings about something that's starting to build in the Admiralty. Dave Caldecott's getting his ducks in a row to go to the Emperor..."

That was the moment when the hatch again swung open, and John's words stopped instantly. Wouldn't be a good thing to have this sort of talk observed. But it was Rear Admiral Marlene Stoll, of the Venus Station, another of the trusted officers.

I should be clear about why these were the trustworthy officers — they were the very top ranking members of the so called 'Fiora ring', officers with a background in serving on the frontier stations. John Fiora had been Admiral Noyce's commanding officer at the Belt Station many years prior, and they'd stayed on good terms. Rear Admiral Stoll had served most of her time from Commander through flag rank at Venus. They all knew the trials and tribulations of being defenders of the distant but critical reaches of the Empire, and they knew that the fancy textbook ideas and the complicated technology to be found on the drawing boards at Fleet R&D weren't always what was needed for fighting pirates.

It probably goes without saying that I was aligned with this group.

Opposing them — and by extension *us* on the Belt Station — was Caldecott's group of officers, the self-dubbed 'Home School' of doctrine (known to us as the 'Caldecott Circle'). They were convinced we were a bunch of frontier warmongering media darlings with no idea of the real finesse that it took to build a fleet. They also felt we were backward and stupid.

The fact that John Fiora was the First Lord of the Admiralty was good for us — it gave us a lot of operational leverage, and shielded Karen and me from too much trouble because of our antics. But Caldecott was still Second Lord of the Admiralty, and he was a trusted friend of the Emperor. Worse, his cronies controlled the Navy Board, meaning they had the ability to give priority to construction projects.

That was why the new flagship was a supercarrier, not a new model, fast battleship, as John had wanted. We had a pretty good grip on the Imperial Senate and the Imperial Commons thanks to the high public profile of the members of our ring, and that meant we got the funding we wanted. Caldecott just had the ability to drag his feet and slow our building.

Overall it was a bit of an organizational mess.

Our latest victory had been the 'repurposing' of the four other supercarriers of *Ark Royal's* class that had just recently started construction under Caldecott's influence; DCNS *Bonaventure*, originally slated as a carrier like *Ark Royal*, was going to be completed as a fast and rather powerful battleship. Dave wasn't so happy about that, but we were.

As Marlene took a seat at the table, nodding to Greg and John in turn, John continued, "Like I was telling Greg, Marlene, Dave Caldecott is getting ready to go to the Emperor with a list of complaints about us."

"What grounds could he have to make a complaint?" Greg frowned. "Surely our record speaks for itself."

John leaned back in his chair and held his hands up before him, "What do you think would give him ammunition in trying to convince the Emperor that we're irresponsible?"

Marlene and Greg looked at each other immediately, then back to John. Marlene said it first, "Ken?"

John pointed to Stoll and nodded, "Bingo. The media loves him, but you know the Emperor, he has a twisted sense of what a Naval officer is supposed to be, and 'on camera' isn't in the definition."

Marlene leaned forward, "He also doesn't seem to think you have to be very good at much."

John laughed and Greg nodded, "He certainly doesn't seem to have a concept of what gets the job done out there. But what is Caldecott expecting to get out of this? The Senate reviews our budget, and you still report to the Prime Minister..."

"He can call an Imperial Commission, can't he?" Marlene glanced from John to Greg, and both paused before nodding almost simultaneously.

They didn't need to explain to each other what the significance of an Imperial Commission would be, but for you readers (who hopefully haven't dealt with one because we had them removed from the constitution) essentially it meant the Emperor could put Caldecott or a chosen crony in charge of an inquiry that would investigate some trumped-up problem. Maybe 'waste of frontier defense resources'. And with the authority of that inquiry, Caldecott could suspend officers, including John, to isolate them for months of testimony. In the meantime the Second Lord could put his own people in our places, essentially taking over.

So my antics were causing problems. I didn't know it yet, of course.

"What do we do?" Marlene leaned back.

Greg nodded at the question and both looked to John, who shrugged slowly, "I've warned the PM, but I don't know if he can convince the Emperor not to do this. There's no threat to Imperial security now that you've finished the Syndicate, Greg. And this report that Ken just sent about Cooper and Yat Sen isn't enough — it'll look like we're trying to make up threats to delay an audit. For now we just need to keep doing our jobs. I'll see what I can dig up as leverage."

Marlene and Greg exchanged slightly strained glances, and John nodded, "I'll keep you apprised. But I just wanted to tell you in person."

Everyone in the room sighed again. Politics was usually just plain bad... unfortunately it was a fact of life, even in Defense Command.

So that was what was going on at Earth. Now let's get back to me. Because my ego is feeling left out. And yes, to answer my editor, egos can feel left out.

CHAPTER TEN
STILL WAITING

One thing I think a lot of people overlook when they're reading about duty in space, and definitely when they see movies about it, is the waiting. A three-day trip to Asteroid Theta, for instance, can go very slowly. It's *three whole days* of travel, all the time wondering if you're chasing wild space geese (a particularly vicious creature, the space goose), and trying to figure out what you'll do if you actually find what you're looking for.

Of course you don't let on that you're wondering any of these things while you make the voyage — as a Captain or a Commodore, you're supposed to have those answers at your fingertips, so if you don't actually have them, you'd better make it look as though you do.

Well, in most company... but then I don't keep most company.

Karen was lying on her stomach on my bed, picking at her dinner. This was the second day of the trip, so we'd arrive at the rendezvous with *Lion* and *Honesty* tomorrow, if all went to plan. For now we were both anxious.

With her legs bent at the knees and swinging behind her, Karen looked like a teen girl chatting with a girlfriend about trivial things.

Actually, following that analogy, I'd be her *girlfriend*, so let's skip that one. Anyway, she was staring at her plate, stabbing at the thawed fish sticks, rice and macaroni, not really that hungry by the look of it.

"You know, you might have more of an appetite if you weren't lying on your stomach," I was shoveling food off my plate from my usual spot in the chair next to my bed, and Karen rolled her head and looked at me.

"You just don't like having my crumbs on your comforter."

I shrugged, "Yeah, maybe."

Two days of waiting had that sort of draining effect on our banter — it couldn't go full bore at all times, despite how much we tried. Karen rolled onto her side to face me, propping her head up on her left arm.

"Wondering what we're going to find?" I kept shoveling food and Karen nodded.

"Exactly. You know I've never liked being in the dark. This could be a trap... could be an embarrassment..."

I nodded slowly, finally laying my fork down for a moment and letting my head fall back against the chair, "Or it could be what it always seems to be: something important and just the right size for us to handle."

Karen smiled thinly, "You want to bet on that?"

I matched her smile and shook my head before looking down at my plate again, "Not a chance. Does feel a bit strange though... you not being on *Lion*, I mean. Nothing against Kris at all, I just feel like I can't get us into as much trouble now without you out there to bail me out."

Karen's smile twitched and got a little bit wider, but almost a little sadder at the same time, "Don't worry. I'm right here to look after you — faster response time and all that."

I kept looking at my plate. It wasn't that simple and we both knew it.

"Well, you know. I just don't want to be as cavalier... not when we could both pay for it."

That meant rather a lot, now that I think on it.

Karen looked back at her plate too, "Yeah, I know. Don't worry about it though, we'll be fine."

Simple words that were comforting enough, and I nodded. It wasn't like Karen and I hadn't done our share of storming pirate houses before she'd come aboard my ship. Ship fighting would just be a slightly different dynamic.

And for the tradeoff — for dining with her every night, and seeing her every day — it was worthwhile. Granted, people like Charlie were getting less of my time because I was spending it with Karen, but they all seemed happy enough.

Besides, I was a bad influence on them. Perhaps they could de-corrupt themselves while Karen monitored my insanity.

"You'd still better eat," I looked up after a moment's pause, retaking my own fork and stabbing some of the thawed food.

"Don't know, have to watch my figure," Karen rolled back down onto her stomach and I chuckled.

"If you like I can do that for you," I grinned. "And it's doing fine."

"Mmmhmm," Karen rolled her eyes, picked up her fork and started poking at her food again. "So, think Rear Admiral Castillo's still running the Martian station?"

My grin slipped to a smile at the change of topic and I shrugged, "You know, she might be. If the Martians have much of a force out here, she'd definitely be the one running it. But I have to say, I'm hoping we don't run into that delightful woman. I'd settle for one of their destroyers and Cooper and Yat Sen. And then we could go in shooting."

"Admiral Noyce mightn't approve of that approach," Karen finally started chewing some food. "A little tact maybe?"

"You know me, I've got all the tact in the world... when I want it..."

Karen laughed, and we finished our dinners.

Chapter Eleven

Rendezvous

Wolf began deceleration procedures the following morning, slowing from the cruising speed of 140 kps that had been selected by Erica Martin in order to get us to the rendezvous just as *Lion* and *Honesty* arrived from their more distant destination.

At around 1700, we finally came to a stop at the rendezvous point, and sure enough, Kris Jacobs had brought her frigate and its consort to just that spot so that we arrived almost simultaneously.

Standing on the bridge of *Wolf*, I watched the icons of the two ships close range with us — it'd take about two more minutes for them to reach realtime communication range, and then we could start the planning for our entrance into Asteroid Theta orbit.

"Feel nice to see your old ship?" Matt Baxter was standing behind Karen's chair at his Operations post, and she nodded once.

"Certainly doesn't hurt. Wonder if Kris changed the carpet in my day cabin yet... you know how she hates reds and all," Karen glanced at Matt, and the black Briton smiled.

"Indeed she does. I'm sure by now the job's done."

I grinned, turning from the screen, "If she's been as bored as we've been, she probably helped install it herself."

That was an idea I seriously remember entertaining for a while — I could redecorate parts of the ship if I got bored. Maybe my cabin could use a makeover. Some new... um... vases. And a potted plant. Made of plastic! Yes, ideas like this actually occurred to me in the bright and airy days just before the troubles began.

"Realtime comm range in a minute now, sir. I'm aligning the dish and looping the grid," Jim Hannigan made his report from behind the bank of Sensors and Communications consoles he oversaw, and I nodded.

"Good, when you can get Kris and Commander Gunney put them on the screens," I linked my hands behind my back and looked to the forward bank of vidscreens as I spoke.

Hannigan didn't need to reply — he'd been with me since the *Friendly* days, it was just assumed that we were on the same wavelength.

Proof of that fact came a moment later as Captain Kristen Jacobs and Commander Mark Gunney appeared on screens two and three, both in realtime as communications lasers carried our vid links back and forth between ships. There'd be a short lag due to the distance, but it was small enough to still earn the 'realtime' label.

"Kris, Mark, thanks for coming," I smiled, and Kris grinned.

"Thanks for having us," Gunney quipped back instantly. This was before his particular style was well known to the whole fleet, but we in the Belt Squadron were already used to it.

"Wouldn't miss it," Kris added with a nod, and then her eyes darted from me to

Karen. "You taking good care of *Wolf*?"

"Just as good as your care for *Lion*," Karen got to her feet with a smile. "What color did you go with for the day cabin?"

"Teal," Kris shrugged. "I helped install it yesterday."

"Told you," I leaned towards Karen and pretended to whisper the words, and the four of us shared a chuckle.

"Anyway, we better figure out just what we're doing," I sobered a little and paid more attention to the screen. "You've both read the briefing notes I sent with that message?"

Kris and Mark nodded simultaneously, and I replied with a nod of my own, "Excellent. So basically we don't know what we're going to run into, and there's a good chance shooting could result. Thoughts?"

"Well as much as I'd like to kick down the door and walk in as if I own the place… might be a good idea to keep something in reserve," Mark Gunney's suggestion was sharp and appropriate, and I nodded.

"Sounds like something I'd say, though I'm dumb enough to think I'd own the place," I smiled. "But I'm definitely in favor of the reserve idea. Kris, I think that means keeping *Lion* back. Chances are they'd expect a drop-in from a frigate and escort but not from two frigates. That's upping the ante a bit."

Karen glanced at me, "Yeah, but we operated frigates in pairs a *lot* when I was in *Lion*, remember. They might be expecting us to keep a frigate out of sight, and have a plan for that."

Hmm, good point. Sending one frigate in to sniff around and then letting the other ride to the rescue was a tactic Karen and I had effectively used a number of times. If Cooper and Yat Sen were setting up a new Syndicate, chances were they'd be waiting for such a move.

They were dumb, but probably not dumb enough to be fooled by the same trick *again*.

"Well," I nodded slowly, "let's change it up then. Mark, you and *Honesty* will be the reserve, and if you can puff up your drive signature to look like *Alberta* or even *Cheetah* that'd probably be a good thing. Kris, you and *Lion* will come in with us."

Both commanding officers nodded again, though my eyes were drifting now to one of the other screens in the wall. The latest scan of Asteroid Theta was being displayed on it — one provided by a merchant we'd paid to keep tabs on the Martian dispositions. It was about two months old, but compared to some of our charts, that was rather current.

"If you two can both have a look at the system map, let's pick some vectors. Kris, what do you think for the approach?" my eyes darted back and forth between their faces and that map, and Kris and Commander Gunney's eyes did the same on their own sides of the link.

"Hmm… maybe straight in on the usual vector from the Belt colonies — use the regular cargo lanes. Nothing like running past a bunch of local ore haulers to make your entrance noisy," Kris' accented words brought a grand assessment of the situation.

Karen grinned next to me, "I think I must have left notes in my office or something — those would be pretty much my exact words."

Kris' smile broadened but I frowned and shook my head, "Careful there Kris, you're getting to be like *her*. Bad business."

Karen rolled her eyes and Kris chuckled.

"My present rank doesn't permit me to express how good I think that'd be," Mark Gunney grinned.

With another laugh we got ourselves back on topic.

"Alright, I agree on that vector," I pressed on. "Two shiny big frigates running down on the Asteroid from the usual shipping lanes… that'll wake them up. Mark, you need to tuck in somewhere and not be seen. Any preferences as to where?"

The Commander glanced narrowly off screen and nodded, "Yes, we can come in from the reverse side and stay out beyond that large rock cluster. We can disappear back there."

My eyes drifted over the map and I found the clump of mini-asteroids drifting beyond the gravity well of Theta; a perfect hiding spot indeed.

"Sounds good. You boost for that location now, be there for a comm burst check in… say… six hours?"

Gunney nodded, "Yessir, you have a nice flight now, boss."

"Excellent," I grinned. "Kris, I guess that means we move in… three hours. That'll get us all into the system at the same time."

Kris nodded, "You bet. So what's the plan when we're in there?"

"Rules of engagement are polite for now. Martians get the usual courtesies, we decide what to do about any pirates we find when we get there. Don't just start shooting, but keep your mags ready to respond if anything comes flying at us."

My words drew still more nods. We couldn't go in with guns blazing on a hunch, and even if we were right, deciding whether or not to deal with pirates the old-fashioned way would be tricky until we could weigh the importance of any pirates we found against the possible offense to the Martians and a whole bunch of other things.

"Alright, we good for now?" I looked between my ship commanders, and both nodded in turn. "Great. Keep in comm contact, text only is fine. Let's move."

"See you in six," Gunney immediately vanished from the screen.

"This should be fun," Kris smiled and disappeared as well.

Taking a deep and well-satisfied breath, I glanced at Karen. She was still smiling, and as she glanced at me her eyebrows bobbed up and down.

The wait was almost over — more irresponsible activities were soon to follow.

And we thought of that as a relief. Because we didn't know any better at that moment.

CHAPTER TWELVE

TO BULLY A MARTIAN

Wolf and *Lion* bore down on Asteroid Theta, moving at over 180 kps through the major space lanes that led from deeper space to the orbit of the inhabited rock. Two frigates cruising side by side was nothing to shake a stick at, that was for sure — entire pirate squadrons had been wrecked by frigate pairs.

We were about to cause quite a stir.

"Closing range now, sir. We're getting sensor readings for the rock..." Hannigan was taking his time as he usually did, pacing from console to console and overseeing the work of his team of sensor technicians. "First scan going up on the screen... *now.*"

Karen and I stood side by side and stared at the display as it shifted from the space surrounding *Wolf* and *Lion* to the space that lay before us, then to the orbit of the asteroid.

There were three large ships in close proximity; two Martian trader ships and a Martian 'destroyer escort' (the Martian designation for what we like to call a corvette).

Not all that much in the system, then, it seemed — two slow-moving luggers and a single DE (shorthand for destroyer escort) weren't a very formidable lineup, though perhaps they were all this relatively out-of-the-way post warranted.

"Focus scans on low orbit, just in case they dropped any pirates low to hide them," I glanced at Hannigan, and he nodded.

The scans pressed out a little farther towards the craters and caverns of the asteroid, but no new icons appeared on the screen.

Hmm, so far nothing obvious. I glanced at Karen, "Got a feeling about this one?"

She frowned as she toyed with the end of her ponytail, "I'm not sure. It doesn't feel right. It's too... spartan around here. Only two luggers? It's as though the traders are avoiding this place or something."

I nodded. Theta was an out-of-the-way backwater... which meant the cheapest and seediest traders should be here in larger numbers. It could just be bad timing for us... or it could be something more.

"Let's get closer then. Jim, as soon as that DE hails, get whoever's aboard up on screen. Maybe I can bully him into answering some questions," I crossed my arms.

Karen chuckled, "Since when have you bullied anything?"

I let my head tip sideways and shot her an unimpressed glance, but she was already looking towards Lieutenant Commander Martin, "Erica, let's keep this velocity until the last possible minute. I want us running down on them at full speed. Might shake them up."

I nodded in agreement — no destroyer escort in the solar system would be glad to be alone while dealing with two *Predator*-class frigates. A fast arrival would just give the crews less time to steel up for the fight.

"They've got a relay drone out here, sir. We can do realtime comms in about a minute," Hannigan reported as Karen finished her orders.

"Good, hopefully we'll get to talk to someone sooner rather than later. Anything in low orbit yet?"

Shaking his head, Hannigan went back to making his rounds and I glanced again at Karen, "Wild space geese?"

Her eyes narrowed slightly and her head shook ever so slightly from side to side, "No, there *are* pirates around here..."

Karen tended to have a good instinct for knowing when the troublemakers were around. I probably did too, I just didn't bother to isolate it from the rest of my brain, so I couldn't be certain precisely which part of my psyche was telling me that trouble was coming.

But it sure was coming.

"The destroyer escort just fired its drives... and again... sustaining them I think. It's heading this way at about 40 kps. Accelerating slowly."

Hannigan's smooth narrative was matched by the movement of the icon on the main screen, and I let my head tip sideways. That ship didn't want us close to the two transports in orbit. Otherwise it'd never be foolish enough to leave the support of Theta's shore-based weapons to go out and meet two frigates.

"Any signal yet?" Karen glanced back at Hannigan and he shook his head.

"Nothing... hang on..."

Hannigan paused at one of the sensor panels, then reached down over the shoulder of the tech sitting there and tapped a couple of codes into the computer. His eyes then narrowed and he looked up at Karen and me, "They've started sending power in large amounts to their forward turrets. I think they're getting ready to bluff the hard way."

Bluff indeed — there was no way a single Martian DE was going to pick a fight with us...

"Let's get ready to receive in case he is in fact an idiot," I said evenly, and Karen nodded, turning instantly to Matt.

"Battle stations. Bring up all mags and get the laser grid ready," Karen stepped back to her chair and sat quickly. It was her job to make sure *Wolf* was ready to fight, it was my job to make sure *Wolf* and *Lion* fought together.

Not something I was used to, I must admit — I had done both jobs at once as a Captain, but then it was more a teamwork exercise. Now as a Commodore I wasn't supposed to worry at all about the particulars of commanding one ship in action. *Wolf* was entirely Karen's job...

This would be a good practice on restraint for me then — no giving orders about weapons and things, not on a one-ship scale anyway.

"Establish a Battlelink with *Lion* please, Jim," I turned to Hannigan. "Put it on screen two."

The Lieutenant Commander nodded, and in short order screen two — one of the smaller vidscreens in the wall next to the main screen — switched from a ship battle schematic to a *WolfNet* screen with the word 'Connecting' flashing across it.

A few seconds later *Lion*'s bridge appeared on the monitor, with the picture centering on Kris Jacobs.

"Looks like we've got a cheeky one, Kris," I nodded to her, and she smiled.

"Yes, we do. We're at battle stations with all weapons charging. Orders?"

"Stay on our starboard beam. Both ships to hold laser fire until I give the order — I don't want us starting an Imperial incident here. Mags only, I want his engines and weapons down at most."

Kris nodded, and as I turned back to Karen she smiled at me, "What, you think I didn't know that already?"

With a smile and a shrug I turned back to the main screen — the Battlelink would remain up but Kris and I wouldn't be talking constantly. It was just there to make sure my orders were clearly transmitted to her when they came.

We were well within realtime comm range of the destroyer escort... was it seriously going to try to stop us?

"They're spinning forward turrets — clearing them to fire," Hannigan leaned over the shoulder of one of his sensor techs as he gave the report. "No targeting sweeps yet."

"He's dead if he tries to fight us. You think he's just posturing?" Kris asked over the Battlelink, and I cocked an eyebrow and half-shrugged.

"No telling. Weapons range?"

Hannigan looked to a different console and took a quiet report from one of his techs, "That'd be... six minutes to main lasers, another thirty seconds after that to mags. His turrets will be in range after that by about a minute."

No way this ship could be fool enough to try to fight with those stats in mind — the bigger weapons on *Wolf* and *Lion* had superior range to the destroyer escort's turreted lasers and mags. He'd be torn to shreds before he even got close enough to scorch our plating.

But the Martians might've been overconfident. We'd heard their boasts many times — how their turret-mounted weapons were much better than our casemate emplacements. The thing they didn't like to admit was that their weapons were lighter because their power systems were cruder, and that the only way they could cover most of their hull was to turret those mags in slick ball turrets.

Sure they were fast-tracking, but a Martian destroyer escort had only a third of the mags of a Defense Command corvette, and only two smaller ports for its laser array.

Not a match for *Wolf* or *Lion* or even *Honesty*.

And yet this fellow came charging with all the insane speed he could squeeze out of his engines...

"Aha... signal now, sir. Realtime vid!" Hannigan was virtually running around behind the banks of consoles he supervised. Hopefully he was wearing comfortable shoes.

"Screen four, please," I folded my arms and turned to glare at the screen displaying Kris and the bridge of *Lion*.

Screen four then went to a *Wolf*Net screen with the 'Connecting' text flashing on it, and finally the face of a Martian Commander appeared. The man was skinny and pale, typical of the Martian stereotype, and his puffy red tunic collar seemed to double the width of his neck. He looked rather like a jug-headed imbecile...

Well, to be fair, I don't know what qualifies one as looking like an *imbecile*... this guy just *did*. Actually, his face was vaguely familiar to me. Maybe I'd had to deal with him before some time.

"You are trespassing in Martian space! Turn around now or we will open fire!"

The kid was *cheeky* indeed. I'd thought only pirates were fool enough to be so brash under such threat, but here I was being proven wrong.

"Commander, pleasure to see you again," I smiled. I was sure I'd seen him somewhere, so now I just had to gamble that I had. The look of shock that slipped unabated onto his face suggested to me that I might have hit a nerve. Didn't matter why, his discomfort was all I wanted now. "Be so good as to disarm your weapons and stand off for parlay, or I'm afraid I'll be obliged to destroy your ship."

He swallowed but tried to hide his nervousness — he was holding a bad hand, and I was coming at him with aces and eights. Er. Bad poker analogy. Ignore it.

Wolf and *Lion* were bearing down on him, and his little destroyer escort wasn't going to be much of a deterrent.

"I will *not* allow you to trample the–"

I held up my hands, "Oh come now, Commander, we're not here to trample anything. Well, anything aside from your illegal arms sales to Cooper and Yat Sen. We may have to put a stop to those, I'm afraid."

His eyes widened further.

I had to be careful now. I couldn't tip my hand too far to reveal how little I actually knew. I'd done that on past occasions, and it wasn't good.

"Uh… what do you mean… how dare you… you have no proof…"

My eyes shifted from screen four to screen two, where Kris was biting down against a laugh. I glanced back at Karen and she smacked herself in the forehead with the palm of her hand for dramatic effect.

"You realize you just as much as confirmed my intel on the pirates and your dealings with them, right Commander?" I turned back to the screen, and the gaunt, pale man turned even whiter. "Here's a tip, practice your lying and your bluffing before you start trying to toy with Imperial interests."

He started to turn red at that comment — his face flooding with blood and starting to match his uniform. I let my grin grow into a smile.

"So, you want to point me to the pirates or are you going to make me turn this system upside down until I find them?"

To his credit, or maybe discredit, the poor Commander tried to bristle against my words, "You have no claims to this sector of space!"

I let my smile fade and tilted my head, "And last time I checked it was in violation of the Venusian Accord for either your Imperium or my Empire to trade with known pirates. Which means I'm treaty-bound to clear all systems under both Martian and Earth control of pirate influences."

"That's fast and loose with the rules, Commodore!" the Commander objected.

"Yeah, that'd be my style. I suggest you help instead of hinder, Commander. Would you be so good as to reverse course and deactivate your weapons?" I wasn't asking for a surrender, just cooperation, which admittedly might get the poor fellow shot for treason if he was made an example of by Martian authorities.

But I honestly couldn't worry about his career until Yat Sen and Cooper were dealt with. After a red-faced huff, the Commander killed the link.

"Weapons powering down and they're reversing drives," Hannigan reported almost immediately.

Alright, that was good.

"So," I turned and looked to Karen, then glanced back up at Kris on screen two, "I guess we just need to find our pirates before they sneak away."

"I'll get my crystal ball," Karen piped up with a smile.

"I'll take some lotto numbers too," I chuckled, but my mind had already drifted out of the discussion as my eyes searched the map screens.

They were close. I could tell...

CHAPTER THIRTEEN

THERE BE PIRATES IN THEM THERE ROCKS

While *Wolf* and *Lion* were scaring the destroyer escort back into orbit around Asteroid Theta, Commander Mark Gunney's corvette *Honesty* was approaching the Martian colony from the opposite direction. Creeping in under silent routine, the ship was virtually emission free, so unless somebody pinged it with active sensors it'd go unnoticed until it wanted to make itself known.

That was Commander Gunney's plan. He'd been with his ship for ten months by this time, and even in that short-seeming span, he had done his share of sneaking up on foes. That was one of the key reasons he was on the rise — in less than a year he'd taken three pirate raiders in short firefights, not a bad tally at all.

And as you might expect, he was itching to teach the Martians about his reputation.

"Time to our covering rocks?" Gunney was standing with his hands linked behind his back, watching the main screen as his own passive sensors took in the minor spectacle of two frigates bearing down on that little Martian DE.

He certainly wouldn't have wanted to be in the destroyer escort's place... but then he didn't have to worry, he'd joined the right navy.

"We're coming into realtime of the rocks now, skipper."

Gunney nodded and glanced at the Ensign commanding the Sensors and Communications section, "Good. Getting anything on the passive sweeps?"

The Ensign looked between screens in front of him and quickly consulted one of his techs, "Nothing that's registering, sir, but we're getting increased radiation reading from the area. Can't pin down where it's coming from without a lidar ping."

Increased radiation? Well that could be nothing at all — one of the rocks could be made of uranium. But it could also be a sign that heavy weapons in unshielded containers were out here. Pirates tended to play fast and loose with transport rules for such weapons.

So it could be nothing or it could be something, and the only way to find out would be to flash the active sensors online and reveal *Honesty's* position.

"Slow us down, helm. Let's spend a little more time checking our passive readings."

No point rushing to cover — *Wolf* and *Lion* had things well in hand.

"I wonder how much latitude we get before he comes back and threatens us again," Karen was standing next to me with her arms folded, her right hand toying with the end of her ponytail again as she examined the vidscreens.

I nodded in reply to her comment, "I don't want to press too hard if we can help it. Last thing we need is to start a war with the Martians when the pirates are organizing again..."

It's actually funny when I look back on it: I was at that very moment worrying that we'd accidentally begin a war with pirates and Martians in an alliance. Oh the painful irony.

"Well I for one want to see what's in those transports," Kris chimed in over the Battlelink. "If they're storing weapons, we'll know the pirates have to be near."

"Mmm, good point. Alright, take *Lion* in for a closer look. We'll hang back here and keep an eye out for any impromptu guests. Jim, anything from *Honesty* yet?"

Hannigan was already at the sensor controls as I asked the question, so he quickly checked the scan boards, "Nothing active out there. I could fire a ping that way to see if Commander Gunney's in behind the rocks by now. It'd probably look like we were just checking the area for pirates."

With an approving smile I nodded, "Sounds good. Get a ping ready."

"Erica," Karen turned to the helm and navigation consoles, "turn us around and head towards those rocks at 40 kps. But keep the maneuver engines spun up, in case *Lion* finds trouble."

Lieutenant Commander Martin replied with a nod and began directing her pilots and navigator. *Wolf* yawed to starboard and then the engines fired, pushing the frigate off its previous course and driving it towards the cluster of floating rocks.

"Sir, *Wolf* just changed course. It's heading this way."

Commander Gunney frowned, "Have they seen something we haven't?"

The Ensign at sensors shook her head, "I don't see how, sir, their passive sensors aren't much better than ours, and they're much farther out..."

A loud ping erupted from one of her panels — the computer inserted the sound as soon as the passive sensors were subject to an active sensor lidar burst. Only *Wolf* could see the actual results of the scan, but the crew of *Honesty* now knew they were being observed.

The Ensign at sensors rushed to the blaring panel and ordered the tech there to redirect passive receivers to listen to the area behind the rocks.

Commander Gunney suddenly got the feeling that something very unpleasant was up.

"Lieutenant Commander Ashby, let's go to battle stations."

"Kris, forget the transports," I was barely able to pry my eyes from the new icons on screen one to Kris aboard *Lion* on screen two. We were just on the edge of realtime range so there was a lag, but I could see Kris' eyes darting to her main screen as the results of our sensor ping reached her.

Suddenly, transports weren't seeming so important.

"Confirmed sir, that's definitely three purpose-built raiders and a converted liner. They were masking their emissions behind the rocks."

I wasn't honestly surprised — hiding behind rocks is a tactic everybody uses to this day, and has been using since space fighting became possible. Remember, it was the very tactic we'd sent Mark out there to use in the first place.

"That's *Honesty* creeping up behind them," Karen pointed at the DCN icon behind the four pirates.

"We better get up there fast. If he has to face all four on his own I don't like his chances... Kris, battle speed..." I didn't look away from screen one that time, but out of the corner of my eye I saw *Lion's* Captain nod.

On the main display, *Lion* abruptly reversed course, then kicked its drives in at full velocity.

"Everything you've got, Erica," Karen glanced quickly at her Helm Master, and the junior woman nodded at her Captain's order.

Wolf kicked forward, climbing from 40 kps to 180 kps in less than a minute.

"They're powering drives, looks like they're getting ready to scatter!"

Mark Gunney smiled and folded his arms, "You mean they're going to try. I like delivering rude surprises, and this seems like a perfect time for one. Jenny, try to track down which one's their flagship. Look for heavy traffic."

As the Ensign at Sensors and Communications began to work on that problem, Lieutenant Commander Ashby stepped up to his Commander's side, "We're ready for action, sir. Forward laser and mags are almost locked on the leading target."

"*Wolf* will be in range in less than a minute, sir — they're making good speed. *Lion's* right with *Wolf* now, too. Second pirate in line looks like the ringleader."

Gunney didn't even look at his Ensign as she offered the report, instead looking from Ashby to the screen and back, "Alright, so we're trying to pick up the second raider. Retrack firing solutions and go after his engine pods. Let's break some legs."

"Yes, sir," Ashby trotted back to the techs at the tactical consoles.

"They've definitely seen us now, sir. Lead ship is running targeting sweeps, looks like energy guns."

Typical. Pirates were always awfully fond of energy guns, usually because the things were easy to build and maintain, weren't as power-consuming as lasers, and were quite destructive to unarmored hull. Think 'buckshot'. Not precise or good at long range, but plenty destructive to someone without protection.

Now, *Honesty* had a layer of armor on its outer hull, but corvette armor was admittedly slim. Enough energy gun concentration could crack even the thickest armor, and with that many pirates loaded for bear, *Honesty's* armor wasn't going to be enough.

But it wasn't just armor that was protecting the corvette: Mark Gunney's weapons were coming online too.

Mags and lasers were the main weapons of every Defense Command ship. Torpedoes existed, sure, but they were big and relatively slow, so much so that *Honesty* didn't even have tubes fitted, and *Wolf* and *Lion* only had two each.

As opposed to energy guns, mags were like space scalpels; long-ranged, focused and fast-firing, they were best employed in overriding an enemy's power systems. The lasers were, of course, the ship-killers, but they were extremely demanding on power plants of ships in which they were fitted. Neither weapon was easy to maintain, but both were much better than the energy guns the pirates were coming forward with.

"Hang on, skipper. I think two of those raiders are armed with Martian EM cannons..." the Ensign in charge of sensors was hurriedly reading the energy signatures on her receivers. Martian weapons drew power at a level greater than anything you'd see from an energy gun, so Mark rightly concluded these pirates had indeed been armed by the Imperium.

"Send to *Wolf*, Martian mags on some pirate ships. Second in line is assumed to be flagship."

The signal was sent by comm laser through the outgoing signal array, and then Commander Gunney turned to his XO, "Targeting solution?"

Ashby nodded in reply, "Forward laser and mags are tracking solid."

Gunney tipped his head sideways, "Fireworks time. Let 'em have it."

Screen three on *Wolf*'s bridge switched to a vid scan taken by one of the ship's telescopic cameras. The enhanced image was rather impressive; *Honesty*'s six forward-mounted mags began firing their long white-blue lances of EM energy, setting a scene like old machine gun fire with tracers.

The target was not there for the camera to see — no lens was wide enough at this magnification to catch both ships — but I could see it in my mind's eye (lucky for you, eh?). The second raider in line fired its port thrusters and began to push itself out of the way, but with computer assistance the casemated mags from *Honesty* tracked the ship.

Half or more of the bolts pounded into the alloy of the raider's hull, their extreme heat scorching the already blackened plating and sending dangerous power surges through its crude grid.

"We're in range in ten seconds," Matt reported, pacing between the tactical consoles behind Karen's and his chairs. "I've targeted the third in line."

"We have number four looked after," Kris added quickly over the Battlelink.

I nodded, "Good work. Let's not let them get out of here. Jim, add Commander Gunney to the Battlelink as soon as we're in realtime range.

"Mag range... now..." Matt looked up, and Karen turned to him with a cool gaze and a smile.

"Say hello for me, will you Matt?" her tone was so sweet.

The Brit smiled, and then nodded to the Ensign at fire control, "Shoot."

Wolf's forward mags erupted instantly, fast-firing and raining electric energy down on the third ship in line as it tried to build up speed to escape the rock's shadow. The pirate was too slow — or, I suppose, *Wolf* was much too fast, already having worked up to maximum speed on the approach.

"Enemy fire!" Hannigan barked, but there was no trademark shudder through *Wolf*'s deck. We weren't the target.

Screen three showed *Honesty* receiving two yellow streams of mag bolts, courtesy of Martian EM cannons (the Imperium's fancy name for mags) mounted on the first raider in line. The energy bolts collided with the corvette's upper engine pylon in a blinding flash and did some scorching, but the crystalline armor that clad the ship refracted most of the energy safely away into space, and what got through was easily absorbed into the ship's grounding grid.

The grounding grid, I should add, was Defense Command's best-kept defensive secret in that era; armor deflected as much of the energy as was possible, but to protect the power systems from overload, the hull of all new ships was laced with a lining of power conductors separate from the main lines. They carried the energy of strikes safely away from the primary systems, and actually stored them in a backup cell, or if too much energy was being carried into that cell, simply vented it out into space.

It was a great innovation, quite effective against mags, and here it was getting a workout. Problem was, if the conductors in that grounding grid burned out, the energy would bounce on through the hull and into the main power systems, same as if the grid wasn't there. In other words, it could overload.

Which in immediate terms meant we needed to relieve *Honesty* before the grounding conductors in its hull were overloaded and burned out.

"Kris, can you get in close enough to relieve *Honesty*?" I turned to screen two, and just as I did, Mark Gunney and *Honesty's* bridge glowed to life in screen four, the realtime Battlelink now established between all ships.

"Don't worry, we've got you covered, sir," Commander Gunney's quip was typical of him.

I smiled, "Glad to hear it. Let's focus on the last three ships in line. Let the first one get past you, Mark, but see if you can't give it a drive leak that you can follow. Once we knock out the other three I want you following it. See if you can find its base."

Commander Gunney smiled, "Heh, kick it hard, let it run home crying, and follow?"

I grinned, "Exactly."

"Understood," Gunney turned away from the screen and started dispensing orders, and screen three showed *Honesty* rolling and turning in place, its drive pods firing to spin it on the spot.

"Kris, let's finish off the rest…"

"Energy gun range, sir!" Hannigan barked the warning, and this time *Wolf* did shudder as the energy bursts from the rough-and-tumble weapons began to spatter against thick armor.

The energy output from these particular guns was so low that it didn't even bleed through the armor to hit the grounding grid. We were bearing down on the armed liner, and Karen was walking back to her chair as the main screen tracked our approach.

"Laser one, Matt. Let's carve off two drive pods," her smooth tone was just as exquisite as usual, and as she turned and sat down in her chair I glanced back and smiled.

She bobbed her eyebrows at me and tossed her head just enough to flip her ponytail back up onto her left shoulder, "Fire when you have the solution, Matt."

There was a pause as Matt and the Lieutenant at fire control ran numbers through the computer, calculating range, vector, speed of light and all the rest, and then Matt looked up and keyed the intercom from his keypad, "Shooting number one laser!"

The warning was necessary; a laser shot wasn't like a mag shot. The entire central core of *Wolf*, from stem to stern, was a giant conduit for the power of the laser bank; the four emitters located around the ship were simply directors for that central feed. Trying to fire two emitters at full power at once was asking to overload the laser bank — and in turn, to possibly overload the reactors and blow the entire ship apart.

Matt, however, was just firing laser one — the bow emitter — and even that shot could shake *Wolf* to the core, and cause power fluctuations, depending on shot angle and duration.

Hence all the calculating and whatnot.

Wolf quivered and then the bright red beam of broad, flat, fiery energy lanced from my frigate's bow. The pirate liner tried to whirl out of the way, but it wasn't fast enough. Sure, ships of its type were menacing when thrown against other liners and cargo haulers, but not when facing a real warship.

The laser slashed into its unarmored hull like a hot knife through butter.

"Erica, keep our bow on the liner. Matt, keep the port mags firing at the raider in second place," Karen crossed one leg over the other and settled her forearms on the arms of her chair.

"Yes, ma'am," Martin was the first to reply, and as she did she stepped over to the helm and tapped one of the pilots on the shoulder. *Wolf* yawed slightly and the beam of the laser stayed in contact with the liner. It was slicing viciously across the pylon that attached the ship's port engine pod to the hull.

"Port mags, aye," Matt nodded to the fire control Ensign for the appropriate weapons and the mags from *Wolf's* port side — a sizable number of mags, it must be said — began spraying a veritable shower of white-green death.

"Kris, take the upper pylon for us," I looked to screen two, and she nodded from *Lion's* bridge.

Seconds later *Lion's* laser three, the port emitter, spewed its red beam, and just as we finished shearing off the liner's port engine pod with *Wolf's* laser, Kris Jacobs was sawing off another one.

Karen remained sitting comfortably in her chair, "Erica, hard to port, please... vector 145, down angle thirty. Matt, keep port mags engaged on the previously established target, add our bow mags to the fourth ship in line."

The fire pouring from *Wolf* was immense. As the second ship in line, the presumed command ship, began to overload under the unholy shower of light that was burning up its outer hull, the bow mags began an onslaught on the fourth ship in line — the raider desperately accelerating around the dying liner.

Lion's bow mags sprayed after it. Over seventy percent of the shots connected, and then Matt poured *Wolf's* bow mags into it as well.

Watching ships shut down under mag fire can be very interesting or very dull. The fourth raider abruptly lost power as its grid burned out under the withering heat of two frigates' mags, but the second ship in line, feeling the weight of *Wolf's* port mags, began to melt, and then as a raw mag bolt struck too close to its central reactor, it burst in a silent explosion.

The liner spun away out of control as *Lion's* laser finished shearing off its upper engine pod, and so all that was left was the first raider in line.

I smiled as I watched Commander Gunney on screen four, coolly directing his corvette's fire. A laser shot lanced out from *Honesty's* bow emitter, clipping the tail end of the raider in what would have been considered a shameful miss... had he been aiming for a kill shot.

As it was, the raider pushed past *Honesty's* port side, trading mag shots and then punching its speed up to a somewhat impressive 188 kps. A long trail of radiation would follow it wherever it went.

Hopefully it wouldn't realize that was what we were looking for, or if it did, hopefully it wouldn't care, and would go back to base regardless.

"We'll give them a bit of time to think they're getting away," Mark Gunney looked back to the screen.

I nodded, "Sounds good. You can probably overtake at will."

Then I paused, my eyes moving between the screens before glancing back at Karen.

"Well, that was very good shooting, everyone!"

I grinned.

CHAPTER FOURTEEN

A COMMODORE'S JOB DESCRIPTION – REVISITED

"Whoa, whoa, *bloody hold it!*"

Heavy footfalls chased Karen and me down the hall — someone was jogging after us and two guesses who that was. I turned and walked backwards down the corridor, while Karen looked over her shoulder, "We'll be *fine*, Matt."

"*Fine* like a damned fox. You're not going to be going off half cocked when I'm in a position to prevent it."

I slowed to a halt and held up my hands, and Karen stopped and turned around next to me, folding her arms and frowning at the taller black man, "So you're going to throw us in the brig?"

Matt's eyes narrowed, "Don't tempt me. No, I have something much worse in store for you. If you won't listen to reason and leave this to SF…"

"What, Matt? What could you possibly do that'd keep us in check to your satisfaction?" I crossed my arms and smiled.

A hand came to rest on my shoulder, "He's sending us with you."

My eyes jerked up from Matt and locked on the bulkhead straight ahead.

"Aww no, come on, that's not fair… he'll keep us from having any fun…" Karen started shaking her head, but Matt's smile broadened.

"Rank has its curses, wouldn't you say, Charlie?" the Briton grinned.

I winced and turned around to see that Charlie Peters and eleven Special Branch officers in black fatigues had appeared from thin air behind us and now stood smiling and brandishing their weapons. They were going to be babysitting us… which, I had to admit (at least to myself), wasn't such a bad thing. I'd ordered *Honesty* to follow the escaping raider, and Kris and *Lion* were headed to Theta itself to have an earnest chat with that Martian commander about arming pirates. That left Karen and me to board the pirate liner to look for intel on just what the Syndicate was up to.

Alright, I know, I know, Commodores are not supposed to board pirate ships with the Security Forces. But again, it's the cavalier reputation — I had to do this sort of work against the pirates, it was the only way to make them worry about me. And we needed them worried. Karen and I had to be the officers they'd do just about anything to avoid tangling with, and there's necessary mythos involved with that.

Of course, Charlie had always boarded with me in the old days, so I don't know why I was making such a big deal of it right now… well, except to keep playing out the joke.

But the joke was dead.

"We probably should stop pretending we mind the help before we miss our flight," Karen leaned towards me, and I nodded.

"Charlie, I'm pleased to tell you that we've decided you can come along."

Major Charlie Peters smiled, "Excellent!"

+++

Adrienne Thompson's fighters formed a protective screen ahead of the two assault shuttles, Karen's fighter and my own. I always made crossings like these in my plane, not with the troops. This wasn't a matter of ego or hubris; flying myself allowed my fighter to stay in as close escort for the transport until it safely docked.

The other twenty planes launched from *Wolf's* deck were directly under Adrienne's command, and they were tasked with taking out any remaining energy guns that might threaten our approach. That was about all I'd want F-194 Starlights to try to do in a situation like this — you probably noticed that we didn't even launch a combat patrol when we entered Asteroid Theta space. People like Second Lord Caldecott would have scoffed at that, but the pilots surely were appreciative. The last thing they'd have wanted was to be left behind if we had to pull out because it was a trap, and frankly, against most armed ships, fighters weren't effective.

So we tended to keep fighters in reserve, using them for ground strikes or assaults on targets like this liner — already badly shot up and nearly defenseless. Such uses kept our pilots alive and our mags well tuned.

Anyway, doctrine can be talked about later. The two assault shuttles were rolling away from each other now, Karen following the one that was going high, me edging my control stick over and following the one that went left. We'd breach from different airlocks, then meet somewhere in the ship — just like in the old days.

"See you in there. Don't get shot without me," Karen called over the radio and then waggled her wings as she pulled away.

"Yeah, thanks for saying that on an open comm. I'll have you up on insubordination char– *whoa*..." I'd been watching her fly off and nearly gone nose-first into the assault shuttle I was guarding. Well not almost — it wasn't really that close.

But anyway, it was now time to pay attention. Like a grown-up.

"We'll hit the lock in twenty seconds," Charlie's voice came over the comm line from the shuttle I'd nearly just hit. "Same old routine, Ken? We'll dock, then you dock with us and we all go in together?"

"Sounds good," I slid my plane into position behind the transport and throttled back in time with it as it approached the hull.

"Ha, well I might just not let you dock, keep you out altogether," the Major persisted with what I hoped was a stifled laugh.

Frowning, I started to key up some preliminary menus on my HUD (head's up display), then started putting the plane into standby docking mode, "Insubordination abounds today. Well if you don't let me in with you I'll just go land in their main bay and work through the ship alone. You choose..."

"I figured. Let's do it the old fashioned way."

I nodded to myself, "Excellent."

I watched then as the shuttle pilot edged her ship up to the side of the liner, found a lock, extended the main boarding tube, and slammed lightly into the side of the pirate vessel. At the same time, from the upper rear of the shuttle, a soft tube began to extend towards me. This was the nifty and surprisingly usable fighter-docking tube these shuttles carried mainly for rescue operations.

Pushing on my controls, I tipped my Starlight forward so the nose was pointing relatively down, then fired two light thrusters and pushed the plane forward onto the magnets of the tube. The flexible chute bonded to the fuselage around my cockpit, first loosely, and then as the operator on the shuttle registered the clean dock and hit the aptly-named 'SEAL' button, the electromagnets in the rim of the tube clutched down hard, pressing a sealing foam against the alloy plane that created a solid airtight bond.

Securing cables with electromagnets were fired from the shuttle next, anchoring my plane in place relative to the assault craft, and then I keyed the flight computer (and in turn the plane) into standby mode and popped the canopy.

Unbuckling from my chair, I floated up weightless into the chute, my hands finding the synthetic rope that hung down one side and using it to pull myself through the four-meter length. At the far end, the hatch to the shuttle was open, and I spun myself weightlessly around and then went through feet first, landing with practiced ease on the gravity plating of the shuttle.

Smiling dashingly at the somewhat amused Special Branch onlookers, I dusted my hands off for symbolic effect, "Not bad for an old Commodore."

Then I straightened up and hit my head on one of the ceiling consoles. To their credit, none of the Special Branchers laughed.

"Dammit, who installed that there... I swear..." I rubbed my head and started grumbling as I drew my mag from its hip holster and checked its power cell. Good spirits were necessary before boarding actions.

I tapped my foot and studied the ceiling of the airlock as the Special Branch officer ran a decoder on the keypad. We'd gone through our hatch into the liner's airlock with no problem at all, but being industrious, the pirates had locked the inner door to slow us down.

Without realizing it, I was also starting to hum an antiquated song — yes I do have rather a fondness for antiquated culture — and I was getting amused stares from the Special Branchers who hadn't before seen me waiting in an airlock to board a pirate ship. Those who had boarded ships with me before now just ignored me... meaning *Charlie* ignored me, and the rest of the team seriously wondered whether I was rather insane.

"Got it, sir," the woman running the decoder on the keypad turned around, sliding her lock-breaking device into a pouch in her vest and slinging forward her mag rifle. These Special Branchers were carrying the fancy and slick new MAG-90s, while the Security Forces were still using the EP-5 personal rifles... you probably don't care, but I was quite impressed by the new-fangled guns at the time. Still am, really... but anyway.

Charlie stepped forward and nodded, pulling his weapon up and pressing it against his shoulder, getting it set to pull up into firing position, "Alright then, Carly and I go through first, then we move by twos. Watch your angles, we'll deploy for defense first and then pick our route. Pilots hold the boat and only close the hatch if it looks bad. Clear?"

There were silent, certain nods from the assembled Special Branch officers, and from the pilot and the co-pilot who'd poked their heads through the hatch from the shuttle. I nodded too, and then in keeping with the plan... er, *my* plan, I reached past the woman at the keypad, thumbed the hatch open, and stepped through.

"Ken!" Charlie leapt after me, lunging through the hatch, grabbing me and nearly tossing me against the wall just beyond it with one hand as he covered a couple of angles with the MAG-90 he held in the other.

Silence.

I cocked an eyebrow, looking around and noting that this airlock was down a very short branching hallway from the main corridor.

"See, no need to get overdramatic, Charlie. They're just *pirates*," I smiled.

Okay, so at this point you're wondering what the hell I was thinking. Look, by that time I'd boarded a lot of pirate ships, and not once had they ever seriously defended an airlock. It's against their nature as pirates to be waiting on the other side of a door as it opens — at least when the ones doing the opening are Special Branch. Much better to let them in and then catch them in a crossfire at the first junction. Surround and destroy as opposed to meet head-on. It's not the way I would defend, it's not the way Charlie would defend, and it's not the way a Martian would defend, but for pirates, that was the game.

And my specialty was manipulating their game.

Charlie knew this, so with an expression that landed on the spectrum between 'frown' and 'scowl', he withdrew his hand from my shoulder and stepped back, leveling his weapon at the intersection between the hall we were in and the main corridor. The rest of the Special Branch officers followed him through, and together they started to creep forward, moving with all sorts of caution.

I leaned against the wall and listened in silence. Obviously there were at least a dozen pirates guarding that intersection from one side or the other… the question was which way… or both?

Well, one way to find out.

"So, my dear pirate scum friends out there, which side are you on? Or do you have both covered?" I called, and Charlie raised his fist to stop his team moving forward before looking back at me and nearly hissing. He hated when I did this.

I held up a hand and shook my head, then closed my eyes and let my head loll back against the wall, "Come *on*. It's not like we don't know you're out there. Might as well just lie to us and see if you can get us pointing the wrong way."

I loved doing this. They never expected you to actually ask them to tell you something, but their natural bravado almost always made sure they replied.

And as if on cue, a gruff woman's voice shot back at me, "Yeah right, we're to the left then, eh!"

There were sniggers from around the corner, and then the sound of something falling to the deck… on the right.

I smiled thinly and pointed right, then left, and nodded to Charlie. His expression managed to mask his frustration and he simply let out a breath and nodded, then did all the fancy professional hand moves that meant things, splitting his team into two lines of black-clad Special Branchers close to each wall.

The front two people — Charlie and Carly, I think he said her name was, tugged magbangs off their vests. Magbangs *were* in service at this time, even though all the movies seem to think we were using sonic grenades. They were basically the same as current ones, detonating grenade-style and releasing a pulse of EM energy that stunned anyone in range. The newest models could actually knock people out, but we didn't have any of those for Charlie's team at this point.

Gritting my teeth, I kept my eyes closed as the grenades were pitched in each direction, and then the loud whine alerted me to the detonation. The broad EM pulses that were released didn't kill, but in the tight space of the corridor they were potent enough to incapacitate any pirate defenders.

The way was open for our little incursion.

In silence, Charlie and his Special Branch officers flooded out into the corridor. I opened my eyes just in time to catch the flash of two mag shots. The "all clear" came shortly after in a low, unrecognizable tone.

Rocking forward on the balls of my feet, I came off the wall and rolled my neck around to stretch it once, then followed, mag in hand.

So far so good.

CHAPTER FIFTEEN

THE FINER POINTS OF DIPLOMACY

Kris Jacobs stood with folded arms on *Lion's* bridge, watching on the main screen as the destroyer escort hovering over Asteroid Theta tried to hide the two transports behind it. As *Lion* got closer to the asteroid, passive sensors were picking up all sorts of radiation coming from those two ships — they were either hauling nuclear waste or weapons, and they sure didn't look like any waste tugs Kris had ever seen.

For one thing, they were actually painted. Waste haulers were never painted.

Nope, these two were carrying micro-power supplies for mags... er, EM cannons, as the Martians called them. And the destroyer escort was trying to hide that fact.

"We're getting a signal now, ma'am," Lieutenant Commander Tony Crycheck, *Lion's* Sensors and Communications Officer, made his report, and Kris nodded.

"Screen three."

While the *Lion*Net screen went to its buffering window, Kris straightened herself a bit, zipped up the collar of her ship-dress uniform shirt, and almost wished she'd decided to put on her tunic this morning — she might have looked more menacing.

But then again, the reason I'd sent Kris to do this job, aside from the fact that I wanted to board the liner myself, was that Kris had the decided ability to charm. She always said it was because she was Australian, so I'll stick with that explanation. Anyway, I'd already given this Martian Commander grief enough for one day — a more friendly approach seemed in order.

So Kris' friendly demeanor and informal dress, combined with a well-timed smile or, dare I say, tossing of her hair as she looked away from the screen, might make the Martian more cooperative. Personability was a hell of a weapon on days like this.

Kris took a deep breath as the buffering completed, then assumed a neutral expression as the Commander appeared on her screen.

"Sorry about the mess out there Commander," she said kindly. "Looks like you had pirates sitting there waiting to attack the arms transports you're looking after!"

That wasn't the greeting the Commander had been expecting — good job Kris for wrong-footing him like that! He stammered slightly before managing to say, "Yes... well, um... we had the situation under control."

Kris smiled, "You're welcome, we're always glad to help our neighbors in the fight against piracy."

His mouth worked again, slightly disbelieving, and Kris took the opportunity to run a hand through her hair, just to throw him something else unexpected. Once upon a time she'd been such a quiet, straightforward officer. Exposure to Karen and me had multiplied her mischief abilities far too much for this Martian's good.

Finally he managed to say something, "Halt your approach."

Kris put on an expression of mock offense, "Well that's rather rude of you, us having just saved you from those mean pirates."

"You didn't *save* us from anything, you goddamned Defcom!" the Commander really was too young and inexperienced to be trying to deal with the best of our Belt Squadron. In retrospect, I should have taken that as a clue. Kris crossed her arms and huffed. She has a remarkable way of looking like a surly twelve-year-old sometimes —mischief again…

"How's that, exactly. Didn't see you out there blowing them away yourself, *mister*."

The Commander's eyes narrowed, "They weren't our enemies, dammit! You just destroyed our–"

To his credit he realized what he was saying and managed to stop himself, but of course the damage was done. In hindsight it really had been an easy concession to get —a sign that the Martians hadn't left their best and brightest out at their Asteroid bases. You might think it too easy, but keep in mind, since Admiral Noyce had taken down the Syndicate, a vacuum of power had let just about anybody get to the higher ranks of power out here… and the Martians, it seemed, had used the new stability to move the dregs of their officer corps out to the frontier.

Kris' expression morphed smoothly into a pleasant smile, "Well that's good to know Commander. Now, I expect you've read the Anti-Piracy Convention of 2206. Under Article Sixteen I'm entitled to confiscate any vessels carrying weapons bound for pirate use."

The Commander was red and huffing with anger. He looked a bit like a bomb about to go off, and though Kris was tempted to push the big red button and watch the splatter, she was well aware that she was treading on very touchy diplomatic ground. The discovery of Martian transports carrying weapons for pirates was going to be diplomatic ammunition enough to stop further attempts to arm a new Syndicate —once the Imperial Diplomatic Office got hold of the evidence, they'd bluster and threaten doom and gloom to the Mars Imperium if the shipments weren't put to a stop.

This Commander would probably be executed by the Martians for his mistake, now that Kris thought about it. Rumor had it they weren't particularly agreeable.

So she wouldn't force the issue of actually confiscating the weapons, "Listen, I'm not in the mood to shepherd those ships back to Belt Two, even if the prize money would be a nice bonus. How about you send them to the nearest Martian Naval base for internment?"

The Commander's eyes narrowed, "Oh I will, you wait and see, bitch."

Oh my, what an amateur this fellow was. Pirates flung insults at each other, but the courtesies of the Naval service held that officers treated each other with respect.

Kris wasn't impressed, and her face tightened, "Watch your language, sir."

He huffed again and then cut the vid feed without so much as a 'good day'. Again, this probably should have been a clue to us —no Martian Commander sitting in his destroyer escort as a *Predator*-class frigate bore down on him would have been so insolent, even if he was incompetent.

Well, he wouldn't unless he knew something we didn't. But he did order the transports to boost out of the system, giving us our PR victory, and so Kris let her arms fall to her sides, and feeling slightly miffed at the discourteous end to her interaction, marched back to her chair.

Lion began to reverse engines.

CHAPTER SIXTEEN

PIRATES, GUNFIGHTS, AND FREE FOOD

Charlie Peters was leading us through the dark but wide corridor towards the bridge of the liner. How did we know where the bridge was, you ask? It was a *liner*, probably a Martian one by the look of the shoddy workmanship, and of course it had direction signage for guests.

The pirates could have changed the arrows on all the signs to confuse boarders, but that seemed unlikely; pirates were, by nature, not very bright, and so while they might think of misdirecting potential enemies by mixing up signs, they might have indeed gotten their own crews lost in the big ship if they did.

You may think I'm being unfair to the pirates, but since Grant Merger had gone down, they'd been nothing but daft. This was probably one of the easiest periods for dealing with them we'd ever had.

And true to form, they weren't being too clever here.

Sounds of a firefight erupted down the corridor and around a corner from us. Charlie did the tactical 'fist-up-to-stop-the-people' hand gesture, and our party stopped in two lines against the walls of the corridors, crouching into the shadows of the darkened hall. The pirates either had turned off the lights for our arrival or they'd lost power to the secondary systems in this section when we took out their engines. Either way, we had nice shadows to cover us as we listened.

Charlie's comm vibrated against his hip. He tapped it to life, its feed actually running up a microfilament through his vest to his headset. As he did this, I activated my own comm and held it to my ear so I could listen in.

"Peters here," Charlie whispered.

"Lieutenant Stranks, Major, we're at their bridge and they've got a barricade set up."

Excellent — that was Kyle Stranks, the new head of *Wolf's* Security Forces (remember him from that boring briefing you better not have skimmed?), and the leader, Karen excepted, of the other assault shuttle's party of regular SF boarders. We hadn't been in regular contact with them in case our comm transmissions gave away our positions —we'd only use the comms when we seriously needed to.

So Karen and Stranks had gotten themselves to the bridge from another direction. And now they probably wanted us to get around the flank.

I pulled my comm from my ear and keyed on its little screen, activating a relative direction tracker... fancy speak for an arrow that pointed towards the source of Stranks' comm unit. It pointed to the wall on the right side of the corridor. So that probably meant Stranks and Karen had approached the bridge from another corridor parallel to this one, and had gotten there to find it barricaded.

Valiant of the pirates to put up a fight under these circumstances, I supposed. But futile.

Charlie was using the same arrow function I was when I looked up, and then he glanced at me and nodded, "We can go the rest of the way down this corridor and hang a right. We'll either come out behind the barricade or in front of another one."

I nodded, "Let's do it."

Doing some more of those nifty tactical arm movement things, Charlie got his Special Branch officers onto their feet and we all continued to creep down the hallway.

One corridor over, Karen sat pressed up against a door frame as energy gun fire flaked some more alloy off the side of the wall that was keeping her alive. This really wasn't going so well for her.

The SF ranker who had volunteered to take point was sitting in the doorway opposite her, gritting his teeth and cradling his right arm. He'd gotten a good graze from one of the nasty energy guns the pirates were using, and it'd done a serious cook job on his upper arm. He'd be in treatment for quite a while when he got home.

Unfortunately, that was just the nature of boarding actions, Karen knew that as well as I did. Whether you went in with black-clad Special Branch elite officers or the regularly trained Security Forces, someone was liable to get shot.

Looking back down the corridor the way she'd come, she could just make out the figure of Stranks in the darkened hall, leaning around the corner of the nearest intersection and spraying a few mag shots back at the barricade. The energy gun fire from the pirates was drowning the boarding party's EP-5 rifles. I shouldn't get this technical, but those old mag rifles lacked the refinement to control their energy output — they couldn't be set to cut through barricades without taking the risk of slicing through hulls.

Karen gritted her teeth and pressed further back into the doorframe. It was about all she could do...

Then something obvious occurred to her. Looking up, she located the keypad for the door, and reached up and hit it.

The door slid open obligingly, and she slid herself into the safety of the room.

Well, safety until the dozen pirates already there all pointed their guns at her head and demanded she drop her mag.

She dropped it and held up her hands.

"Charlie, Stranks again. They've got reinforcements in the rooms over here..."

Lieutenant Stranks was cut off by the sound of weapons fire, and Charlie stopped us again, looking forward, "Check the rooms!"

We hadn't passed many room so far on the walk up here, and those that we had passed had been swept for pirate presence. By this time, though, we were hitting the same section where Stranks and Karen were pinned down, and there were many rooms indeed.

One of the Special Branch officers was near the first upcoming doorway on the right side of the corridor, so he turned immediately and keyed it open and dropped to one knee. Flashlights were switched on and the room was swept instantly.

Empty.

"They probably don't have enough people to fill every room," I said quietly.

Charlie's eyes narrowed thoughtfully and then he nodded, "Sounds about right." He waved everyone onward.

Our party moved in a silent, smooth motion, with Charlie and I leading the way towards the sound of energy gun fire. The intersection between corridors that we presumed would take us to the fight was barely twenty meters ahead, with only one more door between us and it.

Charlie got to that door first, and he did the same thing his officer had done at the last door; he dropped to one knee, lined his MAG-90 up with one hand and keyed the door open with the other.

One of his officers was right behind him covering the wide angles, but as the door opened and I realized the room was full of pirates, I lunged forward from my position opposite him, rolling in dramatic style across the floor and coming up on one knee with my mag leveled in front of me.

The door frame stopped my momentum with a thud — a painful one — but it was enough to straighten my firing posture, and I squeezed down on the trigger. Charlie and his officer were already firing, and let me tell you, those slick new MAG-90s were as good as advertised.

Fast-shooting and smooth, they sprayed half the room with mag fire on full automatic while I plugged away with my sidearm on the other half. This all took about three seconds — the pirates were looking the other way and barely even got to turn around before they were convulsing and dropping.

Lots of prisoners…

Then one guy turned and hauled someone with blond hair up in front of him as a shield. I frowned, holding my fire as he put his gun to Karen's temple. Damn.

"You shoot me Defcom and I start convulsing, I pull the trigger and she loses her head…" he spat gruffly, his grimy hand closing around Karen's throat.

I stood slowly, my mag still lined up on his face, and Charlie swung around the corner, "Put it down!"

The Major's words drew a toothy smile from the renegade, and he shook his head, "No way asshole, you shoot me and she dies."

Charlie stayed in place, and I let my mag drop a little, "Karen, seriously, come on now. He didn't even tie your hands."

Despite the grubby paw on her throat, she smiled. In a flash the gun wasn't at her head anymore, and the pirate was being flipped over her back to land with a very loud thud on his back in front of her. Then, for good measure she dropped her boot evenly on his face, with the crunch and other unpleasant sounds that lead to someone swallowing a lot of teeth.

"*That*," she said looking down at him, "was incredibly rude."

He groaned and coughed, and Karen looked up at us, thumbing towards the corner of the room, "Charlie, the barricade is through here."

With a smile, Charlie came to his feet and waved his team into the room, "Charges on the corner. Let's undermine these bastards."

As his officers hauled the battered pirates out and applied explosive pads to the wall, I walked over to Karen. Recovering her mag from the floor, I handed it to her, "You really need to stop humoring these guys, one day you could get yourself hurt."

She flashed a smile, then her eyes fixed on something over my shoulder, "Well it wasn't today."

She brushed past me and grabbed a muffin off a table that contained all sorts of munchable foods, and I turned in disbelief, "You're going to eat *that?*"

"Hostage situations always make me hungry. I suppose they were waiting for us in here for a while," she started eating.

I could have protested — said it could have been poisoned or whatever — but as I opened my mouth the bulkhead in the corner exploded with the sort of boom that can fracture eardrums. The shaped-charge pads carried by the Special Branch officers blasted the wall out into the pirates in the corridor, and then Charlie led his elite team through the new hole, shooting everyone in sight with methodical precision.

Me, I dropped and covered my head as soon as I heard the blast. Apparently I'd not been paying attention when Charlie yelled 'Fire in the hole'. I still think he might not have yelled it and said he did, just to surprise me.

I waited for the smoke to clear a little and looked up. Karen was standing there eating her muffin, not looking at me or the wall. Typical.

"Women," I grumbled as I slowly pushed myself to my feet.

"What was that?" Karen smiled between chews.

"Nothing," I grumbled again, then we followed Charlie through the blasted hole.

CHAPTER SEVENTEEN

CLUES

I covered left as Karen and I went through the door, and as I entered the dark room with my flashlight brightening some of the din, I saw a flash of movement. Dropping to one knee I squeezed the trigger twice and listened for the thud of a hiding pirate falling to the deck.

It came, and as it did I got slowly back to my feet, keeping an eye out for more movement as I carefully stepped into the office.

"Clear over here," Karen said quietly as she reached the corner on the right side of the room.

I stepped to the left, then came to a stop as a well-dressed pirate twitched at my feet, "I think we've found the skipper. Looks like Mister Cooper, if I'm not mistaken."

Karen brought her mag down to her side but kept her flashlight up, "Our illustrious enemy was hiding in a darkened office? Well that's not going to play well for him in the press."

She took a few steps towards me and then froze in place, hearing, as I had, the sound of boots on the deck behind us. We both silently counted to three — in time with each other without even glancing at each other to coordinate — and then she lunged right and spun, bringing her mag up. I dipped and stepped left, and in seconds both of us had our mags trained on the man in the door.

Poor Charlie had decided to follow me with his MAG-90, and so we were looking down the barrel at each other.

"You two really shouldn't leave the group without telling a teacher," he smiled, lowering his rifle and letting it hang from its clip on his vest.

"Well you should learn which target to track," I straightened up with a smile, holstering a weapon. "You really think it's wise to let *her* have a shot at you?"

Charlie shrugged, "Karen likes me. You I don't trust."

I chuckled at that and then the three of us edged up to Cooper's twitching body.

"So, we get one of the bosses," Karen holstered her mag and shined her light on the pirate's face. "We should get him back to *Wolf* and get someone to stop him convulsing so we can get some information from him."

"Indeed. Let's see if he left anything incriminating lying around," I lifted my light and started to sweep the lavish day cabin for papers.

Now, had this been a Defense Command ship taken by boarding, or I suspect even a Martian ship, there'd be nothing to be found; information security protocol was tight, and you just didn't leave sensitive documents in plain sight, or frankly, intact.

But this was a pirate ship, and at best they were a bit fast-and-loose about information security. Grant Merger had been good at handling his intel, but he wasn't typical, and even most of his Syndicate cronies had been embarrassingly incompetent in this area.

It made our jobs a little easier, I suppose, but then pirates weren't all that good at writing their plans down to begin with. If they didn't commit their schemes to paper or datafile, then there'd be nothing for us to find in the first place.

Charlie and I began shuffling through the few papers we saw on a desk and a rather unpleasantly filthy couch. I winced as a piece of paper I tried to pick up stuck to the upholstery of that seat. Shining a light on it, I was glad to see it was of no value, so I let it drop.

It was a good thing I was wearing gloves, that's for sure.

Karen went to the vidscreen built into the wall and pulled out her comm. Tapping a few menu items on her small screen, she frowned, her features glowing in the light of the comm's display, "This was definitely a Martian-built liner. Looks like it was only taken in the last year; it has all the latest civie Martian OS..."

She was so good at figuring that stuff out. My best strategy for getting information out of a Martian computer was to shoot it, pry it open, and look for paper.

Which is why I didn't often try to get information out of Martian-built computers.

"Hello..." Karen let the word slip as her eyes widened slightly, and then she looked up, "I've got a set of attack plans here... for the Belt colonies. There's also a list of ships that have signed on with the new Syndicate."

Charlie frowned as he stopped shuffling papers, "A bit of an easy find, wouldn't you say?"

Karen looked from me to him, smiling, "Why Charles, are you saying I'm not that good?"

Holding his hands up with a grin, Charlie shook his head, "You know I'd say nothing of the sort, ever, dear Karen."

"Yeah, he never speaks the truth," I smiled, stepping back over Cooper to stand next to Karen, then looked at the information on her comm's small screen. "Well, it's either on the level or a hoax, but I'm thinking that Cooper wouldn't sacrifice himself in here if he was just trying to plant false intel. So let's beam that database back to *Wolf* and get Matt to start dissecting it. Anything else?"

Charlie turned back around and shone his light on a stack of printed papers, "I've got what look like love letters here. Well, *love* isn't quite the word I'd use. Lust maybe."

I cocked an eyebrow, "And we want to know this why?"

Reaching to the ledge and picking up the sizable stack of papers, Charlie turned and held them up to his flashlight's beam, "They're on Imperium Fleet stationary and they're signed by Rear Admiral Kitty Castillo."

I straightened up in surprise at that one, and then my eyes found Karen's as we shared our mild disbelief. Rear Admiral Castillo was the gritty Martian commander out here on the frontier, a real nasty sort of woman who could be called many impolite things. This was incredibly shocking, then...

"Her first name is *Kitty*?" Karen shook her head slowly.

I nodded, "I know, what a surprise."

"And the whole lusty letters to a pirate Commodore isn't shocking?" Charlie frowned.

I looked from Karen to him with a shrug, "She never struck me as very classy, but I suppose that's a clue too."

Karen tilted her head and tugged at her ponytail again as it sat on her shoulder, "Yes, but a clue to what?"

Good question. We'd have to come up with some answers later.

For now, we needed to collect Mister Cooper and get back to our ship.

Chapter Eighteen

Meanwhile, Away From Asteroid Theta

I know it's taking place far from the Belt, but it's best you hear this part now instead of some other time…

Rear Admiral Marlene Stoll flew her flag from the battleship *Sorceress*, a ship aptly named to match her Naval abilities. The Venusian pirates — the pirates who operated in the space around Mercury and Venus, and were based at stations much too close to the sun to be safe — had long decided that Stoll was a witch, because she always, and I do mean *always*, got the drop on them.

Well she was not a witch, or a sorceress for that matter — how very rude of you to suggest such a thing! She was, however, one of the ablest flag officers in the fleet, and now she was heading back to her ships at the Venus Station.

Sitting in her cabin and reading through Admiralty regulations as she tried to figure out just what damage Caldecott could do to the Fiora ring, she looked up when her vidscreen chimed and a new message appeared in her inbox.

She frowned and leaned forward on her couch, grabbing the remote from her coffee table and opening the alert — it was a short notice from the bridge that had been sent in lieu of someone calling her on her comm. By now her crew knew that she didn't leave her comm on in her cabin, but that her message screen was perpetually open.

The message filled her monitor in the wake of a *Sorceress*Net buffering screen, and she was on her feet and out her door about six seconds after she read it.

Emerging onto the bridge, Marlene walked straight up to the battleship's main screen and settled her hands on her hips, "Where did he come from exactly?"

"We're not sure. As far as we knew, nobody else would be trying to make the trip out here, ma'am," the Lieutenant Commander at Sensors and Communications replied evenly.

There was no reason for a Martian destroyer escort to be out here at all. *Sorceress* was heading directly back to Venus on the most direct course possible at this time in the season. It meant cutting across the orbital plane of both Venus and Mercury and taking a course close-in to the sun, as Venus was halfway around the star from Earth just now.

But Mars was the *whole way* around the sun from Earth, and Mercury was as well — it was a perfect travel season for ships going back and forth between Mercury and Mars. So why was a little destroyer escort on this side of the sun right now?

"What distance? Are we in realtime range?" Stoll turned to the Lieutenant Commander at Sensors and Communications and he nodded.

"Screen two then," Marlene turned back to the screen and waited as it switched from a scan display to a buffering screen, and then a Martian Commander appeared.

"Good day, Admiral," the Commander said politely, and offered a courteous nod.

"And to you," Marlene didn't sound impressed, but she was going to keep up her niceties anyway. Rules of the game, after all. "You seem to be in a strange place, Commander, is there any assistance we can render?"

The Commander shook his head, "No thank you Admiral, we're quite alright I assure you."

Oh this guy was *good*. Not at all like the fools they sent to the Belt.

"I see," Marlene's eyes narrowed very slightly. "Would you mind sharing your plausible cover story for being out here?"

The Martian smiled, "We're chasing pirates, ma'am. Which unofficially means we were sent to check your ship's performance on a return run to Venus this close in to the gravity well."

Well that sent Marlene's eyebrows up — he was very good. Of course the first part was the official 'cover' story, and then the second part was meant to sate her curiosity, while making it sound mundane.

But she wasn't fooled... not that she'd admit that right now. I'll explain why in a minute...

Forcing a false smile onto her face, Marlene nodded, "Alright, hope you've enjoyed the show. You'll be on your way then?"

The Commander nodded, "We've got all the readings we need. My compliments to your engineer, we were having a hard time keeping up."

"I'll pass that on. Pleasant journey, Commander," Marlene nodded once more, and then the visual reverted to a *Sorceress*Net screen.

Frowning, Marlene turned to her Flag Captain, "Last trip back they tailed us for drive readings, right?"

The Captain nodded, "And they followed us from just outside Earth's sensor grid. Last four times that's where they picked us up."

"And this time?" Marlene's eyes narrowed.

"He came straight from around the sun. Good liar, but I doubt he realizes that we saw him coming," the Captain's tone dripped with all the suspicion Marlene was nursing.

It wasn't all that uncommon in those days for the Martians to tease us a bit — to track one of our ships taking copious scans, watching speed and maneuverability, those sorts of things. We didn't really do it to them because, well, frankly, their ships weren't as good as ours. As plausible excuses go, then, this Martian had done alright, except for failing to explain away his vector.

Most tails were seemingly pre-planned; they picked up a Defense Command ship in open space and shadowed the vessel collecting data. It was an accepted arrangement that wasn't at all hostile. But this fellow had come from seemingly nowhere, so what did that mean?

Well, those of you who know your history know exactly what that means.

"He's reversing course now, ma'am," the Sensors and Communications Officer piped up.

How very interesting.

"Alright... well we're due back on station, I don't want to divert. But next relay ship we pass, send to Admiralty what we've seen. And let them know I might come back out for a peek myself," Marlene looked back at the main screen as she spoke.

"Yes, ma'am."

Sorceress continued on course, and soon the word of the strange encounter got back to the Admiralty.

Racing to the opposite side of the solar system, we can also check in with Commander Gunney and *Honesty*. Only hours out of Asteroid Theta, the corvette was keeping a discreet distance from the damaged raider it was tailing.

Remaining steadfast on his bridge, Mark Gunney stood with arms linked behind his back, watching the pursuit on the main screen. He imagined it'd be a long run to the pirate base, but at least for the first few hours he'd keep a vigil going from the bridge, just in case anything changed abruptly.

He was actually watching the screen when eight new pirate ships appeared on the edge of sensor range. The sensors were set to passive, but the pirates had their drives at full and were positively hammering towards Theta, which meant their emissions were rather obvious.

"Well, didn't see that one coming. Who's for a tactical 'get the hell out of here'?" Mark glanced at his First Officer.

Lieutenant Commander Ashby nodded quickly. "Helm, turn us around. Discreet burn back to Theta — don't let them see us if you can manage it."

"Yes, sir."

It was entirely possible for a *Noble*-class corvette like *Honesty* to outrun pirate ships without being seen. First of all, *Honesty's* sensors had about half-again the range of just about everything we'd seen the pirates cobble together up to that point, and the ship's engines were much more sophisticated and cleaner burning than most of the beefed-up civilian drives favored by the pirates.

Again, like energy guns compared to mags, we had an edge in complicated and high-maintenance gear, and it did pay off now and then, so long as we didn't get carried away.

Mark Gunney wasn't going to be getting carried away, that was for certain.

"We'll be able to do about 180 kps without being seen, at this range," the Lieutenant at helm reported after a moment's calculations. "The radiation trail that raider's leaving behind will help mask us."

Mark nodded, "Great."

Honesty turned in space and retraced its steps, moving with a sense of distinguished urgency.

CHAPTER NINETEEN

THE SOUND OF THE OTHER SHOE DROPPING

"I've just sent the plans you collected back to Belt Two," Matt Baxter was too wrapped up in serious affairs to scold Karen and me for anything as we dropped to the deck next to our fighters.

Wolf's landing bays were bustling as Adrienne Thompson's fighters landed and the shuttles came back. We'd stripped the liner of information and a third shuttle had come over from *Lion* to pick up most of the captured pirates.

We kept one with us.

Charlie walked beside us at the head of the stretcher bearing the pirate 'Commodore' Cooper, still twitching occasionally, to our medical bay. The entire Special Branch team followed, MAG-90s ready in case the pirate was somehow playing possum.

Matt watched them walk past then looked up at me, "I think you might need that absurdly named torture device you told Jones about to get something out of him."

I nodded, "Yeah. Kris comm'd me a couple of hours ago and said she'd gotten the transports to leave the system with their cargoes?"

Matt nodded again, "She worked her charm. But there's other news. Mark Gunney's on his way back with *Honesty*; he's got at least eight pirates coming this way. Doesn't look like they've seen him, but that raider will have tipped them off about our being here."

"Great," Karen was unzipping her flight jacket and loosening her collar as she spoke. "Don't suppose the Martians are worried about the defense of their asteroid?"

Matt shook his head, "Kris sent a warning at them while you were coming in to land. They're saying nothing. We didn't want to interrupt your chat with the LSO while you were trying to come in."

I bobbed my head, "Good idea. Alright, the Martians are arming pirates and they aren't worried about the eight new pirates coming to town. And the fact that they're coming in the first place suggests they were at a rendezvous point somewhere nearby, and got called in."

"Yes, but by who?" Karen tugged her ponytail out of her collar and adjusted her jacket. "The pirates calling reinforcements or the Martians calling them?"

I didn't say anything in answer to that for a moment, instead clicking my teeth together and staring thoughtfully at the deck. Who'd made the call?

"We need more answers," I said after that brief pause. "Karen, you get us ready to cruise. We'll leave as soon as Mark gets to us with *Honesty*. You and *Lion* finish off that liner… if we're lucky the Martians haven't been paying close enough attention and they won't know we've boarded and taken prisoners, so make it a soft kill. Matt, you and me are going to go roll up our sleeves with old Mister Jones. And with Mister Cooper as soon as he gets up."

Karen nodded evenly and then stepped past Matt, tugging off her flight jacket altogether and handing it to a surprised deck hand. Matt then nodded as well, and we headed for the brig.

"Mister Jones, good news, you were right about the rendezvous."

Jones looked up at my words, and his eyes went wide as my gloved fist connected with his nose.

"Bad news, we've stumbled onto something rather bigger than you suggested. You bastards don't so much as look at each other without boasting about how tough you are, so tell me, what did Cooper promise?"

I walked around behind the man as he cradled his nose, spitting blood and snarling the predictable protest: "You bastard, you broke my nose!"

Unimpressed, I grabbed the back of his head and bounced it off the table with a little more force than I probably should have, "Well, I suppose I don't know my own strength. Now what did Cooper boast?"

As you've probably noticed, my mood had changed. Eight ships coming... well nine, really, with the raider we'd let live, and the time for niceties had passed.

"Alrighty, let's ask him then," I said after a moment of silence, then looked up at the two-way mirror and nodded. The door at the far end of the interrogation room opened and a still partially-stunned Cooper was virtually dragged in by Matt and Charlie. They sat him down in the chair facing Jones, who was still cradling his bloody nose.

Cooper's face became more alive with recognition in that moment, and I stood back and folded my arms across my chest as the two pirates stared at each other. Jones was the first to hold up his hands, "It wasn't me... I swear..."

"Hate to disagree, old chap, but you told us exactly where to find Mister Cooper here, as I recall," Matt said with an unkind smile. "Even told us that the Martians were arming him."

Cooper's expression grew rather intense, and there was a prolonged silence. I glanced from Matt to Charlie, and then Cooper lunged out of his chair, reaching across the table and grabbing at Jones while he emitted a growl and some unfortunate language.

Charlie had him back in his seat with a smooth grab of his throat, and then I locked eyes with the newly captured pirate.

"You've been betrayed, Mister Cooper. But by more than just Mister Jones."

Here came the hasty gambit that Matt and I had figured out as we'd walked from the flight deck to the brig. We were used to putting together wild plans during short walks — the only hiccup in this one had been printing time.

Hopefully we could pull it off anyway.

"Bullshit. I know I shouldn't have trusted this fucker, but you got nothin' else on me Defcom."

I winced slightly, "Be glad Karen isn't here, Mister Cooper. Your language might have earned you a mild concussion."

"*Fuck* her."

Charlie was good enough to bounce the man's forehead off the table for me, and Cooper seemingly decided it was not worth the satisfaction to continue his profanity.

"Interesting choice of words, there, Mister Cooper," I nodded to Matt, and the Briton bobbed his head toward the mirror. The door opened and an Ensign with two stacks of papers entered the room, handed them to Matt, and withdrew.

"Now what have we here?" Matt leaned over Cooper's shoulder and dropped the stacks on the table. "Letters from Kitty Castillo, is it? Why it *is*!"

Cooper's eyes dropped to the stack of copied letters, each with its letterhead shadowed by a *WolfNet* screencap — an indication that the letters had been printed from our comm database.

He examined that pile, then his eyes darted to the letters we'd pulled out of the day cabin on the liner.

"Thought she really wanted you, eh? Thought the Rear Admiral had fallen for the *dirty pirate*," I smiled now, and Cooper looked up at me.

"Nice try. You just scanned and printed 'em," Cooper sounded reasonably certain of that conclusion, so I forced my smile to broaden.

"Yeah, yeah sure. But let's take a step back and think this through, Mister Cooper. You get a dirty informant to kill one who's found out about your arrangement with the Martians. Then you sic us on Mister Jones in hopes that we kill him. But he conveniently survives, and lets us know where your loading zone is for all the new toys she's giving you."

So far that was what I thought I knew, and Cooper's eyes narrowed in such a way that made me think he thought I knew more than that, even though I didn't, but I was still going to look like I did.

Yeah, I was slightly confused too.

"So. You hand us the guy who's going to finger your location? Are you really stupid enough to have thought we'd just kill him because the guy you put on him was packing a tank laser, or did Kitty convince you that it was better to let us do it because it wouldn't arouse suspicions?"

I had *no idea* who had done what in trying to get Jones killed. Obviously they had indeed been stupid enough to expect us to kill Jones when we took that house (we're talking about Chapter 1, if you're lost) and had it not been Karen and I, Mister Jones might indeed be dead.

But I was hoping all this was making Cooper doubt… and by the look that he was trying not to let show on his face, I was pretty sure it was working.

"See, she's been in it with us since Admiral Noyce headed home," I continued, completely fabricating now. "She wanted to set you up just for her side to crush, but we offered to combine forces and take you all out at once. So congrats, you've wandered right into our little trap. Actually, you should feel lucky to be alive, we're not taking any more prisoners today. And your nine other ships are coming."

Cooper's eyes went wide, "But I didn't call them!"

I came around the table from behind Jones and leaned forward, "No kidding, who else would be able to call them in?"

"Those fucking Martians!" he hissed. "They promised me. They said the new Syndicate would be powerfuller than Merger's, and that we could have the Belt when they were done with you."

Ah.

You have to appreciate that at this moment I was thinking a lot of things. My thought process began with the fact that 'powerfuller' clearly isn't a word. Then it went on to marvel at the fact that I'd unsettled this guy enough to get him to spill a bit of information. And then it clicked in to the 'when they were done with you' bit.

Obviously, 'done *what* with me' was the first question on my mind, but I couldn't go that route because of the ruse...

Then there was a convenient knock on the door, and an Ensign leaned in, "Commodore, report from the bridge. Four Martian ships are approaching Asteroid Theta from the opposite side — three DEs and a destroyer. They're forming up with the DE that was here already."

I nodded, "Thank you. Well Mister Cooper, that's my backup. I better go get ready to obliterate your *new* Syndicate. You must be having all sorts of fun thinking about all the lies..."

Cooper looked about ready to spit as his eyes came up to meet mine.

I grinned, "Oh I just have to know — what'd she promise to do to me personally? I mean I know the whole 'you'll have the Belt' angle. Did she start by promising you could flay me alive? And did she actually end up using the 'we'll defeat the Empire' line too?"

His face twisted, "Yeah, she said the Empire would fall. And we were going to flay you. And fucking *space* you. And your whore captain, well she was going to be tast–"

My fist crunched down on his nose, just like it had on Jones', and almost instantly Matt was bouncing his face off the desk again.

"That's no way to speak about a lady," I leaned down further and whispered into his ear. "And thanks for letting me in on Admiral Castillo's deal with you. We printed those off five minutes before you got here — I can still *smell the toner*. Hope you like prison."

He tried to look up to scream something, but fast as ever on the draw, Charlie put his sidearm to the back of Cooper's neck and pulled the trigger.

I stood up with a bitter taste in my mouth as the man started convulsing again. That had been a remarkably productive interrogation.

"Well," I looked from Matt to Charlie, "the other shoe just dropped."

"And landed on us," Charlie re-holstered his mag. "So if I put this picture together correctly, Castillo is arming pirates to attack the Belt with her... as part of a Martian-launched war?"

I raised my eyebrows, "Sounded an awful lot like that. But he's a pirate. I hope he was lying... or that she was playing him like I said she was."

Matt tilted his head, "You think she's that smart?"

I met Matt's eyes, opened my mouth to say something, closed it again, and let out a breath.

"Oh good," Charlie shook his head slowly, then his eyes settled on Jones. "What about him?"

I blinked and looked back over my shoulder at Jones, "I promised to let you go Mister Jones. You can either get that freedom now, so that his friends can pick you up, or you stay with us."

Jones was cradling his nose again, and I could tell he wanted to spit a line of foul language at me, but I think the fear of being caught by his peers was more than enough to dissuade him from aggravating me, "I stay put."

"Good," I smiled thinly. "Gentlemen, we have work to do."

Matt and Charlie followed me out of the room, and I headed for the bridge.

I stopped in the room just beyond the interrogation room and nodded to the Ensign who'd interrupted with the news of the Martians' arrival, "Good instinct, Ensign. That bit about the Martians showing up was just what I needed to close him out."

The Ensign looked up at me with a frown, "Uh… sir… that was a report from the bridge. From Captain McMaster."

I studied the Ensign's face for a moment. Nope, she wasn't kidding.

I ran, quite literally ran, out of the room.

CHAPTER TWENTY
AND THEN I GOT IN A BAD MOOD

Just as a brief aside, I found out much later that it was literally during my run from the brig to the bridge that day that the brave crew of the communications ship *Marconi*, one of the deep range laser-comm ships that floated between Belt Two and Earth, relaying messages back and forth between the asteroids and the homeworld, discovered a Martian destroyer escort closing with it in stealth mode.

Marconi, like all message ships at the time, was not a fully-fitted military vessel but instead a giant receiver and laser-signal array with engines. Its sensors were usually set to passive to avoid interfering with signal traffic, and its defensive systems were virtually non-existent.

Two laser shots carved it in half before the crew knew what was happening, then the Martians magged any pods that managed to escape with survivors.

And *Marconi* was just one of the nine communications ships taken out within a period of ten minutes. Communication between Earth and the Belt went dark. But I wouldn't know this for a few days yet, I just felt the need to recognize the loss of those brave crews when it happened.

I emerged onto the bridge slightly out of breath, and said nothing as I stumbled forward and stood before the main screen. Yep, that was a total of five Martian ships now in local space, and they were coming out from Asteroid Theta in a formation that I guessed would, for them, be counted as militant.

"What's the news?" Karen came out of her chair and stepped up beside me, her eyes never really leaving the display on the main screen.

"From what we tricked out of him, Rear Admiral Castillo promised Mister Cooper *our* Belt colonies for the new Syndicate, and she said something to him about destroying our Empire," my words weren't particularly smooth as I caught my breath, and Karen's face darkened measurably.

"Well, I suppose we can ask her what she meant by that. I think that blip on the destroyer's transponder means she's aboard," Karen pointed quickly at the small red triangle next to the larger icon of the Martian destroyer.

I frowned — a Rear Admiral flew her flag from a battleship, that was just the way it worked. But the triangle did look like a Martian Admiral's pennant, and the uptight Imperium didn't like to toy with its Naval traditions.

Did seem to enjoy toying with us though.

"Realtime when, Jim?"

Hannigan looked up from the console he was hovering over, "About three minutes. Weapons range a minute and a half after that, from what I'm seeing."

I nodded and took a deep breath to try to calm myself down a bit, "And how long until Mark gets here?"

Hannigan turned from the panel to peer over the shoulder of the person behind him, "About fifteen minutes out, by the looks of it."

I ground my teeth together — dammit, I couldn't leave without warning Mark that trouble was coming from all sides.

Perhaps I could delay the intrepid Martian Admiral by talking to her... that or *Lion* and *Wolf* would have to fight one hell of a holding action.

Why, you might ask, couldn't we just signal *Honesty?* Remember, laser comms aren't that good for trying to connect with moving targets. They can do it at relatively short ranges by sensor lock, but over long distances you needed pre-established coordinates to send to. So I could link to Belt Two from here with a long range burst, because the coordinates for its large receiver array were programmed into the computer and changed on a consistent, predictable basis. But a ship moving in the middle of nowhere wasn't as easy — if it wasn't close enough that sensors could lock on and give the comm laser something to aim for, there was nothing we could do.

So we had to wait.

Or...

"Alright, let's get ready to cruise. Give me a Battlelink to Kris," I turned as I said the words, and Hannigan aligned the arrays for me.

Karen, already knowing — as she always tended to know — what I was thinking, turned and nodded to Matt, "Battle stations. Erica, plot an intercept course for *Honesty* and then prepare a full burn turn to reset course for Belt Two after we link up."

The Battlelink came to life in screen two and I nodded to Kris, "We're going to chat for a minute, then go intercept Mark and head for Belt Two at maximum speed. Looks like the Martians want a war with us, and they've signed up the new Syndicate to help them out."

Kris' eyes understandably widened at the words, but she turned away nonetheless and began giving orders.

It was a dangerous plan, going one way and then doubling back. We'd potentially have to fight our way through five Martian warships on the second leg there, but I was willing to bet their crews would be no match for ours.

Willing to bet... because I really didn't have another option. Decision making for Naval officers can be just that easy.

"Jim, send a message to Belt Two, let them know everything I just said, attach our current scans, and give orders to Wes to rally the squadron at base and prepare to receive. I don't know if we'll be followed the whole way, but if we are, I want us concentrated there."

With another nod, Hannigan began giving orders to his staff. I took another deep breath and glanced at Karen, "Was it only an hour ago that I was in a good mood?"

She smiled, "Forty-five minutes."

I managed a smile in return, then watched the Martians draw closer on the main screen.

"Realtime comms in forty seconds now, sir," Hannigan's report was quiet, and I nodded.

At around that moment I realized I was still in my flight jacket, having not bothered to change before going on that nose-breaking spree in the brig. Now as I think of it again, that nose-breaking was a harsh reaction for me... but then what I was hearing wasn't exactly cuddly teddy-bear stuff. Nose-breaking seemed warranted then, and I won't second guess it now... not that you should care, particularly.

We were about to have it out with the Martians, after all.

Trying not to let my mind get carried away with that thought, I pulled off my flight jacket and tossed it to my chair, then tugged at my shirt in an effort to straighten it out a bit. No tunic on hand, but oh well, Kitty Castillo could see me in this state, I didn't much care.

"Twenty seconds."

The Martians were trying to start a war with us? After literally a century and a half of peace. Occasional spats of cold war, occasional border incidents, and a bona fide war scare back in First Lord Fiora's day... but in all my time in the Belt I'd heard not so much as boo from the Martians. The last 'war' we'd fought had been their rebellion in 2110, what they call 'The Glorious War of Freedom From Tyranny' — I kid you not, that's what they call it.

I call it the day in history when they rioted over having taxes lower than Earth's but still 'too high', when fourteen Defense Command SF guards got killed, and over 2,000 civilians on Mars were murdered by the mob, and the Empire decided to pull out because it wasn't willing to spend lives on that money-pit dustball of a planet.

Seems we call that fight different things.

"Linking up now, sir. She seems eager to talk," Hannigan's words came alongside a buffering display to screen two, and I folded my arms and set my stance in front of the monitor.

It took a second for the Martian signal to be properly linked through the system, and then sure enough, the visage of Rear Admiral Kitty Castillo wearing a fierce grin appeared.

"Commodore Barron, it's my pleasure to inform you that you are in violation of Martian territory and Martian law. You are to surrender your ships at once and prepare to be boarded."

Okay, there are a lot of things I could have said at that moment, but appreciate again that my day was riding the express train southward... by which I mean I was getting pretty ticked off.

"Please do shut up, my dear Admiral. Don't give us cause to destroy you."

Castillo's smile faded, "Excuse me?"

"*Kitty*," I started with a surprisingly civil tone, "are you, how do I put this, a complete lunatic? Because from what I've been told you and yours are about to start a shooting war with the Earth Empire, and you're paying pirates to augment your forces."

Her eyes narrowed, "Well, seems you're a keen one. You won't be warning Earth, though."

"I'll be doing whatever I bloody well please, actually. And *you'll* be standing down right now or we're going to have an unfortunate situation on our hands," my eyes settled on hers, and she tilted her head.

"Five against two. Three, sure, when your corvette gets back. But I think we'll do fine, and shortly after that it'll be fourteen against three," the Martian Admiral's smug gaze irritated me.

So I gave as good as I got, "I noticed they took away your battleship, *Kitty*. What, did your Admiralty get embarrassed by the smut you were sending to Mister Cooper? You seriously should have sent that stuff in a brown paper wrapper."

Her lips twisted into a snarl, but I smiled and held up a hand, "Besides, I very much doubt you can bend over as far as the diagram says you can."

Oh that set her off. Boom. Riot blast. Minor nuke. She shot daggers through her gaze. Unfortunately for her, daggers don't do much in a ship battle.

I took two steps forward towards the screen and let my eyes narrow, "Or did they pull your ship to augment their home fleet? I bet you think you're so clever, you'll strike unexpectedly and win great victories, is that it?"

Her lips twitched and she *glared*.

"Well, hate to break it to you, but I'm at the Belt, Greg Noyce and John Fiora are at Earth, and Marlene Stoll's at Venus. You want to win, you're actually going to have to produce some *fighting spacers*, not closet smut stars with piratic hang-ups and overexcited Commanders."

Yes, I was letting it fly. This, you should note, was not wise. I've told many young officers never to lose their cool, never to say something they'll regret. Well, I didn't regret saying any of this, but it would probably have been a bit more courteous not to say it all.

So a word to the wise, do as I say, not as I do... or... well, don't say what I said. Take my advice and keep your mouth shut...

Unless you can back it up with raw firepower. Then let fly. And come to think of it, I was about to back this tirade up.

"You're about to die in our first great victory, Mister Barron," she hissed at last, and my smile broadened.

"I'll feel guilty about beating up on a delusional Admiral, not to worry."

With that I turned away, and Hannigan cut the feed. I found myself staring at a bunch of open-mouthed faces — everyone was staring at me. Karen, who must have stepped back while I was spewing my verbal assaults, moved forward and I leaned towards her.

"Why's everyone staring?" I whispered. "Was I that outrageous?"

I mean, I had essentially just started the first Imperial war in the history of the Earth Empire by implying that an enemy Admiral was a repressed sex-freak... I really should have contemplated how that'd look in the history books before I did it. But at least it did look good in the movies.

It was time to start a proper shooting war...

CHAPTER TWENTY-ONE

HOW TO SAVE ONE'S SKIN

Now, you're probably sitting there thinking we all treated the coming of war far, far too lightly, and you may be right. At this point in time we were still looking at the Martians the same way we looked at the pirates — another menace, another challenge for us to collectively put down... and our default setting for putting down a menace, as you've seen by now, is 'cavalier'. It wouldn't remain so for long, but there it was.

We *did* understand the gravity of the sudden outbreak of conflict and we were shocked by it. It was as though the Martians had been planning this in their back rooms for a while and we'd stumbled onto the plan just as they were bringing it out into the light, but before they were totally ready to launch it. *Totally* ready to launch it.

They were still pretty ready.

Back on topic, though, we weren't just trying to laugh it off. It's sometimes hard for people to understand the sense of humor one needed to have when working the Belt in those days. You might scoff at all the joking and informality, but consider what everyone knew to be going on: we'd been out-foxed. The Martians and the pirates were ganging up on us. We had three ships scattered in unfriendly space and a total of fourteen ships closing in on us. And there was promise of much fighting and misery to come, possibly on a scale much larger than we'd ever seen against the pirates — and even against Merger, who'd attacked Earth in force.

So there were two choices when you looked at that scenario. You could get completely depressed or dramatic or catatonic, and in turn get killed, or you could try to put on a cavalier show like you always did, ignore the panic that was pouring through your veins, and get back to work.

You know which one we picked, and a good thing too.

"Weapons range in one minute," Matt's voice was a little more hurried than usual, but I didn't pay much heed to the change in pace. The Briton persisted, "You want to give them something to think about before we leave?"

I frowned thoughtfully, glancing at Karen, and her brow creased, "We go into laser range and I don't like our chances of getting out without moderate damage."

That was, of course, a very good point. We were days from a friendly port, and even the slightest damage could be daunting with a long open-space haul ahead of us — particularly if there'd be an enemy on our heels.

So getting into range and fulfilling my threats the old-fashioned way wouldn't work.

The carrier experts like Caldecott would have screamed 'launch fighters' at a moment like that, and summarily gotten all the pilots killed or captured for nothing. That certainly wasn't an option.

That left...

"Torpedoes. Matt, plot me a firing solution, and Kris, you get one too."

Kris was still on the Battlelink, now on screen four, and she nodded.

"We'll leave them a little present. Push them out of the tubes, set their drives for proximity activation," I continued, and Karen smiled at me.

Yep, we'd leave the glorious Imperium Navy a little surprise.

"After that, we go meet Mark."

Fireworks time.

Commander Mark Gunney was pleased — *Honesty* was making excellent progress, easily outpacing the pirates whose cruising speed as a squadron was simply no match for the corvette's. Sure, some raiders were faster, but in order to maintain their cohesion, the pirates were staying in a united, *slow* formation.

That meant *Honesty* had a forty minute lead on them, and that'd be more than enough time to warn *Wolf* and *Lion* to evacuate the system.

"We have them on long-range sensors yet?" Mark turned to the Lieutenant at Sensors and Communications.

"Not yet, sir. Another five minutes I'd say, and then two more before I can get a sharp enough reading for a long-distance comm."

Gunney nodded. That was fair enough, there was no rush.

Wolf and *Lion* started to back away from the advancing Martians, and I can only imagine the snide grin on Castillo's face as she watched us move. It was understood that our *Predator*-class frigates were individually each more than a match for her destroyer, but all those destroyer escorts were the problem — we could be overwhelmed too easily by that much fire.

The risk just wasn't worth taking.

Of course, the distinguished Miss *Kitty* probably didn't see it that way; she was looking at this as a glorious reversal for the Earth Empire, even though this incident was clearly a victory for us. Seriously, we uncovered their elaborate trap before it could be sprung — think us claiming it as something of a victory was just overblown spin? Wait until you read the next book and tell me this wasn't a huge event for us...

Different perspectives, different stories, I suppose. Can you believe this all started because Karen and I felt like storming a pirate house, then were grounded by the Belt Nine fighter maintenance crew and went to harass an informant? It's wild, I know, but these things can happen that way. It can actually be rather frightening to look at the number of random occurrences that have played important roles in starting wars in human history. Not to get too far off on a tangent here, but what about the Archduke Franz Ferdinand's driver turning down the wrong street one morning in 1914. If you get a chance, look it up. An assassin tasked to kill the Archduke had missed his window and given up for the day when, by sheer bad luck, his target turned unexpectedly down a side street and pulled up in front of him. Bang: First World War.

Anyhow, enough editorializing.

Wolf and *Lion* were backing off, but we were leaving a present in our bow wake.

For the record, you can't even see the torpedo tube on a *Predator*-class ship. It's so rarely used that it's tucked right behind the forward weapons pod facing down. Looks like a little dot when you're flying in to land your plane, and at a distance you can't even tell it's there.

That, today, was a good thing, I decided. Because the torpedoes from both frigates were gently thrust out of the hull and then lay dead in space, the radiation from their hefty warheads the only way of seeing them… but that radiation had been masked by our drive emissions.

The Martians weren't scanning the space ahead of them too closely, it seemed.

"Alright, time to bow out properly. Karen, Kris, let's get out of here," I was used to being the guy who looked to Erica Martin and told her to fly *Wolf* out of a tight spot, but this time Karen gave the orders, and on *Lion* Kris did the same.

Both frigates turned with well-practiced coordination, their port pods firing one way and starboard pods the other to throw them into a flat spin before firing again to stop the turn.

Then in *Wolf's* engineering bay, Andrew Jenson opened up the conduits and the reactors poured their energy into the drive pods' thrusters. *Lion's* engineer did the same, and both frigates surged away, their speed climbing up past 60 kps in a few seconds, reaching 100 kps in only a minute.

Behind us, the Martian ships began to pour more energy into their drives as well. Their acceleration wasn't too bad, but then they got close to our two dormant torpedoes. Martian DEs can move pretty quickly, but at point blank range torpedoes are faster still.

Both warheads locked onto the same DE, one that was cruising next to Castillo's destroyer. As I eyed its transponder, I realized it was the destroyer escort that had been in the space over Asteroid Theta this whole time. Somehow it was ironic that it became the target.

The torpedoes' engines kicked hard, and I watched them pop up on the main screen. They rocketed in at ballistic speed, and they hit four seconds apart. Number one slammed into the DE's upper drive pod, and in so doing sent a shockwave through the ship and backed up its power system, which in turn started to overload.

The second torpedo flew smack into one of the laser turrets — I'll explain those later — and went off. This second explosion buffeted the little ship, and then it unleashed the overload the first hit had set up.

Short form for what came next reads like this: BOOM.

Sorry to be unsophisticated in the terminology, but for the record, it was one of the mightiest ship explosions I'd ever seen. It wasn't often that torpedoes got into ship-to-ship fighting, at least against pirates (and there really hasn't been anyone else to fight until this day) so the success in having two connect with a single target was a novelty.

A novelty that killed a Martian crew, but there again was one of those things you ignore. They declared war on us, after all. Surely that means something.

As I say, you don't think about those questions.

Wolf and *Lion* had worked up to 188 kps by the time I started paying attention to speed again, and the Martians had elected to drop back, worried we'd left more surprises in their way. I hoped that we'd bought time enough to get to *Honesty* and then to make a run for it.

If not, well, we'd deal with that eventuality when it came.

✦✦✦

"Commander!" Mark Gunney got the harried call a few minutes later, and then *Wolf* and *Lion* popped up on the main screen. He'd been sitting down so he stood up in surprise, advancing towards the screen for a moment before pointing and turning towards the Sensors and Communications Officer.

"What's their vector?"

"Coming right to meet us… hang on, they just pinged us with sensors."

That, when communication wasn't directly or easily possible, was usually an attention-grabbing move by a veteran Captain, so Mark paid attention immediately, and watched as both frigates did something the textbooks didn't recommend.

With momentum carrying both our frigates at 188 kps, we yawed 180 degrees and our drives fired at full. We came to a dead stop in short order, and by the time *Honesty* was about to pass us we were working up to full speed on a matching course.

Mark Gunney got the message, "We're not going to Theta, ladies and gentlemen. Follow whatever course adjustments they make, deactivate stealth mode and get everyone to battle stations."

Honesty, *Lion*, and *Wolf* now fled the area in company. And the pirates and the Martians gave chase.

CHAPTER TWENTY-TWO
FIGURING OUT WHAT WE COULD

I had a headache. It had been a long time coming — after a day like that, I was almost surprised it hadn't hit sooner. As soon as we safely got past Asteroid Theta in company with *Lion* and *Honesty*, I headed to my cabin to take some Adlennol, which probably wouldn't kick in for half an hour.

In the meantime, I stole ten minutes for a quick shower, tossed my clothes into the laundry chute, and tugged on a fresh pair of ship fatigues. There'd be no time to get comfortable in civvies. Besides, it'd seem wildly inappropriate to be wearing civvies at a time like this.

My vidscreen was patched into the bridge sensor feed thanks to Hannigan's efforts, so I could watch the pirates and the Martians merge in our wake and continue the chase, not gaining on us thankfully enough.

We were pulling away from them all, making a startling 196 kps back towards Belt Two.

The question that remained was what we could do when we got there.

I grabbed the remote off my chair and sat on the end of my bed, scrolling through the available charts we had in the *Wolf*Net computer. One of the information screens on the Belt colonies contained the most recent disposition of my squadron, so I pulled that one up in a window over the sensor display.

The ships of the Belt Squadron seemed all too scattered all of a sudden. The Martians had planned this really rather well, I had to admit. Without any sort of warning at all, they would have caught the elite ships of the Belt Squadron in ones and twos, and torn us up.

And that was probably what they were planning to do at the other stations. By now, word of the new state of relations between the Martian Imperium and the Earth Empire should have reached the Admiralty... (remember, I still hadn't found out about *Marconi's* loss, and the loss of the rest of those gallant ships).

So I hoped that First Lord Fiora was quickly bringing the fleet to war footing, that Admiral Noyce was bringing his battleships to full alert, and that Admiral Stoll was collecting her Venus Squadron. Her command was the closest to Mars and Mercury this season, she'd probably get hit first...

But back in this place, now, we weren't exactly in the best shape to deal with nine pirate vessels backed by four Martians. I could only hope that those thirteen ships were the sum total of the combined force the enemy had out here.

No, actually, I could do more than hope. Realizing that I had more information than I thought I did, I pointed the remote at the screen again and scrolled through the file directory in the finder window. Sure enough, Cooper's files from the liner had been uploaded, and I opened two of them — the 'Attackplan.pnss' and 'Availableforces.pnss' files.

Stupid pirates were using Martian OS's alright — who used file extensions anymore?

Anyway, two new windows popped up, one next to my own chart of the Belt showing the attack plan. Unsurprisingly, lots of not-so-subtle red arrows were pointing at Belt Two, the home base of my ships. But dozens of smaller arrows were spreading out from there.

Ah yes, that made sense too. They had expected to hit us with surprise on their side, so they wanted to take out the Belt Two home force — usually three ships — and then hunt for the rest of us one at a time, blasting the Belt colonies away as they went.

I hated it when an enemy actually knew what he or she was doing.

But the question now was whether this plan would survive.

There was a knock at the door and I blinked, looking up with some surprise. I really shouldn't have been surprised, Karen liked to sit in on these thinking sessions whenever we were on the same ship for them, so of course she'd be coming here, now that *Wolf* was safely away.

"Come on in, Karen."

The door opened and Karen, showered and refreshed like myself, stepped in lightly, turning to look at the screen before backing over to the bed and sitting down next to me. She almost immediately matched the slump I'd assumed subconsciously.

"Well. Never been more glad that my fighter wasn't in top form…" her words were abrupt, and I nodded.

If we hadn't gone looking for Carlos, we'd have been blissfully ignorant of all this. Insane how fate smiles on us some days… but I'll not get started on that subject again.

"At least we've accounted for all their ships," she continued after a moment, and my eyes twitched to the other window I'd opened — the one I'd forgotten about in my brooding.

Thank God Karen was paying attention.

My eyes scanned the list of ships there… five Martians and twelve pirates… "No, there are still three pirate ships out there we don't know about."

Karen smiled and looked at me, "History major, not so good at math."

"Hey," I glanced back, leaning against her and pointing at the list, "nine following us, that leaves three unaccounted for."

"How many did we blow up at Theta?" she asked with an innocent smile, and I looked from the screen to her and then smiled and shook my head.

She was gracious enough not to make more of that, so we just sat there and stared at the screens for a couple of minutes.

"I think they'll follow us back to Belt Two," Karen said after the silence. "They've got the momentum, and they're probably hoping we'll only have a small part of the squadron there when they arrive. I mean, if they wait and go after the smaller colonies, they give us time to regroup and coordinate, and that'd be bad for them. They go straight to Belt Two, they only face us and whatever Wes has been able to pull together."

I nodded tiredly in agreement, "And they don't even know for sure how many ships we called in to take our place when we left."

It actually wasn't as bad as I thought now that I looked at it. When we got back to Belt Two, we'd have at least six ships total — three *Predators* and three corvettes, all of the latter being of the *Noble* class. Now I had to do math in my head… if Wes ordered recalls to Belt Two, what would return by when?

Hell, had Wes even gotten to Belt Two yet? I hadn't checked whether he'd arrived at the Base when we were at Theta — we'd been so busy with pirates and whatnot that I'd just assumed he was on schedule. Whoops. Yes, that sort of mental slip happened even to the likes of us.

But he'd definitely be at Belt Two by the time we got there, and if he wasn't there personally the base itself would have forwarded on our recalls. So who could get to Belt Two in time to help us?

Karen, true to form, was already answering questions that I hadn't asked, "I'd say *Alberta* will make it down for sure. Marshal's good and timely about getting to his patrol stations, and he was only at Belt Seven."

I nodded slowly, noting the icon of Admiral Noyce's old flagship, now under Captain Marshal Samuels, another of the Belt Squadron's fine officers.

"*Lady Grace* will make it too," she smiled, and I nodded again. That was Karen's old (aptly if inconsistently named) corvette, also one of the *Noble*-class like *Friendly* and *Honesty*. That'd actually give us a pretty powerful four-four combination; eight ships total against a Martian destroyer and three DEs, plus the assorted pirate vessels armed in a variety of manners.

The odds were actually not so bad, even if the Martians had fitted mags or even lasers on the pirates. We had a nice solid fighting chance.

"So, if all goes as we hope…" I said after a moment.

"We're not going to die," Karen nodded.

I chuckled, "Well that's a relief. I'm hungry."

It wasn't a convincing chuckle — or it sure didn't feel like one. But remember, brave front, cavalier unflappability… these were the requirements of the service.

Karen smiled again, accepting the offer because she knew it needed to be accepted, and glanced at me, "I'm actually kinda full after that pirate muffin…"

I elbowed her and she laughed.

CHAPTER TWENTY-THREE

ALL TOO QUIET AT EARTH

While we were running from Asteroid Theta, bad things were happening at Earth… well, bad for the Fiora ring, at least, which to me means bad for the Empire (but obviously I'm biased).

John Fiora came out of his office at a steady pace, rounded the corner, and leaned down, placing two hands on the Lieutenant's desk. By the time the young woman turned her head he was staring straight at her, and she nearly jumped.

"Still no comms with the Belt and with Venus?" John's question was straightforward enough, and the girl shook her head.

"Nothing yet, sir, but Communications section says it may be due to solar flare activity. They say we'll know in an hour or two."

Frowning, John straightened back up and nodded, "Let me know as soon as they decide it isn't. And signal Admiral Noyce, I want to meet him down here as soon as he's available."

The Lieutenant nodded and then John turned and left her to her work. Pacing back to his office, he closed the door a little more loudly than he probably should have, then rounded his desk and dropped into his chair, wheeling it forward and staring at a blank spot in the middle of the tabletop.

Damn that Caldecott, things were about to get complicated.

John had just heard from a connection of his that there was to be a special address to both Houses of Parliament today — in about three hours in fact. And while the connection didn't know who was speaking, she'd warned him that it was on Naval matters.

So if it was going to the Commons and the Senate, and it was about Naval matters, and *he* didn't know about it, then that left one pretty obvious possibility for him to consider: old Dave Caldecott had been chatting with the Emperor, and had convinced His Majesty to call an inquiry.

The only question now was how bad things would get.

Great timing, you have to admit. To lose communications with the Belt and Venus, and now this… perhaps Caldecott had used his connections to take out comms for some reason. Perhaps he feared a preemptive broadcast using my celebrity or something to discredit his position from the start, at least with the public.

Without comms to the Belt and Venus, though, the Fiora ring was just short of crippled; it was basically just John and Greg in Earth space, with a handful of other junior friendlies and members. Lovely lovely lovely…

John took a deep breath and sat back in his chair.

Admiral Greg Noyce appeared in John's office about an hour and a half later — quite good time from orbit to ground with little notice. Greg didn't know why he'd been summoned, though he didn't expect good news.

He'd been spending his time aboard *Warspite*, drilling his new squadron in battle tactics. Commanding battleships was certainly an adjustment for Greg — he was long accustomed to the swift firepower of the Belt Squadron, and was only now finding his footing with the heavy, slower, massively-armed capital ships of the Heavy Squadron.

If a new Syndicate did indeed pop up, as my reports to him had indicated one might, his ships would be ready to stop a charge against Earth. Nobody would ever get as close as Grant Merger had — not again.

The progress was good for the Heavy Squadron, but based on the First Lord's seeming mood, Greg wasn't certain that the challenge he and the Fiora ring were next going to face would be the sort that could be dealt with using battleships.

Not without a full-blown coup, anyway.

"Thanks for coming, Greg," John waved Greg to a chair, and the Admiral sat quickly.

"Glad to come. What's the news, John?"

John leaned back in his chair and spread his arms dramatically, "We're about to get crucified, I think. Davie Caldecott is going to address both Houses of Parliament in about an hour and a half on Naval matters, and I only found out ninety minutes ago."

Greg's eyes widened, "Is that so? Well that's not exactly good news. Have you been able to signal the Belt or Venus? A statement from Ken released to the media now might help undercut the Second Lord, on account of Ken's celebrity..."

John shook his head slowly, "Believe me, I'd love to try that. But 'solar flare activity' has cut comms in both directions — nothing to Venus, nothing to the Belt. We can't even send to Jupiter and get them to bounce it back."

Greg tilted his head slightly, "That's very suspicious."

"You're telling me," John leaned forward again. "I'm getting set to send frigates out to tell the comm ships to do their jobs, but I think Caldecott must have that whole section in his pocket. We're probably not going to get connections to the colonies back until we've both been relieved."

Greg's expression remained steady, "You think it'll come to us being suspended?"

"If the Emperor's sanctioned a commission on us, I don't see how it can't. You're going to get a lot of golf time with pay, if I'm right."

Greg smiled, "If only I didn't have to abandon my ships to get it. I have an uneasy feeling that the training time we lose is going to be missed."

John shrugged and put his hands behind his head, rocking his chair back, "I hope it doesn't come to that... but I don't like the way this is going."

There really wasn't much else to say — things weren't looking good for the Fiora ring.

And they didn't know half the troubles that were coming.

CHAPTER TWENTY-FOUR

SQUADRON — RALLY!

"*Lady Grace* is coming in now, skipper. That gives us five ships."

Captain Wes Pellew was standing on the bridge of DCNS *Cheetah*, his *Predator*-class frigate, and he smiled at the report of the Lieutenant Commander at Sensors and Communications.

Glancing at the woman, he chuckled, "Thank you Katie, I *can* count to five. All the fingers are on the same hand, so that makes it easier."

She grinned back, "Yes, sir."

It was a good, light moment, and Wes tried to keep those coming as best he could, particularly now that the gravity of the situation was evident to everyone at Belt Two. There were a lot of pirates coming after them, and the Martians were behind it all.

That was still hard to accept, actually — the *Martians* were pushing all this along?

Well, it sounded implausible but it was the only explanation for everything that was happening... including the communications blackout. The relay ships that usually connected the Belt to Earth were no longer on station, and Wes had a sinking feeling they hadn't all gone off on joy rides.

The Martians hadn't been incompetent when they'd planned this.

Unfortunately for them, the Belt Squadron was much better than merely 'not incompetent'.

Sign pirates to fight the Defense Command Fleet, so that the Martians didn't have to die alone? That was cute. But Wes wouldn't be losing sleep over it. The enemy was a day out of Belt Two now, based on when *Wolf* had sent its report, and by the time I arrived, Wes figured he'd have six ships — not five but *six* ships of the squadron — waiting for me.

That meant nine Defense Command frigates and corvettes would be here, waiting to tangle with the best the Martians and their new allies had to offer. The odds had been much worse for us at the Battle of Deep Black... but then, admittedly, the Syndicate at that fight hadn't been armed and escorted by the Martian fleet.

What that confusing sentence means is that Wes wasn't too worried.

Cheetah was here, another *Predator* like *Wolf* and *Lion*, and thus more than a match for any one ship the pirates or the Martians had to attack with. Then there were the *Noble*-class corvettes *Friendly*, and *Lady Grace*, and soon *Generous* would arrive, having caught word of the impending attack by a lucky encounter with a hauler. That made four ships, all of them under ten years old — brand new by ship standards.

Backing up these four ships were two veterans that were themselves no slouches: Admiral Noyce's old frigate *Alberta* under Marshal Samuels was a tough ship, well upgraded and easily a match for a Martian destroyer, and the corvette *Sackville*, a hell of a little ship that had plied the space around the Belt Station for over twenty years, and had a reputation for beating pirates senseless, no matter the odds.

Six excellent ships, to be joined by the barely scratched *Honesty* and the angry *Wolf* and *Lion*. It wasn't going to go well for the pirates and the Martians if they came here... and Wes hoped they would.

As far as the Martians knew, Wes wasn't at Belt Two, and there was no way Defense Command could rally a substantial force of ships on such short notice.

It'd be quite a surprise, then, when they found the whole Belt Squadron waiting for them at Belt Two. This concentration was an unlikely turn of luck for us, but then the last week had seen a pretty impressive run on Imperial luck.

Wes wasn't inclined to look a gift horse in the mouth when it showed up, and neither was I — particularly when the odds were already being tipped in the Martians' favor.

Still, the fight would be pretty intense, with that many ships coming at each other from both sides. There was time to think about preparing the Belt domes for action, and in fact, Wes was about to deal with that...

"Signal now from Captain Stanton on the base, sir."

Wes nodded to the Lieutenant Commander at Sensors and Communications, "Good timing. Let's have her on screen four."

Turning to that screen, he waited as the *Cheetah*Net screen buffered and then smiled as Sharon Stanton, the Captain of Belt Two's Naval base, appeared, "Good day, Wes. I see *Lady Grace* just arrived."

Wes smiled, "We're getting the whole band together for this show. I've got my guitar all polished up and ready to go."

"Right. I guess that makes us the accordion section," Sharon chuckled. "But seriously, do you think you could lend us some more SF for the day? We're moving everyone from the domes into the shelters, but there's looting breaking out and I'm running short on people."

Belt Two had nine civilian domes, and then the base was in a tenth, well-protected and heavily armed dome. Trying to get the two million people from all those domes into the big shelters carved out of the rock under them really couldn't have been an easy job, though, especially for the base's relatively small SF unit.

Well, small compared to a couple of million people, Wes supposed. They still had over 8,000 SF guards on their base, and over 300 Special Branch officers on top of that.

But if they needed some of the squadron's people power to get the domes ready to receive, Wes certainly wasn't going to say no.

"Just tell us where you need us," he nodded. "I'll send ships to the hardest-hit domes and we'll send down all the spare SF and Special Branch we've got... but I'll need them back before the battle."

Sharon grinned, "Thanks Wes, you're a doll."

Wes' brow twisted at that one — sort of the 'uh... alright' look, "Sure."

The vid link flashed off, and Wes frowned and shook his head, looking back to the Lieutenant Commander at Sensors and Communications. She smiled at him, "I think she likes you, sir."

Wes' eyebrows went up slightly, "Everybody likes me, Katie. Get *Lady Grace* on the line when it's in range."

"Yes sir," the Lieutenant Commander kept smiling, and with a shake of his head, Wes turned back to the main screen and crossed his arms.

CHAPTER TWENTY-FIVE

MORE EXCITING WAITING

It probably seems like an odd time to mention this, but one thing that Karen does to unwind when she's under stress is, well, to start dancing. Not ballet or jazz or anything formal like that, she just plays some classic 'disco' music with a beat and starts going at it like a college girl in a club.

Yeah, she kept that one quiet for quite a while, but it's true. I always made a point, in stressful times, of dropping in on her in her cabin — the only place a self-respecting Captain could suspend her sense of reality and start swinging her hips — and let some of her ridiculous enthusiasm wash over me.

Seriously, if you never saw Karen doing this, you missed out. She even let her hair down most of the time.

Now, you might be asking how could she be doing something so juvenile only a day before a huge battle?

Well, I've skipped over the day we spent doing battle drills, and the two three-hour meetings we had about exactly what we could expect from the Martian-pirate fleet's weapons and tactics. Believe me, that would bore you much more than Karen's wiggling around her cabin. And don't worry, you didn't miss anything — you saw how *Wolf* and *Lion* and *Honesty* fought around Asteroid Theta, and you already have all the conclusive information we had about the way the pirates and Martians would pull together.

In other words, you knew as little as we did... well, you probably know much more now that we did then, but I've only said as much as we knew then... more or less. Hopefully that makes sense.

Instead of continuing to dwell on how much we didn't know, our serious, professional, elite, incomparable Captain Karen McMaster was bouncing and bobbing her way around her sizable cabin while loud, centuries-old music accused her of being trapped in some sort of 'boogie wonderland'.

And you thought *I* was inappropriately nuts? This doesn't even get covered under the 'cavalier persona' defense. She was just getting down with her naughty self, as they used to say...

Anyway, I walked in on this sight when I went to confess a few worries I had about the battle to come. She was bouncing and turning and doing those arm-moving things that sort of curled and weaved and went up and down... sorry, I'm not much of a dancer myself, so I don't have the technical terms for you.

Just think of a young woman at a fashionable club... with admittedly old music... getting *down*. And make sure the woman you picture is wearing off-duty sweats and a short-sleeved shirt, with her blond hair unbound and a big smile on her face.

This was my Flag Captain. The day before a big battle. And what's more, this didn't worry me in the slightest, because it was normal.

Actually, it was good sign. So as I closed the door and stepped towards her, I found a spot in the middle of the floor and crossed my arms, letting a slight smile twitch onto my face. Karen whirled and saw me and flashed one of those smiles, doing some of those arms things and whatnot as she did.

"Ken, come and dance with me!" she wiggled her hips and turned around again.

"You know better than that," my voice was monotone — its usual response to these situations. It'd take a very good day for me to indulge her, that was for sure. And while this was certainly proving the high point of the day, I wasn't going to stop being the guy who pretended he didn't have rhythm.

"You're no fun, as usual," Karen grinned and started dancing her way around me, doing all sorts of weavy and twistish thingies and arm stuff and the rest.

Sorry, I don't know how else to describe it. But it was fun to watch, I must admit.

By the time she worked her way back around to my front, she was smiling ear to ear — a very bright sight, that — and the song was fading. Tugging the remote from her pocket, she paused the playback, stopping the next track from coming up, and wiped her glistening forehead with the back of her hand, breathing just a tad more heavily than usual.

"One day you'll dance," her eyes met mine, and I smiled, uncrossing my arms.

"Yeah, one day we will. For now, I'm wondering about the civilians in the domes on Belt Two. Think they're being looked after?"

Despite the move to a more serious topic, Karen's infectious smile went nowhere, "Of course they are. Wes is looking after things, I'm sure of that."

I nodded slowly — she was probably right. Well, there was no 'probably' about Wes; he'd look after things. I was just worried that he wasn't there, I don't know why. You'll find I tend to worry a lot more than I let on. Before a fight, every possible eventuality cruises through my head and panics me... all so that when the battle is joined I don't worry about things any more. I don't know if that makes sense to you, but it's the way I work.

So I'd been worrying about the state of the civilians, and about two other things.

Both of which I'd managed to forget.

Come on, if you ever saw Karen dancing around in her cabin like a college girl you'd forget things too. At least give me credit for remembering the civilian matter.

"Is that it?" Karen had the remote poised, and her shoulders were already starting to rock side to side a little.

I cocked an eyebrow and didn't even try to contain my smile, nodding instead, "Yeah, that'd be it for now."

"Good," she hit play, and the speakers began to vibrate again.

I smiled, instinctively crossing my arms, then frowned, trying to remember one of those old-time turns of phrase. "Um... yes... shake your *groove* thing."

Grinning, Karen turned around and began to wiggle her hips and do arms things again. My foot almost started tapping in time with the music but I positively refused to let such a thing happen just now, so I clamped it to the deck with a strong force of will.

Karen turned around again, grinning ear to ear, "You enjoying the spectacle?"

My eyebrows went up and my smile slipped past my determination to disapprove, "I'll let myself out when I'm ready."

Wolf cruised towards battle.

CHAPTER TWENTY-SIX

SHOOTING ONESELF IN THE FOOT — WITH A MISSILE

Subtle title for a chapter, wouldn't you say? Well it basically sums up the situation Greg Noyce and John Fiora found themselves staring at as they sat in the First Lord's office and watched on the screen as Dave Caldecott pontificated about responsibility and the need for the service to be somber and all the rest.

Basically, he was trotting out moralistic reasons for Defense Command to get rid of the popular Fiora ring and its media-friendly attitudes. The press loved dealing with John, Greg, Marlene and myself — we respected them, kept them alive in tight scrapes, and gave them entertaining stories whenever those stories wouldn't compromise security.

But Caldecott's crowd hated the media, thought the Fiora ring cared more about putting on a good show than protecting the Empire, and wanted us gone.

This was what you'd expect from Dave Caldecott — we were used to him complaining at every turn about the way we handled ourselves in front of the cameras. His most entertaining complaints were the ones he made at *press conferences* — the irony on those days was so thick you could build a bridge out of it.

Unfortunately, my promotion to Commodore and my refusal to conform to his job description for the position had given Caldecott enough puff to get the Emperor to call an inquiry. Hardly the Emperor's fault — Caldecott did a fine job spinning his version of things, and my bad behavior admittedly didn't help.

I mean, what Emperor wouldn't be wise listening to someone who said: 'Gee, Your Majesty, Commodores aren't supposed to storm two pirate houses in a single morning. He might be a liability.' On face it sounds pretty insane for a Commodore to do anything of the sort, at least it does if you don't quite comprehend the need for theatrics when you're trying to make headway on the Belt frontier. Guess what, the Emperor didn't get it.

And if you're sitting there shaking your head at my defense… well, first, I have no idea why you'd buy my memoirs if you disapproved of my behavior, and second, remember that (by blind luck, yes I know) it was my cavalier behavior that had set us onto the Martians' scent before they could strike.

The point of all this was that my actions had given the Second Lord the leverage he needed to get the Emperor to call for an Imperial Commission — an inquiry into the state of Defense Command. And John and Greg sat in John's office and watched, in varying levels of shock and frustration.

John's chin cradled in his hand, his elbow propped on the arm of his chair, and his expression none too impressed, "We're incredibly lucky we don't have organized pirates to fight right now. This is going to paralyze us for months."

Greg nodded, "Let's hope the pirates don't realize we'll be tied up. If they were to figure that out, they'd start causing more problems."

The quietly-spoken words drew a nod from John, and then both were silent as

Caldecott raised his voice a little higher — to the point where the already irritating voice almost broke into a puppet-esque squeal.

"…And it is with great dismay that I declare that, during this period of inquiry, we will have to recall some of our most famous officers from their active duties…"

"Here it comes," Greg looked back across the desk at John.

The First Lord nodded, a look of thorough disgust crossing his features, "His voice gets much higher and my dog's going to be the only one who can hear it."

Greg smiled despite the prevailing mood of dread and looked back at the vidscreen.

"…first of all," Caldecott squeaked at the assembled Houses of Parliament, "First Lord Fiora will be required to suspend himself from command, pending a review of his decisions. We will also have to recall Rear Admiral Marlene Stoll from Venus, and ask Rear Admiral Greg Noyce to relieve himself temporarily of command of the Home Fleet's Heavy Squadron. Most importantly, we must recall Commodore Ken Barron from the Belt Squadron, as his actions *demand* review."

There was no mistaking it: Caldecott *loved* saying those words. You know how vindictive people can be — me, for instance (after this stunt I was rather inclined to get him exiled to the free asteroids as a traitor to the Empire). And that doesn't even compare to what came for me after the war, as you probably already know… Anyway, Caldecott was being vindictive too, he just wasn't as good at it as I was.

"New officers will be temporarily appointed to these posts, and the operations of the Defense Command squadrons across the Empire will see no ill effects," Caldecott squeaked on.

"Hear that, Greg? I guess he doesn't consider 'all activities grinding to a halt and pirates running unchecked' to be an ill effect," John probably sounded a little bitter, and seriously, who could blame him?

I mean, appreciate the scene: the two most decorated officers then in Defense Command history were sitting across a desk from each other, in the First Lord's office — one of *their* offices — hearing that they were a danger to the security of the Empire. And hearing it from a guy who'd only ever fired a weapon on a shooting range, and hadn't even done that in a decade or two.

Politics was, then as ever, tons of fun.

"I suppose I might as well book some tee times with the kids," Greg sighed. "Hopefully they'll let loose cannons like me on the links."

John nodded, "And I've got a house to renovate. Guess we've got nothing more to worry about. I'm sure our friend Davie there can handle whatever gets thrown at the Empire."

"You adding a bomb shelter in your renovations?" Greg asked with a smile, and John chuckled.

"Am now."

They both laughed — it was a good joke.

As far as they knew.

CHAPTER TWENTY-SEVEN

WORRYING (GALLANTLY)

We ended up getting to Belt Two with about four hours in hand — the pirates and the Martians just couldn't keep up with the high-speed run of three of the fastest ships in the Defense Command fleet.

Of course I worried most of the way back — what else does one do in circumstances like that? The important point is that you can't let yourself get *consumed* by worry. You can let your brain run wild with all the crazy what-ifs when nobody else (except Karen) is around, but when it comes to showing your face in public, you project absolute confidence, whether it's authentic or not.

I was very much aware of the fact that Defense Command was suddenly at *war*. Not just 'pirate war', not just skirmishes with raiders or unaligned ships with attitude… this was a *war* war. The kind with a full-time enemy with organized resources and infrastructure on the same level as the Empire. Sure, the Martians were widely seen as incompetent, and then as now, I found their ship quality and their tactics to be inferior to ours…

But they'd planned this to ensure surprise was squarely on their side. And surprise might be all they needed to turn the tide.

It didn't matter how bad their ships might be, or how pathetic their ship-to-ship tactics *seemed* to be: if they caught the Belt Squadron or the Venus Squadron or, God help us, the *Home Fleet* unawares, they'd have the advantage.

Believe me, I'd seen it a number of times: even the most powerful warship was a poor combatant when it wasn't ready to fight and the enemy was.

These were the sorts of concerns that were rolling through my mind for most of the trip back — excepting that interlude where I visited dancing Karen. And those fears were still sitting at the back of my mind when I arrived on *Wolf's* bridge to witness the arrival in Belt Two local space.

I wanted to know how many ships were there for me, and I had a dread expectation that there'd only be one or two. That somehow the Martians had been everywhere at once and had killed my squadron and left us with no chance of holding Belt Two.

Karen was standing with her arms folded as I emerged onto the bridge, and she glanced at me as I arrived beside her, "We'll have long-range scans of the system in about a minute. Good timing."

I tried to smile, "I'd pretend it was magic or something, but I had the feed up on my vidscreen down in my cabin."

"I know," Karen succeeded in smiling, looking back to the screen as she did. "You history sorts, always cheating."

That did actually get me to smile — I know, you probably don't get the joke, but you haven't spent countless late hours talking with Karen McMaster about the epistemology of history and science.

And after reading that description, you're probably *glad* you missed those talks. I don't blame you, honestly.

Anyway, what she said made me smile, and I crossed my own arms, "We don't think of it as *cheating*, remember. We just acknowledge that there are many different ways to get a job done, and even more ways to characterize it."

"We science folks just get the *right* answer," Karen played her counter-card with a grin.

"Yeah, well we believe in relativism, so there are no *right* right answers are there then?" I shot back, actually starting to free my mind from its worries with the inane talk.

Then someone cleared her throat, and I frowned and let my eyes dart between the screens... oh. Kris Jacobs was on screen three, and now she waved at us, "Hey there, we all don't really give a damn about the epistemology of your learning. So kindly shut up."

Karen and I both grinned and quieted down. You might wonder why I didn't dress Kris down for her insubordination... well, my editor says that if you're still wondering at my failure to conform to regs by now, you might want to reread the book to this point.

Wolf, Lion and *Honesty* were racing painfully to their destination, now, so I'd have my answer momentarily... time just seemed so sloooow. Yes, slow enough to attempt to convey the speed with extra 'o's in the word.

Ah, waiting and worrying. What would life be without it — aside from less stressful, I mean.

Looking back over my shoulder I caught sight of Hannigan leaning over the shoulder of the Head Sensors Tech. That must mean he was getting a read on *something*, surely. It actually felt like Hannigan, or maybe a powerful lord of time, or *something*, was slowing the seconds down, making the wait that much more excruciating...

Six icons suddenly popped up on the main screen.

Lost in all that inane musing that you just read through (and more that was so inane I just couldn't in good conscience include it), my mind didn't immediately register what I was seeing.

Karen was smiling, of course, because her damned science brain understood *everything*. Me, I just sort of stared for a moment, and then my mind finally started processing again. The whole Belt Squadron was here.

Nine of Defense Command's very best ships against a flimflam assortment of pirates and Martians. The odds were suddenly tipped in our favor.

But in our favor or not, we could still be annihilated, and with no squadron ships away from the fight, we'd have no Naval support for any of the Belt colonies if our squadron was wiped out.

"Well, that'd be a good reason to not all die, I suppose..." I replied verbally to my own musings, and Karen glanced at me.

"You need a good reason for that now? Guess I better get a personal cause then..."

I grinned, "Yeah, go into classrooms and talk to science kids. Warn them not to turn out like you!"

Karen made the 'oooh' face before she smiled and turned back to Matt, "Deceleration procedure, Matt."

I looked back to Hannigan, "As soon as we get into range, let's do a giant realtime conference, Jim. You can use whatever screens you need; I want to talk to everyone at once, if I can."

Hannigan smiled, "Of course you can, sir. When do I ever say no to you?"

"Let's see, when I'm wrong, when I'm stupid, when the answer's 'no'..." I was definitely feeling subconscious relief as I paced back to my chair. "So how long?"

Hannigan leaned sideways to check a timer on one of the screens his tech was running, "Say... nine minutes."

"Erica, prepare to maneuver us into squadron formation," Karen looked to Lieutenant Commander Martin as she too stepped back towards her chair.

Taking a deep breath, I lowered myself into my seat.

It was going to be a long nine minutes.

CHAPTER TWENTY-EIGHT

TAKING STOCK

Karen and I stepped into my day cabin just as the vidscreen was glowing to life in the wall and dividing itself into eight windows. Each separate mini-screen was faced with a *Wolf*Net loading display.

What you're now going to read is one of the most confusing sorts of tactical meetings fleet officers can have: a vid conference. I'd have loved to get the Captains and Commanders of the entire squadron physically together in one room for a meeting of this importance, but like I said, we only had four hours. It might sound like a lot, but when you're trying to coordinate nine ships it's precious little, even for an elite squadron.

So the next best thing was to do it by vid, but as you can probably guess, trying to watch eight faces on a screen could get confusing — and it was made worse by the fact that body language didn't come through cleanly. Everybody was looking straight at their screens, and thus the vidcameras on their side of the feed were making it look as though they were staring straight at whoever was watching.

In other words, I'd be looking around at eight different people, but each one might think I was looking at him or her when I was in fact looking at someone else.

It may not sound like a problem, but it can be a big one...

Still, no option today.

Kris Jacobs and Mark Gunney were the first to appear, and that made sense since both their ships were still in formation with *Wolf*. We were close to the rest of the squadron, but not in formation with them yet, so it'd take a bit more time to coordinate realtime feeds...

Next came Wes Pellew from *Cheetah*, and Marshal Samuels from *Alberta*. The corvette commanders then began appearing in turn. These were names you'll probably recognize — Andrea Kiley, Isoruku Togo, Katya Romanov and Elise DeWinter. The so called 'Band of Fellows' (a rip off of the old Shakespearian term 'Band of Brothers' which doesn't quite eliminate the male overtones, but don't blame me, the media picked it, and I rarely use it).

So we all ended up staring at each other, and I have to say it was good to see the familiar faces again, even if just on screen. I may not have been able to shake each one of their hands in person, but now I had some real visual proof that everyone had made it back.

"Marshal, glad you made it to the party," I started with a smile, and the elite Captain gave one of his trademark understated smiles.

"Wouldn't miss this show, Ken."

There were matching smiles from all the officers, and then Wes leaned towards his screen with a grin, "The rest of us showed up too, you know."

"Yeah, but you all had a pretty short flight," I protested with my smile broadening, "and besides, let's not get into a praise-mongering match."

There was laughter — I don't know why, in retrospect, because every time I re-read that sentence it doesn't strike me as amusing. Nerves, probably, as I was definitely feeling them. However, we were all on the same screen at last, and it was probably a good idea not to waste time with mindless chatter.

"So, Wes you know our situation?" I leaned back in my chair.

"Just got confirmation of it from Hannigan," Wes nodded, and all the other Captains and Commanders nodded as well.

"Good... so... thoughts?"

I know it sounds like a pretty vague and open-ended way to start such an important briefing, but job one at a time like that is to get the opinions of your very best people. We could start without me bringing my biases to the table... I'd get to that part later, if need be.

"Seems to me the odds favor us," Marshal was the first to comment. "They seriously lack regular ships — I don't care how many guns you give the pirates, they're still undisciplined and not up to our level."

The matter-of-fact statement got some nods, and Mark Gunney chimed in immediately, "I have to agree with Marshal on that one. We did get the drop on the pirates out there, but they still were pretty bad to begin with."

Karen shifted slightly in her seat, then leaned towards the screen, "Very true, gentlemen. Frankly I'm not worried about us as much as I'm worried about Belt Two. With the advantage the pirates have in numbers, they might well be able to attack the domes."

That thought didn't quite come from left field, but I certainly hadn't thought of it. Don't misinterpret; I always tended to consider what harm our fighting could do to the local stationary bases, but that wasn't what Karen meant. She was wondering whether the pirates would take this chance to try to actually *raid* Belt Two.

I better back up for a minute and explain this properly. Pirates didn't just attack shipping in the Belt in these times; there were plenty of Belt colonies around with only small garrisons of SF looking out for them, and so actually sending landing parties to pillage for supplies, slaves, and worse wasn't as uncommon as it should have been.

That said, since Admiral Noyce had taken over the squadron years back, such attempts had become rare and often suicidal, but the pirates still lusted after the booty they could collect from raiding the domes.

Belt Two hadn't been hit by such a raid in almost seventy years — not since it had become the home base of the Belt Squadron. No pirate was stupid enough to try to get around a Defense Command ship to land, and since Belt Two's status as main base meant there was always at least one ship around, that made the colony off limits to raiding.

Hence the size and success of the colony: they had our protection and the persistently rich mining economy of the rock. All that time untouched left Belt Two as one of the richest and juiciest targets for raiding in the entire region... and if the pirates were able to tie up our squadron with most of their ships and then land pillaging parties, that could definitely be a problem.

Now I must be honest: as I said before, I hadn't yet even thought of that particular possibility. This is why I have meetings with my Captains and Commanders when big decisions need to be made — there's absolutely nothing wrong with getting different perspectives on a problem. Ego and hubris are the most dangerous things in situations like these.

Wes, apparently, had thought of the problem too, "We've helped Captain Stanton evacuate the domes to the shelters, but there's still plenty there to loot if they want to. Could be a problem."

I nodded slowly, looking to my desk for a moment as I thought through the potential risks and what resources I had to throw at them.

"Well…" I began to think out loud, "I can't set aside a ship to cover the asteroid, not when we're outnumbered and when they might be overwhelmed. I take it Sharon doesn't think shore batteries can cover all the domes?"

Wes shook his head, "Not enough coverage to deal with the number of landers that might come down. Or to deal with CB fire."

Counter-battery fire is what Wes meant by CB — it's fire that seeks out the enemy's weapons positions and destroys them. Most stationary installations were near indefensible because they lacked enough firepower to defeat a moving target before it eliminated their stationary batteries. Again, don't mistake me — Belt Two was well protected by batteries. The problem was they were designed to cope with only one or two raiders, and to do so in conjunction with a local ship. That was the defense plan for the colony, but now it didn't fit the situation.

But my point still stood, "Even so, I can't separate one of you to watch the domes. You could be singled out and overwhelmed, and we can't afford to be weakened."

There were a number of nods from my officers, and then Kris leaned forward to take her turn… just as Marshal Samuels began to say something. They cut each other off and then stopped, Marshal nodding to his fellow Captain, "Ladies first, Kris, by all means."

Kris smiled, "Good of you, Marshal. Alright, I think we don't worry about the domes. Sharon can look after the shelters with her SF. I doubt the pirates would be slaving today anyway — not with that much posh stuff down there to loot if they want it. Let them have property so long as they're not pillaging people. Leave the domes and meet them in open space."

"That's what I was going to say," Marshal smiled, and Kris shrugged.

Karen glanced back to me, then looked to the screen, "I think that's best. We just need to make sure we don't meet them too far out and let them get around us."

"Indeed," I leaned forward and propped my elbows on the desk, wringing my hands. Then something absurd came to me (surprise surprise). Maybe *this* was the plan… "I'll pick a point for us just off range of the asteroid and we'll form up there… actually, I'll get six of us to form up there. Marshal, you and Isoruku and Katya hide in the nearest rock cluster you can find."

Marshal frowned, "What about not dividing the force?"

I let my eyes narrow thoughtfully, "I still don't want any single ship alone, but you three should be able to stay out of sight and still be in range to assist us… mainly by hitting on the flank."

"Would you rather have the whole squadron in a battle line?" Wes frowned slightly now, and I shook my head.

"No, no they've thought all this through too well, I think. Normally I'd have us all in a battle line, and my guess is that Kitty Castillo is counting on that. So she'll show up and be confident that we six are all she has to deal with, and come straight in with guns blazing… and maybe let more pirates go looting than she should. Then Marshal, Isoruku, Katya, you hit her hard from behind."

I was pretty sure this idea had come out of nowhere, and I had some logical reservations about it, but instinctively I also had a fair amount of faith in it.

And on the Belt frontier, a 'fair amount' was more than enough.

"We'll be like ghosts," Marshal's tone reflected his confidence.

Mark Gunney snorted a laugh, "If you need inspiration, remember the last time you owed me cash."

We all chuckled at that one, but I cut my own laughter short, "Good. Three more items then. First thing: the primary targets will be the Martians. They're the regular warships and thus the biggest threat. Second, fighters all launch on my mark, not before. Don't want them stuck out there without us looking after them. Lastly, don't worry about Belt Two until I say so. I don't care if the pirates are landing on a dome, you keep focused on the space fight until I give the thumbs-up to go help out Sharon Stanton."

A chorus of "aye sirs" and "yes sirs" came as the immediate response, and I smiled, "Excellent. I don't think I'm forgetting anything… Any more news? Wes, you let the Admiralty know what's going down, right?"

Wes' eyebrows went up, "Actually, no. Comms to Earth have been down since before you left Asteroid Theta."

I blinked, "Seriously?"

Wes' nod was somber, "Sorry, I meant to tell you sooner. My guess is our new foe had a hand in it."

I blinked a couple of times — that fact would take a bit of time to process. It meant things were more complicated than I'd thought just a moment ago.

"Alright…" I wasn't sounding as confident, I realized, but I was signing off anyway, "That's it then. I'll have Jim Hannigan send the rendezvous coordinates for everybody but Marshal's group when I get them. Marshal, let the rest of us know where you choose to hide."

"Will do," Marshal nodded.

"Good. Then…" I looked to Karen and she nodded in confirmation, so I looked back up, "Then we're done. Good luck!"

Everyone exchanged pleasant send-offs on screen, but I stopped paying attention almost immediately. No comms to Earth… damn.

Something else to sort out… *after* the battle.

I looked up after a very short pause and nodded to Karen. She smiled thinly, then we both got to our feet and headed back to the bridge.

CHAPTER TWENTY-NINE

SHOOTING WAR

The squadron's performance under the stress of this new war needs more recognition. Remember, this squadron of ships, Captains and Commanders had seen action only against disorganized pirates and then the Syndicate force. They'd only once before been called upon to fight in formation as a single unit, at least in real life, with squadron maneuvers a once-a-year sort of thing, only happening when all ships came in for the annual review.

The fact that we were in formation, deployed, sitting and *waiting* over an hour before the Martian-pirate fleet arrived was something to take pride in.

That last hour, though, passed rather slowly. Belt Two's excellent sensor array caught sight of Castillo's force when it was still half an hour away, so we were able to confirm that it was indeed comprised of thirteen ships; to review it once more, the Martians had three DEs and a destroyer, Yat Sen's pirates had three liners, a converted yacht, a hauler and four small raiders.

We were outnumbered but they were outclassed.

I don't want to bore you with more waiting. Believe me, I was frustrated, stressed and anxious all through that last hour… though because I was sitting on the bridge I didn't reveal that to anyone. You get good at hiding it — at being the picture of assurance and confidence.

As I sat next to Karen and focused very carefully on not making any nervous moves or gestures, the range tracker on the main screen counted down to under four minutes, indicating the amount of time until, we believed, the combined enemy fleet would see us waiting for them.

Battlelinks filled eight of the ten smaller screens surrounding the main screen; those small displays were serving their purpose of keeping me in touch with my Captains and Commanders quite well.

We were ready… I know because I was reciting something of a mantra in the back of my mind: *Deep breath. We're ready. We're ready.*

I don't mean to startle you — I wasn't on the verge of a breakdown or anything. It's difficult to explain my thought process… no that's not quite it. The thought process is as I describe — you're *thinking* in a way that doesn't inspire confidence. And you're thinking jaggedly, which is as awkward as it sounds.

But under that thinking, you're on autopilot. Your mind sits back and wrings its hands and fears the worst, trying to bolster its own fragile confidence with weak words, and at the same time, you're *doing* what you have to do, and doing it well.

Coming out of my chair, I wasn't thinking at all about how I was thinking. I linked my hands behind my back and walked towards the main screen. The icons of the approaching ships were clear and almost moving in realtime. Belt Two's excellent active scanning gear kept us informed of every move.

Almost autopilot.

"Ladies and gentlemen," I addressed myself to the Captains and Commanders on the screens (not to mention the bridge crew behind me), "It'll be a privilege, as usual. Let's make it clean."

There was a chorus of approval for my words. You might think they lack gravitas but we Belt officers can in fact avoid the barn-burning statements when we don't need them. No more time to worry, only time to fight.

Total autopilot.

My eyes narrowed as they drifted over the chart on the main screen. The Martian ships were leading out for the pirates... the DEs flanking the destroyer, all four ships coming forward in an unbalanced arrowhead formation.

Behind them, the pirates had managed to get themselves into a line, but their biggest and slowest ships were all on their left — our right as we faced them — giving their formation a certain unevenness.

"Let's focus on the Martians, as planned. *Wolf* and *Lion* will take on the destroyer. Wes, you and *Cheetah* take *Lady Grace* and *Honesty* and deal with the other three. *Friendly* will stand back and keep an eye on our flanks."

Those ships were the ones with us in open space — *Alberta*, *Generous* and *Sackville* were tucked behind rocks floating not too far away.

My orders got instant nods and a few verbal replies. By the book, the responses should have been scripted, abrupt and immediate, but despite the certain advantage to having some orders repeated sometimes, we tended not to clutter the Battlelink with too much chatter.

Karen came to her feet behind me as I spoke, nodding to Matt as he coordinated fire control from his Operations consoles, "Focus on Kitty Castillo's destroyer, Matt. Erica, plot a course to advance on the ship, coordinate with *Lion*."

I think by this time I was pretty good about not giving such orders myself. Not my job anymore, and that was one part of the Commodore's mandate I took seriously. A flag officer didn't try to take ship command away from a Captain — it went against all good leadership principles.

And when the Captain in question was Karen McMaster, who was certainly (she'd say 'maybe', not 'certainly', but she'd just be being polite) a better ship handler than me, it'd be downright *stupid* to try.

Lieutenant Commander Martin's helm crew tied in immediately with *Lion*, passing coordinates back and forth through Battlelink windows at their stations and choosing their heading. Both *Wolf* and *Lion* began to edge forward in the same second, heading side-by-said for the advancing Martians.

Just about... *now* the Martians should be seeing six ships coming out to meet them.

"We just got pinged... and again... again..." Hannigan looked up quickly from the screen he was hovering over. "They're at full active sensors, and they're strobing fast. Looks like good active sensors."

I nodded once and then unlinked my arms, folding them across my chest, "Indeed. That's fair. All ships keep an eye out for incoming fire, in case their range is better than we expect."

"Energy building in their coils," Hannigan continued, "their mags... er... EM cannons are coming online, and their laser turrets."

Turreted lasers, that's right. Each turret laser barrel had about an eighth the output of one of our traversing beams, but Martian ships installed their lasers in double mounts to try to maximize their abilities. I preferred our fixed (variable angle) weapons, but as you can tell by now, I pretty much preferred everything Defense Command did over the Martian approach.

"We in realtime range?" I glanced back at Hannigan, and after leaning sideways to check a panel he nodded slowly.

"We are.... *Now*. And look at that, signal from the destroyer coming in. You know who..."

I smiled at Jim Hannigan's casual phrasing and nodded, "On screen nine."

Stepping to the smaller display, I waited as the *Wolf*Net screen went through its loading process, then stood still for two more seconds until Kitty Castillo appeared on it. She was smiling a fierce death's-head sort of grin, obviously quite pleased with herself.

"Ken, good to see you made it for our little occasion. Surrender now or die."

I grinned harshly, "It's *my* little occasion, Kitty. So to poach your eloquent and *entirely* non-cliché threat, you surrender or die."

Castillo smiled, shrugging, "Sounds like we're at an impasse."

"Indeed," my eyes narrowed, and then I glanced back over my shoulder. "Matt?"

Kitty didn't need to see more — she looked off-screen and barked 'open fire this instant', then looked back, "You'll see, Barron. Your evil Empire will fall to the democracy of President-for-Life Godwin."

Understandably, I didn't even know where to start picking apart that little statement. Thankfully, Hannigan distracted me.

"I think they're shooting at us, sir," he said loudly. "They don't seem to quite have the range, or the aim, though."

My smile grew again, "Good observation, Jim. Karen, Kris, why don't we show them how it's done?"

I didn't need to look at Karen or Kris, I just listened to smoothly-delivered orders and waited as Matt Baxter pressed a few buttons.

First *Wolf* and then *Lion* fired bow lasers in a stream of glowing red anger. The emitters we carried were, as I already said, just about eight times more powerful than those Martian turrets, and they had a hefty range advantage, by the look of things.

The destroyer took both hits hard, but kept pressing forward...

A shooting war had begun. And we were hitting the ground running.

CHAPTER THIRTY

SQUADRON ACTION

Martian counter-fire was the first to reach us, and I have to say their shooting was better than I would have liked. EM cannons found *Wolf* and *Lion* as we led out for the Belt Squadron, those turret weapons again lighter in punch than ours, but able to track us a little better.

Still, they were predominantly destroyer escort EM cannons — not designed to deal with the sort of protection our frigates had. The destroyer's pods were being shorn off as we closed range, our lasers still firing at full bore.

Lady Grace and *Cheetah* were quickly alongside *Lion*, and *Honesty* came alongside *Wolf* on the opposite quarter. I just stood with folded arms and watched.

"We'll have to discontinue laser shot in fifteen seconds," Matt called from the back of bridge and Karen nodded, looking back.

"Good enough. Get the mags ready to rain hell." She was unflappable.

My eyes narrowed as I watched. Screen nine had flipped to an image of the Martian destroyer as it was slowly carved apart. It was trying to spin out of the line of fire, its laser turrets turning to stay with us.

"We're discontinuing beam, Ken," Kris reported from *Lion* on screen two. "Opening up with mags."

"Likewise!" Matt's report came from behind me, and I nodded.

"Focus on the destroyer, I want it out of the fight."

Both *Wolf* and *Lion* mounted six bow mags, and both ships began pouring energy out through them now that the lasers were no longer monopolizing the power of the ships' reactors.

The screen showed these bolts slamming into the destroyer — it was like golden rain falling on the hull of the ship. Still, the destroyer's electro magnetic shielding seemed to handle the extra fire — unlike laser energy, EM blasts could be shrugged off.

"Looks like it still has three functioning pods…"

I hadn't even noticed as Karen came up alongside me, but I nodded at her words.

"Andrea," I addressed myself to Andrea Kiley, latest commander of my old ship *Friendly*, "come up and get a laser shot in on the destroyer, please."

Cheetah's laser, I noted, was splitting a DE in half, while *Lady Grace* and Mark Gunney's *Honesty* were laying torrents of mag fire into the DEs they'd each selected as targets.

"We've almost got ours…" Wes was on screen three, and I nodded in reply to his words.

"Good shooting, Wes. My compliments to your tac section," my eyes stayed fixed on the screen.

Wolf shook under my feet as I spoke, and my eyes darted back to the image of the destroyer. Laser fire from the Martians was coming back at last.

"They've got a good line on us, sir... Output of both barrels looks like it's about a quarter of what we fire... more incoming!"

I reached out for something to hold onto as *Wolf's* shaking turned into bucking, and I managed to grab Karen just as she found one of the railings behind the helm section.

"Erica, turn us into it!" she ordered as she steadied herself.

Clutching the backs of her two pilots' seats, Martin didn't bother to respond directly to Karen, instead issuing the order to her helm crew, "Four points starboard, increase speed to 95 kps!"

We were trying to angle ourselves to present our slimmest profile to the destroyer — the bow-on profile. The destroyer had drifted out from just in front of us, so now we were lining up on the ship again.

"How long until we can get another laser shot?" I looked back towards Matt, forgetting for that moment that it was Karen's job to ask.

Matt was braced upright against the tac panels, "I can give you one in about a minute. Aligning now!"

"Reduce speed to 75 kps," Martin ordered without being told, and the bucking reduced again to shuddering of mag... sorry, EM cannon strikes as *Wolf* drove straight in again.

"Their fire's shifted to us, Ken," Kris' picture broke up on screen two for just a moment, then came back. "Caught us on a bad angle — reverse starboard pod, present our bow!"

Lion was displayed on screen ten as she gave the order, Hannigan predicting my desire to see just what was happening to *Wolf's* fellow *Predator*. Four Martian lasers were focusing on its upper pod wing... and they were starting to dig their way through the reinforced armor.

Damn.

I forced my eyes back to the main screen at that moment — I don't know why I did, but I did — and watched the icon of one of the Martian DEs vanish, the computer deciding that it wasn't a threat any longer. It wasn't; Captain Wes Pellew had cut the thing in half, and now *Cheetah* was coming around.

"Covering you, Kris," Wes said on the Battlelink. "Try to roll clear if you can!"

Cheetah surged forward and turned sufficiently to present the mags of its port broadside — that's eighteen mag batteries for those of you unfamiliar with the *Predator* class. A torrent of mag fire was unleashed, and the destroyer shuddered under the onslaught, one of its high turrets being cooked by the fire almost immediately.

Lion managed to get around to present a low profile as this distraction arrived, and then from below the frigate a new laser shot found the destroyer; *Friendly*, my fine old corvette, had come up, and now its smaller laser was punching into the destroyer with force.

"That'll finish off Kitty," I managed to say under my breath. I was only just starting to straighten up and regain my footing after the bucking, and my hand was still on Karen's shoulder.

Realizing that, I pulled it away, but Karen didn't seem to notice one way or the other, looking back to Matt instead, "Laser shot, as soon as you can."

"Coming... *shoot.*"

The laser fired its angry red energy again and joined *Friendly's* beam and *Cheetah's* mags in driving into the destroyer. This time the ship visibly bucked on screen nine, and its fire against *Lion* simply stopped. Two more of its drive pods were sheared off entirely, and then it appeared that its systems shut down under the rain of mag fire.

"Reprioritize targets," I said immediately, walking back to a central spot on the bridge and crossing my arms again. "Finish off those last two DEs."

There were again a handful of affirmative responses, and mags immediately shifted targets to the last two unfortunate Martian destroyer escorts. They'd probably expected this to go better for them.

"We can't hold this acceleration," Kris' voice came from *Lion's* bridge. "Our high pod wing is compromised, I've got to cut its acceleration or we could tear apart."

I nodded, "You're the new reserve then. Andrea, bring *Friendly* up to replace *Lion* in line."

"Got a feisty one here..." Elise De Winter, Commander of *Lady Grace*, gritted her teeth as her ship surged under her — she nearly bounced out of the picture on the Battlelink.

My eyes darted back to the screen, "I see it, Elise. Wes, cover?"

"On it," Wes barked orders off screen and *Cheetah* angled around again.

De Winter's foe was causing more trouble than we'd have liked — it had both its single laser turrets cutting into *Lady Grace's* bow pod, and it had already managed to compromise the corvette's bow laser emitter. As a rule of thumb, you didn't try to use an emitter when it was damaged, so Elise was turning her ship hard to starboard.

But things never seem to happen fast enough in battle.

"I've got mine under control — it's trying to run," Mark Gunney wasn't having as much trouble with his target.

"Run it down. Andrea go with him," I looked to both Commanders on screen, and with nods they barked orders to their respective bridge crews.

So *Honesty* and *Friendly* surged ahead of the line, keeping up with the chaotic and desperate retreat of one of the DEs. *Lion* was falling off the pace as repair crews rushed to secure the laser-inflicted damage, *Wolf* was holding course towards the destroyer's dead hulk, *Cheetah* was veering to the starboard side where *Lady Grace* was taking more heat than was proper.

"Kris, help Wes and Elise when you get up here. Karen, let's follow Mark and Andrea."

Nodding, Karen gave the orders without words — a simple glance to Erica Martin resulted in the necessary course changes.

Cheetah's mags opened up on the meaner of the DEs, and the small ship abruptly stopped shooting and reversed course, leaving a badly shot-up *Lady Grace* behind it as it rotated through 360 degrees and tried to boost away.

Lion came alongside *Lady Grace* and slowed, both damaged ships hanging together and covering each others' wounds as best they could. *Cheetah* chased the culprit — this DE tried to work up speed to get away, but *Cheetah's* big engines were already at full burn.

The frigate almost pounced onto the DE, and on the screen I detected a smile on Wes' face, "This'll learn ya... laser shot please."

The mag fire from *Cheetah* fell off in one second, and a red laser beam flew out of its bow emitter in the next. Instead of going for a drive pod wing, this shot — coming from behind and slightly above — zeroed right in on the DE's upper drive pod, and there was a fiery and muted explosion as the laser bored straight through the relatively light protection it met.

With that the DE tumbled slowly forward, its power systems straining to deal with the loss of one pod. The trouble wasn't helped by the torrent of mag fire that Wes piled onto the unfortunate little ship. Every system on the main power grid of that Martian warship was rapidly fried and it tumbled away.

"I'll correct course and drop back to *Lion* and *Lady Grace*," Wes looked back to his Battlelink screen and I nodded.

"Excellent work. Mark, Andrea, how about you try that."

Mark grinned, and Andrea smiled. Shooting a drive pod at these speeds and ranges was no easy thing — even good targeting teams could be fooled by slightly diverging vectors.

But, almost as soon as I made the suggestion, two of the last fleeing DE's drive pods shattered, and the loss of two at once instantly killed the ship's power grid. It drifted away on momentum, but was no threat.

Smiling at that, I let out a deep breath and glanced at Karen and nodded. She smiled a small sort of smile — one of the small victory recognition but not overconfidence sorts. You know the type.

There was still much to do...

"Alright, regroup at *Lion's* position. How far back are the pirates?"

I could have gauged that from the main screen if I'd felt like it, but it was easier to just ask Jim Hannigan, and the man closely checked two panels before looking up, "About two minutes."

Two minutes seemed at that moment to be a lot of time...

In fact, I'd realize as I read the battle logs later on that we'd only been engaged with the Martian squadron for about 110 seconds. Seriously, all that reading you just did *felt* as slow and as long as it reads, but it only took about a minute and a half to go down.

Not bad.

But there was more work to do, so I settled myself again, looked to the main screen, then let my eyes dart over the faces of my Captains and Commanders, "Launch fighters to target their raiders, we'll deal with the rest."

There were still nine ships to fight, and two of my elite vessels were severely damaged.

CHAPTER THIRTY-ONE

SQUADRON KNIFE FIGHT

Fighting Martians is one thing. They've got a Navy, they've got doctrine, they've got discipline.

Fighting pirates is another thing entirely. You've seen us in action against pirates who weren't ready for us, but this was different. These ships were ready, they'd been up-gunned by the Martians, and their only doctrine was the cleverness of their skippers.

So what had been an organized line fight the moment before was about to turn into what I might best describe as a knife fight. Or a bar fight. Think *chaos*, and the only thing that potentially gave the Belt Squadron an advantage was the fact that we had such good unit cohesion — that the skippers of the squadron all got along really well.

You look to your friends in a knife fight. And we were all friends.

"Here we go…" Karen's words were soft, and I glanced at her as she said them, then nodded once and looked back at the screens.

We had four healthy ships in open space, and two wounded. Their three liners, hauler and yacht were all coming straight for us, while their raiders were splitting off on opposite vectors, trying to get around us.

Adrienne Thompson and her fighters were out there to hunt those raiders, as were the squadrons from *Lion* and *Cheetah*, and each wing of ten planes from *Honesty, Friendly* and *Lady Grace*. That meant each raider would get the attention of thirty F-194 Starlights.

This was why we carried the planes. Not to be unkind, but this was all they were good for by the time of this fight — they couldn't go toe-to-toe with ships with a lot of protection and plenty of light weapons to swat them down. I'm a pilot. Karen's a pilot. We know this to be true. Caldecott's folks just didn't get it.

But now's not the time for that rant. The point was that the fighters were doing what they did best: going after the pirates' light and fast raiders.

"Marshal, get ready. Don't engage until we get their attention," I looked to Marshal Samuels' face on screen four and he nodded. He and *Alberta, Sackville* and *Generous* were still unengaged, waiting to get the drop on these pirates.

My eyes shifted back to the main screen, which displayed the regrouping of our open-space force around *Lion* and *Lady Grace*.

"We've got the pylon secured for now, Ken. Just won't be doing anything over 150 kps for a while," Kris reported as we formed up, and I nodded.

"Good news. Elise, how's *Lady Grace*?"

The Commander shook her head despite herself, "We got a surge in the laser array. Engineer's worried we might blow up if we try firing it now."

That drew a muted 'damn' in the back of my mind — not only had we lost the main weapons array on one of our ships, it was *Lady Grace*. I had sentimental attachments to that ship.

"Alright, no worries. Reverse course and head back to Belt Two. See if you can help the fighters deal with those raiders heading that way."

Elise's face was the picture of disappointment, but she nodded, "Yes, sir. Sorry, sir..."

I shook my head, "Hardly your fault. Look after Belt Two for us."

She nodded once, then ordered her Lieutenant at Helm and Navigation to get her injured ship turned around.

That left us in the open with five ships with which to meet the six large pirate vessels; we had three frigates in decent fighting condition and two fine corvettes, they had a mélange of frankensteined warships.

"Range in forty seconds," Hannigan's report seemed to punctuate my thoughts... "And signal coming in from the yacht."

Frowning, I glanced back at Hannigan, "Really? This'll be interesting. Screen nine."

I turned again to that screen as it flashed to a *WolfNet* buffering screen, and then the face of a gruff-looking fellow appeared. I can only describe Jebediah Yat Sen as a Genghis Khan wannabe — he's got the stringy beard and the unwashed look, but he really lacks the menace he seems to think he has.

"Surrender now, Commodore Barron, or be destroyed."

I actually smiled at that. I mean, we'd just taken apart a four-ship Martian squadron, and now he was being daring when he had only five ships coming straight at us, with his other three trying to go on a looting run...

As I was thinking that, something in the back of my mind reminded me that five ships plus three ships made for only eight ships. One was unaccounted for.

I blinked, immediately looking away from Yat Sen, and searching the main screen for the ninth pirate icon. Where was it? Jebediah stared at me from his screen and seemed to grow frustrated as I refused to look at him.

"Jim, find me the ninth pirate. Where is it?"

There was an unusual amount of urgency in my demand, and Hannigan instantly realized the implications of what I was asking. Karen's eyebrows shot up and she turned to the main screen as well.

"Do you surrender?" Yat Sen demanded over the link, and I frowned, looking back to him for just a moment.

"You'll be dead inside ten minutes, Mister Yat Sen. Find some satisfying food and start praying."

The warlord-wannabe grinned, "We will see."

Then he disappeared.

I wasn't paying much attention to him at that stage; instead I was walking over to Hannigan's consoles.

"Where is it?"

Hannigan was moving from panel to panel, frowning and shaking his head, "I can't *find* it..."

See, this was the problem with pirates — they didn't operate the way militaries did.

"Alright..." I turned back to the screens, "Marshal, get out here. Everybody keep your eyes open for our missing friend. Let's dispatch these unseemly fellows as quick as we can."

Marshal Samuels smiled on the screen, "With pleasure. Isoruku, Katya, shall we?"

Three new icons flared to full life, emerging from the space debris they'd been sheltering themselves behind. They were much closer to the pirates than we were.

"Everybody else, let's go get them. Close fast."

It wasn't easy to keep track of everything that happened next. If it hadn't been for the consistent and excellent record kept by Belt Two base's sensor grid, we might never clearly know how the next stage of the battle took place. As the chapter title implies, it was a knife fight — and it was messy.

Cheetah was out ahead of us, Wes sitting confidently on his bridge. Then the hauler opened up on his ship with a laser. A *real* laser, not a Martian one. And at long range — outside our own range.

"What the... *back engines to port, turn us into the shot!*"

The first indication I received about that laser blast were those hurried orders from Wes, and then Hannigan obligingly flipped screen nine to a view of *Cheetah*. The fine frigate was having its lower pod wing cut away... the huge laser, possibly from an old Defense Command battleship, was carving the pod right off. We still have no idea where they got that laser — they shouldn't have had it... that was why *Cheetah* had been caught by surprise.

But Wes' orders were turning his frigate into the blast, and soon the slim bow profile of the ship was presented and it was shifting sideways away from the laser.

Wes looked immediately back at his screen, "Ken, it's bad. I'm sending damage control to secure the breaches now, but I can't accelerate too quickly with that kind of tear..."

His words referred to the fact that the cut across the wing was almost three-quarters of the way through — if *Cheetah* fired its pods up to anything over, say, 120 kps, the pod accelerating on the end of that wing would apply too much stress to the damaged section, and might tear itself off entirely.

It was much worse than *Lion's* wound.

"Understood, stay out of trouble if you can," I looked to Wes' face and he nodded.

The main screen suddenly indicated three lasers flying; *Alberta*, *Sackville* and *Generous* were closing in quickly with the pirate hauler that had fired that monstrous laser shot, and they had all seen what it had done to *Cheetah*. Although two of those ships — *Alberta* and *Sackville* — were thirty years old, their weapons were still excellent, and even though it was big, the hauler wasn't well-protected at all. It started to come apart easily, and so *Generous* veered off to face one of the liners that was turning to attack *Alberta*.

It's difficult to say whether a pirate ship is a match for any Defense Command vessel because each pirate is so irregularly armed, so neither I nor Commander Togo could really know whether he was cruising his corvette into a winning or losing exchange.

EM cannons began firing from the liner, and *Generous* took several very heavy hits as it changed vectors and approached. Isoruku Togo, unsurprisingly, remained a picture of calm on the Battlelink screen, but his ship was taking a frigate's worth of EM fire from that liner.

"Andrea, support *Generous*," I said immediately, taking a step towards the screens (as if that'd somehow emphasize my orders). "Kris, you stick with Wes. Mark, you're with *Wolf*."

Karen was already turning back to Matt, "What can you get a laser shot on?"

"One of the liners right now," the Briton replied immediately.

Karen nodded once, and Matt looked to the fire control technician, "Shoot."

The bow laser emitter was getting a lot of work today; another stream of red energy poured out through it, viciously smashing into the unprotected hull of the liner as we continued to close.

Staying alongside *Wolf*, Mark Gunney's *Honesty* lined up its laser against the third liner, but as Mark opened fire, a flurry of EM fire sprayed back at his corvette. I mean a large flurry — much more than *Wolf's* broadside could put out on its own.

"This is festive... break formation and accelerate six points port," Mark Gunney's orders to his crew came through clearly enough on the Battlelink.

The pirate hauler then exploded fiercely on the screen — from what I could tell at the time, *Alberta* had finished the ship off handily enough. *Sackville*, on the other hand, was adrift with one of its pods missing, firing mag bursts in self defense but not able to maneuver effectively.

"Katya, you alright?" I managed to ask as I realized her ship's plight, and she nodded on screen.

"We will make do... nothing a few weeks of shipyard time won't repair."

That was a good attitude — one common to the Belt Squadron, though admittedly not to the entire fleet.

Wes gritted his teeth and looked straight out through the Battlelink, "We just had a surge in the grid, I've had to take the laser offline!"

"Understood, Kris stay with him..." I looked to the status of things again. The liner *Wolf* had shot was breaking up, but the one Mark Gunney had engaged was keeping *Honesty* back with a veritable typhoon of EM fire.

The first liner — the one that had squared off against *Generous* and done some damage to Togo's ship, was now taking fire from *Friendly* as well, but it was sending back EM fire in torrents too. It was chaotic, all this, but at the time I was somehow keeping track.

"We're closing on Isoruku's liner," Marshal seemed to read my mind as he spoke, and on the screen *Alberta* swung around quickly and its laser lanced out again.

The liner took the hit but, unlike the one *Wolf* had shot, this one took the blast in stride... and then *Alberta* was bounced sideways on the screen as Yat Sen's yacht targeted it with a Martian-style laser shot.

"Cheap shot," Marshal gritted his teeth on the screen. "Roll and get the pods out of his line of fire."

Alberta's protection was lighter than a *Predator*-class frigate's, so the Martian lasers hit a bit harder.

"Karen, let's take him out," I waved my hand towards Yat Sen's ship and Karen nodded, looking to Erica Martin.

"Erica please."

Those were the only words it took for *Wolf* to change course, but one of *Alberta's* pod wings was still cut halfway through by the time our laser trained on the yacht.

"Shoot!"

It's funny how a battle can be reduced to monosyllabic words at times, but Matt's order to the fire control tech was proof enough that things could become just that simple. *Wolf's* laser fired immediately, and Yat Sen's ship found its rear half being showered by red energy. The pirate had clearly added some armor to his flagship as the stern didn't flake away under the intense beam, but the little ship was batted sideways.

On the screen, things were getting even more chaotic. *Generous* was trying to back off, its main hull riddled with holes in the crew compartments section. Hopefully the crew had been quick about their decompression protocols.

Andrea Kiley had *Friendly* throwing mag shots into the liner that was causing them grief, and despite being wounded, Marshal's *Alberta* was hitting the liner hard too. The liner was at last overwhelmed by mag energy, and its fragile jury-rigged power grid fizzled out.

That left the flagship yacht and a single liner, and the four raiders that were not here.

Mark Gunney's voice came over Battlelink, "This liner's making a run for it... Andrea can you come with me to try to catch it?"

"On our way," Andrea Kiley was only too happy to oblige, and I let them chase the thing. A liner with that much firepower would be a serious threat to the space lanes.

In the meantime, I looked to Karen, "Let's finish him."

She nodded and looked back to Matt, "Shoot again, as soon as you have the range."

"He's running!"

My eyebrows went up and I looked back at Hannigan's rather abrupt and admittedly unclear report. Don't blame Jim for not saying *who* was running; sometimes in the heat of action, you stop with the details. It happens.

"He's up to 180 kps already... that thing kicks fast..."

Looking to the main screen, I realized Jim was referring to the yacht — Yat Sen, for all his talk, was bugging out, and fast. Faster than we could catch him, with that sort of speed.

"We'll get him next time."

I actually said that before my brain had accepted the fact that we weren't going to kill the man. I'd get him later.

"Mark, Andrea, stay after that liner, but don't go too far."

Mark nodded and Andrea replied more formally for them both, "Aye, sir."

Trying to cycle my brain around properly, I looked back to Hannigan, "What about the raiders?"

He frowned, "I still only see three. But the fighters are riding them pretty hard."

"Good. Take us back towards Belt Two... I've got a bad feeling."

I certainly did. Abrupt and bad — the worst sort of feeling.

Wolf turned around.

CHAPTER THIRTY-TWO

RAIDERS

Adrienne Thompson was one of the fleet's best pilots, and her unit — Wolfstar Squadron — was probably the best group of fighters the Belt had ever seen (not that I'm biased). With *Friendly's* ten fighters joining them, they were tangling with the pirate raider who'd gone 'high' to get around our squadron.

A raider is basically half the size of a corvette, but it's built more along fighter lines than ship lines, and it lacks the four-pod configuration. It's fast, small and well armed, probably carries about sixty crew, and it can be a real menace, coming out of nowhere and leaving before you can catch it.

But against thirty fighters it was only moderately effective. While bigger ships could easily shrug off fighter payloads, raiders were more fragile, and so F-194s could actually do some damage to them.

At least that's what we expected our planes to do. But reality doesn't always bend to expectations…

Adrienne's squadron wasn't the only one doing the fighting against the three raiders we were tracking just then, but hers is the only story I've gotten in person, and based on the outcome it was typical of what was happening with the others.

"Line up again on the port side," she ordered as she banked her Starlight around the raider. The pirates were pretty focused in their fast run towards Belt Two.

"Coming on line," the reply cackled into her helmet, and she guided her plane onto an attack line, throttling back as her wingman and the rest of her half of the squadron slipped into formation.

The raider's mag turrets began spewing at them again, and she had to jink creatively a couple of times, but she was still doing fine. In fact, since one of her planes had been knocked out eleven minutes earlier, she hadn't lost any.

"Lining up from behind for a run," the flight leader from *Friendly* added to the conversation.

"Very good, let's hit it. We're running low on time," Adrienne slammed her thrust controller forward and her Starlight kicked. I've already mentioned (a while back near the beginning of this volume) that the F-194 is a hell of a dogfighter, and this is true.

As the range dropped quickly, the EM cannons on the raider kicked into rapid fire and seemed to turn Adrienne's approach course into a tunnel of energy, but with the help of her flight computer she danced her fighter right around all the fire. Getting into close range, she started lining up with her last missile — an ambitiously named 'X9 Shipkiller' — and let it fly.

"Shoot Three," she said smoothly as the missile released (in the movies where she says 'Fox Three' it's inaccurate — nobody's said 'Fox Three' or 'Fox' anything since the regulation changes in 2209, just so you know).

The call was repeated by the rest of her squadron, and then they began to peel out of their line and into their two-ship formations to strafe from various other vectors.

Those X9s rode quickly in towards the raider, but they weren't particularly good weapons. The best DCRD (Defense Command Research and Development) could produce, sure, but they were slow and couldn't maneuver worth a damn. The raider shot down over half the warheads well away from its hull, another quarter of them as they got in close, and most of the rest actually *missed* the target because of faulty trackers. The three that didn't fly past the raider exploded glamorously, but only managed to scorch armor.

You see, this is the problem I mentioned about fighters. These days in 2231 weren't like the classic days of space war — the ones filled with legendary pilots like Frank Gulliver. Gulliver flew his most famous missions in 2176, and in those days, ship hulls were very thin, meaning a fighter could kill a big ship rather easily. It was a glorious time to be a pilot, and my fondness for the romantic image of that period in our history was probably the main reason I took my pilot certification.

But by 2231 (let alone today), those trying to be guts-and-glory like Frank Gulliver just got themselves killed, because ship hulls were stronger, armor was plentiful, and large vessels were faster. You could only get a small missile's drive up to a certain speed before you risked cooking off the warhead, and by the same token, the explosive payload could only be of a certain size.

So anybody (like Caldecott) who said fighters were the "Queens of the battlefield in space" needed to actually learn to fly and then try to take out a raider with a squadron of the best pilots in Defense Command.

Adrienne was trying to do exactly that, and the damned raider was just chugging along steadily.

As she clamped down on her trigger and sprayed the raider with mag fire, she heaved a deserved sigh, "Alright, we're getting *nowhere* with this. Let's wave off for now, get out of range. I need to patch in to *Wolf*."

"Signal coming in," Hannigan drew my attention with his words, and I turned to him.

"Sure, who?"

"Commander De Winter," his reply was quick, and before I could frown because Elise De Winter wasn't on the Battlelink, I recalled sending her back to Belt Two — now just out of realtime range.

I nodded then, "Screen six."

The screen switched from a sensor display to Elise De Winter's frowning face just about immediately, "Sir, we just had a raider fly past us. Looks like it's running on very low emissions — we wouldn't have seen it if it hadn't been so close to our base course. Tried a shot at it but our mags just went offline with a surge. We've sent you the vector it's on… looks like it stopped at the Martian destroyer wreckage and now is heading straight for Belt Two base. That's all I've got."

As the screen blanked I felt my eyebrows rise and I looked at Karen, "Stopped at the destroyer?"

Karen frowned and nodded, "And heading for the base. They either want to blow something up... or land..."

Land? Why not. The Martians had planned well enough so far. If they'd managed to arrive by surprise and given us no time to prepare, they'd have expected there to be chaos on the base. Fear of civilian losses and pirate raids would have sent the SF on the fleet base facilities out into the settlement domes to protect against landings and to maintain order.

Meaning if the Martians put an elite team into the base, they might be able to collect sensitive intelligence that could betray the Empire's military situation.

Yes, we had to protect against that rather unpleasant possibility.

"Increase speed to the base. Recall *Friendly* and *Honesty* — the other liner can wait. How are the Starlights doing against the other raiders?" I turned from the screens with my words.

Hannigan frowned and moved to a different console, nodding to the tech there before looking up, "Not well. They've lost nine planes, and haven't so much as tickled the raiders."

"They'll be looking to land at the domes," Karen said in low tones behind me. "Distract the SF, give the last raider a chance to hit the base."

At this point I was mentally cursing them: damned smart pirates... and Martians.

"Signal from Commander Thompson," Jim Hannigan wasn't getting much time to catch his breath between reports. "She's confirming that they're having no luck."

I nodded slowly, taking a precious few seconds to consider my options.

"Karen, let's get to the base at maximum possible speed — see if we can catch the raider. Jim, tell Adrienne to keep hounding her target as long as her power cells can keep her out there, and to make it seem like we're desperate to stop them... well, I suppose we are. Matt, coordinate with Kyle Stranks; get every available SF armed and ready to board the base, and let Charlie know his officers should suit up."

There were nods as the orders were acknowledged, Karen ordering Erica Martin to speed up the ship, Matt getting on the internal comms to the head of SF and to Charlie Peters, and Hannigan sending the message back out to Adrienne.

We now had to deal with a ground fight...

"We won't be able to overtake them at the speed they're going," Martin looked back from the helm and Karen and I both nodded.

She was referring to the fast pace of the raider — it was making 130 kps, and while we could go faster, if we tried to accelerate past the 115 kps that Erica Martin had us doing, we wouldn't be able to decelerate at the base itself — we'd either overshoot or crash into Belt Two. Strangely enough, that didn't seem like a viable option.

Get a signal to Sharon Stanton," I looked back to Hannigan. "Tell her to get the SF in the domes ready for pirate landings, and to get the base ready to receive boarders."

Chapter Thirty-Three

The Commodore's Job Description Is Now In The Trash Bin

"We're approaching the base," Hannigan's report was unnecessary but appreciated. We were all watching the main screen, noting the four raiders that had gotten past us and docked at various points on Belt Two.

In retrospect, we probably should have done more to stop this landing, but then, had we not focused so thoroughly on the space battle, this could have been the least of Belt Two's problems. Four raiders probably meant no more than a total of 300 pirates and Martians; they wouldn't do that much harm.

Problem for us now, though, was that the raiders had each forcibly docked with airlocks attached to their targets — the three raiders that the fighters hadn't been able to stop had gone to Domes Two, Four and Seven, and docked with the large transport unloading columns that connected each dome's commercial district directly to cargo ships carrying merchandise. They'd been docked for about ten minutes, too, so their pirate raiders were already facing off against the SF guards waiting to defend each dome.

Of course, them being docked meant we couldn't in fact destroy them. The raiders were too close to the domes; blowing one up while it was docked might well fracture the docking column, or, even worse, send debris showering down to breach the dome. Neither was a good idea.

But that was actually the lesser problem. The domes were each defended by large SF units. The fleet base, on the other hand, was down to a skeleton crew of security personnel. In retrospect again, probably not the best allocation of SF we could have made, but we had no reason to suspect the pirates would hit the base itself — not when domes full of riches lay vulnerable and well within reach.

The Martian elite strike team was not meeting great resistance in the base. They'd begun their boarding just a minute before we came in to dock, and as the SF reports from the base show, there was precious little in position to resist them.

Considering how completely we were being blindsided lately, I counted this as a 'could be much worse' scenario... and as Matt commanded *Wolf* and edged us up to a lock not far from the one to which the raider was connected, I slapped a power cell into my mag, closed the cowling, and prepared myself for a little more personal shooting.

Matt, as you might guess, hadn't been pleased when Karen and I turned ship command over to him, but because we were going to be boarding Belt Two base with over sixty SF guards and Charlie's full Special Branch unit, he was relatively easy to placate.

Now Karen stood next to me, managing one of those fabulous trademark smiles as she closed the cowl on her own mag and let it drop down to her side. We were all going to breach through one lock, led out by Charlie's team in case the Martians were lying in wait for us.

"So... long day..." I said with a deep breath as we stood there, and Karen's smile broadened just a tad — probably with a ton of effort.

"Not done yet," she said in low tones.

Across from us, Charlie Peters grinned, closing the cowl on his MAG-90, "You kids just stay behind us and it'll be short enough."

I chuckled and then we all stood still and silent, waiting, again, as Erica Martin edged us up to the docking port of the base. We then listened to the thuds as the clamps engaged and the cables were magnetized to lock *Wolf's* position against the docking column.

"Sharon says they're trying to get computer access from one of the secondary operations centres," I repeated our intel once more just in case some of the assault team had somehow forgotten it. "Then we figure they'll either try to get back to their ship or to manual comm control, to send their findings back to an Asteroid."

Charlie nodded, and behind Karen, Lieutenant Stranks leaned forward, "We'll keep them from their ship. No worries, sir."

I nodded to the young Lieutenant, watched him recheck the power cell in his old EP-5 rifle, and then straightened myself up beside the wall, leaning my head back against the alloy. The light over the airlock door went from red to green just as I did, and Charlie had reached out and popped the hatch before I managed to push my head forward again. Leading through with his team, Charlie moved with quiet and quick efficiency, covering one side as his second person in line covered the other. The docking column was wide and open, trailing 'down' into the station before entering a reorientation chamber at the bottom.

That'd be where the Martians would undoubtedly try to ambush us.

As the last Special Branch officer stepped through the hatch I came off the wall and waved to Karen, Stranks and the SF guards, and we all followed the black-clad officers quietly down the corridor. It wasn't too long a walk, and after all the waiting I'd done the speed with which the reorientation chamber appeared at the end of the chute was a bit of a surprise. Essentially, the floor in this room curved 'up' the wall and let you walk from one gravity zone into another...

Sort of hard to explain, but imagine walking up to a wall and then sticking your foot out and walking up that wall, only to find that the wall is now the floor. It's disorienting and the room has 'sweet spots' of both zero gee and conflicting gee. Get caught in either and you're stuck — not a good way to be under fire.

Charlie was leading the way through the room, peering down the barrel of his MAG-90 for any signs of ambush. He was creeping — I could watch him do this from above — and looking in every direction.

And then an EM bolt (even in hand weapons, Martians call mags 'EMs') went right over his shoulder.

The speed and ease with which he and his whole team — two of them still on the wall, so to speak — returned fire was *insane*. Charlie did some tactical hand thingies and they erupted out into the hall, firing quick bursts from their excellent weapons.

"Come on," I said in low tones, and Karen nodded as we stepped up our pace towards the chamber. Charlie darted out of view just as we reached the actual beginning of the large room, and now we aimed 'up' and walked forward... which was down... until we reached the wall which became the floor...

Okay, I'm getting a headache just writing about this part, so let's skip to us getting under cover just outside the chamber door. The Martians had been set up to fire straight into the chamber, but their heavy EM gun had been much slower firing than the MAG-90 in Charlie's hand, and he and his team had thus dropped the Martians instantly.

I crouch-walked along the corridor wall opposite the Special Branchers, nodding to Charlie, "This is the way to the aux center they're holding?"

He nodded, "I do believe it is. Ready?"

Glancing at Karen, I shrugged, "Yeah."

Grinning now, Charlie did his hand thingie with the fist, and the Special Branch officers crept quickly down the well-lit hall.

I followed, but Karen glanced first at Stranks, "You go the other way, cut off the boarding party from the raider. Don't board the raider until we give you the all-clear. I don't want you getting flanked over there."

Stranks nodded, "Yes, ma'am."

"Good," Karen smiled and trotted after us.

"Around the next corner..." Charlie's whisper was barely audible, but I heard it and nodded.

We'd only needed four minutes to get to the auxiliary control center that the Martian strike team had gone for, and we'd seen no Martians on the way. Presumably they knew we were coming, knew that we knew where they were...

So the question then was where they'd go from here, what they'd try...

Charlie pulled a magbang out of his vest and put his thumb on the priming switch, but I held up my hand, "Wait a second. I've got an idea."

He frowned curiously, and then I did something you'd expect me to do.

"Hey, Martians, how many of you are there?"

I actually yelled that. Yep, even after this day of battle and worry and stress, I was still able to resurrect my cavalier idiom long enough to ask that question. And somehow the silence that followed just after my question seemed more stunned than disciplined.

But there was more to my question than just my own eccentricity. I thumbed Charlie in the direction we'd come, then did a curving hand thing that to me said 'flank them'. He frowned at me, rather puzzled, but then Karen kindly translated...

"You flank them," she whispered. "We'll put on a good show."

Charlie smiled and nodded, whispering, "You always do." Then, with a bunch of tactical hand gestures, he silently withdrew back down the hall with his team.

We watched them go for a few seconds, then I met Karen's eyes and grinned, "Just the two of us, again. Go figure."

Karen smiled brightly and shook her head, "I have no idea why I volunteer for this."

"My irresistible charm, of course," I said with as much false resolution as I could muster, then I looked the other way and called out. "Well, Special Branch is going around behind to flank you, so you better look out."

That's right, I told them exactly what Charlie was up to. Why? Because first of all, there was a ninety-five percent chance they'd think I was trying to mislead them, and would thus deploy everything up front expecting a rush to come from Karen and me. And then, in case the five percent chance played out and they believed me, Charlie would deal with them.

I think it goes without saying I was supremely confident in Charlie's Special Branch officers.

Still, the Martian strike team — probably an elite band of special forces, by their standards — was disciplined enough not to take the bait and answer back. Smarter than pirates in that regard, I must concede, but they still were in a bad situation.

Oh and if you're wondering, we weren't getting the internal camera vids of them because they were jamming the feeds. And they weren't able to access the feeds of us, because Sharon had locked them out of the operational database. They were still trying to hack in, which I presumed was why they hadn't left this section yet.

So, we just had to give Charlie enough time to get around the next junction and into position to get the drop on them...

"Now?" I asked a bit impatiently as I sat on the deck.

Karen shrugged, "Sure."

I pushed myself to my feet and got my mag ready in hand.

"Come on guys, turn around and look at the Special Branch guys sneaking up behind you. Seriously."

And then, bless Charlie, I heard, "Yeah jeeze, you all too good to look at us or something?"

I nearly laughed as I swung around the corner. Three Martians were behind cover opposite me, but they were all looking back at Charlie Peters and Defense Command Special Branch leaping out of a room door well behind the barricade. Charlie must have found a way to use the trick we'd used on the pirate liner here — he'd gone room to room instead of through the corridors.

Anyway, Karen and I were around our corner in a flash, and I shot two of those Martians waiting for us, she got the third (yes, I shot better than she did... for once). We moved quickly up to the barricade with our mags trained on them, but that was the end of the resistance we personally dealt with.

Charlie's team swept in and fired cleanly, dropping a Martian unit of twelve. The Special Branchers suffered only three minor injuries in the exchange — not too shabby, if you ask me.

Still, the Martians could be full of surprises, so I was careful as I climbed over the office chairs and the desks that had been crammed together to block the hall, and Karen covered for me as I did. I watched out for her as she came over, and we found ourselves back with Charlie, standing in the middle of a bunch of convulsing Martian bodies.

Then Karen's comm chirped, and she grabbed and keyed it in one rather smooth, elegant motion, "Yes?"

Stranks sounded like he was in pain, "Twelve Martians trying to break through to their ship!"

I frowned, turned to the door of the auxiliary control room, keyed it open, and leaned in. Charlie grabbed me by the back of the tunic and pulled me out, "Idiot, that's my job!" He swept in with an officer covering his side angles, and after a few seconds looked back.

"Empty."

Frowning, I glanced at Karen. Then we scrambled over the barricade and started running.

So maybe we got spoiled by seeing how well an elite Special Branch team handled the Martians. Seems the boarding party had done a great job jamming and misleading base sensors; they were running for their raider and had left a sacrificial team of guards behind to keep us occupied.

Stranks, fortunately, had gotten in the Martians' way… and personally, he'd gotten in the way of one of the Martians' EM bolts with his knee. Poor fellow's leg was burned black and he was in extreme shock by the time Karen and I managed to find a corridor that cut across to his position.

The sound of mag and EM shots seared through the air as we both dropped to one knee against the corridor wall. I managed to count nine of *Wolf's* SFs on the ground, four convulsing and five dead. Dead.

I'd managed not to come face to face with the death so far today. Until now…

Karen checked Stranks' vitals as we crouched next to him, and I edged up behind two of the guards who'd stayed with him and were trying to hold this corridor. We were in one of the hallways that ran perpendicular to the straight-line path to the raider. The Martians had to get down the corridor that crossed this one, but we were in their way… that make sense? Okay, envision a lowercase letter 't'. They were going down the long stalk, we were holed up in the short crossing line.

And we could have been doing better.

"We deployed a ring around the raider," Stranks winced as he spoke, and inhaled sharply as he tried to drag his leg closer to the wall. "Most are still on the way…"

I nodded at him, understanding his words well enough — the sixty SF that he'd taken off *Wolf* were spread out covering all the approaches to the raider. Collecting them all together was going to take time.

But with only about ten guards and Karen and me here to stop them, the Martians might break through before the rest of the SF concentrated.

"Surrender, Defcoms, and we'll let you live!"

At first I was pretty certain I had to be dreaming — that couldn't be…

"That's *Kitty*," Karen had donned a disbelieving expression, and my eyebrows went up.

"So it is…" I turned away from Stranks and edged up the wall towards the corner, tapping one of the guards there on the back and getting her to move behind me, out of my way.

Stopping in place, I waited as Karen slid up the wall next to me, then leaned a little further, just to the edge, so my voice would carry, "Kitty, hate to tell you, but you're not in any position to make threats."

That brought a brief silence, followed by another self-righteous blowup from my counterpart, "Bullshit, you've got nothing between me and the ship."

I laughed — loud enough so she'd hear, "Well, Karen and I are here."

"Commodores should know better than to try ground fighting," she hissed back.

Looking to Karen with a mock air of offense, I called back, "And Rear Admirals are somehow really good at it? I daresay I thought you knew better than to try to handle a gun, Kitty. Not your specialty."

"I'm the only one with the codes for your database, idiot!"

She probably shouldn't have been so forthright about that. Here's a lesson: *never* volunteer information you don't have to unless it helps you. Somehow people never learn that.

"I see, so you've got the information you hacked out then," I yelled back. "Charlie, that means we need her alive. I want to know how she got those codes."

There was a pause, then Kitty came back sounding even more irked, "That shit isn't going to fool me. I heard what you did to my decoys over the comm!"

The sound of shuffling boots from around the corner suggested to me that she'd redeployed some troops to cover any possible angles of approach from behind her.

Charlie, who while I was yelling at Kitty had crept up the hall with us, smiled at me, and went right around the corner, MAG-90 blazing. His team followed smoothly, all tactical and elite.

Me, I just leaned back against the wall, glanced at Karen, and smiled.

"You know, I might stop showing up at these ground fights. They're getting tiring."

She chuckled, sitting back against the wall next to me, "I'll believe it when I see it."

A few minutes later two Special Branch officers walked past us carrying Kitty Castillo's convulsing body.

We waved at her.

CHAPTER THIRTY-FOUR

DEEP, DEEP BREATHS

For the next four hours we cleaned up. Ships made their way to Belt Two base, some more slowly and more painfully than others. Charlie and his team actually went to Dome Nine to help deal with the particularly feisty pirates who had landed there; SF cleaned up the rest on its own.

Kitty Castillo was thrown into *Wolf's* brig, in a cell right across from Cooper. We figured that, after all their corresponding, putting them in the same room… well, that wouldn't be couth at all.

Karen and I hobbled back to *Wolf*, had our showers, and tossed our uniforms in the laundry. It was late enough, but still there was time for a conference with the Captains and Commanders — while everybody cooled down from the battle. Adrenaline stopped flowing, headaches ensued… the usual.

Well, a bit more than usual: this had been the first fight of a *war* that a week ago none of us had seen coming. I suppose now it's hard to appreciate, but back then this was a total shock to all of us, and even after fighting this first battle — now known as the Battle of Belt Two — we were just a little disbelieving.

When we met in the conference room on Belt Two base — we waited until all ships had docked or been towed to the yards so that we could meet in person — we were all sitting around slightly addled.

I'm sure that inspires confidence, learning that some of Defense Command's elite had still not quite come to terms with the fact that a war was on. But, the meeting itself was important and productive.

Mark Gunney was actually the first to arrive and join Karen and me at the table, nodding in his usual style, "You two should throw these parties more often."

I smiled (despite my pounding head) as he sat, "Excellent shooting, as usual, Mark."

"Heh, seriously. From all of us," he nodded back, and then we all leaned back in our chairs and tried to rest our brains in silence until more people arrived.

Andrea Kiley came in next, fairly quickly as *Friendly* and *Honesty* had reached the base at the same time, then a slow trickle followed: Marshal Samuels, Kris Jacobs, Isoruku Togo, Katya Romanov, Elise De Winter, and finally Wes Pellew, who had *not* had time for a shower and was covered in black streaks of smoke.

"That laser shot cooked half my grid," he said with a few solid octaves of frustration, dropping into a chair. "My engineers and I have been over it twice… we'll be in the yard for at least three weeks tearing out the burned relays."

I winced in sympathy and leaned forward, "Very bad luck, there, Wes. But you still did much worse to the Martians."

He shrugged but his mood didn't brighten, "Sure. But that's small consolation."

True enough. Captains and Commanders cared rather a lot for their ships — seeing one damaged was somehow *personal*. For his part, Wes wasn't frustrated at the damage or the enemy, but at himself for giving the orders that got *Cheetah* hit.

Now, you and I both know it wasn't his fault — none of us could have expected a Defense Command *battleship laser* to be on that hauler. But rational assignment and the label 'accident' or 'surprise' didn't help a Captain who was staring at his shot-up ship.

So Wes was preoccupied, as were most of the Captains and Commanders present, because only three ships in the squadron had come through essentially unscathed: *Wolf*, *Honesty* and *Friendly*.

One by one, the rest of the commanding officers reported the level of damage. Marshal Samuels wouldn't be able to go far from base in *Alberta* until he had a week in a slip rebuilding the damaged pod wing, and Kris had to report similar problems for *Lion*, though with lighter damage she only needed half the yard time.

For *Sackville* much more repair was needed; the lost engine pod had to be reattached, or replaced. *Lady Grace* and *Generous* were in little better shape. So that meant most of my squadron would actually be stuck here at Belt Two for quite a while.

Not the ideal outcome, but then considering we'd destroyed or disabled seven of thirteen attacking ships and captured the four raiders (did I mention that we took them once their landing parties were dealt with?), we'd done well. No Defense Command ship destroyed; I wouldn't complain about that.

Deaths among the crew… I wouldn't *think* about that. It'd sink in on the very next day, in fact, that seventy-three people were killed on the day (not including the other side). But that wasn't for worrying about at this meeting.

"So," I said slowly after the litany of repairs was listed, "now we've got some bigger questions to deal with."

My head was throbbing less; the Adlennol I'd taken was finally starting to kick in. I might get sued or challenged to a duel for saying this, but Adlennol does *not* work in thirty minutes like the commercials say. Not for me, anyway.

"First of all, we're at war. Which I don't think is going to fully sink in for a while. But strategically, we have a couple of big problems to deal with. First of all, we need to secure the Belt colonies against anything else that comes here."

There were nods, but everybody was understandably too tired to offer ideas, so I just pressed on with my own, "The information we got out of the liner says we've seen everything they put together, which strikes me as quite likely. But there'll probably be more coming when the Martians realize we're still here. So getting back on our feet is job one, reinforcements are job two."

There were nods, and I kept going, "The second part of job two, though, is warning Earth that a Mars attack fleet might be coming its way… even in the off season. Seems to me that this attack here couldn't just be random timing; they were after our intel, probably as a setup for an Earth attack. They cut our communications and kept them cut so that Earth still doesn't know… and Kitty Castillo was making promises about breaking our Empire."

Again nods — this, as you can see, wasn't our most interactive meeting.

"So how do you want to let Earth know? Hire a courier ship?" Mark Gunney broke the silence, but I shook my head.

"If they eliminated our communications ships, a courier won't get through. And moreover, you know what the political climate is like at home. We send a message saying 'war begun' and only send sensor data, logs and news stories with it, and Caldecott's crew is going to cut it up and blame us for drawing war. So better that... well... that I go back there myself. And get on the vidscreens and make sure we control the message."

I'd thought a great deal about this approach, and I didn't like it. No one at the table needed me to tell them that I'd much, *much* rather be here than dealing with Imperial politics, so me making that suggestion didn't sound like anything but an assumption of a painful duty.

"You sure you can't just send one of us?" Wes leaned forward with a frown. "I know how much you hate dealing with all that garbage..."

I shook my head, "We've got three active ships on station here. I'll go in *Wolf*, which'll pretty much guarantee, I think, that we can get through the Martian blockade, if there is one. The rest of you need to focus on getting your ships ready for war again, before the Martians get back. Mark, Andrea, you two will need to go on mobile patrol, keep an eye on the colonies — especially the ones between us and the Martian asteroids. Wes, you'll have squadron command, especially once you're mobile again. And me, I'll go do what a Commodore must do."

There were a few thin smiles, but that was it. That was the plan.

The meeting broke about twenty minutes later.

CHAPTER THIRTY-FIVE

HOMEWARD BOUND

Wolf departed Belt Two that night at 2358 hours, and by the next day at lunch we were all suffering from the inevitable crash that comes after prolonged and intense periods of action. After the excitement of the past few days, Karen and I both decided to hold off on drills, in no small part because we didn't want to further exhaust the crew when we didn't know what we'd run into in open space.

So we were all collectively wiped out... and nervous. There's a good combination.

I sat in my cabin for a lot of the afternoon that next day, wondering at everything that had happened in the past week. From visiting Belt Nine and grabbing Jones, then going and collecting Cooper from Theta only to uncover a Martian plot to deliver a crushing blow and start a war, and then to fight the biggest space battle in Earth history to that point.

Yes it was the biggest to that point — hard to believe, isn't it? Weird, that hadn't really even occurred to me until the day after. And even then I was pretty sure bigger ones were to come. Was I ever right.

We still had Kitty Castillo, Jones (with a nose cast) and Cooper (also with a nose cast) in the brig, so we could grill them for more information as we traveled. And there were all the files that we'd lifted off the raiders — not much, but something...

There was lots I could be working on, but not much that I *felt* like working on. So I was taking it easy. Trying to preserve sanity (or whatever counts as sanity in my case).

One consistent worry was that we'd get to Earth and find it conquered. I hadn't mentioned that potential outcome to the squadron COs, but it was a real fear in the back of my mind.

My gut was telling me the Martians weren't *that* coordinated. That even after a ten day flight at 190 kps, we'd get there just in time to save Earth. Hopefully we'd tripped Castillo's trap early, and there were still days before the Martian assault on Earth was supposed to be launched...

And surely John and Greg would be suspicious at the loss of communications — be on the alert in case the unthinkable was afoot.

You see, I didn't know about Caldecott yet. That idiot...

So there was plenty on my mind. Plenty to do, and plenty to hope for.

For now, I needed supper.

And as if on cue, there was a knock at my hatch, so I got to my feet and headed for the kitchen, "What'll it be tonight for you, Karen?"

The door swung open and Karen stepped lightly in, closing the door and then jumping on my bed and grabbing the remote, "The usual. Fish sticks, potatoes."

"I swear, you're the only woman I know whose taste in food is as good as mine!" I called back from the kitchen, and she smiled, rolling onto her front to face the vidscreen.

"I am, I know. You should feel incredibly lucky!"

Grinning, I leaned back out through the kitchen door, "Oh, I certainly do."

Karen smiled kicking her legs back and forth in the air and cradling her chin in her hand.

I was lucky in a lot of ways.

AFTERWORD

I believe the first words out of the mouth of my publisher were 'what, you're leaving it there?' I nodded to this, and then explained that the whole point of the series is to try to get people hooked and coming back for more... or to minimize their pain if they hate me (or the book).

So if you really liked this account of my experiences at the beginning of the Martian War, hopefully you'll want more, and that'll come with the next volume.

If you *didn't* like the way I told the tale, then I've only subjected you to about 60,000 words on the matter, and you won't hold as big a grudge against me as if I made you read something much longer. Sound fair?

Well, hopefully you're in camp one. And if you are, what comes next you'll greatly enjoy. You've probably seen the news clips and the documentaries on the whole big mess surrounding Earth and the beginning of the war. Caldecott versus Fiora, and Greg, Marlene, Karen and me in it too for good measure... it's a pretty popular subject, and there's been at least one decent movie on it so far.

But you want to know what it was like for Karen, me and *Wolf*? That's a fun tale to tell, with drama, and action, and humor, and all the other things that make for great stories.

So I advise you to go get it. It'll be out soon, or depending on when you're reading this, it might be out already.

What'll it be called? I'm thinking "The Almost Coup", but the publisher says we should brand 'Rogue' into every title in this series, so that'd make it "The Rogue Inquiry" or "The Rogue Almost-Coup" which to me just sounds odd. We'll see who wins this fight. So long as you buy it. Er... I mean enjoy it.

Anyway, good day. See you next time!

THE
ALMOST
COUP

THE AUTOBIOGRAPHICAL REMINISCENCES OF
ADMIRAL THE LORD KEN BARRON FOR 2231

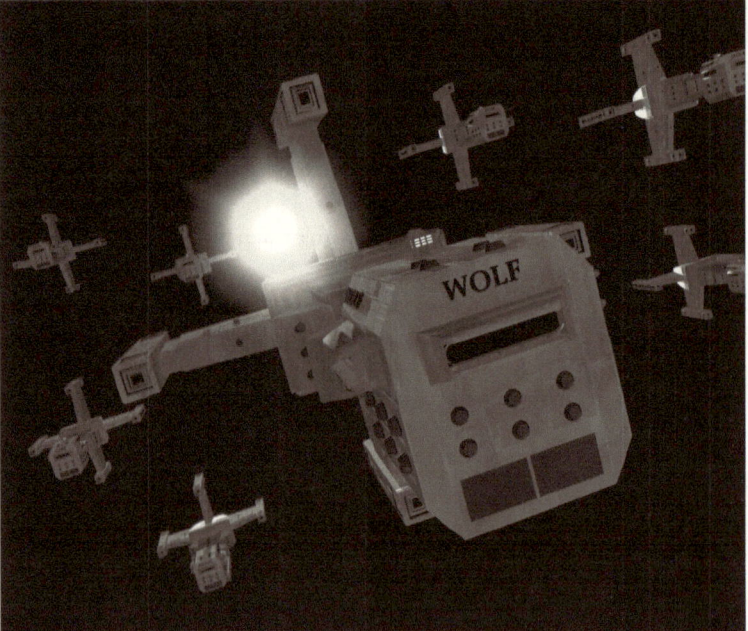

WOLF

THE MARTIAN WAR - 2

KENNETH TAM

FROM THE AUTHOR

Welcome to book two of the Martian War!

In my introduction to *The Rogue Commodore*, I explained where the series came from (*Star Defenders*, *Bonaventure*) and how yes, Ken Barron is sort of based on me. Now I want to explain the unusual style of the series: why, you might ask, did I set these books up as the reminiscences of the main character? A couple of reasons, really.

First, I'm presently studying history, and read sources like this (albeit with less dialogue) all the time. I've always found them interesting, and the biases and issues of historical memory and interpretation, I think, make for interesting additions to the narrative. More than that, though, this format lets me (through Ken Barron) talk directly to you, albeit with you playing the role of a reading audience 250 years in the future. One thing I learned from talking to readers about the *Equations* series is that, when I was actually able to answer their questions in person, I enhanced their reading experience. Well, I'm trying to do that from the start with *Defense Command* — hopefully Ken Barron's explanations of the way the universe works will help you cruise through the story, and have fun in the process.

Once again, many of the characters you'll read about in this book are based on real-world friends of mine, and these characters will be immune from death for the entire series. Given their immunity, and my desire to create suspense, I'm not going to list who they are — they already know who they are. That said, you can probably guess some of their identities if you really want to. My job right now is to thank all those people who've allowed me to poach their personalities — I hope your characters live up to your standards!

Specific thanks again to Peter Caron and Wes Prewer, my good friends who've both offered excellent advice and insight whenever I've needed an outside perspective. Wes also deserves a special nod for all the work he's done on the covers of both the *Defense Command* books and the *Equations* novels.

Finally, the biggest thanks again to my family — Jacqui and Peter, the best parents I could have asked for, and Atlas, my German Shepherd who *Equations* readers will remember from all my acknowledgments there. Without this family of mine, there would be no Iceberg, and no *Defense Command*!

– Kenneth Tam

Preface

What, you ask quite rightly, is an 'almost coup'? It's what the media dubbed our actions around the time of this book, however sensationalist that interpretation may be. I mean seriously, our loyalty never once drifted from the people of Earth or even the Emperor, we just had to trim back some red tape. But that's a biased assessment — I'll let you make your own determination.

So today you're reading my account of what happened in Earth space during the fall months of 2231. My guess is you may have read *The Rogue Commodore* so you already know how the war with the Martians got started at the Belt... Well now we wanted to tell the story of what happened at Earth, and how the Second Lord's antics affected a situation that was already very, very bad.

Same style as last time, I should warn you; these are my memoirs, after all, so I get the final say on how the story is told. Hopefully you'll enjoy it as much or more this time as last! Without further ado, let's get started.

This is *The Almost Coup.*

And here we go, this is me working on the second draft of this manuscript. I was just accused by the publisher of not providing enough context, so here's a 101 entry-level look at the basic structure of the Earth Empire's government and how it works. Or doesn't. That depends on who you ask, really. I might even see if the publisher will spring for an organization chart in the front of this book next to the battle maps and whatnot...

So, how does the Empire government work in 2231? Pretty much the same way today's does — it can be just as frustratingly slow and divided, at times, and often seems incoherent. However, it has the best of intentions, and if you understand where the Empire's government came from, you'll realize the fact that it works at all is quite an achievement.

Remember, Earth went from barely-unified International Federation to 'Empire' in 2057, with the success of then-President Luther Gordon (the Great), but his election by plebiscite to the office of Emperor left a lot of questions as to just how democratic government could be maintained. Working off models from states like America, Canada and Britain, the political leaders essentially slotted the Imperial office into the role of a weak executive, or of a constitutional monarch. Legislative power stayed with the Federation (renamed 'Imperial') Parliament, but the Emperor maintained certain powers.

On the next page, there's a list of the powers assigned to each part of the government. When you look at it, it probably makes the Parliament sound pretty powerful, and indeed, Parliament is that. The problem is that Parliament is very rarely unified. You have different political parties, some of them in the Emperor's pocket, and you have ambition, and media-pandering, and the omnipresent need for everyone sitting in the Commons and the Senate to get *elected*. So while there is a lot of party discipline (meaning parties tend to vote the same way on pieces of legislation most of the time) there's never a guarantee for even a majority government that it can get its job done.

EMPEROR:
- Head of state
- Command of Imperial Army
- Veto Power on Legislation (overruled with majority in both Houses on re-vote)
- Power of Oversight (can launch Imperial Commissions with wide-ranging authority that can only be shut down with majority votes in both Houses of Parliament)
- Ceremonial Duties (grants titles, but cannot confirm them without majority vote in the Commons)
- A lot of unofficial influence, because come on, he's the Emperor
- Palaces and fancy clothes and stuff

PARLIAMENT:
(2 Houses, Senate and House of Commons)
- Legislative/Policy Control (including declaration of war)
- Control of Defense Command
- Power to overturn the powers of the Emperor in all cases with sufficient majority vote
- Imperial Oversight (every ten years they can vote to have the Emperor replaced)
- Diplomatic powers
- Pretty much everything else, aside from what the judiciary handles

So it's not perfect — it's full of loopholes, in fact. But that was our system, and to be frank, that still is our system, despite a few of the constitutional reforms that have reined in a bit of that Imperial influence.

Anyway, that should hopefully get you up to speed on governing issues in this period. Let's get started…

Chapter One

Someone Flipped The Chess Board

You probably remember where *The Rogue Commodore* left off, but in case you didn't get a chance to pick that up, Karen and I were cruising from the Belt Station home to Earth aboard *Wolf*. Belt Two and the entire Belt Squadron had just repelled a major combined attack of pirates and Martians, and now Captain Wes Pellew was in command back there, patching up the squadron and getting ready to protect the Belt colonies at all costs.

Meanwhile, Karen and I had taken *Wolf* and were heading back to Earth to warn the Admiralty and the entire Empire that the Martians had started a war against us, and that we had good reason to suspect an imminent attack on the planet.

That's enough of a start to get us rolling. I'll fill you in on other details as we go, if they come up.

But for now, let's just skip straight to *Wolf*. By the time we were three days out of Belt Two I was getting very, very anxious. Remember how prone I am to secret nervousness — the kind that I hide from everyone but that gets me worked up when no one's around?

Yeah, that hit. Pretty bad, too.

You can probably guess why: I was seriously beginning to digest the fact that I'd played a part in beginning a shooting war with the Martians, even if I just happened to be the guy getting shot at.

So I worried that I'd brought this down on us, and then I wondered if *Wolf* was going to reach Earth too late — to find a fleet of Martian ships in orbit, and laughing Martian soldiers planting their flag on my parents' front lawn. It would have to have been a hell of a fight for things to go down that way, but stranger things had probably happened.

Then there were the lesser worries: what if we got there in time but no one believed us, or if we got there and the Parliament said 'let's surrender' or 'make peace' or 'pretend it didn't happen'. Making peace might sound nice on paper, but peace is a two-way street — both sides have to want it, and the Martians clearly didn't. So if we started trying to negotiate and all they wanted was us dead, they'd get their way.

Such scenarios as these, and many more, were dancing through my head in those first days.

If you're thinking it's not healthy to worry that much, you're right. Karen told me that whenever I got so neurotic, and over the years she'd become incredibly adept at getting my thoughts away from things like this.

Usually with something I thought to be entirely insane.

"Come on!"

I was huffing and already sweating.

"Keep moving!" she yelled back over her shoulder at me.

She was running this course like a winged angel with combat skills. Me... well, I'm a Commodore, I didn't run SF obstacle courses, except for those rare times when Karen cajoled me into doing so...

Karen had convinced me that it'd be a good idea to use physical activity to distract myself, and since *Wolf's* detail of Security Forces had just set up its obstacle course in gym two on the rec deck, it seemed like a convenient place to work up a sweat.

But this was more of a sweat than I quite felt like working up. As I've explained before, I'm in pretty decent shape, but I'm no hunter-killer-ripped-up-super-athlete. And this thing involved festive activities like vaulting oneself over walls taller than, oh, *me*. You get the picture.

Karen, being in excellent physical condition (of course, she just had to be), seemed to elegantly hop over every damned thing in her way. But then she was slim and limber and whatnot — her muscle-to-mass ratio made me look like a barge towed by a seal.

How's that for imagery? My publisher says it doesn't make sense, so we've put money on whether readers will understand it or not.

I was stumbling down to a walk as Karen started climbing a cargo net in front of me, and she looked back over her shoulder again, "You can do it, come on!"

I held up my hand and managed to wave flittingly at her before bending over and propping my torso parallel to the ground with hands on my knees. As I tried to take deep breaths, Karen let go the net and dropped back to the deck and slowly walked over to me, breathing the slightest bit heavily.

"You know you're not in bad shape, you can do it."

I held up a hand over my head while I stared at the deck, collecting my breath and nodding.

She was right, of course. I wasn't a complete wreck — she just happened to be better than me at this obstacle course. And I didn't have a chance of outrunning her, if I played fair.

Now you know me, do you think I'm the sort to just give up when the odds are against me? Nah, I play dirty.

So as soon as Karen looked away, checking to make sure there weren't any SF or Special Branchers around watching my embarrassing display, I launched into a sprint towards the nets.

Her head whipped around fast, "*Hey!*"

I laughed out loud, "I may be slower, but I lack conscience!"

I reached the net with a solid five-second lead, throwing my foot forward to hit the synthetic rope webbing at full speed.

In typical fashion, my foot slid right through the net and I went in face first with so much momentum that I bounced back, flopping upside down and dangling. To my credit, I kept my head from hitting the deck.

So I was pretty badly tangled, with my head hanging upside down from the net, and Karen slowed and came to a stop right in front of me, crossing her arms and staring down at me with a stern gaze.

"Learn your lesson?"

"Get me down," I grumbled.

She smiled, "I don't see why I should."

I'm pretty sure my expressions weren't even close to looking like what I meant them to look like because I was upside down, but I tried to smile, "Uhm... did I mention... that.. I like your shoes?"

We negotiated for my release.

CHAPTER TWO
IMPORTANT THINGS NEARER VENUS

Had I known what I would later learn about the situation unfolding elsewhere while I was running that obstacle course, I never would have started worrying to begin with... well, at least not about the immediate safety of Earth, and certainly not about the Martians getting to Earth before me.

You'll recall (I hope!) that Rear Admiral Marlene Stoll had been on her way from Earth to her command at the Venus Station while Karen, Kris, Mark Gunney and I were stirring the pot at Asteroid Theta. That was all covered in *The Rogue Commodore* if you missed it, but suffice it to say Marlene had run across a Martian destroyer escort where a Martian DE shouldn't be.

Specifically, she'd sighted one in space around the sun — on the course between Earth and Venus, and its Commander had said his mission was just to tail her flagship to gather sensor data on Earth space drives.

Marlene hadn't believed that. She'd arrived on the Venus Station and discovered that communications had been cut between Venus and Earth, just as they'd been cut between the Belt colonies and Earth. After about twenty minutes she'd put two and two together, and she'd lived up yet again to her nickname — 'the Sorceress'.

With all the instinct and poise that made the Venusian pirates hate her, she collected three other ships from her squadron and headed back out into the space between Venus and Earth to keep an eye on things.

So while I was worrying and getting myself tangled in a net, her battleship *Sorceress* and a another battleship, a frigate and a corvette were cruising in the space lanes between Venus and Earth, waiting to see if anything strange started happening.

Marlene was actually in her cabin much of the time, reading and doing the paperwork she was accustomed to doing as an Admiral, when her vidscreen — set as usual to the *Sorceress*Net mailbox display — chimed, and a new message popped into the inbox.

She read the subject and headed straight for the bridge.

"Are we sure that's not some glitch?" her words as she stepped onto the bridge deck were sharp, but her Flag Captain (who I'm pretty sure was Kyle Feldman at this point) was already looking back at her and shaking his head.

"I don't see how. It's all passive readings... *Warlock* and *Kodiak* are confirming," he said evenly, and Marlene nodded, stepping quickly forward to the vidscreens on the forward wall of her bridge.

Those screens were showing something that she definitely *wished* was a glitch. She counted twice to be sure, but the computer was indeed showing twenty-five individual ship signatures... some of them *very* big.

"Well, I think we've figured out what that DE was doing sniffing our heels," Marlene turned back to her Flag Captain. "Still no comms with Earth?"

He shook his head and she frowned, looking back to the screen, "I would've expected John to have done something about the connection by now… we'll have to carry the news ourselves."

"Yes ma'am, but they're making 186 kps by the look of things. We may not be able to get ahead of them."

Marlene frowned and turned to the Sensors and Communications Officer, "They're going that fast this close to the sun?"

The Lieutenant Commander nodded in reply, and Marlene's brow climbed in surprise and she crossed her arms. With that sort of speed, her squadron might indeed not be able to get ahead of them. She half wondered if she shouldn't have sent warning about the dead comms and the strange DE straight from Venus to Earth, instead of waiting out here to find out more.

But then again, as she rightly concluded, if she hadn't been out there, no one would have known for certain that a real Martian fleet was inbound.

"Well, we can try to slow them down," she started thinking out loud. "See if we can give them a reason to be nervous…"

Her Flag Captain cocked an eyebrow, "Ma'am?"

Sure, Marlene had a great reputation for getting into tough scrapes and beating up on foes of the Empire… but usually those foes were Venusian pirates, not a formation of twenty-five ships.

"We make them think that Earth knows they're coming," she looked from her Flag Captain to the screen. "We have to get in close anyway, I want lidar pings on each one of these signatures… and I want to make sure they really are Martians."

That last point was, in fact, one that couldn't be overlooked. They'd come out here looking for a fishy Martian plot, and so they assumed this long column of ships emitting copious amounts of radiation was in fact from the Imperium. It remained to be confirmed, however, that these were indeed Martian ships.

"So we go in close for a look," Marlene uncrossed her arms and turned back. "Perhaps we ask them what they're up to out here. And then we try to slow them down."

Her Flag Captain opened his mouth, then closed it. The Sorceress had spoken, her will would be done… so he turned to his XO, "Move us into realtime range, keep a close eye on them. And bring us to battle stations. Tell *Clever* to get ready to run for Earth with the news if this goes south."

The four ships of her formation turned towards the approaching column of Martian ships.

It didn't take much time to close the range — within four minutes, the Martians clearly had *Sorceress* and its cohorts on their scopes, and their column had slowed and was configuring itself into a line abreast for a fight.

"Realtime range?" Marlene tapped her foot as she watched the deployment on main screen, and after a quick pause the Sensors and Communications Officer replied.

"About forty seconds. Weapons range in a eighty seconds."

She nodded. That was fine.

Her head, she told me much later, was at this point spinning. Don't get me wrong:

the figure you see in all the movies about this — the stoic 'sorceress' standing with folded arms on her bridge, lock-jawed and staring down a fleet six times her number — is accurate enough. She looked calm, cool and collected, much as I did when this sort of thing happened.

But secretly she was starting to hear the little voice that said, "You're *insane.*"

You probably thought the same thing when you first heard about this incident — I sure did... but then I think *I'm* insane a lot of the time. Anyway, as the range closed she was beginning to wonder just how she was going to handle this.

There was a good chance that the Martians would just start shooting as soon as they could, and her four ships would have to be *very* lucky to live through that. But perhaps she could play this another way. Courtesy was a useful tool in those days, and it might just give her an opening.

Or she'd be killed.

Battlelink had been established between the ships of her force, so as these thoughts crossed her mind she looked between the faces of her Captains on *Sorceress*' bridge screens, "Everyone stand by to reverse drives in... sixty seconds. And ready your torpedoes."

Torpedoes, remember, weren't supposed to be particularly useful mobile weapons, and Marlene hadn't heard about Kris, Karen and me using them at Asteroid Theta, so this was a definite out-of-the-box idea for her... just the sort of thing she needed facing odds like these.

The three Captains and Commanders on the small screens nodded and began giving orders, and behind her Marlene heard her Flag Captain repeating the same directives to his officers. Marlene took a deep breath, looked down for a second, and tapped her foot.

"Twenty seconds to comm range."

She nodded, glancing back at the Lieutenant Commander, "Get me their commanding officer on screen five when you can."

Nodding, the Sensors and Communications Officer moved between a couple of technicians around her, pointing and saying technical things appropriate for the moment.

It was a long twenty seconds of waiting. Marlene stood stoically as the time passed, her eyes fixing on screen five as it switched from a secondary sensor display to a loading screen, and then a buffering screen.

"Standing by to reverse drives," the Lieutenant Commander at Helm and Navigation reported as the buffering bar hit forty percent.

Timing was going to be crucial to make this work — Marlene couldn't get carried away...

"Alright," she said to the Captains and Commanders on Battlelink, getting her last orders in as the buffer on screen five hit eighty percent, "Fire torpedoes just before you reverse drives on that mark... but be ready to remotely disarm them if this turns out to be something innocent."

"You think that's likely, ma'am?" Jake Lee, *Kodiak's* skipper, asked with eyebrows up.

Marlene smiled, "No, this is going to be a mess."

The buffer pushed through ninety, and then a hundred, and then the screen went black and then popped back to life to reveal a Martian officer — an Admiral by the look of him — with five round tabs on his rather overbearing collar.

"Good day, Admiral," Marlene's tone was polite, but loaded with an undercurrent of menace, "I'm Rear Admiral Marlene Stoll, Defense Command Venus Station. I must say, I'm rather surprised to see you out here."

"Admiral Stoll, your reputation precedes you. I am Grand Fleet Admiral Garvey, of the Imperium Solar Navy. I must say, I wasn't expecting to see you out here either."

A smile formed on Marlene's face, "I expect you weren't. So, how about you tell me what you're up to?"

"Reversing course... now..." the Lieutenant Commander at Helm and Navigation whispered loudly as Marlene's words finished off, the twenty seconds having elapsed already. Fair enough.

"Torpedoes launching," *Sorceress'* XO, standing back at the ops consoles, reported in an equally quiet tone. Usually the microphones associated with comm screens didn't pick up whispering — it was a convenient feature designed to allow for situations like this one, where the CO needed to hear what was going on in her ship, but didn't want that broadcast to whoever she was speaking to.

Too convenient a feature, you ask? Hey, by this time we'd been using that handy ability to mess with pirates for about a decade, we knew what we were doing. Marlene certainly did.

And as his sensors detected the reverse in thrust from the Earth ships, Grand Admiral Garvey looked away from the screen for a moment, "Oh my dear Admiral Stoll, wouldn't you prefer to come in closer?"

Marlene's smile widened a little, "I'll consider it. Just tell me, will you be asking me to surrender if I do?"

The Martian met her smile and shrugged, "Well, nominally I would have ordered you to be destroyed, but since you've been so very courteous, I'd gladly accept a surrender."

Great, this wasn't just a misunderstanding then. It was definitely war. But at least the Martian was being courteous...

"Ah, so this is war then, is it? Albeit undeclared?" Marlene unfolded her arms and stepped towards the screen, and the Martian Admiral nodded.

"It is, and don't think you can change your Empire's fate my dear Admiral Stoll, the Belt has already been taken by now, and no one can communicate with Earth thanks to our interdiction. Best you surrender now."

Marlene's smile faded — but not in the 'shocked disbelief' style of fading that his Grandness the fool Garvey had wanted. Her eyes were abruptly sharp lasers boring into him, "Really? Think we haven't been waiting for this? I'm just your warmup, we'll see how you like it when you get to Earth."

"Yes, we will," the Martian's smile faded in kind. "And, forgive the cliché, but you won't be there to see it..."

"Turn us around and boost at full speed, please," Marlene gave the orders without removing her eyes from the screen.

"We can run you down at will. You're better off surrendering, my dear."

Marlene's eyes narrowed, "I'm not your *dear*. Time to ballistic range, Commander?"

"Three seconds, ma'am. Drives are just firing up now."

I should explain what this means, as it was understood by Marlene and her officers without being explicitly said. Remember how we laid our torpedoes like invisible ballistic mines at Theta? Marlene's ships did the same thing, except her two battleships had two tubes each, in addition to *Kodiak's* one.

So with the Martians rapidly advancing, the dormant torpedoes Marlene had ordered launched just before Garvey got on the comm had drifted forward undetected. As such, while their distinguished Lord Admiral had been trying to intimidate Marlene, the warheads had gotten awfully close to his ships, and now the torpedoes' drives were firing up.

It all happened rather quickly, really; the plumes of the five torpedo drives appeared on the scope, and the Martian Admiral frowned and looked away.

"Kill the link," Marlene turned from the screen. "All ships break for Earth, maximum velocity. Actually, Kelly, bring *Warlock* back to Venus, we can't leave our station without capital ships with this going on… Jake, take *Kodiak* back too. The Home Fleet will be able to handle this. You two watch out for Martians poking at my base."

The Captains of the respective ships — Kelly Monahan of *Warlock* and Jake Lee of *Kodiak* — nodded over the Battlelink.

"They're starting counter-fire against the torpedoes," Marlene's Flag Captain nodded at the screen, and she frowned and turned back.

Martian EM Cannons began spraying their bolts at the five torpedoes as the weapons accelerated towards the long line of warships with a combined approach speed of over 300 kps. To the Imperium gunners' credit, three of the torpedoes were shot down by this sudden onslaught of counter-fire, but two of the big warheads slammed in.

One battleship took both hits — *hard*, by the look of it. The first warhead blew its upper engine pylon off entirely. The engine pod at the end of that pylon, its thrusters still firing irregularly, spun away from its ship, and then slammed into a nearby destroyer before the smaller ship could get out of the way.

The second warhead rammed the 'tail' of the Martian ship — that (ridiculous, as far as I'm concerned) section of hull that extends out behind the drive pylons on a Martian ship. Up until then, and still today, I'd always told people who said our own ships should have 'tails' that the things were terrible liabilities. This shot proved it. The explosion tore the tail off, and sent such a surge through the powergrid that the battleship burst like a balloon.

Two ships taken out, not so bad.

Of course, the surprise that had allowed Marlene to nail those two Martians was lost, so she wouldn't be able to pull this again, but for now her job was done.

"They're slowing down, ma'am. Looks like they're getting ready to deploy search and rescue, and they're forming up to receive fire."

Marlene nodded, "Excellent. That'll slow them down a bit, so let's get a move on."

The Captains and Commander on *Sorceress'* Battlelink nodded, and then Marlene turned to her Flag Captain, "Let's get to Earth."

Sorceress and *Clever* headed for Earth, with *Warlock* and *Kodiak* splitting off to make their way back to Venus shortly after they got out of the sensor range of the Martians.

Some have asked me why Marlene herself came back to Earth, instead of returning to her station as regs might normally have dictated. Well, I think the reasons for her decision are pretty obvious… but then, I also happened to be heading back to Earth myself at the time, so I may well be biased.

But look at it this way: a fleet of twenty-three ships was heading for the homeworld. As a frontier Admiral (or Commodore), your orders are to look after your station, sure, but ultimately you still have to protect the heart of the Empire. And with no communications ships left out there, and with no immediately clear threats to your station, it just seems… well… *right*, to take the initiative and head to Earth yourself.

Especially when you don't know what the hell else is going on out there.

You can second guess our respective choices with 20-20 hindsight all you like… though I'm not sure why you would. Bottom line is we wanted to go home to make sure Earth was ready.

And go figure, Earth wasn't even close to ready.

CHAPTER THREE

THE VERY (UN)IMPORTANT INQUIRY

I suppose I should put a disclaimer in front of this: sorry if I seem bitter about the inquiry. I just get a bit queasy when I look at all the chaos that came because Dave Caldecott wanted to have his political victory over the real Naval officers in Defense Command. You'll see why, if you don't already know from reading or seeing it elsewhere.

Greg Noyce and John Fiora were sitting on the latter's patio while Marlene was having her skirmish with the Martians. Karen and I were still six days away in *Wolf*, and Marlene was further than that, though she didn't realize it yet.

And, of course, communications between Earth and *everywhere* were down.

"So I read the paper this morning, and Caldecott blamed bitter elements in Defense Command Communications for interrupting the comms," John leaned back in his chair and sipped his drink.

Greg's eyebrows went up and he nodded, "All the news broadcasts I saw showed that statement as well. At least the media didn't believe him completely... but I still would prefer to know what is actually causing the disruption."

John nodded, looking absently up at the sky as he took another sip.

It was a good question. *Nothing* in the past forty years had interrupted all communications between Earth and its colonies. John was tempted to blame Caldecott for the blackout — to keep me and Marlene wrong-footed and unable to defend ourselves before his little drumhead tribunal. But the instincts that made First Lord Fiora the head of our ring of officers weren't accepting that easy answer.

Greg was just as suspicious. He'd been taking advantage of his suspension from command aboard his flagship to spend time on the golf course with his kids, but he'd been more preoccupied of late than he'd admitted to anyone. Something was just *wrong* about this whole thing — beyond the obvious wrongness of the inquiry — and it took officers who'd actually been out on the frontier and who'd faced foes in defense of the Empire to realize it.

So Caldecott, assuming he wasn't part of the problem, probably wouldn't even realize that something sinister was brewing.

"My question is why hasn't Caldecott sent new communications ships out on station to reestablish comms. Or even frigates to check to make sure everything's alright," John looked back at his drink, and then glanced across the table at Greg.

Frowning, Greg nodded, "If it were me, I'd be determined to find out what's actually going on. But according to a couple of friends I have in DCC, there's been a lot of bluster from Caldecott's people — blaming them for incompetence and saying they can't be trusted."

John frowned, "So he won't send other comm ships out because he thinks what, they'll go awol?"

Greg half shrugged and nodded, taking another sip of his own drink, "My guess is he'll send corvettes soon, if he hasn't already. But I don't think he's too concerned — he probably thinks this will pass after we tire ourselves out, and then he'll just have more ammunition to use against us in the inquiry."

John shook his head slowly and sighed, "I can't believe I have… had, I suppose… such an idiot for a Second Lord. Gotta love politics."

Greg laughed shortly and nodded.

They sat for a couple of more minutes staring aimlessly at the sky — two great Admirals unable to do a damned thing because of politics — until John's wife leaned out the deck door, "John, SF here to see you."

John looked over his shoulder and frowned, "SF? What do they want?"

She shrugged and John nodded, looking back at Greg, "We both better see them then. In case they want a fight."

Greg smiled, "I haven't been in a rumble with SF for a long time."

Getting to their feet, the Admirals followed John's wife into the living room adjacent to the deck, and were greeted by three SF — a Lieutenant and two regular guards — standing with stern gazes.

"Well well, you boys want a beer or something?" John smiled as he came to a stop in front of them, Greg standing off to his left flank rather less jovially.

The leading Lieutenant didn't react at all to the joke, "Sirs, you're both being summoned to appear before the initial hearings for the inquiry this evening."

Greg blinked in surprise, and John took another sip of his drink, "Is that a fact? Lovely. Tell Dave we'll be there with bells on."

The Lieutenant again didn't react — except for extending his hand with two blue folders, "Your summons documents. These tell you where to be, and when."

John's boisterous mood notched up one more level, "*Really?* That's great news. Wouldn't want to miss it. Why don't you leave them on the floor before you get out of my house?"

The Lieutenant blinked and his eyes darted to John's decidedly unwelcoming smile, "I'm required to hand deliver them, sir."

"You just did, I'll swear to it. Now drop them and get out," he took another swig, and the Lieutenant blinked one more time, then did precisely as he was told.

John watched the door hit the Lieutenant as he walked out.

"Well," Greg stepped forward and crouched to pick up the two folders after the SF guards left, "I suppose I'm not going to be golfing this evening."

John nodded, "Prospects don't look good."

They'd been summoned.

CHAPTER FOUR

GETTING CLOSE TO EARTH

The next three days were spent with Greg and John under questioning by Dave Caldecott and a handful of his cronies, all broadcast on vidscreen for anyone who wanted to see them... but apparently ratings were non-existent after the first twenty minutes — no surprise there, the questions got procedural *real* quick.

I know I wouldn't be able to stomach watching a chubby, round Admiral with a voice that almost broke when he got worked up, squealing about why John didn't countersign every piece of paper on his desk *twice*.

But clearly, it was a matter of public concern. You all care a lot about it, right? Oh, you don't? Shocker.

Sorry, like I say, bitter. Because in those three days of useless questioning, *Wolf* had gotten three days closer to Earth, and much, much more importantly, Marlene had slowed the Martians to about half their pace. Now, I could write this whole book about the drama that she and *Sorceress* created in those three days, and the five that followed, but since you can go to Marlene's memoirs for that, I'll just review the juiciest bits.

So, day three of the inquiry was also day three of her slow boost. Just about as soon as she'd started for Earth after the incident in Chapter Two, she'd realized her best bet would be to use *Sorceress* as a torment — to keep the Martians nervous and moving slowly — while she sent *Clever* ahead to report. That way she'd get word to John early, and still buy time for him to mobilize.

What she didn't find out until much later, and what we didn't really know until we found *Clever's* wreck about ten years ago, is that the brave little ship, under Commander Gerda Falkenhayn, had run across two of the destroyer escorts the Martians had sent ahead of them to hunt comm ships.

The fight Gerda's little corvette put up must have been worthy of song — one of the DE's wreckage was found drifting near *Clever*, and pieces of the other one were around the wreckage as well. If we ever get into the Martian archives we might learn the details of the fight, but for now I can tell you — from what Marlene's told me of Gerda and *Clever*, and from having seen corvettes and DE's tangling many times — that it was an epic fight.

That said, Marlene was left fighting a holding action to buy time for a courier who'd been destroyed en route. She didn't know it at the time, and had she found out she might have stopped her delaying tactics, but thank God she didn't. If she and *Sorceress* hadn't been out there living up to their combined reputation, we'd all be worshipping the Martian President-for-life as our lord and savior right now.

And my back is too bad these days for me to bow to anyone but the Emperor.

So back on topic here, it was three days after John and Greg were called to the inquiry that *Sorceress* traded shots with some Martian destroyers. And let me tell you, this was a *clinic* in battleship fighting. Cadets should take note.

Marlene was standing in that familiar stubborn pose on the bridge of *Sorceress* when the Sensors and Communications Officer stopped between one of her tech's consoles and frowned, "Ma'am... I think they're trying to send destroyers forward to clear the way."

Well it was about time — Marlene had figured the Martians' first move would have been to send light ships forward to try to clear any Defense Command traps before the capital ships tried to make their way through.

I better explain just what Marlene had been doing to them.

Sorceress had only six torpedoes aboard, and now that the Martians knew she was willing to use them, she couldn't afford to just try to lob them at the Imperium ships every time she gained the range — they'd be shot down and have no effect at all.

No, she was much too crafty for that sort of simple (and useless) plan. So she'd ordered the ordnance from *Sorceress'* three squadrons of F-194s to be crated up into cargo containers. With the very extensive missile reserves the ship carried for its fighters, she'd been able to actually put together sixty-three 'mines' that could be left in the Martians' path — much like torpedoes, just not propelled.

We know that fighter missiles like the glamorously named X9 Shipkiller were nearly useless when launched, but six of them in a box that was almost impossible for even lidar to detect could indeed damage a DE or even a destroyer. Enough of them going off near a battleship could really mess up that ship's day, too.

So Marlene had figured out a handy weapon that maximized the use of her fighter ordnance, and importantly, that significantly slowed the Martian progress. She'd watched on the main screen for each of the past three days as the column of Imperium ships cruised into cluster after cluster of the mines she'd laid, and as the leading ship got close enough, the jury-rigged proximity fuses on the bombs triggered detonation.

Only the first Martian to stumble into one of these crude little weapons had so much as been scarred by its encounter — it had taken some hefty damage to one of its turrets — but since then, fear of the things had forced the Martians to halve their speed, leaving them slowly creeping ahead at about 90 kps as they watched their lidar screens for new little blips that might damage them.

You might ask why the Martian battleships didn't just come to the front and muscle their way through; well, it's simple practicality. This armada was being sent to conquer Earth, and yet it was taking losses before it even faced our Home Fleet. It couldn't afford to be arrogant and to take any damage that would hurt it later — not if it had an alternative anyway.

So for three days Grand Admiral Garvey had been chugging along slowly, taking his time and shooting down every mine his escorts saw before damage could be done.

Now, had it been Marlene in Garvey's position, she'd have sent some frigates... er, the Martians called them destroyers... anyway, she'd have sent some of those forward, and used them to clear the way, so that the fleet could keep its speed over 100 kps. Of course, she could have trusted her frigates to *not* engage the battleship laying the mines, because Defense Command frigate Captains tend to be smart enough to realize it would be a losing fight.

Evidently, Garvey had less *conservative* destroyer Captains.

After three days of slow-slogging (time in which, had Garvey not been slowed, he'd have shown up at Earth), the Martian finally unleashed a few of his destroyers and DEs. And Marlene was waiting for them.

Back to her standing on the bridge: she narrowed her eyes as the icons of the two destroyers and three DEs came forward in a tight diamond. They were clearly in a formation that someone had suggested to them would be good for anti-mine operations, and they took some pot shots at bits of space debris that looked like they could be mines.

Marlene actually hadn't sent any fresh mines at them since that morning — there was no need to waste the things since the mere threat of them was enough to slow the Martians right down.

"Alright, time for some fun. Call the Captain to the bridge, Commander, get ready on your weapons. Lasers and mags I think… let's remind them that we're out here," Marlene turned and nodded to *Sorceress'* XO. The Captain was off duty, so he'd not be up here for about two minutes. For now Marlene would look after this herself.

"Helm, give me a 180, and run down on them hard. We're going to swoop in and then reverse drives just as we enter extreme laser range. I don't want to be in shooting distance of their popguns, but I want a clean shot with our bow beams."

The Lieutenant at Helm and Navigation nodded (the Lieutenant Commander was also off duty this shift, if you're wondering), then started giving orders to the techs around him. The Lieutenant Commander at Sensors and Communications looked up at Marlene just as the Admiral turned to her.

"Ma'am, looks like they're coming right after us. Their acceleration is up to 110 kps and climbing."

Marlene smiled, "I once was told that it isn't smart to *run* to a fight. Particularly one you'll lose. Commander Dozi, time to laser range?"

Sorceress' dark-skinned XO looked up from the tactical consoles he was overseeing, "At present rate of approach, thirty-eight seconds."

As you can tell from that, *Sorceress* was staying *very* closely ahead of the Martians — perhaps dangerously so. Being that close to such a large enemy required a constant and attentive watch of what the Imperium ships were doing, to make sure they didn't leap forward before *Sorceress* could work up the speed to escape.

Well, escape really wasn't a concern in this case.

"We're all set to reverse course, ma'am. They won't get a shot off at us," the Lieutenant at helm spoke up immediately, and Marlene smiled at the young woman's enthusiasm.

"Glad to hear it."

Turning back to the main screen, Marlene folded her arms, "Give me a count, Commander Dozi."

"Twenty seconds."

Slightly out of breath, *Sorceress'* Captain emerged onto the bridge, well inside the usual time it took for him to travel from his cabin to the command deck, "What's going on?"

Marlene glanced at him and then nodded towards the main screen, "We're getting our first taste of the personal stuff. We'll dash in and hit this sweep force with both lasers, then pull back."

The Captain crossed the bridge to stand next to his Admiral, nodding, "Sounds good."

It certainly did sound good, and what's more, it *was* good.

"Ten seconds. Powering the laser grid," Commander Dozi's smooth voice called out the time.

"Standing by to reverse drives," the Lieutenant at Helm and Navigation added right after.

Marlene found her foot tapping on the deck as she watched the approach. She wasn't nervous, or even anxious, so much as eager. That might sound uncivilized or callous, but this was the defense of her home she was dealing with. She was looking forward to doing more good for the people she was trying to protect, and to reminding these Martians why they were the underdogs.

"Stand by..." Dozi's words came slowly... "*Shoot.*"

There was a slight tremor through the deck as both of *Sorceress'* hefty bow laser emitters simultaneously spewed red energy.

Commander Dozi (yes, I keep mentioning him by name because we all recognize him from his later... let's call it *fame*) was an excellent man to have pointing laser beams — both *Sorceress'* shots caught a different DE.

Remember how much carnage that aged battleship laser the pirates had at Belt Two did to *Cheetah*? This was about six and a half times worse. First, neither of those DEs had a commander nearly as good as Wes Pellew to get them out of the line of fire, and second, these new lasers in *Sorceress* were about twice as powerful as the one that had hit *Cheetah*.

Single drive pods were sawed off both little ships in the few seconds that came between Ben Dozi's order to shoot and the Helm and Navigation Lieutenant's order to reverse engines. It might not sound like much damage, all things considered, but with the tight formation those five ships had been keeping, it was messy.

The Martian ships scattered like pirates under fire, two of them nearly ramming each other in the process.

"Nice shooting, Commander," Marlene smiled and nodded to herself, watching on the screen now as *Sorceress* yawed through 180 degrees without losing momentum and then sped away again.

She'd reduced the Martian fleet to only twenty-one effective ships, but it was still quite a threat, a threat she had to keep delaying.

So as *Sorceress* sped away and the Martians slowed down again, Marlene hoped that *Clever* was making good time.

Clever's debris was, we think by that time, already scattering through space.

CHAPTER FIVE
FINDING MARCONI

If you've read *The Rogue Commodore* then you might recall me introducing what we were about to find, also three days out from Earth. I'd been in my cabin when the message came from the bridge — it was Matt's watch, and Karen and I were due to meet for supper about ten minutes after I got the call.

By the time supper rolled around, I wouldn't have much of an appetite. Why? Well, that's pretty obvious.

Karen and I met on the lift heading up to the bridge. As the doors closed behind me, she looked my way, "I'm hungry, Matt tell you anything specific?"

I frowned and shook my head, "I figured he told you."

Her brow furrowing slightly — as much as Karen's brow ever seems to furrow — and she shook her head, "He just didn't sound too happy."

I smiled, "Does he ever?"

"Touché."

The lift was moving pretty quickly through *Wolf's* hull, carrying us towards the bridge at a reasonable pace that still seemed all too slow. I was beginning to wonder, and when I wonder it's like worrying — it gets a little out of hand.

What could Matt have found that required both of us to see it right away, and which at the same time he didn't want to repeat over comms? This was all probably some damn trick, he was just toying with us, trying to keep us on our toes...

Later I'd think back to that musing in the lift and wish things had been that simple. I don't know why, but the loss of the communications ship *Marconi* has stayed with me. Well, that's not quite it — every ship I've seen lost has stayed with me, melodramatic as that sounds, but there's something about *Marconi* that just, well, resonates.

We got to the bridge and Matt pointed us to a debris field displayed on the main screen. We walked forward and looked at it, and ordered Erica to slow us down to confirm what the transponder — the device that had highlighted *Marconi's* wreck on Jim Hannigan's sensors — was saying. Yes, the debris was from *Marconi*. Yes, the little ship had been shattered.

You might think it's something that commonly happens to comm ships. Being out there alone in deep space, you might think they'd be common targets for pirates. Not so. Pirates, as a rule, steer clear of Defense Command ships — attacking any ship under the black sun of the Command is a death sentence. We tend to take things like that personally.

I mean, it's different when we show up and trade shots... not much different, but when it's a run-in and we're doing our jobs and they're resisting getting caught, that's a bit different. What I mean is, nobody — *nobody* — goes out looking to pick on a Defense Command ship, and especially not a virtually unarmed little workhorse like gallant

Marconi. Because when they do, people like Karen and I lose our senses of humor real quick.

Marconi's crew of eighty-six, and its skipper, Lieutenant-Commander Vince Makarov, were doing their jobs out here one day. They were on a 120-day tour between the Belt and Earth, doing nothing but relaying signal traffic back and forth, dreaming about home, staring out at the blackness, and making sure the different parts of the Empire could stay in touch. It's an unexciting but absolutely crucial job. They never make movies about it, they never give medals to comm ship crews, but without them, we're cut off. As we were when we stood and watched *Marconi's* debris drift.

I stared. I ground my teeth. I linked my hands behind my back and breathed sharply.

Marconi was the first ship I knew of that we'd lost in the war, and as losses go, this one had been a cheap shot against a non-combatant.

I'm guessing you know the sort of thoughts that were going through my head at that moment. Thinking in coherent terms wasn't happening so much.

Karen, thankfully, always keeps her composure better than I do, and she realized there was a question that really needed to be answered. We could assume that *Marconi* had been destroyed around the time we lost communication with Earth, four days earlier. But we didn't know who'd done the destroying — which particular Martian bastard had been out here to take out the comm ship, where it had gone, and if it was still hanging around.

Karen, who wore one of her uncommonly dark expressions, looked slowly at Hannigan, "Any sign of who did this, Jim?"

Hannigan shook his head, "I've extended active sweeps to maximum range, but haven't seen anything out there."

I turned towards him then, "Any trails that we can follow?"

It was an off chance — sometimes if a ship got hit, it could vent atmosphere or plasma or *something* that you could track...

Hannigan shook his head again. Of course not. *Marconi* didn't even get a chance to charge either of its two mags. Mags designed for *asteroid deflection*, not *fighting*. The ship was not a combatant, by any definition that I subscribe to... why not just demand a surrender? Disable its comm array with mag fire and take the crew off? Do something civilized?

Sorry. Again, carried away. This will pass, eventually.

My brain at this point was finally starting to work, and I looked back to the main screen, "Never mind, actually, Jim. We don't have time... we'll deal with this later. Note the position in our log."

"Aye, sir," Hannigan's tone, like all of our tones, was grim.

"Full speed for Earth," Karen said quietly, and Erica Martin nodded at her post.

Wolf pushed on past *Marconi*, and kept cruising for Earth.

I just hoped the planet would be alright when we got there.

CHAPTER SIX

STARTING A COUP — SORT OF

The rest of this book, much to the chagrin of my publisher, is essentially the story of one very, *very* long day. You probably know the day I'm referring to — 28 September 2231, a nice enough seeming Wednesday on the face of it. This was when *Wolf* got to Earth, but the day began hours before we pulled in.

John and Greg began the festivities, in fact, meeting on the lawn outside the Parliament buildings in the capital city. Then as now, there were a dozen or two picnic tables on that two-acre front lawn, theoretically so members of the public could come and eat lunch basking in the aura of the great leaders of Earth's Empire... or just to be fogged in or soaked by the rains that are common on the Capital Island any time of year.

Usually overworked clerks used the tables to devour hurried breakfasts and lunches, to curse out their bosses, and to try to remember why they'd gotten into the public service to begin with.

So it was around 0900 hours local time — obscenely late by the standards of the First Lord and Admiral Noyce, who unlike Caldecott, didn't think that duty and war should only take place during the midday hours. As offices had already opened for the day, there were only about thirty clerks and adjutants out at the tables.

John was sitting alone at one of the tables, eating a quick and portable breakfast as Greg arrived, a paper under his arm.

"Lots of company this morning," the latter observed as he stopped at John's table and sat himself down.

Looking up and nodding, John's tone was anything but covert, "The damned like to eat together."

"You got that right, m'lord," a passing clerk sighed just loud enough to be heard, and both Admirals grinned.

Settling down at the table, Greg laid the plastic case with his breakfast MRE (meal-ready-to-eat) before him, then opened the paper, turned it around, and slid it over to John.

"They're starting to turn the media," Greg said quietly. "I think the networks are bitter because we haven't been able to give them the usual attention... and Caldecott's blaming us for the nets being down."

John glanced at the above-the-fold headline for the day: "Fiora Ring Facing Music; Barron Missing the Dance". His eyebrows climbed for a second as he read the first few lines, then he shrugged, "Glad they're paying attention, at least. I was able to talk to Sergei at DCC last night for about five minutes. Caldecott still hasn't done a damned thing about the blackout. He's insisting it has to be sabotage and he doesn't trust any comm ships to go out and take stations — figures they'll vanish too."

Greg leaned forward, opening his breakfast and shaking his head, "In other words, it serves his agenda to keep us blacked out and to do nothing until we've been condemned by the press."

John nodded once.

"Well, I was on with a couple of friends up in fleet last night. They've noticed a total drop off in merchant shipping from both Venus and the Belt, and they can't account for it. Shannon wanted to take a couple of frigates out towards the Belt to see what's going on, but because she's one of my chosen officers, Caldecott put a stop to that, and now is refusing to check things out with his own ships."

Frowning, John swallowed the last of his food and slowly began to collect the various wrappings for disposal, "Civilian traffic has dropped off and he's *not* worried? He's either a fool or he's up to something big…"

Greg gave John one of those 'that's a dumb question' looks and John managed to smile, "Right, he's probably both. But the lack of civilian traffic… that's not good. I mean, we're not in peak season, but now I'm actually starting to wonder. What exactly is he up to?"

Taking the first bite of his MRE breakfast, Greg slowly shook his head, "I'd give a month's pay to know. Shannon is trying to do everything she can up there to get information, but Caldecott put Admiral Michaels in charge of my section of the fleet. She nearly got court martialed for not having an honor guard turned out when he sprang a surprise inspection."

John groaned and shook his head before turning towards one of the garbage cans nearby, lining up his breakfast's case, and hurling it in.

"Nothing but bag," he said to himself with a bit of satisfaction as the case dropped into the bin, then he looked back with a sigh. "So. Everything over our heads is spinning right out of control, and we're here. Again."

Greg nodded again as he chewed, "Indeed."

"And I couldn't find out why they wanted us back today. I thought they finished yesterday, but since Ken's not here I guess we're both on the line for two pounds of flesh," John pulled the paper in front of him, looking down past the lead article and quickly scanning the news.

Greg chewed while John's eyes darted from line to line, and then the First Lord's gaze stopped and fixed on one little article in the bottom left corner of the paper — below the fold.

"The Emperor's coming to his Government Palace today," John's words were quiet, and Greg looked up.

"I saw that. Think it means something?"

John read a couple of lines and then looked up, "If I was going to ask the Emperor to bring charges of treason against senior Naval officers, I'd want him in town for the occasion."

Greg stopped chewing. It was quite an assumption — one of those 'jump to worst possible case scenario' sorts — but it seemed… well, *more* possible at this stage than it would have seemed a week earlier.

You see, in these times (and even today, actually, though it'd never happen anymore), the Emperor could bring charges of treason directly against officers of the government or the military, and the Parliament needed only confirm any charges he made if a death penalty was handed down by an Imperial tribunal in relation to the charges. Nice little loophole for the Emperor, that, though the Prime Minister did have a parliamentary veto to any charges made by the Emperor, if — *if* — he could get a two-thirds vote against them in each house.

I know, that all sounds terribly technical, but suffice it to say that if the Emperor was coming to town to deliver treason indictments, the Fiora ring was, well, very *screwed*. Sorry, hard to mince words when they're dangling a noose in front of you.

Greg took a minute before he started chewing again, and John found himself staring at the paper. Surely, that wasn't why the Emperor was coming to town. And even if it was, could he somehow use this...

"I wonder... who do we have in SF and DCI around here? Has Caldecott purged our people the whole way down?"

With a thoughtful frown, Greg started running over names in his head, "I haven't heard a great deal about this area, but my guess is that would indicate he's left it alone. But then that wouldn't make sense to me — if there are charges about to be leveled, he'd want to know the SF was completely loyal to him. Security reasons."

John smiled thinly, "True. But he knows he wouldn't have a prayer getting SF or DCI on his side... and this article says the Emperor's bringing two battalions of Household Guard with him, for 'exercises' at the Capital Complex."

Greg stopped chewing again — he wasn't going to get through his MRE too quickly at this rate — and his eyes narrowed, "I hadn't read *that* far. The Emperor is bringing a thousand troops to the Government Palace?"

"Yep," John leaned back. "So we're going to need SF and DCI on our side if we're going to pull this off..."

"Pull what off?" Greg laid his food down now. The obvious direction John was heading with this commentary didn't sound good — a clash between SF and the Imperial Army's Household Guard? Not exactly one of the missions either force had contemplated, for the obvious treasonous reasons.

But then, Greg knew John Fiora well enough to know the First Lord wasn't insane. Well, not totally.

John's smile grew just a bit, and he started looking at all the clerks sitting at picnic tables around them, "Any of you want to save the Empire from chaos?"

People looked up from their breakfasts, frowning and staring curiously, wondering whether the First Lord had snapped.

"We all do, sir," one woman from a nearby table said sardonically.

John smiled at her, pulled his wallet out of his pocket, and tossed it to her, "There's five million credit on the platinum Vizorcard in there, go buy some stuff."

She looked down at the wallet in her hands and frowned, "Uh... what? Sir?"

"Sorry to cut breakfast short, Greg, but somebody just took my wallet. I think we should go report the theft at SF Headquarters, eh?"

Greg smiled, standing up, "I wasn't really hungry anyway."

The pair of Admirals left their table and walked away from the Parliament buildings that would be the site of their trials later in the day, and the woman with the wallet watched them go with a rather baffled look on her face. She, of course, was a twenty-four year old Haley Briand, then supposedly clerking for the fifth justice on the Imperial Court.

Yeah. Right. Clerking.

The almost coup, such as it was, essentially started when she caught the wallet.

CHAPTER SEVEN

WE ARRIVE AT LAST

Wolf decelerated in the space just past Luna at about 0840, Imperial Standard Time, that same morning. We arrived in the system just as John and Greg were reaching SF headquarters, actually, but Karen and I had *no clue* what foolishness Caldecott had been up to.

I'd slept a tiny bit on the last night of the approach — not nearly as much as I thought I should have, but what can I say, I was worried my home wasn't going to be there when I arrived.

Karen and I were standing stiffly on the bridge, watching the main screen as Hannigan piped up everything his sensors could tell him about the area. There hadn't been much civilian traffic in the space between Earth and the Belt, and we could only guess that the bastards who'd destroyed *Marconi* had been taking out the merchants as well.

But Luna was there, and to our collective relief, the icons of the Home Fleet began to pop up on the main screen as we got close enough to tap the Defense Command sensor grid.

"Head straight for Earth orbit, bypass the Lunar anchorages," Karen's orders went to Erica Martin sometime before we hit the Lunar zone, so *Wolf* didn't even slow down as it passed the moon's orbital plane.

"We're about three hours from Earth orbit," Erica reported a little while later. Sorry I don't have a better temporal sense of this for you — I actually realized at 0840 that I should probably be keeping a closer eye on the clock... which was maybe twenty minutes after she'd said that.

Anyway, we were cruising in close, and I was very, *very* glad to see that, by some miracle, we'd outrun the Martians.

Perhaps our enemy wasn't as well organized as I'd feared. No, it was actually Marlene being a brilliant ship fighter. But I didn't know that yet.

"Jim, collect my warning messages to the government and the Admiralty and prepare a signal burst as soon as you can line up a dish," I turned to Hannigan, and he nodded, already tapping some of his techs on their shoulders and pointing to images on their screens.

"We've got a relay station in range now, I'll be able to send it off in about three minutes," Hannigan looked up, and I nodded. That'd be good — John would get as much warning as I could give, and we could deal with the Martians.

One of the techs behind Hannigan then called him in a tone that was a bit too surprised for my liking. He turned around to address the question, and as he did I frowned slightly and took a few steps towards him.

Had they seen the Martians on sensors? Were we too late?

"Sir..." Hannigan turned back to me, "we just got an order from the relay station... to *stand down*."

My frown deepened, "What, did we violate protocol not stopping at Luna? Tell them to go to hell, and to pass on our message package."

Hannigan nodded, his own expression no better than mine. Looking back to his surprised tech, he patted her on the shoulder, "I'll take this one, Macy."

He tapped his headset to life, then looked back to me, "Relay Four, this is *DCNS Wolf*. Negative on all-stop. Repeat, negative on all-stop. We have priority eyes-only intel for Admiralty and government, relay immediately on my instructions. Sending now."

He nodded to another of his techs, and the messages I'd spent two days carefully writing with Karen's help launched out through space towards the relay station.

Jim stood quietly, waiting as the time delay dragged out… it'd be about a minute for the reply to come in at this rate.

I turned to look back to where Karen had been, and in the process banged right into her — she'd silently arrived to stand at my shoulder. She smiled now (thank God for some normality at a moment like this) and looked back towards Hannigan.

His hand went up to his ear. His face twisted and darkened.

Locking eyes with me, Jim Hannigan reported on what he was hearing, "Someone's not being too careful with their comm protocol — a couple of four letter words in there… now they're saying we're in violation of Admiralty Order 864.6B… whatever that is. They're saying we should stop and prepare to be boarded."

My head tilted slightly, "Excuse me?"

Hannigan nodded, "Can that be my reply, sir?"

"Indeed. And tell them to pass on my message traffic or I'll personally see the officers in charge over there exiled."

With a fierce smile forming, Hannigan repeated my threat and his own question, and Karen turned back to Erica Martin, "Keep up cruising speed, we're not stopping at this station."

Martin nodded in acknowledgment, and *Wolf*'s powerful engines continued to press us forward as the distance rapidly dropped off.

"They're coming back with more threats, sir… and quoting 864.6B. I can only guess that's a new order, sir… Matt?" Hannigan glanced across the bridge at the XO, and the Briton shrugged from his place at tactical.

"Tell them that Commodore Barron says 'Terribly sorry, but you've damned the Empire. We'll be back to collect you later.' Then kill the link. Erica, get us to Earth as fast as you can."

We weren't going to let some damned bureaucratic appointee stop us for violating approach protocols. Now some people have said to me that if I'd just hove-to then and sent the signal packet through channels, all would have turned out fine *without* the drama of the rest of that day.

Those people are stupid. Sorry, if you're one of them, you're dumb.

About three minutes later, *Wolf* hurtled past a station that was screaming bloody murder back towards Earth. It was about three minutes after we passed Relay Four that we noticed three *Predator*-class frigates separate from Greg's squadron and move to intercept us. At the time, I thought the deployment of those frigates was good news…

Well, it was. But let's put a chapter break here for convenience's sake.

CHAPTER EIGHT
COMMODORE HUNTER JOINS THE FUN

Commodore Shannon Hunter is probably best known for her days as Greg's Flag Captain during various pirate wars. She'd been with him in *Warspite* at Deep Black, and now she'd been promoted to Commodore in command of the frigate group of the Home Fleet.

If you've read the volumes leading up to *The Rogue Commodore* (which, as I write this, I haven't actually written yet... but if you're coming to these in order, later on... well... you get it...) you know what a cool customer she is. Nobody in the fleet has forgotten that boarding she led where she single-handedly beat six pirates senseless in unarmed combat before Special Branch got there.

Anyway, to see her transponder flying from *Panther*, the frigate leading the trio coming out from Earth to meet us, was a good thing. She was one of the Fiora ring, though not as politically involved as me or Karen, as she really couldn't stand cameras.

It took about an hour for her to reach us — her fleet station was approximately an hour from Earth orbit, and we were three from Earth when we passed the relay station, so that meant we traveled at the same velocity towards each other for about sixty minutes.

You really cared about that detail, I assure you.

"I can get realtime in about forty seconds, sir," Hannigan's mood had been noticeably darkened by his exchange with the rude people on the relay station, and really, who could blame him for being displeased?

"Good. Erica, don't slow us down. Hopefully Shannon has them trained to form on a ship moving at full speed," I glanced across the bridge at Martin, and she nodded.

Karen was standing next to me (still), and now she leaned in closer, her tone low, "And what if she's been sent out to stop us for boarding?"

I frowned, whispering back before I fully thought through the answer, "Shannon wouldn't... or..."

"New Admiralty orders out of nowhere, a rude relay station... I'm just saying, better be ready for the unexpected," Karen leaned away again.

Oh boy, was she ever right. I mean, Karen's usually spot on, but this was something that I hadn't honestly even thought of. To me, it was pretty clear: nothing else could be going on at Earth — everyone there was sitting and waiting for me to arrive with day-saving intelligence...

Or *not*. John could have tightly buttoned down the local space... He could be fearing that our loss of communication from the Belt meant we'd been compromised, or infected with an evil space plague, or been attacked by humanoid aliens who'd mutated from wolves, cats and bears, or been turned into people-eating goats with attitudes.

Maybe the relay station had been a bit heavy-handed in trying to order us around, or maybe we'd just been too wired to listen to some common sense.

Well, when Shannon got into range, I'd tell her exactly what was happening.

"Locking in realtime comms. Screen four," Hannigan was, as usual, right on cue.

Turning back to the front wall of screens, I paced forward a few steps and watched the *Wolf*Net loading screen slowly buffer the signal.

"They're beginning to reverse drives and turn… looks like they're going to form an escort wing," Hannigan reported evenly.

Nodding, I kept my eyes on the screen, and then Shannon Hunter popped up there.

I smiled in a friendly fashion, "Good to see you Shannon, you look well. Wish I had good news for you…"

Shannon held up her hand, "Ken, I'm under orders to haul you to *Warspite*. You're to be transshipped straight from there to the inquiry."

"Oh."

Yes, I actually said 'oh', even though I had absolutely no clue what she was talking about. As soon as I realized that I didn't know what she meant, I frowned.

"Um, fill me in here. Inquiry?"

Shannon frowned, her stare changing gears — it felt as if she was sizing me up to see if I was leading her on, or if I really didn't know what Caldecott was up to. I guess I have an honest face… or she realized that, with comms down, I couldn't possibly know.

"The inquiry… Dave Caldecott got the Emperor to call one, Admiral Noyce and First Lord Fiora have been under questioning for days, and you're on the block next. You're their star target, actually," she said quietly.

"You're kidding," my eyebrows twitched. "You *are* kidding."

She shook her head.

I stared at her for a minute.

And then Karen edged over to me and elbowed me, because I was still silent.

So then I said it: "That *son of a bitch!*"

I know, wasn't a good slip for me, but Caldecott had much worse coming.

"He's trying to make political hay, and in the meantime he's not done a damned thing to find out what happened to communications?" I looked back to Shannon, and she shook her head.

"I actually tried to get permission to go have a look at the situation, but Admiral Michaels — she has Admiral Noyce's position until the end of the inquiry — told me that it was Fiora conspiracy and that she wouldn't have me contributing to it."

I think my jaw actually dropped, but Karen was there to sound poised and disgusted all at once, "Are you kidding? Caldecott's cronies are saying we caused the comm blackout?"

Shannon nodded evenly, "You with the Belt, and that Admiral Stoll did the same with Venus."

"Oh my *God*, Caldecott is a complete bag of shi–" caught myself that time. I took a deep breath, trying not to let my anger bubble up too much… like there was a chance of that happening. "Shannon, we've just had war declared on us by the *Martians*. They took out *Marconi*, I'm guessing they knocked out every comm ship out there, too. And I don't see how they aren't coming here next."

Shannon's gaze switched back to that studying mode, trying to figure out if I was lying, insane, or somehow telling the truth.

"Jim, send her the package," Karen had the good sense to provide evidence, and Hannigan beamed the package to *Panther* just as that frigate fell into formation off our starboard engine pod.

Shannon's eyes darted away from Karen and me then, probably checking the data on another screen.

"I've got Rear Admiral Kitty Castillo and her pirate lover in my brig, if you want to see them," I offered, but Shannon wasn't listening any more.

She read for a while — probably about three minutes. That was good; she was taking her time, she was making sure we weren't nuts. I knew for a fact that Shannon Hunter would side with us over Admiral Stacey Michaels any day... let alone Dave Caldecott.

"Well," she said after that pause, "this is a bit more important than politics."

"A tad, eh?" I nodded.

"I'll transmit it on to the Admiralty right away... as far as I know there haven't been reports of activity on our grid so far..."

While she was talking, my brain clicked into gear and began to consider the situation. I didn't know much about it at that moment — we'd spend the next hour trading astonished questions and forehead-smacking answers to get me and Karen up to speed — but one thing was clear: Dave Caldecott was in control of the Admiralty.

The idiot hadn't even sent ships out to investigate a total communications blackout... which either made him incredibly stupid, or meant he was working for the Martians.

You might think that sounds like a big jump, but it was actually the first one made by most news services that covered this: the Martians happen to declare war with a surprise attack, just at the moment when a short, bald, squeaky-voiced prima donna managed to cripple Defense Command with his politics?

"Shannon, don't send that package to the Admiralty," I said it just in time

Of course, this is the second moment all my enemies have pointed to and said 'you could have done it differently —gone through channels!' As I said, they're stupid.

"If Caldecott's in control of the Admiralty, he's going to get the report and assume it's false... or he's part of this whole thing and he's trying to cripple us for an attack. We have to get the word out some other way."

Shannon nodded, "Good point. He's got his people in command of the Home Fleet... we've got some Captains who'd be loyal to us. My frigates are all reliable, but Michaels has the Heavy Squadron, and Sibley has the Light Squadron."

"I bet they sent you to stop us expecting you to turn," Karen said quietly. "They get to say our conspiracy is bigger that way."

I glanced at Karen and nodded slowly, "Great. Guess we're not getting the heros' welcome."

Karen smiled, "You and your ego. Shannon, let's think about this. Who do we have... and how can we get hold of First Lord Fiora, or Admiral Noyce?"

We had a lot to figure out.

And in the interests of avoiding more exposition, and of building some decidedly a-historical suspense, I'm going to make you wait a little while to find out what we decided!

Well, keep turning pages.

Chapter Nine

Meanwhile, At SF Headquarters

The completed 'Theft Report' form was sitting on the table in front of John and Greg. It was all very routine looking — they'd explained how seven young guys wearing gang colors had jumped them, and how'd they'd had to defend themselves with only a rock and a plastic bag with a sock in it. I still have no idea where the sock came from, but if you don't believe me, visit the Martian War Museum; this report is on display (at least it is when I'm writing this) with their signatures on it.

Of course, they didn't even implicate Haley Briand, which probably was better for her in the long run. Well, no probably about it.

Anyway, I know what you're thinking: *Oh no, they filed a false SF report! That's up to six months in the lock up!* You'd be right on any other day; today, though, at 0900 hours, they weren't sitting across the table from an SF officer who'd file their report, they were across the desk from Admiral Tessho Hirobumi (Hirobumi Tessho if you go with traditional Japanese naming arrangement), the head of Defense Command Security Forces, and Admiral Thea Fostopolos, head of Defense Command Intelligence.

Caldecott had left the heads of the Defense Command security services where they were, probably thinking the 'corruption' in those two branches ran too deep — even if he put his own people on top, they'd be powerless to stop loyal (and smart) SFers and intel operatives from helping the Fiora ring. So instead of wasting his time, Caldecott was counting on the Imperial Army to do his dirty work.

That was just fine.

John and Greg had been quickly explaining their own plans and ideas — they had an opportunity with the Emperor arriving in town in three hours, they had to play it right. Of course, playing it any way at all wouldn't be easy with the damned Imperial Army's Household Guard sitting there.

Just to make sure this is clear, the Imperial Army is a completely separate military force from Defense Command. We do all the important Imperial work — we have the fleet, the Security Forces, and the intelligence, communication, logistical, and... well... we have *all* the other networks that can operate outside a planet's atmosphere. The army has tanks, and guns that, if used on a space ship, would blow holes in the pressure hull and cause decompression. Not so smart using such guns in a boarding action.

The Imperial Army served the Emperor, and that was about it. All told, there were about 60,000 of them, and they were well-trained and heavily gunned... and if Caldecott had the Army looking out for him, that meant he had plenty of muscle to back his claims. We had no contacts within the Army, no good relations (actually, we tended to have very *bad* relations with the Army), so there'd be nothing we could do to stop them following his commands.

But John and Greg *had* figured out a way to use the resources that DCI and SF could still give them (admittedly, give them under the table) to take advantage of the *Emperor's* presence.

No, I'm not going to tell you how. On the off chance that you don't know how this goes down, I need to build suspense. And yes, every historian reading this book just cursed my name.

Anyway, sorry for getting very sidetracked. There was a knock at the door while this meeting was going on, and an aide — a trusted aide — poked her head in, "Sorry to interrupt, but *Wolf* is now on the grid, and we just got a coded burst transmission direct from *Panther.*"

They'd heard about *Wolf's* arrival only minutes after we'd been challenged by that relay station, thanks to the DCI operatives network that kept Fostopolos in the know. Now they were about to get the intel we had to offer, direct and complete.

If you're wondering how we knew where to send the information in order to catch John and Greg, you're asking a good question. I'd like to say it was some sort of sixth sense — that we somehow knew John and Greg would be thinking ahead and would be at SF Headquarters just when we pulled in.

Nothing so glamorous as that. It was mainly because I knew Admiral Hirobumi pretty well, and I figured he'd be able to do something useful with the information at hand. He wasn't really part of the Fiora ring at that point, but he was a good fellow — he didn't play politics, he just made sure the Empire was safe.

We'd needed that sort of person today... so that's why I told Shannon to send the burst transmission to SF Headquarters, under the guise of a request for an SF escort for me when I went down to the tribunal or some such thing.

But back on point. Greg and John were there to receive the signal in person, which was a great turn of luck of their own invention.

Tessho Hirobumi nodded to that aide, and she ducked her head back out, closing the door behind her.

"This might shed some light on what exactly is happening," the head of SF said in his studied way, tapping his keyboard until the main screen on the side wall of his office switched from the map of the capital they'd been looking at to my message.

These messages played in sequence, with cuts to footage of the Battle of Belt Two, scans of the letters from Kitty Castillo to Cooper, and some footage of *Marconi's* wreck drifting in space.

They sat and listened and watched for about ten minutes all told, as I quickly ran through everything on that pre-recorded burst. You can actually watch the entire briefing package at the Martian War Museum, if you like. The museum's section covering this day is full of stuff that none of us participating ever thought would get out!

"Well," John slowly looked from the screen to Greg and back as the burst finished playing, "that's a problem."

Direct quote, that — Thea and Tessho and Greg all tell it the same way. John's most violent reaction to the reality of war with the Martians was 'that's a problem'. Small wonder this guy was the greatest First Lord we'd had — at that moment he had nothing under his direct control, but somehow he had *everything* under control.

"We really need to see the Emperor now," John went on. "I suppose this hasn't been forwarded on to the Admiralty because Ken doesn't want Caldecott to get hold of it."

Hirobumi's eyes narrowed thoughtfully, "I am not a political player, Lord Fiora. If we are jeopardizing the security of the Empire for political reasons..."

"I think what he means, Tessho, is that the Second Lord's choice of a moment to paralyze our fleet with his inquiry has been an interesting one," Greg held up his hand. "Until we establish that the choice of time for the inquiry was a coincidence, we can't afford to trust any of Caldecott's people."

"I'd have heard something if the Second Lord was planning to betray us to Mars," Thea Fostopolos — a rather fiery character, I must say — cut in quickly.

"No offense Thea, but you didn't have any warning about a pirate-Martian coalition. And if there's an in-house security problem, then I think we know why," John managed not to sound abrupt with that, and she quieted down.

The four Admirals sat there for about a minute, considering just what they could do in the situation. Their plan regarding the Emperor was predicated on suspicions of Caldecott... those suspicions still held.

Now the timeline was just much more sensitive.

"We need to get this inquiry ended, right now," John said after a moment. "But the only way to have it overturned is to have an emergency vote out of Parliament. And we don't have the votes..."

As with treason charges, it took a two-thirds majority vote in both parliamentary houses to get an inquiry voted down. Had I known John and Greg were at that Headquarters, I'd have sent along an additional message, telling them that Karen and Shannon and I had a pretty good idea of how we'd deal with the inquiry, we just needed someone to get to the Emperor.

I've counted my blessings many times for the fact that they decided to stick to their original plan without me asking them to.

"I don't think this changes anything," Greg said quietly after the prolonged pause. "The fastest way to solve this is still to get to the Emperor. If we bring this evidence to him he'll have to pay attention to it. And if he doesn't..."

John's eyebrows raised and he nodded slowly. This could all end very messily...

But then some said John Fiora's middle name was 'Messy'. It's not. But some say it is.

"Alright. We stay on plan. Tessho, can you have your assets ready at the lunch break?" John addressed the head of SF, and the man nodded once, with force. John bobbed his head in reply and then glanced up at Thea Fostopolos, as she stood with folded arms. "Your people set to go as well?"

"Always," she didn't sound particularly charitable at that moment, but John ignored her tone, instead glancing again at Greg.

"I guess we're going to answer some questions," Greg said with a smile.

John grinned, "Yes, we are."

They stood to leave.

CHAPTER TEN
WARSPITE AND OTHER PROBLEMS

Karen and I had retired to our chairs on the bridge once we'd gotten within ten minutes of the Home Fleet. Shannon was under orders to deliver us to *Warspite* and from there I'd presumably be flown (under heavy guard) down to the inquiry, so that on the way I couldn't blow the whistle about the dangerous situation that was developing throughout the Empire.

I didn't know if Caldecott knew what was going on outside of Earth space or not. But damned if he wasn't going to find out.

"We're approaching realtime range," Hannigan reported as the main screen's sensor display began to zoom in closer on the icons of the Home Fleet.

At least the fleet was here. Led by idiots at the moment, but at least Earth had a solid line of ships to rely on when the Martians showed up. Hopefully we'd have good people commanding them by the time those Mars folk arrived.

"And we're getting a signal from Admiral Michaels on *Warspite* now," Hannigan had his hand to his ear, pressing his headset in close and wincing. "Oof, it's for you alright, sir."

I smiled and nodded, "Screen two, please, Jim."

I wasn't even going to get off my ass for this conversation.

There was a pause as the message bounced down to the screen through the comm buffer, and then Admiral Stacey Michaels appeared on the screen, a smile on her face, "Stand down, Barron. We're sending boarding parties to take you and Captain McMaster off your ship for questioning by the inquiry."

My smile didn't flinch, "Good morning, Admiral Michaels."

Her smile twitched slightly, "You can't play dumb, these are orders from the Emperor. Now come to a complete stop, or I'll order Commodore Hunter to disable you."

"Shannon wouldn't do that to me, Admiral. See, we both happen to know that war has begun with the Martians, so we're going to go get the inquiry stopped."

Tip my hand too soon, you ask? Hardly — I needed to get a sense of whether she knew. I counted the rather inelegant laugh she snorted in a swinish fashion to mean she didn't know; she assumed I was joking.

"You'll have to do better than that, you contemptuous little showboy."

Ouch. I mean really, this was coming from a fellow Defense Command officer. I glanced with some surprise at Karen, and she shrugged.

"Well," I looked back to the screen, "that's too bad. Guess you'll be exiled with the rest of the traitors we run into today. Meantime, you sent the three fastest ships you've got to stop me, and now they're all with me. There's nothing you can do to stop me short of Earth."

Not quite true, but I was hoping Michaels — an officer, I should mention, who was nominally in the Bureau of Personnel — didn't know her ships too well. The gamble paid off by half.

"That's fine, you'll be the traitor. I can't stop you, but I know someone who can."

"Great, I'll pass them too then," I tilted my head slightly, but my smile remained.

Her smile twisted into a hungry grin, "I'm going to love watching you get the noose, you traitor."

"We'll see, won't we now?" I kept my smile in place, and then she had the good sense to kill the conversation signal.

I let out a long breath as she vanished and my smile faded. Looking over to Jim Hannigan, I raised my eyebrows, asking a wordless question.

"She's not even trying to turn her ships to come after us," he said, then leaned down over the shoulder of one of his techs. "Looks like they've got the Light Squadron moving into position to intercept us."

Ah, that was the sound of the other shoe dropping. The Light Squadron, with its light and fast ships and carriers, was firmly under Caldecott's thumb. I imagine the crews of the Heavy Squadron would have been reluctant to get into a fight with their own, but no one in a senior job in the Light Squadron considered *Wolf* or *Panther* or any of us to be their comrades.

So send the loyal ships to deal with the most hated traitors, and use my attitude during this approach to Earth orbit as the final nail in the political coffin of the Fiora ring...

Isn't politicking grand?

"How long until we fall in with our esteemed colleagues of the Light Squadron, Jim?"

Hannigan chuckled, his eyes not moving from the screen he'd been looking at, "Call it forty minutes to comm range. They're about fifteen minutes off orbital space."

I frowned thoughtfully at that — there were too many ships in the Light Squadron for us to fight through (as if fighting was really an option to begin with) and they were fast enough to catch up with us. We'd need to do something to throw them off the scent.

Oh, and for all those people who say this is a vindication of the Light Squadron and carrier concept, don't even start. The fact that they were fast enough to catch up to four frigates is lovely. The problem I have with these carriers is that *Wolf* and *Panther* alone could have destroyed any two of them, if it had come to a gun fight. They cost more than battleships, they don't have any punching power now that defensive technology has exceeded the ordnance a fighter can carry, and they just aren't practical.

But anyway, we'd need to get around them, to avoid things getting out of control.

I glanced at Karen and she was smiling — something I was very glad to see.

"So," I leaned towards her, "what's the plan, then?"

Karen played with the end of her ponytail as it sat on her left shoulder, and she shrugged flirtingly, "I dunno, do you like long flights in deep space in small craft?"

I chuckled, then smiled, "Now that you mention it, I sure do!"

We hatched another plan. Lots of those that day.

Chapter Eleven

Launching...

"Oh, not a *bloody damned chance!*"

Notice how Matt Baxter really can sound like a parent? It was probably one of the few things that kept me alive through all those years, that yell of his. The voice of reason, the one telling me and Karen not to do stupid stuff... who knows where we'd have been without him, because even with him yelling, we still got ourselves into enough trouble.

Anyway, he was doing his usual — chasing us down the corridor outside the bridge as we headed for the lift. We were still about half an hour from running afoul of *Ark Royal* and the rest of the Light Squadron, so we weren't *too* rushed.

"We have to go, Matt," I was walking backwards, as I usually did when he chased us.

"Yes, but take Charlie with you, you're going to be branded a fugitive when you get down there!" Matt's words remained stern, and I had to admit, I could see some reason in them.

"But we can't afford to send out too many small craft or they'll see us," Karen said in a soothing tone.

Matt stopped in mid step and grunted, "Fine. Good luck."

He then turned and marched back to the bridge, and Karen and I stopped in the middle of the corridor and looked at each other with deepening frowns. With him we never won *at all*, let alone won *easily*. What was the Briton up to?

"We'll have to see what he's scheming later," Karen said after a moment. "Let's go."

We got to our quarters about three minutes later, and we moved fast, as pilots sometimes can.

I quickly got out of my duty fatigues and switched to my flight fatigues. They looked quite similar, but there were a number of crucial differences in construction. The flight fatigues were equipped with stronger pressure seals, which were much better suited to a decompression in a small fighter than the emergency decompression weave on duty gear.

I don't know if you really cared to know that. But it's cool.

Anyway, it took about two minutes to switch clothes, and then I sprinted out of my quarters and headed for the lift. When I got there, Karen *wasn't* waiting for me, so I crossed my arms and started tapping my foot impatiently.

Almost a whole minute later, she sauntered down the corridor in her flight fatigues, smiling.

I glanced back at her with a grin, "You women always take *so long* to get ready."

She extended her hand towards me, and my eyes slid down her arm to its contents. A mag in its holster. My eyes then crawled down her torso to the side of her hip, where hers was already clipped to her belt.

My hand reached down to my hip, and I mentally smacked myself.

"Well, of course we're always late, we have to go collect your mag from your room so you don't forget it," her smile was decidedly smug as I huffed a sigh and pulled my sidearm out of her hand.

"I was only *kidding*," I muttered as we waited for the lift to arrive.

"Wolfstar 825, Wolfstar 826, you're cleared. Stand by on my mark. And... 825... launch... 826... launch."

Those were the orders coming through Karen's headset and mine as we taxied our Starlights to the catapults in Bay Two, then launched out of *Wolf's* hull at rather high speed. With our burners firing for about the first thirty seconds of the flight, we were able to charge away from *Wolf's* bow and then vector slightly away from our ship's course, using the velocity of our launch and the momentum provided by the ship itself to speed our acceleration.

Hmm, that's sort of hard to explain more clearly. You know how if you throw a ball forward as you're running, it goes faster than if you were standing still when you threw it? Yeah, like that. Karen and I were flying faster than we would normally have been.

And the best part was, as we cut our drives thirty seconds out, we were giving off no emissions at all. We could see Earth, big and beautiful I might add, just about half an hour away, and we were coasting through space on momentum.

Hopefully we wouldn't have to fire our drives until we were well past the Light Squadron, and after that it would be easy enough to get to the surface.

I mean, if we were going where someone like Caldecott was expecting us to go, then we undoubtedly would have been in trouble trying to get past the patrols, but we weren't. More on that later.

For now we were on our own, coasting through the abyss at a combined velocity of about 200 kps. And Earth was in the window.

Here we come...

CHAPTER TWELVE

OOPS

So I don't drink much alcohol, and that's fine with me. But I know a number of people who are regular partakers of the fermented fluids, and one of them told me a funny story she'd heard from the Academy during this period. Apparently, the heavy-drinking students at the Academy had started a drinking game during the inquiry. Basically, every time Caldecott was speaking, they got set up, and every time his voice cracked and he started talking in ultra-high pitched tones, they downed a shot of their choice.

Apparently this drinking game nearly gave one cadet alcohol poisoning — one of the reasons I advise you all to avoid the bottle! But the point I really should be making here is one at Caldecott's expense: his voice was horrible and got squeaky rather frequently.

I have no idea how Greg and John survived the days of questioning under it, but they did — and at about 0950 hours they were settling into now-familiar chairs behind the witness (or more properly, the persecuted) desk, waiting for Caldecott to arrive across from them with his cronies.

"We need to move around 1200 hours," John said quietly, and Greg nodded. The Emperor was probably getting into town at lunchtime, so it'd make sense to try to get to him before his Household Guard got settled in at Government Palace.

Of course, John and Greg had left the precise timing to Thea Fostopolos, as it'd be her people who did the yeoman's work in this little subterfuge.

"Here we go," Greg abruptly looked back across the open floor to the tables on the other side, and behind those tables the doors had opened and the procession of idiocy, otherwise known as Caldecott and his fellow inquirers, filed into the room, all decked out in fancy braid and carrying thick stacks of papers.

John shifted in his seat, and Greg leaned forward slightly, elbows on the table. The schedule called for the sessions to run from 1000 to 1800, but with a lunch break at 1200 when the move would have to be made.

Glancing up at the clock, John kept his frustration in check through force of will, refusing to look directly across at the squat, smug, round, grinning figure of his Second Lord as the latter sat and began shuffling through papers.

It was 0956...

"I know I should wait four minutes, but I think it's in the best interests of the Empire for me to start sooner. We have all the evidence we need now."

John's eyes darted down to Caldecott and he glared, "And what's that supposed to mean, Dave?"

Caldecott squeak-laughed, "Your protégé Barron showed up this morning, and he's inciting mutiny in the fleet with a false story of *war* with the *Martians*. He's trying to claim that the Martians are launching a secret campaign against us, that they destroyed our comm ships, and that they're coming here right now!"

John's eyebrow went up and he straightened in his chair, "Really? So what are you doing about that, Dave?"

"Laughing. You think a ridiculous story like that is going to save your hide? You're ridiculous."

Greg tilted his head slightly, "Lord Caldecott, you just used the word ridiculous twice. Would you like to put that a different way?"

Caldecott's face soured, "Insolence will get you nowhere. Along with all the trouble you two have been causing for me and this inquiry over the past week, Barron's stunts are all the evidence I need. You're both to be arrested under suspicion of corruption."

John's eyes widened slightly, "Excuse me?"

"Guards!"

Hang on, let me pause here, because you might be asking the same thing I did the moment I heard this: how the hell did me arriving with news about a Martian War along with some less than cordial verbal exchanges amount to treachery? Apparently Caldecott had framed these things in such a way for the Emperor that it had looked like John and Greg were trying to hide something — something corrupt. We're still unsure of just how he managed that, but, well, it made for some cheap drama.

John pushed himself to his feet, "I object to this — you have *no* authority!"

Greg was on his feet too, his hand going behind his back and waving subtly to the DCI agent who was supposed to have been planted in the audience.

"I have the authority of the Emperor. Good luck getting it overturned. You're a traitor. Not even your political lackeys will touch you now, *John.*"

John opened his mouth to slam the insolent little fellow with sharp words when the doors behind Caldecott opened, and through them came a file of *Imperial Army troopers.* That's right, Caldecott knew no real Defense Command SFers would dream of taking John Fiora or Greg Noyce into custody on such baseless charges, so the Imps were getting the job.

Greg gave the quick thumbs-up, thumbs-down sign, and the agent in the audience came to her feet slowly, drawing a mag from the waistband of her jeans. That was the sign for the Special Branch team, waiting in the custodians room next to the gallery, to get out into the open — before they'd even had a chance to set up all the listening equipment they'd brought along to record the morning's goings on. Well, they wouldn't need it, by the look of things...

The intel agent shuffled past other audience members in the room and stepped into the aisle, mag swung forward, and as she did, the door next to the gallery swung open and a full Special Branch team of a dozen officers under Major Carrie Walsh swept into the room behind John and Greg.

Now, this, of course, didn't look so good. About twenty Imps had come into the room from the doors behind Caldecott's table, and they were all packing their usual overpowered energy guns. Personally (because Carrie Walsh is a great tac officer) I know the blockheads didn't stand a chance if things got ugly, but then, they were Imps. They didn't know a damned thing, but they thought they knew a lot. And they thought they were invincible.

Caldecott thrust himself to his feet (if you watch the recordings of this it's funny, because the camera guy that day watched him get ready to stand, so he moved the camera up with him, but moved too far and so all you see for about twenty seconds is the top of his head). The Second Lord was squealing with rage, "You Special Brancher police, you get out of here this instant! Captain Neider, secure this room!"

That was to the Captain of the Imperial Army troops, a sour looking blockhead. He stepped forward around the table, brandishing his sidearm and bellowing in the red-faced manner that the Imps like to use, "You there, get out of this room. The building is under our jurisdiction."

"You're in violation of all orders, get out!" Caldecott continued to squeak.

John stood his ground, glaring unphased at Caldecott and then shifting his stare to the Captain of the Army, "Captain *Neider*, get your men out of this building. You're in violation of the Articles of Empire — Imperial Army personnel are not allowed to make arrests."

I don't think I could have been calm under those circumstances, but John was. And equally calm, Greg turned around quickly to wave the Special Branch officers forward, then nodded to the DCI officer, and she tugged a comm out of her jeans and spoke into it.

"Stop talking into that comm immediately!" the sound of an energy gun whining to full charge filled the room and the army Captain steadied himself into his standard shooting stance. "You only get one warning, ma'am!"

John stepped into the aisle in front of the DCI officer and crossed his arms. Greg leaned back over the partition between the witness seats and the gallery and took the mag sidearm one of the Special Branch officers was offering him.

"Now, Captain, you are not authorized to make arrests. These Special Branch officers and the intelligence officer you just threatened will take Greg and I into custody. Understood?"

The army officer, finding his bulky gun lined up with the face of a First Lord, paled slightly. Sure, he was a blockhead, but John has a good way of being personally persuasive, and he was also a rather famous officer.

"No!" Caldecott shrieked — literally shrieked. "You can't do that, that's not acceptable! You clearly own the SF, you're throwing a coup, right now!"

Greg was holding his mag down at his side, but his eyes locked on Caldecott's, "I'd be very careful throwing around that word, Second Lord. You're the one who just deployed *Imperial Army* troops into a Parliamentary building, and gave them illegal authority to arrest officers."

For those not up on their constitutional law, the Articles of Empire hold that the Imperial Army is a tool only of the Emperor, for his personal security and for defense of the Empire from outside threats. In practice this means they're a rather beefy security force with a lot of pretentions (with a few choice exceptions, as some I met later did prove competent). None of the blockheads in this room were exceptions. Defense Command, on the other hand, was constitutionally the only force allowed to provide security to Parliamentary buildings, and to make arrests or bring criminals to trial.

Caldecott's face twisted and his eyes darted away from Greg, taking in the scene again.

The army troops had fanned out, their big bulky energy rifles slung forward into awkward firing positions, each of them trained on one of the Special Branch officers or on Greg or John. I should mention, too, that every trooper looked like he'd received a swift kick to the groin before storming out here — every man (all men, by the way, as the Imps tend to prefer) with gritted teeth, looking slightly maniacal.

Carrie Walsh and her Special Branch officers were standing or crouching with practiced cool, their MAG-90s sleekly lined up on one or two blockheads each. The numbers were against Special Branch, but numbers were *always* against Special Branch. The intrepid black-clad officers had long ago learned how to make up for numbers with training.

It probably occurred to Caldecott in that moment that shooting would be the worst possible outcome — if Caldecott ordered his troopers to start the shooting, his story that the Fiora ring was trying to stage a coup could be tainted (he'd be the one trying the coup). And yet, if Caldecott let John start the shooting, Caldecott himself might be killed, which obviously was the first fear in the round man's mind.

But if he let John and Greg be 'taken into custody' by their own people, well that'd be a press windfall for Caldecott. This standoff was itself proof enough that John and Greg considered themselves above the law.

So the runty Second Lord wiped his forehead with the sleeve of his tunic and fumbled his screechy words, "Ahumm... er... Captain Neider... let them go."

"Sir?" the blockhead Imp looked back over his shoulder in confusion, and Caldecott flailed his right arm.

"*You heard me!*" that came out of the Second Lord's mouth in such a panicked pitch that the words were again nearly inaudible, but the Captain nodded once and took a step back.

"Let's go," Greg called quickly, sliding out into the aisle with John, covering the Captain with his mag as first the intel agent John had stepped in front of and then John himself backed out of the room. The Special Branchers followed slowly, peeling off to the aisle one by one, at all times watching the Imps for a single inappropriate movement.

Carrie Walsh was last to leave, and she offered a friendly salute to the Captain before closing the door behind her.

Outside the room, the Special Branchers formed around Greg, John and the agent, leading them quickly to an SF bus that had been called over from headquarters.

"Well, that didn't go the way we planned," Greg said quietly, handing his mag back to the officer who'd lent it to him.

John nodded, "Let's see if we can get still get to the Emperor — before the entire Army goes on alert."

"We won't have much time," the DCI agent said quietly behind them, and they both looked back at the same time. Neither had actually been introduced to the agent who'd been planted in the audience. The plan had been for her to cause a scene at the lunch break, and for Special Branch to sweep in and remove all the officers from the room in case of threat of assassination, giving John and Greg a chance to slip over to Government Palace.

Well, that hadn't happened. But now, as John looked back at the young woman, he frowned as he tried to place her face. She smiled in a friendly fashion, and then reached out to give him something.

He looked down at her hand and recognized his wallet — because of course, it was Haley Briand (the girl who'd been tailing them at the park benches).

"You!" Greg was duly surprised, and she shrugged with a twitching smile.

"Yeah, Admiral Fostopolos has had me tailing you both all week, in case Caldecott tried something funny."

John smiled broadly, "I guess this qualifies!"

They rushed into the bus.

In the back rooms of the Parliament Building, some Imp blockheads who'd evidently wanted to do some killing kicked over garbage cans and flipped chairs in frustration. They'd actually ventured into one of the clerk offices to throw their tantrum, and three of the clerks — two who'd actually seen John and Greg out at the picnic tables that morning — overheard Caldecott engaging in a high pitched screaming rant. He was chewing out his loyal 'yes'-men (all men again… Caldecott's gang is rather backward, just like the Imp Army).

"We have to have a press conference! Get the camera footage! We have to have a press conference! God dammit, those bastards! We have to—"

Caldecott stopped in mid-yelp and collapsed, ending up face first on the ground with an abrupt thud. Everybody panicked, figuring the little lard bucket had finally had a heart attack, but no, his implant was still keeping his heart going. He'd just managed to work himself up so much that he'd passed out — something I wish I'd seen.

Sorry, as you can tell I really don't have any sympathy for the *thing*.

No, I can't think of a better word than 'thing' right now. Cut me a little slack, I'm trying to be polite.

While one of his aides called for a doctor, another commed back to his central office, and made the most fateful decision of the day: he scheduled a press conference for 1500 that afternoon.

That's right, knowing his esteemed Second Lord as he did, this aide figured he had to give Caldecott the morning to recover from the stress, or his implant would probably overload and he'd have heart failure. So that meant a five-hour wait for the press conference.

No harm done, surely? John and Greg *were* under arrest, after all…

Ha. Hahahaha!

Chapter Thirteen

Actually It Was Only 10:40

Wolf and the three frigates under Shannon Hunter had slowed their progress as they neared the Light Squadron, delaying interaction as long as possible so Karen and I wouldn't be missed until we were nearly over Earth's atmosphere.

Of course, there wasn't much that could be done to hide our absence once the four frigates got into realtime range of the Light Squadron; Matt walked to the front of the bridge and simply nodded to Hannigan.

He wasn't even going to try to let Shannon take the heat for this one: this was going to be all him. Matt's a great guy that way — he delivers on all the big moments.

As he stood and waited for the comm links to *Ark Royal* to be established, he kept himself steady on the deck and just stared, unimpressed, at the buffering screen.

It took about a minute for the feed to complete, and Matt squared his shoulders and looked stern — not a difficult thing for him, believe me — and stared right into the eyes of Admiral George Parks-Dawes.

I'll talk more about George later, for now just try not to get too distracted by his last name. I'm not saying it was a bad name, just that it's a... *memorable* one.

Parks-Dawes was not, at least, looking as smug and pleased with himself as Michaels had been, "Commander, I need your ship to heave to immediately. Please summon your Captain and Commodore to the bridge."

Matt's eyebrow slowly climbed, "Oh, but of course."

I've seen the recordings, and know he sounded patronizing, but Parks-Dawes didn't seem to notice. Keeping to his fiction, Matt looked to his left and nodded to Erica Martin, "Bring us to all stop. Stand by reverse drives. Jim, signal the squadron to form on us. Tactical systems remain on standby."

Parks-Dawes managed not to change his expression through the series of orders, even though Matt had overtly mentioned tactical systems. Old George Parks-Dawes was in the Caldecott circle, but remarkably enough, he wasn't a blustery fool.

Wolf slowed smoothly as its reverse drives fired, and *Panther, Jaguar* and *Tiger* — the ships of Shannon Hunter's force — slowed in kind. The maneuver was handled as smartly as if the Belt Squadron had been executing it.

"Your Captain and your Commodore, please, Commander," Parks-Dawes repeated the second request.

Matt's face remained blank, "I'm not sure I understand you, sir."

"Captain McMaster. Commodore Barron. Commander, they must come aboard *Ark Royal* immediately, to be transported to the inquiry."

I suppose it goes without saying that Parks-Dawes hadn't yet heard about John and Greg and that little mixup with the blockheads. Wait for it...

"Oh, they'll probably make better time if they don't come all the way back here before going to Earth again, sir," Matt managed to sound helpful that time, and Parks-Dawes frowned.

"Excuse me?"

Matt's eyebrow cocked again, "Sir, they've already been dispatched to the inquiry. In the meantime, Commodore Barron asked me to suggest that you order your squadron to prepare to receive the impending Martian attack."

Now in point of fact I'd suggested no such thing — I would have done, but I'd never have believed a Caldecott officer would have listened. I'm rather glad Matt used my name without authorization, though, because for all my dislike of his politics, Parks-Dawes actually paid attention to those words.

"Excuse me, impending attack? Are you serious, Commander?"

Matt nodded once, his expression quite frank, "I am, sir. Jim, send him the files, if you please."

I honestly can't say I'd have had the perspective or patience to do this, but now I suppose you can see why Matt's considered the grown-up of our ship's company. Parks-Dawes looked off screen as the transmission began to come in, and he paid attention to it.

It took about five minutes for Parks-Dawes to go through enough of the files to be satisfied that it wasn't all fabricated.

He looked in a different off-camera direction and nodded to someone on his bridge, probably his Flag Captain, Marcel Maddox, "Alert the squadron to stand by for intense action. Have *Yorktown* and *Hornet* launch scouts to do a wide sweep of vectors towards Mars."

That was no small step, though it's often thought to be a slightly bigger one than it was. What I mean is this: the approaches the Martians could have been coming in on were countless — they could be coming from any side in a three dimensional battlefield. Fighter patrols were good, but they'd have to be incredibly lucky to run right into the Martians as they came...

Though it was something, and I tipped my hat (not that I ever really wear hats, but you get the point) to Admiral Parks-Dawes for being bigger than his boss' politics.

Now the Admiral looked back at Matt, his expression still neutral, "Now, Commander, you say Barron and McMaster are on their way already?"

Matt nodded once, managing to contain what he later told me was shocked surprise at Parks-Dawes' compliance, "They're on their way, sir."

"My orders are to make sure they're delivered to the inquiry, Commander. I need their vector please."

Matt frowned and shook his head, "I'm sorry sir, can't say that I have that."

"This is a direct order, Commander."

I'm not sure if Parks-Dawes thought that last statement would actually have an effect before he said it, but as soon as Matt folded his arms and shook his head again, I imagine the message was pretty clear.

The Admiral looked off-screen, "Track back along their vector, look for any anomalies, and send to Earth Defense the likely approach vectors."

Matt's frown deepened, but he remained silent until Parks-Dawes looked back to him.

"Sir, you won't be stopping them," the Briton said evenly.

"I hate to say this, Commander, but your insubordination is requiring me to relieve you of command. Turn the bridge over to your next officer in line and remove yourself to your quarters."

Credit again to Parks-Dawes for actually sounding like he didn't want to give the order, and props to Matt for smiling and nodding, "Aye aye, Admiral. Lieutenant Commander Hannigan, any orders before I depart?"

Jim Hannigan stepped down from the console bank he'd been standing behind and into the view of the screen, "Yes Commander, I order you to assume command. And I order you to order me to end this communication."

Matt nodded somberly, "Very well, please do."

After this ridiculous little theatre, which I really didn't know Matt had in him, Parks-Dawes flinched in surprise, and then he disappeared as one of the techs listening at communications killed the feed.

"Jim, send to Shannon that we better get moving before they try to disable us. Erica, they're bloody fast ships. Can you get us around them?"

As Jim Hannigan returned to his post, Erica Martin looked back over her shoulder and flashed a broad smile, "I think I can."

Matt nodded, "I've heard that works for little engines. Let's go. Take us on a vector out towards… oh, say Venus. Jim, suggest to Shannon that she split her ships, send one with us and take the other on a vector towards the Mars approaches."

This, I remind you, was not *Commodore* Baxter, but *Commander* Baxter, outranked two grades by Shannon Hunter, and still giving veritable orders — *excellent* veritable orders. Small wonder Shannon followed the 'advice' and turned one of her frigates, skippered by a full *Captain* (Wen Luong of *Tiger*) over to the charge of a *Commander* on *Wolf's* bridge.

Well, big wonder, I suppose. But she had an irrational trust in Matt's ability to deliver, and it was well rewarded.

The frigates fired their drives in unison, spinning in various directions and spiraling upward at full burn, passing over the Light Squadron and working up to full speed while Parks-Dawes tried to turn *Ark Royal* and the other carriers around in formation.

The frigates pretty much got away.

CHAPTER FOURTEEN

RE-ENTRY... ER... WELL, JUST ENTRY

"So, you're sure this is still the best way to get the job done?"

The question was Karen's and it wasn't an unfair one. As you'll see (if you haven't already found out somewhere else) what we were about to do defied the laws of common sense. But then that's pretty par for the course for us, now, isn't it.

No, there was no need for a question mark at the end of that last sentence. It was a statement of fact, not a question.

I nodded a couple of times in response, and looked sideways out of my canopy at her in the next plane over. We were flying absurdly close together, hoping we'd slip through the passive sensors of the Earth defense grid as we came in on ballistic approach.

As you're probably guessing, there was little chance of that. Whatever I say about the Caldecott circle, the officers and crews of the orbital defense stations, generally themselves separate from politics, were (and still are) just damned good. My HUD flashed red almost at the instant I finished nodding, and the active sensor pulses started washing over my detectors about a second later.

"It's all we can do, my dear Karen!" I probably sounded more hurried and less gallant than I'd have liked, but oh well.

"They just scrambled two squadrons from the local stations to intercept us," Karen's voice came over the headset again, and I nodded, watching the icons of just about forty Starlights pop up on the HUD.

Great.

"Kinda wishing we'd asked Adrienne along right now," I muttered, and heard a short laugh from Karen (Adrienne Thompson, CO of *Wolf's* fighter squadron, if you're wondering who I'm referring to).

"Better that we focus on evading, I don't want a fight with these guys. Word is they're as good as we are."

I frowned and tapped a couple of my flight controls, bringing my main systems online, "Well that's not setting the bar very high."

We stopped our nattering for a moment as we reactivated our fighters' main combat systems. We'd been coasting on momentum with the minimum of power emissions to get this far, just firing the main engines every five minutes or so for about thirty seconds. Our speed had remained high, but now the combat systems were cool.

"Intercept in seventy seconds... mark," Karen was getting tactical, and that was a good thing. For me, not for them.

I glanced her way as she said it, and I swear to this day I saw her flash a smile. She was wearing her flight helmet, though, so I'm not sure how I could have seen that...

Anyway, I went back to firing up my main systems. The engines and mags came online in a rush, and my defensive and countermeasures followed right after. It all sounds pretty simple, though I recall the process being rather button-pushing-intensive... such was the nature of fighter craft, I suppose.

"So, I'll go right, you go left?" Karen's voice came in again, and I nodded once.

"As usual, you get to go conservative while I go liberal."

There was a pause, and I glanced at Karen just as her head turned to me, "*What?*"

"Sorry, historical politics joke. Ignore me."

There was a laugh, "Roger *that.*"

I smiled to myself and then settled down into my seat, keying the strap-tightener to make sure I was belted snugly in. We were close enough over Earth now — if they chased Karen and me into the atmosphere, I could be pulling some serious gees.

"Hang on, did you say Starlights? IFF is reading these folks as Starbursts," Karen's voice crossed the space between our fighters again, and I frowned, my eyes darting across the HUD.

Sure enough, IFF transponders were coming up with a 22X4G suffix. which probably means nothing to you, and was a top secret code until about four years ago. But that wasn't the Starlight suffix. (I can't tell you what the IFF suffix for an F-194 Starlight is because it's still in use by some of our ships, believe it or not.)

Anyway, these weren't F-194 Starlights that had been sent to intercept us, they were F-184 Starbursts. For all you ship-spec keeners, this'll be review. For everyone else, the F-184 Starburst was the fighter model that was front line before the F-194 Starlight (Karen's and my planes) were adopted by Defense Command. What many people don't realize is that when Defense Command adopts new gear, the old stuff usually stays in circulation for a while. Remember how only Special Branch on *Wolf* was carrying the shiny new MAG-90s by this time? Same idea — we only have enough money in peacetime to adopt new kit in stages.

So, the Starlights, new and shiny and cutting edge as they are, were deployed to front line units where their advantages would do the most good. The Starbursts on orbital duty were among the last to be slotted for replacement because, frankly, the Admiralty and the Navy Board expected the fighters over Earth to be least likely to see action...

Well, whoops. Who could have known, eh?

The reason I'm prattling on about this is simple: Karen and I had the advantage. Starbursts were fine planes, head and shoulders better than the rickety but charming old F-174 Sunbursts they'd replaced (hey, don't complain to me about the similar names and numbers, I had nothing to do with the naming). That said, the F-194 Starlight was the best fighter in space, without exception.

In my publisher's words (after reading that little tirade) Karen and I had faster and more maneuverable planes.

"Well, I'll take small favors when I can get them. Stand by to break formation," I smiled inside my helmet, then narrowed my eyes as the Starbursts appeared in visual range ahead.

We were getting very close indeed...

"Break... now. Tally-ho!"

People think saying 'Tally-ho' is stupid. It probably is, but I do it anyway.

With a flip of the wrist, I rolled port and with my free hand, threw the throttle to full. In a smooth motion, my plane kicked forward on an oblique angle across the approaching vector of the Starbursts. Karen rolled the other way, her fighter taking a course that mirrored my own in the opposite direction. We were following a route that was basically like the two arms of a 'V', trying to get around the defense force.

And of course they didn't want to let us pass.

"Attention unauthorized craft, join our formation immediately and accept escort to *Orbital One*. You will not be warned again."

I frowned at the no-nonsense order, and replied with my own nonsense reply, "Terribly sorry, can't oblige. And you fine people really shouldn't try to stop us."

Now, you ask, with forty planes coming out to intercept us, what the hell was I thinking being so brash. Well first of all, if you don't get that I can be rather cavalier by now, you might want to re-read the book to this point. Secondly, though, we weren't looking to fight them, we were trying to break through their formation and to speed out the other end, too fast for them to get us.

Sounds unlikely on paper, sure, but we're talking about two planes, and two planes only, trying to make the break. And Karen and I (mainly Karen) weren't bad pilots at all.

There was no more comm chatter, the Starbursts just lined up in attack wings (five-ship diagonal lines of planes) and split in an effort to envelop us on the approach.

"Seems like they don't want us to get through," Karen's voice came over my helmet speakers again.

"Yes, seems like that..." I was starting to pay too much attention to flying to be witty.

Twenty of the planes — one whole squadron — was coming at me in four attack wings.

I watched the closing distance on the HUD, and waited for the warning tone to start chiming. They'd have to get a lock on me with their missiles. They couldn't possibly expect to disable me with direct mag fire... Starbursts were just too slow to stay on me if they tried...

Or maybe that was why they'd sent *twenty* Starbursts for each of us.

"Look out for mags, they probably don't want us dead."

Karen chuckled, "Glad we're all on that same page then. Roger."

My fighter continued its sprint, the throttle open all the way, the plane making almost 193 kps in the vacuum.

Get ready... get ready...

I should say this: for me, flying isn't like planning for a battle. You know how I overthink things leading up to a fight in a ship? I don't do that in a plane. It's a different level of interaction, it's something I'm directly handling. It's virtually instinctive, at least for me... for better or worse.

The bolts of mag fire started to slice past my cockpit and the wings of my Starlight, and my eyes narrowed.

"Taking fire, going nuts," that wasn't official speak, but Karen knew exactly what I meant when I said it.

I pulled back on the stick and kicked in the accelerator, feeding a short burst of speed into my drives as I arched over the fire. It was an easy follow for the pilots coming at me

— they needed to only adjust very slightly on their approach to get their weapons to follow my quick 'climb', but the move bought me seconds.

And I'd need more of those seconds. With me racing towards them at 193 kps, and them coming at me at around 188 kps, our combined approach velocity was a huge 381 kps. That meant they wouldn't be in front of me for long, and once I got past them they wouldn't be able to keep up.

The fire stopped for a second, and I banked port and dropped back onto my old course just in time for the mag bolts to start splitting the space I'd just been traveling through. It was a somewhat satisfying feeling to be staying out of the way of that much mag fire... but something felt a little hollow about it.

Of course, I didn't know it then, but commanding those two squadrons was Commander Simon Rhee, and he was more or less on our side — he was a protégé of Admiral Hirobumi, and he knew exactly what was going on. He was making sure to put on a good show of shooting at us, but his planes weren't really trying.

Still, I didn't know that at the time, as I took a deep breath and kicked the accelerator to life again. The HUD reported that I had just about ten seconds before I raced through their formation...

Wow, that was a *short* ten seconds, I remember my mind editing in a dramatic 'woosh' sound as I watched the Starbursts slam past me in a blur. Of course there was no such sound in the vacuum, but it almost seemed to be necessary — I mean, stunt teams aside, not many people do that sort of high speed pass *through* another formation.

I thumbed the accelerator again, pushing my Starlight a little further ahead while the Starbursts fired their wing thrusters and flipped over. Their engines struggled against momentum and began pushing them back after me, but even at top thrust they couldn't do a damned thing.

"Well that was fun," I said with a smile as I watched the Starbursts accelerating in their vain attempt to catch up to us. "ETA about sixteen minutes on the destination. I think I'm starting to feel gravity already... should've skipped the big lunch."

Karen laughed over the comm, "Yeah, probably. Let's hope that's your biggest problem today."

I wasn't sure the 'that' she was talking about was my lunch or the Starbursts, but either way I 'mmmhmmmed' in agreement — that had been easy, relatively speaking. Despite what you've seen in *some* of those movies, there was no dogfight, and I certainly never screamed "WHO'S YOUR COMMODORE, BABY?!" If you haven't seen the movie I'm talking about, don't bother. It's trash.

Karen and I were set to dive into Earth's atmosphere, and from there, it would be time to save the Empire...

We dove.

CHAPTER FIFTEEN

UNDER ARREST

Greg lowered himself into a chair facing Admiral Hirobumi's desk and sighed as John dropped into another chair next to him.

"Well, that was... not good," Greg's tone was low but even.

Admiral Hirobumi was taking his seat as Fiora and Noyce settled themselves. Of course, both men were technically under arrest... yes, it was a formality, though admittedly a limiting one.

"You caused a stir, yes," Hirobumi said sharply. "How does this impact your overall plan?"

John raised an eyebrow and glanced at Greg, "I'm trying to figure that one out for myself. What do you think?"

Greg frowned thoughtfully and leaned back in his chair, "Well, we wanted to be taken out of there under Special Branch escort, so the parts of the plan that stem from that shouldn't have been too badly impacted. But..."

His voice trailed off and John nodded, "But now instead of being under protective guard from a potential assassin, we're prisoners."

The original plan, I should explain now, was for Haley Briand, the agent in the audience, to start waving a mag around and threatening to kill the traitors, then to have Special Branch burst in to save the day and get John and Greg out of there.

Clearly hadn't worked out that way.

"What I find immensely troubling is Caldecott's choice of security," Hirobumi's mind was clearly tied to that topic, his carefully chosen English words revealing his displeasure. "He certainly is not willing to trust Defense Command."

John laughed shortly, "Well, I suppose he's not as dumb as we think. He knows most of the Command has identified him as a liability, but the public is going to be seeing this live on the lunchtime news. And if Caldecott has any brains, he'll be holding a press conference then too."

Remember, now, that Caldecott's out cold, under short-term sedation as per doctor's orders to keep him from having a serious heart incident. Greg and John didn't know it — and even Hirobumi didn't — but they all had a bit more time than they realized.

"So we'll be criminals in the media in a couple of hours time, assuming the news didn't go live and break into morning programming," Greg released a sigh of his own. "That'll make our life interesting."

John and Hirobumi both nodded, staring at the desk between them. It had to still be a bit of a shock — having stood in the middle of a gun-toting showdown between Special Branch and Imperial Army blockheads...

John later told me that he'd been cool in the moment, but the near-deathishness of the affair began to hit him as he sat in the chair in Hirobumi's office. But remember, this is

John Fiora — neither Greg nor Hirobumi saw a sign of his nerves, I've asked them both. Still, it was starting to hit him, so he was slow on the planning at the moment.

"We could try going to the media first," Greg suggested after a long pause, "tell them what happened, control the message."

Hirobumi's stern eyes narrowed thoughtfully, but John shook his head, "No we can't. We're prisoners, and prisoners don't get air time. If we do it'll be evidence of the corruption that Dave's accusing us of…"

"Ah, I suppose so," Greg nodded.

It really was a bad situation for them — their plan (which I still won't ruin for you) was seriously in jeopardy, and they couldn't use all the resources available to them to get control of the situation because if they did they'd make Caldecott's case for him.

Incredible how much damage one politically connected and motivated idiot can do, isn't it…

Around this moment something hit John, though — something beyond the muzzles of the Imperial Army energy guns. They were dealing with the fate of the Empire here, it wasn't a career battle anymore.

"But what we're dealing with is the fate of the Empire. I think our political battles have to take a back seat…" he said slowly after that pause, and Greg leaned forward slightly and nodded.

"I agree. We take the chance of being called out as traitors and exiled… but we really must take that chance."

We all know the story of what came of these two fellows, so it's perhaps hard to grasp the gravity of this decision at the time. They were facing the possibility of being condemned individually — of being labeled conspirators against the Empire, and thus being either exiled or more likely *hung*, if no one believed them.

There was no way for them to know how things would turn out, all they knew at that moment, as they made their decision, was that they needed to act lest the Empire fall. And if it didn't fall, and they — and I — were proven grossly wrong by some strange confluence of events, it would be bad for all of us.

So don't underestimate the courage it took to keep with the plan.

In my case it was fool's courage, and I was acting on a different plan they didn't know about at the time. But for them it was sheer guts — the stuff that made them great fleet officers.

"We stick to the plan then," John's voice by now had its confidence fully restored — a fast turnaround to say the least.

Greg nodded, and then Admiral Hirobumi leaned forward in his seat and keyed his intercom to the receptionist outside, "Send for Admiral Fostopolos, please."

They'd have to adjust their plans very slightly, though. That they knew.

"Let's call a press conference for noon. We'll get the local lunch broadcasts, see if that gets us anywhere," John looked to Greg, but the junior Admiral frowned and shook his head.

"Maybe we shouldn't give the conference. Get one of Thea's press officers to release the information we received. If the Imperial Army sees us live on camera, they might be able to move to cut us off from the Emperor."

John's eyes narrowed in thought, and after a moment he nodded, "Yes, that's good. Means the warning about the Martians isn't as politicized, gives us more latitude..."

Then the critical idea came to John — I don't know if I was somehow beaming telepathic signals about the harebrained mission Karen and I were on, but somehow he knew it was crucial to get to the Emperor quickly.

"Tessho, can you get that convoy together for us to get over to the palace in the next hour?"

Hirobumi blinked in surprise, then nodded in a sharp jerk, "Yes."

John smiled, "Do it. Road trip time."

The Emperor would be dealt with before the people actually knew what was going on.

Chapter Sixteen

"My Grandmother Seduced My Husband Before He Left Me For My Best Friend"

You know, I'd like to think you're offended by the title of this chapter, but I get the sad feeling that you might be laughing and remembering the episode of the *Geraldine Coilier Show* I'm referring to. Or maybe you've seen some of the other episodes along those lines that Geraldine Coilier has done. Lately, the successors to her brand of live daytime trash vid have gotten even more daring, and censorship has virtually vanished…

Of course, that's getting slightly ahead of the story.

Karen and I angled our planes across the North American continent, not towards the capital but to the live Toronto studios of the *Geraldine Coilier Show* — the highest rated live vid show for weekday mornings on the entire planet Earth.

It was so popular it was even watched in late-night and primetime slots in other parts of the world (those parts in different time zones watched it live, no matter what time of day it was for them). This delightful bit of family programming was our rather unorthodox target.

If you don't know this story from history, you're probably getting the gist of our plan by now.

Going after this unusual media outlet at 0900 in the morning (Toronto was two time zones earlier than the Capital Island) was a strange but good decision for us, and it let us land unopposed. Days after Karen and I did the run, we got to see the scramble logs for all the defense fighters sent up to find us in Earth's atmosphere — had we been near the capital, or a major military installation, we'd have been cooked.

As it was, the North America Number Four Squadron was nearest to us, and its pilots were still flying Starbursts, notoriously even slower relative to Starlights in the atmosphere than in space — Karen and I were doing about mach six, they were barely over mach four.

Anyway, we got to Toronto rather quickly, and then we cut our speed sharply and dove straight into downtown at subsonic speed. With Karen leading the way (she says she was showing me the safe flightpath, I say 'ladies first!') we weaved our way through the buildings, scaring the hell out of a few hundred thousand morning commuters.

The studios for *Geraldine Coilier* were in the north of the city, one of the oldest sections of buildings left standing after the superstorms of 2144. We got to them in a blur, and as we came over them I cut my turbines and switched to directional thrusters for flight control.

I won't bore you with the technical processes too much, but the old Starlight (the model we were flying then) was still a bit choppy under thrusters in the atmosphere — the ride lacked the smoothness of a turbine, particularly when I flipped the switch that dropped my gear.

My point for bringing this up is… well…

Karen landed smoothly on the lawn in front of the old warehouse studios. I only landed on top of Geraldine's car by accident — the thrusters bounced me sideways and the back landing foot crushed her sporty little silver mid-life-crisis hover roadster.

I swear, I meant nothing by it. She's a wonderful lady.

Who profits on human misery and hysteria…

Sorry.

Anyway, I pulled up, moved forward slightly, and dropped onto the lawn next to Karen's fighter. We'd done enough weaving back in the downtown to hopefully lose the Starbursts coming after us for a while, but even when they did find us, they wouldn't be able to land to pursue — well, they physically *could*, but they'd be under orders to call in SF, not to land and deal with us themselves.

So we had a bit of time, but I still rushed to pop the canopy of my plane, and scrambled over the side, checking for my mag in my holster as I dropped to the grass and turned around.

Karen was standing with a frown and folded arms, and she pointed with her thumb at the crushed car in the "RESERVED FOR GERALDINE" spot.

I shrugged, "Whoops."

A smile spread on her face immediately — thank God for small favors like that smile — and then she waved towards the studio door, "After you, Commodore!"

"Oh no, I insist Captain!"

Her smile broadened. And then we turned to the door. And saw the security guard and the half dozen office workers who'd come outside to see what the noise was about.

"Uhm… hi folks. We need to crash the show."

My words were met with jaws hanging open.

Karen and I walked slowly towards the door, trying to avoid eye contact.

"So that bitch stole my man from my granny!"

"Booooooooooooooooooooo!"

Geraldine was swelling at the loud boo as it came, and then she rushed with her wire indicator to a woman with a question, directing the parabolic microphones to collect her brilliant comments.

"Yeah, I got a question… so old granny, what the hell you doin' with your granddaughter's man? My granny always said I had to share, but she asked first."

The crowd dutifully began to chant, "Gerald-*ine*! Gerald-*ine*! Gerald-*ine*!"

See, I think this sort of exchange says something very very *bad* about society — not only the fact that more than one person can compare notes on infidelity and grannies (in the same sentence, those two words) but worse that they do it on live vid.

I mean come *on*, we're the Earth Empire, the shining beacon of civilization in the solar system, and we're dealing with this?

It has struck me as very ironic on a number of occasions that it was this show we had to crash — one that so fundamentally works against my sense of propriety, one that frankly makes me gag.

But this was the job, and I suppose I *seriously* shouldn't complain: John and Greg were at that moment in the capital getting ready to risk career, limb and life for the Empire. I just had to stomach listening to this tripe.

Well, I didn't listen for long.

The studio for the *Geraldine Coilier Show* was like all the stages you see for these shows — theatre style arrangement for the studio audience (with about 200 people in the seats) and a cheaply decorated stage with chairs on it for the victims. Er. Guests.

Karen and I came from the side of the stage in a flash. The fight-breaking security guards — big burly women and men well-trained and with the formidable ability to claw apart twin sisters battling for the love of the same tree — saw us coming and tried to stop us, but Karen and I were approaching with mags drawn.

The six security guards thus went face first into the filthy carpet, twitching as the mag energy bled off.

"What the fuck!?" Geraldine's choice of words... well, I'd say it displeased me, but I don't need to beat the point to death: I hated being on this set.

"Sorry to interrupt," Karen was far better able to cope with her own disdain, as always. "We need to do an unconventional broadcast."

There was a shocked murmur from the crowd, and Geraldine stood open mouthed for a long few seconds.

I figure everyone was taking a few seconds to recognize that we were actually *us* — our faces had been splashed all over the news in past years, what with the excitement in the Belt. Lately Caldecott had been running up our pictures as enemies of the Empire... and here we were, holding up Earth's favorite live show.

"Uh... ladies and gentlemen... welcome Commodore Ken Barron and the luscious Karen McMaster!"

If I hadn't heard the playback of the recordings a few dozen times, I wouldn't believe that anyone would not only call Karen 'luscious', but that they'd leave out 'Captain' in the same breath.

Karen's eyes narrowed but she kept a painted-on smile — this was bigger than both of us. We couldn't start shooting civilians.

Then I felt a bony fist jab me in the kidney, "This is my time you young git. Off with you, I want my fame!"

It was one of the grannies. Again, consult the footage if you don't believe me.

I turned, determined to be polite, "Ma'am, please. This is crucial to the security of the Empire."

Of course, by now Geraldine had gestured for her crew to put the parabolic microphones on Karen and me, so my whisper was broadcast to the world, and to the audience. I got an 'OOooooOOOOOoooooohhh.'

"Bullshit, you sort always say that. Dave Caldecott says you're evil!"

Now, thankfully enough, my next actions have never been seriously questioned — I guess you all sort of agreed with my thought on the priorities here. Telling off a crazy and promiscuous old woman probably would have gotten great ratings for Geraldine, but Karen and I didn't have that much time before SF busted down the doors.

"Ma'am, sit down," I leveled my mag at her nose, letting it hover about six inches from the tip of her old beak. Er. Distinguished... beak.

Her eyes went very wide, and she shut up and sat.

Karen was already pulling her comm out of her pocket, tying it into the building network, "Can the techs in the control room please go half-screen and run what I'm about to send. Just run it raw, it's all been compiled for you."

That was the data package we'd sent to Hirobumi, and that (still unbeknownst to us) Matt had used to convince Parks-Dawes to go on alert.

"Ladies and gentlemen, you know who we are. I understand that Second Lord Caldecott has been trying to impeach the so-called 'Fiora ring', a euphemism, I think, for the fleet officers who know what they're doing. Well what Karen's playing for you right now in the screen window next to me is data from the *Martian-pirate combined attack on Belt Two*. That's right, just under ten days ago the Belt Squadron was in action against a Martian fleet, and now we believe a second Martian force is on its way to Earth. *Wolf* came here to warn Defense Command to prepare, but guess what, Dave Caldecott has the fleet sitting on its hands."

I actually believe I heard a pin drop.

Everyone in the audience — and even on the stage — had their eyes glued to the monitors. Hopefully this would be convincing, but I didn't have time to let everyone just digest it.

"Now I know SF is going to be here to collect Karen and me in a minute, but here's what we need *you* to do. That's right, we're here with the warning, doing some pretty edgy legal stuff to get it to you, but we're still under orders to report to the inquiry. We can't *stop* the inquiry without a military coup, which would be bad..."

Eyes slowly started to drag their way back to me.

"So here's the plan: the Parliament can overturn the inquiry right now if a two-thirds majority passes the motion in both houses. So get on the comms, start sending messages to your MPs and get them to vote. Do it now. We need an avalanche of mail getting to them. They need to overturn the inquiry and restore Defense Command to working order immediately, or we'll be in serious trouble."

Some people in the audience were pulling their comms out, which was good. Many more, though, were just staring at me.

I glanced at Karen and we shrugged almost simultaneously. She looked back to the crowd (and the cameras), "Well, look, if we're lying, it won't take long to figure out, even if we mobilize the fleet for defense in between. And seriously, if we were acting against the interests of the Empire, why do you think we'd be asking you to comm your MP?"

There were a few nods in the crowd, more comms coming out.

Indeed, all across the planet, panicked viewers, watching a pirate ship fire a battleship laser into Wes Pellew's *Cheetah*, began opening their comms and sending notes to their Members of Parliament.

Apparently, both Houses of Parliament — both were sitting at this moment — were hit by a sudden cacophony of 'new message' pings on their consoles. Of course, those consoles only got the mail that was forwarded to them by the parliamentary secretaries, but apparently the secretaries were taking the panicked mail seriously.

Thank God for that *large* favor.

The vote was being introduced in the Commons *seconds* after Karen and I finished our pitch. Now that's quite good for government work.

But Karen and I were still on that wonderful stage, staring at a silent audience.

"So…" I ventured the fatal words, "any questions?"

A hand shot up, and Geraldine rushed to the side of this woman, and the microphone kicked in, "So, like, are you two, like, you know, sleeping together?"

The audience laughed. My face blanked, and, well, words can't describe the thundercloud that formed around Karen. It was like the room got darker.

I mean come on, we'd just announced the impending Martian attack on Earth, and all the crowd wanted to know was this?

"Ma'am, you *seriously* need to change the subject—"

And then (thankfully, I'd say) the doors burst open, and we had new guests for the show.

CHAPTER SEVENTEEN

STANDOFF ON THE GERALDINE COILIER SHOW

Now, Karen and I had been expecting to get ourselves detained for our stunt — it'd probably take a few minutes for any motions on the floor of Parliament to get out of the way and for a vote to end the inquiry... assuming, of course, that our plan worked at all.

And even I wasn't crazy enough to just assume it would work. Karen and I were trying to play off our celebrity and to mix in a bit of common sense. We hoped that would get the people on our side, and the politicians would thus toe the line.

So the plan looked really good on paper, and we figured we had a decent shot — otherwise why would we have come all this way?

Anyway, I digress. Back to the point of being detained: the studio doors were flung open, and who walked in? You guessed it, not SF or Special Branch, but *Imperial Army* blockheads. Apparently Caldecott had thought to dispatch some of his troops to the other cities where Karen and I might come down if we broke with procedure.

And our little broadcast, combined with the rather obvious sight of our fighters on the lawn, were pretty clear signals of where these idiots could find us.

"Drop the weapon! Drop the weapon! Imperial Army! Drop the weapon!"

Karen already wasn't too impressed by the audience's candor. Let me tell you this: it takes a lot of discourtesy to get on Karen's bad side, but if you end up there, well, you might want to find a new identity. Change your passport.

Not that she's vindictive or anything. Just... er... not a good person to annoy. And blockheads bellowing at her like a broken record after she'd just had to listen to the height of discourtesy, well, not smart.

For my part, as soon as I heard the order for her to drop her weapon I had my mag out and turned on the Imperial Army Captain's head. The man was another smug looking beefy guy with no neck and a voice that was a bit too high pitched for his size, and he stretched his big energy gun out at the end of his chunky arm and glared at me down its barrel.

"Surrender in the name of the Emperor!"

The audience actually *booed*, which for some ridiculous reason I found gratifying at that moment. Then one of the Sergeants from the army detachment fired twice over their head, and they *freaked*. That's a technical term. They screamed and dove out of their seats onto their hands and knees, trying to shelter behind the chairs in front of them.

Their reaction was entirely understandable — energy guns weren't like well-tamed mags, every hit *killed*. That's why Defense Command had elected to stick with the mags years back, that and energy guns could easily blow holes in ship hulls, making a firefight when boarding a pirate ship counter-productive.

Anyway, sorry. The crowd had panicked with good reason, and my eyes narrowed.

"He just threatened the safety of a public audience with an unchecked energy weapon," Karen's tone was steely as she trained her mag at the Sergeant.

"Drop your weapons!" the squeaky beef-Captain yelped again. His men — again, all men — fanned out behind him, about twenty from my quick count, all leveling their big energy rifles at us.

The door behind them opened again.

By this time I have to say I was starting to get somewhat... tense. I mean, Karen and I were good with mags, no question. Not as good as the likes of Charlie Peters and his Special Branchers, but we were still pretty good.

That said, twenty blockheads with the collective mental power of a prodigious camel were still going to be able to *kill* us both before we extricated ourselves, unless we surrendered. Worse, any sort of firefight would have caught people in this crowd and on the stage, and as abhorrent as their morals might be, they still qualified as innocent. Dammit.

I glanced quickly at Karen, and her stern scowl reflected similar frustrations. We could surrender ourselves and just be released when the inquiry was nixed. Yes. That.

Or...

"Captain, order your men to drop their weapons. Now."

And that wasn't me of course, but Major Charlie Peters.

I'll back up and explain: remember way back (well not that far) to how in the corridor on *Wolf* Matt had been pretty quick to let Karen and me argue him out of insisting that Charlie and *Wolf*'s Special Branch detachment came along? Well, this is how he got around our objections — he just sent Charlie without telling us.

But what about all those fighters we had to dodge? Well, being rather clever, and owing to the fact that a Special Branch assault shuttle is packed with all sorts of clever electronic warfare kit, Charlie had set himself up to look like a civilian shuttle carrying a private businessman coming back from a meeting on Luna. With all the stir Karen and I caused with our usual abrupt and obvious arrival, he'd slipped right through the grid.

And then he'd picked up our feed, probably shook his head and cursed our stupidity, and come down after us.

You say it's all too convenient. I believe my words for it (the ones I didn't say out loud) were "Oh, thank God." Here's a tip, when a Special Branch team shows up out of nowhere to save your backside, don't complain about how unlikely it seems. That's their job, they're unlikely.

Anyway, the Captain looked over his shoulder and realized rather quickly that a dozen black-clad Special Branchers in full tac gear — meaning they were wearing the vests with sufficient plating to absorb a single energy gun strike — were looking down the barrels of MAG-90s at him.

Standoff — the second one between Special Branch and the Imperial Army in about ninety minutes. See why they say this morning was almost a coup?

"Captain, you really should do as he says," Karen's words were decidedly unsympathetic. "Your men don't have a chance."

She was right. Sure, she and I would go down first if the shooting started, but the blockheads wouldn't last a minute against Charlie's team...

Then the door *behind* Karen and me opened, and the heavy claps of SF boots burst onto the stage behind us.

"Oh for..." I managed to stop myself from saying anything more as I glanced back over my shoulder. An SF Commander with mag drawn, followed by another dozen SF guards, piled into the room.

The Commander's mouth dropped open as she saw the scene, and her guards, automatically making choices based on training and loyalty, leveled their rifles — old EP-5s — at the blockheads. Of course, the SF were as unarmored as Karen and me, so their chances of living through a gunfight didn't look so good.

"Sir?" the Commander slowly approached my side, her mag waving towards the army boys, not me — something that I rather appreciated just then.

"Commander. Um... what can we do for you?"

"Uhhmm. I was under orders from Captain Chikai, the regional SF chief, to make sure you weren't held up by our Imperial Army colleagues, actually."

Oh.

Well that was definitely good news — I later found out from Admiral Hirobumi that Deng Chikai was one of his best Captains on Earth (another turn of luck for us — feel free to keep a running tally) and that orders had gone down the pipe from SF headquarters to not let the Imperial Army do *anything* that might interrupt a vote in Parliament to abolish the inquiry. This order was actually tied more to John and Greg's plan than Karen's and mine... but hey, it worked out. Chikai's surveillance had shown the blockheads rolling after us, and he'd dispatched a team to watch them.

To this day, people argue whether this thus constituted a coup... but anyway.

The Commander, I have to mention too, was Nadira Khan, just before her promotion. She was already confirmed for the promotion before she bailed Karen and me out — she did *not* get her commission for helping us, as some have said.

"Glad to have you then, Commander," I smiled and nodded, then looked back to the blockhead Captain. "I am *so* tempted to ask you if you're feeling very lucky, there, Captain, but I don't think you'd get the joke. So what're you and your men going to do?"

The Captain was sweating — which for a guy his size didn't seem like it'd be a rare thing — and his eyes were darting around from Karen to Commander Khan's SF guards and then to the Special Branchers who'd rounded his flank enough for him to see.

His blockheads were in a bit of a panic, turning and aiming and then turning again and aiming again, as if they were trying to cover two opposite directions at once. Didn't make them look too professional, but then, they weren't. At *all*.

"We... uh... you should surrender, sir. It's your duty."

He'd stopped shouting, but he still wasn't seeing sense.

Karen glanced at me with a frown and I bobbed my eyebrows and shrugged. Looking back to the Captain, I slowly shook my head, "What, you want me to peel off the roof of this place and put a couple of Starlights over your head, just so you can be *sure* you're totally outclassed?"

I shouldn't have tried such a 'clever' answer. He just stared at me, not quite understanding that I was kidding.

"How about this, Captain," Charlie spoke up from behind the meathead. "You and your boys walk out of here through the door behind the stage. We won't stop you, and then you can call for reinforcements."

The Captain turned around for the first time and got a good look at Charlie, "I can't do that."

This was starting to get less funny and more frustrating and a hell of a lot more dangerous. If we couldn't talk this guy down, the studio and all its innocent grandson-in-law stealing grannies might get shot up.

Wow, that didn't sound half bad in hindsight.

But it wouldn't do.

Still, despite being seemingly crazy in everything you've seen me do so far, I wasn't about to start shooting. Karen and I and the SF guards under Commander Khan wouldn't have survived energy gun fire, and so we couldn't be too brash.

I wasn't ready to lose lives over this yet, which just happened to make for boring vidcasts.

Someone actually heckled from behind the seat they'd been sheltering under, "Come on, shoot the bastards!"

Thankfully no one with the guns decided to follow that line of thought.

And so we just stood there, weapons leveled at each other, waiting and watching…

CHAPTER EIGHTEEN

GOVERNMENT

I wasn't witness to any of this, and I didn't have any of my trusted friends from the Fiora ring on the ground in the Parliament Building, but from the people I *have* talked to (and the vids I've watched after the fact) this is more or less how things happened in government, literally in the minutes while Karen, Charlie and I were staring down our barrels at the blockheads.

If politics bores you to no end, you can skip the next couple of pages, but I promise, this is probably the clearest explanation of goings-on in our Parliament that you'll get anywhere.

First, the Senate was hearing debate over a motion regarding trade with the Belt colonies — specifically, if you really care, it was proposition 4181.6, that all shipments of goods sent to the Belt colonies should be subject to three percent less taxation, in order to lower prices. Big debate from the Belt delegation about how that'd stunt the development of local manufacturing operations out there... all sorts of economic stuff.

The Senate, I should mention, was only about a third full. It wasn't a crucial debate, and more to the point, voting on the proposition wasn't due until after lunch. Most Senators were in their offices catching up on early morning messages.

So, according to Howard Duffy, one of the Senators for Belt Five, it was a hell of a surprise when almost 150 panicked politicians sprinted through the many doors at the outer ring of the Senate chamber and clomped down the stairs to their desks. It was pretty much a race to call the point of order that'd end the debate — I'd thought for the longest while, that was because the politicians cared deeply for the safety for the Empire.

Well, many did, but some were more interested in getting his or her name in *Hansard* (the Senate official record) as being the one who'd stopped the debate and put forward the point of order that saved the Empire. And by some, I mean Senator Gustav Stryker of Luna, who campaigned on the slogan "I Saved the Empire in the Senate" three years later.

In any case, Stryker raised the point of order and the vote to call for an abolition of the inquiry by Dave Caldecott and this house was carried with an eighty percent majority. Dave Caldecott was popular with some of these people, but the evidence Karen had put up on the screen was scary enough.

And besides, consider the risk-reward calculation for these politicians: if they'd dawdled and wasted time, and the Martians had shown up, they'd have had no careers. At least this way they'd have a chance if I wasn't lying, and if I was, they could tar and feather me later.

Parliament's lower house, the Commons, was much more entertaining, if you find politics entertaining.

The Prime Minister was in the middle of Question Period, and with his usual elegant but somber tone, Mister Gabriel Pope was handling the opposition with ease. I should mention that I've had many opportunities to meet with Gabriel Pope over the years, more now that he's retired to Washington, and he is indeed as formidable in person as we all would like to believe he is. No question that we were in great shape in terms of political leadership for this situation, at least in Parliament.

In any case, at the moment we're talking about, Pope was responding to a question about prejudice against the Belt colonies with a quip about his own African-American ancestry, and then a panicked MP — Henri Joubert of South Africa — burst into the chambers, having stopped on the way back from the washroom to watch Karen and me give our little broadcast.

He called the point of order immediately, and also demanded that everyone turn on their vidscreens and switch to a news network. By this time, Karen and I were in a standoff, but the news wires that watched everything on the vidnet had picked up our feed and were replaying it gleefully.

Pope sat down immediately, and looked at his Deputy Prime Minister (then Olivia Bennington) with rather a surprised look on his face. His exact words, according to what he's told me lately, were "Well, seems that Dave Caldecott is indeed a dangerous son of a bitch."

He then stood up, "Madame Speaker, given this evidence it seems prudent to raise a point of order to interrupt Question Period and call for a vote to end the inquiry that has lately been commissioned by our Emperor."

The Speaker of the House, Kim Tuz (of Hungary, not Kim Tzu of China as is sometimes wrongly recorded), rose and immediately called the vote, herself having just watched the same feed on her screen. Everyone sat down, watched the yay-nay voting screen come up on their monitors, and then almost every single MP hit 'yay'. The resolution to end the inquiry passed.

Standing back up immediately, Pope addressed the Commons, "Based on this information, I think it necessary to issue Parliamentary orders that First Lord Fiora be immediately restored to his position, and that Defense Command be mobilized to Defense Condition Three, as a precaution."

That vote went through as well, and then was passed up to the Speaker of the Senate, who called the vote there and saw it passed.

Thus, in about five minutes, the political allies of the Fiora ring, combined with all the panicked members of the opposition, voted to restore order to Defense Command.

Now, it's an often-asked question: how the *hell* did two houses, both of them divided with their own political worries and factional infighting pull together and deliver such shockingly effective votes in that short a space of time?

Well, first of all, remember that Gabriel Pope had a majority government in both houses — his New Whig party held between fifty and fifty-five percent of the seats in each house, which helped. But if you look at the vote count, you see that over ninety percent in the Commons and eighty percent in the Senate sided with us.

I'd love to take credit for somehow persuading such a large segment of traditionally opposed political factions to join our cause, but really I think most of the work had been done already.

These people had by now heard of Caldecott's little incident with the inquiry, and though it wasn't being debated officially in either house (you don't debate that sort of thing until you know all the facts, and it had been less than two hours since John and Greg had been pulled out of the showdown by Special Branch) there was unrest. What the hell was Caldecott doing with Imperial Army troops?

Combine that with the fact that, even for the opposition, Defense Command was a fairly popular and well-accepted organization, and that the exercise of Imperial power — such as the calling of an inquiry by the Emperor to investigate Defense Command — was seen as an uncouth flexing of the Emperor's political muscle, and you can probably read a sentiment of bitterness among the MPs and Senators.

Basically, the Emperor had gone over their heads and given an unpopular small man the right to question Defense Command, an organization they considered to be their purview, and worse, the little man was using Imperial troops to do his will.

Keep in mind, Defense Command is *not* supposed to be answerable to the Emperor at all; it's a tool of the Parliament, and thus the government. So, all in all, any decent excuse to end the inquiry probably would have been backed up.

Throw in some flashy pictures of shiny Defense Command frigates getting cut into by pirates and Martians, and you get the response time down under five minutes.

The gamble Karen and I had gone for had paid off.

Only problem was that the Emperor could technically veto the resolutions, so our work wasn't done.

Well, by 'our' I don't mean Karen and me. We were in a standoff, remember.

Chapter Nineteen

Off To See The Emperor —The Wonderful Emperor Of Earth... Too Much?

The Imperial Army troops at the front gate of Government Palace were getting word through their earpieces that something was going on in the Senate and the Commons — something that endangered the power of the Emperor.

I've actually heard recordings of the warning the Brigadier in the palace sent out to his men, and it's pretty cryptic: "The government has voted, and the power of the Emperor to police the corruption in Defense Command has been torn down by fear and cowardice. Be on alert for unrest."

Now that's pretty bloody cryptic, if you ask me.

And the timing could only have been marginally worse.

A Defense Command hover truck was pulling up to the front gate as the warning finished, and the army boys swarmed it — their whole detail of twenty guys surrounded the truck with leveled rifles while the Sergeant in charge clamored up to the driver's side window.

"What the *fuck* is your business here, Defcom?" he hissed at the darkened glass as the window began to roll down.

As you probably know, he hissed those rather impolite words at the young, innocent and pretty Haley Briand, who was wearing an Ensign's uniform and now turning red and starting to well up with tears.

Haley Briand wasn't a great DCI officer for no reason: the Sergeant went white as a ghost. Even a blockhead doesn't like to make a young girl, probably on her first assignment as a driver for Defense Command, bawl her eyes out. And Haley Briand could do that on order, if need be — as a preface to shooting you and taking all your stuff.

Of course, that wasn't her goal just now...

"I'm *sorry*," she pleaded, "Second Lord Caldecott told me that I had to take these prisoners into your custody, or Defense Command would let them go. I... he... I mean he told me it'd be okay..."

The Sergeant was taken aback — Haley's 'chin-quivering, almost-sobbing innocent' routine is unashamedly devastating — and he stammered, "Uh, yeah. Prisoners. In the back?"

She nodded, sniffling (in a way no serious Defense Command officer *ever* would, but the Sergeant didn't know that), "Yeah, in the back... he said I should leave them with you, or take them in, or do whatever you said I should. What should I do?"

The Sergeant looked away and waved one of his Corporals to open the back of the truck, and that man and his detail ran around the truck's rear end, and opened the unlocked hatch. Greg and John sat in restraints glaring at the army blockheads.

"There's First Lord Fiora here, sir! And the other one, Noyes or however you says his name!" there was no accounting for grammar in the Corporal's reply.

"No one else?" the Sergeant hissed the question, then tried to smile at Haley. It was quite amusing, the way he was trying to be nice to her and still an authoritarian ass to his men, all at once. Oh and we've got this all on the button camera that Haley was wearing, if you're wondering how I'm being so descriptive.

"Nobody, sir!"

The Sergeant kept his anxious smile, "Alright... uh... check their restraints. Make sure that they isn't faking!"

Even Sergeants lack language skills in the Imperial Army.

Then the Sergeant looked at Haley, "Uh... not that we doubt you Miss officer... ma'am... but just to be sure they haven't gotten out of their bindings in the back, you know."

Haley made a good show of recovering from her 'near breakdown' and nodded, "No, it's okay. You want to take them in yourself, or should I bring the truck in?"

The Sergeant looked back to the Corporal, just as the junior non-com swung around the back of the truck and gave a thumbs-up to his senior.

"You take the truck on in. Stay around if you like, get some... uh... food. The mess is always happy to see a lady of your... character."

I don't really want to know what he was thinking when he said that, because the character Haley had put on wasn't a particularly useful one for military affairs. But anyway she nodded, and sniffled, then smiled, and as the gate opened, she throttled up and the hover truck pulled into the courtyard of the palace.

Now, Government Palace is the least spectacular of the Imperial palaces — it's really only a huge mansion with a number of outbuildings and lots of lovely green stands of trees, blue ponds, and paved foot paths. It's not like the Imperial Palace with all the gothic spires and whatnot.

That said, there were huge numbers of Imperial Army troops in the compound, camped out on the parade fields near the tall wall that surrounded the whole complex — remember, the Emperor had brought two Battalions of the Household Guard with him.

Haley left her window rolled down, and kept her semi-sob expression going as she drove, even as she stopped and asked an army Major for directions to the Security Center. She's *sooo* good.

The truck came to a stop outside the Security Center (which she would have known how to find blindfolded in the dark with both arms tied behind her back anyway, I should mention) about ten minutes later. Long enough to be seen by everyone, to make sure no one would be surprised by the presence of a hated Defcom vehicle within the walls. It's sort of like hiding in plain sight, I suppose...

Anyway, the Security Center is in a quiet corner of the palace complex, isolated from the rest of the compound by a stand of trees. This makes less tactical sense than it might — had Defense Command designed the place, it would have been surrounded by open fields so that it stayed in plain sight at all times. But the Emperor mightn't want to see the gloomy business of looking after grounds security, I suppose, so the army had kept it out of sight of the main building.

Which Greg and John had noticed as soon as Admiral Hirobumi and Admiral Fostopolos had rolled out the orbital photos of the palace. Opportunity, big time.

As the truck idled on its hover cushion, Haley opened her door, swung her legs out, and dropped to the ground, pulling her mag off her seat and tucking it (spy style) into the back waistband of her pants and shuffling her tunic awkwardly to cover it.

There were a few gaggles of army blockheads standing around outside the security house, and thus there were wolf-whistles and catcalls as she walked *around* the outside of the security building. Her semi-sobs were gone, and a rather hippy swagger in their place.

Look, if you think this is all very shameless, you're right. But it's what was necessary, and while she'd have gotten nowhere using these tactics against Defense Command personnel, the blockheads were susceptible. And when you're saving the Empire, you take what you can get.

The blockheads watched her swagger out of sight before realizing she'd left her truck running out front. One of the more sensible Corporals among them tapped his comm earpiece and called inside the small security building, reporting the strange arrival. A few more guards wandered out of the Security Center to investigate, and about two dozen army troopers eventually formed a ring around the truck.

One was then ordered to open the back hatch, and so he stepped forward.

Then the magbangs went off.

The truck had one of these magbangs affixed to each side — they just looked like cylinders to anyone who didn't know what to look for — and now John triggered them with a remote from the inside.

It was an almost silent blast, and the EM energy released did as advertised: all twenty-five guys went down.

Hearing the quiet hum of the grenades, Haley sprinted back around from where she'd been sheltering behind the building, tugging her mag out of her waistband. In the back of the truck, John and Greg got out of their restraints (they had been legitimately locked in, but they also had voice authorization to open them with the truck's computer), then collected MAG-90s from the truck's arms box and opened the other hidden compartment.

Come on, of *course* there was a hidden compartment. This was a DCI truck with grenades mounted on the outside, you think the R&D crew wouldn't add a hidden central section that housed two (admittedly small-statured) people?

So as John and Greg opened the hatches, Carrie Walsh and another small-figured Special Branch woman pulled themselves out of an uncomfortably tangled state, drawing MAG-90s for themselves.

Each of them was wearing a regular Defense Command uniform, not Special Branch kit, but now they all hauled protected Special Branch vests out of the arms box and pulled them on. These were the vests that could stop an energy gun bolt — the ones Karen and I didn't have at the studio. At the very same time this was happening, we were still in our standoff, by the way.

Greg then grabbed an extra vest and MAG-90 for Haley, and without a word, the two Admirals popped the hatch and jumped out the back of the truck.

Carrie Walsh and her officer got out and then rounded the truck to its driver's cab, landing the craft on the pavement.

"Alright, so that worked…" John was quickly checking the power cell in his MAG-90 as he spoke. He wasn't accustomed to this new gun — he'd gotten past using major personal arms back in the days when the first model EP-5s were still front-line. That said, it's a user-friendly gun.

Greg was handier with his own gun, having checked its cell already, "Yes it did. Hopefully the rest of the plan will as well…"

He was walking towards the front door of the security house as he said the words, and now he stopped and dropped Haley's vest to the pavement, laying her own MAG-90 on the vest.

She'd gone inside.

John and Greg stood and waited, tapping feet and humming as the sounds of surprised yells and weapons fire erupted from the Security Center. It was only the size of a small house, really, and there were seven people left inside, including the Brigadier commanding the two Battalions that were in the compound.

Haley was vicious. I mean, you know how good Karen is with a mag? Haley is better. Haley's day job includes use of a mag, so she's necessarily better. She made Karen and me look like slow old folks (and I suppose compared to her we probably were, even then), rolling and diving and doing all sorts of wild shots to drop the army blockheads.

I can actually say that, of all the things the movies get wrong about this whole episode, the way Haley Briand can wield a gun is continually right. Or close, anyway — she's faster than most of the actors you see, but the movies slow down her shooting to make it more believable and easier to follow.

John and Greg stood outside and did the stereotypical (even comical) waiting sort of things.

"Nice weather," John said, looking skyward.

"Yeah, good day for golfing. We should do eighteen holes after we finish our meeting."

"You and the kids go, I think Anne and I'll go for a picnic."

"Presuming we're not on a gallows."

"Oh yeah, I mean if we've already got plans…"

A smiling Haley Briand stepped lightly out of the Security Center and stopped to collect the MAG-90 and vest Greg had brought for her, "All set, I tripped the silent alarm, and located the tunnel."

"Excellent, off we go then!" John got his MAG-90 into a comfortable position, then the two Admirals and the DCI officer went to see the Emperor.

CHAPTER TWENTY

'AUDIENCE' WITH THE EMPEROR

In these days, the Security Center and the Central Building of Government Palace were connected by a tunnel network, to allow for evacuation of the Emperor under dire circumstances. Some of these tunnels may or may not still be in service, I can't confirm or deny that for security reasons. But John, Greg and Haley were pacing through one of them, weapons raised and ready.

Back at the Security Center, Carrie Walsh and her officer were waiting to receive the blockheads who'd reply to the silent alarm. If you're wondering, *no*, the two battalions didn't know what had happened — Haley shot the Brigadier before he could warn them. This has been doubted in some histories of the event, but you can check her button-cam footage if you don't believe me.

So the first responders would be people thinking that maybe one of the prisoners had made a break for it, or that they were holding the Brigadier at gunpoint, or something like that. The hope was that this distraction would keep all eyes focused on the security house.

And so far the tunnel was empty, as promised.

"So, how much further do you think, Haley?" Greg was at the rear of the line of three, spending most of his time looking back towards the security house end of the dark corridor, in case they were being followed.

"Rough estimate… we're here."

The way she said it drew a smile from both John and Greg, and sure enough, they'd reached a hatch marked 'Main Building'. Of course, that meant the fun was just getting started, because the three of them — one superagent and two Admirals who hadn't so much as boarded a pirate ship in years — were about to go up against the entire household guard of the Emperor.

Not promising.

If you're wondering, the orbital photos didn't give any hint of where the tunnel came out in the Main Building. The deep pulse scans were able to see that a tunnel ran between the Security Center and the Main House (and tunnels connected all the buildings, in fact) but it couldn't be precise about where the tunnel hooked up with a given building.

So this was basically where everything could fall on its backside — they could arrive in the guard room of the Main House, with sixty blockheads to deal with (or surrender to).

But this was the fate of the Empire, so they had to try.

"Ready?" Haley took a quick breath, and with two short 'Yeps' from Greg and John, she keyed the hatch open.

In a cheap bid to build a little more suspense, I'll tell you that while they were doing all this exciting stuff, we were still standing in the studios of the *Geraldine Coilier Show*, in the same standoff. For half an hour by the time they opened that hatch, we were just *standing there.*

At one point, a producer leaned out of the control room and screamed, "Hey, Parliament has ended the inquiry and ordered Defense Command to DefCon Three! Fiora's back in charge!"

A wash of relief rolled over me when he yelled this, and I looked at the army Captain, "Come on now, surely that's enough for you to stand down and leave."

The neckless man shook his head, "Nope, the Parliament is your boss. And the Emperor can overturn that declaration any time he likes."

Clearly, the fool wasn't too adept at politics, but he still had many guns.

So the standoff continued.

Haley leapt through the opening hatch like a bloody cat, rolling up to one knee in a single fluid maneuver, and leveling her MAG-90 at the dark room.

John and Greg, much more distinguished (meaning older) weren't going to be doing any somersaults, so they just stepped through and quickly covered various angles.

There was no one there. No guard.

And indeed, there was nothing in the room except for a set of stairs — one of those metal spiral staircases that wrap around a pole and thus don't take up much floor space — and a hatch with a very small window in it. Haley quickly stepped over to the window and glanced through before whipping her head back.

"Guard Room!" she hissed, and John and Greg stepped hurriedly away from any line of sight that small window could offer.

We found out later that the opening of the hatch Haley had just dove through had caused a security alert. But the alert had to be routed through the Security Center, which was for all intents and purposes abandoned, so no one knew the three of them were there.

They didn't know that no one knew, though, so they were sweating rather anxiously. Well not Haley — she once informed me that sweating isn't in her nature, so I'll propagate that myth.

"Stairs, I think," John bobbed his head toward the narrow spiral staircase, and Haley and Greg nodded.

Haley fit easily onto the narrow clanking metal case, and she led the way up, covering the dark chamber it led to with her MAG-90. John and Greg followed with more difficulty, their broader bodies less well-suited to the very narrow stairs than the waifish superagent who'd preceded them.

"Clear... I've got an unmarked hatch!"

As John and Greg managed to untangle themselves from the stairs, Greg was the first to say it, "Well, no choice but to open it."

Haley nodded, waiting for both Admirals to get themselves into flanking positions.

"When you're ready," she said evenly, bringing the sight of her MAG-90 up to eye level.

John looked at Greg, and Greg took a deep breath.

Not just to build suspense, I want to pause for a minute and point out again how much of a risk these two great old heroes of the Empire were taking. They might be shot dead and die as traitors — there was no way for them to know what they were about to find.

"Let's go," John gave the final word and Haley opened the hatch.

To say they lucked out would be a pretty substantial understatement.

The Emperor, Luther Gregory III, was standing in his bathrobe, leaning over the bathroom counter and peering into his luxury bathroom's mirror, shaving, when the wall next to his towel rack popped open and a slim superspy launched herself through.

"Whhaaa!" may not sound like a distinguished cry for an Emperor to make as he dropped his razor and leapt back from the wall, but imagine what you'd say if your wall was flung open and people climbed out while you were freshening up.

John and Greg stepped through after Haley, and immediately the three of them lowered their MAG-90s.

The Emperor was wild-eyed with surprise, and his hands were up, "Don't hurt me!"

Yes, he said that. We have it on tape.

John frowned, "Farthest thing from our minds, Your Eminence. We have evidence that Dave Caldecott hasn't shown you. The Empire is facing an eminent, imminent threat!"

The Emperor, in his bathrobe, went to put on some new clothes.

Chapter Twenty-One

Oh Really, A Threat From Mars?

The Emperor sat at his desk in his chambers, his jaw set, watching on the main screen opposite him as *Cheetah* took a heavy beam in the wing. It seemed that the scene from our battle with Kitty Castillo's combined force was the most effective one — Wes Pellew's *Cheetah* was one of our newest, finest, best-skippered ships, so watching it take a solid hit woke people up.

"Commodore Barron thinks they're coming here next?" the Emperor asked quietly, looking from the screen to John, and the First Lord (still in tac gear with his MAG-90 dangling from its vest harness) nodded.

For those of you wondering, yes, the Emperor did already know the answer to that question. I don't know if he's a regular viewer of the *Geraldine Coilier Show*, but word had gotten to him. Why he didn't own up to that from the start, wait and see.

"Yes sir, and the timing couldn't be worse. With the inquiry ongoing we're in no position to–"

The door to the Emperor's chambers swung open behind John, a panicked aide rushing in, "Your Majesty! Defense Command personnel have taken the Security Center..."

Sliding to a stop, the aide found himself staring down the business end of a MAG-90 with a smiling Haley Briand behind it.

"Guards!" he yelped before the Emperor could raise a hand, but as the first blockheads rushed into the room, His Majesty thrust himself to his feet.

"Stand down, guards, immediately!"

The three blockheads who'd rushed into the room skidded to a halt, their weapons still aimed at Haley and Greg who were now standing shoulder to shoulder with MAG-90s leveled.

"I'm being briefed, get out!" the Emperor boomed in Imperial fashion.

The blockheads looked at each other and then slowly began to back away.

"Schneider," the Emperor glared at his aide. "First of all, knock. Second, order the guards not to attempt to retake the Security Center unless I expressly order it. Third, put a call into Dave Caldecott and ask him to report to the Palace immediately."

The aide nodded, mouth still hanging open in shock, and then he backed slowly away before turning and fleeing from the room.

"He was kinda cute..." Haley smiled, glancing at Greg.

Frowning, venerable Admiral Noyce shrugged, "You know, I really couldn't say."

"Your Majesty, it's essential we mobilize Defense Command, move to Defense Condition Three and end the inquiry," John persisted in cordial tones, and the Emperor cocked an eyebrow and sat.

"I suppose you were too busy breaking into my palace to hear, First Lord, but Ken

Barron went on the *Geraldine Coilier Show* and presented evidence to the viewing audience of just this. Parliament voted down the inquiry and reinstated you, *and* moved Defense Command to DefCon Three over twenty-five minutes ago."

John stood very still at those words. He'd just broken into the Emperor's palace, risking execution for treason and attempting an almost coup just to accomplish what Karen and I had pulled off by crashing the set of one of Earth's finest daytime programs.

Well, that was what ran through his head first.

The Emperor leaned back in his chair, adjusting his white jacket — he was wearing one of his all-white, silver-trim Emperor suits (instead of a bathrobe) — and eyed John closely, "You see, First Lord, I was just showering and shaving to make myself look presentable for a press conference in which I was going to veto those two moves. But now it seems I have a problem."

And that changed John's line of thinking rather abruptly.

"*Excuse me*, Highness? What the hell did you think you were going to do, exactly?"

The Emperor's eyes narrowed, but John didn't so much as think twice about his choice of words or tone. He was single-mindedly focusing on the defense of his Empire… and if the Emperor got in the way of said defense, John was going to do something about the Emperor.

Yes, that was more or less a treasonous thought, but in point of fact, if the Emperor was abandoning the well-being of the Empire for the sake of political gain, he was libel for impeachment and thus it might not be treason.

John's hand twitched towards the handle of his MAG-90, but the Emperor shook his head. By now both Greg and, importantly, Haley had turned to face the Emperor, so the dark-skinned man smiled ironically.

"Look, it's politics. I didn't think it was necessary for you to take over to defend the planet. Your behavior here proves well enough that you're a wreckless fool, John. But since you were able to mobilize Defense Command forces to get yourself in here, I'm going to bet your ships won't fight for Dave Caldecott."

The smug tone, somewhat unexpected in its snide quality, stung as it hit John.

"So I'll approve the overturn, in the interests of the defense of the realm. But Dave Caldecott's going to stay your Second Lord. And I'll have as much say in your operations as I like."

Now, I don't know about you, but when John later told me that he'd seen the Emperor, my first reaction, my *expectation*, was that His Majesty had been simply played by Caldecott, and that when the truth and the evidence were revealed, His Highness would have a good old-fashioned revelation, thanking us copiously for our efforts.

This smug son of a bitch wasn't quite living up to those expectations.

But at this stage, beggars couldn't afford to be choosers.

"I don't care about Dave Caldecott right now," John leaned forward and put one hand on the desk before him, letting the other rest on his MAG-90. "You order all the Imperial Army men back to bases. You take Dave with you as an advisor and you get back to your Warsaw Palace, or wherever you want. You let me and the *government* take care of our little problem. And you and me, we'll talk about our little disagreement here, later."

"I'll have you executed when this is done," the Emperor grinned.

"Don't you think, Your Majesty, that Dave Caldecott launching this inquiry at just the moment the Martians were poised to strike was a little convenient?" Haley asked the question in a sweet tone, and both Admirals glanced at her in surprise.

The Emperor looked up at the young superagent with his grin fading, "Excuse me?"

She stepped forward, then sat down on the far corner of his desk, "You see, I'll bet he came to you with all sorts of reports and stories about the incompetence of Defense Command, under these Admirals here. And he said that now was the perfect moment to clean house, Admiral Noyce having just defeated the Syndicate and so forth. Right?"

The Emperor stared at her, his smile gone and a look of suspicion creeping over his face. He didn't actually answer.

"And now the Martians happen to move just when he removes, or tries to remove, our front line of defense. You sure he's not after your job, Your Highness?"

Slightly taken aback, the Emperor glared at Haley, "He said there might be some risks to the Empire, but risks are just risks. And frankly, to get rid of you all, and your idiotic methods, I'd *risk* the Empire."

Whoops, what a thing to say.

"But maybe you're right. Maybe Caldecott was working for the Martians. God knows how that'd be sorted out, but yeah, he knew I hate you showboating idiots… he might well have tried to use that to hurt me…"

By which he surely meant 'hurt the Empire', right? Idiot that our Emperor was. Have I mentioned that he was an idiot yet? He was.

None of us to this day know just what the Emperor's grievances were with us — he didn't like showing off, probably. Thought we were darlings of celebrity, or that our popularity was dwarfing his…

I don't know, he's the commander-in-chief of the Imperial Army, maybe their idiocy rubbed off on him. Maybe he was a power-hungry, self-serving autocrat who hated us because we reinforced the system that existed — the system that kept executive power split between him and the Parliament (and that put the final word with the *Parliament*).

Whatever his reasons, anyway, we couldn't do much about them, for the time being. We were slightly more worried about the Martians coming.

"Order your troops back to bases, *now* Your Majesty. Get yourself to Warsaw and get in your bunker. If you want Dave Caldecott arrested, then when he shows up call my officers. Now, in the meantime, get a car down to the front steps to take us to the Security Center and then out of here. Understood?"

Hell *yeah*, that was John Fiora, First Lord of the Admiralty, being rather straightforward with the Emperor of the Empire he was sworn to defend.

The Emperor glared at him for a moment before hitting the intercom and giving the appropriate orders.

"You better hope the Martians come, John, or you and your Admiral and your pretty little girl here are going to get executed. And hell, you might get executed even if they do. Borrowed time now, John. Borrowed time."

John's eyes narrowed but he said nothing. Greg led the way and the two of them headed for the door. Hopping off the corner of the desk with an unusually jaunty smile, Haley stood at attention and saluted, "Pleased to have met you, Your Highness."

The Emperor stood up and smiled at her, "Now I couldn't execute something that looks like you. Better use attributes like yours for…"

You know, I'm not going to repeat what he said next, because it's rather unbecoming of anyone with a sense of personal dignity, let alone an Emperor.

Haley took it in stride, "Well, I think I'd prefer execution, Your Highness. Good day!"

She turned and raced out of the room after the Admirals. As she ran, she pulled her comm out of her pocket and checked the feed from the button cam she was wearing. Yes indeed, she had it all recorded in color.

"Your Majesty, I'm blushing," she said quietly to herself.

Our superagent is good.

She, John, Greg, Carrie Walsh and the other Special Branch officer pulled out of the palace a few minutes later.

CHAPTER TWENTY-TWO

WE WERE STILL STANDING OFF

Karen and I hadn't so much as taken a step for almost forty minutes, and I was getting rather irritable. The Parliament had done what we needed them to do, and that meant I should be able to get to Admiralty House so we could sit down and quickly plan our moves to deal with the Martians.

But I had an *idiot* of a blockhead in front of me, believing against all reason that somehow his precious Emperor could change the situation for him.

Then, by some wonderful providence, the Captain heard something in his earpiece. He reached up and pressed the small item deeper into his ear, frowning as he did.

"Alright," he said quietly in reply to whatever was said (that recording I *haven't* heard) and then he waved to his men, "Okay guys, listen up. We're heading back to base. Stand down."

Almost mechanically, the blockheads lowered their weapons and began to file towards the door behind the stage. The grannies hiding behind stage furniture threw things at them, but as the SF guards with Commander Khan and Charlie's Special Branch officers slowly lowered their mags, the Captain of the blockheads came over to me, weapon down.

"I just want to say, sir, I'm a *big* fan."

I was still holding my mag on this guy for some reason, though I elected to lower it at that moment, "Uhm. Thanks. Glad we didn't have to kill each other."

"Yeah, that'd have been a *big* downer for me."

This is all on live vid, remember. There are recordings if you don't believe that it happened. And then he looked at Karen.

"And Captain, you're *hot*. He's lucky to have you around."

The blockhead gave a 'knowing wink', implying something that he shouldn't have.

Karen stared at him, but she *didn't* lower her mag, "Leave, Captain."

The audience, their heads poking up over the backs of their seats, 'Ooooohed.'

The blockhead went on his way, and I holstered my mag and glanced at Karen, "Um. Let's leave."

For the first time since we got to the studios, she smiled, and then I waved Charlie over.

Major Peters, in his typical style, paced casually towards us, keying on the safeties of his MAG-90 as he came. Arriving next to Karen and me, he looked up with a grin, "So, you a fan of the *Geraldine Coilier Show?*"

Karen gave him one of her 'not-funny' smiles, and I grinned, "I'll be a fan of this episode. The rest... well, I have strange vid tastes. Liked the part today where the cavalry showed up though..."

Charlie grinned, "I swear, if there's a day I don't show up to save your ass... well..."

you won't be in a good way after it."

We all just stood there after that comment. Not that what he was saying wasn't true — Charlie Peters had, by this time, saved my life on many occasions, and kept my life out of danger many more. If he ever stopped doing that sort of work, I'd be due in for a meeting with the grim reaper.

No, it wasn't what he said, just the lack of a witty punch to the line.

"That was pretty flat, wasn't it?" he frowned after a moment's silence.

"Yeah. Not snappy enough."

"Indeed… hmm… Well, you better book a dinner table at the reaper's favorite restaurant for the day I quit," he put out the follow-up with a thoughtful frown. "How's that?"

I smiled, "A little over thought, but it'll be the one they'll use in the movies. Snappy!"

Charlie nodded, "Glad to keep the repartee standards up."

As you might have noticed, every last movie about this event has skipped straight to the dinner with the reaper remark, and that's a pet peeve for me and Charlie both. It takes *work* to sound witty and carefree after riding out that sort of intense situation. It's not like a movie where you can just use the take that works, sometimes you say something that isn't… well… *sharp*.

And the surprising thing is sometimes we care if something doesn't sound good. We like to keep up a healthy repartee — like dark humor and cavalier actions, it's one of the things that keeps us going out at the Belt. But *anyway*, I'm sure you care less about why we cared about sounding witty and are wondering about the coup and the impending Martian attack.

"So, we'll head over to the capital and catch up with Greg and John," Karen pushed past our irrelevant banter and got on to the important matters.

"Sounds like a plan. I'll get my team back up to *Wolf*, I imagine the fleet will be rallying in orbit soon enough."

I nodded, "Done. Tell Matt we'll be up there as soon as we can be."

Charlie nodded, then turned away and started throwing some of those tactical hand gestures to his officers, pointing them towards the doors.

One question my publisher actually asked me about this part is why hadn't Karen and I asked Charlie "why the devil" he was on Earth. Well, simple: we'd put it together. Knowing Matt and Charlie both, we didn't need to ask him to know that Matt had let us go only with a secret proviso. Besides, was this really the time to waste on irrelevant conversation?

No comments about trying to be witty or sharp, please.

I waved to Commander Khan and she stepped over quickly as Charlie was leaving, "Sir?"

I nodded to her with a smile, "Thanks for showing up, Commander. My compliments to your Captain as well. I'll be sending more proper thanks later, when we're out of the woods."

Commander Khan smiled and nodded, then looked between Karen and me, "Is it really as bad as you've said?"

That question surprised me slightly. Think of the implications — an officer not totally convinced that Karen and I were telling the truth was willing to put her neck on the line in a near-treasonous standoff with the Imperial Army...

Karen, thankfully, wasn't going to be surprised into silence by such an innocent question, "It's bad, indeed. You might want to tell your Captain that civil defense could become a priority very quickly."

Khan nodded, "Very good, ma'am. If that's all..."

Karen bobbed her head, at last sliding her mag into its holster, "Dismissed, and thanks again."

Commander Khan and her SF Guards filed off the stage, and Karen and I followed at the end of their column.

"How long do you think we have?" Karen asked quietly as we walked.

I was staring straight ahead, not exactly focusing on anything as I did, and I slowly shook my head at the question.

"I don't know, I half believed the Martians would be here when we arrived. So... well... soon. Soon or they're not coming."

Karen started to nod but then stopped, her gaze jerking straight ahead, "Wait, if they don't show up, the Empire's saved... but we're...?"

"We're going into exile. Or the gallows."

Karen's brow had been creasing, but at my words her expression neutralized, "So we have a conflict of interest."

"We seem to," I nodded.

We walked to our fighters.

The crowd applauded our departure, and the show went on.

CHAPTER TWENTY-THREE
DON'T FORGET MARLENE!

As the chapter title implies, that four- or five-hour diversion on Earth wasn't the only thing going on that morning. Admiral Marlene Stoll and *Sorceress* were getting closer and closer to Earth local space as she continued falling back ahead of the Martians, and things weren't looking spectacular.

Sorceress had run out of those improvised mines about ten hours short of Earth, and after expending another torpedo, Marlene had been forced to order a full-thrust fallback. Her great (and thankfully fast) battleship was running, four pods full, from a twenty-one ship Martian fleet.

"ETA ninety minutes. Still no sign of comm ships, ma'am."

Marlene was standing, still ever-stoic, on *Sorceress'* bridge, with her hands linked behind her back and a serious stare taking in the situation on the main vid screen. All that she could think about at that moment was the prospect of finding Earth defenseless, not ready for a fight.

Now, she didn't know that *Clever*, and its warning to Earth about the impending attack, had been destroyed in transit… she just had the worrying feeling that the corvette might not have arrived in the system yet… or that it hadn't been believed… or that it had met with misfortune.

Hey, they don't call Marlene Stoll the Sorceress for nothing. She has *amazing* instincts that way.

Anyway, at a hair-raising-for-a-battleship 192 kps, *Sorceress* was running for Earth.

Meanwhile, in Earth local space, *Wolf* and *Tiger* were running towards Marlene, going full drives ahead in an arc extending out towards the Venus approaches. The two *Predator*-class frigates weren't being pursued now by Parks-Dawes' own ships — that stern chase had been ended as soon as Parliament had voted down the inquiry.

So Matt was in the clear… right?

Well, yes, but look at it this way: if *Wolf* had been chased by a couple of frigates, those frigates would have turned into backup when the Martians were spotted. Instead it was just *Wolf*, with *Tiger* nearby and *Panther* and *Jaguar* out on a vector more towards the direct Mars-Mercury approaches. If worse came to worst, it'd be just those four frigates together, over an hour away from the support of the Home Fleet.

That wasn't good.

But Matt didn't know what was coming at him. Of course he, like Karen and I, had an idea the Martians must be sending something pretty hefty towards Earth, but he had no idea precisely what 'hefty' would translate into. That was why he was out there with Shannon Hunter, cruising far away from Earth: he was taking *Wolf* out to be a picket ship.

"Matt… I've got… a *battleship*. Coming into extreme passive range, its drive signature is *big* — running at 192 or so," Jim Hannigan was leaning over the back of the chair of one of his operators. "No IFF yet."

Matt has an imposing way of standing on the command deck. He's a tall, broad dark-skinned fellow with a rather regal air — when he wants a regal air — so him with folded arms and a stern frown is about as impressive as it gets.

Now he turned that frown on Jim Hannigan, "Keep me apprised, and send to Shannon and Earth that we've got something coming in fast."

"Aye," Jim nodded and began giving quiet orders to his techs, and Matt turned towards the helm section.

"Erica, angle us towards the incoming ship, stand by to reverse drives," Matt's tone was even, and Lieutenant Commander Martin nodded in turn.

Wolf redirected itself towards the incoming unknown ship, messages flying from its signal array and persistent sensor pulses firing out towards the newcomer.

"Got a frigate coming into sensor range on scope!"

Marlene's eyes darted to the section of the main screen that would hold the sight of a frigate coming out from Earth, and sure enough, an icon slowly glowed to life.

"No IFF tags yet, but we'll be in long-range comm range in about forty seconds."

That was good news, and Marlene told me later that after that realization, at least one of the seventeen knots in her stomach was undone. That still (doing my math here) left sixteen knots.

What could she assume from seeing a frigate over an hour out of Earth space? Did it mean that *Clever* had arrived at Earth and provided warning? Did it mean a second Martian force had gotten around her and hit Earth already? Was the ship just on maneuvers?

Clearly, there were many different possibilities, and like all fleet officers, Marlene was compelled to run through all of them in seconds, coming up with alternative ways to handle things she hadn't already thought of, and applying solutions she'd thought of in her many hours of pondering to that moment.

Ours is a job of persistent, hidden panic.

"Ready to record a burst message," *Sorceress'* Sensors and Communications Officer interrupted Marlene's thoughts, and she quickly said her piece.

"Signal coming in… and IFF too…" Jim Hannigan stood up and looked at Matt with some surprise. "It's *Sorceress*, message going to screen two now."

Matt nodded and turned to the screens at the front of the bridge, just in time to see a *Wolf*Net buffering screen turn into Marlene Stoll's sober gaze, "To incoming frigate, we have twenty-one Martian ships inbound, target Earth. Form up with us as possible, and pass on warning to the Admiralty as soon as you have the range. Admiral Stoll out."

Well, that answered the 'how many' question.

Matt Baxter took a single deep breath — not a huffed sigh or anything, just a single, calm long breath — and looked again to Jim, "Send that on to Admiralty House and to Shannon. Let's get her frigates together with us and form up on *Sorceress*. Ship to full battle stations."

Klaxons kicked in immediately, Lieutenant Stranks keying them from the console he was occupying at operations.

"Stand by to return a message," Matt turned to the main screen as he said the words, and after another short pause Jim Hannigan nodded.

"Recording."

Matt nodded again, "Admiral Stoll, this is Commander Matt Baxter, in *Wolf*. Commodore Barron and Captain McMaster have gone down to Earth to end an inquiry that Caldecott was using to cripple the Admiralty, and we don't have word on how that's going. We've passed your warning on to Admiralty House, we will form on *Sorceress*. Commodore Hunter and *Panther, Jaguar, Tiger* are out here as well. We've sent to them to join our formation as soon as possible. I can't speak to the readiness of any other ships. See you on Battlelink."

Matt looked to Jim and nodded, and Hannigan in turn nodded to the appropriate technician. The message was cut and sent out to *Sorceress*.

Things were coming together quickly out there, just over an hour from Earth.

They were about to get much, much worse.

CHAPTER TWENTY-FOUR
BIG OLD HAPPY REUNION

Admiralty House was reasonably close to Defense Command Security HQ in the capital, and that wasn't too long a haul for our Starlights. With a short sub-orbital hop, we were over the Capital Island in barely twenty minutes, and we were just coming down to cruising altitude when a comm chirped through my helmet.

"Ken, this is Charlie. We're not going to be going back to *Wolf*."

I frowned, "Why not?"

"Um, Matt's over an hour out on picket duty."

See, in the real world, we overlook or *forget* details like that sometimes.

"Oh. Well. Um… come on down to the capital then. Karen and I are heading for Admiralty House, you can meet up with us there."

There was a pause on the line and then a short, "Sure."

The comm cut.

Steadying against some turbulence, I smiled to myself. I mean, sure, the world was about to come under attack, but funny little things like that still happened. I say funny because if, then or now, I let myself be frustrated by trivial little complications, I'd go mad.

Part of our job really is just making light of whatever we can afford to make light of — if we don't, there are snapping sounds, raving, screaming, drooling, and straight jackets.

"Foggy today," Karen's voice cut across the comm between our fighters as we dove below cloud cover.

She was right, the fog was thick and the winds were up — it was a lovely day on the Atlantic. Made me homesick, really. It also required a bit more focus as we cruised over the Cabot Strait — the waterway separating the Capital Island from the mainland of North America — at only mach two. Civilian and government air traffic over this island was common enough, and not all aircraft had the same advanced navigation sensors our Starlights boasted. We could see through this soup, or at least our sensors could, but some poor fellow in an old plane might get caught in our slipstreams.

"Homesick yet?" I smiled as I keyed the range on my sensor panel up to maximum. There was a chuckle on the other end of the comm.

"Very. I bet it'll be a lovely day when we get to town, too."

Just as she said it, we pushed out of the fog bank and found ourselves hurtling through a sunny day over the jagged forest island that had been adopted as the capital of the Empire. I'd actually been born on this island, which many people take (wrongly, I say) as some sort of sign that I was meant to rule the Empire or something. Karen was born just on the other side of the Cabot Strait from here, so we'd actually come through the same Defense Command Academy in our younger days.

Actually, that's where we'd first met, oh so long ago…

Yes, nostalgia was beginning to set in as we dropped lower, out of the civilian traffic lanes, and began cruising up and down over the undulations in the forest.

"Wolfstar 825, Wolfstar 826, this is Admiralty House traffic control, reading you inbound. Maintain course, we've cleared field two for you."

The interruption was a good one — my nostalgia ceased, though my smile broadened, "Roger that Admiralty Control, you want us to buzz the street and do a victory roll?"

"We always say no, Commodore Barron. You never care."

You might think that a cheeky traffic controller is a bad thing, and I've actually been asked if, when that comment is played out in movies, it's a fake add-on. Again, it's not: a sense of humor and good relations between pilots and air traffic control is never a bad thing, so long as it doesn't impede efficiency.

"Ladies first," I glanced out the side of my cockpit and bobbed my head at Karen. She gave a thumbs up back, then yanked back her throttle and surged forward.

Over the next crease in the land, Terra Nova appeared, and Karen surged down low towards the city's open street that led right down to the harbor and Admiralty House. Quickly cutting her speed as she came over the main street, she made sure she created more than enough noise to get everyone looking skyward, then threw her plane into a graceful roll before dropping her landing gear and descending behind the great old Admiralty House building.

I followed doing the same thing, but of course, Karen's move had been far more graceful.

John and Greg were in the Admiralty House C&C when we arrived. It's strange, I hadn't been there for over a year, and yet when I walked in the front door and waved to Gerald and Betty — the civilian receptionists who'd been working the entry desk since I was a cadet, and who probably have higher security clearance than I do — I didn't even stop to take in the pleasant atmosphere of the building.

I should explain that: Admiralty House has a certain atmosphere that makes it the most welcoming place for Naval officers (well, good ones anyway).

The fact that Dave Caldecott and his officers usually stayed out was a help.

Now, Karen and I waved to Gerald and Betty and stepped quickly to the corridor on the right, taking the first set of stairs on the left down to the bank of elevators that carried people through almost a hundred meters of rock into the C&C bunker.

I should admit this: that's not actually the way down to C&C, but I'm hardly going to betray the blueprints of Admiralty House, now am I?

In any case, it was a quick elevator ride with a stiff-lipped SF Guard working the buttons, and then Karen and I stepped out of the lift into the core of Imperial Defense.

The C&C bunker is big, bright, and covered with wall-to-wall vid screens. It makes the bridge of a battleship look spartan, which is saying something. There were probably eighty techs and junior officers moving around, talking in low voices, handing out clipboards and all the rest of the things you see in movies that make military rooms look busy. Yes, I am in fact too lazy (and too bound to secrecy) to explain it all.

"Still no readings on the Martian force, sir, but we have *Sorceress*' scans up on the screen now."

Those words were called across the room by the Captain of Earth Sensors and Communications Intelligence, one Ronald Davis. They didn't make sense to me at the moment — Martian force? *Sorceress?* I still didn't know any of what Marlene had been up to.

For now, though, I glanced at Karen, and with a rather elegant shrug from her, we proceeded forward from the elevator bank, our eyes scanning the busy bunker for the figures of our Admirals...

"Ken!" John was waving from a map table in the middle of the room and Karen and I headed his way.

As we arrived at that table — basically a horizontal vid screen built into a table top — John reached across to us with an extended hand, "Thank God for you!"

"Hey, I didn't infiltrate any palaces and convince any Emperors to not veto things," I smiled, taking his hand.

John grinned, "It was fun to be tactical, but more credit goes to Haley Briand than to Greg and me."

Just as he said it, Greg's hand landed on Karen's shoulder, and she turned with a smile to shake the Admiral's other hand, "Good to see you again!"

Greg, of course, had until recently been the Admiral of the Belt Squadron — right up to the Battle of Deep Black and the weeks of fallout after. We'd all fought together for years, and we knew each other all too well.

Smiling, Greg shook Karen's hand and then mine, "I hear you two got the air time this morning. John and I were left to creeping through tunnels."

Karen shrugged, "You weren't victimized by a crowd of daytime vid viewers though."

With a laugh, Greg nodded, "I think the chance of being shot for breaking into an Emperor's bathroom was probably less fearsome."

We chuckled and nodded, and then with the requisite (and yet all too brief) reunion babble out of the way, our eyes dropped back to the table we were standing around.

"Oh, good grief."

Yeah, I said that. Not so snappy or cool, eh? Sorry, sometimes it just comes out like that.

"I know..." John's smile faded out of necessity. "We just got these in from *Sorceress*. Apparently Marlene ran into a Martian advance scout on her way out to Venus last week, and she decided to bring out *Sorceress* and *Warlock* with a couple of escorts to make sure nothing was brewing."

Greg nodded, leaning forward and pointing to the Martian fleet, "She's destroyed or disabled several of their ships with torpedoes and lasers, but that's still twenty-one. And no carriers, all conventional warships."

I nodded slowly, staring at the screen and the scan readouts for long seconds. It was a great, *great* thing that these ships hadn't arrived any earlier, or we'd have been smashed without recourse. Even so, the situation wasn't spectacular. The Home Fleet, between its Heavy and Light Squadrons, had twenty-eight ships, and with *Wolf* around we now had twenty-nine, and Marlene made thirty. People say "oh, well, clearly we were fine, then!" That's just not the case.

The Home Fleet was, first of all, not fully mobilized, nor was it expecting battle. Worse, and what people often don't seem to realize, is the fact that taking any severe losses to the Home Fleet — the Fleet that is the strategic reserve for the Empire — would cripple our war effort, even if losses were under ten percent. Everyone likes to think of the glorious "100%" annihilation of an enemy force as the only victory you can get, but even at our recent Battle of Belt Two — which had gone very well for us indeed — total-kill wasn't the outcome.

There were also practical concentration problems: the Heavy Squadron was almost an hour out from Earth in the *opposite direction*, meaning it was two hours or so from where *Sorceress* was coming in. That meant the sixteen ships of the Light Squadron were the logical first responders — they'd be the ships to go out and support *Sorceress*, *Wolf*, *Panther*, *Jaguar* and *Tiger* as they fell back.

So, you say, that's great: sixteen ships plus five equals twenty-one! We'd be sending out as many ships as we'd be facing! Er... *no*. I'll explain in a minute, because John's next comment helps.

"Parks-Dawes, despite his affiliations, listened to Commander Baxter's warning, Ken, so the Light Squadron is on alert. He's just commed us requesting authorization to go out to support *Sorceress*."

Greg frowned at that prospect, "Do you think that's wise?"

Here's the problem they (and Karen and I) were thinking of: basically, the Light Squadron is, as the name suggests, quite light. Exact disposition of the force was as follows: *Ark Royal* (supercarrier, tough ship); *Yorktown*, *Hornet*, *Essex* (carriers, very fragile); *Indomitable*, *Invincible* (battlecruisers — the same size as battleships but with no armor protection so they can be faster); *Hawk*, *Eagle*, *Shark*, *Falcon* (*Predator*-class frigates); *Witty*, *Charisma*, *Virtue*, *Droll*, *Charm*, *Pride* (*Noble*-class corvettes like *Friendly* or Mark Gunney's *Honesty*). Total sixteen ships, and have a look, not a *single* battleship.

Ark Royal could put out approximately as much fire as a battleship, and take that much punishment, but *Indomitable* and *Invincible*, despite their names, were glass-jawed — they could shoot as many guns off as a battleship, but a solid hit that would bounce off a battleship would blow them apart.

You can appreciate our dilemma, then, in sending a force built around battlecruisers, carriers and *frigates* against twenty-one Martian ships, of which nine appeared to be battleships. It's like sending gymnasts out to play defense in an American football game.

Splat.

"Well... I don't want them to get all the way here unopposed. If we call in the Heavy Squadron now, they can be in position over Earth in an hour, you can join them, and you can go out and finish the Martians off..." John was looking at Greg as he spoke, and with a slow sigh Greg nodded.

Here's the way the thinking goes: you're always — *always* — better off stopping an enemy force short of a planet. The amount of damage they can do to a planet is immense, if they can get into range, so there's no utility in hiding under the guns of orbital stations unless you have no choice.

That's why we have the Defense Command Navy. So of course we're going to go out and meet them, and while it would be much better for the Light Squadron to wait for the

Heavy Squadron and for both to go out together, there was no time for that.

The Light Squadron would have to do what it could to slow the Martians down, and then Greg would finish them off. That was the plan.

"Karen and I can fly out with Parks-Dawes and rendezvous with *Wolf* out there," I pointed to the space between Earth and *Sorceress*, and John and Greg both quickly looked at us.

"Your planes are being fueled up right now," John nodded. "Take command of all Parks-Dawes' frigates, I don't care who's senior. Shannon has the other three?"

Greg nodded, "They're from the Heavy Squadron."

John looked back at the screen and nodded slowly, "Alright, you two work together — *Wolf* can command the four Light Squadron frigates, Shannon keeps hers. Do what you can... Greg, you get back to *Warspite*. Let's order Parks-Dawes out and the Heavy Squadron in."

If you had a hard time following everything that John just said, don't worry, you'll get used to volleys of orders. I won't stop to explain it all right now — let's just get moving.

"Sounds good. Parks-Dawes stays in command of his ships then," I looked up at John, and he nodded.

"Yeah. Yeah they've been his ships the whole time, and he did have the presence of mind to listen to Matt's warning. We'll give him a chance... but actually, if you think you need to, you can tell him I gave operational command to Marlene. I'll beam an order to your fighter saying that... use it if you need it."

I nodded again, "Done."

There was a pregnant pause, the four of us standing around the map table in still somewhat stunned disbelief. We were about to accept an attack on Earth — the first serious attack on our home planet, with the exception of the Syndicate raid.

The Martians had declared war against us. We'd nearly thrown a coup.

What a day.

I looked at Karen, and thank God, she smiled, "Ready then?"

With a short nod, I smiled back, "I am. Gentleman, good luck to you!"

I extended my hand to John, then Greg, and Karen did the same. We left.

Apparently, after we left, John looked at Greg and grinned, "You hear what they were getting asked on that lovely show this morning?"

Greg chuckled, "We're all so morally out of step with popular culture."

"Yes, we are. Alright, I guess we need to find you a ship to take you out to meet *Warspite*... and Admiral Michaels might not like being relieved. Do we have any Special Branch assault shuttles on the island?"

Karen and I were going up one elevator when John asked the question, and sure enough, the doors of another elevator opened just at that moment, and Charlie Peters stepped out, "Anyone seen Commodore Barron?"

Greg looked back at the question, smiled as he saw Major Peters — another Belt Squadron veteran he knew quite well — and smiled.

"I think we might just."

They waved Charlie over and let him know he was about to be borrowed by the Admiralty for a mission.

CHAPTER TWENTY-FIVE

RUNNING TOWARDS A FIGHT

"Wolfstar 826, this is communications for *Ark Royal.* I have Admiral Parks-Dawes for you."

Karen and I had climbed off the Admiralty field in our freshly fueled planes, pointed the noses upward, and thrown open the throttles. We broke orbit within six minutes, and were cruising with throttles open to maximum cruising speed out towards a rendezvous with *Wolf.*

And right now, we were passing the Light Squadron, as its ships turned around and began firing up their drives to follow our intercept course. I'd hoped Parks-Dawes would ignore us, as I really didn't want deal with a Caldecott person right then, but sure enough…

"Wolfstar 826, roger that. Put him through."

There was a pause — just long enough for me to look sideways at Karen and for her to give an exaggerated shrug from her plane — and then the voice of Admiral Parks-Dawes pitched in.

"Commodore Barron, have orders from Admiralty here. I understand you'll be taking over my frigates?"

The tone was actually pretty neutral — not surly or petulant, as I'd almost expected it to be. I didn't know George Parks-Dawes that well you see, but he was one of the Caldecott circle, so I had certain expectations.

"Yes sir, that's what's been ordered."

"I see… Commodore, our training to date has produced formations that rely on the close integration of my frigates with my battlecruisers. We're much more effective together than apart…"

Now, I'll admit I should have thought of this back at Admiralty House. John and Greg and Karen too. Here again, I suppose, is proof that we're not all-mighty and all-seeing (we're generally 'mostly-mighty' and 'mostly-seeing', as Karen once put it to me). Parks-Dawes was right, his squadron would probably be much more effective intact than split to merry hell by me.

Now, in my defense, and everybody else's, for that matter, this was the wrong day to try to get us to trust a Caldecott circle officer on the first go. I mean, after we nearly threw a coup to get rid of that idiot's inquiry, it wasn't so natural to, in the bunker at Admiralty House, just simply believe that Parks-Dawes would be fit to command all the ships he had in his squadron.

Hardly a fair or frankly *logical* lack of trust, but there it was. So now I decided to remedy it.

"Alright, Admiral, I'll leave them with you for the moment. If things look like they're getting out of hand I'll take command of them, but if your ships are used to being integrated, now's not the time to change their routine."

There was a short pause and then a genuinely appreciative tone in the reply, "Thank you Commodore. Good hunting!"

Hunting with what? I just gave up four frigates. That was actually the thought I remember running through my head, foolish as it sounds.

"And to you, Admiral. Good luck."

The comm cut out, and I glanced back through my canopy at Karen, "So, let's hope all the maneuvers he's been doing have… well… been good."

Karen bobbed her head, "We'll find out with a bang if they weren't."

I nodded in reply, and the tension began to tug at my muscles. This was going to be much, much worse than Belt Two.

"Sorry about the rough ride, Admiral. We're not really used to Flag Officer passengers," Charlie Peters made his apology as he sat down in the seat next to Greg, but of course Greg Noyce just smiled and shook his head.

"I used to fly F-174s, remember. This is a magic carpet next to a Sunburst."

Charlie grinned and nodded, "So I've heard."

They were both in *Wolf's* assault shuttle, racing away from Earth in the opposite direction from Karen and me. The Heavy Squadron had been ordered to rally at Earth (with the exception of the frigates already out with *Wolf* and *Sorceress*), so the idea was that *Wolf's* shuttle would meet *Warspite* (the Heavy Squadron flagship) about halfway to Earth, giving Greg at least half an hour to get aboard and to undo any chaos caused by the temporary command of Admiral Michaels.

I don't know if half an hour sounds like a lot of time, but it really, *really* isn't.

Actually, let me refine that. It's a very long time indeed, if you're waiting while your small craft or fighter cruises to a rendezvous. Once you're aboard a warship that isn't ready for a fight but is going to be in one… well, then half an hour of preparation time seems like no time at all.

When they got to *Warspite*, things weren't going to be fun.

But they were flying that way, nonetheless.

Marlene's stare remained fixed on the screens before her. Someone actually asked me once (and I don't know why they asked *me* this) whether Marlene really stood and stared so stoically in those minutes while the squadrons were all moving — if she didn't have a nervous twitch or anything of that sort.

Since I wasn't there, I can't confirm this with impunity, but my understanding is no, in fact she did *not* have a twitch or anything of the sort. She stood and stared, rather intensely, and her mind clocked through tactical scenarios like a machine.

I don't think some people fully understand that this is why she's known as the *Sorceress*. She's intense, and she makes things happen that, according to the normal rules, just can't happen.

And today we'd need that ability in large, unsubtle doses.

"The Light Squadron seems to be coming out now, ma'am."

That wasn't actually someone reporting sensor readouts from *Sorceress'* bridge, but

Matt Baxter from *Wolf* over the Battlelink.

"Well that's something… any sign of the Heavy Squadron?"

Matt looked off screen for a moment at Jim Hannigan, then was forced to shake his head, "Nothing in range. But ma'am, when we were on our way in, the Heavy Squadron was under Admiral Michaels, and it was an hour in the other direction. They may not be able to reach us in time."

Marlene's gaze shifted back to the main screen, "Really. So that gives us one battleship, *mine*, a handful of carriers, a couple of battlecruisers that I'd gladly trade for a good sandwich, eight frigates and a half-dozen corvettes to try to stop a battleship-heavy fleet with?"

As she finished her list, her eyes darted back to Matt on the screen, and with a very thin smile, the Briton nodded, "Bet you'd give your pension to have your squadron with you just about now."

Marlene smiled, "Well I wouldn't give *my* pension for anything, but if you're offering yours."

Matt grinned, "I'm sorry, signal breakup, didn't catch that bit, Admiral."

Nothing interesting happened in the next half hour. It's eerie the way these things go — the waiting is murder. You almost start wishing the enemy could develop teleportation beams or some such thing, just so that you could get into action sooner… but they don't. You sit (or stand) and wait, watching the clock, wondering if everything everywhere is going to plan or not. Wondering if you don't know something, or if the enemy doesn't…

And at the end of half an hour, you're really glad to hear your own ship's LSO in your headset.

"Wolfstar 825, Wolfstar 826, welcome back. We're going to have to do this at high speed, so be ready for it."

"Roger that, give us the line LSO," Karen's smooth tone floated through the comm, and we both watched on our HUDs as *Wolf* drew closer at 192 kps.

This landing would indeed be tricky; *Wolf*, now in formation with both *Sorceress* and *Panther*, was running at close to full speed — a speed that Starlights could match and *slightly* exceed, but only under afterburners.

Karen and I were only very slightly ahead of the Light Squadron, so soon *Wolf* would be decelerating to form up with Parks-Dawes' force, but neither Karen nor I wanted to wait that long… so we'd have to do an afterburner landing.

It's often been suggested that Karen and I are exceptional pilots. Karen is, I'm not. I'm good, but I'm not some sort of uber-pilot. So for Karen, this'd be easy, surely enough. For me… well, you know me, I made it my business to do stupid, low-percentage things.

And it hadn't killed me yet — none of the stupid things I did killed me, because (as you've no doubt noticed) I happen to be writing this.

But it was going to be tricky.

"Approach on the 1-1-5, Wolfstar 825. Wolfstar 826, you get the 1-1-9."

In simple speak, that meant we were coming in on slightly different approach angles — we'd actually be angled in differently, one ahead of the other. I know it sounds complicated, but it works.

A grey dot out in space slowly began to grow through my canopy, and then two more, smaller dots appeared flanking it. My HUD told me *Wolf* was the smaller dot on my left — *Sorceress*, obviously, was the big one.

Within seconds, though, they weren't just dots. At the closing speeds Karen and I were using, the distance between our planes and *Wolf* were being eaten up at around 400 kps. That's *very* fast.

"Turning over and counter-accelerating, 1-5-0 kps," I said as soon as my HUD prompted me. I pulled back on the flight controls, and the plane turned over 180 degrees, the engines cutting power. Karen did the same.

Now, what was happening was basically this: Karen and I were now pointing in the same direction as *Wolf*, and moving slower. We'd up-throttle to keep up with the ship as it approached us, and as it got just ahead, we'd kick in the burners, climb to an obscene 206 kps, and enter the flight bay on the port side.

Sound daredevil? That's why nobody in peacetime really ever tries it — it's *nuts*.

But, it wasn't peacetime... so we did it.

Come to think of it, there's really no reason for me to describe it all again — Karen landed first, and I followed closely after, albeit with a much rougher landing overall. Like I said, Karen's the star pilot, I just know how not to kill myself in a plane.

We were on our ship, though, so as our planes were taxied to their deck slots by the deck carts, we were both popping our canopies and starting to climb out.

I actually jumped down from the canopy and landed wobbily on the deck before they wheeled over a ladder for me. Tweaked my knee too, dammit. So much for haste. Karen sensibly waited for her ladder, and then we headed for the bridge — she walking smoothly, me hobbling slightly and cursing my stupidity.

Wolf was soon to be in one of the biggest fights in Imperial history.

Chapter Twenty-Six

Here We Go

Karen and I went straight to the bridge, not even stopping to change out of our flight suits. Matt smiled at both of us as we arrived, and I put on a look of mock sternness as he passed me on his way back to his usual post at Operations.

"We'll be chatting about going behind my back later, my dear Matthew," Karen said in a surprisingly matronly fashion, and he chuckled.

I got to the front of my bridge — the place I really wanted to be at a time like this — in time to see Battlelink flash to life for Admiral Parks-Dawes and his three Commodores of the Light Squadron. Shannon was already up on screen three, Marlene on screen one.

"Marlene, hear you're saving the Empire again," I grinned as I came to a stop and folded my arms. "Like, does that ever get old?"

Marlene's eyes flicked up from off screen and she smiled, "Did you just ask me if I'm getting old?"

"Said nothing of the sort!" I protested with a smile. "Now, you've brought twenty-one ships to play. We tangled with a small Martian squadron under Kitty Castillo last week, cleaned their clocks, but they were only backed by pirates. Suggest we start by hitting them with torpedoes."

Parks-Dawes, a little uncomfortable with the familiar humor Marlene and I shared as members of the Fiora ring, picked his moment to jump in, "We could send out quite a spread from all ships. Eight frigates with one each–"

Marlene, not privy to all that had already gone on at Earth (and thus not necessarily inclined to be friendly to Parks-Dawes, a known Caldecott circle officer) frowned now at the Admiral, "Well I've used up my torpedoes and a bunch of makeshift mines, I'm afraid. They're getting quite good at shooting them down."

"Still, my squadron can stand off and fire a total salvo of… fourteen, in one shot. That might overwhelm their defenses."

Marlene cocked an eyebrow, "Be my guest, but you're only going to have about three minutes before they're on top of us. My scans say they're accelerating."

Parks-Dawes looked slightly miffed by Marlene's tone, but he simply looked away from his screen and gave some orders, then looked back, "All Light Squadron ships, deployment pattern beta. Launch torpedoes in sixty seconds. Launch combat patrol, and stand by all bombers with anti-ship loads."

I'll interrupt with a little more explanation here: carriers didn't just carry Starlights, they also carried the F-288 Sunbomber, a dual-pilot craft that was painfully slow, and which carried a 'powerful' payload of X-14 Apocalypse missiles. They were supposed to give the carriers the ability to wipe out squadrons of enemy ships. Unfortunately, in tests and exercises, the bombers seldom got to their targets, and the X-14s proved no more effective than the X-9s carried by Starlights.

However, Parks-Dawes was working with what he had. And who knew, maybe he'd figured out a way to make his planes and bombers count...

"If it suits you, Admiral, I won't get in the way of your squadron operations," Marlene's words were curt. "Ken, Shannon, if your frigates join *Sorceress* in formation, we can form a second combat group to your first."

She really wasn't giving Parks-Dawes much of a choice; she'd take the ships that were loyal to the Fiora ring, he could have his ships, and we'd work together.

So Parks-Dawes nodded, "Very good. Target selection prospects?"

The Martians were coming up on *Wolf's* main screen now — not just their icons from the long range sensors, but better lidar silhouettes that came as they rapidly closed range on us. All the information that we had on their fleet composition — which I will admit wasn't all that much — was run against these lidar findings.

"We need to target their battleships first and foremost," I said, still staring at the screens. "When Greg gets out here, if we can have leveled the battleship field he'll be much better off..."

"No chance our X-14s will get through battleship protection," Parks-Dawes said frankly. "We can wipe out a half-dozen destroyer escorts, keep their destroyers back, but I'd be inclined not to try anything against the battleships."

It's hard to lock eyes with someone over Battlelink, because everyone thinks you're looking at them. Even so, I'm pretty sure Marlene and I managed to trade a mutual glance on that comment — it was refreshing in its honesty, but troublesome in its content.

In short, we didn't have the teeth to take on the real threat.

"Well, they either know what we've got coming at them or they're lucky in their deployment strategy," Shannon Hunter bobbed her head towards something off-screen, presumably indicating her main screen.

My eyes darted back to the main screen on *Wolf's* bridge, and sure enough, the Martians were rearranging their formation. A wall of nine Martian battleships was deploying — five in the top rank, four in the bottom.

"They're putting the battleships out front?" Marlene frowned.

"My torpedoes are launching now, we might get lucky here," Parks-Dawes looked away from his screens, and part of me hoped he was right.

I looked away, "Time to weapons range, Jim?"

I hadn't even really had a chance to say hello to any of the bridge officers, but Jim Hannigan didn't skip a beat, just nodding to someone and then pointing to the main screen. Looking back, I realized he'd put the respective weapons ranges of each ship — ours and what we knew of theirs — up around the icons in dashed-line rings.

"Little something I put in after Belt Two," he added helpfully.

Believe it or not, no Defense Command tactical display had ever used the (now standard) icon rings to show weapons range. Jim Hannigan wasn't just a great officer, he was a pioneer!

As much as I'd like to have dwelled on that innovation, the icons were showing the Martians to be about forty seconds away from weapons range... no, about fifty — they were slowing down as they formed up.

Torpedo icons now flashed up on the scope, but they'd take almost thirty seconds to plunge into range, so I took the brief opportunity to look to Shannon, "*Wolf* can take top spot, Shannon, your ships bottom and flank?"

She nodded, "You and your ego, always have to be on top of everything..."

I grinned, "Yes ma'am, that I do."

With that I nodded to Karen, who was standing with a thin smile a little ways across the bridge, and she nodded to Erica Martin. Without any further need for words, Erica moved *Wolf* to bring us up over *Sorceress'* high drive pod. At the same time, Shannon spoke to her two other Captains — Wen Luong and Conrad Benwah, if I haven't mentioned them already — over Battlelink, and *Panther*, *Tiger* and *Jaguar* slid into positions off each of *Sorceress'* other drive pods.

Then the torpedoes closed to terminal range, and the Martian destroyers and destroyer escorts leapt forward and shot all of them down.

Just like that.

Whatever you say about the Martians — and I've said many rather disrespectful (albeit deserved) things — they weren't complete idiots. The same tactic wasn't going to get them every time, and Parks-Dawes' torpedoes proved that.

"Looks like we're going to have to do this the old fashioned way," I said quietly.

The battle was about to begin...

An hour behind our position — 'behind' meaning in the direction of the Belt approaches — *Warspite* accepted *Wolf's* assault shuttle at just this moment. Charlie's pilot put the craft into the battleship's bay with regular authorization, and Greg and the Special Branch team disembarked without incident.

"Guess they have no idea you're aboard, sir," Charlie smiled as they descended the ramp to the deck of the battleship's main flightbay.

Greg smiled and nodded — that seemed quite likely. Admiral Michaels hadn't been informed she was being relieved of her command of the Heavy Squadron for the coming fight, though I personally was surprised that she'd suggested she should keep command of a squadron that she had absolutely no experience commanding during the biggest battle in the history of Earth local space.

I mean, really, was her ego that big?

Well, not to put too fine a point on it, but yes.

As Greg was escorted to *Warspite's* bridge by Charlie's squad, the crew and the officers they passed were all very pleased to see their Admiral back aboard — *Warspite* had fought at Deep Black, the crew was thoroughly loyal to Admiral Noyce, and rightly so.

Having him back gave them a shot of confidence that, given the situation, was sorely needed. As for Admiral Michaels, well, they wanted her off the ship before she got them all killed.

Greg arrived at the bridge after several minutes of hurried walking, and apparently none of the crew bothered to inform the bridge that Admiral Noyce and a detachment of elite Special Branchers had come aboard to relieve Michaels of command. When the bridge doors opened, Michaels didn't even look back at them.

She was, in fact, busy yelling at Commander Xi Zelin, the ship's XO and Operations

Officer, for her 'inefficiencies in preparing for battle'. I have no idea what she was referring to, but since Zelin years later took over the Venus Squadron, I'm going to guess Michaels had no clue about her quality as an officer. Hard to believe, I know.

Charlie and his squad spread slowly across the rear of the bridge, Charlie making a point of locking eyes with the battleship's Lieutenant Commander in charge of security, letting him know that all was well, that there was no threat from the Special Branchers to the security of the ship…

"You really should keep your voice down, Stacey. It's rude and disrespectful to throw tantrums on the bridge," Greg was pleased to be back on his ship, and it showed.

Michaels whirled on the source of the comment, apparently not recognizing the voice as Greg's, and then she froze just as she opened her mouth to start bellowing out a snide reply. Charlie waved, then raised his MAG-90 with one arm, angling the muzzle towards Michaels.

"I have orders from the First Lord, Admiral Michaels. You're relieved and confined to quarters. Please leave my bridge now."

Michaels' face apparently flushed bright red, and a sudden wave of rather impolite laughter rolled over the bridge crew as she started to sputter angry half-words.

Can you *imagine* what would have happened if this imbecile had been commanding our battlewagons (that's a colloquial term for battleship, by the way) when they ran down on the Martians? Best not to think about it.

"Admiral, you've been asked politely. I'm afraid I'll have to remove you if you don't comply," Charlie added with a courteous smile. Charlie's good at sounding all-business, even when he's about ready to break heads. It's the cool professionalism that you get when you're trained to single-handedly defeat a roomful of pirates with only, oh, a shoe and a box of thumbtacks in your arsenal. Half a box of tacks, even.

I'm not kidding, Charlie could do that.

Anyway, Michaels sputtered on, but she also had the good sense to move towards the exit hatch. Charlie did a couple of quick tactical hand-wave things, and two of his officers stepped into position behind the Admiral, determined to tail her right to her quarters.

Sputtering Admirals running loose aboard ship aren't good, so Charlie's team would make sure this one behaved.

As Michaels exited the bridge, Greg stepped down to his chair and smiled, nodding to his Flag Captain, Val Rodriguez, and to some of the other nearby officers, "Looks like I got back just in time. What's our status?"

"Laser range in fifteen seconds… mark."

Jim was reading off the time for me, even though the new icons were up on the screen. I nodded and glanced up at Marlene on the Battlelink, "What're you going to focus on, Marlene? We'll focus on its escorts."

Marlene's eyes narrowed slightly as she appraised the targets on her screen, "Let's go after that battleship on the right of their line… make that on *our* left. Indicating it with a red tag on my screen…"

As she said the word 'tag', her Sensors and Communications Officer actually tagged the battleship she meant with a red marker, and sent that information across the Battlelink so all ships with us could be sure we were attacking the same thing.

"Roger that, Shannon, looks like we've got four DEs and a destroyer to play with then," my eyes shifted to Shannon Hunter, and she nodded.

I paused and quickly gazed over the screen again, "Alright, Rach, your ships take the DEs, we'll handle the destroyer."

"Confirmed…" Shannon began repeating attack orders to her Captains, and I have to say, things on the screens started to get a little confusing as flag officers from both our little group and Parks-Dawes' Light Squadron started giving out orders.

I'd hear a Commodore giving orders to three or four different Captains at the same volume level that I'd hear someone trying to talk to me — the Battlelink system at this time still didn't have relative screen muting, which we added after this battle proved we needed it.

Still, Shannon and Marlene and I were well in tune; our ships all moved with the combined confidence of old compatriots, despite the fact that *Wolf* had never so much as been on maneuvers with *Sorceress*.

With only about ten seconds to laser range Karen looked back to Matt, "You getting a good solution on the destroyer?"

The black Briton nodded with a thin smile, "Have it zeroed, all batteries."

I took a deep breath… without the Belt Squadron (or other cruisers for that matter) for me to directly command, I actually didn't have a whole lot to do in this action. Karen gave the orders that moved *Wolf* around, so I'd just keep an eye on the bigger situation.

"Range… *now.*"

"Fire forward laser," Karen's tone was smooth and cool.

"Shoot!" Matt translated the order to action, and there was the slightest tremor as *Wolf's* bow laser sliced out with angry red heat.

One of the smaller screens switched to an enhanced vid of the external situation. The destroyer was a tiny gray smudge, the red laser trailing from a huge beam in the near side of the vid frame to a thin line rubbing up against the smudge.

That's what we see of space battles in our ships — not a whole lot. Not like the movies where the omnipotent camera angles fly you around and show you all the hot fighting in gruesome detail…

But to give you some of that detail (since these books I'm writing hardly seem to be limited by point of view), we hit that destroyer hard. It was already spinning up its turrets to take a shot at one of Shannon's frigates, but we clipped it first, and clipped it good. Normal strategy for us is to weaken the drive pod wings, to cut down maneuverability in our opponent. This is actually an anti-pirate tactic, keeping their quick little raiders from escaping us.

Now we caught the destroyer's port pod wing near the base, and as the laser dragged along the wing towards the hull, Matt was able to angle it to take a severe chunk out of the ship. Excellent shooting.

Laser shots were flung back from this destroyer, but they'd been thrown out of alignment by our hit, so we lucked out and didn't take a single blast.

"Good penetration on that shot," Matt reported immediately.

"Definitely losing some speed," Hannigan confirmed, and Karen nodded, looking back to Erica Martin.

"Get us in close. Matt, keep the lasers boiling to close range, then finish the job with mags."

"Roger that…" Matt started giving orders to his operations crew, and the gunnery teams started new sets of calculations on their computers as *Wolf* pressed closer to its foe.

I kept watching the big screen, and on it Shannon Hunter's frigates clearly were coming up with us. Shannon followed the same doctrine that Karen and I did — lasers first, then close and finish with mags. Lasers could do a lot of harm, so we always led out with them and tried to weaken the foe before we came to closer grips.

The escorts that were attached to the destroyer *Wolf* was engaging immediately got raked by laser fire from three frigates. Shannon's ships shot as well as Matt — it's often suggested that we exaggerate when we claim all four of our frigates made direct hits with our first laser shots. It's true, we did. Remember, four frigates skippered by pirate-hunting Captains, with crews skilled with the laser batteries: the Martians got more than they bargained for.

One of the DEs got away from its laser shot with little damage, turning past it too quickly for *Jaguar's* gunner to correct the solution. Both other DEs took heavy hits to drive pylons, dropping their speed by as much as twenty percent.

So out of the four destroyer escorts and single destroyer that were coming forward to try to screen for the battleship Marlene was going after, we'd smacked four ships pretty hard in the first round.

Now, I'd continue with the narrative of what we did, but as you probably know, something much more dramatic started at just this moment. So since it's impossible to tell two things at the same time, I'm going to go over and tell that whole story first, then come back to finish this off. I figure it's the best way to explain how Marlene, Shannon and I reacted in our own little battle.

CHAPTER TWENTY-SEVEN

YORKTOWN, HORNET, ESSEX, INDOMITABLE, INVINCIBLE

I once lectured about this fight in Defense Command Naval Staff College, and the first question I was asked after giving my talk was an excellent one, from then-cadet (now Commander) Jack Szekeres. The question went like this: "Why the *hell* were Admiral Parks-Dawes' carriers so far forward, sir?"

Yes, the 'hell' was in there, despite my rank at the time, and indeed, the 'hell' belongs in that question.

Well, I have to say right now that the insults that were slung by many at Parks-Dawes for his choice of deployment are *not* warranted — and remember this is me saying it. I don't like the Caldecott circle, obviously, but for all his faults when it came to judging associates, George Parks-Dawes wasn't a fool, or a coward.

So let me explain what his plan was.

Under a new doctrine he'd been working up for a few years prior to this fight, a new concept of 'constant strike' had developed. To distill this down to understandable concepts, think of it this way: we all knew by this time that the weapons carried by Starlights and Sunbombers just weren't up to cracking ship armor on one pass. At this time, too, it was doctrine for the carriers to stay back from a fight and to send their planes forward to do the fighting. Well, the result in that case is pretty self-evident, I think: the carrier sends its planes, they attack, everything they shoot with bounces off, and they come back to their motherships.

Parks-Dawes wasn't satisfied with writing off his carriers as useless, so he got to thinking about what his planes actually *could* do, or how he could improve their odds, and it occurred to him that repeated strikes against single targets might cumulatively inflict some damage. One wasp stings you, it's not so bad, but if dozens keep coming for an hour, you're dead.

But here's the problem with that idea: if the carriers are far back from the fight, then the planes they launch go in, strike, and then aren't back in position to attack their targets for at least an hour — the planes have to fly back to the carrier, rearm, turn around, and fly back to the attack.

George therefore decided to take the risk of moving his carriers right up to the front, and to rotate each carrier's fighter force in three stages. One group of fighters and bombers would attack, a second group (the one that had just attacked) would cover it (create a diversion) and the third group would go back to the carriers, which would be very close by, to rearm. In this way, Parks-Dawes figured he could keep his planes on a constant attack.

This, of course, was a huge risk for the carriers — not so much for his own ship, *Ark Royal*, as it was a supercarrier, a one-of-a-kind with a battleship's armor and weapons as well as planes. *Yorktown, Hornet* and *Essex*, three gallant ships, weren't so well protected. Parks-Dawes knew those carriers would be vulnerable, though, so he put a battlecruiser with both *Hornet* and *Essex*, and kept *Ark Royal* next to *Yorktown*. The idea was that the big ships would look after the carriers, protect them from harm.

It looked good on paper, and what most people forget is that it worked well in three separate simulations in the year prior to this fight.

Yes, John, Greg, Marlene and I would have said flatly that the strategy wouldn't work in a real action, but then before this battle we'd have been saying that with no proof to back us up. So Parks-Dawes wasn't a fool, an idiot, or anything like that. He put his ships in harm's way, knowing it was dangerous, probably not quite realizing *how* dangerous, but still determined to make the absolute most of what he had. Caldecott circle or no, he shouldn't be criticized for this deployment.

My God, though, it was... shocking, I think is the best word. It was shocking to watch. Because as you probably know, it went so terribly wrong.

I've gotten most of this part of the narrative from *Ark Royal's* XO, if you're wondering, Commander Yolanda Burke.

Parks-Dawes watched us engage the battleship on the flank, and at the same time the fighter-bomber wings from his carriers were launching. The carriers were up close, with the Light Squadron's frigates and corvettes maneuvering forward to make sure Martian escorts didn't slip in to attack them.

"*Ark Royal's* assault group to focus on the battleship on the right of the line, *Yorktown* to take the next one in, *Hornet* the third, *Essex* the fourth," Parks-Dawes' style was calm and reassuring, and he settled himself in the command chair on *Ark Royal's* bridge.

The crew, who'd been with their Admiral for over a year now, and truly respected him, were calm as they passed those orders on, and he watched on the screen as the Starlights and Sunbombers hurtled from their motherships' line, past the battlecruisers, and plunged towards the Martian battle line.

You'll notice that the frigates, corvettes, and battlecruisers hadn't launched their own small fighter wings — they were being kept as the strategic reserve.

The Martian ships all launched what we've come to call their 'Interceptors'. They're short-range but heavily-armed fighters, and they rushed forward and started tangling with the Starlights escorting the Sunbombers.

So far, nothing seemed too unexpected; Admiral Parks-Dawes sat still in his chair, his gaze cool and yet alert. The bridge crew remained calm — there was no reason to panic.

The Starlights did a good job tying up the Interceptors — we still don't have exact numbers on how many each side shot down, but we think it was about even in terms of lost planes. But then the Sunbombers closed to launch range and started releasing their Apocalypse missiles.

I should be more specific, here: virtually *all* the Sunbombers attacked at once — not the three-waves system they'd trained for. I can't explain why they did this; they'd trained for over a year on this strategy, but it can be different when you're in your cockpit taking fire, believe me. They all launched (without orders) inside about a minute of each other, and then peeled off to get back to their ships to rearm.

That was the first problem.

The Apocalypse missiles raced towards their targets — the four battleships Parks-Dawes had ordered — at high speed, but many were shot down. Of a total of sixty or so launched, a little over half got past the Interceptors, and only half of those got past the close-in defenses of the battleships and their escorts.

As the missiles plunged to impact range, the Starlights broke contact with the Interceptors, hooking back up with their bombers (none of which had been lost, thanks to the excellent fighter cover), and they all cruised back to the carriers.

Twelve missiles struck the Martian battleships, and not a single one did so much as slow them down. In fact, the missiles almost seemed to speed them up.

Apparently Parks-Dawes was on his feet by this time, calmly asking his Captains over the Battlelink to broadcast to the carriers to remind their flight leaders to break the next attack by wings.

Then his jaw dropped.

Mine sure did. I was only paying partial attention to the Light Squadron from *Wolf's* bridge, but, well, it's hard *not* to notice four battleships and six escorts leaping forward at about 195 kps in what I can best describe as a lunge.

They moved fast, breaking from their line and boosting forward with an acceleration I don't think our own battleships of the time could match. They were chasing down the wakes of our bombers, and before our planes could get close to their hangers, these battleships were in extreme laser range of the Light Squadron.

It's really hard to describe the stab of terror that went through all of us who were watching, because we all knew exactly what was about to happen. I remember Karen taking a second from her own orders and looking at me. She moved her mouth to silently say the words "Oh God," and I nodded once, my jaw hanging slack with pure shock.

Marlene tells me this was the one moment that day when her resolve fell away — she gasped out nearly the same words: "Oh God no..."

Battleships had gotten into gun range of carriers, and that was never supposed to happen. Never. Carriers were fast and light specifically so they could avoid that sort of challenge.

Parks-Dawes only paused for a short few seconds, he looked back to his Captains on the Battlelink, barking orders with a whole new urgency: "Get the carriers back *now*! *Indomitable, Invincible*, move up to interdict."

He then turned to his own Flag Captain, "Get us forward, we have the best guns in the squadron."

That, for anyone who calls Parks-Dawes a coward, should be a rude reminder of the truth: he ordered his own *carrier* into a fight with four battleships, trying to save the more vulnerable ships he'd brought forward.

It was all, of course, too late.

Yorktown, Hornet and *Essex* reversed their drives hard, and quick ships that they were, their forward momentum dropped off instantly. But they were still coasting towards the Martians for long seconds.

"Come on, come on..." I remember hearing Parks-Dawes' urgent plea to the fates over the Battlelink, and I nearly cringed. They were desperate words, said with the eerie-half-calm of a pilot in a crashing plane.

A pilot who knows he can't save himself.

Invincible and *Indomitable*, Captains Rory Falkner and June Barrett, were the first to engage by guns, and they got off scathing shots. Battlecruisers have guns as big as a battleships' (but no armor) so their lasers were powerful. Turning to present broadside angles, each ship maxed out its power grid and sprayed *three* laser beams at the Martians.

In the same instant, the Light Squadron's frigates and corvettes dove into the fray, taking up the attention of the six escorts that had come up with the Martian battleships.

None of the Light Squadron ships shot as well as *Wolf*, or as Shannon's ships. The battlecruisers each hit one battleship with two of their three beams. I remember watching this on one of the screens, and for just a moment I hoped it'd be enough to scare off the Martians.

One of the battleships actually took a pretty hard hit, too, its speed falling by over twenty percent as a beam weakened its starboard drive pylon.

Ark Royal fired now, and I gritted my teeth. The huge supercarrier had lasers bigger than the battlecruisers', and much more armor, but it was also a gargantuan target. The beams of Parks-Dawes' flagship cut into the closest battleship — another painful hit by the look of it...

Apparently Parks-Dawes (standing out of the Battlelink camera shot by now) didn't look hopeful at this. In fact, he closed his eyes and said a quiet prayer. Probably pleaded for forgiveness with his maker. I surely would have — it's nothing peculiar to him, any commander who realizes his or her loyal people are about to die would trade his or her immortal soul to save them. Any good one would, anyway.

Prayers like that don't get answered, though.

I remember watching *Invincible* explode. Just like that. Two of the Martian battleships got the battlecruiser in a crossfire less than ten seconds after *Ark Royal* fired. The seven much lighter laser beams fired from the Martian turrets dragged across the fragile battlecruiser, and then it exploded.

I'd never in my life thought I'd see a warship that big just *explode*.

I literally could not respond verbally to the sight. That was 2,100 crew dead, in one fiery flash. And if that wasn't bad enough, *Indomitable* went up immediately too. Just seconds later. I can imagine what it was like for Parks-Dawes, looking at the faces of Captains Barrett and Falkner on the Battlelink screens as their ships were blasted apart.

Staring into the eyes of subordinates you ordered to their deaths — *as they died...*

But he kept his wits about him. He was a good commander, and he cared about his crews. *Ark Royal* took one hit in that volley that destroyed the two battlecruisers — only one double-turret of Martian battleship lasers hit the assault carrier. Those hits cut the starboard number three recovery bay wide open, and Commander Burke was ordered from the bridge to see to damage control.

About a minute after she left, the bridge of *Ark Royal* was incinerated in a crossfire. Parks-Dawes wasn't standing in front of his Battlelink camera in those moments — I didn't see his face or hear him speak in the last seconds.

But he died with his loyal bridge crew. And so whatever you say about his politics, and I've said plenty, you better respect him as an officer. Yes, he made a tactical mistake — a massively costly one in terms of lives and units — but it was a mistake that was based on what he thought was the best doctrine and tactics available at the time. And while almost 10,000 officers and crew of Defense Command paid for it with their lives, so did he.

The carriers were next.

The Light Squadron frigates and corvettes did everything they could to try to interdict on behalf of the carriers — to buy time for the fragile ships to get away. Starlights and Sunbombers, all still in space and without ordnance after their first massed strike, began hopeless strafing runs on the battleships. Their mags could do nothing to the big Martian ships, but they tried. And over two thirds of the planes from the original strike were shot down in those moments.

Then the carriers got hit simultaneously. They went up like the battlecruisers; first *Yorktown*, then *Essex* and finally *Hornet*.

Ark Royal was still staggering forward, actually passing the Martian battleships with a scathing exchange of fire that did some serious damage to one of the Martian battlewagons, but its bridge was gone, so the assault carrier was being commanded from Auxiliary Control.

Marlene sent the general retreat order to it and the remaining cruisers and planes within a few dozen seconds, and for whatever reason — perhaps slightly awed by their rapid success — the Martians just let the survivors of the Light Squadron go.

As this was going on, *Wolf* got into mag range of the destroyer we were tangling with. Now, you need to understand that as this was happening on the big screen, I was the only one paying a great deal of attention to it — most of the crew members on the bridge were too occupied by their particular duty to pay much attention. And even if they did, they were professional enough to stay focused for the moment. Succumbing to shock could get you killed.

"Mag batteries… shoot."

Matt's clipped order unleashed a shower of mag energy on the destroyer as it dragged itself towards us, and our fire was on target, slamming into the Martian ship and bursting through its plating.

"Two points to port," Karen ordered evenly in that second, and *Wolf* handily angled to the port side, presenting half the mags on the starboard side to the destroyer. Matt was already giving orders to the gunnery section, and in seconds those batteries were adding to the storm of concentrated electro-magnetic energy.

The destroyer seemed slow in replying — seemed, at least, in the context of the moment. It took about three seconds for return fire from their EM cannons to start fighting back against the torrent we so easily poured on it. It was too little too late.

As we'd seen at the Belt, Martian ships didn't have sufficient protection against large amounts of EM energy, and the ship overloaded within about twenty seconds of the onslaught. It was a sharp victory for us, but, well, it was nothing compared to the destruction the Light Squadron had been subject to.

Sorceress was shooting too, and Marlene's gunners were spot on. Lasers from the battleship were severely cutting into the Martian battleship she'd sought to challenge, and I remain convinced to this day that, had *Sorceress'* gunners not been so completely perfect in their shooting, that battleship would have jumped forward the way the other four had, and that we'd have had it in our laps without warning.

As it was, we couldn't risk trying to hold out against the entire Martian line.

"Shannon, cover us with torpedoes — all ships withdraw towards Earth, full burn!" Marlene's tone was slightly more urgent than before — the 'slightly' being no mean feat at all, given what she'd just seen.

She assures me that her head was spinning about as much as mine was at what we'd just seen, but again, we couldn't afford to let that sort of thing get to us.

You might think it strange, I suppose: neither Karen nor I worried too much about rushing Earth's orbital defenses, hijacking a talk show, or standing off against blockheads while a near-coup was staged. But something like this stung — and badly — for reasons that should be painfully obvious.

Watching five of Defense Command's most prided ships, with a total combined crew complement nearing 10,000, get annihilated in seconds, and our fleet flagship get virtually destroyed in that same time… well, I defy anyone to take it lightly.

That's why we have to find humor in as much as we can when we can. Scenes like this one don't leave you.

But, at that moment, we were leaving those scenes; *Wolf*, *Sorceress*, Shannon Hunter's frigates, and the cruisers of the Light Squadron, along with the surprisingly fast half-wreck of *Ark Royal*, all boosted away from the Martian line, with only three meager torpedoes from Shannon's frigates to delay a pursuit.

For whatever reason, the Martians gave us almost five whole minutes to get moving before they collected themselves to chase.

CHAPTER TWENTY-EIGHT

COUNTERPOINT

Greg received the feed that was relayed from *Sorceress's* bridge through Admiralty House as *Warspite* cruised past Earth on its way out to rendezvous with us. The Heavy Squadron was moving quickly, we weren't quite as fast, and the Martians were slower still, so it seemed we'd all meet about fifteen minutes from Earth space.

As the feed from Admiralty House loaded up on the main screen on *Warspite's* bridge, Greg was busily speaking to the Captains of his battleships and the remaining corvettes.

"We'll need to integrate as best we can with the Light Squad–"

He was actually saying that, ironically enough, when the *Warspite*Net screen switched over to a copy of a video feed from the Light Squadron frigate *Shark*, which had survived the destruction of the carriers to join us in our retreat.

The bridge brightened as two battlecruisers filled the screen with bright white light and then shattered.

Greg's words trailed off, and Charlie Peters, who'd elected to stay on the bridge since he didn't have anywhere else to be, found himself staring. Charlie didn't see much ship fighting up close like that — his combat experience was plentiful, but he was Special Branch, so he tended to see more shooting and stabbing.

Watching the epic scene of five capital ships being turned into debris inside a minute... well, no one was ready for that. Hopefully, no one ever *will* be. If it gets so bad for the Empire that losing ships so grand becomes commonplace, then...

Anyway.

"Lord Fiora is sending up a message from Admiralty House," the Sensors and Communications Officer interrupted Greg's thoughts — or, as he told me later, his thoughtless state.

He'd been thinking about how to integrate his ships with the Light Squadron for greatest effect. It hadn't even occurred to him that the Light Squadron might be essentially *gone* by the time he arrived.

But he was Greg Noyce, and I can't overstate what that means in terms of command ability: he blocked the shock from his mind with practiced and determined force of will and nodded to the Commander who'd interrupted him, "On screen fourteen."

He turned to that screen just as the signal from Admiralty House — in realtime range for only another moment or two — buffered up, and then John appeared. John has this stare he wears when very bad things happen, and it covered his face as he locked eyes with Greg.

"Well, I almost wish we were back storming a palace right now," the First Lord said evenly.

"Strange, but I agree..." Greg paused as the vid feeds ended and sensor data started scrolling across two of the bridge screens in front of him. "So, that gives me eight battleships, eight frigates, and nine corvettes to stop them with... and they're still at nineteen operational ships?"

John nodded evenly, "You've got a battleship deficit... not sure what I can suggest. I've never fought a battle line action before. Just keep your ships moving, Greg. Don't let them double-team you..."

The signal dropped out at that rather aptly-timed moment — *Warspite* surged out of realtime range. Greg took a deep breath and nodded to himself, his eyes dropping to the deck as he thought through John's words.

To explain, a battleship deficit was, theoretically speaking, a guarantee of death, and it had been in Naval tactical thinking since, oh, the twentieth century. See, it's not so easy as, to phrase it the way one reporter once did: "eight against ten... the numbers are almost the same, so eight is still in with a chance". The reality isn't anything of that sort.

Think of it like this: if Greg went line-to-line with the Martians, two Martian battleships would not have a one-on-one engagement. They'd have a two-ship advantage, allowing those two ships to double-team two of our ships, destroying ours twice as fast. Once the two of our battleships they double-teamed were gone, all four of those ships could go on and double-team four more of ours, and we'd be dead after killing maybe two of theirs.

The mathematics of destruction, to paraphrase a great old book.

So Greg had a serious dilemma. How exactly could he make eight battleships somehow equal ten? You might think his solution would be to get the frigates and corvettes he had the advantage in to attack those last two Martian battleships, but remember, the Martians still had nine escorts for us to deal with, and that all frigates had less armor than battlecruisers.

Ships like *Wolf* were powerful, but we didn't belong in a slogging match with battleships.

"Sir, follow-up message from the First Lord... loading on screen fourteen..."

Greg blinked and looked up at the screen again, just in time for John to reappear (not in realtime any longer), "I got cut off, sorry. Do what you can, I'm mobilizing the ground reserves right now. We'll have SF ready to counter any landings, and the Imperial Army is warming up its tanks. God help us if we need them, but based on what we see down here, they don't seem to have troop transports with them. That could be good or bad. I'm keeping back half Earth's fighter umbrella to counter any landing shuttles; all Sunbombers and Starlights are going up with you right now. I hope they help."

John paused, digesting what he'd just said. I've seen a copy of this message, and I have to say that never before or since have I witnessed him so grim. And who could blame him? I was grimmer than hell by this point.

"Listen, Greg, all I can say is Godspeed. Go get 'em."

The screen flashed to black, and Greg breathed a deep sigh. Even with half Earth's fighter umbrella — just about 450 planes, he reckoned — he wasn't sure what he could do against ten battleships.

But there was only one way he could find out.

Warspite surged on towards battle.

+++

What remained of the carrier fighter and bomber wings were rushing back to Earth, planning to rearm on the orbital stations and prepare for planetary defense. I watched them go and decided not to count how many were left.

I know the number now, though. I counted after the battle was done, and only about a quarter of the planes launched from carriers that day managed to survive. And though I feel strangely wrong for saying it, I have to admit I'm glad I wasn't asked to fight that battle from my Starlight. Because I'm not nearly as good as some of the hundreds of pilots who died.

Wolf was now the center ship in what was turning into a long line of frigates. Shannon's three frigates were off our starboard bow, the four frigates of the Light Squadron under Commodore Shamus Czarnecki off our port: I'd become the acting force commander for an eight-frigate squadron.

Why me, you ask, and not Shannon or Shamus (both of whom were I believe senior to me at the time — in terms of date of commission)? Because I was the only one with experience commanding a squadron in a fight against another squadron. Remember Belt Two? That was my experience in leading a squadron action. That was *all* of my experience.

As you might expect, staring across space at nineteen operational Martian ships as we fell back (some of the damaged ones we'd shot up were holding formation), I wasn't wild about having to command a squadron of ships that had never fought together against an enemy more professional and concentrated than any I'd ever seen...

But that sort of panic can't be revealed. Not to the bridge crew, not to the Captains of the other seven ships as they now popped up on Battlelink, and certainly not to Marlene.

"Rendezvous with the Heavy Squadron in seven minutes."

I blinked at Hannigan's helpful interruption but didn't look at him. I was staring at the screen, watching the well-organized line of Martian battleships as they came forward. We'd underestimated their military prowess, certainly... though I still remain unconvinced of their strategic ability. But that wasn't a thought I was having then — at that moment I didn't doubt any Martian abilities...

And I was starting to get slightly lost in my thoughts. That sort of thing didn't happen to Marlene, Greg or John — they were well past it. But the gravity of what I was looking at was stalling me, and for many long seconds I couldn't think.

Karen, of course, snapped me out of it, and with nothing more than a casual — accidental, she always claims — brush of the arm as she walked past me towards Jim Hannigan's station.

I blinked as her shoulder slid past mine, glanced at her, and she smiled at me.

Well you know what effect that has.

I was able to kick my brain into forward motion, and I started seeing more than a menacing line of icons on the Martian half of the screen.

"Shannon, they're leading out with their destroyers and DEs... looks like some of them are pretty badly banged up."

Shannon's eyes flickered off screen, and Shamus Czarnecki looked as well.

"You thinking we try to split them off from the battle line?" Karen was abruptly standing beside me, and I glanced at her and nodded.

"Best option I can see right now — eight top frigates against a mixed bag of Martians, it's the only advantage we have."

Her eyes narrowed, and she raised her hand and pointed to the sensor display on the big screen, "On the left, that's the fourth DE Shannon didn't get to before we had to withdraw. I think it's the lead-out ship if we hit that side."

My eyes narrowed and I nodded, "You hear that, Shannon?"

"I did. Leave the corvettes to cover Admiral Stoll and Admiral Noyce and see if we can get a little interference run?"

"I'm game. Shamus?"

Commodore Czarnecki wasn't one of the pirate-fighting veterans, but he was a capable enough officer, "Agreed."

Marlene, listening to us chatter over her Battlelink, nodded once, "Go get them. If you can pull that escort aside we might be able to manufacture something…"

I nodded, then took a moment to smile at Karen before looking across the bridge to Lieutenant Commander Martin, "Erica, plot me a course that can get us across the bows of the Martian cruisers without exposing us to their battleships. It'll have to be pretty oblique."

"Aye sir," Erica Martin stepped quickly over to the plotting consoles, and with two navigator techs, quickly began running numbers.

"We'll stay in the middle of the line, Shannon. You lead out with… *Jaguar*," I said evenly, perhaps confidently. Conrad Benwah's *Jaguar* was the cruiser on the extreme left of our own line, anchoring our port flank, so it'd be the natural ship to break course first.

Erica plotted our course, and we waited.

Before I go on here, I should mention something that is perhaps funny. I wouldn't have found it funny at the time. In fact I would have likely committed a felony had it even been mentioned to me.

Dave Caldecott woke up from sedation, and staggered out of the office he'd been placed in to rest in the Parliament buildings. John had, by this time, called an emergency press conference from those buildings to announce the civil defense situation, and he and Prime Minister Gabriel Pope were actually addressing a tense room full of reporters and Parliamentarians about fallout shelters, Home Guard units, and SF and Imperial Army deployments, when Caldecott stumbled through the back door onto the stage.

I don't know if his aide had somehow told him he had been booked for a press conference that afternoon — remember, he'd been planning to announce the condemnation of the Fiora ring on Imperial vid when he'd had that heart incident? Well, I don't know if he thought the stage was set for his announcement, of if he was just being himself. But you'll probably recall the vid clip.

Second Lord Dave Caldecott hobbled up onto the stage, stabbed a finger at John, and squealed, "*You traitor to the Empire! I'll burn you!*"

With the squeal, the cameras in the room all turned to Caldecott, and then they sensibly went back to John. John looked at Dave Caldecott once, his gaze ever so briefly being overcome with venom, and he looked back into the cameras and continued what he was saying, "…all sky and orbital traffic is now being grounded. If you see anything without a black sun on it airborne, get on the comm immediately to the Defense Command tip line and file your report. We'll have fighter response squadrons, SF and Special Branch ready to deal with any Martian landings. The Imperial Army will be on standby to expel any strong Martian forces that come to ground…"

As John went on with his rather important instructions, Dave Caldecott screamed something unintelligible — I can only assume he was still slightly out of his mind, either due to his sedation or his character. After that a few SF guards tried to escort him away. When that failed, Major Carrie Walsh of Special Branch, then overseeing the improvised defenses being set up around the Parliament buildings, arrived to drag the small monster of a man away by the collar.

Had I been anywhere in the room, I'd have shot the Second Lord of the Admiralty. It was well that I wasn't. I was elsewhere…

CHAPTER TWENTY-NINE
BATTLE OVER EARTH

Few people these days have ever heard of the ancient sea battle at Cape St. Vincent, and really, this fight that we were about to join bears little relation. But I always felt a certain strange connection between that engagement at sea and this stage of the Battle Over Earth. Anyway, that's of no great importance to what happened, just how I remember it.

Jaguar led the dive to port, as all eight of the *Predator*-class frigates followed Karen's plan and tried to pry the escorts off the front of the battleship line.

Crossing the path of the advancing Martians on an oblique angle and with a relative closing speed of over 200 kps, we certainly got their attention.

"All ships, stand by laser batteries. Slice up that fellow on the left end of their line."

It was already understood by all the Captains who'd now directly interfaced with *Wolf's* Battlelink that shooting our lasers into that poor destroyer escort was the plan: I was just formalizing the order.

What were we trying to accomplish? Well, as you can tell, we had a decided advantage in escort ships — they had nine, and when Greg's ships joined those covering Marlene, we'd have a total of eighteen. Now, doing your math you might say that the combined Defense Command force thus comprised twenty-six ships to the Martians' nineteen — surely that meant we could win!

Nope. Remember, they had the advantage in battleships. Trying to stop their battleships with our eighteen cruisers would have been like trying to stop the offensive line of a North American football team with the kids from a *high school chess club*.

So all we frigates could hope to do was get the Martian escorts off the front of the Martian battleship line, to keep them from screening our fire — that is, blocking our targeting solutions, shooting down torpedoes, or even taking hits for their capital ships. Under the circumstances it didn't seem like much, but we had to try.

"Range in four, three, two..."

"Ready... *shoot.*"

Simple words like that get the job done on a frigate like *Wolf*. 'Ready... shoot' was Matt, and his British-accented words sounded decidedly civilized as they ordered *Wolf's* starboard lasers into full-throated and silent roars.

Every frigate in our line was opening up as its lasers came into range, and the destroyer escort we'd chosen to focus on came apart neatly. If killing a ship and its crew can ever qualify as neat... but again, that's a question we can't ask at times like those.

"Course correction to starboard at the appropriate mark, please, *Jaguar*. Call it as you make it," I folded my arms across my chest as I gave the orders, and I watched Captain Benwah of *Jaguar* on screen eleven as he nodded to himself. Erica Martin's course called for us to loop around behind the Martian battleships, or at least look as if we were planning to.

You see, the real job of screening vessels is to keep littler ships like our frigates from firing torpedoes into battleships — remember how all the torpedoes Parks-Dawes had launched from the Light Squadron were shot down? Well the destroyers and destroyer escorts with the Martian battleships hopefully couldn't know that all our *Predators* were out of torpedoes, so presumably they'd have to turn back and match our course, in order to prevent us torpedoing their battlewagons from behind.

It sounded pretty thin to me then too, but it was what we had to work with.

"Mark," *Jaguar's* Captain said the word, and then looked off screen, "Starboard by fifty points."

"All ships keep line," I gave that order too, confirming the agreed-upon plan. "Any movement from our counterparts, Jim?"

I glanced back over my shoulder at Hannigan just as Karen stepped past me and gave Erica the order to alter course to stay in line. Hannigan was peering over the shoulder of one of his techs, watching the radiation emissions from the Martian ships — rad readings always foreshadowed ship movement, but in those days we could only really see them from up close.

"Not yet. Wait… there's timing for you, they're reducing drives — they're probably going for a fly-past."

In English that means they were going to slow down their ships and let the battleships go by, thus getting between our Earth frigates and the Martian capital ships. That'd suit us just fine.

"Continue on planned course until my mark, then designate targets for yourselves and get ready for close action," I looked from Jim Hannigan back to the vid screens, and the Captains and Commodores of my provisional frigate squadron nodded almost simultaneously.

"Integration in fifty seconds."

Marlene stood stoically on her deck as *Sorceress* reversed drives to allow for a smooth tie-in with Greg's advancing battleships, and the great battleship that she'd long flown her flag from began to shudder slightly at the reverse thrust. Greg's head then flickered to life in one of the vid screens before her.

"Sure glad you're clairvoyant, Marlene," Greg nodded to his old comrade, and Marlene raised her shoulders in a shrug.

"Wish I had more sorceress-like powers than just that. Eight to ten… got any ideas how to win this one?"

Greg's eyes were narrowing thoughtfully as the question came, "Can we get torpedoes in to weaken them?"

Marlene let out a very short sigh and shook her head, "Don't think so — I played that trick one time too many, their escort is watching for it."

Greg began to nod, and then he looked off screen for a moment and looked back again, "I'm sorry, *what* escort?"

Marlene's eyes jerked back to the sensor display, just in time to watch the battleships pass their escort screen, and to see the dotted lines marking laser shots begin to pass between the frigates with *Wolf* and the nine Martian small ships. By this time *Sorceress* was far enough back for me to no longer be on Battlelink, so she hadn't been getting realtime information on what we'd managed.

"They still have clouds of defense fighters around them, a few hundred at least," Marlene was saying that as the icons of the fighters launched from Earth blinked up on her display.

She looked from the sensor display to Greg's face on the nearby screen, back to the sensor display and then back to Greg, "Well, apparently I *do* have the power to magically summon up fighters. You thinking what I'm thinking?"

Greg smiled, "I think so, yes."

For the record, this pair saved Earth.

Wolf was dancing in a tight spiral, but thanks to artificial gravity none of us aboard felt much at all. Karen was commanding the ship in battle, and, as had been the case at Belt Two, I felt slightly useless.

We'd walked right into the Martian screening forces, and now they were trading shots with us and most of the squadron. The particular destroyer *Wolf* had chosen to deal with wasn't shooting very well — or, perhaps to be fair to that ship's crew, Erica Martin was throwing *Wolf* around with poise, speed and unpredictable grace. Laser and EM cannon shots flashed right past us, and Matt Baxter hammered back after them with a determined and accurate fury that I'm glad I've never had to receive.

All this, of course, was guided by Karen's smooth orders, given comfortably with a reassuring tone that kept everyone on the bridge relatively relaxed.

Other frigates weren't doing so well. Shannon's ships were handling themselves admirably, but the Light Squadron *Predators* were having problems. One was getting badly mauled by a destroyer escort (a ship smaller than itself).

Hawk and *Falcon* were tag-teaming a DE, much in the way we expected the Martian battleships to tag-team Greg's, but the feisty little Martian was trading shots at a rate of three to one. *Falcon* was abruptly forced to pull back when one of these shots punched a hole in the forward thrust vents of its starboard drive pod, launching it into an uncontrolled spin.

Shark then lost a drive pod to a DE. That was bad. No reflection on the crew of *Shark* — they were doing the best they could, given their lack of experience — but this wasn't going to do.

"We need to get them thinking multi-directionally..." I was thinking out loud with those words, and then paused for what felt like minutes. It was, evidently, only a second-long pause, but in it I weighed the risks, and the situation seemed to warrant my next order: "All frigates, launch your fighters. See if we can't add a new threat to the rear of the battleships, get them looking both ways."

As was standard procedure for any ship going into what the manuals call 'Type Four' action (Ship-to-Ship Action: Multiple Major Combatants), all our fighters had been being kept on standby for a crash launch throughout the battle. I don't like to launch fighters prematurely because I've had it done to me — a ship launches you, then is forced to pull back leaving you out there with just your wingmates and usually a world of hurt barreling down on you.

But the world of hurt in this case was big enough for me to be justify putting Lieutenant Commander Adrienne Thompson, the elite Wolfstar Squadron, and the Starlights of the squadrons from the other ships, into space.

And no, I didn't at this point know what Greg and Marlene were planning. I wish I could say it was more than incredible luck that led to this coincidence in thinking, but it wasn't. No great plan, no secret tactic that we in the Fiora ring debuted in this fight. Nothing like that. At best it was great minds thinking alike... or fools failing to differ.

The Starlights and Sunbombers from Earth rushed across the gap between the quickly-formed and now-slowing line of Earth battleships and the Martian battlewagons. The 450-odd small craft crashed into the Martian Interceptor perimeter within seconds, and they did so almost at the same moment the fighters from our frigates appeared at the battleships' rear.

Now, you'd naturally think nothing of this — and the Martians surely seem not to have. We'd already seen how ineffective fighters and bombers were against battleships, so what was the use of this?

Well, that was about to become apparent. I talked to Adrienne about this the day after it happened, and she'd never seen *anything* like it. Because the fighters couldn't hurt the capital ships they're often overlooked, but the actual fighter-to-Interceptor battles out there were the most vicious dogfights recorded in the annals of space warfare.

Hundreds of planes going at each other between Martian battlewagons, with turreted Martian point defense EM cannon hammering out bursts at Sunbombers as they made attack runs...

Wolfstar Squadron hurtled into this mess from the rear, and Adrienne was able to sneak our planes in fairly effectively, as all the Martian Interceptors had been drawn forward to meet the oncoming craft from Greg's side.

She slammed her own plane forward, "Break up and mix in, stick with your wingmen."

I've seen Adrienne dogfight before, and I can tell you without a doubt that she made many of the Martian Interceptor pilots regret their career path that morning. We got the inter-pilot transmissions from Wolfstar Squadron piped into the bridge, and I listened intently even as Karen continued to order *Wolf* against the same, persistent Martian destroyer that we'd started the fight against minutes earlier. This destroyer wasn't giving so easily as the one we'd faced earlier.

"Holy hell, what's that?!"

That was a scream over the Wolfstar comm line. We hadn't lost a single plane from our own squadron yet — I know, sounds farfetched, but it's true. I'm not sure how, but Adrienne's pilots were keeping themselves alive in the biggest dogfight in the history of spaceflight.

And then another exclamation, this one from Adrienne, "Break and climb, full burn. *Move*! All frigate Star squadrons, get the hell out of here!"

Then one of the Martian battleships exploded in a massive maelstrom.

Having been warned ahead of time, Greg's fighters had known to expect this, and they and the Sunbombers peeled away without a loss; some of the planes from the Light Squadron frigates, and three from Shannon's frigates, were crushed by the debris cloud that erupted from the bright explosion.

And then a second one went.

By this time my eyes had shot up to the vid screens and were glued on pictures coming back through the reverse angle cameras mounted to the tails of our Starlights; a *second* battleship had been blown to bits.

Believe me, I was confused.

Then the lasers cut in, and not in a charming dance floor sense of 'cut in'; Greg's battle line opened up with bow lasers at extreme range, choosing three particular Martian battleships — two of them already damaged by encounters with the Light Squadron and *Sorceress*, as I later found out — and slinging red beams of energy into them.

The Martian line shuddered and instantly began reversing drives. Within seconds — just as the destroyer *Wolf* was fighting finally succumbed to mag fire — the escorts reversed engines in a massive retreat as well.

"Pursue?" Shannon's sharp question ripped over Battlelink, but I was already shaking my head.

"No, they're pulling back to the battleships, we won't have a chance to get at them until the battlewagons get us in range."

What the *hell* — a deserved 'hell' — had happened?

Greg and Marlene had used the conflagration of a huge dogfight to send torpedoes through. *Very* risky, but under the circumstances quite necessary. Between them, the seven battleships of the Heavy Squadron fired fourteen torpedoes in a single salvo, and targeted only two Martian battleships with those warheads.

With the escorts out of the way and the Interceptors tied up with the Earth defense squadrons, nothing but the battleships' own point defense batteries were left to shoot down incoming torpedoes.

It should be said that of fourteen torpedoes fired, only three ultimately hit home. Nonetheless, the three were sufficient, because Greg and Marlene followed them with that massive laser salvo off the bow emitters of their combined battleship force.

The momentum changed in that single combined firestorm.

Seven Martian battleships backed off, meeting up with their escorts, and we let the collected Martian squadron, now only fourteen ships, withdraw in good order. One battleship was too damaged by the laser fire to fall back, and Greg immediately broadcast an order for it to surrender.

The crew self-destructed that ship. We did *not* destroy it in cold blood, contrary to some accusations.

We watched in mild disbelief as the Martians backed off, then turned and boosted away.

"Shannon, go after them, get hold of the Heavy Squadron's corvettes and take them with you. Keep us apprised of what they're up to," I gave the orders entirely without thinking.

Greg hadn't established Battlelink with me by the time I gave that order, but I figured (correctly, it proved) that he wouldn't push his luck by going after them today.

We'd gotten through this, the biggest battle in history to date, and Earth was safe for the moment.

But we didn't know if the Martians had anything else up their collective sleeves, so we recovered our planes and formed up with Greg's battleships, falling back towards Earth to deal with whatever came next. By mid-afternoon, we figured we were safe enough to rotate crews from action stations, but we stayed on alert for the rest of that day.

Too bad history doesn't ring a bell to let you know when it's finished for the day.

CHAPTER THIRTY
CALM DOWN

I sat in my chair on the bridge as we all slowly plied our way back to Earth late that evening. We'd stayed out there and waited and watched, wondering if the Martians were only feinting their retreat. Our shuttles were out constantly, grabbing lifeboats and pulling pilots out of their ejected cockpits, if they were still alive. Search and rescue after a battle is a grizzly business, and usually it means collecting both enemy survivors and your own.

That day, I've heard, many of our search teams passed right by Martian life pods, even if they seemed to be bleeding atmosphere. I can't say I condone it, but I understand it. Our survivors came first, not theirs... it's wrong, but you have to understand, it's just the way it is.

We collected over 3,000 Defense Command survivors, too, which I think is nothing short of remarkable. There had been over 12,000 people aboard the ships we'd lost, and add another 1,000 pilots and bomber crew to that: we'd lost a massive number of people. More people than Defense Command had lost altogether in every major battle up to that day.

After we found every Earth-built escape pod and cockpit we could, we started hauling in the Martians. And fair or not, the Martian crews pulled out of their life pods and onto the decks of the ships that recovered them had a rough time. A few were laid out pretty solidly when they complained about their treatment, two were actually shot when they got into a brawl with deck crew who started spewing insults at them. Shot with mags, that is — non-lethal. None of them died on our decks.

We got them under lock and key, and we started looking for officers among them who might be useful. All told, we had about 1,100 prisoners.

The rest got away.

And why, you ask, did we let the Martians run when they had only fourteen ships to our total of twenty-four; couldn't we have wiped them out?

Yes, we probably could have, but it would have cost us a couple of battleships, half our frigates and half or more of our corvettes — and we'd already lost the Light Squadron, more or less.

Contrary to popular thinking, a victory in space doesn't come only when you annihilate the entirety of the other force — one hundred percent destruction of the foe is rare indeed. It was pure fluke that we got close to it at Belt Two; here we took the destruction of three of their battleships and five of their escorts as victory enough.

Besides, we really didn't know that they were finished with us, or that they didn't have a second force standing by somewhere ready to attack Earth if we got dragged away giving chase to that battered force we'd sent running.

And we were all very tired.

Greg, Karen, Marlene, and me especially — Marlene hadn't slept well while she tried to slow the Martian advance, Greg had been dealing with the inquiry for all that time, and I'd been worrying about what I'd find at Earth. We were all very fatigued going into this day, but we'd done what we'd needed to do — peaked at the right time.

Now we were exhausted. That was it, no more toying with the Martians — we'd get them next time. For now we were going home, to repair our damaged ships, get our wounded to hospitals, and to sleep...

Remember too that this all happened on the same day. It was one of the turns of fate that seem to boggle the mind — one of those sorts of days where everything came together in such a tangled mess that if I wrote it into a fiction book nobody would ever believe it. Things don't really happen like that, people would say, but the strange reality is that days like this (albeit on a much smaller scale) happen all the time. Pardon the cliché, but it seems warranted: when it rains it *pours*.

This was a very long day for all of us. For me it was the second-longest day in memory. The only one that's ever seemed longer was that very black day, years later, when they put Karen into intensive care. I suppose you can understand why that'd be darker.

So I sat on *Wolf's* bridge as Karen ordered us back towards Earth.

We spent the night counting our dead.

CHAPTER THIRTY-ONE

THE DAY AFTER

What's the first thing you do after a big battle like the Battle Over Earth? I mean after you're pretty certain it's actually done — that the Martians are running? By the next morning, Shannon had commed in from her pursuit, letting us know that the Martians were making no moves to turn back for another attack. She was recalled after that, with only *Jaguar* ordered to pursue the fleeing Martians for another day to be absolutely certain.

So the next morning we were on to the first post-battle step, and what would you guess that to be? You're right: the press conference.

We hadn't been certain of enough the night of the battle to let the media know anything concrete — they had reporters in the Parliament press pool taking regular updates, but there was no detail given in those briefings as we weren't about to betray our situation over public broadcasts that the Martians could watch.

The next morning... well, we still would have liked to stay off the air about what had happened, but the media can't be ignored. The day of the battle they're understanding, and rightly so, but as soon as we've had time to collect some of our thoughts, they want to hear them.

So I stood next to John, Greg, and Marlene on the stage in the main Parliament Building and explained what we'd experienced at Belt Two and Asteroid Theta, then Marlene summarized her section about the gallant delaying action she fought, and Greg and John gave an edited version of the visit to the Emperor. You know what happened so I won't repeat what we said.

Then we opened up for questions, because that's what you do at press conferences. I'm fairly accustomed to dealing with the press by now — the number of media outlets I deal with at the Belt has well acclimated me to that particular task. John's happy to answer questions too, so Marlene and Greg usually let the two of us handle it, just for those reasons.

So as John called for the first question, from the Imperial Wire Service reporter Harry Yates, I edged slightly forward on the stage, to make sure I took the brunt of any answer that I could.

"Was Second Lord Caldecott conspiring against the Empire to make sure we weren't ready to receive this attack?"

It's funny, despite all the commotion that the media drummed up around this question after the events of that day over Earth, none of the four of us on stage had honestly spent much time reflecting on it. We'd lost too much in the fight, and we weren't at the stage yet to start worrying about pond scum like Caldecott again. So that look of slight surprise you might have seen on all of our faces on the vids of the press conference was a legitimate one. Was he conspiring with the Martians?

John opened his mouth to answer the question, but found himself at a loss for words — and understandably. He had to be incredibly careful what he said here, because technically he could be called out to a duel by Caldecott if he accused the Second Lord of being a traitor without evidence.

Yes, the new dueling regulations were on the books in those days (they came in 2227, if you're wondering), and though they were rarely used, Dave Caldecott just might prove himself fool enough to try.

With that delicacy in mind, I launched quickly into one of my patented non-answers, "Harry, we really don't know. It's no secret our ring of officers and his really don't get along, but he's still a fellow officer — I really can't imagine him conspiring against the Empire. Our disputes are always ultimately over what we think is best for the safety of the Empire... so... well, I don't think Second Lord Caldecott would ever consider Martian rule best. That said, there are plenty of real things that I can't imagine, so we'll have to launch an inquiry and wait for the outcome. Our focus for the present is consolidating our defensive position and finding out just how much damage the Martians have done. Then we'll be hitting back. We'll worry about Second Lord Caldecott when we know the Empire is out of danger."

I'm good at the comforting non-answers.

The next question came from Jessica Qing (at this time, she was just arriving at the level of fame she's known for these days), "So, Admirals, Commodore... what exactly do we know about the strategic situation? You've briefed us on this battle, and the state of local defense... what about the Empire?"

John leaned forward on his lectern, "Well Jessica, they've clearly planned this out pretty well, at least in terms of disrupting our communications, so officially, I don't have any information for you on what exactly is happening. However, early estimates of the size of the fleet they sent after us, compared with what DCI tells us they have altogether, suggests that they can't have much out there. Ken reported no battleships coming out of the Asteroid colonies, and when Marlene left, Venus was quiet. My guess is they focused their effort here, and that gives us time to redeploy our forces outward. We'll meet them wherever they turn up."

Another not-quite-answer, and that's no knock to John. His assumptions were good ones, and obviously he couldn't be too specific without communications between Admiralty House and its many outposts. Such are the dangers of losing communications.

"So you're taking steps to restore communications?" Jessica Qing followed up quickly, and John nodded.

"We lost our entire 'Rotation Two' communications unit, by the look of things. We're going to be sending out 'Rotation One' starting tomorrow, but we'll begin with establishing only the most crucial communications links. We're not going to be restoring non-military communications until we're certain we can defend the comm ships that are out there. The Martians might still be hunting, so I'm concentrating escort groups to defend those that we do send out."

I actually should pause here to explain this: back in these days, there were no private signal companies — there was no EmpNet or Comms Imperial. Those private signal companies were started after the war, with major government subsidies, to produce redundant signal capacity and make it harder to knock out our comms the way the Martians had. Before the war, it had been seen as too expensive for private corporations to get into the signals business, so all traffic (civilian and military) went through the Defense Command grid (the same way some of you might still be on the Defense Command Public Comm Plan as opposed to one of the private ones).

The press conference went on, but I really don't think anything else that was brought up is critical to this book. As you might expect (or remember) the first press conference after something like the Battle Over Earth was full of questions and concerns. We didn't know then what we know now, that the Martians had fired their biggest shot for the campaign opener, and that we'd more or less survived. They had plenty left to fight with, though.

We just needed to figure out how to reply. And that's what matters next.

CHAPTER THIRTY-TWO

WHERE NEXT?

I have to be honest, we had no clue what to do next when we all filed into John's office in Admiralty House later that morning. Well, not *no clue*, but no great ideas. We knew we needed to do the general things we'd said in the press conference — make sure we could secure the Empire, and then take the fight to the enemy. But those sorts of goals are exceedingly easy to put on paper, and not so easy to realize in action.

"You think Dave was working for the Martians?" Marlene asked quietly as she settled herself into one of the chairs facing John's desk.

John tilted his head and half shrugged at the prospect, sitting as well, "You know, I really don't know."

"He's not smart enough," my own reaction was abrupt and rather unsympathetic, but then as now, that was my thought on the subject.

"And," Greg rapidly rode in to keep me from sounding too brusque, "if he'd known the Martians were coming, he'd have been expecting them days ago. For all the time that Marlene held them up, he'd have been in a blind panic, not maintaining this inquiry smugly and seeking power."

"Ah yes," John nodded. "So probably not his planning, unless he's very cool under pressure…"

He let the comment trail off — we all did. Our political enemies couldn't be the focus right now. We had gotten rid of them, more or less, at least for the present, so now we had to protect the Empire.

"We need plans. We've lost the Light Squadron, but honestly I couldn't imagine sending them out anywhere even if we still had them. Marlene, you've got one battlewagon at Venus… Ken, I should send you one…" John trailed off again. It's hard to figure out where to start at a time like that, believe me — there are so many different things to consider.

"The independent cruisers in the Belt need to be collected too," Greg filled the silence, and John nodded.

It's often forgotten that the majority of Defense Command's older ships were out on independent cruises in ones and twos in the Belt, looking after our trade interests, showing the flag, and keeping piracy down. We tried to be as friendly towards the independents as we could be, but that meant our frigates and corvettes (and one battleship) out in the asteroid belt were scattered all over, and vulnerable to Martian attack.

"It's been over a week since we lost comms… that's two check-ins with command. Some of them may already be collecting at friendly ports," I crossed my arms, tilting my head thoughtfully.

Standing orders were that, if an independently cruising ship lost contact with command over the course of ten days, it should put into the nearest friendly port to make sure things were alright. Now, the problem with that regulation was that, in the century since it'd been on the books, no ship in that situation (having missed two comm linkups with Defense Command) had ever found a war on when they got to a friendly port, and Captains now tended to be lax in their obedience of the order, following it when it suited their cruise schedules, but not always.

You really couldn't blame them, it was just a *very* inconvenient practice right now.

"True. We'll have comms with friendly ports back in a couple of days, and they might already have gotten word through the Belt. Still, we should show the flag out there, so Ken, why don't you visit the Protectorate on your way back to the Belt? Marlene, you should drop in on the Coalition. If you find any of our ships there, parse them at your discretion, and hopefully you'll find some. Right now I'm looking at the bottom of the barrel in what I can send out to support you. We need to focus on looking after the comm ships we send out."

"And with only seven battleships to do it with too," Greg added quietly. "How long will it take to reactivate mothballed ships?"

John looked up with a frown, "I only had two minutes on the comm with the Comptroller this morning — she's on her way out to the mothball yards now. She thinks she can get us another ten ships in about two weeks, but we're talking *very* old stock, not upgraded. We'll have to press them into service, though."

"Can we rush completion on the new construction in the yards?" Marlene leaned forward slightly, and John's eyes darted down to her.

"I talked to Ray Fletcher for about three minutes this morning. He figures he can get *Bonaventure* out of the docks in three weeks, but it won't be fit for service away from Earth local space for another two months. *Bonavista*, *Hibernia* and *Terra Nova* will be another month each."

Those (of course) were the new battleships in our yards, each of them bigger and tougher than *Warspite*. Originally, *Bonaventure* had been laid down as an assault carrier, but we'd wrangled back control of the contract from Caldecott's people, reengineered the keel as a battleship, and then laid down three more. They were due for launches beginning in 2232, but now they'd be coming out of the docks with all possible haste.

"Well, if you've got them in local space, you can release some of my battleships to the Belt and wherever else we need them," Greg was thinking out loud (as we all obviously were).

John nodded, "Let's make that the plan. In the meantime, Ken, Marlene, get back to your posts by way of our allies. Show the flag and make sure they're being looked after, try to collect some reinforcements and assist any cruisers you feel you safely can. Once we get comms back, we'll be able to properly coordinate this thing."

It probably sounds like a horribly vague plan to you. It sounded even vaguer to the four of us at that moment. But you have to understand, we really didn't know what was going on out there — we didn't have hindsight, and we didn't even have actual intel on what our enemy was doing.

John couldn't afford to weaken Earth's defenses — it was arguably too much to send me and Marlene away. But we had to get back to our posts — Marlene could look after Venus, and I could look after the Belt, and on the way we'd get in touch with our allies in the independent belt. Hopefully we could collect reinforcements from the independent cruisers and establish some sort of war footing.

And then, once comms got restored and we could find out what had been hit, when and where, we could move to respond. Consolidate first, then counter — no point swinging back in the dark with no idea how much harm has been done to you.

"I'll leave tonight, then," I said slowly.

Marlene nodded, "Yes, me too."

"Good," John let out a sigh and looked at Greg. "And we'll hold down the fort."

"Yes, we will," Greg added his own nod.

And then we four sat silently for a couple of minutes, just absorbing all that had happened. It was a mess — a real mess. But we'd deal with things as they came, and hope that the Martians weren't as ready for us as they seemed to be.

You might believe that line of thinking is too defeatist, but we prefer the term 'realistic'. War requires a lot of luck, and I was half afraid we'd exhausted all of ours just stopping this attack short of Earth.

But what I 'half-thought' didn't matter. Our job was to do everything we could to protect the Empire. And that's what we were going to do.

I got back to *Wolf* later that day, having taken a few minutes to stop and visit my parents at their house on Capital Island. I felt bad about visiting when the rest of the crew wasn't going to have the chance to get planetside to see anyone, but I was down, and their home was a short hop from Terra Nova.

As my fighter came down easily on *Wolf's* flight deck, Karen appeared in front of the nose and delivered a wave, then stood and waited for me to get myself up over the side and lower myself to the deck. My knee was still tender from when I'd tweaked it coming down the day before, so it was a slow process.

"So, we're off again?" she had her arms folded and was smiling, not the slightest bit tense at the prospect of going back out into a potential fight.

I tucked my helmet under my arm and nodded, "Back to Belt Two by way of the Hawke Protectorate. We'll see if any independent cruisers berthed there, and if they did we'll round them up and bring them back to the Belt colonies with us."

"Ah, so I finally get to see the Protectorate," Karen's smile twitched. "Meet the infamous Lady Hawke too, I expect."

I grinned, "The two of you coming into personal contact will probably cause some sort of rupture in the fabric of the universe..."

Karen tilted her head, "How's that work, exactly?"

I chuckled, "When you meet her, you'll get it."

You certainly know who Lady Hawke is, and what the Hawke Protectorate is, but believe it or not, up until this time, Karen had never been there, whereas I had (obviously with Charlie Peters). But that's not important for the moment — you can pick up the next volume in this series if you want to know what happened.

"Well, we're fully functioning and ready to boost. I've had the comms open and the crew's been getting in touch with family and friends, so they're ready to go. We have a couple of scorches on the hull I'd like to scrub out, but that can wait," Karen recited the status of *Wolf* as we began to walk from the deck.

"Excellent, we'll boost tonight. Should take us about five days to get to the Protectorate, I figure. Comm ships should be deployed and online soon after we arrive, so we'll be able to properly coordinate our next move with everyone. As soon as *Bonaventure* gets out of the yards, we'll apparently be getting a battleship at Belt Two, so that's good news…"

Karen nodded as I spoke, then glanced at me just before we stepped through the hatch at the opposite side of the deck, "Any idea what we're going to find at Hawke?"

I shook my head, "Hopefully a bunch of our independent cruisers waiting for orders. And if Wes warned Lia, then she'll have the Hawke Navy ready to assist."

With a second nod, Karen fell into step with me, "Let's hope so."

We headed for my cabin.

CHAPTER THIRTY-THREE

AND THE POLITICS OF IT

I don't want to have to finish the political story of what happened in later volumes of these memoirs. I want to wash my hands of the Caldecott situation here and now, so we can worry about telling only the important stories in the coming books.

First of all, the most obvious thing (that I managed to leave out of the first draft of this chapter, embarrassingly enough) is that, by a *unanimous* vote in both Commons and Senate, the Empire was declared at war with the Mars Imperium the morning after the Battle Over Earth. It happened right after our press conference in fact, timed by the government PR people so that the vidcast would pick up right where we left off, and Prime Minister Pope would be able to build upon our very high ratings.

The declaration put the Cabinet on a war footing, and John was immediately voted broad powers over military areas (with less oversight than he was accustomed to in peacetime) and was also given a lot more power over other key sectors, including industry and economy. That proved quite crucial as the war went on.

Then there was the Caldecott situation.

Six weeks after the Battle Over Earth, Dave Caldecott was put before a Parliamentary inquiry into his conduct. He was stripped of rank and any title he might have had the chance to gain as a former Second Lord, and his case was forwarded on to the courts.

Despite an appeal on the part of the Emperor, Dave Caldecott was found by the Justices of the Privy Council (that's what it was called before we renamed it the Imperial Supreme Court) to be guilty of 'possible treachery', and was exiled and declared an enemy of the Empire. The important element of that sentence was the 'enemy of the Empire' part, which as you probably know means that, should Dave show his face in Imperial territory again, it was the obligation of every Imperial citizen to *do him harm*. That clause was apparently lifted from ancient Roman law by the writers of the Articles of Empire, for exclusive use in situations like this one. If Caldecott was arrested in Imperial territory, he'd be sent to the gallows.

Now that probably sounds harsh, but had the Privy Council found him guilty of definite (not 'possible') treachery, he would have been executed.

Rumors have circulated that John was responsible for the exile sentence, and the rumors are right — but the context is often misunderstood on this subject.

You see, the Emperor was making public appeals on behalf of his loyal servant, the Second Lord, vowing that the man was of good character and could not have possibly been conspiring with the Martians. Behind closed doors, the Emperor was pulling strings within the Privy Council to try to get Caldecott executed.

Huh?

My first reaction exactly, but think of it this way: if the Emperor defends a man as being innocent, and then Defense Command sees him executed rashly, the Emperor gains some ammunition against us. Particularly when that Emperor wants to declare a vendetta against the First Lord later in life, and tries to accuse him of creating a conspiracy that framed Caldecott.

But that is indeed a later story that I'll have to cover separately.

John, believing that Caldecott was indeed merely an idiot, not a traitor, pulled enough strings, and did enough press junkets to get the people and Parliament on his side, and Caldecott was exiled as opposed to executed. So, eight weeks after the Battle Over Earth — eight weeks from the day when he'd thought he was about to take over the Admiralty — Dave Caldecott was put under the charge of Captain Liam Singh aboard the battleship *Empire*, and under the escort of Shannon Hunter's frigates, was delivered to the Coalition of Unaligned Asteroids, where he apparently used his personal funds to establish himself.

As the CUA was (and still is) quite a good ally of the Empire, we put watching him in the hands of their excellent intelligence services.

Another story for another time. As I once said to Karen, Caldecott had the character of an ancient Greek named Alcibiades — a man who led Athens to disaster in war against Sparta, then joined Sparta and had an affair with the King's wife, then joined Persia, before joining Athens again. His loyalties were to whatever power he sided with, right up until the moment they kicked him out. That's Dave Caldecott for you…

Caldecott's circle was deprived of its last leadership when Admiral Michaels, the last big-name flag officer, was cashiered from the service on the charge of having exceeded her orders. She had tried, remember, to keep command of *Warspite* until Greg came aboard… but the problem is she never actually *exceeded* her orders. She wasn't relieved until Greg boarded his ship, so her actions up until that point were officially authorized.

But then the inquiry into Caldecott dirtied her already poor reputation, and the people were screaming for blood, so Admiral Michaels was lucky to get away with a mere cashiering.

The only real regret John, Marlene, Greg and I share about the political fallout is the disgrace that was piled onto George Parks-Dawes. As I stated repeatedly back in the chapters he was involved in, the man wasn't politically on our side, but he was duty-bound to Earth and he did his very best and gave his *life* for the Empire. And contrary to the media's later claims, he wasn't incompetent — he was unlucky, and damned from the start by the type of ships he was fighting with.

If you go back and listen to the interviews we all gave about the Battle Over Earth, none of us — not John, Greg, Marlene, nor I — ever once criticized Parks-Dawes' character, or even his judgment. Yes, his tactics didn't work, but he couldn't have known that they wouldn't until the disaster actually befell him. While some say he shouldn't have used untested tactics to deploy so many large ships, I have to wonder what else he could have done at just that moment. It was a desperate fight, and he fought with gallant innovation that just happened to fail. If his tactic had worked, what do you think history would have said about him? That he was as good as the rest of us, or better.

It's about time the media goes back and corrects the wrong impression that was created of this officer. He doesn't deserve to pass into history in ignominy.

CHAPTER THIRTY-FOUR

ON THE WAY AGAIN

I knocked on Karen's cabin door around noon of the day after we boosted from Earth orbit. She wasn't on watch for the first day out, Matt was taking command so that Karen could get a bit of rest. We weren't running drills immediately — there was little point, as the crew had done so marvelously in the Battle Over Earth. We'd do more exercises in the days of the trip to the Hawke Protectorate, but for the first day, we'd all get some rest.

There was no answer when I knocked, so I wondered what she might be up to. Dancing away her stress? Well possibly... or sleeping, perhaps. It might not sound very heroic, but we officers do need the same occasional sleep-in you do to keep sane. Relatively sane, at least.

Well, whatever it was, I'd find out.

Keying her combination into the door pad, I listened to the clunk as the hatch unlocked, then I opened it and poked my head in. Sure enough she was out like a light on the bed.

Karen prides herself on being an early riser most days, and while her need to sleep in was completely understandable under the circumstances, I wasn't about to pass up the opportunity to give her a bit of grief about it.

Creeping in and closing the hatch behind me, I edged around to the side of her bed and settled myself into the chair next to it. I then leaned forward to tap her on the shoulder, but as I did she started to roll over, her face turning my way. I leaned back and waited — maybe she'd seen me...

When her eyes remained shut, I decided she was indeed still asleep, so I leaned forward again to tap her on the shoulder... but just couldn't do it. She was sleeping peacefully, and that's not something I could bear to disturb, given how late she'd been up the night prior and how much we'd had to do in the past two weeks.

Remarkably enough, it had really only been two weeks. And come to think of it, Karen hadn't been sleeping much over those long days. On the way from the Belt colonies to Earth she'd had one good night's sleep, but she'd spent a lot of perfectly good sleeping time being on call to listen to my worries about what we'd find at Earth.

Now that Earth was safe and we had a better idea of what was going on across the Empire, I was in much better shape mentally.

Yes, things were better... I leaned back in the chair and started thinking about how things really could have been a great deal worse. Luck had thus far allowed us to save the Belt Squadron from piecemeal destruction, and had delayed the Martian strike on Earth (which we assume was supposed to be delivered shortly after the strike on Belt Two) until just after we could arrive with warning.

And now Karen and I were playing cards at a table in the middle of an open field on a nice day.

"Got any eights?" she asked.

"Ha, go fish."

She picked up a card, tucked it into her hand, looked down at her cards, then back at me, "Blackjack."

Laying her cards down face-up, she revealed her royal flush.

"Damn," I threw my cards to the table again, "you always win this game."

Then I stopped and contemplated how I'd gone from Karen's cabin to the card table...

I'd fallen asleep in Karen's chair. And sure enough, as I opened my eyes, there she was, smiling at me, "You came to visit?"

Trying to straighten myself in the chair, I blinked a couple of times, "Well you looked like you were having so much fun..."

"I was, until you started snoring."

"You know full well I don't snore!" I objected, and she sat up in bed and shrugged.

"Well I wasn't, so it must have been you," she said playfully.

I shook my head, leaning forward, "Nah, you dreamed it."

She chuckled, "I was *not* dreaming about sleep, believe me."

I cocked an eyebrow, "You don't say."

"I do say," Karen smiled. "Hungry?"

"Definitely. It's time for lunch or some other meal. Let's get food."

Pushing myself to my feet, I headed to the kitchen while Karen got herself out of bed. We then ate food and talked about the Hawke Protectorate, and passed most of the first day of our trip to that ally doing nothing productive...

But then you can't always be productive. That's the one big advantage of these long hauls between colonies: you have time to slow down, relax a bit, and recover.

And we both needed to do that.

So as *Wolf* drove through space towards Hawke One at 190 kps, we ate potatoes and fish sticks.

AFTERWORD

The Rogue Commodore was about 60,000 words, and this book is nearly the same length. Hopefully you're fine with the fact that you have to wait a little while to find out my version of what happens when *Wolf* arrives at Hawke One.

Of course, you may have seen either of the movies about it, but neither is very good, in my opinion. I'll probably get challenged to a duel for saying that, but, well, bring it on.

Next book we get to add Lady Hawke to this narrative, and I know there's been much whispering and gossip about that — people want the inside dirt on Lia Hawke, for whatever reasons. As you'll see, what you'd expect is what you get. *The Hawke Mission*, as I'm going to call it, will be out for your reading pleasure soon enough.

Incidentally, it's a great failure on my part, but I'm not really going to get to explain what Marlene found when she got to the Coalition of Unaligned Asteroids, let alone what she faced when she got back to Venus — those stories should be books all their own, so I can point you to her own memoirs for the detail, or suggest the official history of the war.

I'm actually trying to convince a rather good historian I know to get working on them, but to avoid spoiling the chances of getting him to agree, I won't mention his name here.

Anyway, that's been *The Almost Coup*, I do hope it's been enlightening.

Thanks for reading — and see you next time!

THE
HAWKE
MISSION

THE AUTOBIOGRAPHICAL REMINISCENCES OF
ADMIRAL THE LORD KEN BARRON FOR 2231

THE MARTIAN WAR - 3

KENNETH TAM

FROM THE AUTHOR

Welcome to the third installment of the Martian War series! In my introduction to *The Rogue Commodore*, I explained where the series came from (*Star Defenders, Bonaventure*) and how yes, Ken Barron is sort of based on me. In *The Almost Coup*, I explained how this reminiscence style came about. Up next: the Earth Empire.

So what's up with the Empire? It seems to be a force for good in the solar system. That's a bit of a switch from the Empires we're used to hearing about — the sorts that collapse Republics and are ruled by tyrannical robed Emperors who desperately need dermatological care. Well yes, the Earth Empire is a departure.

I set out to present a different sort of Empire in these books — one you actually might be able to root for. Essentially, it's based on the British Empire of the late nineteenth century, but with modern enhancements. The Earth Empire, for instance, is *not* dominated by the scientific racism that marked the old British Empire, and it doesn't disrupt any indigenous peoples (all humans out there are newly-settled colonists). The better aspects of the old British Empire were adopted though: the Earth Emperor's power is checked by Parliament, and every adult in the Empire has a vote.

What about Defense Command officers being celebrities? It might seem odd to us today that combat officers could be big-time celebrities — that's a status we reserve for movie stars and such — but if you look at the British Empire of the late nineteenth century, military heroes were indeed big-name celebs. Instead of celebrity magazines, there were popular books full of color portraits of people like General Roberts ('Bobs of India'), General Wolseley ('our only General'), or Lord Kitchener ('Kitchener of Khartoum', 'K of K'). And I suppose that makes sense: these fellows were promoting the glory of the British Empire in a time when Imperial glory was very popular. As it turns out, in 2231, things aren't all that different... well, except for the presence of 24-hour news.

Anyway, that's just a little background on where the ideas for the Earth Empire came from. On to the usual acknowledgments...

Once again, some of the characters you'll read about are based on friends of mine, so thanks to all of them for letting me steal their personalities!

Peter Caron deserves a very special thanks in this book: he was instrumental in helping me develop the character of Lia Hawke, much to everyone's benefit. Specific thanks as well to my good friend Wes Prewer, for his continued support (graphical and otherwise) on this series.

Finally, the biggest thanks again to my family: Jacqui and Peter are the best parents I could have asked for. I keep saying that and I mean it. Those of you who read many of my acknowledgments pages will expect me to next thank my German Shepherd Atlas. My dear friend Atlas passed away last summer; to him I owe the greatest thanks of all, for the lessons he taught me. I hope that, in some small way, his legacy lives on with all my books.

– Kenneth Tam

FOREWORD

So, based on the kinds of comments I've been getting, these reminiscences seem to be pretty popular, and that's neat. I guess I'm not entirely crazy... or at least if I am indeed insane, I'm an entertaining sort of insane. If that's the case, thanks for enjoying my insane ramblings.

If you're reading this then chances are you've already picked up *The Rogue Commodore* and *The Almost Coup*, but if for some reason you haven't, go buy them. In the meantime, let me explain to you where we are in chronological terms: the Martians have launched a surprise war against us, and the Belt Squadron under my command beat them and their pirate allies senseless at Belt Two. After that we rushed to Earth, and with the help of Admiral Greg Noyce and First Lord John Fiora, undid the inquiry of Second Lord Dave Caldecott that had paralyzed our defenses. Then Admiral Marlene Stoll arrived... with the Martian battle fleet on her heels, so we beat them back at the cost of all the Light Squadron's big ships.

Good, now that you're caught up, this book takes *Wolf*, with me, Karen and Charlie Peters aboard, to none other than the Hawke Protectorate. Based on the feedback I've been getting, this part of the story is highly anticipated — people seem to love stories of politics and combat in the Belt.

That and there seems to be a bit of an interest in Lady Lia Hawke. Go figure.

Let me tell you right now, though, Lia Hawke probably isn't what you're expecting her to be, and while we do have some adventures while on this Hawke Mission, the movies truly get it wrong. You'll see what I mean.

Anyway, I won't prattle on any longer.

This is *The Hawke Mission*.

CHAPTER ONE

WE DO A LOT OF TRAVELING

Wolf was plying the space between Earth and the Hawke Protectorate when I left you in *The Almost Coup*, so let's pick back up with that... just four days later.

Wolf was in the last full day of its cruise to the Protectorate. Like our earlier cruise from the Belt to Earth to warn about the Martian attack, this particular voyage wasn't too exciting. We did locate the wreck of another communications ship, which again angered me, but I was better able to control my reaction this time.

Knowing we'd thwarted the main Martian attack on Earth gave me a little less reason to be incensed, but make no mistake, I was still *not* pleased when we ran across the communications ship *Oki*, Commander Joan McClusky. The small ship, like *Marconi* and the rest of that rotation of communications ships, had been destroyed by Martian cruisers before their attacks on Earth and at the Belt.

Hopefully the communications ships of the next rotation, hastily called out of the servicing yards to reconnect Earth to the Empire, were already heading out to their stations...

But anyway, as I start this book we were only about a day from Hawke One, the capital asteroid of the Hawke Protectorate. Then (as now), the Hawke Protectorate was one of our closest allies, and at that time it was still at least partially run by its original patriarch, Lord Ian Hawke. Now, sorry to start piling on historical context in the first chapter, but for the sake of those who don't know their history, let me explain who Hawke was, and what the 'Protectorate' meant.

Lord Hawke was, of course, the First Lord of the Admiralty for Defense Command just before the turn of the century — a little more than thirty years before these events. He'd beaten the pre-syndicate pirates to such an impressive pulp in his term as First Lord that the Emperor had perpetuated his title of 'Lord' beyond his term (something that happened only rarely in those days) and gave him a reward... a *Protectorate*.

Basically, the Protectorate of Hawke was Lord Ian Hawke's personal fief of six asteroids — and they were (and are) very well stocked. Those six rocks had been on the list of asteroids the Empire wanted to colonize, but for years we hadn't been able to pool sufficient funds to seed them, and we were afraid the Martians would snatch them up in the meantime.

So we gave them to Lord Ian Hawke. He had plenty of corporate connections, and combined with his reputation, his personal fortune, and the force of surplus warships we sold him, he was able to set up colonies in no time. The understanding, of course, was that he would trade his resources with us — not the Martians — and that as an 'independent' player in the Belt, he'd build alliances with other unaligned asteroids, giving us diplomatic opportunities to secure more markets for our goods.

And you know what? It worked. Big time.

The boom in the Imperial economy beginning in 2210 can be credited to a couple of things: the rise of the last Belt colonies to their full economic potential, and the massive export trade we started with a dozen unaligned asteroids.

So that's the brief history of the Hawke Protectorate. I've probably left things out, and I'll mention them if they become relevant...

As for Lord Ian Hawke... well, he was a bit of a curmudgeon. Some people use words that are much less polite to describe him, like 'ass'. Suffice it to say he was old (over 80 when this all happened, and still hanging on), he was an advocate of his own legend, and he kept what you might describe as a harem... under the guises of polite court.

Yes, he ran *court*, just like the Emperor. If that doesn't tell you something about him...

Anyway, he was one of the people we were going to see.

How does this relate to day four of *Wolf's* cruise towards Hawke One? Well, I was in the process of laying out my court dress (not an actual dress, as my editor laughingly suggested, but pants and a jacket that composed court attire) on my bed.

You see, regular dress uniform isn't good enough for Lord Hawke's court, he likes all courtiers and guests to wear the court dress that was in vogue when he was First Lord. You've probably seen the pictures. This stuff was ornate, impractical, and utterly useless in a decompression scenario. It wasn't even self sealing, and it had *braid*.

Having been to Hawke a number of times before, I owned a set of acceptable court wear.

It needed brushing up, and I had to add the fifth bar to its collar — I was a Commodore now, after all — before it would be fit to wear.

I was actually fighting with that bar on the right collar when there was a knock at the hatch. I looked up, and before I said anything, it popped open and Karen poked her head through, "Hey-hey."

"Karen!" I was already frustrated with the rank bar, so apparently I was sounding slightly testy, "What're you doing sticking your head in here like that? I could've been naked!"

In retrospect, no, I have no idea why I said something so ridiculous.

Karen's eyebrows climbed and a smile twitched onto the corners of her lips, "Um. Right."

"You want to come help me with this damned rank bar thingie, or not?"

Karen's smile extended to full breadth and she stepped into my cabin, closing the hatch behind her. Sauntering over, she seated herself smoothly on the bed next to me, leaning over my court uniform with a frown.

I leaned back as the blonde back of her head interrupted my sight of the collar, "Getting a good look?"

"Is this what I think it is?"

I cocked an eyebrow, "Well, if you think it's court dress, then yes. If you think it's something else, then no."

Karen leaned back, sitting upright on the bed and looking at me, "This is *court dress*. Does that mean I need it?"

I looked at her, and our eyes locked in one of those 'uh-oh' moments.

"Um. Yes."

Karen's eyes shifted back to the suit and she nodded twice, very shortly, "Really. Well. That's a bit of problem."

I have to say, I was slightly frozen. I could just picture Karen showing up in Lord Hawke's court in her regular dress uniform — if she somehow got past the dress code guards at the door, he'd certainly start spitting wheezy insults at her. Stuff about women and pants...

Yes, in case you've never seen the pictures, court dress from the period Lord Hawke preferred demanded gowns, and *only* gowns, for women — not like the stuff that's worn today (or even the dress uniforms worn to Imperial Court in and around 2231). To put it rather bluntly, Lord Hawke was a dirty old man, and as he got older he increasingly reverted to the old attitudes of the 2150s.

"So nobody told you that Lord Hawke was old fashioned about court dress?" I slid that question out rather awkwardly — awkwardly because there were only two people aboard *Wolf* who'd been to Hawke's court before... me and Charlie Peters.

"No, you didn't mention that..." Karen bit her lip for a second, and I got that sort of disembodied guilty feeling — you know, the one you get when you realize you forgot to tell someone important to you about something important.

Well *I* get that feeling, anyway. If you don't, then you don't know what I'm talking about. And there's an open chance that you're a horrible person.

But Karen, remember, is Karen McMaster. The incomparable and unflappable.

She looked back at me, "Well... I guess I'm going to cause a sensation."

And then she smiled her 'mischief' smile.

That instantly got rid of the guilty feeling, and I grinned, "I'd be shocked if you didn't."

Wolf cruised on towards Hawke One.

CHAPTER TWO

MEANWHILE, IN INDIANA

DCNS *Indiana* was a second-generation *North America*-class frigate — a ship of the same class as *Alberta* from the Belt Squadron, but about fifteen years older. That class of frigates was pretty long lived, mainly because within the same hull design, their kit and electronics and whatnot had all been improved over time.

Basically, *Alberta* might look the same as *Alabama* (the first of the *North America* line of frigates), but there were numerous advancements built into *Alberta's* hull that *Alabama* just didn't have.

And keep in mind, even *Alberta* was by this time already about ten years old, meaning *Indiana* was twenty-five, and *Alabama* was thirty-three. These sound like long periods of service, and in reality they are, but that was the nature of naval building these days — it wasn't like some periods in history when navies turned over ships every fifteen years... it was more like other periods in history where floating ships just weren't decommissioned.

Wow, like the precision with that historical allusion? Yikes.

Well, anyway, for its age, *Indiana* was being very well cared for, and it was still an effective combat vessel, especially for the duty it had been assigned. Like twenty-six other ships in the Defense Command fleet, *Indiana* was an independent belt cruiser, one of the ships that plied the trade routes between the free rocks, showing our flag and hunting piracy wherever it could be found. Ships like *Indiana* very seldomly returned to Earth or the Belt colonies; resupplying with our allies, they usually stayed out for a year, two or even three before returning to an Imperial port to rotate personnel.

That last part probably doesn't matter for the present context. *Indiana* was in the middle of one of its long cruises out behind a charming backwater hellhole called Caligula when it lost contact with Earth. Captain Elsie McKinnon didn't think much of that at first — the usual weekly comm check-ins between independent cruisers and Earth got addled now and then. These things happened.

It was when the *second* check-in didn't go through that she started worrying.

The space through which Elsie McKinnon was cruising at the time — all the area 'behind' Caligula — was relatively lightly traveled by Earth traders, and that's why she was out there. Her sources on Hephaestus Rock had tipped her off to the presence of pirates in these little-traveled sectors of the Belt, and she was sniffing around. She was on to something, but I'll get to that later. The important point to make right now is that she hadn't run across any civilian shipping that could warn her of the war that had been going on for about eleven days.

So with no word of what was going on, and no friendly shipping around to tell her, Elsie McKinnon decided to do the logical thing: she headed for Caligula. Let's now pick up with her just as her Helm and Navigation Officer was maneuvering her ship to connect with Caligula's main dome dock.

"We'll have hard dock in a minute now, ma'am."

McKinnon nodded at the report, then folded her arms with a frown, glancing at her XO, "Think I should be worried about not getting to speak to our mission?"

When *Indiana* had come into comm range of Caligula, the first comm call McKinnon had placed was to the Earth Empire mission to Caligula — our mini-embassy, so to speak. But Caligula CommNet had blocked the call for reasons unknown.

The XO shrugged and then shook his head, "I doubt the Caligulans are going to mess with us. Probably just comm trouble."

Caligula was a tiny colony of 50,000 people in four small, filthy domes, all set up independently and only one of them supposedly Earthgreen (for those of you, like my editor, who don't know what 'Earthgreen' is, it means simulated sky, day and night, etc... you know, like every belt colony... and here I thought it was a common everyday term, like 'perspicacity'). The colony's economy was based on mineral extraction and the selling of those extracted minerals to the Empire — they'd be fools to disrespect a Defense Command ship.

Oh, and I should mention that Caligula signed a treaty with the Empire in 2224, which gave our ships — both civilian and military — favored status, and required Caligula to side with us in any formal war that might take place. Standard clause for the trade deal.

You're probably getting the idea of where this is going.

"Hard dock... now."

McKinnon glanced back across the bridge at her Helm and Navigation Officer and nodded, "Thanks Jack. Comm, try to get the mission for me again. And if you get blocked, I want someone in government." Glancing back at her XO, McKinnon shook her head slowly, "I'm not in the mood to deal with crap."

Then the boarding alert alarms began to sound.

McKinnon frowned and turned quickly to the operations consoles at the rear of the bridge, her XO quickly rounding them and stopping to look over the shoulders of their operators. Boarding alert in a friendly dock didn't make a lot of sense...

But McKinnon wasn't a fool, "Security, assemble anti-boarding parties. Get the Special Branch team to the bridge. Just in case."

Keep in mind, McKinnon had no idea there was a war on. And even if she'd known, this wouldn't be what she expected at all...

"Ma'am..." her XO looked up, then bobbed his head at the main screen. The display at the front of the bridge flashed from a local space map to an internal camera feed... from the docking airlock.

Two of *Indiana's* crew were standing against the corridor wall; grimy looking soldiers with heavy weapons were standing in front of them. A file of similarly grimy soldiers was coming aboard, and as screens two through nine started putting up separate internal camera feeds, it became clear there were a lot of grimy soldiers. And they were extremely grimy (hence the repetition of that word).

With them, though, was a well-dressed man.

"Lock us down, all sections but the ones they're in. Warn the crew to prepare to repel boarders. Wait for my order," McKinnon had been out in the independent belt long enough to know that starting by picking a fight, even in situations as clearly inappropriate as this, was not a good idea.

I know, your Imperial pride might be burning right now, and hers certainly was, but if she immediately started shooting at these people, and one of them got on the comm to the defensive gunners of Caligula, *Indiana* could be disabled before its drives worked up enough strength to break away from the dock.

Talking had to be an option in such a scenario.

"They're heading for us, I think," the SF Lieutenant barked rather sharply, tapping each of his techs on the shoulder and handing them mags from the arms box as he spoke.

"No kidding. Any sign of them heading for other secured areas?" McKinnon asked the question as she crossed the deck to the arms box and pulled out a mag for herself.

The XO had yet to arm himself, as he was leaning over the shoulder of one of his operators, "Negative on that, ma'am. They're only coming here. We're guessing about fifty so far… and more coming in."

Were it me, I'd have been thinking '*Dammit all*' about then.

"Boarding teams one through six are ready and positioned to protect engineering and the technical sections, ma'am. All personnel have reported in from their repel-boarders stations…" the SF Lieutenant looked up from his bank of consoles.

"They'll be up here in about a minute at this rate," the XO reported, then collected a mag from the arms box as well.

McKinnon nodded to both reports, then turned to the bridge door, "I can't meet them in here. XO, the bridge is yours. Keep an eye on me and be ready to block the door. Helm, get the drives ready for emergency breakaway."

The bridge door opened just as McKinnon took a step towards it, and Major Ted Jieshi stepped in — *Indiana's* head of Special Branch (and incidentally, a friend of Charlie's), "We're set up to defend out here, ma'am. What's going on?"

McKinnon headed to the door and shook her head as she passed him, "I'm going to try to find out. More than fifty soldiers are aboard my ship."

Jieshi frowned, "Only fifty?"

From the perspective of a Special Brancher (or anyone who knew that *Indiana* had a crew of over 300) that number seemed rather… inadequate.

McKinnon kept shaking her head as she stepped out of the bridge and Jieshi closed the hatch behind them. He and his team were, to their seeming misfortune at this moment, still equipped with EP-5 rifles, not the shiny new MAG-90s that were Charlie's glee at this point. One of the problems independent cruisers often faced was a lack of the most current supplies.

But there were still a dozen black clad Special Branchers in the corridor, standing imposingly in two files, one against each wall. McKinnon and Jieshi marched between them, then came to a stop at their head, and squared themselves, looking rather menacing.

You might be thinking it stupid for the Captain to put herself in the line of fire like that, but I'd have done it in this sort of situation, and so would Karen. Sometimes independent rocks got overconfident, and the only way to get them to see sense (without declaring war on them and thus alienating the rest of your independent allies and partners) was to talk tough.

Elsie McKinnon was ready to do that...

And on cue, the column of grimy soldiers (apparently these fine specimens were, in dramatic style, called the 'Caligula Guard') came around a corner a ways down the corridor.

They slowed down as they caught sight of the Special Branchers and McKinnon, but they pressed on up the corridor towards the roadblock until the distance was down to about ten meters. Then they stopped.

McKinnon's eyes narrowed, and her hand noticeably moved to the handle of her mag (this was all recorded by the cameras on deck, if you're wondering about my narrative detail), and Ted Jieshi kept his right hand on the handle of his EP-5, then patted the top of the barrel with the left. Such unsubtle signs of strength are often needed when dealing with less... *refined* members of the independent belt population.

The Caligula Guard troopers puffed up (rather goon-like) and started brandishing their own rifles (very old EP-3s that we'd probably sold them in the 2220s), but before things took a messy turn, the tall, gangly, gaunt, supposedly well-dressed man who'd come aboard with the troops sauntered around them, coming to a stop in the gap between the two parties.

"Violence won't be necessary if you cooperate, Captain. You are ordered to stand down your ship immediately, for internment in our neutral port, or you will destroyed."

Huh?

Um.

Yeah.

Elsie McKinnon scowled at this man, "Who exactly are you?"

It's interesting, all the self-important officials of every insignificant rock seem to expect Defense Command officers to know them by name. This one looked almost offended as he answered, "I am Ambassador Jack Croft, of the Caligula government. You are interned, Captain. I'm here to order you to stand down your ship, and if you don't our batteries will disable your drives. I want your reactor offline before I go."

Impudence is bad, and this order seemed to smack of a great deal of it, but McKinnon was actually in a tough spot (as history, and the brief after-action inquiry, have both done well to recognize). With a large body of soldiers having surprised the technicians at *Indiana's* lock, she faced two problems. If she attacked the boarders, it'd take time and cost lives to get them off her ship, and worse, her drive pods would probably be blasted apart before she could get up to power.

So despite the fact that, under power and free to maneuver, her frigate would be more than a match for this rock's defenses, she was quite trapped.

Then something else occurred to her, "You said you're *neutral*? Neutral in what?"

Croft smiled in a rather sinister fashion — you know, the cliché way bad guys always seem to smile, "Mars and Earth are at war. Pleased to be the first to tell you that. Now order your reactors offline and I'll leave your ship in peace."

Once a ship's reactors were completely shut down (not left on standby idling), it took about four hours to get back up to drive power, and during those four hours, the energy output was massive and impossible to miss. In other words, with reactors offline, *Indiana* would be defenseless against space attack, and if McKinnon tried to restart them, her drive pods would be shot off before they were even close to being ready to make thrust.

But she had no choice.

"I'll inform my government of this," she gritted her teeth as she said the words. "If you know what's good for you, you'll leave my ship before I'm forced to do that."

"No, you'll shut down your reactor, and *we'll* send word out for you. Or do you want your ship destroyed?"

It's hard to explain the frustration McKinnon had to be feeling. She'd essentially lost her ship without a fight — she'd been blindsided because she hadn't been suspicious of a treaty-bound 'ally' of the Empire. Now, to you and to me it sounds like she couldn't be blamed for not being a paranoid panicker, but at a moment like that, as she reached for her comm and gave the order to shut down the reactors, she was mentally going through all the 'mistakes' she'd made.

Good Captains have nightmares about days like this one. McKinnon, as far as I'm concerned, was a good Captain indeed — she lived through her nightmare, and she kept her head together.

"Now," her eyes had been locked on Jack Croft since he'd stepped forward, "get off my ship. *Now.*"

Jack Croft nodded in that polite-but-sneering way bad guys do, then turned on his heel and waved his soldiers back down the corridor.

McKinnon stood still, and next to her Ted Jieshi's grip on his EP-5 tightened, "So what now?"

She didn't know what would come next, so she just remained silent.

Indiana was interned.

Chapter Three

Cyclops And Banff

In a separate sector of the free belt — but one not too far from Caligula in relative terms — the battleship *Cyclops* was cruising for Hawke Six (the furthest-out rock in the Protectorate). *Cyclops* was the only Imperial capital ship in the Belt — remember, we didn't even have any at the Belt colonies any more. Its job was to travel around showing the flag, and theoretically, to be ready to smash any pirate bases that were found by the cruisers we had out there.

But, as Captain Christian 'Mik' Mikaelsen would tell you (and as he told me several times over his two years on patrol) the pirates were always far too smart and far too quick to get caught by a ship with *Cyclops'* laser power. He did a lot of menacing, and was able to protect entire colonies by simply being in the area, but for the two years of his command, Mik hadn't seen a single fight.

The last ten days, however, were threatening to change all that. Having lost contact with Earth, Mik had done the sensible thing before heading for a friendly port: he'd commed ahead to the Protectorate — the ally nearest to his cruising sector — to see what was going on. You might think this was a common-sense approach to a comm blackout situation, but believe it or not, not every Captain with the opportunity to contact an allied port did so. In *Indiana's* case, there was no communication because the ship was out of range of any rock other than Caligula, but with exceptions like that aside, a number of Captains simply didn't contact friendly ports by comm when they lost touch with Earth. I don't know why, but they didn't.

That's not true, actually. I heard one such Captain's excuse on this subject — he thought it would have been detrimental to Imperial security to reveal his inability to contact the Admiralty. I don't know if I buy that, but whatever my judgment, he certainly didn't comm an ally to see if they had any information on the silence... and of course, every one of our major allies in the Belt could have explained it to him.

Wes Pellew had spread word of the war — remember, Caligula had known about it.

Anyway, pardon that minor rant. Christian Mikaelsen had called Hawke Six, and so he knew about the threat. His ship was now cruising at best speed to Hawke Six to link up with whatever Defense Command ships rallied there, and he was personally spending many long hours on his bridge, just in case there was trouble.

And, go figure, we join him as trouble arrived.

"Sir... getting a distress call... urgent..."

Mik was sitting in his chair staring rather intensely (he can get this intense stare sometimes), but he blinked and looked up at the report, "Really? Helm, stand by for course correction. What've you got, Finn?"

The Lieutenant Commander at Sensors and Communications was frowning and leaning over one of his technician's shoulders, "No double check that... one moment, sir..."

Mik got to his feet and walked slowly towards the bank of consoles, watching the seemingly baffled Lieutenant Commander with a patient but eager gaze. In two years of cruising so far, *Cyclops* hadn't so much as received a distress signal — such was the uninteresting life of belt cruising in a ship too scary to tangle with.

The Lieutenant Commander abruptly looked up, "Sir, it's from *Banff*, they're taking fire from a squadron of unknown ships..."

Mik stopped in his tracks.

Yes, he'd been warned in his last message from the Protectorate that open hostilities had begun with Mars, but somehow intellectually knowing that didn't equate with being ready to hear that one of Defense Command's ships out here was taking direct fire.

Mik nodded after that very brief, thoughtful pause, "Confirm that. And pass coordinates to helm."

The Lieutenant Commander nodded to his technicians, and now two of them rechecked the feed, making sure it was marked with all the right transponder codes. The information was then passed on to the helm.

"Coordinates received, Captain. Should we adjust course?" the Helm and Navigation Officer turned back from his consoles.

Mik nodded, "Head toward the signal source, maximum thrust. What's our ETA?"

"About... forty minutes, sir."

Hopefully that would be time enough. If this was some sort of Martian attack, forty minutes could be far too long, but a call like this could also be a baited trap. Caution was definitely in order.

"Confirming, sir. *Banff*'s tags, correct sending protocol... the signal looks legit."

Mik's expression tightened, and he nodded once, "Get us there, redline the drives. Finn, signal Hawke Six and inform them of our situation. Ask them to pass word on to our embassy and to distribute a warning to all Defense Command traffic that there might be hostile ships in this area. Then send to *Banff* to hold on, we're coming."

The Sensors and Communications Officer nodded, turning to his techs again and slotting them to various duties encompassed in Mik's command. The Captain then turned to the officer of the watch, "Let's go to general quarters."

Cyclops turned hard to port, and its powerful drives pushed hard, getting the big battleship up from its leisurely 165 kps cruising speed to its maximum of 193 kps. It may not sound fast compared to a frigate, but for a battleship that was pretty good indeed.

Captain Christian Mikaelsen rode to the rescue.

But *Banff* was destroyed, entirely, within minutes of sending the signal. One of the corvette's data recorders did survive, though it wasn't found by a salvage crew until almost a year after this incident. What we learned from it, though, was that Commander Fred Herwig had been heading for Hawke Six to check in, much as Mik had been.

Herwig had only been three months into his cruise of the Belt, and on his latest route he'd been poking around space not far from where *Indiana* had been — just a little further down towards the Protectorate. After two failed comm check-ins, he'd been heading for a friendly port, though we don't know if he knew about the state of war. He certainly didn't check in with Hawke Six before heading there, because their comm records show no communications with *Banff* after war was declared... but he could have found out elsewhere. The recorder we salvaged told us nothing about Herwig's signal history.

We did get a good look at *Banff*'s sensor data.

Four ships had appeared on its scope, cruising in formation, and before Herwig was able to react to them, his ship had lost one drive pod to enemy fire. *Banff* put up a good fight, but there wasn't much it could do to save itself. The distress signal went out, and the ship died.

And *Banff*, we found out later, wasn't the only victim of this sort. But I suppose I'll get into that more later.

By the time *Cyclops* hurtled into sensor range of the debris field, there was... well... nothing but debris.

On the bridge of the battlewagon, Mik wasn't at all comfortable with what he was seeing. Pacing back and forth before the main monitor, he kept his eyes moving between his officers and the displays of wreckage.

"Come on, Finn, any survivors?" his question sounded frustrated, but I don't think anyone could blame him for that.

For the record, Defense Command ships had not been attacked during their independent belt cruises since the fall of the Syndicate, and even in that time it was rare for them to be hit, and almost impossible for them to be completely destroyed.

"Not seeing any beacons from life pods. No active drives from small craft..." the Sensors and Communications Officer shook his head as he moved between the consoles he oversaw.

Mik let out a sharp breath and shook his head. It was tough to accept that no one got off that corvette alive.

"Any sign of the attackers?" his question was again sharp.

A pause ensued as Lieutenant Commander Finn Yaalon consulted his technicians, and then he looked up, shaking his head, "We've got nothing on scope, sir. Not so much as a drive wake."

"Right," Mik rasped the word almost under his breath, then turned to Helm and Navigation. "Heave to, prepare SAR operations. Launch both fighter squadrons, put Star Squadron on recon — I want a three-hour sensor buffer around this area. Burst Squadron will assist with the search for survivors."

The orders came quickly, and Mik's well-trained crew began executing immediately. He was counting on the fact that *nobody* dared mess with a battleship, and using that fact to allow for a search for survivors. His Star (F-194 Starlight) Squadron would fan out away from the wreck site, watching for a return by the original attackers, while his Burst (F-184 Starburst) Squadron would help sift the wreckage to see if anyone had lived through *Banff*'s loss.

"Signal Hawke Six and request support of any Defense Command ships in port," Mik turned back to the main screen and stroked his beard (I know beard-stroking might sound cliché, but Mik pulls it off).

Cyclops hove to and looked for survivors. None were found.

CHAPTER FOUR

THEN WE ARRIVED

I received some complaints about the unimaginative chapter titles in *The Almost Coup*... sorry, I lack imagination... and the will to try to acquire imagination. Look forward to more bland or painfully corny chapter titles.

Of course, that has nothing to do with *Wolf's* arrival at Hawke One. We were on final approach about eighteen hours after *Cyclops* had halted to look for survivors from *Banff*; Karen and I were both on the bridge, sitting in our chairs and waiting.

Waiting, go figure...

"We're about to hit safe comm range," Jim Hannigan reported (he was still the Lieutenant Commander of Sensors and Communications, just like last book). "I'm ready to send up the briefing package."

I nodded, "Good, send it... let's hope they already know most of it."

There were all sorts of different ways to pass information through the solar system — messages carried by traders, comm bursts, and... well... messages carried by other ships that weren't traders. Right, didn't think that paragraph out before I started... wonder if the editors will leave it in. Well, they did, but they took out the comment I wrote into the first draft about what a hack I am.

My point *is* that Karen and I had talked about it and we hoped Wes Pellew, then commanding the Belt Squadron in my absence, had spread the word of war to our allies.

"Sending the package... now," Jim tapped one of his techs on the shoulder and she in turn hit her send key, firing the comm package out through *Wolf's* transmitters and through space at maximum velocity.

We were, at that point, about an hour's flight from Hawke One's orbit, but thanks to the network of comm satellites that were scattered in space around the rock, we would be able to establish two-way comms with them while still cruising at full speed... we just wouldn't be able to go realtime.

Alright, I know this will bore most of you, but to answer the inevitable question of 'why couldn't you do that from much farther away', here it is: we *could have*. We could have successfully sent a signal straight to Hawke One from about two and a half days out, but unless we stopped in space to wait for a return signal, we couldn't get a reply — we'd be moving, and their signal wouldn't find us.

Worse, though, was the prospect that if we sent a signal at them from two days out, a Martian would get hold of it, find out that the famous *Wolf* was heading for Hawke One, and then send a large number of ships to blow us apart. Such things happened against the Syndicate too many times to count, and so it became unwritten policy not to reveal your destination until you were nearly there. This is different, I should add, than a cruiser skipper not checking in with an ally for information (as I ranted about earlier) — that sort of communication isn't revealing the intended destination.

So, for all you comm-obsessed technophiles, that's why we didn't use the generous range of our 'Spectra-Flux ENcomm ST Mk 5.6' sooner.

For the rest of you who didn't care why we signaled when we did, I apologize.

Karen leaned over towards me in her seat, "Is there anything in that package that tells anyone I have *nothing to wear?*"

I smiled and leaned towards her, "I've sent a note to a friend."

Karen raised an eyebrow and straightened back up in her chair, "Oh my, a lady friend at Hawke One. What will the people say?"

I chuckled and straightened back up, "Nothing appropriate."

"Signal received," Jim reported as he paced behind his techs.

"ETA on Hawke One orbit is fifty-eight minutes," Erica Martin piped in with a report from helm, and I nodded.

"Very good, keep an eye out for the answer, Jim," Karen offered a verbal reply to the reports.

Then we sat for a few minutes, so I tapped my foot on the deck and Karen drummed her fingers on the arm of her chair. I think I heard Matt — Commander Matt Baxter, can't remember if I've mentioned him so far this book — humming behind us at operations.

You might think it absurd... but... well... we were waiting...

"Incoming reply signal. Jack, align the array, Trish stand by with decoders," Jim nodded to a couple of his people, then frowned as he came to a stop behind another. "Make that *two* return signals, one with a fleet stamp and another with a government stamp. Fleet stamped one is marked private."

I smiled and looked sideways at Karen, "That'll be her."

Karen's eyebrows both went up, "And a private message too."

I shrugged, "Discretion is a great thing."

A smile crept onto Karen's face, and she looked away, "Can't disagree with that."

"Government signal in the decoder," Jim looked our way at that moment. "Main screen?"

"You know it, Jim," my smile remained as I nodded to the man, and he smiled too, tapping another tech on the shoulder.

"So who do you think we're dealing with?" Karen straightened in her seat slightly.

"I'm pretty sure I know who..." I let my words trail off as the *WolfNet* loading screen appeared on the main monitor, and the progress bar scrolled across the bottom.

We had another fifteen seconds to wait as the signal worked its way out of the decoder and up to the monitor, and then a huge head-and-shoulders shot of Lady Lia Hawke burst onto the screen.

Lia was done up in court dress, by the looks of her gown and the vertical hairstyle that appeared to have been machined... but she was still able to take our call. Which was a very good thing.

She smiled just after appearing, "Ken, nice of you to show up. We were sitting around here wondering if you were going straight back to the Belt, though I kept telling people that there was no way you could resist the Hawke charms. Oh, hi everybody on the bridge... let me guess, still Erica, Jim and Matt, and some new faces probably... Karen? Well I look forward to embarrassing you all immediately! And congratulations on the Commodore thing by the way, Ken, that's awesome. Anyway, we knew about the war — Wes Pellew passed on word from the Belt and we've sent it to everyone who'll listen, and some who won't. We're sheltering a number of DC independent cruisers, but we've gotten word of trouble from Martian shipping out here, so watch your back on final approach. I'll meet you at gate six on the Capital Dome — you're preapproved to come right in. That's it for now. See you at the gate. We'll talk…"

Then, for the first time in that entire tirade she paused, "Guess I didn't really embarrass any of you with that. I'm sort of disappointed now."

Then the signal cut, and I chuckled and glanced at Karen, "There you have her."

Karen smiled, "The infamous Lady Hawke. Why do I get the sense I'm going to like her?"

"I don't know, when you meet in person you might rupture the fabric of space time…" I muttered, and Karen laughed.

"I've got the other signal decoded, sir. You want to take it in private?" Jim was being very helpful and discreet this morning, but I shook my head.

"Nah, I keep nothing from my bridge crew!"

Karen stopped laughing and looked at me, "Really?"

I shrugged, "Private from Fleet HQ down there? How bad could it be…"

Lia popped up on the screen, "Oh and tell Karen she can borrow any clothes she likes. We'll deal with that when you get here."

Karen's eyes slid sideways and grabbed me, and I just sat there slightly awkwardly.

"Oh, I. Um."

I stopped talking.

The members of the bridge crew exchanged some curious glances, and *Wolf* pushed on towards Hawke One.

CHAPTER FIVE

MEANWHILE, BACK AT HAWKE SIX

While *Wolf* was about an hour out of Hawke One, *Cyclops* was docking with Hawke Six's main dome, and Captain Christian Mikaelsen was getting on the line to the Imperial consulate on the rock.

Sitting on his bridge, Mik wasn't in a terribly good mood — as I'd alluded to earlier, there were no survivors from *Banff*, and that displeased him greatly. He's the sort of fellow who believes in the ability of Defense Command to protect the Empire from the darkest elements in this solar system, so it goes without saying that he hates the idea of the protectors getting so thoroughly destroyed.

Now, that sort of feeling is one most of us commanding officers in the DCN generally share, but the diplomats tend to take a slightly different approach.

As the main monitor on *Cyclops'* aged bridge glowed to life and revealed Ferdinand Tripp, the Consul to Hawke Six (we had an Ambassador to the Protectorate on Hawke One, and Consuls at each of the other five rocks), the diplomat was scowling.

Mik wasn't in the mood to deal with scowls...

"I'm still waiting for your report!" Tripp yelped. He was a youngish kid of a diplomat, at that point on his first posting outside Earth orbit, and all too concerned with protocol. "I want your report immediately."

Mik leaned back in his chair and laced his hands in his lap, "I sent you a report."

"What you sent me was ridiculous! I want it in a written file, and I need to know where you've been on this cruise. Immediately! I have to know who the Foreign Office has to contact to make sure our alliances have been activated..."

Reversing the move he'd just made, Mik leaned forward, "You know, I just spent about eighteen hours sifting through the wreckage of one of Defense Command's ships."

"Irrelevant. One ship is of no consequence right now — we're at war and we need every ally, and you're jeopardizing relations by–"

"By *what*? By being more concerned with the fact that there seem to be organized squadrons hunting our independent cruisers? Our alliance with the Brown Rock Colony and its squadron of eleven barely serviceable Sunbursts is definitely more important than *that*."

Tripp opened his mouth to shoot back some retort, but Mik had a good head of steam going.

"I can't believe you, you think our cruise is more important than passing on a warning to all ships that we're being hunted? Get off my line, and get me an open conduit to the rest of the Hawke colonies."

By this time the Consul was getting flustered, "You... they... they've all been warned already. We sent out your message. Now I want your paperwork."

"I'm useless at paperwork, but I'm better at diplomacy than you, kid. What do you think you're going to do if I tell you where I've been? Send them a reassuring signal that the Empire hasn't forgotten them? Or are you going to be asking me and whatever ships I can scrounge to get out there and show the flag?"

Tripp didn't have an answer for that one.

"Open a channel to the Hawke rocks, *now* Consul. We've got tactical information to pass on, and a rally to send out. Or if you *don't* want us to collect a force to go out to show the flag for you, then you can just keep jamming this line. Seriously."

You might think this happens a lot — that we in Defense Command, particularly in the Navy, tend to strong-arm the politicians and other civilians into doing what we say... and I suppose that's true to some extent. But those people who say this means the Empire is becoming a militarist state need to reread *The Almost Coup*. We throw our weight around, but we do so only with the support of the Parliament. If we get too pushy and the Parliament turns on us, we have *nothing*.

So I've always patted Mik on the back for this little exchange. Couldn't have dressed the kid down any better myself!

Consul Tripp keyed off his personal feed and, after a moment, opened access to the Consulate's High Priority Diplomatic channels to *Cyclops'* Sensors and Communications Officer.

"We're in," the Lieutenant on watch at that post smiled, looking up at Mik. "Sending your signal package now. Do you want to add a header message, sir?"

Mik pushed himself up out of his chair and nodded, "Sure, let's record it..." he paced up to the front of his bridge and squared himself off.

"Alright, this is Captain Christian Mikaelsen, *Cyclops*, to all embassies and Defense Command ships. According to what we've been told here at Hawke Six, we're the first Navy ship to bring in proof that we're being hunted out here... and we are. We've just found *Banff* destroyed, we believe by an organized Martian squadron. I suggest that nobody go outside the Protectorate on your own if you can help it, and I request any ships without orders from command join me at Hawke Six so we can get out into the independent rocks, show the flag, and find these guys. If orders superseding this request are bouncing around out there, please make sure they get to me. I'm at Hawke Six, and will probably remain for around six days from the sending of this signal. Look at the time stamp in the corner and do the math. Alright, good luck everybody, see you soon."

Mik turned from the main screen and the vid recorder, nodding to his Sensors and Communications Officer, "Edit it and send it."

"Yes sir," the Lieutenant nodded, moving to hover over some of his specialists.

The signal hit the Hawke comm grid — even then it was as good as the grids in Earth local space and the Belt — and so within an hour, it was all the way up the chain to Hawke One.

On the way it caught the frigate *Ohio*, at Hawke Four, and the corvettes *Amherst* and *Nanton* at Hawke Three. Those ships immediately headed out for Hawke Six to join *Cyclops* and *New York* (the latter frigate was at Hawke Six and helped with the search and rescue... I think I left that out, sorry).

So that meant a force of five ships, including a battleship, was assembling at little old

Hawke Six, and this all before Karen and I had even arrived to start planning. Defense Command's doctrine of independent action by commanders had certain advantages, no doubting that.

CHAPTER SIX

SLIGHT PLAN CHANGE

Erica Martin was maneuvering *Wolf* into position over the Capital Dome of Hawke One when Jim looked up from one of his technicians' consoles, "Sir, signal with our codes being forwarded up to Hawke One from Hawke Two… I'm scooping it."

I'd been sitting in my chair, listening to Karen give the smooth orders that brought *Wolf* into perfect synchronized orbit over Hawke One, and it took a few seconds to shake my mind back into reality, "Let's see it when you get it, Jim."

"Yes sir, it'll be a minute."

I nodded and glanced at Karen just as she turned to me and smiled.

"Well, soon I'll be trying on clothes. That'll be fun," her tone was sardonic enough to force me to smile, and I nodded.

"I look forward to it."

Still smiling, she shook her head and looked back to Lieutenant Commander Martin, "Give me a count on soft connection, Erica."

"Aye… make it forty seconds to soft contact."

"Sir, I can give you the signal. Screen two?" Jim looked up with his report at almost the same moment.

"Very good," I offered a nod in reply. "Let's see it."

The buffering screen popped up on the second monitor, and since it was much smaller than the main screen that was displaying docking data, I slid forward off my chair and crossed the floor to get a better look.

Just as I came to a stop before the screen, Captain Mikaelsen's message flashed up, and Mik delivered his warning. I won't repeat it — go back and read it in the last chapter if you can't remember.

Karen was abruptly beside me, "Jim, they send telemetry with that?"

"Screen's three and four now, skipper," Hannigan's answer came just as those two screens quickly began buffering visual data.

I stood still, and then for whatever reason I folded my arms. The smile that I'd been wearing vanished almost immediately, and Karen's own enthusiasm for finally being at Hawke One seemed to chill.

We were watching the debris field that had previously been the *Canada*-class corvette *Banff*. And seeing quick flashes of Search and Rescue unit reports that said there were no survivors, and no signs of the attackers.

Mik's warning that there were organized hunting units out here struck home, too. You might think it was a bit of a leap to assume the destruction of one corvette was evidence that we had hunter squadrons to deal with, but it was the first assumption we made — because *no single ship* would dare take on a Defense Command vessel…

Well, let me qualify that: a Martian battleship would likely not tremble before a

Canada-class corvette, but a Martian battleship wouldn't be able to catch any corvette. Defense Command very much subscribed to the 'be bigger or be faster' philosophy — if a ship couldn't stand a chance in a gunfight against its adversary, we believed it needed to be able to outrun that adversary.

Seems logical, I know, but you'd be surprised to know how many warships haven't lived up to those requirements.

Anyway, I found my eyes trailing down from the screen and landing on Karen, "I'm thinking we'll skip court for this visit."

She nodded, "Quick stop, indeed."

"Soft connection, ma'am," Martin's report interrupted our thought processes, but it accompanied a slight shudder as the clamps of the docking chute connected with *Wolf's* hull. "We're locking it in."

"Matt, square us away and get the hatch open," Karen turned and delivered her orders, and Matt Baxter nodded immediately, barking orders of his own. *Wolf* had to go through proper docking procedure before we'd be able to leave for our meeting with Lia.

"We should get ready to head down there," I looked back to Karen, and she nodded.

We left the bridge a moment later.

I'd hoped that my reunion with Lia Hawke, who I hadn't seen for a couple of years, would have been under better circumstances. Hell, even with the war on, I'd hoped we'd have been able to meet without a pressing warning like Mik's looming over us...

But you know how life is. Sometimes things work out wonderfully, other times they work out okay-ish, and sometimes they just hit the fan — as they very nearly did with Dave Caldecott's inquiry. But I've promised not to dwell further on that fiasco. Moving on.

Karen and I were just heading through *Wolf's* lock and into the chute that carried us down to the dome when the sound of hurried footfalls erupted from behind us in the corridor. Someone was running, and of course I knew who that was...

Stopping, I tapped Karen on the shoulder and shook my head, "Hang on a minute, we should all go together."

She frowned, "We who?"

Charlie Peters (Major Charlie Peters, our Special Branch guy who you'd better remember from all the times he's saved me from certain doom) began to decelerate as soon as he burst around the closest corner in the corridor.

"Don't leave without me..." of course he wasn't winded even though he'd been sprinting. Stupid ultra-fit Special Branchers. Well, I suppose that's only stupid until it saves your life...

Karen frowned, turning around, "Um. We expecting trouble?"

Charlie looked at me and did an eyebrows-up eyebrows-down 'doesn't she know' sort of look, and I shrugged, looking back at Karen, "You never know when you'll run into trouble. And Charlie's been down here with me many times. We know the lay of the land."

"And I know precisely where and how to get him out of trouble," Charlie added, convincingly enough. As if *I* was the one who caused trouble on this rock.

Karen's eyes narrowed ever so slightly, and her head tilted a tiny bit, "Alright. Let's not waste any time then."

"Good," I turned back to the chute and started walking.

Now, this chute was one of the low-capacity zero-gee ones, so we had to get hold of the wall ladders and pull ourselves down to the bottom. I don't really like sustained zero gee (don't start on the irony of that, *please*) so it was a bit of pain for me… but then I was used to it by now, and particularly used to this chute, because it was the one that *Wolf* had been assigned on previous visits, and that *Friendly* used to dock at in those long bygone days.

I kept my feet facing 'down', and once I got towards the bottom and gravity began to bite, I started locking them into rungs on the ladder and climbing down the old-fashioned way. Then I jumped onto the deck.

Yeah, I know that was boring. You try to make climbing a ladder sound exciting. It was a *ladder*.

With my feet firmly planted on the deck of the Capital Dome's special reception deck, I turned around to see the reception lobby, and as Karen and Charlie landed on my flanks, they did the same.

Sure enough, a squad of Hawke Household Guards — the 'Household' part meaning these were the Protectorate's *ceremonial* infantry — were waiting for us, with a rather serious looking Lia Hawke at their head.

"Atten-*tion!*" the gruff word brought a bunch of Hawke Guard boots down to the deck simultaneously, and the squad of well-dressed infantry crisply snapped to parade-ground poses.

Lia looked back over her shoulder at the sergeant who'd barked the order, "Jeeze George, use your inside voice."

I don't know if I successfully contained my smile, but it didn't matter. The lobby was empty except for these troops, Lia and us, so there wasn't a lot of chance of sending the wrong impression.

"So you finally show up, and you bring troublemakers?" Lia looked back at me, her hands landing on her hips in an overblown parody of a particularly angry stance… or whatever kind of stance it is when she throws one hip out with her hands in that position…

"I figure the three of us combined might get halfway to being as bad as you," I shrugged.

A smile slowly crept over Lia Hawke's face, and she began walking toward us, hands still on her hips as she threw one leg jauntily in front of the other. She was acting all heiress-like, just for our benefit.

I should mention, actually, that her brunette hair was back down in a ponytail and she was wearing a Hawke Command uniform — the blue tunic and black pants that were trying very hard not to look tailored, but clearly were, as nothing off a fleet supply rack would meld to a person's shape the way these clothes did. Why am I talking clothes? You'll find with Lia, the way she acts is often governed by what she wears… or, well, that makes it sound very superficial. What I mean is that her clothes are often an indication of the 'mode' she has to be in, so when she's wearing court dress, she has to be formal, polite, some might even say *submissive*. When she's in uniform, she has to be tactical and responsible, and when in civilian dress… well, she's *nuts*, but not in the air-headed way you might expect of an heiress.

Though a little of that civilian-dress insanity does seem to seep through into her fleet persona.

Anyway this was uniform-mode Lia, albeit a special 'reunion edition' of uniform-mode Lia. As you can tell by the walk, that includes a bit of random outrageousness.

She stopped right in front of me, her head angling one way and then slowly turning to the other in a movement that I only hope you can picture as being rather farcical, and then she did the smile-and-bite-her-bottom lip thing that's all mischief, "Glad you're back."

"That makes one of us," I got the words out before her arms launched around me for a huge hug that I happily I returned.

Withdrawing from the hug pretty quickly, I pointed Lia towards Karen, who was standing back with folded arms and a smile of her own.

Lia sidestepped and extended her hand, "You're Karen McMaster."

Karen nodded with a pleasant smile, taking the hand immediately, "Yes I am… though I don't think you get many points for not mistaking me for Charlie."

Lia's eyebrows played, "I don't think he'd appreciate that too much."

"But it would be pretty funny," I tried to keep the knowingness out of my smile, and Karen — still in the dark about the inside joke — simply shook Lia's hand and stepped sideways to get out of Lia's way.

"I take it you two are already acquainted?" Karen nodded towards Charlie.

Now, you have to appreciate that, for a woman somewhere around thirty years old (I'll never admit to her age, I'd be killed if I did), Lia had a certain way of acting much, much younger, usually with the goal of making mischief. It's not something that she often reveals in public, but it's rather fun when she does it.

She did that now: her eyes narrowed to slits and she grinned widely as she approached Charlie, rather in the mode of an excited high school girl. This was about the time when I managed to grab Karen's eyes with mine and wave her gaze away from Charlie.

Curious, Karen let Lia pass her and then slid over to my side, leaning in to whisper, "Problem?"

"Um. No…"

Lia and Charlie got their arms around each other pretty quickly, and Karen turned towards them at the all too familiar sound of lips meeting in a movie-worthy passionate kiss. Karen's eyebrows hit the top of her forehead (figuratively speaking, of course), and she turned back to me.

"I guess that's not the greeting she gives everyone," she whispered again, and I shook my head.

"Well I got away without one. And if she'd tried that on you there'd be a bit of a scandal."

One of Karen's eyebrows stayed up while the other dropped, "So Lady Hawke and…"

I shrugged, then nodded.

Karen opened, then closed, her mouth, thinking very carefully about her next question, "Should they be doing this in public?"

"Probably not, but it's been a couple of years since they last saw each other. And besides, it's just us and them," I bobbed my head towards the Hawke Guards, who were all politely staring over our heads.

Karen tilted her head and a half smile twitched onto her lips.

Behind us we could hear Lia breaking their rather long kiss, "Hi Charlie."

Charlie Peters, *Wolf's* ass-kicking, enemy-killing, Commodore-saving, tough-as-nails Special Brancher just smiled back, "Hi Lia."

We left the lobby a few minutes later.

Chapter Seven

Catching Up

"We've redecorated since you were last here," Lia walked out into the middle of the floor of Hawke Command and Control, raising her arms and waving to show off her rather posh strategic operations centre as if it were a game show prize.

Smiling, I slowed to a stop beside Karen and took in the large chamber that looked rather like Admiralty House on Earth — just with fancier trim.

"I like the finishing touches," Karen said with an unusually domestic tone.

Lia shrugged, "We don't have to run our expenses through Parliament. If I want new trim, I just buy one less torpedo for the year."

I started to chuckle, shaking my head, "I always knew you'd be positively dangerous as a fleet commander."

Lia strutted — there's really no other word for the jaunty walk she was using today — back towards us with a widening grin, "I'll have you clapped in irons."

Karen rode right to the rescue, "Now now, I believe Charlie's here to stop that from happening. You can keep her preoccupied, can't you Charlie?"

Charlie didn't really turn red, because he's a Special Brancher and therefore too cool to blush. He still shifted his weight from one foot to the other, though, and that was worth it. You might think it mean of us to pick on him, but seriously don't pity the guy. Come on, he was with *Lia Hawke* and they were nauseatingly happy to see each other — even if they weren't physically displaying that fact at the moment.

Lia passed Charlie and bobbed her eyebrows, "Well if anyone could stop me."

But Lia wasn't *just* sauntering around flirting — keeping her strut going, she arrived at a plot table and waved us over.

"I have pretty pictures to show you!"

Karen smiled and shook her head, "I'll never turn down *pretty* pictures, I suppose."

We quickly gathered around the plot table, and Lia leaned over the vid-lined tabletop, keying a few buttons on the controller to bring up an active map of the Protectorate and surrounding space.

"So, we're obviously here," her tone iced over instantly (that's the sort of thing court life taught her to do) as she pointed to Hawke One. "You got a copy of Mik's warning before you came down, I believe, so I don't need to repeat that for you. What I can tell you, though, is that three ships are responding to his call: *Ohio* from Hawke Four and *Amherst* and *Nanton* from Hawke Three. *New York* is already out with *Cyclops* at Six."

I leaned over the plot table with my eyes narrowing. There were about a dozen Defense Command ship icons on the display, several of them ghosted. I looked sideways at Lia and she smiled, "Ghosted means we haven't had word from them since the war started. This is all that was operating in our sphere of influence when the big bad Martians started poking you."

"The rest of our cruisers are over in the Coalition sectors?" Karen asked, her eyes bouncing from icon to icon.

Lia nodded, "I've got a signal going through the secure network over to Todd at Coalition Fleet Ops to see what he's got on his scope, but word is you sent Marlene out that way."

"Yes, we did. She has the high rank, she gets to pick the polite company," I was pretty pleased with that friendly jibe.

"So that's why I have to deal with *you*?" Lia, as always, fired back like... something that... fires back... quickly.

Ignore my last dialogue descriptor.

"So we know where *Argentia, Kentucky, Waterton* and *Vermont* have docked..." Karen pretended to just be interrupting with a sensible question, but I think she was saving me from a losing battle of verbal repartee.

Lia looked past me to Karen, maintaining her consistent smile, "We're keeping in six-hourly contact with them for you. Word is they're alright, but if I were you I'd want to get out there to pick them up as soon as you can get moving. They're not exactly holed up in the toughest ports I've ever seen. *Kentucky's* at Joe's Colony. I didn't even know *Joe* had a colony until *Kentucky* called from there. And I'm pretty sure I've had stronger defenses in pillow forts."

Charlie — usually silent in fleet talks, so don't think his silence odd — nodded at that remark, "You do have excellent pillow fortification skills."

Lia opened her mouth to say something flirty and probably a little too revealing, so my hand shot up, "No mental images I don't need while we're trying to save the Empire, *please*."

"Awwww," Lia's look of mock offense was funny.

Karen's eyes settled on one of the ghosted icons, and she glanced at Lia, "Why's *Indiana* out of contact?"

Lia's mock disapproval was immediately reshaped into one of those gritted-teeth looks that people get when they think the listener isn't going to like the news (hope you know which gritted teeth look I mean!), and she leaned back, "You really don't want to hear about that."

I frowned and straightened up as well, "I want to hear most things you have to say, Lia."

"How about my pillow fortification skills?"

"How about you tell us what's up with the ghosting," I folded my arms and bobbed my head towards the icon.

Lia crossed her arms, "You're not going to like it."

"When has that ever stopped you from talking?" it didn't sound as mean as it reads, and she took it in the right spirit.

"Fine. *Indiana's* been interned. By the Caligula government. Apparently they want an end to free trade, a few tariff guards for their exports..."

I think I was frozen by that comment. In fact I know I was.

The thought process goes something like this: *Excuse me? One of our... allies is interning one of our frigates because they... want to... negotiate trade policy when we're in the messiest… war we've ever been in…*

There are some four letter words that fit into the places where the '…' things [ellipsis marks] go in that paragraph, but you only think those words, you don't write them.

Karen, of course, wasn't flapped at all, being that she's unflappable, "I'm sorry, they're trying to kick the Empire while we're down?"

Lia nodded, "They're trying to stomp you while wearing uncomfortable high heels."

"I hate heels," Karen shook her head slowly.

"You'll have to borrow some of mine for court then. My esteemed father with the 50s mentality won't let a woman in without them. But let's worry about that another time, because I'm guessing you don't want to stay that long right now…" Lia turned back to the plot table.

I unfroze, mainly due to the 'heels' reference, since it seemed exactly like the sort of comment that just *belonged* in a Command and Control centre. That was sarcasm.

"No. No we won't be staying. I suppose we'll have to rendezvous with Mik and take six ships out to each of these ports that's sheltering one of ours. Show the flag, promise to protect them from pirates, and make sure our ships get out in one piece…"

My eyes had been following a course from friendly port to friendly port, stopping at Caligula. That four-letter-wordy (six-letter-wordy if you double the 't' to add the 'y' at the end) little rock was at the extreme edge of the Protectorate sphere, so I had half a mind to wonder why *Indiana* was out there to begin with.

That aside, I was slightly incensed, but I won't harp on why, because I do that much more effectively later and I shouldn't repeat myself… not too much, anyway.

Lia caught me looking at the *Indiana* icon again and shuffled a bit closer to me, donning her quieter, somber tone, "I've got our Foreign Office doing everything short of declaring war on them to cut *Indiana* loose, and I've got two ships ready to go in case you want to split your forces and take *Wolf* straight out there."

I looked sideways at Lia and she smiled reassuringly at me, "See, I learned. Not a total hack over here. A partial hack maybe. Not a total hack."

I smiled my 'thank you' smile, and then glanced the other way at Karen, "I don't know, she seems like a hack to me."

Karen shrugged, "Well you'd be able to tell, wouldn't you?"

My smile immediately dropped into a mock frown, "Hey, I thought you were on my side!"

Shaking her head slowly and with a smile of her own, Karen straightened up, "I dunno, seems like girls should stick together in situations like this."

Oh, that narrowed my eyes, "Charlie, sidearm. Lia, I'm going to want your ships ready to join our cruise… we're leaving in four hours. We'll send Mik out to get the other ships, *Wolf* and yours will head for Caligula."

Lia was beaming at Karen, and Karen was having way too much fun.

"I'm coming along," Lia jauntily sauntered around me towards Karen, "and, since I have to leave my flagship here to defend Hawke One, I think we just might have to be shipmates."

Karen looked directly at me, "Oh, this will be fun."

Lia was nearly skipping around to Charlie, "I know. And Ken can hear *all* about pillow forts, and how much rolling you have to do on the pillows to get them just right…"

"Charlie!" I barked the word — I can't deny that, I *barked* it.

He nodded and we both broke for the door, but it was no use. They followed.

Chapter Eight

Hawke Six

Cyclops was docked at Hawke Six, and Mik was still working commendably to contain his anger as wet-behind-the-ears Consul Tripp kept harassing him for paperwork. There's no question, the Foreign Office is a partner of Defense Command in the Belt — but whether it's a good partnership or a really, *really* bad one tends to depend on the people involved in a specific scenario.

Mik's a great skipper, and he even has a good diplomatic sense, but Consul Tripp was a disaster on two legs. So Mik was not having any fun at all...

"Skipper, we're detecting a warning ping from one of the Hawke Command buoys out there."

Mik was actually writing his report by hand on a clipboard that was propped precariously on his bridge chair arm. His handwriting was terrible, and that's probably why he was doing his report this way — if Tripp wanted to give him this much grief, that was fine. He'd follow the rules, and let the Consul deal with what was handed to him.

That piece of poetic justice isn't really the point of joining the story here (though I find it immensely funny and poetic in its sense of justice). No, this sensor ping is the reason we're back at Hawke Six, mainly because so much attention is paid to it by later commentators (and movies) on the subject of this mission.

Looking up from his chicken-scratched report, Mik frowned at his Sensors and Communications Officer, "An unusual ping?"

The Lieutenant on the half-staffed watch nodded, "Yes, sir. Special alert ping indicating a military unit."

Mik clipped his pen to the clipboard and dropped it next to his chair, stroking his goatee as soon as his hand was free of the report. What was this ping? Well first I better explain what a Hawke Command buoy was.

Basically, the Protectorate of Hawke had six rocks within its borders, and the Hawke Command Fleet simply wasn't large enough to be everywhere at once. In order to ensure the best possible coverage of the rocks, a massive network of passive scan buoys had been scattered out on the open fronts around each rock, at a cost that was plainly stunning.

The idea was sound enough, though — these sensor buoys could track ship traffic in the space surrounding the six Hawke asteroids with a level of precision that Defense Command could only dream of (we had the technology, but there was no way that we could convince a peacetime government to let us build over a hundred thousand of these buoys to protect the Belt colonies).

Anyway, Hawke had been seeding space with them for a while, and now they were paying off.

"Really? Intercept the feed and let's see what those nifty things are showing..." Mik climbed out of his chair and paced towards *Cyclops'* main screen.

The Sensors and Communications Officer actually had to seat himself in one of the empty chairs near his techs — with *Cyclops* in dock, the crew rotation had been halved to allow for some R&R.

"I'm scooping it... hang on, sir, Hawke Command C&C is forwarding it straight to us."

Mik smiled — that was indeed rather considerate of them. Mik told me later that, if he'd had his choice, he'd have been dealing with the Commodore running Hawke Six's defenses, not Tripp... but probably better that we don't pulverize this dead horse. Oh dear, that was a cliché. My editors hate clichés. Terrible.

The buffering screen popped up on *Cyclops*' main screen before Mik, and he waited patiently until the sensor data started streaming... and then stream it did.

Stroking his beard, Mik paced in front of the big screen. Even with the benefit of years of hindsight, we're still not sure exactly what he was seeing. If you pull the log of the sensor feed, you'll see three icons seemingly moving in formation, each with a drive signature that looked like it *could* be Martian... but that was as much detail as he got. The passive sensors on the buoy weren't capable of scanning for a silhouette to confirm the actual identities of the ships.

This sort of incomplete information is pretty common for Defense Command work — sightings like this, inconclusive at best, are a regular part of the life of a Belt cruiser. In fact, we usually didn't get this much detail. Either way, we were used to seeing incomplete information, and using judgment and common sense to fill in the blanks.

So, three icons that look like military ships in formation, that aren't broadcasting a friendly IFF, and that are on the prowl on the vector towards the location of *Banff's* destruction... well, do the math.

"I think the perps are returning to the scene of the crime. Ops, how long would it take us to break dock and get out there?" Mik turned to his Operations Officer, already fairly certain he knew the answer.

The Lieutenant who had the ops watch looked up and shook her head, "About ten hours to get us there, assuming engineering can fire up our reactors right away."

Mik nodded, turning back to the screen. It might be hard to understand from an outside perspective, but when a ship is stood down in a safe port, it's not exactly ready to respond rapidly to a blip that far away.

"We could see if *New York* can get out there faster..." the Sensors and Communications Officer suggested, but Mik shook his head.

"No, let's not set up a three-to-one fight for them. But get the CFG up here, I want a flight of Starlights to go out for a closer look."

As Mik gave the order to get the Commander of *Cyclops*' fighter group up to the bridge, the officers on deck reacted with appropriate speed. Some people (political enemies of the Fiora ring, I should point out) have suggested this was the wrong call — that somehow Mik should have magically transported his battleship across six hours of open space with a cold reactor to destroy these three ships.

I'm not sure what fantasy land they live in, but that wasn't physically possible. Unless they have a time machine and matter transport technology, that won't change. So sending Starlights to find out exactly what the icons were was a great option — they were fast, they had the range, and this was what they were built for.

And then there are those slightly more sophisticated critics who want to know why Mik didn't have Starlights out in that area on patrol. I'll tell you: because his ship and *New York* were stood down in a friendly port, and thus they were relying on the excellent defenses of Hawke Command to protect them. It'd have been rude and redundant to send out Starlights under that protective umbrella.

Anyway, there are more criticisms, but they're all flawed. Trust me when I say Mik made the right call.

And so a few minutes later, four F-194 Starlights scrambled from *Cyclops'* fighter bay.

At the same time, the Hawke Command combat fighter patrol in that area — four F-195 Starhawkes (rebadged Starlights ordered from Imperial factories and fitted with extra mags instead of missile racks) were heading for the area.

Eight fighters went out to sniff around these three icons, but none were closer than four hours away from the unknowns.

Returning to his chair, Mik settled himself and reluctantly grabbed his clipboard.

"Ops, alert all crew that are on R&R on Hawke Six. And engineering, let's fire up the reactor in case they decide to come this way. Send to *New York* to do the same. And pass on word through the Hawke rocks that we're seeing some unknowns out here."

Settling the clipboard on the arm of his chair, Mik sighed again.

There was still paperwork to be done.

CHAPTER NINE

WHO WOULDN'T WANT A SHIP NAMED AFTER THEM?

Let's get back to Hawke One, and the question you're probably asking (or you might not be, but no matter, I'm asking for you if you aren't): how would Lia Hawke get off Hawke One and then ride out of the Protectorate on a Defense Command ship without getting in hot water?

Well, I actually put that question to her as we walked down to her cabin in the Capital Dome, and found her two large duffles packed and ready to go.

My exact question was, "So, um, Lia… how're you getting away with this?"

Her precise answer (as she handed Charlie one duffle and gave me the other) was, "Magic."

To which I said, "Must be pretty powerful magic."

And she said, "Yup."

That was the end of the conversation. Help answer your question? No? Go figure, it didn't answer mine either.

But with the benefit of hindsight (and many grilling sessions for this book), I've found out a bit more. See, it sounds slightly wistful and very irresponsible — Lia being Commander-in-Chief and yet piling off for a road trip with her Defense Command buddies, leaving behind her flagship and the protection of her Protectorate. As it turns out, though, her flagship, despite having been listed as active during this period in every official record you might take a look at, was experiencing major drive problems. It was fine for puttering around an asteroid, but the ship's engineer was quietly telling the Captain that, should the drives run at cruising speed for more than twenty hours, the ship might explode. Obviously, with a war on and pirates in the vicinity, you don't advertise quaint facts like that. But that's only the first reason.

The second reason… well actually, let's say the 'rest of the reasons', were much more political. To begin with, Lord Ian Hawke had been getting huffy after the war started, demanding he get to do some combat command (despite his age and girth and obsession with mistresses) because he hated the Martians — so having Lia leave would be fine, he could take operational control for a while. Ian Hawke had also temporarily deformalized court when word of war had reached Hawke One (meaning it wasn't mandatory for several weeks, thus allowing all the nobles among the courtiers to get back to their fiefs within the Protectorate to review local defense preparations) — so Lia's attendance wouldn't be required.

Then there's the fact that Lia hadn't seen Charlie or me for two years, and a twenty-minute visit just wasn't long enough after that amount of time.

And really, what it all comes down to is that Lia wanted to go. Now, I'll be the first to tell you that Lia is no bubble-headed heiress like the ones you're used to seeing in the media and on reality shows — she's very, *very* smart, and she has the combat instincts of a pack of wolves. But she *is* still an heiress. She gets her way. Though, again to make sure you don't misinterpret this, she gets her way *because* she's smart, not because she's spoiled. Her father had learned it was better to let her do what she wanted, even if he disagreed… because by that time, she knew the system he created better than he did. He had a certain control over her when she was in his presence, but increasingly in the years up to 2231, she'd been gaining far more influence outside his presence than he'd have probably liked.

So. That's why she was boarding *Wolf* with us about an hour after we'd left the ship.

Getting to the top of the zero-gee chute that connected *Wolf* to the dome, I planted my feet against a wall and heaved Lia's bag into the lock, where it dropped to the deck with a mellow thud. Charlie then floated up next to me, shaking his head, "I can't believe we let her make us do the lifting."

I have to say, I turned rather incredulously towards him, "You shut it, you're hers. I'm a *Commodore*. This is very wrong."

Karen tugged on my foot and pulled herself up to be shoulder-level with me, wearing a 'tut-tut' finger-wagging sort of expression, "Well, next time *I'll* ask you on her behalf."

I scowled, "Playing dirty."

"Stop complaining, you two. I sent the heavy trunks up with the Household Guards already!" Lia interdicted as she floated up past us, sliding her foot into the lock and pulling herself into the standard-gravity chamber. "Thank God. I forgot to put on a zero-gee bra — that was uncomfortable!"

I'm not really sure if your jaw can drop in zero gee, but mine sure tried.

"Um, too much information again, there, Lia…" Charlie pushed himself across the gap at the top of the chute and then stepped in after her.

Karen just smiled, "Should never forget a zero-gee bra, Lia."

I just started to shake my head, "She's a bad influence on you."

"So now I have two bad influences," Karen turned and pulled herself into the lock.

With a sigh, I followed, and as my feet planted on the deck I realized, with a resurging smile, that Matt was standing at the *Wolf* end of the lock, his arms folded and his expression… stern. If you haven't read *The Rogue Commodore* or *The Almost Coup*, let me fill you in on Commander Matt Baxter: he's *Wolf's* mean dad. Mother hen. Wet blanket. All rolled into one. And he's not intimidated by *any* rank. Well, not in this company.

"Matt!" Lia swept forward and threw her arms around him.

Matt stood rather awkwardly as she squeezed him. She loved doing this, because it really used to get under the black Briton's skin.

And still did, apparently, "Lia, you do *not* discuss *those particulars* of your attire in public, especially not in front of the crew. The rumors will be flying now, there'll be no stopping them."

Lia stepped back with a grin and a girlish shrug, "I guess I like a memorable entrance."

"Some things just don't change," Matt sighed and shook his head, patting her on the shoulder and then stepping sideways to get a straight-on look at Karen and me. "Well, you didn't lose any limbs, at least. I take it we're boosting?"

Karen nodded, "For Hawke Six, and then on to Caligula. Get Andy to fire up the engines."

Matt nodded, "Very good. Any squadron orders?"

"I'm getting to those," I sounded grumpy. "Send a signal up the chain to Hawke Six; Mik is to wait until he has five Defense Command ships and then he's to go out after all our ships that have reported in from friendly ports, except for *Indiana*. Tell him to move as soon as he's collected, and that he should contact Hawke Six from every port he visits to make sure there haven't been new movement orders once he gets out there."

Another nod from Matt, and the Briton started to turn on his heel to head for the bridge... but Lia got him (literally) with a light grab of the hand, "*And* signal the Hawke corvettes *June* and *Emily*, they're spun up and ready to cruise with us. Let them know that I'm aboard and *Wolf* is their flagship."

Matt cocked an eyebrow, "Very good then."

With that, he marched off.

Lia turned back to us, positively beaming, "And I was worried things would have changed since my last visit."

I shrugged, "It's Matt. He doesn't change."

Something else had tweaked Karen's interest, "*June* and *Emily*... relations of your father?"

Somehow, Lia's smile didn't change when she said this, "Nah, mistresses. My father calls it an incentive to perform — he's named all our latest corvettes after his concubines. Mistresses. I mean mistresses."

Charlie and I looked at each other. We said *nothing*. I leaned down and grabbed one of the duffles, Charlie grabbed the other, and then we walked very quickly out of that airlock. Karen followed us. But, because she's evil and unflappable, she shrugged as she passed Lia, "I suppose that makes sense."

Lia fell into step with Karen, "I know, who wouldn't want a ship named after them?"

CHAPTER TEN

BACK TO HAWKE SIX AGAIN

I didn't plan to be jumping from Hawke One to Hawke Six this much, but it seems to be the best way to go now that I'm actually writing this. So let's skip ahead by about eighteen hours — *Wolf, June* and *Emily* had left Hawke One approximately sixteen hours before this chapter begins. No, you didn't miss anything exciting.

Mik, on the other hand, was dealing with some excitement. Of course, having watched the recordings he laid down in this period, I can tell you he didn't seem tense at all — Mik, like most of the good officers in the fleet, just didn't reveal that sort of thing. That said, he's since told me those were a long and painfully slow eighteen hours.

Painful because, by the time the Starlights launched from *Cyclops* and the Starhawkes that had been on combat patrol out on the Hawke Six perimeter got to the location of those blips, space was empty. The ships that had created the sensor blips were gone, and despite three very thorough sweeps, the fighters had turned up no evidence of just what the blips had been.

Now, this might not sound stressful — the fighters got out there and found nothing, so it was probably nothing…

Well, no, we actually can't say things like that in time of war. Mik, quite rightly, had spent eighteen hours figuring out just how bad the three blips could have possibly made things for his situation, and trying to determine just what he could do about them.

For instance, the first thing he considered was obviously that the blips were Martians — a squadron of ships that was out hunting Defense Command independent cruisers. That opened the possibility that there could a battleship or more than one battleship with them, meaning *Cyclops* might be outclassed in any fight it joined. Unlikely though that sounded, he had to consider the possibility.

And aside from the many different combination of ship classes the Martians could offer, he also had to contemplate the possibility that the blips were pirate ships, or a combination of Martian and pirate ships. In that case they were less formidable but likely much more adept at disappearing when found. And they'd be much more vicious when cornered… or when they hit a free port.

You might ask yourself why a Captain would start wondering about all of these possibilities (and I've only named a few of the ones Mik ran through — pick up a copy of his own papers from the war if you want to see the rest) when he actually knew nothing. Well, excessive worry, to the point of panic, definitely isn't good for a Captain. But this wasn't panic, this was prudent contemplation. Same sort of stuff I was doing in the same period.

When there's an absence of information and lives are on the line, you get very speculative. You just temper your guesses with common sense — that is, you don't act rashly… most of the time.

So anyway, Mik had been contemplating all of these things for eighteen hours, and now that his Starlights were landing after their long patrol flight, he had a decision to make.

On Battlelink with him now was Captain Taya Prescott of *New York*, and they were waiting for two other people to join the conversation.

Mik was standing with his hands thrust into his pockets, not quite looking frustrated… yet. Taya Prescott's mood was a little less neutral, "Where the hell are they?"

Looking up at his fellow Captain with a shrug, Mik shook his head, "They'll get here when they get here. No point getting bent out of shape over it."

Captain Prescott, who was well known for her lack of patience, huffed. She was a bit of a by-the-book sort, not that we should really hold that against her. Anyway, she didn't have much tolerance for delays…

Fortunately, Commodore Rolph Yambi, the head of Hawke Command's base on Hawke Six, appeared on the link almost as soon as Mik said his quieting words.

"My apologies for being late," the well-dressed black man was still visibly settling himself in his seat. His eyes then darted around on the screen, and he frowned, "Why isn't Consul Tripp here?"

Mik shrugged, "We're waiting for him, sir."

Yambi shook his head slowly, "No offense to the Empire, but I really don't approve of that man."

"We don't either," Prescott jumped right on that train.

"Seriously," Mik smiled at the frankness and turned away from the screens. "Finn, we getting anything from the Consulate?"

Lieutenant Commander Finn Yaalon had the watch and he looked down and then up again, "No sir. Looks like their comm array's in receiving mode, though."

"Hang on…" Yambi looked off screen. "Alright, we're seeing a signal coming down the chain from Hawke Five. Looks like it was garbled by interference on the way. It's going through your embassy."

That was, in fact, the signal I'd told Matt to have sent down through the Hawke rocks, coming almost seventeen hours after it had been dispatched. It took so ridiculously long because, apparently, our embassy on Hawke One got hold of it, and demanded that Hawke Command not forward it for us. Instead, our amateur diplomatic comm network had sent it… and it had thus taken quite some time to get out as far as Hawke Six.

Mik frowned, "Fleet traffic?"

Yambi nodded, "It's got a Defense Command stamp on it… from seventeen hours ago. Why didn't they just send it through HawkeNet?"

Mik shrugged as Yambi looked at him, "Don't ask me, though if I had to guess, I'd say whoever sent it did try. Sounds like the sort of thing an embassy would get hold of and not let go."

He certainly called that right.

"It's coming in. Hopefully that means…" Yambi's words trailed off as the final player for this meeting appeared with a satisfied smile.

"I have orders for you, Captain Mikaelsen," Consul Tripp sounded condescending. His tone was dripping so much arrogance I had to wipe off my vidscreen after reviewing the comm log. *No*, not literally.

Mik smiled, "Thanks, message boy. Send them up to my ship and Captain Prescott's."

Tripp's smirk didn't fade, "No, I'm giving you the orders. Right now."

"Really," Mik cocked his head. "You're going to broadcast secure fleet orders over an open comm channel?"

In fact they were on secure Battlelink, but Mik was gambling on Tripp not realizing that. And he won the gamble.

Tripp's face soured, "Fine."

"Indeed, fine. Load them up, then we'll talk about what we're doing next."

Mik turned away from the Battlelink, nodding to Lieutenant Commander Yaalon, "Put it up on the main screen."

The *Cyclops*Net buffering screen popped up on the bridge's main monitor, and Mik turned again and watched, waiting for the information to come up. It only took a few seconds, and then a slate of orders in text ran up on the display, saying everything I'd told Matt they should say — that *Cyclops* should wait for the arrival of three more ships and then head for the independent cruisers holed up in free ports between Hawke Six and Caligula.

"I see…" Mik began stroking his beard. "Well, seems like there isn't a great deal to discuss."

He turned back to the Battlelink, "So, Taya, I guess we're waiting?"

Prescott nodded slowly, "Looks like we've got our orders. I'll stand down my crew."

Commodore Yambi nodded, "Good indeed. Our frigate *Whirlwind* will be here by the time you're set to depart. That will leave us with sufficient protection after you leave."

In case you're wondering how one frigate would be 'sufficient' should three turn up, the fact was it might not have been. However, odds were that if three ships showed up, they wouldn't all be battleships, and so combining its fire with the fixed defenses over Hawke Six, *Whirlwind* (a modified *Predator*-class ship) would be more than a match for most threats.

"Sounds good. I'll be standing down too. Commodore, you might want to reply to Hawke One to let them know what we're doing."

Yambi cocked an eyebrow, "You can use my channels yourself if you need to."

"No, all signal traffic has to go through the diplomatic posts! We can't have foreign governments taking possession of confidential signal traffic!" Tripp, of course, as much as explained why it had taken eighteen hours for a simple signal to get to Hawke Six.

Mik smiled, "Of course, how could I forget. Send word on to your own people, Commodore Yambi. And if they want to pass their information along, that's just fine."

"That's not–"

Tripp's Battlelink mysteriously failed at that moment, and the fool vanished.

Shaking his head with a sigh, Mik nodded to Prescott and Yambi, "I'll be in touch. For now, let's all get some R&R. Commodore, let us know if you need anything."

"Many thanks indeed," Yambi nodded, then vanished.

"I'm going to eat a large meal," Captain Prescott killed her link.

Mik heaved a good-sized sigh and headed back to his chair. He wasn't sure how he'd pass the time between now and the arrival of his new squadron, but some planning of its operation was probably warranted.

So he'd do that. After he sat down.

CHAPTER ELEVEN

WORK WITH LADY HAWKE

So we're at the traveling stage again, which means not a whole lot is happening to advance the so-called 'plot'. Again, I'm going to beat the point to death: there's a *lot* of waiting in our business. We don't get to magically flip a switch and be at the next destination, there's a great deal of cruising around, wondering and waiting. Hopefully I've made that clear enough over the past couple of books, but I just wanted to reiterate it again.

It would be about a two-and-a-half day cruise down to Hawke Six from Hawke One, so Karen made sure Matt was drilling the crew on the first day. On the second day, she and Lia and I spent most of the morning locked in a briefing room, running over all the local political situations for the free rocks out beyond Hawke space.

In peacetime (and frankly, in any time) our job is to focus on the Belt colonies. I knew every Governor of a Belt colony by name, knew his or her spouse's name and kids' names where applicable. I knew their tempers, their hobbies, everything. It was part of the job — I had to be able to get them to cooperate with me.

But it had been years since I'd had a prolonged assignment out in the free rocks, and even back in those days I'd only had limited political interactions. Now that I was a Commodore, and one who'd be showing the Imperial flag to a lot of loosely-aligned allies, I needed to get a better sense of what I'd be dealing with.

And, thank God, Lia was there to help. This was her backyard, and while her father still insisted on doing most of the diplomatic work for Hawke, she'd been carefully watching his every move, waiting for her chance to take over.

So here she was, the resident expert, and being Lia, she took far too much glee in that role.

She was sitting in the chair at the head of the table, leaning way back with her boots up on the briefing table, hands laced behind her head and a big smile on her face.

"No," she was saying, "Anderson's Colony is an *oligarchy*. I like oligarchies. Well, I like the sound of them anyway. It's a really funny word, I find. The people running the show... well..."

Karen was sitting across from me further down the table, her face mashed in the palm of her hand as she used her arm to prop up her head. It had been a long morning, "That's terrific."

"So the oligarchs are Romero Kim and Ellen Anderson?" I was trying to stay focused, and Lia nodded.

"Yes, they are. And they've been pretty good supporters of the Empire since you crushed the Syndies."

'Syndies' meant the Syndicate of Pirates — it was a common short form for them in the Belt at the time, though I've always opted for 'the Syndicate', because it sounds more impressive to have defeated 'the Syndicate' than it does to have beaten up 'the Syndies'. Call me superficial, sure, but I do happen to know how to give a press conference, so trust my judgment.

"Human rights record?" Karen heaved a sigh and pushed herself back into her chair, rubbing her eyes.

"Well I wouldn't want to live there, but I'm spoiled. There are no summary executions, only a few questionable imprisonments, so overall not so bad," Lia gave her brief sketch of the status of the rock, and Karen and I both nodded. "Defensive situation isn't great, though, aside from the fact that one of your frigates is docked there... I think it's *Vermont*, but I can't remember now. But that aside, their static defenses aren't in great shape."

I nodded, "Mik can help them organize better when he passes through. Next."

Lia looked down and frowned, "Your interest in this area of space is waning."

"No, not waning. Just not growing," I let my chin drop forward. "How many of these have we done now?"

Lia pulled her hands from behind her head and laced them in her lap, "Oh, probably fifty."

"How many more?" I pressed my question, and Lia pursed her lips thoughtfully.

"Well, ours and theirs, I'd say... another sixty or so..."

And with that I was standing, "Yup, just what I thought. I'm not even going to try to learn them all..."

Karen nodded, standing as well, "With you there. I'm pretty sure my brain just staged a coup."

I frowned, "Really, going through the frontal cortex again?"

"Yep. It really needs to get a new coup strategy. It's no challenge for me to stop it any more."

"Oh ha-ha, you're both funny. Am I really that boring?" Lia huffed her question, and I looked at her.

"Not you personally, just everything you have to say."

Lia folded her arms, "Oh really? Well why don't we make learning this a game. I can make some sock puppets and you can get candy if you get the questions right... or... ooh! How about we make all of them into a song. The 'free belt rock'! If it's good enough I could get us vid play on HawkeNet..."

Karen and I sorta just stared at Lia after that.

She stopped, looking from Karen to me and back, "What? Too much?"

My eyebrows went up and I bobbed my head, "Yeah."

"Fine, what're we going to do now? I've got five hours before Charlie finishes drilling his squad. Then there might be some more dri–"

"Don't finish that sentence," I shook my head, turning for the door. "How is it you still can be so..."

"Clever?" Lia smiled broadly, swinging her feet off the desk and hopping up rather bouncily. "I'm just happy to be with people who I can make uncomfortable and who'll tell me to shut up. You can't imagine how boring life is when you only have serving staff and military officers around to joke with. They're all like 'uh, yes, haha, very funny milady.'"

"We're military officers, I do believe," Karen's tone was dry, but Lia was still smiling.

"Yes, but you don't have any hang-ups about telling me off. It's fun!"

Karen tipped her head and smiled, "Well that's one way of putting it."

"Good!" Lia then somehow got around me and out through the door first. "So, like I said, now what? Want to go to the gym? Shooting range? How about some ballroom dancing? Or maybe gardening?"

Now, you'll probably agree that I wasn't imagining the… 'overeager kid' attitude that Lia was projecting just then. I mean, come on, she sounded like an eight-year-old at a carnival…

And she knew it, because as soon as I looked at her and opened my mouth to voice a protest, her eyes twitched narrower and she grinned, "Or, maybe lunch, and then a briefing on the ship-to-ship tactics I've been working on with the Hawke Fleet."

I closed my mouth and let out a breath before nodding, "You push it right to the edge, you know."

Lia shrugged, "Wouldn't be any fun if I didn't, now would it?"

Karen came out of the briefing room behind me and slid round me with a smile of her own, "Well as long as *you're* having fun."

"My thoughts exactly!" Lia turned her back to us, "This way to the galley?"

"Probably," Karen shrugged, and I glanced at her with a frown — one of the 'what do you mean *probably*' sorts of frowns. *Wolf* was her ship, she'd better know where the galley was…

But she patted me on the elbow with a smile, shaking her head. Of course I wasn't supposed to take that literally… yikes. I did need food.

So we headed for the galley.

CHAPTER TWELVE

GO FIGURE, BACK TO HAWKE SIX

While Karen and I were stumbling towards *Wolf's* galley, being led by the chipper (if not *giddy*) Lia Hawke, Captain Christian Mikaelsen was sitting down at his meeting table with four Defense Command Captains. And I do mean sitting with them — this wasn't one of those digital meetings like a Battlelink conference where everyone was on their own ship, no sir. See, Mik had a bit of a traditionalist flare about him — he liked (heaven forbid) to actually sit in the same room as his peers when he was trying to get things done.

And since they were all docked in a secure, friendly port, it seemed safe enough to collect the CO from each of the ships that had arrived — the frigate *Ohio* and the corvettes *Nanton* and *Amherst* — for a meeting on *Cyclops*.

At the table with Mik were thus Taya Prescott of *New York*, Evelyn Sherman of *Ohio*, Guy Vivar of *Nanton* and Nikhil Jones of *Amherst*. Let's see, Sherman was a solid officer, Guy Vivar was a bit… flighty, to be honest, and Jones was tough as nails. I point these characteristics out for a good reason: remember back during *The Rogue Commodore* (if you've read it) when I was apologizing for saying that every one of my Belt Squadron Captains was pretty much the best at what they did? This is why they were.

Belt Squadron is the plum assignment in the fleet, at least as far as I'm concerned. I mean, for people of flag rank, moving to Home Fleet is the next step up, but for Captains, being appointed to the Belt Squadron means you're the best, and you're serving with the best. When picking the ships for the squadron (and by extension, the Captains) we have the whole independent belt cruising force to choose from, and so we get a lot of the best… and leave behind many undesirables.

Now, that's not to say all the Captains we've left on independent cruising operations are bad — far from it. Look at Mik, for instance… well, he's a special case, because he commands the only independent cruising battleship out there. Obviously we wouldn't give a job like that to an idiot.

But someone like Nikhil Jones, whose name is probably familiar to many of you, is a good skipper, and Prescott and Sherman were both solid enough. Those last two just aren't on the level with the likes of Mark Gunney, Marshal Samuels, Kris Jacobs or Wes Pellew.

Anyway, that little piece of perspective aside, Mik was sitting around a table with the Captains he was going to be taking with him to the free rocks.

"I spent yesterday pulling together a course for our cruise. We're going to have to make a wide arc out there, picking up *Argentia, Kentucky, Waterton* and *Vermont* in that order… meaning our first stop is Paradise, then Joe's Rock, then Furnace Colony and we finish up out at Anderson's Colony. After that we'll have a nine-ship squadron, and I figure we can take a meandering route back here to Six. We'll see if we can find some of these hunting squadrons and get a little payback. Sound good?"

Now, I was about to open up a salvo about how, at a meeting of Belt Squadron Captains, everybody would have contributed something to the discussion with that offer, and how the silence at this table was just another mark of their not-quite-as-sharpness... but then I realized that, with such a sound plan laid out, there wasn't a whole lot to say.

So good job Mik, for having such a sound operation put together.

And anyway, with the silence, Mik looked around at his Captains, "Alright. I'll be exercising squadron command from *Cyclops*, as per Commodore Barron's orders. I did check, and none of the Captains we'll be picking up have seniority, so I guess it'll be me for the duration. Anyone have a problem with that?"

Silence again — and prudent silence, since it's probably not a good idea to tell the CO you think you're smarter than him. Particularly since, at this table, I can't honestly say that anyone had the right to make any such claim.

"Good. Questions?"

Mik tells me that, by this time, he was starting to wonder about the value of actually having a face-to-face meeting. He'd gone to a lot of trouble getting everyone together, and now he was getting mostly blank stares.

"We're cruising in squadron order?" Prescott finally delivered a question, and her tone was none too cordial as she did.

Nodding, Mik, tapped a couple of keys in front of him, and the screen on the wall at the opposite end of the room glowed to life, "I want you leading up front with Guy in your wake. I'll keep *Cyclops* in the middle, and then I want Nikhil and Evelyn right behind, in that order. Single line ahead, with *Cyclops* in position to move against trouble at either end of the line."

"I'd prefer if you referred to me as Commander Vivar."

Mik froze at the rather self-important and snarky remark, and then his eyes fell to Guy Vivar, "Really? Sorry to offend you."

Vivar nodded with some satisfaction, and Mik just stared at the presumptuous little fool. You have to understand, there's an unwritten etiquette code between fleet skippers — if you're in a meeting or a social situation, you tend to refer to any that you know by their first name. Mik had met each of these skippers a handful of times, even the new ones, at various encounters throughout the free belt... that was more than enough qualification to earn him the first-name right.

But, well, Vivar liked to remind people... or at least *himself*... that he was now a big fancy Commander. As Mik said to me, "That's definitely worth blowing the trumpets for." Anyway, this rant really has no point — except to give me (and I suppose, indirectly Mik) the opportunity to vent a little.

"So, are we alright with the cruising formation then?" Mik got back on topic, and there were a few dull nods, and a surer one from Nikhil Jones.

Mik kept his eyes moving between his Captains, hoping (fruitlessly) that someone would have something to say. He really didn't want this meeting to be a waste, but most of them were simply ambivalent, and the only sharp one — Jones — agreed silently (that's his style). Made for dead meetings though.

"Great, well, we'll talk over comms if you think of any issues down the line. Until then, Taya, Evelyn, Commander Vivar, Nikhil, have safe journeys back to your ships... we leave in six hours," Mik began to stand but Vivar interrupted rather incredulously.

"We're not waiting for Commodore Barron? Shouldn't we wait to meet with him?"

Mik slowly lowered himself back into his seat, "We're following his orders, Commander. We leave in six hours. Good day."

He then stood up, turned and walked out of the meeting room, crossing the 'face-to-face' meeting right off the list for future dealings with these Captains. Not everyone in Defense Command was as elite as the ads and press conferences implied.

But Karen and the Belt Squadron and Marlene, Greg and John were and are all great.

Just wanted to make that clear. Don't you think otherwise.

Six hours later, *Cyclops* led this newly-assembled squadron out of Belt Six space.

CHAPTER THIRTEEN

MORE HAWKE SIX

The next day, *Wolf* led *June* and *Emily* into Hawke Six local space.

Karen, Lia, and I watched the approach from the bridge, and while Karen and I stood in our usual spots before the main monitor, Lia slowly made the rounds, arms folded but a bright smile on her face as she actually wandered *through* the various stations, not around them.

At one point I looked back at Jim Hannigan to check realtime comm range, and saw him leaning over one of his tech's shoulders while Lia leaned covertly over his. He looked up at me as I turned to him, and I bobbed my eyebrows and pointed.

As he dragged his head around to look at her, she smiled broadly, "Your comm procedures are faster than ours, I think."

Jim smiled politely and nodded, "Thank you, m'lady."

Lia straightened up with a frown, "Ken, he wounds me with my title!"

"I know, shameful. Next time I expect at least a maiming, Jim. Now realtime ETA please," I turned back to the main monitor to avoid Lia's look of mock offense, and Jim didn't skip a beat.

"About thirty seconds until we hit their grid, sir. Their outer buoys have already relayed a system overview to us... putting it up..."

I nodded as Jim made his report, and then screen two switched to a buffering display followed by a scrolling text file with accompanying pictures.

Mik had put together his squadron and was heading out to collect our ships from friendly ports. That was good.

Lia was abruptly beside me, "They had suspicious visitors..."

Her jubilance was instantly muted as her eyes quickly darted over the text and the sensor data regarding the three unknowns that had probed the Belt Six detection grid, "Friends of yours?"

I frowned, glancing at Karen, "Don't think so."

Karen shook her head, "Looks like they came in for a sniff to test your grid."

Lia nodded slowly, taking a deep breath and biting her bottom lip, then looked back at Jim and put on her southern belle guise, "Oh James, could you ever possibly connect a Lady to her Commodore as soon as you get into range? I'd be ever so grateful!"

Jim looked up with half a grin and Karen glanced back, "Never turn down a Lady, Jim. Screen four as soon as we're in realtime range."

We stood and waited just about thirty more seconds as *Wolf* crossed Belt Six's realtime threshold and Jim Hannigan sent a message ahead to the Hawke Command Commodore's HQ.

"Reply coming in now," Jim's report was quick, and I'm pretty sure Karen, Lia and I all nodded at the same time.

Commodore Yambi was on the screen fairly quickly, smiling brightly as he recognized Lia (I doubt he'd be smiling for me, though maybe Karen would earn that response, being beloved and all…), "Lady Hawke, it is very good to see you again."

"You lie so well, Rolph," she tipped her head sideways. "Everything quiet here?"

"Since Captain Mikaelsen left, it certainly has been," Yambi nodded, then his eyes seemed to noticeably drag sideways towards Karen and me.

"Commodore Barron, I believe we've met once or twice before," Yambi nodded my way, and I smiled too.

"And here I was hoping you'd block out those traumatic memories. Thanks for looking after our ships, though, Commodore. I don't believe we'll be stopping, unless Lady Hawke needs us to — we're aiming straight for Caligula."

Lia nodded immediately, "If you don't need anything, Rolph. We just had a look at those guests who dropped in on you a couple of days ago… you want me to leave *June* with you in case they come back?"

Yambi shook his head, "You'll need her out there more than we need her here, m'lady. *Whirlwind* is due through here on regular patrol in a few days anyway, so we'll be looked after."

With another nod, Lia smiled, "I'm leaving you in good hands, then."

"Yes indeed m'lady. Though not as good hands as your father gets from some of the corvettes' namesakes, I'm guessing…" Yambi released an irreverent laugh, and Lia shrugged girlishly.

"You know way too much about how things work at the top," she grinned. "We'll check in intermittently on the way out and back, just let us know if there are any problems at all."

"I will, of course," Yambi ended his laughter, then directed his words (if not his eyes, because I can never tell who's looking at who over Battlelink) at me, "And Commodore, do look after her Ladyship please. We want her back just the way she is."

I grinned and glanced at Lia, "Well, I sure as hell don't want to keep her. Good luck, Commodore Yambi."

He chuckled again, "Good hunting, Commodore Barron, m'lady."

The screen blanked, and Lia turned on me with a 'how could you' expression.

"Hey," I shrugged, "if I tried to keep you, Charlie'd kill me."

Her eyes narrowed, "Good save. Though I think he'd have to get in line behind some other people I know…"

She looked over my shoulder and I turned, following her gaze around until my eyes settled on Karen's back. Karen, being Karen, was paying us immature kids no heed while she ordered Erica Martin to adjust course for a straight boost on to Caligula.

I looked back over my shoulder and sighed at Lia, "You and your mischief."

She just smiled, and *Wolf* hurtled past Hawke Six with *June* and *Emily* in tow.

Now, I'll just briefly add here, I had completely forgotten about contacting the delightful Mister Tripp and the Foreign Office mission out at Hawke Six during our flyby. I ended up catching a surprising amount of flack from the Foreign Office for that oversight, because apparently I was supposed to stop, bring *Wolf* into dock, pay my respects directly to the Office, and let everyone know what was going on… or something like that.

And, in my rush to get out to the independent belt to save lives and bring home more fighting ships that could help stave off the Martian attacks against our Empire, I forgot high tea with Consul Tripp.

So, to everyone at the Foreign Office who complained to me about this: a thousand pardons for my lapse. Oh, and by the way, go to hell.

Chapter Fourteen

The Lia Hawke Traveling Show

So I'm getting worried — I hope Lia isn't coming off as a stuck-up, irresponsible, crazy *kid* with lots of money and ships and no sense of the gravity of the situation we were facing. I mean, that's probably how she wanted to come off — she's told me many times that her best defense against all the slander and attack she gets for being an heiress is to appear to live up to some of the stereotypes, and to keep her considerable abilities a secret.

That never made a lot of sense to me, but I chose to accept it because I know all too well what it means to have a 'public face' to bring out for the cameras or even the crew when I'm panicking but can't afford to let anyone see.

So I want to make sure I make it clear, gallant readers, that for all her antics, I would definitely trust Lia Hawke with my life, as surely as I'd trust Charlie Peters or Matt or Karen. That's a hefty vote of confidence if I've ever heard one.

Now, that all said, Lia's antics are pretty damned entertaining.

And I have to say, having her aboard made this trip towards Caligula, which lasted three days, not too bad at all.

Mik was off picking up ships at Paradise and Joe's Colony (running a course that was roughly parallel to ours, in fact) but while he was being productive, Lia was keeping us all entertained.

"I can do this as a puppet show if you like," she made that offer sound serious, and Karen and I perked up almost immediately.

"Really?" I leaned forward in my chair.

Oh, we were *definitely* back in the briefing room, hearing more about the Belt political layout.

Lia nodded, "I'll just need to borrow your socks, then I could act out the meeting in which Governor Sanders tried to throttle the Guild negotiator. That was really the first public sign of the problem… but I don't think the vid captures it as well as a couple of sock puppets would."

Karen raised her eyebrow, her chin planted firmly in the palm of her hand as she leaned over the table, "Well it wouldn't, obviously. But do sock puppets have appendages they can use to throttle each other?"

With a frown, Lia huffed and lowered herself into a chair, "You're no fun. Use your imagination."

"I'm imagining a throttling right now," I assured her in the driest of tones, and she smiled.

"Then my work is done. So that's the situation on Egesta. So much fun it makes you want to tear your eyes out."

Ah yes, this was actually my introduction to the problems on Egesta. I think there are going to be at least two books in this series dealing with what happened there, so I won't get too deep into it here, but so you know, this was the first I'd heard of the Egesta colony, and its societal problems. I couldn't have imagined what sort of nightmare was going to happen there... well I could have, but we'll deal with that in chronological order (next book). For the moment, we thought Egesta was just a laughable rock fit for a sock puppet treatment.

Lia was leaning back in her chair now, propping her boots up on the table, "So, I think that covers most of the independent belt on either side of the Protectorate. You're good to go for your meeting at Caligula..."

I blinked a very long blink and straightened up, "Really?"

Lia nodded, "Oh yeah, you know everything the average grade sixer would about the situation. That means you could qualify for the Foreign Office!"

I should point out that Lia dislikes our Foreign Office and its poor patronage bureaucracy as much as Defense Command does.

"We do need to talk about what exactly you're going to do when you get to Caligula, though."

I glanced at Karen and then both our gazes turned back to Lia.

"You implying it's going to be tricky?" Karen sat back in her chair, pulling her ponytail over her shoulder and toying with the end.

Lia shrugged and nodded, "What do you know about the political situation out there?"

I frowned, "What you told us... Governor Gerald wants higher tariffs on our trade so he can develop domestic industry, but he signed a treaty to the contrary years back."

"Yes that's true, but how do you plan to deal with him? You going to walk in and put an offer on the table?" Lia leaned forward, lacing her hands and propping her elbows on the table as she studied my expression.

I cocked my eyebrow, "That's exactly what I'm going to do."

"What kind of offer? Are you going to meet his demands, promise negotiation, offer flowers? I hear he likes the drink, you could get him scotch and a gift certificate to a brothel..."

"I keep the brothel gift certificates for myself, thanks," Karen shook her head and managed to keep a straight face, but I cracked a smile.

"No, that wasn't the offer I was planning to make, Lia. Have you any offers in mind?"

She put on a cat-that-ate-the-canary smile, "Well, I'd promise him an inappropriately good time if you don't mind Charlie killing him as soon as he steps toward me. Barring that, I might be able to promise some defense and trade deals with the Protectorate."

I chuckled, holding up my hand, "No, no we won't need to ask you to make any deals with him, of *any* sort. I wouldn't want to put the Protectorate in an awkward position."

Lia shrugged, "I don't like awkward positions either. Word is that he prefers the−"

"*My* offer will run something like this: turn over *Indiana* or I wipe out your defenses and broadcast the fact that I've done it on every open channel I've got."

A frown immediately creased Lia's brow, "Well that's not very nice."

I shrugged, and almost immediately her frown leapt back to a smile, "I *like* it."

"Knew you would. I take it we've got your support on this?" I put the question casually, actually not *positive* of the answer (ironic, I suppose, given all the later history I have with Lia, to think she'd be against me here). Lia's smile grew, "Well I might have a more sophisticated idea to help you bully him."

Karen leaned back, glancing from me to Lia, "So you'll remember to bring your own socks for that, right?"

Watching Lia's expression change is… well… I can't think of anything to compare it to. Her expression transforms on command, and her ability to choose any guise she likes is scary. It's the skill of a courtier, one I don't think I ever truly perfected.

But at this moment, Lia was putting on an expression-changing clinic, with an open-mouthed aghast gape, "An heiress never uses her *own* socks, Captain McMaster. How dare you imply such a thing?"

Karen let her own smile emerge (yes I know, we were all smiling a lot), "I'm horrified to have offended your Ladyship."

"Good," Lia folded her arms and leaned back. Then she frowned, "Is it just me, or do we get incredibly pointless incredibly quickly?"

I nodded evenly, "You're a bad influence."

She did another fast expression switch and started beaming, "Only when I try hard."

CHAPTER FIFTEEN

THE NECESSARY BREATHER

"Fish sticks. Potatoes. Now!"

Karen flopped face-first onto my bed and I grinned as I headed directly to my kitchen.

Charlie had finally relieved us of Lia about ten minutes before, and that was, I must admit, much to Karen's relief. And mine too, I suppose.

You have to understand, I loved Lia like a sister then and still do to this very day… but damned if she can't be high-energy when she's excited… and she was still very excited to be on this trip. While I couldn't blame her for being happy to get out from under her father's scornful eye, I just wasn't as ready to deal with her high energy as I'd have liked.

And if I was in need of a break, I can't even imagine what was going through Karen's head. Well, probably something suitably elegant and quippy, being that she's Karen.

I pulled two plates out of a cupboard and rapidly dumped the frozen fish sticks and potatoes onto them, popping both into the mini-oven. Turning back to the fridge, I collected two bottles of water with one hand and pulled a tray off the mag-shelf with the other. I dropped both bottles onto the tray and turned to the mini-oven, opened the door and pulled out the hot food, then was leaving the kitchen in… oh… forty seconds.

Oh yes, naval cooking at its finest — fast and simple!

Karen had rolled onto her side by the time I returned to the main room, her head still lying flat against her outstretched arm, "Ken, don't take this the wrong way… I mean, she's delightful…"

"Just eat, the dizziness will pass," I smiled, laying the tray down on the bed.

Karen smiled a winning smile, "You do know how to charm a girl."

"Is that what you are?" I chuckled, collecting my plate from the tray and dropping back into the chair beside my bed. "And here I was thinking 'goddess' the whole time."

Karen somehow shrugged despite her awkward position, then propped herself up on her elbow to eat, "Now that's supposed to be secret, how'd you figure it out?"

"Well, for one I've survived enough to be sure of divine intervention. And then you don't wear burlap sacks and refrigerator boxes to hide the obvious clues," I started shoveling food into my mouth, and Karen frowned.

"They have regulation burlap now — I could wear it on duty?"

I shook my head, "Secret's already out, you might as well just stick with the uniform. Don't think the burlap will save you in case of a decompression."

Karen's frown ended as one of her eyebrows rose, "But if I'm a goddess, then decompression won't really worry me."

I stopped chewing and looked at her.

She smiled, and I gave up. This exchange was unproductive enough as it was… damned if I didn't enjoy the diversion though.

We ate quickly, for no particularly logical reason since we had nowhere to be. Lia was probably quite busy occupying Charlie's time, we still had days to Caligula, and there was no activity report from the bridge... it was just habit.

Eat fast, in case trouble arises.

So, when we sat and lay in our respective spots, still not having moved half an hour after finishing our food, we shared a strange smile.

"I was waiting for a dramatic development... a comm message or something," Karen shifted slightly, cradling the side of her head in her open hand.

I nodded, "Yeah... this is strange. Usually when we get the feeling we need to eat fast, something happens..."

Karen nodded again... and that was it.

We looked at each other.

And our expressions remained pretty much blank.

Now, I'm belaboring this point because I want to remind you again of just how boring some of these cruises could be. The movies always compress timelines and make it seem like every moment of every trip is somehow crucial to the Empire's fate.

Well thank God that doesn't happen to be the case. Not *every* moment. There has to be a little time when the war isn't first and foremost in your mind. There have to be moments, hours even, that you can enjoy.

So Karen and I just stayed where we were, appreciating the lack of somewhere else to be, absently chatting the evening away.

"I don't know how Charlie deals with her, really. I mean, I'd never have thought her his type," Karen wasn't taken to gossip, but in this case I could understand the topic of conversation.

I chuckled, "Is that the jealousy beast raising its head? Oh Charlie will feel so awkward when he finds out!"

Karen's expression slipped right into its 'unimpressed' mode, "Indeed, awkward as he tries to make it seem like he thinks you're funny."

"Oh I can sell it... 'Charlie, she's been so preoccupied lately... I don't know what's going on...'" a pillow careened at my head and I duly dodged it with a laugh.

Karen continued talking without skipping a beat, "Well anyway, I just never would have thought Charlie would end up with someone like Lia..."

With a nod, I leaned over and picked the pillow up off the floor, tossing it back to its rightful place on the bed, "Yeah... yeah I think she's a very different person with him. She trusts him with a lot of things she wouldn't trust other people with, even me. She really feels safe with him... he's not a political player or a brute... she can let her guard down around him and never worry..."

Karen's expression slowly neutralized, and she nodded, "Ah, I do understand then. Rather well, in fact."

Wolf hurtled on towards Caligula.

Chapter Sixteen

Furnace Colony

On the morning *Wolf* and our consorts were approaching Caligula space, Mik and his mixed squadron — strengthened by the joining of *Argentia* and *Kentucky* — were arriving at Furnace Colony to collect *Waterton* from its port of refuge.

Mik was on his bridge, as you'd expect when he was about to enter the local space of a friendly port in wartime, but he was admittedly preoccupied, reading through a stack of complaints. Annoying complaints. And not complaints from the leaders of the colonies he'd just visited — Joe's Colony and Paradise had both been very happy to see his ships. No, these complaints were from none other than Guy Vivar.

Now, Mik's a patient sort of guy in a lot of ways. He handled the face-to-face with his Captains quite well, didn't get too annoyed, kept a level head. As he and I concluded later, this polite behavior must have been misinterpreted for his *caring* about whatever gripes Commander Vivar had about... oh... everything.

Apparently Commander Jones was crowding too tight in formation, or the speed selected for the cruise between independent rocks was too fast for *Nanton's* most efficient reactor output, or the lack of fighter sweeps ahead of the squadron (a squadron moving at 190 kps, no less) was not "responsible according to the tactical manuals of 2228".

Yes, he wrote that into one of his messages.

I don't think I'd have handled this sort of griping nearly as well as Mik did. For instance, Mik didn't have Vivar relieved of command and locked in a cabin, or a brig. There was no shooting, flogging, or physical harm at all.

Nope, Mik just kept his peace, and didn't respond to the ridiculous complaints.

I say that's prudence, he says that's just because he hadn't figured out what to do about (or to) Vivar at that point.

And, of course, he was going to forget the problem pretty soon.

"Skipper... trouble."

Mik blinked and looked up from the stack of pads on his lap, "Trouble?"

His Sensors and Communications Officer was already routing the data streams up to main screen, and Mik frowned as the display changed and revealed just what was happening... or had happened.

Waterton was in pieces — not destroyed, but with two pods sliced right off by lasers. Furnace Colony had clearly taken mag fire on its domes, and one of the four was open to space.

This scene, of course, is one that we were all too familiar with... well, except that it's usually not a Defense Command ship in pieces. Usually it's the local defense ship that's limping when we arrive.

Pirates.

"All ships to general quarters," Mik stood up immediately, dropping the stack of complaints onto his chair. "Scramble all fighter squadrons, combat patrol to be run by Sunbursts, all Starlights get out there and find some pirates for us to kill. Prep SAR craft to check that dome, and get me realtime with *Waterton* immediately."

That string of orders set the crew into hurried motion, and Mik paced up to the front of his bridge. Settling into a squared-off stance, he folded his arms and watched the screens as new incoming data lit them up.

"Dammit," he began stroking his beard.

"Battlelink coming online with squadron… *Waterton's* not responding, but it looks like their long-range dish is out of action."

Mik nodded at the report, his eyes remaining locked on the sensor readouts on the main screen even as the faces of his skippers appeared on the lesser monitors mounted all around it.

"This is a mess," Taya Prescott was by no means subtle in her introductory observation.

"Not seeing any signs of who did this yet, sir," Nikhil Jones added his own report in a stern tone, and Mik nodded.

"Well, it sure looks like a pirate hit," Mik finally let his gaze sweep over the screens with his squadron officers, "but let's not trust looks. The Martians could have done this, tried to make it look like a pirate hit…"

He was really thinking out loud with that, but the concern was apt — it was easy to assume things were exactly what they seemed, but he wasn't about to find out the hard way that this rock was bait and that there was a proper Martian fleet in the neighborhood, waiting to pounce on him.

"Signal now from one of Furnace's arrays," Lieutenant Commander Finn Yaalon was rushing around behind his consoles, taking the reports from his techs.

Mik glanced back his way and nodded, "Whatever screen you have free for me, Finn."

"Fourteen, sir," the Lieutenant Commander was already doing something else when he answered the question, and Mik simply nodded and tipped his head towards the monitor as a *Cyclops*Net loading screen flashed up.

The loading time was long, which almost inevitably is a bad sign — it means one side or the other is having transmitter trouble, and *Cyclops'* kit was definitely fine.

A haggard, bloodied face appeared on the monitor, and Mik avoided a wince at the unknown person (we later discovered she was the deputy mayor of one of the domes) as she glared at him, "We need help… medical supplies. Doctors. We've got three thousand dead at least… get down here. Fast…"

Mik lowered his arms tactfully to his sides, trying not to seem as if he were in a standoff with the woman, "Help's on the way ma'am, SAR teams from all my ships, under escort. Who did this?"

"Who the fuck do you think?"

Mik's eyebrow wanted to climb at that remark, but he stopped it. He could hardly blame her for her attitude at this moment.

"Pirates, ma'am?"

"Pirates and fucking *Martians*. Pirates we could have handled. But because we're your allies, we got Martians too. Thank you very fucking much."

Swallowing rather awkwardly, Mik turned his head slightly, "Help's on its way, ma'am. Please, do you have any telemetry from the attack? We need to get a good idea of what might still be around..."

"Ask your fucking ship. Lot of good it did us. The skipper was sure she could protect us from *anything* bad that could happen. Bitch didn't see this coming, now did she..."

Mik held up a hand — a hand the woman didn't see — and cut her off, "We'll consult *Waterton,* thank you ma'am. Our Search and Rescue teams are on the way."

With that, Mik turned to his Sensors and Communications Officer with a look that got the feed cut. Yes, that was probably rude, but he had no time to deal with someone in shock and feeling bitter about the Empire when the fleet that had done this damage could still be nearby.

"We need to get in touch with *Waterton,*" Mik turned back to his Captains and Commanders. "Anyone near enough to patch us into close-range realtime?"

"We'll be up in just a few seconds," Commander Jones was, unsurprisingly, the first on the scene of the fight. "Patching in the relay to flag... now."

Mik crossed his arms again. He needed to know exactly what had attacked this colony...

And, of course, because he's in this business, he had to wait. The loading time on the Furnace Colony feed had been slow, but this signal, coming through *Amherst* from a very badly shot up *Waterton* was painful.

"Get formed up in divisions, I want to be ready to respond in any direction," Mik took the interceding moments of silence to get his Captains and Commanders onto the same tactical page. "Nikhil, keep *Amherst* with *Cyclops,* we'll stay in close to *Waterton* and the colony for now."

The Captains and Commanders of the mixed squadron began looking away from their screens, barking orders and getting their ships ready to split up in sections of two or three depending on what had been discussed during the trip thus far.

Unlike a unified squadron — the Belt Squadron, for instance — these ships were not accustomed to working with each other, so there was no smooth and intuitive understanding of where ships needed to go, what they needed to do, or how the ship ahead in the line would react. With that all in mind, Mik had elected to divide his ships into divisions of two during combat — two ships were much more likely to get along than a whole squadron at once.

Better to lose some concentration of force if it kept his ships from literally colliding.

The buffering screen finally cleared, and a fuzzy image of a Lieutenant Commander looking very much the worse for wear came up, "Rachel Sanchez, sir... XO. Commander Schultz is dead, I've assumed command."

Mik nodded to her once, "What happened here?"

Commander Sanchez heaved a weighty sigh — she looked like hell, and the sigh reflected that. I learned after debriefing her that she and Commander Helga Schultz had been quite close, together since academy days. She took the loss hard, but was still doing her job... and that would be why Rachel Sanchez is a flag officer today.

"Seven ships: three Martians, four big pirates... and it looked like there might be another one or two staying out of range, watching to see if help was coming our way,"

Sanchez's words were raspy.

Mik started stroking his beard — that thing really comes in handy for him. In a situation like this I'm not sure what I could do to avoid looking shocked. He appeared to have everything under control, though he tells me he was immediately starting to... well... call it 'panic'.

He had with him *New York, Ohio, Kentucky, Argentia, Nanton,* and *Amherst*... three frigates, three corvettes, and of course *Cyclops*. That gave him good odds against a seven-ship force if he stayed concentrated, but he still didn't feel too comfortable.

Not with skippers like Guy Vivar controlling some of his units.

Mik had already written off *Nanton* as useless in a fight because of Vivar's idiocy, and while the rest of his skippers were relatively or completely reliable, collectively they weren't up to the same sort of standard that the Belt Squadron might have demanded.

Indeed, the only real stars on his force at this stage were Nikhil Jones of *Amherst* and Diane Richardson of *Argentia*, with Jason Collette of *Kentucky* being another obvious candidate, but for the vintage of his old ship (*Kentucky* had been due for retirement after this tour, and it didn't even have *Starbursts* aboard, let alone up-to-date armor or well-tuned drives).

If the pirate-Martian force was to turn up again, he didn't really want to have to test the likes of Vivar in a fight... but he might not have a choice...

This was why he was stroking his beard — he needed to figure out his options.

More questions were needed: "How long ago did they leave? And what vector?"

Sanchez's head was starting to tilt to the left, the bags under her eyes almost seeming to grow darker as she focused to answer the question, "They've been gone about six hours, heading towards Anderson's Colony. I think that's where *Vermont's* holed up... I wanted to send a signal that way to warn them, but we don't have anything left to send with."

Mik nodded again, letting out a short sigh, "We'll have to do something about that..."

But the question was *what*. There were, in fact, many questions. Too many to stick into the end of this chapter, so instead let's flip to Caligula, where the other half of the day's fun was about to begin.

CHAPTER SEVENTEEN
DIPLOMACY IS FUN

Karen, Lia and I were standing shoulder to shoulder on the bridge as Erica Martin slowed *Wolf* down over the dark rock that had been so charmingly named Caligula.

"We're being queried," Jim Hannigan reported over my shoulder. "They're demanding that we reverse drives and stand by to receive diplomatic communiqués."

I think I started smiling in a very unpleasant, hungry sort of way at that. Lia glanced at me, and Karen glanced at her, and we all actually chuckled at the same time. Which I have to admit was rather weird.

But that's of little consequence.

Karen looked to Erica, "Alright, take us in full speed. Matt, have the solution yet?"

"Of course," Matt's reply was clipped.

He had our bow laser trained on one of the defensive batteries outside the main dome of the Caligula capital — we could burn away a quarter of the rock's defenses with about fifty seconds worth of shooting, if we so wished.

"*Emily* and *June* report they're in position. Doesn't look like they've been seen," Jim's reports continued, and Lia smiled a little more broadly.

"My girls got skills."

Karen glanced back at Lia with an eyebrow climbing, "Let's hope they have more militant skills than their *namesakes*."

Lia grinned now, "My girls got many skills."

I wasn't going to touch that one, "Jim, send to Caligula that we're coming in and that we'd very much like to see *Indiana* released, and their President—"

"Governor," Lia cut in with the correction.

I frowned, "Yes, *Governor* Gerald, tell them I want him on the line with me immediately. And that we should set up a meeting."

"Aye," Jim was leaning over the sender consoles and pointing at screens to confirm the message with his people.

"They'll be able to see our lasers warming up," Matt's words were something of a warning, or perhaps more of a reminder.

"Counting on that, I think," Karen glanced back at her XO, then looked to me again. "You're in an abrupt mood today."

I shrugged, "What can I say, Lia has this maddening effect."

"It's true," Lia nodded instantly.

"Signal coming in now, from *Indiana*," Jim was moving around behind his banks of consoles rather hurriedly. Strangely, I actually noticed how much moving he was doing then, when I usually didn't notice him rushing around back there at all. "Loading it up to screen two for you. It's realtime via one of the Caligula relays... it's probably being tapped."

That was a handy warning — and one that we could certainly use to our advantage.

"That's my cue to hide," Lia turned and stepped out of the area at the front of the bridge that could be captured by the comm cameras. She actually sauntered over to Jim's bank of consoles and sat up on the edge of one, folding her arms and smiling mischievously at him, "Hiya James."

Jim, thankfully used to Lia's evil ways, simply shook his head, "Don't give Major Peters a reason to maim me."

Karen came to stand at my shoulder, folding her arms and putting on a neutral expression. I tried to look properly serious…

Captain Elsie McKinnon — who at this point I'd never met in person — appeared on screen two, looking rather worse for wear. I should clarify; she didn't looked as though she'd been in a fist fight or anything, but the stress of having been interned like she was, and of now having to face the music for it… well, that'd make any good Captain look rather unsettled.

Fortunately for Elsie, neither Karen nor I blamed her for getting stuck out here — she *had* been tricked and betrayed, hadn't she? Hard to blame someone for getting blindsided like this… so the music Elsie was facing was friendly enough.

"Commodore Barron… I hadn't expected *you* to come…"

I shrugged, "I like to handle these sorts of problems myself, usually."

That got me a look — Elsie's eyes narrowed ever so slightly as she tried to figure out just what 'problem' I was referring to (was I here to shoot her or the Caligula folks).

"Start warming up your reactor, Elsie," Karen's words were nice and smooth. "We'll make sure you don't get any trouble from the locals."

Having been stuck in one place for so many days, Elsie had been thinking a lot about what she and *Indiana* could do when help arrived. She was definitely tied to her dock, but she told me later that she'd expected some sort of cutting-out expedition, with SF and Special Branch landing quietly at the Main Dome on Caligula, to take control of the anti-spacecraft batteries, evacuate the Earth Empire mission, and let her break dock.

That was a really, *really* good idea. I, of course, hadn't thought of it.

No, our plan was much less sophisticated… let's call it crude… and she wasn't going to be immune to Caligula's shore batteries…

Yes I know, compared to the cutting-out plan, mine's sounding pretty bad right now. Give it a chance.

"Caligula government calling now, sir," Jim Hannigan looked back over his shoulder to deliver the report, and ended up almost nose to nose with Lia, whose smiling face was hovering right there as she leaned next to him.

"On screen three," Karen nodded in reply, and Lia turned towards the screens but kept out of sight.

The buffering graphic popped onto that display, and I immediately assumed a properly stern stare, "Stay on the line for this one, Elsie. And get that reactor warming up… think you can be ready to bring engines online in fifty minutes?"

That was asking for a whole lot from the power plants of a *North America*-class frigate, but speed was of the essence.

"Aye sir, we'll work on that…" she looked off screen just as a sour looking face appeared on the display right below her.

"You will halt your approach immediately, or we will destroy *Indiana!*"

I think my eyebrow went up at that little remark, and I crossed my arms, "Sorry, who am I speaking to exactly?"

"Ambassador Jack Croft, of the Caligu—"

"I want to talk to your superiors, Mister Croft."

That one always annoys the diplomats. It's like asking to see the manager in a store; the person you're dealing with immediately proves his or her mettle in his or her reaction (my editor made me be grammatically correct saying 'his or her' instead of 'their' there, even though it's tougher to read).

"*My superior?* The *Governor* has no time for the likes of *you!*"

So we had a testy one here; how fun.

I glanced at Karen, "I don't have time to deal with this idiot. Captain McMaster, fire your torpedoes."

Now *Wolf* didn't have torpedoes (plural), and indeed, we hadn't even set up a firing solution for the one tube we had, but at that moment we weren't in laser range, and presumably only a torpedo could have reached Caligula to do some harm. So I was bluffing…

I'm pretty sure Croft knew that, too, but he couldn't take the chance, "Alright wait. Stop your ship and order *Indiana* to remained powered down. But I'll… I'll…"

"Put the Governor on. Yes you will. We'll hold. Captain McMaster, let's stop."

Karen nodded to Erica Martin, and the hum of *Wolf's* drives changed as we increased our approach deceleration thrust.

"There, we're stopping. Get the Governor now, please, Jack. Hurry there, don't want to be responsible for an incident yourself, do you?" I laid on the patronizing tone, just to get under the self-important idiot's skin a little more.

He clearly didn't enjoy my sub-dermal jibes, and he hit the hold button. The Caligula flag popped onto the screen, with some annoying synthesized classic rock… how *tasteful.*

I let my smile reform, and Karen chuckled, "I think he likes us."

"Well he'll *love* me," Lia was already turning back to Jim. "Oh James, would you tightbeam a signal to *June* and *Emily* for me?"

Jim was fighting hard not to smile, "Of course, *ma'am.*"

"Flatterer," she hopped up onto the edge of one of the consoles of his bank, "Send: 'Continue approach to laser range, plot solutions on shore batteries threatening *Indiana* and prepare to fire upon my order. Remain unseen at all costs. Love and hugs, Lia.' Quietly please, James…"

I don't know how Jim Hannigan kept a straight face, because I didn't.

"I should end my orders 'love and hugs'," Karen looked back at the hold graphic on screen three. "Think that'd go over well?"

"Well, you don't order me around much, so I don't know what I'd think," I said it just as I realized that Elsie McKinnon was staring at us.

We remained quiet for the next few minutes, until Governor Lester Gerald (I don't think this man's parents liked him) saved us from the delightful 'on hold' music of the Caligula screen. Gerald was the typically surly-looking, poorly-shaven, puffy sort of man he's often made out to be — self-important, rude and generally not that bright.

"I'm Governor Gerald, and I hold your ship as collateral against our new trade deal," his greeting, if you can call it that, was quite smug.

I frowned, "Really? You sound like a drug dealer… or a loan shark. Which do you think he sounds more like, Karen?"

She scratched her head thoughtfully, "I think loan shark. He has that look, you know?"

"Yes, that unwashed look. I'm glad we can't catch whatever odor he's putting off…" I nodded somberly.

You want to make a puffy Governor look like he's going to pop? This is how. This stuffed sausage looked like he was about to get a pitchfork in the gut…

"You cannot speak about me in such a rude way!"

My eyebrows went up, "Oh, sorry, you heard that? Well you're a Governor, a powerful one according to your ambassador, why don't you get a trainer?"

"Or a liposuction… or six?" Karen added helpfully.

Boom.

"*How dare you speak to me in such a manner, I should destroy* Indiana *immediately for your insolence!*"

I looked at Karen with a concerned frown, "Wait, if Governor sausage destroys *Indiana*, what keeps us from wiping out his colony… our higher moral sensitivities?"

"Well, if we had any of those, would we be making fun of his weight problem?" she asked the logical question, and I smiled and looked back at the screen.

"So, you were saying, Governor sausage?"

Now, as you've probably figured out, we were playing 'make him insane' with this petulant little egomaniac. I hope you understand our reasoning: he was scum who'd gone back on a legally signed and sealed *treaty* for no other reason than personal ambition, and was in the process threatening the women and men of one of Defense Command's ships.

Not something to get anyone into my good books.

But what were we going to accomplish by making fun of this man? We could have done the obvious thing: arrived and in very formal and threatening tones informed him that, if a single man or woman aboard *Indiana* was harmed, he'd be in an untenable position. Instead, we took some rather unkind and otherwise inappropriate personal shots at the guy, and still got the same result.

Yes, we lost any goodwill we might have had coming into the negotiations, but come on, do you think there was any goodwill to begin with?

Getting back to Lester Gerald, he was stammering, trying to come up with something to say. He evidently hadn't thought through the course of action he was undertaking very well — he knew that taking one of our ships hostage would get our attention, but he didn't seem to have realized until this moment that it left him pretty much without options.

"I… I…"

"I'll tell you what you're going to do, Governor. You're going to release *Indiana* right now, you're going to transport all personnel from the Imperial mission aboard ship, and you're going to let Captain McKinnon boost out to my position. Then we'll be on our way. After hostilities have ended, I'll personally make sure a diplomatic mission comes back here to address your concerns... though after this stunt, I don't know how receptive they'll be."

Governor sausage... sorry, I do mean Governor Lester Gerald, huffed heavily, "You are in no position to dictate terms. You can't afford to risk the loss of a frigate when you're going to war with the Martians. You can't afford to lose *Indiana*..."

Well, he did have that right, the bastard.

"You're willing to risk the destruction of your colony on that?" Karen was quick with a question in reply, and I nodded in the 'yeah, so there' manner.

The Governor squinted — trying to look mean, I expect — and smiled, "You're Defcom, you'd never destroy an innocent colony, even in wartime."

I bristled at 'Defcom' — it's the pirate word for Defense Command, and it's derogatory. Usually I don't get bothered by it, but somehow it seemed more foul than usual in this context...

But then, Karen and I had just labeled him Governor sausage. Either way...

"That's true. We are, however, quite willing to strip you of your defenses, and to let all the pirates around know that we did. Our hands stay clean, yours... well... not so much," any mocking humor had drained out of my tone, the threat being delivered quite clearly.

Some people have asked me if I'd really do that, and the answer is *probably*. If Gerald had eliminated *Indiana* with his shore guns, we'd have wiped them out as we cruised in to take away any survivors. Then we'd have sent the action report on an open signal to Admiralty House, which means the pirates with good listening posts might be able to pick it up. So, perhaps less intentionally, yes I would have done it.

"You're in no position — we can cut your ship up badly before you destroy all our positions!" the Governor hissed. "We're not hicks or roughers, Commodore. My gunnery crews are trained very good!"

You have to love it when the way something is said contradicts its message. And so aptly timed too — diction falling apart at just the wrong instant.

But that wasn't something to dwell on at the moment, we needed to let the other shoe drop, and if there's one thing Lia Hawke loves, it's shoes.

Her head popped up between mine and Karen's almost at that instant — she'd evidently tip-toed up behind us while puffy sausage Governor (yes I know I'm being terrible) was saying his piece, and she leapt up now with a big smile, "Surprise!"

Governor Gerald actually sputtered, "Er... Lady Hawke... what're... uh... hi... nice... uh... hello..."

And he's not a hick, remember.

"Well hello there Lester, I'm loving the rosy-cheeked look, really suits your chins! Now, you were saying something about us not being in a position to do anything about your 'good-trained' shore guns, right?"

The Governor visibly swallowed, and Lia shrugged in as ditsy a manner as she could, "Gee, I might actually have to contradict you there. Sorry about that... oh James, tell my ships to drop their stealth, would you?"

Jim Hannigan nodded to one of his technicians, and the signals went out instantly.

A few seconds later, as the icons of the newly-detected Hawke ships appeared on a panel near him, sausage began to quake. I think that meant he was mad... or maybe he was testing the durability of this colony's seismic activity detectors.

Sorry, am I being too mean?

"I... we... I... uh..."

"You're going to release the Defense Command ship now, Lester, because if you don't, I'm going to make you," Lia sounded so sweet when she was threatening people.

Eyes bulging out of his head in anger, the Governor's arm began to flail. For a moment I wondered if we'd given him a coronary, but he was actually trying to paw his screen off. He succeeded after a few seconds.

Karen and I shared a quick glance, and then we both looked back at Lia.

"James, tell my ships to fire on the shore batteries if they so much as sweep *Indiana's* position with targeting scans," she was already passing on prudent orders.

"Well, that's our hand played... nothing like insult and intimidation..." I looked from Karen back to the screens, and realized as my eyes fell on Elsie McKinnon that she was unusually red herself.

I frowned, "Elsie, you alright?"

She bit her tongue and nodded.

I didn't find this out until years later when I saw the vid logs, but she and her entire bridge crew had been laughing very hard during our exchange with Governor sausage. It hadn't occurred to me that our antics were going to entertain anyone over Battlelink, as *Wolf's* bridge crew is so accustomed to my idiocy that none of its members laughed at all.

The bridge crew of *Indiana*, however, had just come through days of high stress when they'd been facing possible death, its members were evidently willing to laugh at us. You can probably understand their good humor — ever been in one of those stressful laugh-or-cry situations? That was them at this point, and understandably so. So that was one of the reasons for our joking approach to situations like this — we always preferred the laughing to the crying.

The other reason, of course, is that cavalier reputation I keep mentioning. When Governors talk and hear that *Wolf* rode into this situation with me and Karen so confident that we were making fun of the hostage-taker, it makes leaders of free rocks either like us or loathe us.

Either way, they don't take hostages.

And, I should add here on cue, the moorings were released almost immediately: *Indiana* was freed from its dock.

Job done.

Well, we thought so, anyway.

CHAPTER EIGHTEEN

TRIAGE IS NOT FUN

While Karen, Lia and I were venting on Governor sausage, Mik's SAR teams were scouring Furnace Colony's domes for injured and dead. The attack by what we now know to be a well-outfitted pirate force with Martian escort had killed over 4,000 people. We don't actually have a final number of dead because, like so many independent rocks, Furnace didn't have a comprehensive census.

So we stick with 'over 4,000', which is, as far as I'm concerned, disgusting enough. These are civilians I'm talking about. Furnace had and has a Defense Force, but mainly it's a militia made up of the miners who work the rock. There were, at the time of the attack, only 133 full-time professional military personnel working for Furnace's government, all of them mercenaries from Boscawen Corp.

As is tradition for Boscawen Corp women and men, they died to the last person defending their client. Their commanding Colonel apparently went out in a blaze of glory, trying to ram a pirate ship's bridge with a requisitioned *mining tug*.

I shouldn't ever endorse mercs, but if you need to beef up your colony's defenses and can pay, Boscawen's people honor his name (he being the former-First Lord who started the company).

Of course, all that means is that, of the over 4,000 dead, 133 were professionals. The casualties among *Waterton's* crew aren't included in that number; they amounted to forty-one dead and over 100 wounded — out of 206 crew. If that daring little corvette hadn't been at Furnace, the colony would have been stripped bare.

As it was, Furnace was a bloodbath, and the people there were understandably bitter with us for having brought this down on them. I don't know if *Waterton* being on station actually drew the attack, but either way, the Furnace folks had stayed true to their alliance, and they'd paid for it.

That never sits well with a Defense Command officer, least of all Christian Mikaelsen, himself a Belt native.

Mik was still trying to determine how to divide his forces, which I should say was by no means an easy decision to make. He could be reasonably certain that the pirates and Martians wouldn't return to Furnace, but then, he really didn't know what their objectives were. If, for instance, they'd attacked Furnace to set up a trap, then they could be floating just out of sensor range waiting for him to split his force, so they could pounce on separate halves.

In an ideal world, then, Mik wouldn't have split his force at all...

But the risk-reward equation definitely required him to send help up the line to Anderson's Colony, not only for the sake of *Vermont* interned up there, but for the sake of the civilians on that free rock.

Help had to be sent, but neither half of his squadron could be left so weak as to be vulnerable to the seven raiders (and any possible reinforcement they might have).

And now, less than an hour after his squadron's arrival at Furnace, he was going to have to leave again.

"All our fighters and SAR teams to remain behind," he began his orders abruptly, so it took a minute for his Sensors and Communications Officer to register the fact that Mik's words would need to be broadcast. "I don't see how they could do us any more good in a fight than they could here helping the rescue efforts. They'll operate out of Furnace docks. *Cyclops* will pursue the attackers towards Anderson, along with..."

This was the big choice, he needed to pick the right people...

"Commander Jones in *Amherst*, Commander Richardson in *Argentia*, and Captain Sherman in *Ohio*. Squadron command here falls to Captain Prescott; she's to defend the colony until she hears otherwise from a superior. Send that, Finn, and also send warning ahead to Anderson's Colony... let them know what's coming their way."

This, I will say, was a very good set of decisions on Mik's part.

"Ships to boost on *Cyclops* immediately. Helm, mark our course."

Returning to his chair, Mik took a couple of moments to think on just what he was leaving behind as he resumed the chase. First of all, he'd stripped his ships of fighters — all fighters were now assisting in patrol and search and rescue. More than that, he was pulling a battleship off the defense of this rock, leaving two frigates and two corvettes... well, one corvette and what was left of *Waterton* to defend it in case of a return of pirate forces... and he was leaving behind the idiot Guy Vivar.

As *Cyclops* boosted away from Furnace and worked up to its maximum cruising speed, that tradeoff seemed altogether not bad.

I'll be quite honest as I switch to the 'enemy' viewpoint here... we still aren't certain what we were dealing with. We have the official Martian take on these incidents, but the pirates, oddly enough, never sent us logs or anything of that sort to explain their deployments, or even to tell us how many ships they actually had out there. When Wes Pellew destroyed their base long after this, the records section was found to be woefully empty, so we're still scratching our heads.

Based on the Martian logs (which are only good for telling us what the Martians themselves saw) there were nine ships moving between Furnace rock and Anderson's Colony; four of their own and five pirate. They evidently had held two out of sensor range when they hit Furnace, so Mik was outnumbered by over two to one as he cruised after them.

If you're asking why the Martians and pirates attacked Furnace first, your guess might be as good as mine. The logs are decidedly useless in explaining the 'whys' of anything — unlike our own log books, that explain in some detail who issued what orders and the official reasoning behind activities, the Martian logs are much more timeline-based. They explain none of the whys, just say when things happened.

My thought is they were out to scare our allies into hating us, and to do that they were targeting the obviously most 'loyal' — the rocks that had harbored our ships. If the Martians could make the people on those independent asteroids feel bitter about their alliance with us by killing thousands of them, the Empire's position out here could be damaged considerably.

That, I think, would be a smart plan.

The problem with that line of reasoning, though, is that it assumes pirates were smart and capable of planning, which we can't take for granted. No, this could just as easily have been glorified plundering, taking advantage of Martian naval support to hit rocks that had for years been too strong for the pirates to get anything out of, and maybe to get some satisfaction from beating up a Defense Command corvette in the process.

Either way, we know now what Mik didn't know at the time: nine ships were causing trouble in the area, and he'd just split his force to try to stop them.

The day's fun continued.

CHAPTER NINETEEN

CHANGING DIRECTION

Indiana was cruising away from Caligula at long last, due to rendezvous with *Wolf* in about four minutes. *June* and *Emily* were slowly backing away, making sure Governor sausage, in his bitterness, didn't have something up his sleeve to throw at us. I was feeling pretty good about things at that moment — Karen and I were sitting in our usual chairs at the rear of the bridge, and Lia was occupying a chair ostensibly set aside for the XO (Matt didn't mind).

"So, that worked out nicely," Lia was still quite pleased with herself, and both Karen and I nodded.

"Your timing and delivery were top notch, I have to admit," I offered a grin, and Karen nodded her approval.

"What do you think now — straight back to Hawke Six, or see if we can catch up with Mik first?" Karen was, of course, thinking about practical and prudent matters, not self-aggrandizing like Lia and me.

I 'hmmed' thoughtfully — it's not that easy to rendezvous two mobile forces in space, owing mainly to the fact that space is *big*. Our only chance to catch up with Mik would be to meet him at one of the rocks he was destined to visit, which meant he'd either be at Furnace or Anderson's Colony by this time.

Obviously I didn't know then what was going on along that string of free rocks.

"Jim, fire comms off to Joe's Colony, Paradise, Furnace rock and Anderson's Colony. See if you can figure out where Captain Mikaelsen is, and where we could catch up with him," I glanced Jim Hannigan's way, and he nodded.

"We going to do anything else about Caligula?" Lia asked in a slightly more somber tone, her giddy smile beginning to fade. "Trade sanctions or a pox, maybe?"

I smiled, "Oh I'd like to… but no, no I don't think that'd be sensible. They played ball and gave us back *Indiana* without incident, so we logically can't punish them too badly…"

"Just a little pox?"

"No poxing," Karen interrupted, then came to her feet quickly and paced up to the forward screens, putting on a frown. "Jim, when *Indiana* gets into range, give me realtime. Something just occurred to me…"

My eyebrow went up and I climbed out of my chair, following Karen's course and stopping beside her, "Something Elsie can help us with…"

Karen glanced at me, staying silent for a moment to let my own brain wake up to what I should've been concerned about from the beginning. Once again, leave it to Karen to be right on top of things.

"What *was* she doing out this far… yes…" I recited the question as soon as my mind pushed it forward, and no sooner did I say the words than did Captain McKinnon appear on screen two.

"Commodore, Captain, we're out safely with the personnel from the Imperial mission offices. We're ready to cruise," she reported with a nod, obviously quite pleased to be free of her predicament.

"Sorry, Elsie, but before we leave, what were you looking for out here — before you were interned, I mean. What trail were you on?"

I alluded to this question back in the first or second chapter when I was introducing *Indiana* to you, I'm pretty sure.

Elsie wasn't exactly surprised by the query, but she wasn't as prepared for it as she would have been for cruising orders. She blinked a couple of times, redirecting her mental resources, "Ah, I... sorry, we were out here because of some tips I picked up from my sources on Hephaestus Rock — there were rumblings about a pirate buildup in the space out here. It's a blind spot for us in many cases, sir, because our traders don't spend much time out past Caligula. Thought we might run across a base or some such thing, then call in the Independent Squadron."

I'll get to the Independent Squadron — its lack of a real battle record, its disgraceful discipline and humanitarian record, and its bastard Commodore Sean Cook — in the next book. Don't worry about that unit for the moment.

The possibility of a pirate concentration out here was of more concern, though.

Remember, when Elsie had come out here looking for the pirates, there had been no war on — no reason to expect that a pirate base would be particularly dangerous to a Defense Command frigate. Now, with the war, news of a new pirate base in a position to menace a number of our free-rock allies had many more negative implications.

This was the Martians' counterpoint to the Hawke Protectorate — they were using pirates to battle our Hawke-based positive influence in this area.

"Did you have any luck tracking down the whereabouts of the base?" Karen asked quietly, keeping the information flowing.

Elsie shook her head, "We were on a lukewarm trail when I decided we'd been out of touch with the Admiralty for too long. What signs we did have were pointing us in the direction of the Barbary Cluster."

The 'Barbary Cluster' made my eyebrows go up, owing to my historical knowledge. I hadn't known that there was even a 'Barbary Cluster' out here in the asteroids, but the fact that there was one, and that the pirates were apparently using it, was almost a historical *joke*. If you're so inclined some day, look up the Barbary Coast. You'll get it.

"Did you see any pirate ship activity while you were cruising?" I added my question to the fray, and Elsie shook her head.

"Nothing... nothing at all, actually. I was honestly quite surprised — usually if you look hard enough out here, you can find someone to tail. We looked closely and found nothing."

"They were probably consolidating for an attack," Lia was suddenly behind Karen and me again, and I glanced back at her and nodded.

"Yes... yes they were probably collecting a force, with Martian support... maybe they were the ships that probed Hawke Six?" I was beginning to frown as I suggested it.

"I don't know, it's quite a haul to Hawke Six from here, and compared to a lot of the targets along the way, Hawke Six is heavily protected. I don't think the pirates would waste their time," Lia's eyes narrowed thoughtfully.

She was right. Regular Martian forces might have attacked Hawke Six to make a point or do some strategic damage, but I couldn't see militarized pirates being so forward-thinking as to bypass all sorts of juicy free rocks to hit a strong target — why risk getting destroyed when the free rocks were closer and more vulnerable?

But we weren't sure at this point.

About three minutes later we were *very* sure.

We were still talking to Elsie (I've not given you all the dialogue because it gets technical and not particularly helpful for advancing the plot — the vid records are in the Fleet Archives if you desperately want to see them), when Jim Hannigan turned to look over the shoulder of a tech whose panel was beeping.

A text message scrolled up on that tech's screen, and then a new window opened and the face of Captain Jack Gomez of *Vermont* appeared. There was no audible volume — all sound behind the Sensors and Communications consoles tends to run through headsets into the ears of the operators.

So I didn't hear what Jim heard. I instead heard: "Sweet Jesus, pipe this to three right now!"

'Three' was shorthand for 'screen three', and as I heard the uncharacteristic outburst from Jim's consoles, I looked back at him, saw his finger starting to stab at screen three, and looked back to that monitor just as the sensor display that was covering it flashed to black.

Then Jack Gomez, a good skipper who I'd dealt with a number of times over the years, appeared on screen: "Ken, glad to hear you're out here too. We heard from Mik about an hour ago; he's coming our way with his battleship and three other vessels because he thinks a force of at least three Martians and four pirates is going to try to take out Anderson's Colony. He's coming from Furnace, which apparently was blown to hell seven hours ago, despite *Waterton* being there to assist in the defense."

You could have heard a pin drop on *Wolf's* bridge. At least our questions about possible pirate concentrations and targets had been answered…

"I'm coordinating with the Anderson rock government right now, getting a defense set up. They've got four fighter-bomber squadrons and a couple of trade policing ships with mags aboard, but I'm not optimistic. Mik's going to try to catch the Martians and pirates in space between Furnace and here, but again, not sure if he'll be able to. Sounds to me like the bastards are running a fast raiding group… so would you mind stopping by? Quick as possible, Ken, we're going to get wiped out."

I released a sigh and folded my arms at the words. Jack wasn't being over dramatic: he'd get his clock cleaned by seven ships, no matter what the Anderson Defense Forces did to back him up.

"Hope to see you soon… *really* hope, actually…" Jack Gomez's message ended, and I was already looking over to Elsie on screen two.

"You get that Elsie?"

She nodded, "Your SCO patched me in on it. We boosting for Anderson?"

Sorry, SCO is a shortform for Sensors and Communications Officer. I didn't use it much because I tended to call mine 'Jim'.

"Five against seven is definitely better than one against seven," I nodded, then paused, glancing back at Lia, "that is, if your ships are…"

"James, patch *June* and *Emily* into the realtime," Lia was already turning to Jim.

He nodded, despite his rapid movement between consoles.

"Getting a feed from Joe's Colony now… and we just got from Paradise as well…" he reported to me even as the buffering screens for *June's* and *Emily's* feeds went up on screens four and five. "Both report no activity. We're sending situation warnings back."

June's and *Emily's* Commanders appeared on *Wolf's* screens for the first time, but as Lia stepped around me to address them, I was turning fully back to Jim, Karen right with me, "So no word from Furnace?"

Jim shook his head, "Afraid not… my guess is their comm array was the first to go in the attack. I can realign slightly to see if any of Captain Mikaelsen's other ships are still there."

I nodded, "Do that, just tell them we're on our way to Anderson. And send back to Anderson that we're on our way. Tell Jack to hold on."

Nodding, Jim moved to the appropriate consoles and started delivering orders to his staff. As that bustling action continued, I turned back to Karen, tipping my head closer to hers, "What do you think in terms of transit time?"

Her eyes were very sober, her expression in one of its darkest forms, "We're at least thirty hours away, I think. And it's about thirty-five hours from Furnace to Anderson's rock at 190 kps."

Karen had been doing more homework on the transit times out here than I had, but then I'd expected as much.

"They have a two hour advantage on us, with that seven hour head start…" I said very quietly, and she nodded once.

You get a very sinking feeling in moments like that. It doesn't last, because you tell yourself 'oh, they might be slowed by battle damage' or 'oh, we can redline the drives…' but you still get the feeling. You're the cavalry, and you're going to be *just* late enough to show up *just* when the domes are open to space and the rape and plunder is finished.

But even while you're feeling that, you're turning back towards the front of the bridge. In the same instant, Karen and I issued orders to different people.

Karen nodded to Erica Martin, "Everything we've got, Erica. Mark course for Anderson and *go*."

"Elsie, I hope your drives are feeling well-tuned, we're running at top speed," I looked up at screen two, and *Indiana's* skipper nodded back at me.

"We're with you, sir."

Lia turned to me then, screens four and five blanking behind her, "My girls are fast too, and they're all yours."

At any other moment, I'd probably have joked about that phrasing, and Lia would have too.

Just now, though, neither of us was smiling. Well, that's not quite true…

"Thanks for sticking with us," I did smile.

Lia looked at me very seriously for a moment — the look she gives when she's not putting on a show, when something very serious is happening, "We're not bailing out when our allies are at stake. You and Anderson's Colony both."

I nodded, "Never doubted that for a moment."

She smiled somberly, and as she did, *Wolf* turned fast and began to boost at full military power.

We were on our way.

CHAPTER TWENTY

EVENTFUL TRAVELS...?

Most of the time in these books, I tell you about how boring and damning the waiting on these cruises between rocks is. The first draft of this chapter had me saying that our flight to Anderson's Colony was an exception — that there was activity.

Upon reconsideration, I have to say the trip was boring and damning, just like all the rest, though perhaps more frustrating.

Mik was about six hours behind the force that was heading for Anderson's Colony, but he was doing everything he could to catch up.

Now, you might be wondering how he expected to be able to do that with a battleship weighing down his force. Some people have even been gutsy enough to suggest that Mik made the wrong call in chasing this force with *Cyclops* at all.

Gutsy critics. And quite wrong.

The only advantage Mik's four ships had against seven pirates and Martians really came in the big lasers *Cyclops* carried; he needed those guns to have a chance of saving Anderson's Colony.

And, despite what you might think, the forty-year-old *Cyclops* was damned fast. You're about to get a dose of technical history, so if you're happy just knowing that *Cyclops* was fast without knowing why, skip down about five paragraphs. For all the ship buffs out there, this one's for you.

Cyclops was an old *Odysseus*-class battleship, meaning it was of the class that came before the *Warlock*-class (Marlene's *Sorceress*), which came before the *Empire*-class (Greg's *Warspite*), which in turn was about to be succeeded by the *Bonaventure*-class ships (being finished in a big rush). What that means is by 2231, *Cyclops* was three generations old. Indeed, of the original class of nine, only two *Odysseus*' were still in service — *Cyclops* and *Medusa* (Captain Zhukov's ship attached to the Heavy Squadron at Earth).

So old means slow? Well, if left to the old specs, then yes, old means slow. As designed, *Cyclops* couldn't do more than 178 kps on a prolonged cruise, and in practice, most of the *Odysseus*-class never cruised above 165 kps — not up to the standards by this time. But Mik had been in an interesting position when he'd taken over command of the ship in 2228: he was given the post just as *Cyclops* was going in for a sizable modernization project.

Modernization of really old ships happens when Parliament slashes the Admiralty's budget, and in 2227, this had happened to John Fiora as he'd lobbied to get the *Bonaventure*-class set up. He'd wanted six ships, he was budgeted for four, so two *Odysseus*-class ships that were set to be decommissioned were slated for much cheaper modernization projects. When Mik was appointed to command *Cyclops*, he got discretionary control over some of the modifications being made, and knowing as he did that he was going to cruise the independent belt, he managed to get some particularly interesting enhancements approved.

The modernization included the fitting of new engines and heavier weapons, along with new, lighter armor (our alloys by 2231 were much lighter than the armor plating used when *Odysseus* was built). Mik kept the lighter armor and the better engines, but he ditched the new weapons — he stuck with the smaller heavy lasers *Odysseus* had originally mounted.

In a gunfight with another battleship, then, *Cyclops* would be in trouble — its shots probably wouldn't do a lot of damage. But against smaller vessels, even forty-year-old battleship weapons were merciless (remember, the laser that carved up *Cheetah* in *The Rogue Commodore* was about the same vintage... we think). So, the net result of all this was a lighter ship with more powerful engines: *Cyclops* could cruise at as much as 193 kps over moderate distances. That wasn't fast enough to allow the battleship to catch single raiders in peacetime, but perhaps a damaged squadron of pirate and Martian ships would be moving just a tiny bit slower than a single ship.

Which all leads me back to this trip.

Mik was trying to catch the attack force. Standing in the main engine room buried back in *Cyclops'* aft section, he had his arms folded and was waiting for his Chief Engineer, Georgina Yamagawa, to come down one of the service chutes from the left engine pod.

"She'll be here in just a minute, sir, she called in five minutes ago..." one of the nearby engineers stopped to address the skipper, and Mik nodded.

He was down there because it was the only place aboard his ship he could go with any hope of squeezing more speed out of the drives — standing on the bridge and looking over the shoulder of his Helm and Navigation Officer wouldn't do much good — all the pilots did was read the speed dial when they pushed the throttles up to full.

He wanted more speed, and for that he had to make the long trip to engineering.

Lieutenant Commander Georgina Yamagawa arrived within a minute or so, her tunic off and her undershirt, face, hands and pants all streaked and smeared with coolants and greases of various colors. She appeared at the far side of the engine room and started barking orders to her people, until one of them pointed at Mik, standing stoically as he was, and she sighed and hurried over.

Georgina Yamagawa was a fiery sort of woman then, and she still is. These days you can find her in Fleet R&D, not that that really matters in this context. She pulled a rag from her pocket and in very stereotypical engineer's manner, began wiping her hands as she stopped in front of her Captain.

"You find any more speed for me in those pods?" Mik's question was direct, and her eyes narrowed.

"Just a little, I think I might be able to give you 195 without completely crippling us in the long run," she sounded almost disinterested.

"I'll take everything you have," Mik nodded.

With a nod of her own, Georgina left her Captain behind and got to work.

Mik wandered out, heading back to the bridge. He'd just have to keep waiting.

"Andrew's pulling out every stop he can," Karen was lying on her stomach on my bed. "We're up to 198 cruising, and *Indiana* is just barely holding on to our wake."

I nodded slowly, trying to sink back further in my chair. As waits on trips went, thirty hours actually wasn't all that bad… usually. But this time the pleasure of the short trip was soured by the fact that we were still going to be late to the fight, despite all of Andrew Jenson's engineering wizardry and *Wolf's* ultra-modern GL994 'Reliant' military reactors.

There was nothing more for Karen and I to do than sit and wait. Well, she was lying, but we were both waiting. Drills, you ask? At this stage we weren't going to tire the crew with tedium. The women and men aboard were already very well honed, there was no point wearing them out the day before a fight just to prove that they would have been good in that fight… had they not been so tired out by drilling for it.

No, we were just cruising and waiting.

"When we get there," Karen's hand absently toyed with her ponytail as it flopped over her left shoulder, "we're going to have five ships, they're coming with at least seven… three frigates and two Hawke corvettes…"

We had talked about this four times before, but that really wasn't a reason not to repeat it one more time.

"Yes, and we don't know what classes of Martian ships we're dealing with because the pirates took out the sensor arrays at Furnace and on *Waterton* before our red planet friends got close enough to be properly assessed," I was nearly muttering.

Karen made a frustrated noise and let her face fall into her hands on the bed, "I don't usually let this stuff get to me."

"You're entitled, you stay calm way too much," I said before heaving a sigh.

There was nothing we could do but wait… and somehow —and I can only guess as to why this is — this timing issue was worrying both of us as much as the run to Earth in *The Almost Coup*. That trip had seen me in well-hidden (from everyone but Karen) nervous spells, but this one had *both* Karen and I fit to be tied. I don't know if there's a better way to say it than that.

My guess is that it was the scope of this situation that made the difference: if we got to Earth too late in *The Almost Coup*, it would mean a Martian fleet was probably pounding our homeworld from orbit. Nothing *Wolf* could do about that, we couldn't have done anything to stop it…

But here, where the stakes were much smaller, *Wolf* and our fellow ships could turn the tide of a fight, if only we got there in time. This wasn't a race to get a message to Defense Command in time for them to mobilize the Home Fleet to beat the Martians back… this was us bringing enough firepower to save a whole colony… but arriving late…

We could be decisive, but we probably weren't going to be. And we had to wait to find out.

So as *Wolf* drove through space, and as *Cyclops* did the same, no Captains or Commodores were feeling too restive.

CHAPTER TWENTY-ONE
UNFASHIONABLY LATE

I could give you all the gruesome detail of what I saw at the battle for Anderson's Colony, but I didn't actually *see* anything: I wasn't there. Neither Mik's force nor Karen's and mine made it to the colony in time. The Martians and pirates moved very fast indeed, probably realizing that we were hot on their trail.

Here's a summary of what *Wolf* found when we showed up 100 minutes late.

Jack Gomez had been paralyzed from the waist down — the nature of the spinal damage made surgery at that time impossible, though a couple of years ago he regained the ability to walk. *Vermont* was missing three drive pods, but drifting next to the battered frigate was the wreckage of two pirate raiders. Anderson's Colony was in rough shape, with two domes open to space.

Total dead: 972.

Now, that's less than a quarter of the casualties seen at Furnace, and I chalk that up to three factors: first, Jack and the Anderson Defense Force (which lost all its fighters and armed police vessels) had been warned in advance by Mik's transmission from Furnace. Second, *Vermont* was a frigate, inherently tougher than *Waterton*, the corvette that had defended Furnace, and thus able to do a lot more harm to the attackers. Third, and finally, the pirates apparently never got to land their plundering units.

When pirates attack domes, they tend to crack them and then send in assault teams, some in EVA gear to raid homes and shops for property, and others out of EVA gear to rape and pillage the people hiding in pressurized shelters. Now, the stripping of property in EVA suits doesn't take long, but the raping and plundering requires a lot of time — they have to break through ground defenses, heavy doors… anything the colonists throw at them.

With that comes a lot of horrendous killing. People who romanticize pirates should watch some after-action tape Defense Command photographers have shot of this sort of thing. I make light of a lot of the pirates we come across in these books because they're idiots, but I can do that when it's us they're going up against.

When they decide they want to have a good time with civilians, that's where the lightness stops. Not all pirates go that far, but go figure, the independent bastards the Martians recruited to their force were all for it.

But. *But.*

They hadn't landed at Anderson's Colony. My guess is the combination of the Anderson shore batteries, fighter and police ship defenses, and the hot fight *Vermont* gave them, delayed them too much to be able to insert their fast-strike teams and to still be able to collect them before *Wolf* and Mik arrived.

I doubt the Martians and pirates knew exactly how far behind them Mik was or how close we were in *Wolf.* However, given the state of prepared defense they faced when they arrived at Anderson's Colony, my guess is they knew help was on the way, and they bolted.

Of course, the Martian logs, ever useless, don't confirm or refute my suspicions.

But as *Wolf* and *Indiana* decelerated near *Vermont*, and *June* and *Emily* parted company to run quick sweeps all around Anderson for hidden enemy ships, I didn't yet know any of this.

Karen had to put a calming hand on my forearm to keep me from going off. I was in an intense mental place.

"Signal coming in from the colony," Jim was quite busy again, dealing with all the incoming sensor data as well as the signal traffic. As usual, he was able to parse out the key things — like the arrival of a that message — without difficulty. "Screen six."

I nodded, getting quickly to my feet and heading to the front of the bridge, Karen and Lia suddenly appearing on my flanks as I stopped before the appropriate display. After a long buffering pause, a grainy feed started up, with two figures in the shot.

"Commodore Barron, is it?" the man on the left recognized me, "This is Romero Kim…"

"…and Ellen Anderson," the woman on the right added.

These were the oligarchs of Anderson's Colony. I vaguely remembered them from Lia's briefing…

Lia was already talking, though, while I tried to place the names, "Romero, Ellen, you're alright?"

Their eyes turned to Lia's familiar face and they both nodded, Ellen doing the talking, "We didn't get off too badly, in the end. Much better than what we've heard about Furnace. *Vermont* gave the bastards a hell of a fight, though. I've never seen that sort of ship-to-ship killing."

Lia nodded, "Did they land any strike teams?"

"None. *Vermont* kept them too busy, and they seemed like they were in a rush. One of the Martians was staying far out from the fight, watching the vector you guys just came in on — they may have known you were at Caligula. They boosted over half an hour ago, heading out towards Pemberton Station."

I don't know if there's a Pemberton Station on any British train or bus networks, but if there is, that wasn't the one Ellen Anderson was referring to. No, the Pemberton she meant was a rather modest space port floating over a rock that had been first settled by scientists on the Pemberton exploratory mission. It was a small trade port now, mainly serving as a stop-over point for merchants and personnel carriers heading out into the deeper belt, where Defense Command ships tended not to go.

If you could draw a straight line from Joe's Colony through Furnace and Anderson's colonies, it would carry right on to Pemberton Station before heading out into the deeper belt. Caligula, for reference, was not on that line… well, it's really not easy to describe, so I'll just hope I can convince the publisher to stick a map in the front for you. Seems necessary.

By this time, I'd found my voice, "Are you in need of search and rescue assistance?"

Anderson shook her head, "We have it under control. You should get after the raiders. The attack force totaled nine ships when it came in, now it's down to seven — that's four

Martians and three remaining raiders. One of the other pirates is pretty badly shot up too, but Captain Gomez focused most of his shooting on the two that you can see floating in pieces."

I nodded, "Sounds like Jack. Is there any communication with *Vermont?*"

"Their array is offline, we have rescue teams aboard. Captain Gomez is alive but in critical condition. There are many dead..." Romero Kim obliged me with the information.

"You're looking after them?" Lia's question was almost a command, and both oligarchs nodded simultaneously.

"They definitely made the difference here. We're looking after them alright."

I can't avoid stopping here to point out the obvious to all the nay-sayers who think that Defense Command doesn't *care* that this is our job — *this* is what we do. Jack Gomez and his crew could have run from Anderson's Colony and saved their ship, but instead they'd stood their ground, and paid dearly for it. You can scoff or grumble about imperialism and the dangerous 'jingos' of the Defense Command Navy, but I suggest you pay attention to that example. We try to protect innocent people, that's why we signed up, and even my cynicism bows before that mission. Not all of us do it perfectly, and I'll admit that some of us, like Sean Cook (next book, remember) don't do it at all... but most of us do.

Jack Gomez got the Emperor's Black Sun Medal for Gallantry and Distinguished Service for his part in that fight, and *Vermont* received a commendation. They did their *jobs*, and to the cynics out there who choose to think our job is to make life miserable for those who don't agree with us... well you're partly right. The pirates didn't agree with Jack Gomez, so he obliterated a whole lot of them. I'm sorry, I'll stop ranting.

Lia glanced at me, and as she did I realized it wasn't a casual glance, so I looked back. She had another earnest expression on her face — one that I took to be a vote of confidence in Anderson Colony's ability to care for our people.

We couldn't afford to stop to look after *Vermont*. Pemberton was another forty hours up the line... and in that time we might be able to catch the bastards, give them a bloody nose and convince them not to try this again.

Of course, four against seven was not an ideal allotment of forces, but that didn't matter. Pemberton was another civilian target with minimal defenses, and while it hadn't signed a treaty with us, it was still a friendly independent — that is, it didn't deal with Martians.

"We'll boost after them, then," I returned my gaze to screen six. "If you don't mind, we'll leave a message with orders to follow in your care. Please pass it on to Captain Mikaelsen when his ships get here."

Both oligarchs nodded, and then Anderson leaned towards the screen, "We're feeling good about the alliance we have with your people right now, Commodore. You people really do seem to care about your allies."

That was a political positioning statement... I think. As I just said, *Vermont* and Jack Gomez had damned near died saving this rock, and the oligarchs were thankful for that, but at the same time I got the feeling they were making sure they positioned themselves as loyal friends of the Empire. Maybe they wanted goodwill from our Foreign Office in the longer run, maybe they wanted to create a positive, welcoming reputation in the minds of

Defense Command officers who might defend them in future...

Or maybe I was just too cynical.

Either way, I nodded a single time, "You're loyal to your treaty, and we're loyal to you. Take care of your people, and ours. We'll send back good news soon, I hope."

"Good hunting."

The screen went blank and I took a deep breath. Karen was already ordering Erica Martin to bring *Wolf* around again, Lia was talking to her two Commanders over the Battlelink (sorry, I failed to mention that Battlelink had been open this whole chapter — that's why the oligarchs were on screen *six*), and Elsie McKinnon simply ordered her Helm and Navigation Officer to follow *Wolf*.

Two things ran through my head, then. They'll sound cold, but these were my thoughts:

We were late, dammit.

And now we have to wait another forty hours.

Wolf turned and accelerated again.

CHAPTER TWENTY-TWO

A HOT TRAIL

Wolf was almost two hours out of Anderson's Colony, and I hadn't left the bridge. The trip to Pemberton was going to take just under two days, but we could potentially overtake a damaged Martian-pirate force any time along the way. I felt as though I needed to wait on the bridge, to see if there'd be any indication of how soon we might catch up.

I suppose this is as good a place as any to answer the question that several people (non-Defense Command people, I should add) have asked me about this whole affair. That question: *why* go to Pemberton, or more accurately phrased, why go with only four ships? Outside observers have — perhaps rightly — asked what good four ships could do in a fight against seven. More likely than not, all four of our ships would be crippled or seriously damaged far from a major friendly dry-dock... so why give chase to these pirates and Martians when their target wasn't an ally of the Empire?

Well, I think I've already covered the part of this answer that goes 'Pemberton was a trusted friend, we wouldn't leave it out in the cold'. As for going with only four ships, I've thought about those sorts of decisions a lot. I mean, at Anderson's Colony, five against an assumed seven enemy ships, along with the support of the Anderson Defense Forces tipped the odds our way. Pemberton wasn't well armed, and we were down to four against seven... so why bother?

Because.

Sorry, that's a kid's answer to the question, but it's the one I keep coming back to. Look, maybe it's an arrogant belief spawned from years of Defense Command being more than a match for most threats in the Belt (Grant Merger and the Syndicate excepted) but it had long ago become Defense Command policy that, if there was trouble, you headed towards it, and did whatever good you could do when you got there.

Didn't matter how many ships you had as opposed to how many they had, you went. You helped. This might sound "stupid" — and that's a quote — to the uninitiated, but, well, that's what we do. The pirates have to know that wherever they cause trouble, no matter how many of them there are, any Defense Command ship in the area will respond.

And we will hand them their asses. Pardon the colloquialism and the crudeness, but that's the way they put it, that's what they have to know.

So war or no war, we weren't going to back down. It didn't make the best military sense, but that was the way of it. And besides, in this case, if we caught them and slowed them down at the expense of our drives, Mik would come up with *Cyclops* and put the survivors down.

That was why we were going.

But back to affairs of that moment...

"*Vermont* must have cut one of those pirates up pretty badly," Jim Hannigan was muttering to himself, but I was close enough to his bank of consoles to hear it and look up at him. It took him a few seconds to realize I was looking at him, and then he realized and pointed at something on one of his tech's screens. "I'm getting a trail of intense radiation, looks like the ruptured core of a laser or a fracture in the ship's reactor casing."

I cocked an eyebrow, "Really? We must be close if we can still track it…"

"Very. Half an hour or less from sensor range," Jim looked back down at one of his panels, and I turned away from him.

I ended up nose-to-nose with Lia as I turned, and she smiled a very small smile, "Sorry, I like looking over shoulders these days."

My smile was small and thin to match hers, and Karen appeared behind Lia, "We might be able to overtake them soon, then. Hands to battle stations, Matt."

Matt Baxter was only too happy to oblige, and *Wolf's* crew was alerted to the likelihood of impending battle by the whine of klaxons.

"I guess they left their attack too long — they should have cut and run earlier," Lia took a step back and turned so as to put the comment to both Karen and myself.

Somehow, neither Karen nor I quite agreed. That was, of course, a very logical assessment of the situation, and I'm by no means criticizing Lia's abilities as a naval officer by not agreeing with it… it just *felt* wrong.

Usually when something like that feels wrong, it's because the situation as a whole is somehow sickly. That in mind, Karen and I locked eyes for a moment and neither one of us felt fully convinced… this trail was awfully handy…

"Okay, bad feeling about this?" Lia quite easily read our uncertainty, and with a sigh I nodded.

"Not that we mind bread crumbs… the question is why the Martians would let a ship that easy to track stay with them," Karen frowned, pulling her ponytail over her left shoulder and toying with it as she thought.

There wasn't much we could actually say to articulate our concern — we just had an unsettled feeling.

Jim was working in more literal terms, thank God.

"The sort of radiation we're seeing here… I don't know, it doesn't make sense."

We three uncertain command officers turned towards Jim Hannigan with curious gazes, "Why James, is there a problem?"

Managing a smile at his tormenter (Lia), Jim looked up from one of the displays, "Well, I'd need to talk to Andrew about this, but the kind of radiation we're seeing here looks an awful lot like the sort a drive reactor would spill if it was fractured."

I frowned, "Alright… so…"

Jim switched over to a thoughtful frown, "Well, we've been tracking them for two hours now…"

Looking back, I can't believe that between us, Karen, Lia and I didn't realize the implications of what he was saying by this time. Jim, being a classy guy, contained his surprise at our slow reasoning.

"So," he offered helpfully, "with a fractured reactor, why haven't we overtaken this ship yet? Again, we need to check with Andy, but I don't think there's any way for a ship to keep up 198 kps or better with a reactor spewing this kind of radiation."

Oh.

I turned around and looked back at Karen. She shrugged and nodded, and Lia smiled, "James, I should kiss you."

He cocked an eyebrow, and — totally deadpan — said, "You'd condemn me to death by Major Peters for helping you out?"

That earned him a chuckle, and Lia shrugged, but before she could add more to that little bout of repartee, Karen interrupted with a logical question, "So Jim, do you think this trail might be artificial... left for misdirection?"

"That'd be my best guess," the Lieutenant Commander nodded.

Of course it was. The Martians and the pirates, as much as I do love to disrespect them both, weren't completely inept. They knew we'd be able to track their drive trail... the question was where else they might be going while they led us down the proverbial garden path.

And for all the usefulness of Jim's revelation in helping us realize we were being tricked, we still had no idea where they might be headed. They probably wouldn't be going back to Anderson's Colony — turning around and passing us would be needlessly risky...

So there were a couple of other things to consider. They might be returning to their base to lick their wounds... they could be headed somewhere else to raid an unsuspecting target... or they could have dragged us out this far into deep space so they could destroy *Wolf* and its consorts.

If this was an action movie — a particular action movie in which Lady Hawke was presented as a ditz who liked gaudy jewelry and went everywhere with a manservant who had inappropriate duties that would have led to his dismemberment by Charlie Peters had he been real — then the Martian-pirate ploy would obviously have been to trap *Wolf* in open space. What I mean is this: only in the movies would you find Martians and pirates with enough omnipotent knowledge to realize that it was me, Ken Barron, chasing them, and thus have created this ploy as a trap. That makes for a good movie... well, no it was a bad movie... but it's not the way things happen. Only one man was ever willing to destroy entire colonies just to get my personal attention, and these Martians and pirates were not even close to being in Grant Merger's league of evil.

No, in reality the identity of the chaser probably had no bearing on what the Martian-pirate force did...

All of that said, we still had no idea what they were doing. Yet...

"Jim, can you manage a signal to Anderson's Colony at this speed?" I looked up at our enterprising Sensors and Communications Officer, and he nodded.

"I can pull one off."

"Good, send new orders to Captain Mikaelsen... hold station at Anderson's for the moment. We'll send new instructions asap."

Jim nodded, looking over to one of his techs to confirm that my message was being transcribed.

Mik was still a little over two hours out of Anderson's Colony, but when he got there I didn't want him heading the wrong way...

The signal was fired out of *Wolf's* comm laser seconds later, and we raced on after the bread crumbs.

CHAPTER TWENTY-THREE

TRAIL'S TOO HOT — WE GOTTA STOP!

That chapter title is terrible, and I apologize… but, well, I find it amusing, so it stays.

Another hour passed and we remained on course with the radiation leak lighting up our sensor displays. *Wolf's* chief engineer, Andrew Jenson, confirmed for us that what we were seeing was reactor-type emission, and that unless it was being purposely simulated by a cruising ship, there was no way it could be coming from a vessel moving fast enough to stay away from *Wolf*.

But the problem of where the rest of the ships might be, or might be *going*, remained.

Jim Hannigan was the go-to guy on this, so Karen and I were standing eagerly in front of his bank of consoles… Lia was sitting on one of them, watching him walk back and forth.

"Well," Karen was thinking out loud as we tried to determine the Martian-pirate intentions, "if they're heading for another allied colony, who around here would qualify?"

I frowned at the question, and looked up at Jim, "Local space map pleas–"

Jim's finger pointing at the main screen stopped me, because, of course, as soon as Karen had asked the question, he'd had the map put up.

"We're pretty far out now," Lia noted as she eyed the map (from her seat on some poor guy's console… though to be shallow and honest, I don't know if he disapproved).

Matt Baxter was pacing behind his operations consoles, but as his eyes fell on the star map he had the golden idea of the day, "What about Caligula?"

I shook my head immediately, "No, Matt, they'd never… never…"

I stopped talking and stared.

At this point the words going through my head sounded something like this: *You have to be freakin' kidding me.*

Yes, I did in fact think the word *freakin'*.

Karen had been toying with her ponytail again, now her hand gripped the end of it and held on in surprise (that's very amusing to me, for some reason). She looked at me with one of her rare, genuinely disbelieving looks, and Lia punctuated all our thoughts, "They're going to pop Governor sausage?"

You'll have to flip to the map that better be at the front of this book to see why Caligula was pretty much the only port they might be hitting, presuming they were indeed going after a treaty port and not really going on to Pemberton. Basically, if I can attempt to describe the relative positions, Caligula and Anderson's Colony were the only rocks treaty-bound to the Empire out this far, and Caligula was all on its own now.

"Ellen… or maybe it was Romero… one of the oligarchs said there was a Martian ship watching the Caligula approaches," Lia added after a moment.

I nodded immediately, "They might have an informant in the Caligula government… but why wait until we got *Indiana* out… why not pounce on us when we arrived to bail

Indiana out? Hell, with reactors down *Indiana* would have been an easy kill."

We've never found a satisfactory answer to that question, much to my frustration. Of course, the Martian logs we got are of no use to us in the 'why' questions, so my best guess (here we go again, I know) is that Caligula was on their way out, and thus convenient.

"Caligula," Karen said simply, her tone carrying with it an implied 'for crying out loud'.

"Is our guess enough reason for us to abandon Pemberton?" Lia's next question was the logical, important one, and I actually had to stop to think about the answer.

Well, why would the Martians and pirates hit a small station that wasn't allied to us? It didn't make sense for the them to want to attack anyone who wasn't on the side of the Empire — I mean think about it, a neutral who isn't helping or hindering either side gets attacked suddenly by one side, and what does she or he logically do? That's right, she or he immediately joins up with the side fighting his or her attacker.

My guess then and now remains that the pirates and Martians were on a mission to scare our allies out of their loyal positions, while doing nothing that would hurt their chances of getting other free rocks over to their side.

Raping, pillaging and destroying would probably hurt those chances, so they'd save that for our allies...

And dammit, that meant Caligula.

Actually, writing this, I've just realized there might be another reason (wow, this is odd, usually I know what I'm going to rant about before I start the writing). Think about it: Caligula had been interning one of our ships, which meant it wasn't firmly in our camp. Karen and Lia and I had forced Governor sausage into abiding by his treaty... and only then was his colony made a target.

Other neutral rocks could see our diplomatic heavy-handedness in getting sausage to play ball as the direct reason for his rock's destruction... and thus would hate us even more. I don't know how aware the Martians and pirates were of the events at Caligula, but this would add up, certainly...

Well, only took me decades to realize that. I'm slightly embarrassed — I imagine a number of scholars and veterans have already come to that conclusion. Ah well.

Back on point, I nodded in reply to Lia's question, "Our guess is all we have to go on right now. Jim, send new orders to Anderson's Colony for Mik: he's to head straight for Caligula and prepare for incoming."

Karen let go of her ponytail and turned to Erica Martin, "Change our course, bear for Caligula."

Lia passed on the same orders to the Commanders of *June* and *Emily*.

We got off the too-hot-trail, and headed back to Caligula.

An hour after our little revelation, Mik's ships pulled into Anderson's Colony ready to deal some hurt (as Mik likes to put it). *Amherst* and *Argentia* led the way, the two corvettes sniffing around carefully for any sign of the enemy before *Cyclops* committed itself to an approach vector. *Ohio* was bringing up the rear, watching in case an ambush fell from that direction.

But there weren't any pirate or Martian ships in the area, except for the tattered wrecks of the two ships that *Vermont* had shattered in its defiant last stand.

Mik was standing on his bridge, stroking his beard as his eyes took in the information from the various scan feeds *Cyclops* was receiving — both from its own arrays and passed on from Nikhil Jones' and Diane Richardson's corvettes. The battle hadn't been as bad here at Anderson as it had been at Furnace, but that didn't make things any easier…

"Signal coming in from the Colony's government…" reported *Cyclops'* Sensors and Communications Officer.

"Screen twelve," Mik replied as he moved down the wall of screens to twelve, then waited as the signal buffered.

A few seconds later — in a vid feed that was much less grainy than the one that had reached *Wolf* only hours before — Romero Kim and Ellen Anderson passed on word of what had happened, and then sent over our latest orders from *Wolf*.

The orders packet took their place on screen twelve, and it included all *Wolf's* sensor readings of the radiation trail and a brief outline of my reasoning behind picking the destination for Mik's force.

"Caligula, great…"

Mik didn't like the rock, its Governor, or the way it had decided to enter the war, interning one of our ships and all… but then he didn't have much of a choice but to go help Lester Gerald prepare his pitiful asteroid for heavy attack.

And besides, as Mik pointed out to me the last time we talked about this, if I was right, then defending Caligula wouldn't just be about protecting those delightful people who passed their lives in that hole. No, it would be about killing the bastards who'd pillaged Furnace and severely hit Anderson's Colony — two places very much deserving of a little retribution.

"All ships turn for Caligula, maximum speed. Let's try to beat them there this time!"

Of course, there was no way to tell whether the thirty-hour trek from Anderson's Colony to Caligula would be fast enough — we didn't know where along the way the main body of the Martian-pirate force split off from the decoy… they could already be ahead of Mik, or they could be *behind* him.

There was nothing else to do, then: it was a race to Caligula, a traitorous but still-allied rock that needed Defense Command protection.

Led by *Amherst* and *Argentia*, Mik's force of four ships launched themselves into space once again.

CHAPTER TWENTY-FOUR

GREAT RACE IN SPACE

Because I tend to compress the travel portions of this narrative, the actual time that was passing here might not be obvious to you, so think about this: we'd arrived at Hawke One *nine days* before the moment when we turned back for Caligula. More dramatic: the attack on Furnace was almost three days old.

Sometimes I fear that I'm coming across the way those movies I rail against do, making it seem that Mik's arrival and departure from Furnace and our arrival at Anderson's Colony were all within fifteen minutes of each other or some such thing. Not so. It took days to get places, and as you're used to hearing me say by now, days inevitably led to worries and concerns.

Interestingly, and perhaps insensitively on my part, I was actually less worried about the trip back to Caligula than I had been about the trip to Anderson's Colony. Take that to mean whatever you like — maybe I'm a bastard who cared less about Governor Lester (sausage) Gerald and his citizens than I should have, or maybe I was just more confident that we'd figured out the Martian-pirate plans. Maybe a little of both.

Either way, something that occurred to me on this trip was, well, why should I tell you like this? Much better to let Karen say it.

"You haven't been dancing much lately."

That wasn't the revelation, that was what I said to inadvertently get to the revelation.

Karen and I were back in my cabin, because apparently that's been designated the 'almost a nervous wreck' clubhouse, and as she lay on my bed, kicking her legs behind her, Karen turned her head towards me, "How would you know?"

Sitting in my chair, I paused thoughtfully, then shrugged, "Well, I assumed."

"Aha," she said simply.

We were silent again for a while, both staring at my wall vidscreen, and the ETA countdown clock that was glowing in the middle of it. Each second ticked by very slowly. *Very* slowly.

Tick.

Gee, I wonder whether one day I'll write books about everything I've done. Or maybe novels. Maybe an alternate history of Earth, I like those. Have humanity wiped out by an intelligent bio-weapon and replaced by mutant animals... hmm...

Tock.

Or maybe I could take up interpretative dance...

You get the idea.

"You know, it's odd," Karen was actually having the revelation I was alluding to earlier, and I looked at her. With my eye contact secured, she continued, "Well, this ship's been in action everywhere so far. We held Belt Two, fought in the Battle Over Earth, now we're out here... I don't imagine many people will be able to tell stories to their grandkids the way we'll be able to."

I smiled, "Yes, but we'll probably spend most of our time telling our grandkids how the movies about us are wrong."

Karen smiled, "Oh that's ambitious, movies. Maybe one, I say."

Boy was she ever wrong. Not that I knew that then...

"Oh I don't know, either way it'll be entertaining. I can't wait to see what voodoo they try to use to put you on the screen..." I grinned, and Karen tipped her head forward (sideways because she was looking at me side-on).

"Meaning?"

I chuckled, "Well, they're probably going to kill a few actresses when they try to cast you — all the plastic surgery they'll do to beauty themselves up combined with training to do all the stunts you do, the anorexic ones will be dropping like flies."

Karen's smile broadened (I suppose that's a horrible reaction to the promise of dying celebrities), "The Karen McMaster actress body count... that's probably all history would remember me for."

I nodded with mock sincerity, "Oh definitely. The movie will end with you and me making out in an escape pod, having just saved the whole Empire by loading up a computer virus into the Martian mothership, and also infecting them with a plague that they have no natural immunity to..."

If you've had any experience with twentieth century film (I know, it sounds boring but it isn't) then you'll get that joke.

Listening to the string of circumstances, Karen laughed, "A *mothership*, eh? Everyone will know that's made up."

I smiled and leaned further back in my chair, "Yeah, that'll tip them off. I'll probably have to break down and actually write books about this stuff. I am the only one here qualified to write books, Captain math-lady..."

"Oh don't even start that," somehow she got a pillow from beside her feet and hit me with it... without seeming to move off her stomach. She has crazy abilities — that, I should point out in hindsight, have not killed any of the actresses who have tried (and failed miserably) to portray her.

Well, there was that one actress, who I obviously won't name, who had the psychological breakdown and tried to space herself on set, but I've been assured that had much more to do with the 'acid she was dropping at the time'. Not sure what that means, but it must have been rather bad.

Anyway, as you can tell, passing the time on this trip back to Caligula was proving marginally less painful than it had been on the way out to Anderson's rock.

It was, of course, still a process of waiting, and wondering. The very real possibility existed, though, that we were actually hot on the heels of the Martian-pirate force, and that we might somehow overtake them en route.

That possibility pretty much kept us from sleeping, or at least sleeping deeply, because if action came, we'd have to be on the bridge in very little time. Naps were all we got that night, as we drew closer to Caligula...

CHAPTER TWENTY-FIVE

"WELCOME TO CALIGULA, YOU DEFENSE COMMAND BASTARDS!"

Look at that chapter title. Just look at it. Want to know what it is? That is the greeting — the *greeting* — that Governor sausage gave Mik as soon as the comm link was established between *Cyclops* and the Caligula Government mansion.

It's on vid, you can look it up at your leisure. Said Governor Lester Gerald, "Welcome to Caligula, you Defense Command bastards!"

Now, not only is that rude, it's poorly phrased. And for Mik, who hadn't heard exactly how we'd humiliated Governor sausage, it was somewhat out of the blue. Not that Mik had much sympathy for Lester Gerald; even though he didn't know that the Governor was now known to us as the sausage, he did know that *Indiana* had been interned here.

And to add to that, he was slightly on edge, because *Cyclops* had arrived in the space around Caligula to find no Martian or pirate activity. He had limited time, then, to set up a defense, but he did have time to set up a defense — he'd gotten ahead of the bastards, and he was going to catch them as they came calling.

Then this was his welcome.

His reply was off the cuff and rather uncharacteristic for him — he's usually stingy about language, just like me.

Said Mik: "Well <<bleep>> you too."

Now you're wondering. I've included the four-letter words elsewhere in these books, why not here? Well, here's a story that had me laughing for a very long time. Mik doesn't like to slip up in his word choice any more than I do, and worse, he doesn't like it on the record. In a pub or at a game, sure, he's happy to, but not on vid that goes to the Admiralty records office...

So after all this was over, on his cruise back to Hawke space, he quietly went into every copy of the ship's vid log, opened up the appropriate time code, and edited in an actual <<bleep>> over the word. I don't actually know which expletive he used because of this — though I imagine you and I both can use our deductive reasoning to figure it out.

Nevertheless, look at *Cyclops'* video log and there it is, "Well <<bleep>> you too."

That's just brilliant, absolutely great...

Anyway, for all its brilliance, that shouldn't come off as more important than the obvious fact: *Cyclops* and its ships had reached Caligula first, and as Governor sausage puffed up red and began to bluster, Mik held up his hand.

"Look, you can choose to believe me or not when I say this, but there's a powerful Martian-pirate force on its way here, and it's going to rape and pillage to its heart content unless we stop it. So either shut up and let us do our jobs, and use your shore batteries to help us, or I'm walking right now."

Total bluff — I would have known it then, and Mik's since confirmed it with me. There was no way Governor sausage's protests would have kept Christian Mikaelsen from getting the bastards who'd so brazenly torn up Furnace and Anderson's colonies.

But it was enough for the Governor, who stopped his sputtering, "We heard form Anderson that there were probably forces coming our way…"

"And *that's how you greet your only backup?*" Mik was slightly incredulous. Slightly.

The Governor didn't answer so much as huff twice, "Do what you have to do, then!"

And then the sausage killed the link. Have to love how he made it sound like Mik was going to pull his teeth or something.

Glaring at the screen for a few seconds, Mik took a deep breath of his own, then nodded to his commanding officers who were already connected by Battlelink. They didn't know how much time they'd have to prepare for the attack, so plans had been laid out in transit. The best of the ships were with *Cyclops*, all Mik needed to do was say 'go' and they'd all take their positions.

So, Mik looked at the three heads facing him over the Battlelink: Commander Nikhil Jones, Commander Diane Richardson, and Captain Evelyn Sherman.

"Go."

"Going."

"Aye aye."

"Yes."

You can play 'match the affirmative to the commanding officer' if you like — can you guess which response was Nikhil Jones'? If you do, you win a prize! (I'm lying, there are no prizes.)

Mik turned to his Helm and Navigation Officer as the quartet of ships began to maneuver apart, their progress being tracked on *Cyclops'* big bridge monitor.

"Alright, take us around behind the rock. XO, we're silent running, but keep weapons and drives ready for military power."

"We're sticking with you, Mik," Evelyn Sherman said over the Battlelink, and he nodded in reply — that was the plan.

Nikhil Jones ordered *Amherst* into position on the rough approaches from Anderson plus three hours… that is to say, on the expected vector of approach *Wolf* would take. Diane Richardson put *Argentia* on the vector of approach direct from Anderson's Colony, so the two corvettes basically faced the two likeliest paths the Martian-pirate force could take as it cruised in.

Neither ship attempted to hide its presence — they were going to be obvious from the beginning of the fight, and their sensors were active and reaching out to maximum range.

It was around now that Mik — for *once* — seriously missed his fighters. If the ships' fighters hadn't all been back at Furnace for SAR work, they could have reconnoitered outward and broadened the detection net. But such was life, he'd make do.

And no, he wouldn't ask Caligula to provide its corroded old buckets of planes for scouting. He'd doubtless be rescuing the pilots of these malfunctioning old crates if they went out on patrol — rescuing pilots *before* the enemy showed up, that was.

Cyclops pushed steadily towards Caligula, with *Ohio* in formation aft of its port drive pod, and together the ships slowed at the rock, then reversed directions in a lateral spin and pushed themselves down behind the colony.

They were hiding behind the asteroid; hopefully that must be pretty clear.

As they settled in, Mik took a few deep breaths. His heart rate was up a bit, but he didn't pay it much heed. Now it was time to wait…

Wolf was still two hours out, but Karen and I were on the bridge, sitting rather quietly in our chairs. Even Lia, for all her energy and antics, was sitting very quietly in her chair. Our good spirits of the day before — if you can call them good spirits — were dimmed. We were close to Caligula, but yet again, we got the feeling that we were going to be late to the party.

"ETA is 118 minutes now," Karen whispered the words to me so quietly I barely heard them.

I looked at her, "I know!"

She smiled, "Yes, I know you know. But you were going to ask anyway."

A smile crept onto my face, "Yes, I was, actually…"

"Glad to help," her smiled broadened.

"Hey, watch it or you'll make the kids uncomfortable with this naughty whispering!"

Lia was hovering over Karen's shoulder all of a sudden, and I dramatically flipped my hands up into the air, "What?"

She waved her finger between Karen and me, "Whispering makes me nervous!"

Karen cocked an eyebrow, "So you mean you actually say nothing when you're not supposed to be talking?"

Lia smiled, "No, I should have said whispering *by other people* makes me nervous."

I frowned, "Leave us be, or I'll call Charlie to come get rid of you."

Lia's smile broadened, "Well, if you don't mind people making out on your bridge, go for it…"

I released a long sigh and sat back in my chair. We waited and watched. Hopefully we'd get to the battle in time.

CHAPTER TWENTY-SIX
BRINGING THE HURT

Mik was sitting quietly in his chair, anxiously watching and waiting as the sensor feeds came to *Cyclops* around the rock of Caligula. He'd already been in position for ten minutes... how far behind were these damned Martians and pirates? He didn't have all day...

Well, that's what he was thinking at the time, but as he pointed out to me after the fact, he *did* have the whole day. However, that sentiment wouldn't sound as dramatic or impatient, and he was definitely getting impatient.

Stroking his beard, he started to pay a lot of attention to the chronometer on the main screen. Remember how the numbers were running slow for me when I was sitting in my cabin with Karen? They were doing that.

The waiting, as I've said before and will say again, is the killer in this business. You wait, you watch, you wonder. Then the thought occurs to you, not for the first time, but now more powerfully than ever before: what if the guess was wrong? What if they're actually going to Pemberton, and the leak was legitimate and the damaged ship had a miracle worker for an engineer?

Mik could picture it: a smoky engine room with a loud rumbling... then a guy with a long beard, floppy hat, robe, and wooden staff walking in... raising his hands over the engines... uttering an incantation in ancient Babylonian... a light spreading over the chamber... then suddenly the engines are fine.

That development would really be bad news for Defense Command. We'd have to hire our own miracle workers... the Corps of Mages... they'd be self-important and expensive, and they'd constantly be turning people aboard ship into lizards of one variety or another...

"Got them on scope, skipper!"

This is one of those times you thank God for forcing your mind back to reality. Not that daydreaming about Babylonian mages (there are so many things historically wrong with that concept) isn't entertaining. At least to me. And Mik. Sorry, back to our story.

Mik got out of his chair and paced to the front of his bridge, "Alright, let's do this."

The Martians and pirates numbered six ships — the seven survivors of the attack on Anderson's less, no doubt, the decoy ship — and they were coming in on a vector between the two corvettes out on picket duty. Essentially, we've taken that to mean that the combined enemy force turned off the course it was leading *Wolf* along before we turned to give chase, but at least an hour out of Anderson.

No matter, Commander Jones immediately asserted his control as the senior corvette commander, and *Amherst* and *Argentia* were rapidly maneuvered together to face the oncoming vessels. The pirates actually only supplied two of the ships in this force; the Martians had two destroyers and two destroyer escorts leading the way.

Evidently they weren't intimidated by the two small corvettes they faced.

They should have been worried about two corvettes, at least in my opinion, but they weren't. As we found out later (from the nearly-useless logs), it was these Martian ships, not any of the pirates, that had actually done the heavy lifting when it came to taking out our ships defending both Furnace and Anderson's colonies. The pirates led the way, got their noses bloodied, and had made it much easier for the Martians to cripple our softened-up *Waterton* and *Vermont*.

Now, evidently, the pirates had been sufficiently taught their lesson. The surviving two ships probably only wanted to raid and plunder, the Martians would be expected to deal with the Defense Command vessels.

That plan suited Mik just fine.

"They'll have us in weapons range in about four minutes," Diane Richardson said over Battlelink, and Nikhil nodded.

"Very well, we will fall back to the asteroid and gain the support of the shore batteries."

The two Commanders were playing it as though they had no battleship and frigate waiting to pounce, just in case the Martians had a way to read the Battlelink feed. We don't think the Martians ever broke Battlelink coding, but especially at a time like this, it cost nothing to be cautious.

Mik's plan was relatively simple — convince the Martians they had the edge in numbers, that all we'd been able to rush to Caligula were a couple of quick little corvettes, not the big lumbering battleship that plied space out here.

To take advantage of that subterfuge, though, Mik had to make sure the Martians were well within *Cyclops'* laser envelope before he jumped up from behind the rock and started firing — if he came up too soon, the Martians would have time to cut and run before *Cyclops'* lasers could stop them. The trap couldn't be wasted — we didn't want to leave these ships in any condition to do battle in the future.

Making that happen properly required more waiting, though. Not something Mik was eager to do… but he had to. There was no other option.

No, there actually wasn't.

My publisher read those last sentences and seemed to think that it was casual misdirection — that something else would happen in the next ten minutes that would cause Mik to reveal himself early. Well, nope.

The Caligula shore batteries, our bane only days before, now started to put their 'trained good' skills to use, spinning up their admittedly pathetic (against a moving target) lasers for action. *Amherst* and *Argentia* drifted backward at varying paces, matching the speed of the oncoming attack force the whole way back.

The Martian ships were decelerating evenly — they knew how to handle their ships, as much as I'd like to bash them. Their weapons were online and their turrets were spinning expectantly. Very flash, very 'look at us we're great because we have turrets and you don't'. I don't know if the Martians say things like that, but given the number of times I say the opposite, I expect at least one of their more annoying officers boasts about their turret systems. Idiot.

Mik had his arms folded and was still stroking his beard.

"They're now in weapons range," his XO reported from behind the tactical consoles.

"Wait for it. Helm, get ready to pop us up. Evelyn, you too — we go together, but you be ready to give chase if one of them breaks for it," Mik split his orders between his own bridge crew and Battlelink, and he got affirmative replies from both places.

"Targeting priority?" his XO put the next question, and turning back to the Commander, Mik stroked his beard more thoughtfully.

"Hit the nearest destroyer with everything, try to slow it down, then switch to the other destroyer. Evelyn, when we slow down the first destroyer, you move in and finish it off. Nikhil, Diane, you focus on the DEs. Ignore the pirates for now — if they know what's good for them they'll run. They're not much of a threat without naval support anyway..."

The orders drew nods and more affirmative sounds from all over the bridge and Battlelink, and Mik refocused himself on the main screen. *Cyclops* had a very big weapons envelope, relative to the speed the Martians were using as they decelerated to bombard Caligula.

He'd give them another minute.

"We're beginning to exchange fire," Nikhil Jones reported over the link, and Mik nodded.

"Don't get hit," were his exact orders.

On the main screen, the icons of *Amherst* and *Argentia* began to slide sideways, then up and down. A vid feed captured from the Caligula satellite grid added some dramatic pictures, showing the two corvettes twirling and spinning with a handiness only corvettes can ever manage, bright energy shots lancing from one side to the other and back.

"Prepare to go to full military power," Mik nodded to his Helm and Navigation Officer. "Targets all set?"

"Yes, sir," the XO replied evenly.

Mik stroked his beard twice more, then he let his arms drop to his sides, "Alright, up we go. Hit them as soon as the shot's clear."

I can only imagine the look on the Martian commander's face. Of course he didn't record his expression in his log book. Slack-jawed would be most probable. Screams of terror are much less likely, but they'd have been most entertaining.

As *Cyclops* cleared the shadow of Caligula, the battleship's old lasers flared, long beams of angry red energy hurtling across space in a wicked lance that caught the first destroyer — not the flagship, evidently — right amidships. The huge battleship beams were more than a match for the destroyer's armor, and the ship began to shudder and list sideways as the power to its drive pods imbalanced.

The beams dragged off the side of the ship as *Cyclops* began pressing forward under full military power, and the XO killed the shots to begin plotting his solution on the next destroyer. That ship — the flagship — was already reversing course and running. Apparently the Martians are very good at running away... yes, I know that sounded like a dig at them, and it was, but it was deserved.

Nikhil Jones' *Amherst* lunged forward with crisp lethality, its smaller lasers trimming two of the turrets off the nearest Martian destroyer escort, just as it too attempted to reverse course. The second destroyer escort, slightly behind the one that *Amherst* hit, was able to target its weapons more effectively, and the laser shots it fired from its leading turrets rammed into *Argentia* with some force, decompressing a crew section and destabilizing the small ship's flight profile.

"Losing some speed," Diane Richardson stayed cool on the Battlelink. "Returning fire."

The second destroyer escort, like the second destroyer, was already turning fast and hard to run. As Mik had expected, the pirates were already long gone.

Ohio accelerated past *Cyclops* now, the frigate's lasers sawing into the wounded destroyer's upper engine pylon. The destroyer escort Jones was targeting then lost its tail and began to spin, its power systems failing.

"Try to get a hit in on the other destroyer," Mik turned to his XO. Already, two Martian ships had been dealt with without loss on the Defense Command side, but Mik wasn't going to waste the opportunity.

Cyclops' lasers burned outward again, this time trying to catch a piece of the small stern profile of the retreating destroyer. One of the battleship's two bow beams cut across the destroyer's low drive pod, but didn't stay on it long enough to do crippling damage.

"I'll pursue the fleeing destroyer escort, Diane, please finish off the wounded one..." Nikhil Jones was right on top of the situation, and *Amherst*, still undamaged, continued its high acceleration in pursuit of the other destroyer escort that was trying to work up to escape velocity.

Too late, *Amherst* was already making full military speed, almost 200 kps for the little ship, and the Martians were doing about 170. A laser shot hurled from *Amherst's* bow punched a hole right through the Martian's port pylon, and the ship's acceleration topped out at around 172 kps.

"Mags, please," Nikhil's cool words were sharp, and his corvette began an onslaught of mag bolts that simply couldn't be weathered by the Martian ship. It took about six minutes for the Martian to be completely fried by the electromagnetic energy, but in that time, only two shots from Martian EM cannons hit the corvette, neither doing any damage to speak of.

Of course, while that was going on, Evelyn Sherman and Diane Richardson were finishing off their targets.

Mik's eyes narrowed as the destroyer *Cyclops* was chasing desperately tried to accelerate away. It was doing about 184 kps now, which normally would have given it enough of an edge to out-leg a battleship. But no, as fast as the destroyer was accelerating, *Cyclops* was in fact getting towards its top speed faster; it was already doing 189 kps.

And they were still well within laser range.

"Focus on the upper pod," Mik turned to his XO. "Let's cut their speed by a quarter and see how the word 'surrender' sounds to them."

The XO nodded with a hungry smile, and the bow lasers cut out again. Both shots only slid across the upper pylon of the Martian ship, but it was enough; the upper pod's relays must have been fused, because the ship began to slow.

"Mags now, take out its power grid," Mik followed up his orders quickly, and he watched on *Cyclops'* own high-zoom camera feed as a small speck in the distance received a shower of golden energy pulses.

About three minutes later, the destroyer's systems were overloaded, its acceleration died, and it began to drift helplessly away from Caligula. It wouldn't be allowed to drift far.

"Ready boarding parties to take all ships. After what these bastards aided and abetted at Furnace, I think we'll see some public trials when we get them to an Imperial Court."

There were stronger sounds of agreement at that.

That was the Battle of Caligula. The pirates were allowed to run, as they weren't nearly as dangerous as these four Martians, and Mik had single-handedly wiped out a very strong Martian presence in the independent belt.

And, as you might have noticed, *Wolf, Indiana, June* and *Emily* were nowhere to be seen.

That's because, unlike in the movies, we actually *weren't* everywhere at once, Karen and I. Shocking, isn't it? This was Mik's big win, and it was a very good win at that.

We showed up in Caligula space an hour and a half later.

CHAPTER TWENTY-SEVEN
SO MUCH FOR PUNCTUALITY

Mik was smiling when he appeared on *Wolf's* Battlelink, and because I'm me, I immediately looked at Karen, "Quick, check on the ship's canary! He looks like he just ate it!"

Now, I thought that was pretty clever. Karen just stared at me, and Lia's mouth hung open, "Oh my God, did you think that was funny?"

I stand by my joke. These people were all clearly just ignorant. So there.

Shaking his head, Mik laughed (at least he reciprocated there), "No, I just ate *four Martian ships* for breakfast, with the help of these great COs I brought with me. First time I get *Cyclops* into a fight and we come out right on top."

I smiled, "I wish I could have seen their faces when you popped up."

At that point I hadn't seen the battle logs, so I didn't know how right-on the 'pop up' wording was, but Mik simply nodded, "Well, we got to see their faces when we boarded. We got all four as intact as can be after they've been knocked out by weapons fire. Fleet R&D will want to have my babies when they see what I've got for them to study."

"Sure. Well. Um, Karen and I saved Earth from an attack fleet, so don't let four ships go to your head there," I crossed my arms with artificial indignation, and Mik laughed a very hearty, belly sort of laugh.

"Yeah, comparative feat lists are going to be interesting," he nodded, and I grinned before sobering back to my job.

"So, you have a firm grip on each of those ships?"

"Well, not as firm as I'd like — I want to move their crews off immediately, get them into brigs somewhere. I'm almost tempted to drop them off at Anderson to let the locals put them to trial..."

"You mean put them to death," Lia popped into the conversation for the first time, and Mik laughed again at her comment.

"Seriously, won't be doing that, so guess we're stuck with them for a while. Hi Lady Hawke..."

"Mik," she nodded back. "Well, get them to Hawke and we can look after getting them back to Earth or Belt Two for some vid trials and POW camps."

"Yes ma'am," he nodded back.

"Otherwise things are well?" I looked from Lia back to Mik, and he nodded.

"Caligula didn't even fire a shore battery once, and that Governor of theirs has been silent since we cleaned up the mess for him. I'm hoping he's learned the perks of an Imperial Treaty of Alliance."

"Governor sausage? He'll never really learn that lesson," Lia's expression was deadpan, and Mik disappeared from the screen — evidently he was doubled over laughing at the sausage nickname.

The joke really works on a lot of levels if you see this guy. It's mean, yes, but Lester Gerald had it coming. And besides, for all our slander of the sausage, we had just gone out of our way in a panicked rush to save him and his filthy rock from some very unsavory characters. Making fun of the idiot didn't stop us from doing our job, so I have no trouble with it.

If you do... well... challenge me to a duel if you like. You wouldn't be the first, believe me. And I'm still here.

Mik reappeared on the camera after a couple of minutes' laughter. Some have told me a Captain shouldn't be so enthusiastic in a post-combat situation — there should be no laughing. Well, if a post-combat situation finds many dead, then I agree.

But, and I probably didn't make this clear enough back in the chapter about the battle, there had been no loss of life among Mik's crews. A section of *Argentia* had certainly decompressed, but with the crew at battle stations, nobody had been near the breach. And as for the Martians, we didn't know casualty statistics then, but Mik's boarding teams weren't finding very large numbers.

We later learned that exactly fourteen Martians died in the fight, with ten times that number being burned or otherwise injured — not a whole lot, if you think about it.

You might say that fourteen dead is still no laughing matter, and you're again probably right. But, well, we're not perfectly nice people, and these bastards hadn't stopped the pirates from killing over 4,000 civilians at Furnace, or almost 1,000 at Anderson's Colony.

If we'd been laughing at either of those scenes, I'd be appalled.

Here though, no. No, I was fine with us laughing. We all were.

"Alright, well you'll need extra Special Branch and SF teams with you to deal with the crews of the ships... I suppose we'll tow them back to Hawke Six. *Cyclops'* drives will be handy for that," I was talking more seriously, and with his laughter spent for the moment, Mik nodded.

"I don't think we could trust Caligula to hold them for our research teams, so definitely. I'd suggest sending the rest of my force back to Anderson's Colony to help with the repairs there, I already left a solid force at Furnace. Then your ships and *Cyclops* head directly for Hawke Six together, with these catches in tow."

I nodded at Mik's recommendation, "Very well. Issue the orders to your ships, and send them my congratulations while you're at it."

Karen hadn't been part of the conversation until this point, but now she stepped in next to me, "Think we need to leave anyone here to watch Caligula?"

I paused and thought about that for a moment. The most tempting answer was, of course, to let Governor sausage look after himself, but temptations like that really can't be realized.

So...

"Mik, there any skipper you really don't like?"

There was no need to have an expert Captain wasted on this backwater's protection.

Mik's eyes narrowed thoughtfully, "Guy Vivar on *Nanton*. I left him at Furnace. He's useless."

I smiled, "Send him orders to come up and take over security at Caligula until further notice."

Mik matched my smile, "Will do. And if that's it, I'm going to start making tow arrangements. I think we'll actually have enough drive power to haul all four ships at 160 kps. You can leave *Indiana* with me and speed on back to Hawke Six with Lady Hawke's ships, if you think that best."

I smiled, "Sounds agreeable. You look into the details, we'll talk later."

Mik nodded once, and the screen flipped back to its sensor display.

"So we missed the fight," I looked at Karen. "I thought we were fated to be in every engagement that went down in this war, but I guess not."

She smiled and shrugged, "I guess we used up all our luck getting to Earth in time."

"Worth the trade, I suppose," I nodded with a manufactured sigh.

Lia looked between us both with her eyebrows up, "You two want to be in every fight in this war? You're sick. Just plain sick."

She was joking… I think.

For effect, though, she stormed back to her chair, and Karen and I simply drifted towards each other, sharing smiles.

"I suppose she's right," Karen whispered as we got close enough. "We really should focus our energies on more productive things."

"Love, not war!" I whispered back with a grin.

"No whispering, dammit!" Lia hollered from the back of the bridge.

We chuckled to ourselves.

CHAPTER TWENTY-EIGHT

WAIT, THERE'S MORE!

It was reasonably late that evening when there was a surprise knock at my door. Karen and I had just finished our supper, so it probably wasn't her again — not at this hour. I was sitting in the chair next to my bed, doing the paperwork that comes with being a Commodore (paperwork I hated then as I do now, and which I continue to try to shield you from, dear readers!).

There was a lot of paperwork, I must say. Now that we'd had a chance to stop at Caligula for long enough to catch our collective breath, Jim Hannigan had gotten back in touch with Belt Two for comm exchanges, and there were all sorts of forms for me to sign and thumbprint, as well as a few nasty messages from the Foreign Office and Mister Tripp about how I was negligent in not stopping and taking high tea with him. Those were all in a special file I had set up of comm messages I was reserving to send to John Fiora when I got back to Belt Two.

'People to Destroy' was the folder title, a cathartic name and admittedly not a completely accurate one... Ferdinand Tripp's assignment as chief Foreign Office representative at Caligula three weeks after this wasn't 'destruction' as such...

Anyway, I was moving pads systematically from a high pile on the left side of my chair to a growing one on the right, scanning the documents briefly before signing them, trusting that my clerks were doing their jobs and not getting me to sign inappropriate things. The amount of administrative work, though, was truly annoying.

My mother once asked me why we didn't put all the forms on just one pad. And I have to say, I don't know. Later, about ten years after the war, we started using fewer pads for all these forms, but at this point in time we were strictly 'one form, one pad'. Looking back, the fact that it didn't occur to me to ask that all my forms be consolidated onto one pad sort of bothers me. Just goes to show, though, that you should *always* listen to your mother. She's always smarter than you (yes, I know I don't set the bar very high, but my mother's very smart indeed). At least in the movies, piles of pads look dramatic. Maybe I had movie-friendly foresight...

And you don't care. Sorry, forgot the rule of not getting off on a rant about paperwork. So where was I? Oh yes, there was a knock at my door.

"Come on in unless you want to kill me. In that case go find Major Charlie Peters and tell him you want to kill me."

The hatch swung open while I was frowning at the title of one of the pads I'd picked up — it was a Torpedo Requisition form, which had come from the Supply Section with Karen's thumbprint on it. As Commodore of the Belt Squadron, I actually had to okay the requisitions for torpedoes and most other supplies... something I'd have to change. Something I did change, actually. By 2231, the Imperial supply situation was hardly spread so thin as it had been when the requisition regs had previously been updated (2211). In the earlier times, every torpedo and crate of supplies was precious on the Belt frontier... now we had *tons*.

I thumbprinted the pad anyway, then tugged the stylus out of its top right hand corner and initialed the appropriate line. Sliding the stylus back into the pad, I managed to forget that someone was coming in...

Until Lia Hawke did what I can only describe as a belly-flop onto my bed in front of me.

My surprise was such that I temporarily levitated out of my chair... yes, that sounds much better than 'nearly hit the ceiling'.

"Doing paperwork? It looks like you're doing paperwork."

I was half-incredulous, "Well if it looks like I'm–"

"Why do you think they call it paperwork these days? As far as I know nobody uses paper forms anymore."

"It's a criminal oversight, and there should be an Imperial Inquiry," I dropped the Torpedo Requisition pad onto the 'done' pile and Lia smiled at me.

"Loving the inquiries lately, aren't you?"

My eyebrows went up, "You know how I love pain and frustration."

"You do love me! Can't wait to tell Charlie..."

I settled my hands on the arms of my chair, "He knows. It's our secret, we're going to fight to the death for you in your father's court."

"Been nice knowing you then," Lia assumed much the same position that Karen usually does — on her front with her legs kicking behind her. Apparently I missed that memo on proper lying-on-bed posture.

"Is there a reason you're lying on my bed, Lia?" my question was flat, but I think there had to be a hint of 'amused' in there.

Her smile broadened, "Why, are you expecting company?"

One of my eyebrows sunk, leaving the other behind, "Well as a matter of fact, Karen will probably be by later..."

"Aha," she said that a certain way.

You know the way.

"Oh, don't you start. We have to figure out some logistics for getting back to the Belt colonies, and who we should take with us..." I probably sounded defensive.

Lia put on her instantly-earnest expression and nodded quickly, "Oh sure. 'Gee Karen, who do you think should come back to the Belt colonies with us?' 'Oh I don't care, Ken, just make sure you're one of them...' 'Of course I will be, I'd never leave my ship... or you...' 'Will the time ever be more right for us than right now?' 'I don't know, could any time not be right...?'" She started making kissy sounds.

Now, I've re-read that passage a couple of times, and I'm not sure how it comes off without Lia's absurd voices backing it up — because if I hadn't been attempting to appear staunch and unaffected by her words, I'd have been laughing myself to death while she was doing it. Lia knows me well, knew what I thought of Karen from pretty much day one, and was always teasing me like this, with scenarios from the truest to the (obviously) most ridiculous. It was part of the game, and of course, I always got her back. Poor Charlie took a lot of heat on that count.

So when you read that, don't run to your vid, print off a picture of Lia Hawke, and start hurling darts at it. It was well-intentioned and funny.

But…

"First off, your dialogue needs serious work."

With her usual perfect timing, Karen was standing just inside the door with her arms folded and her 'ha-ha, that was so funny I might shoot you repeatedly and then lock you in the brig for a month and also sow salt into the soil of your carefully-manicured garden and rent your house out to a rock band' look. Patent pending.

Lia looked back with absurdly down-curled sad lips, "I practiced so much!"

"Secondly, you need to check some of your facts," a smile was twitching at the corners of Karen's mouth when she said that, and I didn't bother hiding mine.

Lia huffed, "Oh fine, indulge an heiress in her happily-ever-after-fantasies, would you? I have to live vicariously through someone!"

Karen let her smile appear, "Charlie's busy?"

Nodding, Lia rolled onto her side and sat up, "Apparently Special Branchers have to train to keep their lethality. I find that depressing, somehow. He'll be finished up with his team in an hour, but I wanted to come talk to you two in the meantime."

Stepping in, Karen closed my hatch and crossed the short distance to sit on the edge of my bed, "You came here expecting to find me?"

Lia cocked an eyebrow, "You say that as if you didn't just walk in and prove me right."

I chuckled, and Karen shrugged, "Well then. What's to talk about?"

Lia rubbed her hands together expectantly, "Excellent! I'm still worried about two things. The second one is much worse than the first…"

"Tell us that one first, then," I laced my hands together and settled them in my lap.

With a frown, Lia shook her head, "No, I'm the one giving the info, I do it in my order…"

Karen nodded, "Alright."

"Good, first of all, I've been wondering if the three ships that poked their noses into our grid at Hawke Six aren't still out here somewhere…"

Now that was a very serious concern. Remember those three unknown icons Mik had seen in Hawke Six space way back when he was waiting for authorization to go out collecting? They hadn't been accounted for, and while we'd just seen the Martian-pirate force broken by his trap, there was no guarantee we'd encountered all the bad guys there were to be found out here.

Indeed, I rather expected we had only seen a portion of the entire force the Martians and pirates were going to throw at this area and at the Hawke Protectorate. As we'd find out, and in particular, Wes Pellew would find out later, my expectation wouldn't be wrong.

"Worried for the cruise home, or that there might be an attack on Hawke Six before we get back?" Karen's tone had sobered entirely with the serious concern, and Lia let out a short sigh.

"Either, or both. Mik just did a great job of shoring things up out here, but… well, I worry that this Martian-pirate tandem was bait, getting our ships into the open and vulnerable, or stripping the Protectorate…"

I nodded, "And your father's going to give you a special lecture about security."

There are a very few things that can make Lia's face drain of color and strain so completely as mention of her father in that sort of context. She nodded once, "That's coming either way. He still doesn't really approve of you and me working together on anything."

A lot of history had led to this… let's call it *mild disapproval* of my methods by Lord Hawke. You know how Caldecott didn't think cavalier action had any place in the service? Well, Lord Ian Hawke was of similar mind, despite having been in his day even more theatrical and ruthless than I ever was. The number of times Charlie and I had arrived in Hawke Court to receive a friendly wink from Lia and an icy glare of doom from Lord Hawke was… well… we'd seen it a lot.

And Lia was used to getting her share of heat for continually associating with us.

Actually, that might mean Ian Hawke was a good and responsible parent, and that he didn't want his daughter to turn out like him so he was trying to keep her safe from us idiot-types but, well, too bad.

Anyway, Lia shook herself out of her dark thoughts, "Yes, so there's that… and then there's the worse problem."

Her face remained bland, and I looked from her to Karen and back. Both Karen and I leaned forward just a little in our concern, and with a deep breath Lia looked between us.

"I don't know," she almost whispered, "if Karen is my size."

CHAPTER TWENTY-NINE

RACCOONS AND THE FATE OF THE EMPIRE

There are some things that make getting out of bed in the morning very much worthwhile. If you ask people what different things inspire them to look forward to a day, you'll get many different answers... well, I imagine you will. I was actually far too lazy to ask anyone what sorts of things inspired them to get out of the bed in the morning, but let's assume.

The second day of *Wolf's* cruise back to Hawke Six was, for me at least, one of these days worth getting up for. Charlie too, in fact.

Why?

Because we're shallow men... and Karen and Lia spent a good part of the day trying out different types of court dress that Lia had brought aboard in the heavy trunks Charlie and I *hadn't* had to lift.

Now, let me explain this again — it was mentioned back in the first couple of chapters, but for clarity's sake here it comes one more time. Lord Hawke still held court, and by his order all attendees of his court were obliged to wear formal court dress. Defense Command officers couldn't simply arrive in their dress uniforms, they needed to wear more extravagant, thoroughly impractical clothing that couldn't self-seal or pressure-hood in a depressurization situation, and which was generally delicate and uncomfortable.

Go figure, Karen owned no such clothing. Charlie and I had both been to the court of his Lordship before, so we had our appropriate court suits with their braid, tails and gilt, and Lia (obviously) had enough court apparel to allow her to wear a different dress to session every day of the year.

So she and Karen were trying to figure out what from Lia's wardrobe would work for my intrepid Flag Captain. And this, I have to say, was highly, *highly* entertaining.

Now, the reasons it was entertaining are twofold, and I want to make it clear from the beginning that they weren't all as superficial as some people have assumed. Yes, it's pretty much evident to anyone who's ever seen Karen, or even a picture of her, that she'd make court dress look *good*.

I mean, court dress is generally designed to magnify the virtues of its wearer, at all costs... so Karen wearing it is sort of like adding petroleum gas to a fire (sorry, another historical reference — look it up!)

So yes, everyone thinking "Oh you dog" or "Oh you superficial bastard" go right ahead; I won't lie and say that seeing Karen dressed up like that was displeasing.

However, that wasn't the reason the day was so entertaining.

You see, Karen's never been the sort of woman to get over-dressed for anything. Ever. She likes the cut of her dress uniform and occasionally, at important social functions, she's been known to wear a gown, but then only the most practical self-sealing gown she can get her hands on.

So the world of tiaras, flex-corsets, and 'bosom-push-up' wear was brand new to her. As such, her reaction to things that pressed and bound and pulled and compressed were entirely hilarious.

Charlie and I were sitting in my cabin, me in my chair next to the bed and him in my desk chair, wheeled over to the other side of my bed. We were both working on paperwork (well, he was reading a few new information and user manuals for the MAG-90 that had come when we'd coordinated our comms with Hawke Six), but neither of us was being particularly productive.

"I still say they're cute and industrious. You're just paranoid."

That was me, and Charlie threw his hands up from his pad at my muttered words. We were having a bit of an argument.

"You have to be kidding me. They're fiendish and destructive. All their worst work is obviously done at night, but apparently they've got you wrapped right around their—"

I was shaking my head, and I cut him off, "You're kidding, right? What could they possibly do that would cause us any harm? Seriously, we're absolutely superior to them in every way imaginable, all they really have going for them is their cuteness. How could we hold those looks *against* them?"

Charlie's expression twisted to the incredulous category, "Are you kidding? They're clever, probably smarter than we are. And all the garbage they dig up, that's terrible!"

"Oh come on," I dropped the pad I'd been looking at onto the 'unfinished' pile, "it's not as though they're going to use that stuff against us. They'd never be able to…"

"How do you know? They're slick, they're dangerous. And what's up with that mask of theirs, seriously. Why would they need that if they weren't up to no good? No, my friend, let me tell you, they are the *biggest threat to the Empire*. Forget Mars, forget pirates, the biggest threat is from within!"

Charlie was getting pretty worked up about this, and I simply couldn't understand his bias. Couldn't then, can't now.

"Charlie," I looked directly at my friend, "they're *raccoons*."

"With shifty eyes!" he insisted.

I really, honestly do not understand Charlie's problem with raccoons. Maybe it's because I grew up in a part of the world that they weren't native to, maybe I'm just more in touch with my inner child. Probably not that latter one, actually. But Charlie Peters truly hates the critters, and owing to his ability to kill a man with, oh, a cotton ball, I'm pretty sure the raccoons are much worse off for his disdain.

Whether you agree with him or not, though, you might be wondering what the *hell* Charlie Peters and I were doing wasting our time talking about the evils of raccoons. Well, as you know, transit time is boring time, and Charlie and I had long ago fallen into a pattern of conversations such as this. There'll be plenty of them to be read when I go back and record our days aboard *Friendly* and the times before Karen arrived on *Wolf*.

What can I say, we're nuts. No better word for it.

Anyway, it was all too inevitable that we'd drop into this sort of mindless conversation when left with nothing to busy us but paperwork.

"You seriously need to find a new nemesis; your killing talents would be wasted as an exterminator," I looked away and picked up another pad.

"Yeah, wait 'til you open your hatch one day and find a squad of raccoons waiting on the other side, you won't be laughing then," he went back to his MAG-90 manual.

"Oh I imagine I'd be laughing rather a lot if I found a bunch of masked rodents outside my hatch one morning. What next, talking and walking wolves? Or how about cats. Or bears…" I muttered just loudly enough for him to hear.

"Actually, I once read a series of books about…"

Charlie's words trailed off as my hatch, which was wide open, was abruptly filled by Lia Hawke.

Oh, I should explain how our fashion show was working. Charlie's squad was actually set up at either end of the section of corridor that Karen's cabin shared with mine, keeping out bystanders. Karen and Lia were thus changing in the Captain's cabin, then coming up the corridor (in apparently impossible shoes) to show us what they'd put on, while Special Branchers with backs dutifully turned dissuaded any random crew members from wandering into the area.

Karen wouldn't even trust Matt Baxter to see her in some of the getups Lia stuck her in that day. I actually had to use my command codes to deactivate local security cameras to make sure the corridor was safe.

And *yes*, I'd told her dozens of times that her crew would have to see her leaving the ship in whatever she wore to Hawke's court. She just didn't want to be seen in all the disastrous outfits she tried on before deciding.

Well, the word 'disastrous' is the one she used. As you can imagine, I didn't find anything she wore that day to be a disaster. And though I'm hugely, hugely biased, I think anyone with eyes would probably agree (Karen herself excepted).

All of that explained, we can get back to Lia stepping into my cabin with the sort of poise and grace in uncomfortable shoes that comes with many years of court experience. She was wearing the same thing she had been for the past couple of visits — presumably she had settled on it and was now getting a little bit of practice wearing it again after so long in a comfortable, practical uniform.

Lia, of course, was a real pro at wearing these sorts of things, and I imagine pictures and vids of her traipsing around court in her lavish gowns are the central elements of courses on poise, carriage and lady-like behavior in all those finishing schools for the very, very rich. She thus wore her pale blue dress — with its very open neck, curious (to me anyway) sleeves, discreet gold trim straps and ribbons, and high collar that rose over the back of her shoulders — in a way that doubtless made its pricey designer drool.

Or any man who saw it and didn't know Lia personally (or Charlie personally, for that matter).

No drooling for me, of course, as I was staring at Karen.

Now, see, Karen had been up and down to her cabin at least a half-dozen times by this point in the morning (it took a long time to get in and out of these getups) and there'd been no luck. Sure, everything she'd arrived in was, not to mince words, flatly stunning, but it's amazing how uncomfortable Karen gets with something strapless stuck to her torso.

It's not self-consciousness, that, but old instinctive worry about decompression. Everything Karen wears in her day-to-day life aboard *Wolf* is self-sealing. Even those delightful shirts she wears bouncing around in her cabin when she's dancing have microfilament hood-and-bag rigs stitched into them, able to burst out and wrap her body in a temporarily-pressurized cocoon if the room was opened to space.

Despite what some of the movies have reported, almost every piece of off-the-rack clothing in the Empire by 2231 was similarly equipped, except for these ultra-expensive gowns that were not to be burdened with such technologies.

Yes, it makes no sense to me either. I mean, for the Emperor's court, which is held on Earth and is thus not susceptible to decompression, it's fine. But why not be prudent when you're holding court in a dome on a rock? Well, my guess about that comes in two parts: first, Ian Hawke really liked to drum up legitimacy for himself by imitating the Emperor's court practices, and second, he was quite a womanizer. With this sort of court dress being enforced, he's guaranteed to see everything he wants to on a daily basis. I'm sure it made him feel powerful or some other such thing.

But we were playing by his rules... and getting back to Karen, she wasn't much liking the rules over that first half-dozen dresses. She felt awkward without some fabric reaching up over her collarbones, and with the pushing up and the squeezing down and the awkward binding. As I've said, watching her tug disapprovingly at dresses that cost enough to pay my salary for a year was great, and funny.

Seeing her find one she was happy with, well that was much greater.

"I think we have a winner," Lia announced happily, and I dropped the pad I'd been working on over the side of my chair.

Karen stood rather stiltedly, not sure what to think and holding herself in the sort of tentative manner of anyone trying on a new piece of clothing — unlike anything she'd ever worn before — for the first time.

I started to nod slowly, and Charlie, impervious to Karen's radiance, pitched in, "Looks good."

It did look good. I don't know if you've seen a picture of Karen in this gown (there's one floating around, but it wasn't in the fleet archives when I looked). It was fleet green with a long dress that rose up into a flex corset, then kept going right up into what looked to me like a mini-suit jacket, with full sleeves and lapels that actually lift up into a very tall collar that circled around Karen's head.

Just a very modest area of uncovered skin — indeed, between the small size of the collar opening and the huge collar, it looked to me like this dress *could* be microfilament-bagged.

Of course, I wasn't saying anything, or even thinking very much. Karen looked very good in this dress. I mean, she looked good in everything, we've established that, but for the first time she was looking at least somewhat comfortable in a gown she'd never be caught in under any other circumstances.

"So," she was suddenly looking right at my glazed-over eyes, "thoughts?"

"That's. Great."

Notice how I punctuated that answer.

Charlie, having gotten past any stammering idiocy when Lia started coming back in the same gown every time, was being prudent and thoughtful, "Not sure how to ask this, but His Lordship will let you get away without baring more skin?"

Lia shrugged, "I wore a white version of this to court once, he was fine with it. That said, he doesn't expect to get the same show from his *daughter* that he wants from the other courtiers, but, well…"

"Then it's settled." Oh, look at that, I got motor functions back.

Yes, I know, you're all thinking I'm a blubbering idiot. Glad you woke up to that fact, only took the better part of three books to clue you in.

"Does everything… fit…?" I waved my hand rather blandly at Karen's flex-corset, and she shrugged slightly (as much as the huge collar floating around her head would allow).

"It's the loosest and least uncomfortable yet."

I nodded a couple of times, "Um, that's good. Yeah. Good."

One of her eyebrows climbed just a little, and then she *smiled*.

You know how ships we're attacking can be shut down by an onslaught of mag fire overwhelming their systems? That's what happened to my brain functions, and I'm not ashamed to say it.

Karen, perfect at reading me as usual, turned to Lia, "It's settled then. Let's go put on real clothes now please."

The Lady and my Flag Captain turned and left my cabin.

I watched them go, and then as brain functions returned, looked at Charlie, "You know what, raccoons definitely aren't the biggest threat to the Empire."

CHAPTER THIRTY

MORE FUN AND GAMES

Not much else happened on the flight back to Hawke Six from Caligula — Charlie and I did threat assessments of cute, harmless rodents and Lia and Karen tried on dresses. Clearly we were all in very serious moods…

Arriving at Hawke Six two days later really did little to change the prevailing atmosphere.

As *Wolf, June* and *Emily* decelerated smoothly through the massive sensor net beyond the rock, Lia, Karen and I waited on the bridge, watching the distance tick down to realtime range with Commodore Yambi.

"Looks like you have a corvette here… frigate moved on?" Karen glanced at Lia. The two were chatting a great deal more since their little fashion show — guess dress-sharing is one of those bonding experiences, much like raccoon talk.

Nodding her reply, Lia rocked up onto the balls of her feet and came back down, "Yeah, *Whirlwind* should still be on patrol cruise. *Shauna's* a good ship. Namesake is my age and rather moody whenever I see her coming out of my father's quarters, but the ship's good."

The delivery of that quip wasn't as smooth as I was used to hearing from Lia, and that tone, combined with her rocking on her feet and her considerable fidgeting made it rather obvious (at least to me) that she was more than a bit nervous.

She *had* been gone for days, and though she had the authority to do what she liked, her father might well begin to chew her out again when he discovered that two of his precious ships had been committed to a very dangerous operation under the orders of a self-important media-darling (me).

Lia had great steel when it came to resisting stress, and even to resisting her father's railing, but now and then the real agitation those things caused seeped through the powerful wall she put up to hide them.

She'd been having too much fun over the past few days, and now it was coming to an end as the cold grip of her heiress reality threatened to close around her again.

"Realtime with Commodore Yambi in about one minute," Jim Hannigan reported as he moved behind his communications technicians. "And we're getting a signal from the Foreign Office mission… Consul Tripp wants a realtime chat when we get into range."

Speaking of cold grips of reality. A dull ache started to form over my forehead as I thought about the delightful Consul Tripp. This was before I got my wish to 'destroy' him, of course… what could I do to dodge this?

Karen turned slightly my way, "I can deal with Tripp, if you like."

My left eyebrow went up and I glanced her way, "You'll make it look like an accident?"

She smiled, shaking her head, "I'll just take the griping."

A noble sacrifice, but one that really wasn't hers to make: Tripp had bones with me, best that I dealt with him.

"No, I'll deal with him. But thanks."

Her smile broadened, "No problem. Glad you didn't make me do it, actually…"

I switched my expression to 'surprised shock' and prepared to deliver some mocking words when Lia tapped my arm and nodded to screen two. The *WolfNet* buffering screen was already up, loading a feed from Hawke Six Naval HQ… and there was Commodore Yambi.

"Glad to have you all back safely," the man said with a pleasant smile, and Lia immediately shed any visible signs of nervousness.

"Well, we're happy to see you again, Rolph. Any more visitors since we left?"

She was referring to the three unknown ships that had probed the system when Mik had been waiting to move out. Immediately following the line of thought, Yambi shook his head, "Nothing as yet, m'lady. *Whirlwind* came through a few days ago, and *Shauna* pulled in yesterday. She's planning to stay around just to make sure we're alright, but so far nothing."

Lia nodded, "What I like to hear. I'm going to head back up the line to One with *Wolf*, but I'll leave *June* with you just in case. We ran into a lot of pirates and Martians out there."

"Yes, your reports have been making quite a stir in the news, and they were the first thing we forwarded to Earth when comms opened again…"

Now, my mother taught me it's rude to cut people off… well, no she didn't. Actually, no one ever did, which explains why I cut Yambi off, "Excuse me, sorry, Earth comms are back?"

Yambi nodded again, "Yes indeed, since two days ago. Apparently there's been trouble with Martian and pirate attacks on the comm ships that were sent out, but three have gotten into position and are safe for the moment."

Well that was good news — I was already turning to Jim as I processed its importance, "Jim, in my public folder there's a folder marked 'Earth – pending'. Send it."

The folder was mainly filled with paperwork, reports and of course the 'People to Destroy' file — things John Fiora at Admiralty House may have already been forwarded (since at least some of the reports had previously been sent to Commodore Yambi to forward up to Belt Two). Nonetheless, I wanted all the information I had to get to Admiralty House as soon as possible. It was about time Defense Command got back on top of the Imperial security situation after the Martians had so thoroughly blinded us.

Jim nodded and started giving orders, but as Lia began asking Yambi about something (I don't recall what, it was rather Hawke-specific I think), Jim stopped moving behind his consoles, put his hand up to the earpiece of his headset, and let his expression go sour.

"Consul Tripp demanding to speak with you," Jim looked back at me. "He wants a private chat."

The *private chat* comment was actually the crucial part of that statement; Tripp wanted to use his self-important weight as a Consul to dress me down. Now, if you're wondering, the status of Consuls in 2231 was no different than it is today; Consul is a nice word for 'Junior Ambassador'. That's not to downplay the work good Consuls do — on many of our larger allied rocks, Consuls serve in a full and quite effective Ambassadorial role, just get paid a hell of a lot less for it.

But to become a Consul on a rock like Hawke Six takes a special sort: it takes someone of mediocre talent whose mommy or daddy is connected six ways from Sunday. Don't know if that comes out clearly, but think of it this way. Hawke Six is one of the *least important* Consulates the Foreign Office maintains, because the Protectorate is such a good ally of ours. Our Ambassador to Hawke has a huge role, and that's why she's a highly capable lady, but the Consulates we have set up on each Hawke asteroid are there mainly to help our tourists in case they lose their passcards.

So Tripp, who seemed to think himself a big player in the Foreign Office, did virtually nothing of importance. Indeed, his demands for high tea were significant only in the annoyance they caused.

All of that begs the question, I suppose: why didn't I just tell the idiot off? Well, part of that is respect for the good people in the Foreign Office, a number of whom have helped me out of scrapes all over the place, but mainly it's just bad form for Defense Command and the Foreign Office to appear to be at odds. Looks sloppy.

Guess that means I was about to crawl into the trough...

"Screen three, Jim."

My tone drained of anything warm or friendly; the *private chat* demand did that. I wasn't in the mood to be talked down to.

Ferdinand Tripp appeared, his gaze smug... until he realized he was looking at *Wolf's* bridge, with Lia and Karen standing next to me.

"I demand a private chat!"

It only occurred to me at that moment how ridiculously like Governor sausage Tripp was behaving. Bad manners and poor use of diplomatic power seemed to manifest itself the same way across the board... or put another way, bastards are bastards, no matter whose flag they're working under.

"Shut *up*, Mister Tripp. We're busy, and we're leaving soon to go to Lord Hawke's court. I have no idea what you think is so important about me coming to sit with you for tea, but first thing, I don't drink tea, and second thing, I avoid sitting down with complete incompetents. So for the love of God, leave me alone."

Consul Tripp's mouth began opening and closing almost comically, and much as Governor sausage had, he began to puff up and redden.

And then the feed was clouded by static and died.

Raising my eyebrows in surprise, I looked back at Jim. He shook his head, "Wasn't me... Penny, scan local space for anything that could have jammed the signal."

As I turned back to the screens, I realized Commodore Yambi's smile had broadened, "No need to run scans, Commodore Barron. I've just heard that there was a mysterious power failure in your Consulate's communications array. It's as though Central Power just flipped the switch and cut them off. I also have just heard that Consul Tripp's car has been impounded. It apparently was tagged for speeding two days ago, and I suppose my security services didn't read the brief on diplomatic immunity."

Well that did put a smile back on my face.

Lia was grinning proudly, "See, all my top officers have my same sense of justice, isn't that right, Rolph?"

    Commodore Yambi bowed his head quickly, "Of course, m'lady."

    I looked past Lia at Karen, and she bobbed her eyebrows and smiled.

    About an hour later, *Wolf* and *Emily* boosted for Hawke One.

CHAPTER THIRTY-ONE

ONWARD TO HAWKE ONE (NOW WITH EXPOSITION!)

The two-and-a-half day cruise up to Hawke One was destined to be another rather sedate one. This time I had a pile of mail to look over — messages from John at Admiralty House and from Wes Pellew up at Hawke Two being among the most interesting. And lots of messages and no action to further the plot means one thing for this chapter: exposition!

That's right, I get to fill you in on all the goings on elsewhere in the Empire. Bet you're excited!

I'll try to make this as painless as possible.

First were updates about the situation of the Empire: it was still there. Marlene Stoll had made it back to Venus after some interesting times out in Coalition space, only to find that the Venusian pirates had gone into a frenzy of action and were now actually attempting to menace a Defense Command research post that had been taking sun activity readings. She was dealing with that.

Greg had what was left of the Light Squadron of the Home Fleet (still without *Ark Royal*, which reports said would be out of the fighting for as long as eighteen months while its damage was being repaired) folded into his Heavy Squadron, and the entire Home Fleet was thus operating as a single, hugely powerful force.

That said, there had been no more Martian activity around Earth. Based on the deep probes by some of the frigates of the Home Fleet — notably *Tiger* (Commodore Shannon Hunter herself), and *Jaguar* (Captain Conrad Benwah) — the Martians weren't coming back, and had vectored their retreat to Mercury. We were in no position to go after them, but we could hope they'd be licking their wounds long enough to let us finish regrouping — and to finish *Bonaventure*.

The new, massive battleship *Bonaventure* was being rushed into service at speeds we could only hope weren't dangerous; work crews would still be on the ship finalizing tertiary systems (showers, doors, lifts) for weeks after its launch, but the ship was due to join the Home Fleet in only twenty days. That was pretty good.

And, as John Fiora explained to me in his vid message, he'd convinced Prime Minister Pope to let him take personal command of active fleet operations. John, like Ian Hawke and Eddy Boscawen before him, was going to be a 'fighting First Lord' — he'd take personal command of the Home Fleet from the bridge of *Bonaventure*, and turn the administrative aspects of his job over to the Third Lord — the Second Lord position was still open, as Dave Caldecott was in a cell awaiting his fate by this time.

So while Third Lord Diane Pena (no I never bothered to even ask why she or any of the other women in the Admiralty weren't addressed as 'Lady' instead of 'Lord' — nothing's perfect, okay?) took over running the central administration from Admiralty House, John was going to move his office up to *Bonaventure*, though by the nature of his job, he'd probably still spend plenty of time planetside, just with a two-seater Starlight always standing by to carry him up to his ship on a moment's notice in case an attack was found heading Earth's way.

Why is that important to this book? Well, actually, it isn't, but it will be rather important to a great many books I still have to write. And more important for the moment than John's new post was Greg's forthcoming job — one destined to have a huge impact on everything that followed for *Wolf*, Karen and I.

With John taking over the Home Fleet personally, Greg — along with *Warspite* and Captain Becky Afflighen's *Goliath* — was coming out to the Belt Squadron. As soon as *Bonaventure* was launched (with the promise of that ship's sisters to follow promptly) two battleships were going to be detached from the Heavy Squadron and assigned to reinforce the Belt Squadron. *Warspite* was coming back to the Belt, which would be a great return, and Greg would be back where he'd been only months earlier, guarding the most important possessions in the Empire.

Of course, that'd mean I'd be second-in-command, but contrary to what everyone seems to have expected about my ego being wounded or some such thing, I was elated at the promise of both the capital ships and the elite commander who'd be heading them up. The Belt colonies needed far more protection than *Wolf* and our existing squadron could provide.

So that was all the good news I'll share with you — quite a lot of good news, too.

I won't get into the news Mark Gunney and Andrea Kiley were dealing with right now. I was going to leave that all for the next book, but I'm pretty sure I'll discuss what Mark and Andrea ran into within the next fifty pages or so. Actually, I shouldn't really be coy about it right now either... but I will be coy because so many movies leave it out that I don't know how many of you will actually know what they were facing.

I should remind you, though, (because it was a book and a half ago when you last saw them) that Andrea and Mark are Belt Squadron Commanders who'd been sent out to track down surviving pirates after Belt Two. They stumbled, of course, on much more than just piracy. They found Sean Cook's handiwork — the bloody footprints of the Belt Anti-Piracy Force, or as we all call it, the Independent Squadron. We'll talk about it presently.

Anyway, going over all of these messages in my inbox pretty much occupied my two-and-a-half days. I didn't catch Karen dancing on this leg of the trip, but I'm willing to bet she did at least once. We kept our usual routine, though, while Lia and Charlie mysteriously disappeared for much of the time.

We were going to be leaving the Hawke Protectorate behind soon, and those two deserved some alone time together. As far as we knew, it'd be another two years before they got to so much as trade words. I don't think anyone can fault them for spending the last couple of days together, particularly with a war increasing the danger to both their lives.

But Hawke One was coming up fast, and with it came the specter that none of us really looked forward to facing: Lord Hawke himself.

CHAPTER THIRTY-TWO

HAWKE ONE

Wolf arrive in Hawke One space with no fanfare — not that we were expecting any. The colony was clearly getting itself onto war footing, though, as the fighter patrols had doubled since last time we'd come in, and the Hawke flagship *Zephyr*, that frigate of a modified *Predator* design, had been thoroughly overhauled and was running patrols.

Zephyr was an interesting ship (if you like technical background — if you don't, skip ahead past this blurb). Built to a modified *Predator* design, it had actually been laid down as the *Predator*-class ship *Lynx*, but Parliament had yanked funding, forcing us to cut down the original order of twelve *Predators* to just eleven. Instead of breaking up the perfectly good (albeit half-finished) frigate, word was sent to Lia that we'd be willing to sell it to an ally, and with her father's approval, she snatched it up, and ordered another from our yards. Such was the birth of *Zephyr* and *Whirlwind*, named after historical pilot and carrier call signs Lia had heard in a twentieth century war movie about the battle of Midway. Much better than mistress names, I must say.

Of course, the *Zephyr*-class varied in some considerable ways from the final *Predator*-class, most notably mounting slightly lighter lasers and two extra mag batteries on either side of the bow pod... but the Hawke ships and *Wolf* looked related.

That really doesn't bear at all on what happened when we got to Hawke One, but as you by now must be aware, I like to include those tidbits for your enjoyment. If you want more ship history and such, check the Archives on defensecommand.net. Yes that was a shameless plug.

"*Zephyr* is hailing," Jim Hannigan reported as Erica Martin slowed us down to prepare for docking.

Lia was, of course, on the bridge again, and she nodded evenly at Jim, "Screen two."

You might think 'well shouldn't she ask you or Karen to order him to do that?', but by this time we'd been together on *Wolf's* bridge long enough not to worry about such formalities. I'm not sure if we ever had *worried* about them, come to think of it.

Lia took a step forward towards the screen, and Karen stepped deftly sideways behind her, ending up next to me.

"She nervous?" my dear Captain whispered.

I had a good sense for Lia's nervous state — I'd known her when she was a much younger, much less confident heiress who was nigh-terrified by the job her father was going to dump on her. She'd come so very far over the years, but I could still tell when she was putting on a calm facade.

She wasn't to be faulted for that, I did the same thing, as you well know if you've read *The Rogue Commodore* or *The Almost Coup*.

But Karen, who'd only known Lia for a little under two weeks, was still refining her sense of Lia's mindset, and she was certainly bang-on with this call.

Lia was anxious at her homecoming, for reasons I hope I've already clarified for you… well, *reason*, in the singular. There was one major thing that still got Lia's nerves working overtime, and that thing was her dear papa.

The *WolfNet* loading screen flipped to the face of Rear Admiral Latisha Genda, the senior officer in the Hawke Fleet aside from Lia herself. I've only had limited dealings with Rear Admiral Genda; I had worked a great deal more with her predecessor, Hanlon Fitzpatrick, but that was years back.

"M'lady," Genda nodded to her commander-in-chief, "safe journey?"

"Entirely. What have rumblings been like here?" Lia's voice was a little tighter than usual, a sure sign of her anxiety.

Genda frowned very slightly, "We had three unknown ships probe our outer net two days ago. Since then nothing."

That got my attention, and I looked Karen's way in time to see her eyebrows climb. Was the Protectorate being scouted for an attack?

Well, we all know the answer to that question now… sort of…

"Two days ago? Hawke Six had a three-ship probe last week… any other systems report the same sort of appearance?" Lia pressed on with questions, and Genda shook her head.

"None. I've positioned *Zephyr* to deal with any incoming threats, though, and doubled our combat fighter patrols. With *Emily* back I imagine we'll be safe here, though everyone from Two through Five could be vulnerable."

The Hawke Protectorate had a modest nine-ship fleet, with three additional older ships in mothballs that (and I hadn't checked on this at the time, but I know now) were being rapidly modernized to join the fight. With two ships at both Hawke One and Hawke Six, though, that left only five to cover Hawkes Two, Three, Four and Five — not an ideal arrangement given the strength of the Martian-pirate forces we'd been seeing.

"I'll get back to HQ and have a look at that," Lia nodded to her subordinate. "We're coming in to dock in a few minutes now, and we'll be attending this evening's court. Take over *Emily* for local space patrol, I'll have more orders for you later."

"Yes m'lady, good to have you back," Genda vanished.

Turning to me, Lia frowned, "That woman never has good news for me…"

"I'm sure it's just a random drop by," I tried to sound reassuring. "I mean, three ships could mean anything — cargo haulers on their way back to the Belt colonies confirming their vectors by using you for signposts, *anything*…"

"Yeah. Anything…"

We milled around in an awkward silence for a couple of minutes.

Court dress is not comfortable. It's not practical, it looks a bit silly, and it's not comfortable. Well, now, I shouldn't be so unkind… I'm sure by some standard it's comfortable, just not when compared to the standard Defense Command dress uniform, let alone a flightsuit or ship fatigues.

It might come as a surprise to you, but Defense Command's uniform line consists entirely of comfortable, practical clothes, the idea being that people in comfortable clothes can indeed work longer and harder than those wearing stiff, uncomfortable, stilted garbs.

Not pointing any fingers here *cough*IMPERIAL ARMY*cough*, but suffice it to say that ship dress and even our dress uniforms are practical and wearable.

Court dress has a different emphasis. As it was once explained to me, 'at court a man must to appear as a statesman, and a woman should *take her place as a quiet lady who is appealing to look at*, so one's attire must reflect these roles'. I put those italics in to emphasize just how archaic this practice is, and as you might expect, the rules of court didn't sit well with, oh, Karen for one, and Lia for another. The Earth Imperial Court had moved beyond that sort of blind chauvinism decades earlier, but old Ian Hawke... well, I don't need to beat this horse to death. The man liked his ladies beautiful, flex-corseted and quiet (except when laughing at his jokes).

And yet somehow he raised Lia, despite all that...

Anyway, sorry, I get caught on tangents like this, as you well know, but let me get back on track. I was busy belting on my trousers, tucking in my rather ornate shirt, and then clipping my sidearm holster to my belt. With all that done (over the course of about twenty gruelling minutes) I finally turned to the last item on the wardrobe list: the coat.

Now, you may have seen pictures of this coat — I've only ever owned one court coat, and this was the same one I'd picked up when I visited Hawke the first time in *Friendly*. It was ten years old, and to be quite honest, I was a slightly different shape now than I had been when I purchased it — the shoulders were binding more than ever before.

Pulling it on carefully, I closed it, zipped up its front panels, adjusted its tails (ugh, tails) and turned to the mirror in my cabin.

Well, there I was, done up again like a Defense Command peacock.

How manly.

Then my eyes narrowed as I examined my shoulders again.

Oh *damn*. See, this coat had been in storage since, well, since last time I'd been to Hawke One as *Wolf*'s skipper, years prior. And while Karen and I had fixed the collar tabs, the bars on the shoulder leafs were still those of Captain, not of a Commodore.

"Well dammit..." I reached across my chest with my left hand, trying to touch the bars on my right shoulder, but the jacket stopped me. You may know the delightful feeling of having a giant green blanket trying to crush your shoulders like a boa constrictor.

I released the breath I had in my lungs — no need for oxygen when it interferes with court dress, of course — and managed to grab my shoulder bars. Well, I had fifteen minutes to fix this.

And right on time, there came the knock on the door.

As I turned with an awkward shuffle, the hatch swung open, and a bright, warm light filled the room.

Sorry, that's my subconscious muscling in on the narrative. What actually happened was Karen stepped in.

I don't remember everything that occurred in the next fifteen minutes, since it took about that long for the first impact of seeing her done up again wore off (yes I know, some hero I am — at least I'm owning up to it), but what I do remember starts about two minutes before we headed to the lock.

Standing behind me in the mirror with a blinding smile, she brushed off the shoulders of my jacket — now somehow adorned with Commodore's bars — and then tugged at the shoulders of my jacket.

"You're going to need this altered, your shoulders are bigger than when you bought it..."

I nodded without so much as hearing what she said (she repeated it later, guessing correctly that I'd been turned into a vegetable when she walked in), and then we paced uncomfortably out my cabin door.

We were off to see his Lordship, the wonderful Ian Hawke...

Chapter Thirty-Three

Seeking An Audience

Charlie and Lia met us at the lock, and with the grim silence we usually reserved for serious combat situations, the four of us went down the lock chute into Hawke's command dome. I will not describe the amusement of watching Karen and Lia going through the reorientation chamber (where the gravity starts coming from the wrong places). Suffice it to say court dress for ladies generally needs one point of gravity to… um… function properly. More than that complicates things.

After sorting that little challenge out, our escort picked us up in the same arrivals lounge we'd been through days earlier, and we were led to a fancy hover limo.

We raced through the darkening streets of Hawke One's capital — a prosperous, clean, nice place to be, much akin to Belt Two… well, except for the slum on the north side that we had to cruise over in the last leg to the Lord's 'manor'.

"That's a big house," Karen whispered to me as we made our final approach, and I smiled.

"I'm sure if I could breathe I'd have a witty retort," I whispered back.

She chuckled, and then we both glanced away from the window towards Lia. Charlie's hand was resting calmingly on her knee, offering small comfort as her face began to drain of color and her hands began tangling with the hem of her jacket.

As much as I didn't like my jacket, or Karen didn't like having to dress up for show, Lia *really* didn't care for this. You might think her reaction surprising, as she does deal with it quite regularly…

Let me put it this way: you've seen by now how irrepressible Lia is? Well there's one person I know of who can crush that positive attitude at a whim, and it's her father. You might think it's foolish, you might say she should just ignore him as she does other nay-sayers, but for all his faults, Ian Hawke is still Lia's father. In a way, she cares about what he says, even when she hates it.

Hopefully you understand what I mean.

We came down on the west pad just outside the manor, drawing the attention of a procession of court-goers just across the lawn as they shuffled their way up the walk to the front entrance, where they were received with pomp and ceremony. As was customary, Charlie and I climbed out first, offering our hands to help Lia and Karen out. Then all four of us ambled together across the grass towards the long line on the receiving path.

"Do we have to wait in line?" Karen asked quietly, her eyes dragging along the lengthy line of fussily-dressed dignitaries.

"No," Lia's flat, frank answer was another sign of her mood. She was shutting off her charm for a moment, while she was still in safe company, fortifying herself for what was to come.

We made a turn just short of the receiving line, heading up to a secondary door near the main entrance. Hawke Household Guards snapped to attention at our arrival, and one opened the door for us.

"Welcome home, m'lady, and welcome back Commodore Barron, Major Peters, and..." the Guard at the door, who I recognized but whose name I never remember, paused in his friendly greeting as his eyes fell on Karen. It took a second for him to place her face (by now she was frequently in the Hawke media, not least because of our visit to the Geraldine Coilier show), "Ah, Captain McMaster."

We all nodded in turn as we filed into the secondary entrance, and then Lia led the way at a hurried pace through the winding back corridors of the manor towards the court room. She needed to get to that lavish chamber before the courtiers were allowed in, and then we three Defense Command officers would be received early as special guests of His Lordship.

Lia was moving with more speed than her dress and shoes should have allowed — it was quite obvious in those moments that she wore the stuff all the time, because Charlie and I, reasonably experienced in court dress movement, couldn't keep up with her experienced gait. She just knew how to shuffle in those heels better than Charlie and I could cope with the complete lack of padding in the dress boots we were wearing.

"My feet are going numb," I muttered to him as we followed with zombie-esque stiffness.

Charlie smiled, "I've done worse. Ever spent forty hours on your feet in combat boots?"

I grumbled something as he shuffled ahead, and I dropped back to help Karen navigate a particularly narrow passageway lined on either side by very expensive and easy-to-knock over crystal.

By the time the three of us arrived at the private receiving chamber, Lia had already gone in, and the two Hawke Guards standing at attention on either side of the door seemed to be having a tough time hiding their amusement at our mobility problems.

Charlie gave them what I call his "I'm Special Branch and I could kill you with a cotton ball and three paperclips" look, and they smartened up.

Then we waited.

For long enough to put a scene break, here, in fact.

While we were standing and waiting, Matt was sitting in his chair behind the operations consoles on *Wolf's* bridge. I bet you didn't even know Matt had a chair there, did you? He rarely uses it because he's Matt — he prefers to stand at all times.

Much like a horse. Yes, I've said that to him (and somehow I didn't lose any teeth).

Now, though, he was sitting, battling one of those migraines that attack him when he's least expecting them. Despite what the commercials on vid say, none of the anti-migraine pills out there *really* do the job, at least not for Matt, so he was toughing it out as usual, waiting for his shift to end and Jim Hannigan to relieve him as officer of the watch.

Then the Ensign running Sensors and Communications for Jim this shift shot out of her chair.

Migraines tend to leave Matt hyper-aware (painfully so), so as soon as the Ensign — it was in fact Connie Lev, in her first posting — was on her feet, Matt was getting to his.

"What's wrong there, Connie?" he moved gingerly out from behind the operations consoles, and she had already begun moving between the consoles of the technicians in her section, getting reports.

After about fifteen seconds, she turned back to Matt, "I'm seeing three unknown signatures out at extreme range. They're coming in slow and steady from a vector just off base course to the Belt."

By 'Belt' she meant Belt colonies (that confused my publisher the first time).

With a grunt, Matt nodded, "Hawke grid sees them?"

Connie nodded, "They must, if we did. *Zephyr* and *Emily* haven't moved off their patrol routes yet."

Matt nodded, "Send to Hawke Command C&C, check to see if they know something about those ships that we don't. Let's get to standby alert…"

Moving to the front of the bridge and wincing slightly, Matt let out a breath. His evening was suddenly looking more complicated.

And I bet you know why. Or at least you know how this goes in the movies.

CHAPTER THIRTY-FOUR
KEN, KAREN AND CHARLIE GO TO COURT

"Presenting Commodore Barron, Captain McMaster, and Major Peters!"

We ambled through the private receiving door as we were announced in that grand fashion. I took a centering breath as I came to a stop before Ian Hawke's great chair, noting Lia sitting quietly in her own seat at his side, but down one step from his elevated platform.

Karen and Charlie stopped on either side of me, and together we all bowed. Karen didn't curtsy.

"Ooh, so I finally get to meet Karen McMaster. You don't know how to curtsy, there, Captain McMaster?"

Karen's eyebrows went up as she straightened, "No, m'lord, I'm afraid I don't. Particularly not in this dress."

You know that look people get on their face when their best friend insults someone standing right behind them? Charlie and I both got that look.

I mean, it's *Ian Hawke*.

Ian Hawke bellowed a laugh, "You're lucky you look like an angel and have a reputation for fighting, Captain."

I let out a breath. *Phew.*

"Must be nice to have her one cabin down from you, eh there Ken? Commodore rank must give you some privileges!"

You'll notice that Ian Hawke spoke to us with no particular refinement. When dealing with most courtiers, he maintained an air of ostentatious class, but I suppose he assumed that we Defense Command personnel could somehow relate to his more gruff personality.

Things had changed a lot since he'd left the service, though. And I'm willing to bet that even the service he was a part of never fully shared his… uh… perspective.

"Karen's the best Captain in the fleet," I answered his challenge with a flat tone. "Better than I ever was, better than you ever were."

Whoops, don't know where that came from. Said it though, and I can only assume my courtesy slipped because I didn't like the way Karen was getting painted here. Lia's eyes were wide, giving me the wave off, but it was too late…

Hawke must have been a good mood, because he laughed again, "Five bars stiffened up your spine, boy? That's nice. That or your Captain has you whipped."

See, now, how was I supposed to let that go…

But I did, because as soon as he said it, he shifted his eyes from me to Charlie and offered another great question, "Charlie, still fucking my daughter?"

From the mouths of Lords.

I was ready to go ballistic after some veiled shots at Karen, but immediately visions of

Charlie leaping across the floor and 'accidentally' severing Ian Hawke's old head from his shoulders flashed through my mind.

Thankfully, Charlie's Special Branch, which means he has the ability to decapitate with his bare hands, *and* the discipline not to do it, or at least not without much graver provocation.

"Pleased to see you too, m'lord."

Just like that, Charlie completely brushed off the question.

"That didn't answer my question," Hawke's good humor was fading.

"I noticed that too," Karen cut in instantly, detecting — as she explained later — the Lord's weakness (women). "I can't imagine why he wouldn't want to answer such a reasonably asked question, could you, m'lord?"

Basking in Karen's cool attention, Hawke grinned and looked away from Charlie and back to Karen.

"Honey, I really should *name a ship after you...*"

Karen's smile was so icy I was getting cold, "You should invite in your other courtiers."

Smiling as he gave up on his propositions for a moment, he nodded slowly, "Yeah, yeah I should. We can chat some other time."

He nodded to his personal chief of affairs, who set about giving the orders to let the other courtiers in through the main guest entrance. Karen, Charlie and I shuffled to the side, taking up our places as honored guests of court.

How honored we felt, let me tell you.

As you'll probably read when I go back and write the earlier books about the other visits Charlie and I made to this court, we had for years survived Hawke's scrutiny without this sort of abrasive exchange. A couple of things had changed, though... and first among these was Karen's presence.

I didn't like the old bastard prodding at her that way. Not that she needed me to stand up for her (obviously), I just... well, my self control wasn't what it should have been. And that set the tone to start the volleys flying back and forth, and instead of me being able to run interference for Charlie on the Lia issue, I was fuming in my own corner and... well...

Yes, I was worked up enough to be analyzing my courtly errors as I stood there and watched a bunch of courtiers parade in, showing off the work of their pricey cosmetic surgeons and tailors. It was going to be a long night.

Or *not*. Because this is where the movies kick in.

What do I mean by that? Well, if you've seen either of the two films on this subject, you know what happens next. The alarms in the court chamber start blaring.

Let's make something clear right off the top: there aren't any alarms in the court chamber, because that'd be disruptive to the important goings-on of court. A man did run in through the back door and whisper something in the ear of Ian Hawke's personal chief of affairs, who then whispered in the Lord's ear.

I'll go with the movies' dramatic account of what happens next: the courtiers began to scream and huddle together, cowering before the non-existent alarms (seems a bit overdramatic to me) and Hawke announces that we have three incoming Martian destroyers, guns armed and all set to obliterate Hawke One. And worse, they've already crippled *Emily*.

You know what comes next, then. I give Karen an urgent look, and Lia leaps out of her chair.

"We have to change our clothes!" Karen shouts in stilted fashion, and so she and Lia run an impossibly short distance to a chamber were they cast off their court dress in an absurdly fleshy manner and put on some non-regulation civilian clubbing clothes, because that's all the heiress had handy.

Then Charlie and I lose our jackets, and we all run (skip the limo) back to *Wolf*.

We get to the bridge and take our chairs (in the movies there are invariably chairs for *everyone* on the bridge, I think it helps when the shot is being framed) and Matt, migraine-free, bellows, "Incoming fire!"

Here again is the movie process of compressing time. A *lot*. I mean, to begin with, when Connie Lev detected the three unknowns at the edge of sensor range, that put them an hour away. So to be taking fire already... well, it's like running back to *Wolf*. Not possible.

Then I look at Karen and say (in one version): "Guess Hawke's not going to be naming a ship after you after all..." which is a line that makes no sense to me. Or, in the other movie, I say the much more likely, if rather melodramatic, "Let's do this."

Karen starts giving orders, and Erica Martin, Matt and Jim Hannigan begin fighting the battle under her orders, while I completely undercut Lia's authority and 'assume command' of the Hawke Command ships (because apparently Admiral Genda and Lia weren't up to it).

So then it's three destroyers against *Wolf* and *Zephyr*, and it's a messy and brutal fight. *Zephyr* explodes in the first movie version, though for accuracy's sake (the fact that *Zephyr* is still around today) the second movie just assigns the Hawke frigate 'heavy damage'.

Leaving *Wolf* to single-handedly take on three Martian destroyers.

Now, I told Ian Hawke, and I'll tell you: Karen was the best skipper in Defense Command history to then, and since. Combine her with *Wolf's* crack crew and yes, I would agree that we'd have a chance of mauling three destroyers. I could even imagine us destroying them somehow... maybe.

But to do that, we'd pretty much lose *Wolf* in the process. Completely and totally gone. There's no *way* three competent or even *barely competent* Martian crews would let themselves get eliminated by a single Defense Command frigate without so much as scratching us.

Except, as you probably well know, that's how it plays in both movies. They sail *Wolf* through the battle without absorbing so much as a serious hit. And in the process we shatter three destroyers.

I suppose that's a flattering portrayal — it's great to see us do such an impressive thing in a fight and somehow not be left with crippling damage and hundreds of dead.

Too bad it's fiction.

Complete fiction.

I don't know why the producers of these movies decided to go with that story, when it's so blatantly untrue... and particularly when so many of the principal players in the plot they're manipulating are *still alive*. Granted, they don't slander us, they make us out to be heroes and that's lovely, but I'd much rather they told the end of this story the way it happened.

Sorry, but that's what I'd prefer.

So let's back up to the point where the fiction took over in the movies, and see what actually happened.

Ian Hawke's personal affairs man leaned down and whispered in His Lordship's ear, and Hawke's expression twisted into one of distant surprise, "Well, Ken, seems like you and the best Captain who ever lived might have some business to go deal with."

I blinked — I was still pondering angrily the exchange I'd just had — and looked at him, "Indeed?"

I was trying not to get my hopes up, because I *really* wanted out.

"Yes. Three ships inbound now, two big haulers that say they're packed with refugees being guarded by one of your corvettes, *Honesty*. They're saying they're from Egesta, and they're requesting immediate assistance."

What, not three enemy destroyers? No, not at all. That was Mark Gunney coming in like a bat out of hell, trying to organize help for the Egesta situation... well, the first iteration of it. We'll deal with that in a moment, but you're probably scratching your head right now — what the hell... what about the three enemy destroyers?

I can only guess that the movie writers on the first film about our Hawke mission wanted to end on an action 'beat', so they found out about the sensor ghosts we were seeing at Hawke Six and Hawke One (neither of which were *ever* explained), and then saw an opportunity to use them for a satisfying gunfight ending. The writers of the second movie probably just followed what the writers of the first movie did... I don't know, because it was easier?

Why not stick with the truth, and end on Mark arriving with the first wave of Egesta refugees? Well, 'Egesta' today is synonymous with a lot of bad things, not least mass murders, organized crime, raping and pillaging, and the botching of an Imperial intervention. It probably wouldn't be the positive end moviegoers wanted from a light and fluffy action flick about Ken Barron, Karen McMaster, Charlie Peters and Lia Hawke.

The movie makers probably adjusted history just so they could end without invoking the ghosts of Egesta — they leave that to the plethora of 'socially conscious' commentators, many of whom have gotten Egesta entirely *wrong*. Yes, another gripe from me. I'll be fighting many duels when this gets published, I bet.

But sorry, that's a long aside about things that didn't in fact happen. Standing in the court chamber, Karen and I looked at each other, then we both nodded to Charlie and shuffled out the private receiving door. Charlie stayed to look after Lia for the night... well, look after her as best he could.

We caught the *limo* back to *Wolf's* lock, so we could find out what Mark Gunney was bringing us.

CHAPTER THIRTY-FIVE
FIRST WORD OF EGESTA

When we got back to *Wolf*, we learned that Matt had already been in touch with Mark Gunney aboard *Honesty*, and our venerable Belt Squadron Commander had told Matt he had no intention of talking about the situation on Egesta over comms that could be intercepted. It was an apt sentiment, considering just what had happened there — the press was going to find out eventually, that was inevitable, but there was no reason to let word start flying far and wide before the Admiralty had been informed.

The refugees would tell the tale anyway, as soon as they were successfully moved down to temporary housing in Dome Three of Hawke One.

Karen and I headed to our cabins to change while *Honesty* and the haulers full of people made their final approaches to the Hawke One domes.

Standing in the lift on the way up, she glanced at me and smiled, "Guess I get to stop being eye candy."

I chuckled, "Pulling the refrigerator box out of the closet, are you?"

She smiled, "You implying I'm always eye candy?"

Donning a self-righteous look, I gave an exaggerated shrug, "As I recall, the *Belt Nine Informer* crossword thought you were 'sexy', and that Belt Nine reporter wanted to know what designer you were wearing."

Karen's smile widened slightly, "That was weeks ago."

"Oh that's true, and you've really let yourself go since then…"

I have no idea why we were flirting — yes *flirting* — but we were. I wouldn't even mention it except I think it's a good juxtaposition. Most people hear 'Egesta' and immediately go dark, and assume that even before it happened, everyone had a sense of foreboding about that independent rock.

We didn't.

We had no idea what was going to happen there, and we had no reason to assume the worst. So for all those people after the fact who attacked the Foreign Office for overlooking a 'human tragedy in the making', remember that two of the 'heroes of the Empire' about to hear of the first problems on Egesta knew nothing about the rock — or at least nothing beyond what Lia told us in that tedious briefing.

The lift stopped, and Karen and I exited in good spirits, happy to be escaping court dress and looking forward to seeing one of our top Belt Squadron officers again.

It was about an hour later when Mark Gunney arrived on the bridge of *Wolf*. Karen and I were there, having relieved Matt so he could get to his bunk and try to kill that damned migraine.

When Commander Gunney stepped onto the bridge, I turned to him with a smile and a wave, "Mark, damned good to see you."

He actually stopped in place coming through the hatch, looking up at me with what I suppose I'd describe as surprise, then visibly thinking about his response — something Mark Gunney never usually has to do.

"Yes. Definitely. We should talk. It's serious."

That was a sober and chilly greeting from the Commander who was well known for his brusque humor.

"Let's go to my day cabin," Karen's own bright mood had been equally dampened by the introduction.

The three of us headed quickly there, Karen taking a seat at her desk and me sitting on the table's edge. Mark collapsed down into the couch opposite us and heaved a long sigh.

"Sorry," he said. "Shit."

I frowned, folding my arms, "Egesta? Something bad?"

Mark nodded once, "Situation is *fucked*, excuse me for saying it that way. Andrea and I stopped there on our way back... remember sending us out after those raiders? We tracked them out far, thought we were getting a bead on some sort of base out beyond Hawke, and Wes told us to keep going. All's been quiet at the Belt for now, and he wanted to know where the pirates were based..."

I'll explain that, based on what I now know. Remember after the Battle of Belt Two, back in *The Rogue Commodore*, I sent Mark in *Honesty* and Andrea in my old ship *Friendly* out after the pirates who'd escaped destruction? Mark and Andrea are two of the best skippers you could ask for when it comes to hunting pirates, and they'd kept one of the speedy raiders in their sights for over a week.

Checking in with Wes Pellew in charge at Belt Two, they'd received authorization to keep tracking the pirate back to his base, hoping to find out just where the pirates were operating from. That base, in case you're wondering, is the same one Elsie McKinnon had a bead on out Caligula way, and that Wes was going to focus on after this.

With trackers on both flanks of the Hawke Protectorate sniffing for it, it seemed pretty evident by this time that the base had to be located directly 'behind' the Protectorate, but that's not important. The base isn't the matter at hand...

"We ended up losing the pirate around a rock cluster out near Basil's Rock, so after a couple of days of searching, we gave up and turned back. Decided we'd make the run back through our friendly unaligned rocks, show the flag, kiss some babies..." Mark shook his head. "Then we hit Egesta five days ago."

Karen and I glanced at each other — we couldn't imagine what could have happened on that rock to make Mark Gunney so distressed...

Then something occurred to me, "Where's Andrea, Mark? Where's *Friendly*?"

He looked up, "Still there, still trying to help."

My frown deepened, "Alright, that's better than being destroyed. Can we get some elaboration?"

Mark nodded, realizing he hadn't quite delivered the real thrust of the grim news yet. I can't blame him for having to work up to it; I'd need a while to fully absorb it as well.

"I didn't know much about Egesta before I got there, but basically you're looking at a government that's fighting a turf war against the local mining Guild... and by Guild I mean *mob*. Bunch of criminals, I'm not kidding. These guys are Syndicate types. I think some of their enforcers are actually ex-Syndicate — they'd do Grant Merger proud."

My heart rate started increasing with the mention of the Syndicate, as you can appreciate, I'm sure, knowing my past with Grant Merger. We'd broken the bastard's fleet and his bases, but many of his personnel had inevitably escaped... and of course they'd turn up looking for jobs with anyone who wanted brutal, heartless enforcement...

"From what I found out, the government was keeping the Guild in check. It had our moral support, a good trading relationship, and enough cash to hire Boscawen mercs in sufficient numbers to stop any insurgency."

Boscawen Corp mercenaries, remember, from Furnace rock.

"Then Commodore Cook stopped there, about eleven days ago. Stayed for two. Changed every damned thing."

At the time, as you'll appreciate, this came completely out of left field for me. What the *hell* was Sean Cook doing at Egesta? I think I mentioned this earlier, but here it is again: Commodore Sean Cook was the commander of the then-infamous Belt Anti-Piracy Squadron, or, as we all called it, the Independent Squadron. His job was to take six frigates and two corvettes out into the unaligned belt and stop whatever piracy he could, and to try to snuff out the new bases and organizations that were rising in the wake of the fall of the Syndicate.

In fact, the Independent Squadron had a very long history — it had been out in the Belt fighting the Syndicate and its predecessors since Lord Hawke's time at the Admiralty. All through those decades, though, it had never managed to match the success of the Belt Squadron when it came to pirate-killing. The Independent Squadron's ships were always chasing pirates, but they seldom *caught* any, while the Belt Squadron was defending the juiciest target around.

That's why *we* crushed the Syndicate. That's why *we* heard about the *new* Syndicate that Cooper and Yat Sen had put together to assist the Martians, and that still had to be finished off.

Sean Cook heard about *nothing*, defeated *no one*. Part of that was because he was useless, and part was because his squadron was... well... rough around the edges.

I'm sorry, call me old-fashioned (I obviously am) but I've always believed that Defense Command should hold itself to a higher standard. Don't get me wrong, I'll shoot a pirate in the head if I have to, that's the job, but I'm rather above using their actual tactics against them.

For instance, I wouldn't organize the gang rape of a pirate's wife and three children to get information out of him. Sean Cook, as we found out, couldn't say the same. He wrapped himself in the Articles of Empire that said all pirates were considered enemies of the Empire and thus it was his duty to do them harm... but... well, I don't really need to explain what kind of man it takes to organize such a thing, do I?

It's something Grant Merger had orchestrated on occasion. That should say it all.

In any case, I didn't know about Cook's use of tactics at this point, and while I knew he and his skippers were cut from a much less professional cloth than the officers and crew of the Belt Squadron, I didn't have any idea of what he'd done at Egesta.

Mark enlightened me: "When he put in, he filed a request, at gunpoint. He wanted the night club district opened to his crews for recreation, by which he meant he wanted the people in the clubs held at gunpoint while the authorities looked the other way. Then he wanted all the spare food and medical supplies the government had to fit out his squadron for the cruise to Belt Two."

I looked down at Karen again, and her face was taught.

"The Governor said no, obviously, and when Cook put SF on the ground to try to force his way into the warehouses and the club district, the Boscawen Corp guards killed four of them."

"*What?*" I came off the table. Such a thing was unheard of.

"It was in the middle of a home invasion, the Boscawen boys were in the right, believe me. I saw the vid feeds. The SF opened up on them while trying to get away with jewelry and booze."

"You *can't* be serious," Karen came to her feet and started rounding the table.

"I joke about a lot of things, not this. After that incident, Cook apparently pulled out his SF. He didn't attack the domes from space, which is what the Governor was afraid of, but he did something much worse. He went to the Guild, got a bunch of the supplies — and by supplies I mean *contraband* — he wanted from their black market, in exchange for fourteen pallets of EP-5s and power cell chargers."

I was frozen in place. I'm not kidding, I went catatonic for a few seconds. I don't know if civilian readers will quite grasp how monstrously abominable this sort of action is, but it's up there with killing your parents, at least in my books.

Defense Command's job out here was to try to make things safer, to use the vast resources of the Empire to help. Cynics always said we were trying to take over for our own ends, and I always railed against such accusations, but here was one of our own doing exactly what the anti-Empire folks claimed we did.

And that realization came over me and pushed the catatonic response over the edge into silent rage.

Cook had not only loosed SFers who obviously had been removed from any strictures of discipline onto a civilian population against the wishes of a friendly government, he'd then supported what I guessed immediately would become an insurgency by arming it with *modern weapons.*

I know, sure, I panned the EP-5 in both *The Rogue Commodore* and *The Almost Coup,* but that's as a military weapon. Compared to a baseball or cricket bat and a kitchen knife — all the Guild could have really armed itself with on Egesta until Cook's arrival — it was a serious weapon.

And fourteen palettes? That's over 700 guns. As we later found out, he'd decided to make the trade in part hoping that supposedly 'losing' those weapons would get him MAG-90s for replacements. Wow, so smart.

Bastard.

"By the time we got there," Mark went on, "the Governor was dead, the Lieutenant Governor was running the government out of the barracks of the Boscawen guards, and the Government Dome was in total chaos. We commandeered two cargo haulers that pulled in to refuel and loaded as many civvies into them as we could manage, and Andrea stayed on scene while I came to call for help."

Karen frowned, "Why not call ahead?"

"Didn't know where Cook went. Didn't want him finding out what we'd discovered, in case he showed up to clean up the mess. I'm *very* glad I found you here. I was half expecting to have to bullshit some story to Cook about pulling survivors off some unknown rock..."

"Well, you don't have to. And we've got Admiralty comms back, so I'll get this word up the chain to John. We'll have a noose around Cook's neck as soon as he stops in at one of our ports," I nodded grimly.

"It may not be that easy, he's got the whole squadron concentrated. We may not have the force to take him if they all stay loyal when we try to make the arrest. I can't see how anyone in those ships wouldn't be complicit in the atrocities... they could all go renegade," Mark's warning was particularly apt. Whoever handled this would have to do it delicately, so it was good it didn't turn out to be me.

I'd have shot the bastard on sight.

But, as we all know, I wasn't destined to deal with Cook. We were Egesta-bound.

"Look, guys, that's not our biggest problem. Andrea's at Egesta now, and she has all my SF and Special Branch, and she's armed volunteers from both our crews and put them on the ground. She was trying to stop a lot of massacring going on in their Government Dome, but there's no way she has enough people. We need to get there, with as many boots and guns as we can find."

And that, of course, was it. The beginning of the Empire's humanitarian intervention on the rock of Egesta. It would have its low points and its lower points... well, you know, and if you don't, you'll find out.

"We'll pull everything we can together now," I nodded instantly, my mind abruptly beginning to take hold of the situation. "I'll call Lia and see if she has any ships or Hawke Guards we can borrow... I'll check with John at the Admiralty, see what he can send up too. But other than *Wolf*, Mark... Christian Mikaelsen has all our independent cruisers on the other side of the Protectorate, and there's been a lot of damage done to independent rocks on that side. I don't think we can afford to pull him off there."

That's where that idea began. It's been roundly criticized for years. Why, you ask, didn't I jump in the air and say 'we'll call in all ships and go fix this problem once and for all'?

Because, remember, over 4,000 dead at Furnace rock. Attacks stretching from Anderson's Colony over to Caligula, and who knew where else new Martian strikes might come. I know the numbers pale next to the death count at Egesta, but at that time, I couldn't be so sure. And pulling Mik's ships off that patrol zone was a bad idea.

To the critics I say this: guess what, we *don't* have a shiny crystal ball. Thankfully, though, most people seemed to understand the decision that I recommended and John ultimately made. Egesta was a disaster, but if we'd pulled ships from the other side of the Belt and from Hawke, there could have been many, many more disasters.

Enough of me standing on a soap box. For now, anyway.

"Alright," I took a step towards the door, "I'll start making calls. Mark, get back to *Honesty*, we'll boost soon. If you're shorthanded, I'm sure Karen can lend you some *Wolf* crew."

"We're good. But I'll give a lift to any Hawke Guards who need it," he got to his feet.

Karen and I shared a grim stare for a few seconds, and then I left the day cabin.

Chapter Thirty-Six

Preparing To Move On

John Fiora was sitting in his office with Greg Noyce when my signal reached his screen. The two great Admirals watched the feed together, taking in my report about the occurrences out towards Caligula, Mik's great contributions and my recommendations about his deployment, and then my report (and Mark Gunney's logs) about Egesta.

As he told me later, his office got very quiet very quickly as Sean Cook's antics... no, let's call them what they were, *atrocities*... were reported.

Once the transmission ended, Greg looked across the table at John, "I think I should get out there as quickly as possible."

John nodded, "Definitely. Advance your departure time, Captain Pellew might need you at the Belt."

So that was taken care of.

"My father's not going to let me take any ships out of the line now, not after what we saw at Furnace and all the sensor ghosts we seem to have following us. Sorry, Ken..." Lia was sounding unusually somber as she reported her findings over the realtime link.

Standing on *Wolf's* bridge the morning after Mark's briefing, I was getting things coordinated to ship out for Egesta. It was pretty evident by this point I was only going to be able to bring *Wolf* back with *Honesty* — the only Defense Command ships nearby were ones I wasn't willing to release from their other duties. We've talked about why that was.

"What I *can* give you is 150 Hawke Guards, good ones. I pulled three companies from the Capital Guard — these are some of the troops we have trained to deal with urban combat. Should be exactly what you need."

Lia was sure right about that.

"Alright, that's good... thanks Lia. Sorry we have to leave you behind."

Sort of a funny apology, given what we running towards, but at the time it seemed the thing to say.

Lia smiled, "I'll be here when you get back. Don't let Charlie get himself into trouble out there, please."

Matching her smile, I nodded, "Because *I'm* really the guy who could save his ass in a firefight."

She chuckled and nodded, "Exactly."

Our festive words trailed off after that, and we stared at each other for a couple of seconds. I have to say, I didn't want to say goodbye to Lia, but then I never did want to. She might as well have been the little sister I used to think I never wanted.

I still don't know how Charlie survived coming and going over all those years, being so much closer to her.

"Oh James, James could you hang up for us please," Lia called loudly over the link, and smiling, Jim Hannigan leaned into view of the main screen she was occupying, offering a nod.

"Nice to see you again, m'lady."

"Of course it was," her smile broadened, then she looked back at me. "See you!"

Jim cut the link.

Later that morning, Mark Gunney was on the same screen, talking to Karen.

"I've got them all squared away now, not a lot of room left and I probably won't have space to carry them all back along with the crew I collect when we get there…"

He was speaking of the Hawke Guards, who'd boarded his ship an hour after I'd spoken to Lia. *Honesty* wasn't a large ship, so carrying 150 extra personnel wasn't going to be *easy*, but Mark did have the extra berthing space left vacant by all the volunteers he'd left on Egesta.

"You'll be ready to boost soon, then?" Karen was taking a status report pad from an Ensign as she spoke, and Mark nodded.

"Give me another twenty minutes, then we can mobilize."

"Sounds a bit too exciting for me, I'll just leave," Karen said absently. "Call when you're ready, Mark, I'll make sure Ken's up here."

With a nod, he cut the link.

Down at Belt Six, Captain Christian Mikaelsen had returned to his cabin to scrounge some lunch while he worked on his annoyingly large stack of paperwork. As he was quickly pulling a sandwich together in his kitchen, he heard his vidscreen give the 'priority message' chime so he dropped the bread, strode curiously back into his main cabin and grabbed the remote.

The message screen revealed that the signal had come from Admiralty House, so he selected it and then waited as the *Cyclops*Net buffering screen rolled. He tried to restrain his hunger — he wanted his sandwich, dammit — and finally the screen flipped from the buffering screen to…

John Fiora.

Now, it's not all that common for a Captain to get a message direct from the First Lord, not unless the Captain's a problem case like me. Mik wasn't a problem case, his confessed hatred for paperwork notwithstanding.

So he was surprised to see John Fiora on the screen, and even more surprised when the First Lord nodded somberly and said: "Captain Mikaelsen… it's 'Mik', right? Mik, Ken Barron says you're the go-to guy in the independent belt and around Hawke, so I'm promoting you to Commodore. Take over all formerly independent cruisers between Hawke and Caligula, and use them to help defend our allies and Hawke. More detailed orders are enclosed in a file attached to this message. Congratulations, Mik! Good hunting, and call me if you need anything."

The screen went blank, and because he wasn't quite sure what to think, Mik went back to making his sandwich.

+++

I was sitting on my bed with a muffin as I watched my own message from John.

"...Mik will take over the sector between Caligula and Hawke, and he'll be our senior officer tied into the Hawke defense. That should hopefully seal that flank. Marlene's been able to stabilize things around Coalition space, and we're setting up a similar force of independent cruisers over there."

Recall that Marlene was getting back to Venus via the Coalition? I won't even get into the trouble she ran into, I'd need a whole other book. Read her memoirs, or send me many messages demanding another history of the little-known incident there. I'm accosting many good historians to try to get books written.

"Right now, Greg's boosting for the Belt colonies to support Captain Pellew's position. I sent orders to Wes to take Commodore Cook under arrest if he can safely do so, but I'm worried, as you no doubt are, about the amount of damage Cook and his squadron could do if they decide not to go quietly."

That was definitely my first concern about the Belt colonies' situation. Cook had six specially-fitted *North America*-class frigates and two specially-fitted *Canada*-class corvettes, no mean force to deal with, particularly if the entire Belt Squadron had been spread out.

And what many people don't understand is that the modifications Cook had built into his ships made each of them very nearly a match for its successor class — so one of his *North Americas* could conceivably beat a *Predator* in a gunfight. It was a very powerful force, that Independent Squadron.

But that's for next book.

"I'm looking into getting you a large contingent of troops for Egesta, but I'm not sure I can pull an SF battalion together in less than a month. If it's as bad as Commander Gunney's logs indicate, we're going to need boots on the ground sooner than that... so I may ask General Cuthbert for some of his urban combat battalions."

I was opening my mouth to bite my muffin but I froze.

"Hope you weren't trying to swallow when I said that," John smiled. "I know the last thing you want to deal with out there is Imperial Army, but if it means we can nip this civil war in the bud, I'm not above using the blockheads. Alright."

Now, of course, this decision of John's is often said to be a mistake, and though he's never blamed for the tragedies to follow at Egesta, I want to explain his thinking, to make sure you all understand it. We were looking at a civil war in its earliest stages, and the idea was that, if we could get enough heavily armed troops on the ground, we could convince both sides to back off. A couple of corvettes and a frigate didn't carry enough armed personnel to really make that impression, but put down a battalion or two of the beefy Imperial Army blockheads and both sides might decide the fight wasn't worth making.

Anyway, that deployment process was just getting started when John sent me this message.

"I think that's it for now," John said, and I unfroze and took that bite of my muffin. "Safe journey, keep in touch."

The screen went blank.

+++

Captain Wes Pellew was in his day cabin, watching the message John had sent him. My warning of the night before about the possibility of the Independent Squadron's arrival had already tipped him off to the potential seriousness of the situation at hand, and he'd met with his Captains and contacted Admiralty House himself. Now he had orders from the top of the fleet: if Sean Cook showed up, he could put the bastard in a noose on sight, if he so chose.

He'd contemplate his response to Cook's arrival in due time...

That's what he tells me he was thinking when the comm chimed, and his Sensors and Communications Officer, Kate Levec, came on, "Skipper, we have a squadron inbound. Knowing our luck, I bet you can guess who, too."

Wes sat back in his chair.

"Well timing's a great thing," he muttered.

At about the same time, *Wolf* and *Honesty* boosted out of Hawke One.

Everything was set up for... the next book.

CHAPTER THIRTY-SEVEN

TRAVELING AGAIN

Karen and I were eating our dinners in silence. As usual, she was on my bed, her legs kicking back and forth behind her as she used an elbow to prop herself over her food, spearing bits of fish and potato with the fork in her free hand.

I sat in my chair next to the bed, staring over her shoulder at a patch of wall.

In retrospect, I think we were both in a certain state of mental exhaustion. While the Hawke Mission, as I've always called it, wasn't as stressful as the start of the war or the Battle Over Earth, it had been... grim.

We'd won at Belt Two, we'd won at the Battle Over Earth. Yes, we'd lost an astonishing number of men and women with the Light Squadron's capital ships over Earth, but over the past couple of weeks the war had turned itself back into a fight against enemy civilians — or at least, that's how the Martians were playing the game. They weren't just partnering with pirates for the sake of expanding their forces, they were fighting pirate-style...

But then, that wasn't the only problem. Our own people were fighting pirate style, and that wasn't acceptable by any stretch of the imagination. We had a lot to fix when we got to Egesta.

"So," Karen's word seemed abrupt, and my eyes bounced down to look at hers, "I guess we're both feeling pretty sickly about this."

I nodded slowly, "Yeah, that'd be a fair assessment."

Letting out a long breath, Karen nodded, "Well, I suppose it was bound to happen. We've been coasting through this war so far."

I smiled and bowed my head slightly. I had to agree with her — absolutely. There had been fighting, of course, but fighting other combatants is... well, it's preferable to fighting civilians. At least I prefer it.

What we were cruising towards was a civil war that, based on Mark's reports, had civilian insurgency and organized crime as a driving force. And hell, it hadn't even been the Martians who'd caused this problem, it had been one of 'our own'.

I know I keep dwelling on that, which probably speaks a lot to what I actually saw at Egesta, but even before I got there, my over-active 'worry engine' was hitting high stride. We could be cruising straight for a quagmire, a real nightmare, where you can't tell innocent children from bomb-carriers...

How was the cavalier attitude going to hold up under that kind of pressure?

Usually when you're hunting pirates the civilians who side with the pirates aren't hostile. What would happen if the civilians were hostile? Was I going to shoot them in droves? What exactly could I do...?

"Hey."

I blinked, my gaze drifting back to Karen's face after her sharp word. Our eyes met, and then she did the magical sort of wordless thing that always, always snapped me out of

my helpless worries.
    She smiled.
    And thank God for that.
    Wolf cruised towards Egesta.

AFTERWORD

So that was *The Hawke Mission*. Whenever I think back to it, I fail to understand why so much hype has been tied to it by the press and the movie companies — we lost a lot of innocent people in the free rocks, we dealt heavy-handedly with Caligula, and Mik Mikaelsen made his name in the media for the first time. But overall, not so stressful as the start of the war.

Nonetheless, it's been a popular incident for ages, so now you have my perspective on it, and we can move on to Egesta…

The Independent Squadron, the book coming next, is going to tell you just how we dealt with Sean Cook and his ships, and about the fallout of his visit to Egesta. When I explained to my publisher just what I was going to cover in that book, he looked at me and said "Oh God, you're going to kill the series. Every protest group out there will be sending duelists to get you." He was and is concerned for my welfare on this one, and I appreciate that, but I really don't care. As I pointed out to him, for all the heavy-handed assessments of the situation on Egesta we've seen so far, none have really come from the people who mounted the intervention. Readers deserve to see that perspective — I'd argue one of the more accurate perspectives, though of course I'm biased.

I should warn you, though, that this next book isn't going to be nearly so light and enjoyable as our romp through the independent belt with Lia. Hell, I feel bad calling it a 'romp' given the losses at Furnace rock and Anderson's Colony, but compared to Egesta this was indeed a romp. *The Independent Squadron* will be the darkest book I've written so far in this series of reminiscences.

That said, the books that come after will start to bounce back. Not entirely, of course — Egesta cast long shadows — but don't fear that I'll spend the rest of these reminiscences brooding about mayhem. I couldn't have survived the war if I'd done that. You'll see what I mean when we get there.

So anyway, that's enough from me for now. See you in *The Independent Squadron*.

THE
INDEPENDENT
SQUADRON

THE AUTOBIOGRAPHICAL REMINISCENCES OF
ADMIRAL THE LORD KEN BARRON FOR 2231

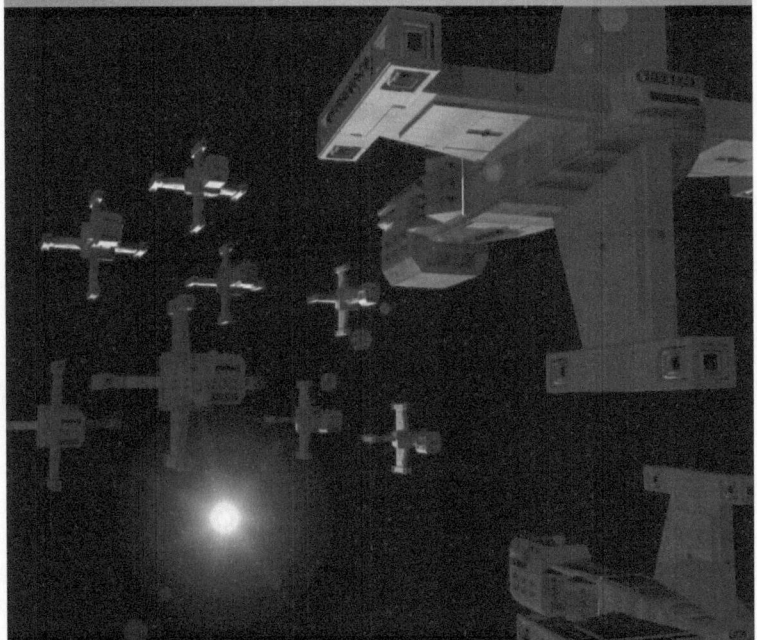

THE MARTIAN WAR - 4

KENNETH TAM

From The Author

Here comes the fourth volume of the Martian War. This book is darker than those before it, and I thought I should talk about that. While writing it, I was asked why I'd decided to include such a grim book in a series that stayed so often on the lighter side. My only answer was, "Um... because that's what happened next." I don't know if that's a good answer, but it's all I have.

As you're about to read, Egesta (named for a Sicilian city-state you can read about in Thucydides) is a mess — a humanitarian crisis involving attacks on thousands of innocent civilians by savage armed fighters. It's the sort of scenario that we see too often in our own times — the sort of crisis the UN sends peacekeepers to stabilize. Lately the stories of such peacekeeping operations, their successes and their failures, have begun to gain more attention in public. I guess, in my own small way, I'm trying to contribute to the understanding of them.

There's no way that, in fiction, I can capture the true horror of present day crises like this, nor can I truly understand or convey the real states of mind of those military personnel trying to stop real-word slaughters. My hope is just to provide a plausible glimpse into what these missions could be like... to help readers think about some of the many horrific challenges our brave peacekeepers can face.

I've based the story of Egesta on a plethora of humanitarian crises I've learned of in my study of history, and particularly on the ways in which the armed forces personnel dealt with those incidents. My imagination and our characters' personalities have filled in the specific details for Egesta, and if I've done my job right, the story will explore some issues that must be faced by all peacekeepers.

Ultimately my hope is that, by putting our beloved characters into this mess, we can all learn something... And that in some small way, I can honor the real men and women who do this job in our present times.

What can I say, I'm ambitious.

As you know, a number of this series' characters are based on real-world friends of mine. My thanks to all of them for allowing me to borrow their personalities for these books.

I need to thank Peter Caron again, for his insight into some of the very specific events that take place. My good friend Matt Gurney also helped me construct a particular memorable incident, and Wes Prewer similarly helped me come to grips with the challenges of Egesta. Wes must also be thanked for the omni-present graphical support he offers this series, and the *Equations* novels.

The last and greatest thanks go again to my family: my elite parents Jacqui and Peter (I'm running out of creative ways to call them great, but great they are). Atlas, my dear German Shepherd, has passed away, but I owe him for the many lessons he taught me. I hope his legacy continues on, in some small way, in the books I write.

– Kenneth Tam

FOREWORD

Well, welcome to *The Independent Squadron*. I made sure to warn my regular readers that this would be the darkest book they'd see from me for a while, and so it will be. That shouldn't be a surprise to anyone familiar with history, though... or even with current events, for that matter. Everyone knows about Egesta. Everybody knows how badly this situation turned out.

I'm not going to make any excuses for that... quite frankly, it's not my place to. I'm pleased — or at least as pleased as I *can* be — that the Fiora Ring didn't cause the problems on the ground at Egesta. But I remain to this day disgusted by the fact that *other* Defense Command personnel played integral roles in turning Egesta into the horrific problem case it is today.

And I won't even start in on the Imperial Army — that's a discussion for a later book.

No, I'll be talking about the beginning of the Egesta crisis, with the actions of Commodore Sean Cook and the Belt Anti-Piracy Force (known to everyone as the 'Independent Squadron'). I think that squadron, while under Cook's command, was the single blackest mark on Defense Command's history, even including Dave Caldecott's disgraceful contributions.

Sean Cook was a savage, and his fate befitted his actions.

At about this point I was going to say 'alright, let's get the narrative started', but as my publisher has pointed out to me, this book is probably going to get a lot of attention in future, from students, scholars and politicians trying to learn more about the Egesta crisis. These people may or may not have read the first three books in my Martian War reminiscences, or they may not have done much background reading on Egesta itself, so let's fill in some blanks before I go further.

Egesta is a free rock in the Belt between the Belt colonies and the Hawke Protectorate, and up through the beginning of the Martian War, it had remained a generally agreeable state. We weren't bound to it by any treaties (our last trade agreement before the war lapsed in 2212) but Egesta had, at the same time, never been anything but welcoming to Defense Command and Imperial shipping.

The main challenge with Egesta had to be its socio-governmental makeup. While the governor and most of the small administration of the rock were pro-Empire, the mining Guild that represented almost sixty percent of the asteroid's population was squarely against free trade, fearing its miners would be put out of work by cheaper imports.

Well, that was the official Guild line. The reality was much less noble: the Guild was the only outfit an Egesta miner could work for, and it was taking huge deductions from its members' pay cheques for services it seldom delivered. It didn't want another Imperial mining company to get settled on Egesta, because (as you probably know) all Imperial mining companies are legally obligated to pay Imperial minimum wage and offer certain benefits without charge. This sort of competition would have been a problem for the Guild, for obvious reasons — an Imperial company would steal away the Guild's workforce in weeks, and still turn a greater profit because of its multi-asteroid assets.

All that in mind, the Egesta Mining Guild painted the Empire to be an evil profit-hording force, and used that threat over its workers to create unrest that in turn kept the asteroid's government from renewing proper diplomatic relations with the Empire. It was a rather awkward situation, then, that only got worse as the Guild continued to drive its workers further into an impoverished state with crippling wage deductions. You'd expect the workers to turn against the Guild for that sort of treatment, but unfortunately, the Egesta government took the heat for their losses.

Not being as politically astute as the administration of the average Belt colony, the Egesta leadership didn't simply sit back and allow the Guild to fold in on itself: it locked horns with the Guild, raising taxes on all Guild operations, and requiring special identity cards for Guild employees. The government thus made itself a target of much rage, and relieved the Guild of its obvious responsibility for the poor condition of the miners. The situation just before war broke out was unstable: as Lia Hawke warned Karen and me during the events of *The Hawke Mission*, things were rapidly running towards civil war when the Martians came to blows with the Empire. The Egesta government's only advantage was its monopoly of force: it had a sizable contingent of Boscawen Corp mercenaries defending its interests, and no domestic combatants were well-armed enough to deal with those professionals.

Until Commodore Sean Cook traded fourteen pallets of EP-5 mag rifles to the mining Guild in return for a weekend of whoring for his crew.

The tailspin started the minute he left, and by the time Commanders Andrea Kiley and Mark Gunney of my Belt Squadron happened upon Egesta, things were *bad*.

That's where I'll join the narrative, roughly speaking. If you're coming to this book having read *The Hawke Mission*, you'll notice that the beginning here very slightly overlaps with some events in that book. I decided to do it this way so all the matters directly pertinent to Egesta would be united in one volume, not spread over two (the first of which really has little to do with Egesta at all).

So here it is, *The Independent Squadron*.

CHAPTER ONE

THE SITUATION AT BELT TWO

I begin this particular book not with Karen and me at Hawke One, where we were scrambling to assemble troops to bring to Egesta for peacekeeping operations, but at Belt Two, where Captain Wes Pellew was supervising the restoration of the last of the Belt Squadron's damaged ships.

This actually warrants a look all the way back to *The Rogue Commodore*. At the Battle of Belt Two, which you might remember, most of the ships in the Belt Squadron suffered some sort of damage in a standup fight with the combined pirate-Martian force that Kitty Castillo had brought to attack us. We won by quite a margin — we lost no ships — but many of our frigates and corvettes did need time in the Belt Two yards to get fully patched up.

On this particular morning (the previous night Karen and I had briefly attended Ian Hawke's court), Wes was actually overseeing the return to full service of the last of these damaged ships.

That last ship was the plucky and irrepressible little *Sackville*, Commander Katya Romanov, which had lost one of its drive pods entirely in the last exchange of fire during the battle. Gleaming bright silver with a new pod and an overhaul to its main power systems, *Sackville* was edging its way out of the repair slip as Wes settled himself into his chair on the bridge of *Cheetah*, his *Predator*-class frigate.

"Commander Romanov's signaling the all clear from moorings, skipper. She's now out of dock and free to navigate," Kate Levec, Wes' Sensors and Communications Officer, reported.

Wes simply nodded; that was very good news. He was temporarily in overall command of the Belt Squadron, owing to my and Karen's departure to Earth after the battle there, and he'd spent the past few weeks on pins and needles, trying to figure out exactly how he and a shot-up Belt Squadron could protect all the Belt colonies against further Martian and pirate attack.

But no attack had come.

Wes has never been the sort to look a gift horse in the mouth, but he still had been eager to get all his ships back into fighting trim — just in case his luck ran out.

Now the entire Squadron was active again, and he had received word that Admiral Greg Noyce, former Belt Squadron commanding officer and the man who'd commanded these very ships to victory at the Battle of Deep Black, would be returning to Belt Two to assume overall command.

So Wes only had to hold out for a short while longer.

I suppose that makes it sound as though Wes didn't want the command, so I should explain more clearly. Wes wasn't afraid of command, never has been. No, he was understandably anxious about a very unsettling tactical situation in Belt Two space: he had no idea where the enemy was, or when it would attack again, and he had only three frigates and three corvettes left at hand to protect all twenty-nine Belt colonies.

Were it me, I'd be climbing the walls. It's a testament to Wes' focus that he was sitting still in his chair.

Oh, and you might be wondering why I say *three* corvettes, not the five that had been with the Belt Squadron at Belt Two. Remember, Wes had sent Mark Gunney's *Honesty* and Andrea Kiley's *Friendly* out after the pirates who had escaped, and had authorized them to keep up their chase, hoping they'd locate the pirates' base and give him a better idea of what he was up against.

They didn't end up having any luck with that, but the decision proved important nonetheless: if they hadn't been out there looking, they'd never have come across Egesta and alerted us to the situation there.

Of course, cynics will say it would have been better if we never found out about the Egesta situation... well, I won't comment just now.

Wes was glad to have *Sackville* back online, that's all I really need to say.

"Give me Katya on realtime comm when she's ready," Wes nodded to Kate Levec, and the Lieutenant Commander nodded evenly in reply.

"Aye, sir."

It took a few minutes for *Sackville* to maneuver away from the yard station orbiting Belt Two and to get into orbital formation with the four other Defense Command ships there. *Cheetah*, *Lion*, *Generous* and *Lady Grace* were now the vessels holding Belt Two; Marshall Samuels had taken *Alberta* out to Belt Fourteen to settle a panicking governor.

Sorry, I realize this must all sound like a flood of ship names that you may only vaguely remember, so let me just say it clearly once and for all: with Wes at Belt Two were *Cheetah* and *Lion*, frigates, and the corvettes *Generous*, *Lady Grace* and now *Sackville*. The corvettes *Friendly* and *Honesty* were the ships out at Egesta, and the frigate *Alberta* was headed to Belt Fourteen.

These deployments will prove important in a minute...

"Hang on... skipper, Belt Two just received an unscheduled comm burst from the vector of Hawke One."

Wes tells me he'd been going over at length in his mind many of those deployments I just mentioned; Kate Levec's words dragged him out of his musing.

"Unscheduled comm burst? Is it being forwarded up here?"

Comm traffic between Belt Two base and Hawke One was generally carried out on a pre-established schedule, necessary to ensure that communications arrays were ready to send and receive when critical communiqués were coming through. For Hawke to send a signal ahead of schedule suggested something quite serious.

Coming to his feet, Wes strode towards the front of *Cheetah's* bridge, frowning and folding his arms across his chest as he did.

Kate Levec was checking with her staff behind the communications panels, and then she looked up, "Not being forwarded... no, hang on, she's sending now. But I have Captain Stanton on realtime for you."

Sharon Stanton was the Captain commanding the Belt Two base (you might recall her from *The Rogue Commodore*).

With a nod, Wes bobbed his head towards screen two, "Put her through. And get that signal cued up on screen three when it comes in."

Buffering displays came up on both screens, with Sharon Stanton appearing first, "You're loading up the message?"

Wes nodded, "Got it on the next screen down from you, but it's still loading. Mind giving me a preview?"

"It's from Ken, and by the sounds of it, we're in for some complicated trouble."

Now, a warning like that really doesn't daunt someone like Wes Pellew.

"Complicated? That's the best kind…" Wes, like the rest of us Belt Squadron officers, had a flare for the cavalier before the war — a necessary boon to the reputation that allowed us to intimidate pirates and blaze noisy trails across the Belt colonies.

Sharon knew this, but she guessed — rightly — that 'cavalier' would be going out the window in this instance, "No, Wes, I mean it. This isn't good…"

Wes' face darkened noticeably and his eyes narrowed, "Alright, stop being cryptic."

Then screen three flashed to life, with my face on it.

I explained the situation: "Wes, looks like Commodore Sean Cook and his esteemed Independent Squadron have managed to start a civil war on Egesta rock. Handed EP-5s to the local criminal guild, and it's turned into mayhem… government's fallen, rape and murder. I'm heading there now to see if the situation can be stabilized, but as the logs I'm attaching to this message will show you, Cook seriously did a number on the asteroid. He's committed some serious violations of regulation, and some atrocities and war crimes, as far as I'm concerned. We don't know where he and his outfit are headed, but if they come your way, watch out. No telling how he'll behave. I don't have orders for how you should deal with him — I'll leave those to John at Admiralty House. I've sent this to him, he'll probably have a signal in the grid to you within a few hours. In the meantime, I'm taking Mark Gunney with me back to Egesta, and Andrea Kiley's already on site. I'll keep you apprised… good luck there. Keep looking after the Belt for me."

And then I disappeared.

As you might recall from *The Hawke Mission*, I could scarcely believe what Cook had done when Mark Gunney had told me of it. Now it was Wes' turn to stare at a blank screen with his jaw hanging open in surprise.

That surprise, of course, paralyzed him for only a handful of seconds, and he looked back to Sharon, "We had any sightings of the Independent Squadron?"

She shook her head, "None of our posts report having had a visit. Either Cook's gone elsewhere to find his fun, or he's coming straight to Belt Two."

Wes blinked once, his mind processing options.

He had five ships concentrated, not enough to convincingly overpower the Independent Squadron's eight specially-equipped vessels. And while Greg was destined to bring two battleships out here, they were still probably ten or twelve days away.

If Sean Cook came to Belt Two, what could he do?

"Complicated," Wes said simply after a second, then looked up at Sharon. "I hate it when you're not kidding."

CHAPTER TWO
HEADS TOGETHER

With the five ships of the Belt Squadron so near each other in Belt Two space, it only took an hour for the four other commanding officers Wes had with him to come aboard *Cheetah* for a meeting. This was the kind of impending crisis that warranted the sort of face-to-face meeting that was all too rare in Defense Command operational life.

Sharon Stanton flew up from Belt Two base to join the Belt Squadron skippers as well, so six people gathered in *Cheetah's* briefing room, sitting around the large table in somewhat stunned silence for a few minutes after they settled in.

At the head of the table was Wes, and as he looked around at his fellow skippers, I'll take the opportunity to reintroduce you to them all. It's been a while since *The Rogue Commodore*, and although I imagine many readers will recognize the names of this elite band of fellows, a refresher is probably wise.

On his right side, Wes had Captain Kris Jacobs, that fiery redheaded Australian. Next to her was Elise De Winter of *Lady Grace* (Karen's old corvette), then Isoruku Togo of *Generous*, with Katya Romanov of *Sackville* opposite them. At the far end of the table sat Sharon Stanton, her brow creased deeply.

"If Cook shows up here... we *should* arrest him," Sharon said finally, and Wes nodded slowly.

"That's exactly what we *should* do, but if we try... I don't know if everyone here got a chance to skim Mark's logs on the way over from your ships, but I did. Believe me, any crews willing to commit those sorts of actions for recreation are going to stick with the Commodore who allows them such latitude. And that means any attempt to arrest Cook could lead to a gunfight between us and the Independent Squadron."

The logs he was referring to were Mark Gunney's, still some of the most graphic and disturbing I've had the displeasure of coming across. Mark was merciless in assembling vid feeds and personal accounts of victims of Cook's visit to Egesta, and his logs were the prime evidence against Cook, even after we gathered more during our subsequent arrival.

All around the table, the Belt Squadron skippers nodded in agreement with Wes' assessment. There was no question in the minds of any of these elite officers that a gunfight with the Independent Squadron would not be a good thing. Many social critics since have ironically suggested it would have been the *right* thing, but reality in such complicated circumstances seldom lends itself to an easy answer.

Let me explain it to you the way Wes later explained it to me (and the way I would have thought in his place): Cook and his people were inciters of atrocities, and if backed into a corner, they might take advantage of their powerful squadron to escape prosecution. The five ships then at Belt Two *might* have been able to handle the eight older Independent Squadron vessels, but there was no question that the fight would badly cripple the Belt

Squadron, or even destroy it outright.

That would leave all the Belt colonies completely defenseless, not just to any Martian and pirate attacks that might be coming, but also to the vengeful spite of an Independent Squadron that would no longer have any reason to respect Imperial law.

While Cook was a bastard and his crews had much to answer for, no one could deny they were battle-hardened combat professionals. Not as good as our Belt Squadron crews, in my opinion, but still well-trained enough to be exceedingly dangerous. So realistically, then, a gunfight with the Independent Squadron was not an option.

The direct method was out. No immediate arrest.

And, sorry, if you're wondering why none of the skippers at the table was actually saying this, it's because they all knew it already. This wasn't like the movies, where the characters had to explain everything for sake of exposition. There was instead a dark silence as minds worked through options.

There didn't seem to be a great many viable alternatives, though...

"Does he know we know about his actions?" Kris Jacobs leaned forward in her chair, casting a glance at Wes.

Frowning, Wes shook his head, "I don't see how he could."

Kris' eyebrow went up, "Could we use that against him? Do you think we could lead him on and buy some time?"

Wes' eyes narrowed and his head dipped slightly, "Keep him quiet until we can split his ships into manageable divisions... or until reinforcements can get here?"

Kris half-shrugged, "If you can't beat him, make him think he's still on your side?"

Sharon scratched the side of her neck, "Is that really viable? Can we really keep all our crews quiet about what we've found out?"

"Well, most of our crews don't know yet — only bridge crews and comm staffs..." Elise De Winter put in thoughtfully, but Wes shook his head.

"No, no the rumors will already be flying. There's no way word of Commodore-sanctioned rape and pillage wouldn't be making its way through the lower decks. We can't pretend we don't know..." he looked back at Kris, "... and I won't pretend I *approve*... but..."

"But we don't have orders to do anything about it. And as long as we don't have to confront him about what he's done, we're less likely to have to fight with him. And with all the press around, he's going to abide by Imperial law in Belt space — as long as we don't give him a reason not to," Kris finished his thought.

Wes nodded slowly.

As you might imagine, this idea left a very bad taste in his mouth, but then it was just about his only option at the moment. There were too many lives at stake, both in the Belt Squadron itself and more importantly in the Belt colonies... he couldn't pick a losing fight to satisfy his own anger. It would have simply been irresponsible.

"So we pretend to be the disapproving but helpless-to-act Belt Squadron?" Katya Romanov asked quite softly, and Kris and Wes nodded simultaneously.

"Until we can divide their ships, or until Admiral Noyce or Ken can get here with sufficient reinforcements to allow us to arrest Cook and his officers," Wes said with a sigh. "I really don't like this plan. But."

Slow nods were the response of the Belt skippers, and the matter was thus settled. They'd return to their ships and be honest with their officers and crews — atrocities had been committed, but there were no orders to do a damned thing about it, and not enough ships present to do anything even if there *were* orders.

And if orders came before reinforcements did… well… Wes would have to deal with those under his own initiative.

Indeed, that's exactly what he'd do.

CHAPTER THREE
INTERLUDE TO EGESTA

To give you a sense of what was going on while *Wolf* prepared to leave for Egesta and while Wes was in that meeting, I've gone back over the logs Andrea Kiley was keeping on the asteroid. One of my test-readers suggested I should wait until *Wolf* arrived at Egesta to begin telling the story there — that somehow I was losing dramatic impact by showing just how bad things were before I arrived… or some such thing. But I think it's important to explain to you the full horror Andrea was coping with. I didn't end up having to deal with quite this kind of gruesome reality myself, thank God.

So, Andrea Kiley was holed up in the Government Dome of Egesta, but her position there wasn't what any military operator would call secure. If you don't remember much about then-Commander Kiley, let me reintroduce you to her: she's the famed Irish Belt Squadron skipper, a hell of a ship-handler and another history specialist like myself. I mention that last fact not out of historian's hubris, but because it applied to her reaction at Egesta. She knew the long history of the Irish insurgency in the twentieth century.

Now, you probably don't know what I'm talking about, but you might want to look it up. Suffice it to say Andrea was well-versed in the history of urban combat and terror strikes… she was the sort of person who understood the nature of the problem being faced by Egesta. One of the few who actually *got it* at the time, in fact.

That she was crouching in the open back of a moving pickup while Wes was in a meeting might be proof of that. Commander Kiley had *Friendly* — my old ship — in orbit of Egesta, and she had every volunteer she could scrounge on the ground trying to maintain order in the Government Dome. To answer my editor's question, no, she hadn't ordered all available people down — she couldn't, in good conscience, force her loyal crew to watch these atrocities, so she only took volunteers. But remember, Andrea's ship was *Friendly*: every man and woman aboard volunteered.

No, I'm not exaggerating in an attempt to romanticize the crew of my old ship. All of the Belt Squadron crews would have been similarly inclined. Mark Gunney's people from *Honesty* volunteered to the last as well.

But even with all that turnout, it wasn't proving easy.

Around the time Wes was closing his meeting, Andrea was hurling herself over the side of the pickup and bolting across an open street with her mag in hand, diving for cover behind a parked and abandoned vehicle.

"Jameson, Hong!" she demanded quietly as she came to a stop, and her Special Branch escort — two officers, because those were all she could spare to move with her — rushed behind the car and dropped to the ground next to her.

They weren't expecting to be fired upon, but instead were trying to remain unseen as they headed for a so-called 'safe house' where a report said a dozen people were hiding out. Hiding out, you ask?

I'd better back up and offer some explanation here: Andrea had six major complexes within the Government Dome under her control, but only six. Government House and the Administration Building were the first two, both large and fairly secure, though they were hardly assault proof if the situation destabilized. Both the Egesta Colonial Hospital and Kauffman High School were also under her control, as was a government ore warehouse (and its space dock — her lifeline to *Friendly*) and the Egesta Colonial Stadium.

Sounds like an impressive set of buildings, and it was, but scattered as they were across a commercial district of the dome, they weren't easy to defend, or to move between.

But defending wasn't at this point the precise problem, because Andrea wasn't taking a side in what was turning out to be a nasty civil war. No, she was letting the government and its Boscawen mercs operate against the Guild as it pleased (though by this time the Guild had driven the mercs from the streets, and it was Guild fighters who were doing the horrible harm). Her self-appointed task was to try to keep non-combatants out of the middle of the urban fighting.

For this job she had — wait for it — just 204 SF, Special Branch, and volunteers from *Friendly* and *Honesty*. You guessed it, that's not *nearly* enough.

With just over 200 women and men, Andrea was desperately trying to keep six buildings secure, convince the Guild not to attack her (or else), and to go out into the Government Dome (the only one seeing any sort of serious fighting) to bring in civilians who were hiding.

She had, moreover, no logistical arm, no transport units, no armor, no urban combat equipment... nothing that SF would usually send into a situation like this one.

Hence the pickup she'd used to travel to this section of town had been requisitioned (stolen from in front of a burned-out house) and hastily painted green with Imperial black suns marked all over it.

This was one of the best people-moving vehicles she had.

And Andrea herself was leading some of these search missions. That's how desperate for warm bodies she was.

So with that explained, let's return to the car behind which she, Jameson and Hong were taking cover. Andrea looked at these two officers and waved her mag-holding hand towards the alley they'd arrived at.

"This is the one, Gwen?"

She was addressing Captain Gwen Jameson, and the Special Brancher nodded, "That's what the message says."

This was all being recorded, by the way, on what we came to affectionately call 'Dead-cams' — small cameras that her Special Branchers and many of her volunteers and SF guards were wearing on earpieces. No, they weren't standard Defense Command issue... Andrea actually 'requisitioned' a shipment of about 200 of them from an electronics store that had been looted. It was a very good idea — we got hours of footage of what happened during this week of the debacle, and though it has not been released to the public, it has been used to convict some people of crimes against humanity.

It has also helped me assemble this narrative of what happened before I got there.

Andrea nodded with the confirmation, then shifted herself into a crouch so she could move out from behind the car. Both Special Branchers mirrored the posture change, and

Gwen Jameson waved Lieutenant Mikka Hong forward. Straightening slightly, Hong covered the opposite side of the street, gazing down the barrel and sight of her gun as she panned it around the trashed street.

With another nod, then, Andrea began a crouch-run out from behind cover, her mag leveled in front of her, and after a suitable pause to cover the Commander, Captain Jameson followed (for anyone confused, Special Branch 'Captain' roughly equates with Fleet 'Lieutenant Commander', so Andrea was senior here). Hong brought up the rear a second after.

Andrea stopped just short of the alley, behind a wall put up to conceal dumpsters from the owners of the townhouses on the side of the street they'd come up. She took a few deep breaths, expecting the very worst, and then nodded again to her two escorts.

"I'll lead out," Gwen Jameson said firmly, and though Andrea opened her mouth to protest, she stopped herself and nodded.

Jameson nodded too, then did some of those delightful hand tactical gestures that silently informed Hong of her intending deployment. The junior Brancher nodded, and then in a flash they were going around the corner into the alley at a trot, MAG-90s leveled. Andrea followed immediately, her own battered pistol leading the way for her.

This, I should mention, was early evening on Egesta, and the Earthgreen dome was simulating the setting of the sun as they moved into the gloomy, stinking alleyway. This place would have once been home to drifters and whores, now it was shelter.

Welcome to Egesta.

Jameson was moving quickly, her ponytail bouncing as she trotted, and Andrea kept up only with some difficulty. She was exhausted and battered, but she told me later she was keeping herself going with a simple thought: 'If it were me needing this kind of help, I wouldn't take *tired* as much of an excuse.'

"One on the ground up here," Jameson hissed the whisper for that report solely for Andrea's benefit — she could have communicated in hand gestures if she'd only needed to tell Hong.

The trio slowed as they neared a body face down in a puddle. Blood was pooling around the man's head, and he wasn't breathing.

Then came the scream. Jameson had been crouching to check the corpse for vitals, but as soon as she heard that sound she was on her feet and running further down the alley as quickly as good movement tactics would allow, Hong and Andrea close in her wake.

Another scream, closer this time. Jameson spotted a door at the end of the alley, open a crack with light spilling out of it. Then another scream, but this one simply didn't stop — it turned into a sob with begging.

Jameson looked back for instruction, and Andrea nodded, "Let's go."

This was what they were out here to stop.

The three rushed forward again, Jameson reaching the door first and flattening herself against the wall next to it. Hong arrived beside her, with Andrea third in line.

"I lead," Jameson whispered, and with two nods as acknowledgment, the Special Brancher swung forward, collected momentum, and drove her foot into the door. As it was already open a crack, it slammed into the man who had been standing 'guard' on the other side, giving Jameson room to enter.

With typical Special Branch presence, she rushed into the room, covering as many directions as she could with her MAG-90, while Hong followed and did the same. Andrea was last in, and she came in bellowing.

"*Defense Command, these are non-combatants under our protection!*"

She stopped abruptly just inside the door. The room was best described as a rape room, there's no way to sugar coat it. Bloodied and bruised men, women and children were huddled in a corner, and other things I won't describe. It was a horror.

And there were about fifteen Guild fighters in there, some missing their pants, but most of them leveling Cook's EP-5s at Andrea, Jameson and Hong.

Andrea's mouth went dry. I can't even *imagine* what was going through her head.

"Get out of here now, these are non-combatants and I'm extending Defense Command protection to them," her voice on the vid when she says that is stern and confident. I know for a fact she was neither at that moment.

I think some of the civilians in the room realized that their salvation was at hand, though.

"We disagree," a woman who'd clearly just had her turn and hastily dressed herself approached Andrea with rifle up. "*These* had Government House passes on them. They're part of the government, and thus combatants."

Such a sneer, that was said with.

"Not by my definition," Andrea turned her weapon on the woman, but the Guild fighter just laughed.

"Well my definition's backed by fifteen guns."

Jameson and Hong both had sweat dripping off their brows by now, but neither had so much as exchanged a panicked glance. They were Special Branch, and if they were going to die, so be it. They'd take as many of these bastards with them as they could.

Andrea... well, like I said, I have *no* idea what she could have been thinking. I can only imagine that, were it me, I'd be staring at the civilians in desperate need of help, and trying to figure out if there was any possible way three of us could take this room.

But whatever her thoughts, they were interrupted by the sounds of boots outside the door.

Reinforcements, that changed things.

"Oooh, Defcoms come for a turn?"

Andrea didn't move at the crude words from the alley.

Then from behind, a hand reached out and cupped her backside, and her head whipped around and the butt of her mag drove into the temple of a newly-arrived Guild fighter. The gruff man laughed as he straightened up.

"You're a pretty one. Too bad the uniform's on..."

Another dozen Guild troopers had arrived, and Hong had turned to cover them... well, as best she could.

"Time to go, honey. Before you join the wrong end of the party," the Guild woman sneered.

Andrea swallowed.

And then staring at the civilians huddled in the room, she slowly lowered her mag and backed past the man who'd grabbed her, then out the door.

Hong and Jameson backed out in turn, and then at a quick, stunned walk, they moved back down the alley.

The screams started again.

Now, you're probably in shock as you read this. You might be thinking 'how could she leave them'? Well believe me, no one has asked that question more than Andrea Kiley. I know her very well, I know about the suicide contemplation, the sleepless nights and the death wish that came after this, and you'll read about some of it. It took her a very long time to get over what she saw at Egesta — not just this incident, but a hundred more.

And if you think you could have done better, I suggest you get over yourself.

What choice did Andrea have in that room, exactly? She had *two officers*, that's it. What the hell was she going to do with almost thirty Guild troopers around her, except join the victims?

She was lucky, indeed, that the Guild troopers were under orders not to directly engage Defense Command personnel — if a Defense Command man or woman suffered *anything* at the hands of the Guild, the unholy wrath that the fleet would rain down on Egesta was expected to be apocalyptic, so we were all 'hands-off'.

But then, what if Andrea *started* the fight? Would the 'wise' Guild superiors be able to control these roughshod troopers if we killed dozens of them? Not likely. Andrea had only 200 people on the ground, they had almost 800 well-armed fighters, and thousands more with mixed weapons. She'd be driven right off Egesta if she actually started a fight, and then all the civilians she was trying to protect would be doomed.

All of them.

Jameson's hand clasped Andrea's shoulder as they walked slowly out of the alley, "We had no choice. We can't..."

Andrea held up a hand and cut the Captain off, "Yes, I know."

There were only three of them, they had to stay alive to help whoever they could. Those civilians in that room were beyond helping, but they'd find others that night who could be brought safely back to the stadium.

It was all they could do with the resources at hand.

This was what Andrea was dealing with.

Welcome to Egesta.

CHAPTER FOUR

BACK AT BELT TWO

Let's turn back to some brighter affairs, though what qualifies as 'brighter' after that chapter is not exactly glowing…

Back at Belt Two, Wes Pellew was sitting in his day cabin, watching John Fiora's newly-arrived message. John was just getting to the critical part of the orders: "…so, Captain Pellew, if you have the opportunity to safely do so, you can take Commodore Cook under arrest on my authority. He's got a trip to the gallows ahead of him, by the look of it… and if he resists, you can use any force necessary to contain him. Given the state of war, we need his ships — if you can save the hulls that would be perfect. Right now, though, my main concern is bringing him to justice. Use your judgment, your actions will have the full support of the Admiralty."

Wes was nodding to himself as he heard this, so he'd report back to Admiralty with the plan he and his skippers had put together — still their best option despite these new orders — and hopefully things would hold together until Admiral Noyce arrived with the battleships.

Now, as I recall, I included what happened next at the end of *The Hawke Mission*, so it'll be no surprise: the comm chimed, and Wes' Sensors and Communications Officer, Kate Levec, came on, "Skipper, we have a squadron inbound. Knowing our luck, I bet you can guess who, too."

Wes sat back in his chair and muttered, "Well timing's a great thing."

"Uh, sure," Levec sounded awkward on the line, and Wes shook his head and came to his feet.

"Alright, before they get into realtime range, I need to send a signal back to Admiralty House, Kate. Make sure the station transmitter is cleared for us."

"Will do, skipper," the comm cut, and Wes turned to the wall screen, picked up the remote, and opened a vid recording window.

He recorded his plan for John's benefit.

Standing on the bridge about half an hour later, Wes had his arms folded and was staring at the sensor track on the main screen. The whole Independent Squadron had indeed come to Belt Two.

Battlelink was active, the five ships of the Belt Squadron ready to fight if Cook's intentions were untoward, though Wes' ships were officially only on standby alert, so the readiness to fight was hopefully not detectable.

"Another minute more," Kate Levec quietly offered the report, and Wes nodded.

"Okay. I'll take Cook on realtime as soon as he's ready."

Wes had told no one about John's orders — as far as anyone in the crews of the Belt Squadron ships knew, Cook and his men and women were monsters not fit to wear the uniform, but nothing was being done about it yet because there was a war on.

Thirty seconds passed quickly, and the *Cheetah*Net buffering screen came up on monitor two just long enough for Wes to turn to it.

Then Sean Cook appeared.

Now, Sean Cook doesn't look much like a monster — monsters rarely do. Take Grant Merger for instance.

But his genuine-seeming smile and his sandy hair weren't going to win Wes over.

"Captain Pellew, good to see you. We're reporting in; apparently you've started a war and not told us?"

You can find the recordings of this conversation in the fleet archives, and I have to say, I was surprised by Cook's genuine geniality. If we hadn't heard about what had happened at Egesta, he'd have come off as friendly and professional, just like most good Defense Command officers.

But we knew. Wes knew.

"The Martians started the war. Something we hear you know something about, *sir.*"

You can argue that Wes should have played his hand more delicately — he'd likely be the first to agree that a little more self control at this point could have worked to his advantage.

But if you think about it, Wes was using up most of his self control simply in *not* opening fire, so this exchange was probably going about as well as anyone could have realistically hoped.

Cook's smile faded, "What do you mean?"

The response sounded innocent and even confused enough, but Wes wasn't buying it.

"Reports are coming in about Egesta. You created a living nightmare."

Something indescribable about Cook's expression changed right then and his gaze hardened as he sensed a serious challenge coming.

"Well that's too bad for them, but we're bound to Egesta by no treaties. You have a problem with me preserving the morale of my crews?"

That's what he called it — how he *justified* it.

Wes' eyes narrowed, "I have a problem classifying *rape, looting and pillaging* as R&R. Call me old-fashioned."

"You are old-fashioned," Cook said distantly. "I could get into it with you right now, explain to you the need to fight with the pirate rulebook if you want to stop them–" at this point on the vid record, you can see Cook making a subtle gesture to his XO, and the energy output of both his flagship, *Nova Scotia*, and the rest of his squadron started climbing "–but I'm not in the mood. What're you going to do, try to arrest me?"

My guess is Cook had thought through the various possible outcomes of his actions being revealed, and had contingency plans to deal with a number of them.

But he'd have no need for the extra energy — Wes wasn't going to force him to use it.

"It's a time of war."

Cook frowned at the response, "What's that mean?"

"It means the Admiralty knows what you did out there, but in First Lord Fiora's words, we need your ships."

Notice that Wes didn't say 'no I won't arrest you', and Cook should have realized that, but I think the relief at having been found out and yet not disciplined was potent enough to cloud his mind.

"Welcome to Belt Two," Wes' tone was arid. "I *will* be limiting your crews' R&R opportunities on Belt Two rock, though."

Cook's eyes narrowed, "Will you, indeed? As senior officer, I say my men and women can roam, gamble, drink and fuck whoever they like."

From the mouths of Commodores.

Wes' tone didn't change, "You're not in command here. You can take on stores and get in touch with Admiralty for orders, then go about your business. We're not rolling out the welcome mats."

A grin crossed Cook's face, "Fine. We'll continue with our independent cruises as soon as I get my supplies aboard. We'll find a Belt colony that's happy to see us."

"The Admiralty will have new orders for you," Wes shook his head.

"Well, the Admiralty orders I've got say that, in time of war, I can use my discretion."

That was true, actually — even were war to break out, the Independent Squadron was supposed to be able to continue its immediate mission, on the discretion of its commander. The assumption was that, in the highly unlikely (we thought) event of war, a good Commodore about to crack a huge pirate cartel, should have the option to delay his or her rejoining of the fleet.

Understandably, we didn't expect this particular combination of events.

"If that'll be all."

Cook cut the transmission, and Wes stood grimly at the front of *Cheetah's* bridge.

The Independent Squadron moved into orbit over Belt Two.

CHAPTER FIVE
FLYING TOWARDS CRISIS

I was staring at my wallscreen, my left hand propping up my head and covering my left eye. I let out a very long breath.

To be honest, the entire trip from Hawke One to Egesta is a bit of a blur to me: I read notes and stats, looked at log entries and reviewed as much of what Mark Gunney had brought along as I could bear.

I have to say — and this might sound incredibly strange to you — I much prefer regular war and even pirate hunting to civil war. Civil war is nasty. It may have shocked you when I wrote 'rape room' in that chapter with Andrea — you might have said to yourself, "In our civilized solar system? Never!"

Well, sorry, the solar system isn't as civilized as we'd all like. Sure, the Empire itself, and places like Hawke, are very nice and pleasantly civilized, but a lot of the free rocks out in the Belt are as roughshod as their names imply.

And while all the movies always make the settlers on those rocks into cowboy and western-type homesteaders who are being victimized by pirate bandits, those of us who've been out there and spent time hunting through those rocks know better.

Some people out on the independent asteroids truly are the homesteading sort. Many are migrant workers, though, living paycheque to paycheque and sustaining themselves with a diet of booze, purchased sex, and bad food. In that order.

So was I shocked that Egesta had descended into chaos? Yes. Was I asking myself 'how could this happen'? No. My line of thought was more in the 'not Egesta too' range. Liberia syndrome, I suppose, though it's centuries out of date and not a particularly good historical parallel.

Anyway, that's a glimpse into what I was thinking as I watched the vid feeds and read the reports. What chance did we really have of fixing this without support? It felt like it was too much for us to handle.

Indeed, it was too much, as history proved, but at the time I believed — or at least hoped — that it was something that could be fixed. If I made the right moves when I arrived.

Today we know better — that there was nothing I could have done — but at the time, I was worried that I was going to mishandle things, and that the situation was going to get *worse*.

Ironic? You bet, but I'll save my rant about the irony of that fear until later.

For the moment, I stared vacantly at the screen.

As you can hopefully understand, I was in no way looking forward to this. There were no pirates to outwit, no Martians to bully... *nothing* redeemable about the situation, even as it stood in that early state.

But part of the job in Defense Command is helping in situations like this, like them or not. And to all the anti-Empire crowd out there, I want them to remember that we went in to help because *nobody else could*. Egesta went bad, but we honestly tried to help because the Empire was the only power with the muscle to make a difference.

Again, I'll stop myself short of that tangent. Suffice it to say I was dreading this mission from the first seconds, and my attitude was in freefall for the whole flight up to Egesta.

Fortunately, I wasn't being left alone to dwell on my reluctance.

Karen was on my bed, and now she rolled onto her side and let out a long sigh, "I prefer it when saving the day is easier than this."

I nodded slowly — she definitely had that right. I'm sure at this point in any movie some needlessly pretentious dialogue would be inserted, some statement on the cruelties of war or the horrid nature of humanity.

Karen, however, is so much better than that. She helped lower my heart rate, helped ease my mind just enough so I didn't get swamped by the gravity of the problem. She kept perspective alive.

And, of course, she did all of this without saying a thing. As I looked at her and her eyes locked with mine, her unshakable calm and wisdom just seemed to carry through her gaze.

How about that, eh — not only is she a ship fighter and a ground combatant, she can send messages with her eyes that would put many philosophers out of work.

I'll say this now and probably many times again in this book (and of course beyond): I really wouldn't have survived this without Karen. Not a chance.

My eyes drifted back to the main screen after a few moments… or maybe it was seconds… of meeting Karen's gaze, and I let out another sigh.

We were flying straight into a civil war. One day out.

Wolf and *Honesty* raced through space.

CHAPTER SIX
WELCOME TO BELT TWO

"You *cannot* take these supplies, sir."

That was Lieutenant Commander Fiona Kellerman, one of Sharon Stanton's senior staff officers for Belt Two base, and she and two regular-duty spacers were standing with arms folded, blocking the hatch to Belt Two base's arms storage bay.

Captain Dwight Bahim was nose-to-nose with Fiona, and he, of course, was the skipper of Sean Cook's frigate, *Yukon*. Behind Bahim were a dozen of his squadron's SF guards, each of them carrying only a sidearm because they'd left all their EP-5s with the Guild.

"We're entitled to those weapons, we filed the paperwork. Stand aside Lieutenant Commander," Bahim's tone was stern, but those of you who know Fiona Kellerman's reputation from later life will know his tone did nothing to dissuade her.

"Your paperwork is being processed," Fiona's tone was dead. "You take them, that'll be a criminal act against the interests of the service."

"*That* is blatant insubordination, Lieutenant Commander," Bahim boomed, and Fiona tilted her head with a rather unimpressed gaze.

"*That* wasn't insubordination. Now, if I was calling you a rapist and a murderer, *that* would be insubordination."

It's funny, now that I think of it, this incident was the first one that ever brought Fiona to my attention — and what an entrance.

"Lieutenant Savilla! I am placing this officer under arrest for insubordination!" Bahim was being creative with his intimidation attempts; one of his SFers stepped forward and drew her sidearm, not raising it but certainly trying to stare Fiona down.

Fiona wasn't armed, nor were the two young loading dock supervisors with her, but the three stood their ground. Word had gotten around about the character and actions of the Independent Squadron's crews, and barely-contained rage was the general response from Defense Command personnel all through Belt Two.

Such would have been the reaction I'd have expected, to be honest. Belt Two base, like the Belt Squadron as a whole, is generally populated with the very best officers and crew — to be working at Belt Two, every woman and man needs more than a few solid recommendations.

None of the people on the base, then, were going to be high-fiving the men and women of the Independent Squadron. It might shock you to think that *anyone* would be impressed by what Cook's people did, but in those early days, before Egesta really got out of control, I did hear some supportive rumblings from the darker corners of the fleet.

That's not important for the moment, though: Fiona and her two supporters were unarmed and Bahim was threatening to arrest her for insubordination.

+++

Imagine how well that went over with both Sharon Stanton and Wes, who were watching this exchange via the base internal cameras (the feed I've since watched).

Sitting in the C&C center for the base (Wes was watching from *Cheetah's* bridge), Sharon was the one who could actually react to the situation, so she tabbed the intercom and huffed a short sigh, "Marcus, Fiona will be needing your help."

"Understood."

Getting back to the standoff, Fiona had elected to lock eyes with Lieutenant Savilla, her steely glare attacking the Independent Squadron officer with relish, "What, you think you can play fast and loose, Lieutenant? You're out of line, get back with your SFers."

Savilla's mouth twisted into a bit of a snarl, and starting to raise her mag, she stepped closer to Fiona. That wasn't the best move; Fiona got a hold of Savilla's wrist, and while the Lieutenant struggled vainly, Fiona managed to wrest the gun out of her hand.

Now that must have been embarrassing.

The SFers behind Bahim bristled as their Lieutenant was disarmed, but they didn't unholster their own weapons.

"That's an action against a direct order in wartime, Lieutenant Commander. You're now in line to be shot," Bahim stepped forward, and Fiona stared right back at him.

This was only destined to get worse, which is why it was fortunate that Major Marcus Atallah, of *Cheetah's* Special Branch (of course), arrived on scene with his squad. The clomp of their boots was enough to draw the attention of *Yukon's* SF guards, and glares were exchanged between the Independent Squadron personnel and Atallah's officers.

"Is there a problem here, Lieutenant Commander?" Atallah was clearly playing the formality card, addressing his own officer before acknowledging Bahim.

Fiona straightened up and kept Savilla's mag dangling at her side, "Major, Captain Bahim here is attempting to draw fifteen palettes of MAG-90s from our stores without an order signed by Captain Stanton and Commander Liebgott."

Major Atallah nodded severely, his grip on his MAG-90 tightening as he turned to Captain Bahim, "Sir, I'm sorry, but until I see a countersigned order by the Captain and the XO, I cannot allow weapons to be released from this storage facility."

"You're in no position to give me orders, Major," Bahim boomed again.

With a barely visible nod, Atallah ordered his officers to raise their weapons, and the SFers behind Bahim tensed. These weren't panicky sorts — you can't be panicky and rape and pillage, I suppose — but they weren't fools when it came to the odds in a situation like this. They had no chance at all of beating a deployed Special Branch squad.

Bahim's eyes narrowed, sweeping quickly from Atallah to Fiona and then across a couple of the Special Branchers.

"So you *are* in a position," the Independent Squadron Captain said after a pause. "Not for long. Lieutenant, we're returning to *Yukon*."

With that, he about-faced in a smart maneuver and marched away.

Marcus Atallah lowered his weapon and turned to pat Fiona on the shoulder, "Nice work."

Fiona Kellerman let out a sigh and nodded, the adrenalin rush ending and fatigue starting to creep in. She'd made one hell of a stand...

+++

Sean Cook was annoyed. The very thought of that bastard being annoyed gives me some pleasure, though he wasn't the sort of man to allow his annoyance to go unanswered.

This meant, of course, that he was in Sharon Stanton's office next to the C&C of Belt Two base about an hour after Bahim clumped back aboard *Yukon*. And he was throwing quite a tantrum.

"As a *Commodore*, I have superior authority. I have requisitioned stores and you have no authority to overturn that requisition!"

Sharon cocked an eyebrow at the repetition in that exclamation — she was recording this conversation to protect herself against future accusations, and she figured I'd get a kick out of Cook's childish idiocy. As much as I got a kick out of anything to do with Egesta, I suppose I did get a kick out of that.

Sharon, I should say (because I really haven't spent enough time talking about her yet this series) was hardly intimidated by Cook. She'd been a combat officer, skippering a frigate with the Belt Squadron until the year before Deep Black, when a shrapnel fragment had clipped the base of her spine and she'd nearly been paralyzed. It'd taken her the two years since then to complete the requisite surgeries and to learn to walk, and though by this time she was on her feet and in her estimation ready to take combat duty, the doctors had kept her on Belt Two base, where the gravity was consistent and light enough to allow her to heal properly.

As you probably know, she was due back in space soon enough.

That all considered, it should be no surprise that Sean Cook was failing to intimidate her at the moment.

"I command this base, and I'm under orders from the Admiralty to retain those weapons until they are requisitioned by *central command*. You'll have to put your paperwork through Admiralty House, and probably explain just what happened to all your squadron's EP-5s," her tone was frosty, and Cook's eyes bored into her.

Or, as she told me later, they *tried* to bore into her.

There was then a knock on the door, and the hatch swung open before either Cook or Sharon could look towards it.

"I hear somebody tried to steal fifteen palettes of MAG-90s," Wes Pellew stepped into the office and said the words while staring directly at Cook. "Who exactly would try to pull something like that, I wonder?"

Cook's sharp stare turned on Wes, and our Belt Squadron veteran returned it with interest.

"It seems insubordination and lack of respect for the chain of command is a chronic problem around here," Cook spat the words.

"We don't like rapists and murderers flying our colors," Wes' flat retort forced Cook to take a step towards him.

"I'm sorry, let me ask again, have there been any orders that stripped me of my rank, or are you still junior to me, *Captain* Pellew?"

Wes nearly snapped, but he kept himself in check through an epic force of will, "You're still standing there a free man, aren't you?"

"I am. And I'm officially going to petition the Admiralty for command here, since you two seem incapable of putting your jobs above the wellbeing of a rock that was asking to be used for a little recreation."

This is on a recording. I wouldn't have believed he said it either, but then, by this time in my career I should have been used to the idiocy of some of the people in the service.

I guess you never get used to some things.

"You're not going to get command," Wes shook his head slowly. "Sharon, why don't you open a message window to First Lord Fiora right now. Let's see what he says."

Sharon smiled thinly, "That sounds about right."

Turning to her desk, she grabbed her remote and used it to open a new message window.

Cook's nostrils had begun to flare, and he let out a long breath, "Well, seems you've drawn a line in the sand. Can I expect my ships to receive any supplies from this base?"

Sharon's thin smile twitched, "Of *course*, Commodore. I'll give you everything you could ask for, as long as I get the right paperwork from Admiralty House. Do they have a rape requisition form?"

You might think that the 'rape and murder' card is being played too much. Did we really have to keep hitting these bastards over the head with it in every conversation, slide in as many references to it as possible? Well, *yes*. We Defense Command officers at this time were still just getting our heads around it.

I mean, our *job* is to defend (hence the name) and so when we hear about our own service doing something as ghastly as what the Independent Squadron had done, we make a point of calling them on it. Sharon and Wes were both ready to lock Cook up as soon as they could safely do so, but in the meantime they'd just embarrass him or make him feel as uncomfortable as possible.

It was all they could do, so they were beating the 'rape and murder' horse right to death.

Back to the conversation, Cook took the insult and turned red, then grunted and spat more words, "We'll be breaking dock in the morning, then. I'll go somewhere I can get support. And you two will be remembered for jeopardizing the war effort for your petty reasons."

He then stomped out.

"Petty," Sharon muttered the word. "*Petty*."

Wes' harsh gaze had followed Cook as the Commodore stormed out of the office, so now he turned back to face Sharon, "Sure. I suppose to him the law is petty. But now we have a new problem."

Sharon frowned, "Uhm…"

"Think about it," Wes said quietly. "Where can he go to get help? There aren't a lot of Belt colonies with the firepower to keep him in check…"

Sharon's eyes widened ever so slightly, "And Belt Fourteen base…"

Wes nodded.

They did have a new problem.

CHAPTER SEVEN

PLANNING

Karen and I were sitting in *Wolf's* briefing room, waiting in silence for the rest of the people due at the meeting.

I hadn't slept at all well the night before — this was the day before we arrived at Egesta, and as you might have guessed from the state I was in when last we visited my cabin, I wasn't in sleeping mode.

Karen was herself looking slightly ragged (all things being relative, of course, because her ragged is, well… well it's not *ragged* in my book), and we were both wary of what we were walking into. My hope was that this meeting would help take the edge off for both of us.

You see, Karen and I had spent the trip to this point reviewing Mark Gunney's logs, looking over the data from Egesta and essentially plunging ourselves headfirst into a very nasty civil war. Being smart officers (yes, I know it's an ambitious claim to say I was smart), we were able to foresee hundreds of horrid possibilities, things we might find, things we might not be able to help.

This meeting, I hoped, would put some of those rampant 'what-ifs' to bed, and replace them with more definite 'this is what we can dos'.

I was reflecting on this when I realized Karen was staring at me, so I looked back at her. For a little while then, we just stared. We couldn't talk anymore — there was nothing encouraging left to be said. All I knew was I was damned glad Karen was on *Wolf* with me. If she hadn't been… well, you can guess how much of a wreck I'd have been already had she not been aboard *Wolf* at the beginning of the war. It probably won't really come across until I write my pre-war memoirs for you, but these were by far the most stressful times of my life to that point. But we were going into this together, and I could take some comfort in that.

The hatch opened after a few minutes, and we broke our eye contact immediately, turning to watch a few people step in: Matt Baxter was first, then Kyle Stranks, Charlie Peters and finally Veronica Choctaw, the Lieutenant Colonel in charge of the Hawke Guards that had joined us. Each of these fine people nodded to us in turn before settling into chairs all around the table, and Karen and I turned our seats to face them as they settled.

Matt, whose reservations about this operation were the greatest (not because he didn't want to help — he was desperate to lend a hand at Egesta — but because he knew Karen and I would inevitably be in harm's way) started us off.

"We think we've got this worked out," he said quietly, and I frowned thoughtfully. "I've taken roll, and between SF and volunteers, we think we can arm and deploy approximately 350 of the crew, not including Charlie's team."

Stranks (remember, just recently Matt's replacement as head of security forces

2231 · MARS AGAINST EMPIRE

aboard) leaned forward, "Yes, and I checked our weapons stocks, we can equip at least 200 of that force with EP-5s. The rest will be carrying sidearms only, but we're thinking that for security duty at the docks and maybe inside some of the complexes, that'll be sufficient."

I nodded slowly, glancing at Karen — the crew of *Wolf* was hers, after all.

"Sounds good. We'll maintain standard skeleton watch aboard ship," she said softly. "Just as though we were sending the crew down on shore leave..."

There were slow nods at the ironic remark, and then our eyes turned to Charlie.

I don't think I've actually devoted any time so far to Charlie's reaction to all this. When last I left him in *The Hawke Mission*, he and Lia were about to part at court, ready to go their separate ways once again. I still don't know how they survived doing that repeatedly, but anyway, the important thing now is Charlie's state of mind.

Let's see. While Karen and I were near despairing at the mess, Charlie was coldly getting ready to go in there to clean it up. You have to understand Charlie's state of mind when it comes to things like this: he doesn't get hung up (as I tend to) on the whys and hows of the origins of something. That's not to say he doesn't understand how a problem started — on the contrary, he knows all too well. No, he just has the ability to avoid getting caught up in the horrendous beginning, and to move straight on to finding the bad guys and, well, hurting them. So his face was a picture of coolness and professionalism.

"My squad is ready to go in. Between *Honesty* and *Friendly*, they put a single squad on the ground. When we arrive, I'll be able to double that. Hopefully it'll give us some flexibility with what we do," even the cadence of his speech seemed unflapped.

"And that's where we'll hope to be useful. No offense to you, Lieutenant Stranks, but many of your volunteers aren't going to be cut out for forward operations. You need field work done in an urban setting, my girls and boys can get it done," Veronica Choctaw spoke for the first time.

I can't say I've ever gotten to know Veronica all that well, but she's as good as they come — Lia doesn't let just anyone into the top ranks of the Hawke Guards. You know how big troopers often bellow what they're saying as if they have something to prove? None of that from Veronica. The woman's words were tough, but then, so was she, and so were her 'girls and boys.'

And she was right, too: the 150 Hawke Guards she had aboard *Honesty* turned out to be a huge offensive... if 'offensive' is the word for it... asset.

"That's true," Stranks agreed with Choctaw's assessment, and Charlie shifted in his seat.

"Though if I'm reading this situation right, we won't be playing a strictly 'offensive' role in any capacity, will we?" he asked, looking my way, and I nodded.

This, of course, was the more complicated part of an intervention like this: what exactly were we going in there to do?

"The way Andrea has it set up — and I have to agree with her on this — we're not actually on either side; we're in the middle trying to keep civilians out of harm's way while the two rival governing bodies hammer away at each other."

And that was all I had to explain to these fine officers; they understood the implications that lay therein. It's pretty straightforward when you think about it — we obviously weren't going to help the Guild, and we couldn't help the Egesta government without making it look like a puppet administration and killing its credibility.

That left us in the middle with no enemy...

"Is there any chance of us getting enough firepower together to take control of the situation?" Matt asked the question evenly, and I shrugged very slightly.

"John is looking into getting a battalion out here and that might work... but that'd probably be a week away. In the meantime, we'll have to stabilize the situation as best we can."

This meeting was, in fact, helping me feel a little better about the mission — not *much* better, but as I'd hoped, the actual discussion about our options was a good thing.

"Now, we're presuming we're going to dock at the commercial cargo locks *Friendly* is holding, and that means we're going to enter the six-building defensive pocket Andrea has put together," Karen leaned forward and tapped a few buttons on the table, waking up the wallscreen and bringing up a map of the Egesta Government Dome. Six buildings highlighted themselves.

I'd seen this map before, and so had the other officers in the room, but now as we all looked at it together it seemed to take on slightly more gravity. Those six buildings — the ore warehouse, the government building, the admin building, a stadium, a hospital and a high school — were all that Defense Command ostensibly held in the dome, and they were more spread out than any of us would have preferred.

As I learned in *The Rogue Commodore*, maps probably aren't going to be appearing in the front pages of this book, so imagine a curved line, starting at the eastern edge of the dome and curling in towards the center. Basically, that was the layout of those six buildings, with government and administrative buildings at the center, the ore warehouse on the edge (unsurprisingly).

It was fifteen kilometers from one end of that line to the other, and we weren't carrying any hover vehicles that we could use to cut down travel time.

"Those six buildings are the only safe places for civilians in the Government Dome," Charlie said quietly. "And I don't think Andrea can have more than twenty or thirty guards at each. They have to be our top priority."

He was saying what we were all thinking.

"I think we rotate Andrea's volunteers out as soon as we can — pull them back to the ore warehouse as a defensive reserve," Karen glanced at me and then Charlie. "They're going to need to rest after all they've been doing. Put fresh bodies at every building, use our *Wolf* volunteers and SF to secure them, and keep Veronica's companies back for rapid deployment to trouble spots."

Charlie nodded at her suggestion, "That's what I'd do."

"That's what we're doing then," I affirmed their words with a nod. "And when we land, I'm going to have to go after the head of the Guild and the President... Governor... I can't remember which. I'll find out and go after both of them. I need them in a room together, and they're not leaving until I get a ceasefire."

Karen nodded once at my ambitious words, and the others at the table repeated the motion.

"And longer term, we stabilize the situation and wait for the cavalry to roll in to take over," Charlie looked back at the map. "Not how I imagined the first major ground deployment of this war."

I nodded, "Let's just hope the Martians are back on their heels. The last thing I want now is to have a Martian squadron drop on us while we're trying to save these people. We'll have to keep looking over our shoulder while we're there..."

That was something that I may not have sufficiently repeated yet: the war was still on, and while we were racing to quickly fix the damage caused by one of our own, we had to contend with the possibility that we were about to be hit by the Martians. As you probably know, the Martians didn't come after us during these weeks; by all accounts, the failure of their first blow out at the Belt had left them disorganized. But we didn't know that, so we were obliged to worry.

Indeed, that lack of knowledge about the Martian military situation in the region played a considerable part in the Egesta crisis as a whole.

But that's enough of that for now. As we officers sat in *Wolf's* briefing room, considering the mess we were about to dive into, there were further developments at Belt Two...

CHAPTER EIGHT

THROW A TANTRUM, RUN AWAY

That chapter title essentially explains my perception of just what Sean Cook did after the MAG-90 incident. It's perhaps too juvenile a characterization for a man of Cook's obvious *maturity*, but there it is.

You see, the morning after he returned to his flagship, *Nova Scotia*, the unpleasant fellow began warming up his reactors, and his squadron's ships began to break Belt Two orbit under maneuvering jets, aligning themselves in cruising order.

Arriving on *Cheetah's* bridge, Wes headed straight for the front monitors, then looked to his Sensors and Communications Officer, Kate Levec, "Any idea where they're angling for, Kate?"

He already had a pretty good idea — Belt Fourteen base, with its small arms depot, was a likely spot for Cook to find his MAG-90s. In case you're not too familiar with the layout of the Belt colonies, Fourteen is the rock on the Hawke-side flank of our Imperial possessions, so aside from Belt Two, it's probably the most visited port of call for Defense Command shipping. We don't know exactly why Cook didn't go straight there to get his supplies in the first place — no one could've stopped him — but I suppose the man was just eager to report in at the much posher Belt Two base, to be heralded as a hero by the media or some other such thing.

In any case, Wes was fairly certain Belt Fourteen was his ultimate destination, he just needed confirmation...

"He's not logging a flight plan," Kate began evenly, pacing behind the consoles of her technicians, "but the vector they're angling out on is consistent with either the Protectorate or Belt Fourteen."

Wes let out a grunt and nodded, "Of course."

"They'll have their reactors hot in about fifteen minutes, by the look of these readings," Kate Levec continued.

That drew a surprised glance from Wes — and rightly so. Driving reactors from idle to hot was (as you might remember from the plight of *Indiana* in *The Hawke Mission*) a generally much more lengthy process. Fast-warmup was just one of the many modifications the *North America*-class frigates and *Canada*-class corvettes of the Independent Squadron had been fitted with, to improve their pirate-hunting abilities.

It'd take *Cheetah* (or any other *Predator*) at least twenty minutes to spin up from the orbiting standby status they were being held at... a regular *North America* frigate would take at least thirty...

But those numbers weren't hugely important at the moment.

"Alright, I'm going to need to consult with the brass on this one," Wes folded his arms and turned to screen two. "Kate, I need a priority message to Admiralty House."

◆◆◆

First Lord John Fiora was sitting in his office with a pile of pads that he says would've broken the back of any single Ensign who tried to move them all at once. His task at that moment was to rush through the recommissioning of about a dozen ships from the mothball yards. Battleships and frigates, mainly — antiquated ships that were slow and not particularly powerful, but that could *probably* fill out the ranks of the Home Fleet if John needed to take the Heavy Squadron and what was left of the Light Squadron out for offensive work.

This sort of thing *always* takes a lot of paperwork.

But when the message window on his office's main screen chimed with that special 'high priority' ping, he looked up. Of course, the ping didn't mean that just Wes had flagged the message as a top priority — most skippers sending signal traffic to Admiralty House label it high priority (why else would it be sent to Admiralty House?). No, the chime meant his staff had glanced at the dispatch and had forwarded it on.

And as John tapped the message up and watched Wes Pellew appear on his monitor, he agreed with the assessment.

He couldn't afford to be worrying exclusively about Egesta and Sean Cook at this moment — it might be easy in hindsight to assume that our First Lord was spending every waking hour thinking only about the crisis, but remember again that none of us knew how bad it was going to get. And John sort of had an Imperial war on his plate — I hear those can be rather distracting.

Nonetheless, he laid the pad he'd been reading back down onto his desk, then hit play.

"Good morning, sir," Wes began (he told me later he'd realized as soon as he'd finished it that it was actually afternoon on Earth, but didn't have time to change the message), "Commodore Cook yesterday attempted to draw fifteen palettes of MAG-90s from Belt Two stores, but we turned him away. He's since threatened to break dock, and as I speak to you now, he's started warming his reactors and is lining up his ships for a run to Belt Fourteen base. I have one ship, Captain Samuels' *Alberta*, out that way sir. But because of the situation, I don't want to give chase without your orders."

This might sound odd to you — a squadron commander calling home for permission to chase down a menace like Cook, but remember a few things: first, this wasn't Wes' squadron by assignment, he was just ('just') the senior Captain commanding, so he had no Admiralty-appointed authority to act entirely on his own. Moreover, there was a war on, and it would be entirely reasonable to expect that John would take a look at the overall Imperial defensive situation and say, "No, no we can't risk Belt Two by having all our ships abandon it."

So checking in was, as far as I'm concerned, a wise and considerate move by Wes. This wasn't an uncomplicated situation, and Wes knew full well he was only seeing a slim slice of the Imperial defense picture. He wasn't going to put the entire Empire at risk just to chase Cook, no matter how much he wanted to nail the man to a wall.

John thus listened, with a frown, to the situation, then looked at the pile of paperwork on his desk and let out a long breath. Things had been quiet at the Belt colonies since *Wolf* had departed… the independent rocks on the outer flank of the Hawke Protectorate were still potentially vulnerable, but Mik Mikaelsen was looking after them. Marlene Stoll was seeing unusual raiding activity in the Venus sector, but even if that turned into something, it wouldn't affect the Belt too much…

And Greg was on his way, with both his own *Warspite* and Becky Afflighen's *Goliath* — two battleships that had left Earth about seventy hours before this message was sent… meaning they had at least another seven days' travel to get to Belt Two.

There really wasn't an obvious option here, as you're probably (hopefully) realizing; there was no way John could cover everything at once, the question thus came to how badly he wanted Cook to stand trial.

And to go to the gallows.

Well, John tells me that was a relatively easy answer.

Tapping his controls, he opened a reply window, rolled his chair slightly sideways to make sure he wasn't being eclipsed by his pile of pads, then looked squarely into the monitor, "Wes, go get the bastard. Leave a corvette at Belt Two, take the rest with you. If you get the chance, arrest him. It's imperative you don't get into a shooting fight with him… if you can help it. I want his ships intact when this is done, so if you could avoid blasting them to pieces that'd be helpful."

He paused, deciding that was as much as Wes needed to hear, "Alright, good hunting, Wes. Good luck."

You, like me, are probably pleased to hear this, and rightly so, but you may not be aware of just how much flack John caught for this move at the time. Parliament wasn't too inclined to be sympathetic to John's position — questions went something like 'you stripped our biggest Naval base outside Luna of its defenses during a time of *war* to arrest an officer who hadn't committed crimes in the Empire?'

Don't condemn Parliament for asking those questions. I'll keep harping on these sorts of points, because to be honest I'm fed up with people today judging every action we took back then through the bitter (or 'enlightened') lenses of hindsight.

We know today that Cook's actions were the catalyst for a massive tragedy, but again, at the time there was a war on. Bigger fish to fry, or that's how Parliament (not wrongly) saw it. Many thought that sending a sizable force to deal with our own while the Martians were still prowling out there was dangerous, and their concern was valid. But John, thankfully, had a great deal of foresight… and he was as eager to get his hands on Cook as the rest of us.

As John's message exited his send buffer, he briefly leaned back in his chair and let out a sigh. He was distinctly aware of the fact that his confident words to Wes were rather ambitious — there wasn't much chance that even two *Predator*-class frigates and two *Noble*-class corvettes from the Belt Squadron could by themselves intimidate and arrest Cook and the Independent Squadron.

Perhaps, though, the odds could be leveled. Given orbits at this time in the late (Imperial Standard Season) fall of 2231, Belt Fourteen was actually considerably closer to Earth than Belt Two.

So John opened a new message window, and you probably know the rest.

CHAPTER NINE

PREPARE TO PURSUE

The faces of the Belt Squadron COs appeared on *Cheetah's* bridge screens about three minutes after Wes finished watching John's message. The Independent Squadron had, by that time, already boosted out of orbit and was quickly working up speed on a vector for Belt Fourteen, moving at a clip faster than any normal *North America*-class frigate should have been able to manage.

As Wes stepped up to the front of his bridge, he nodded in turn to Kris, Isoruku Togo, Elise De Winter and Katya Romanov. Sharon Stanton appeared last from her C&C on Belt Two base.

"I've got orders straight from First Lord Fiora," Wes began evenly. "We're not letting them out of our sight. But I'm ordered to leave a corvette behind, and that'll have to be you, Katya."

He was saying that venerable old *Sackville* wasn't going on this chase, and you can probably guess why: these specially modified Independent Squadron ships could well be a match for the newest ships in the Belt Squadron. It seemed almost inevitable that they would thoroughly outclass old *Sackville*.

Katya, always a classy officer, simply nodded — everyone in the Belt Squadron desperately wanted to at least *try* to get Cook under arrest, but practical realities didn't allow everyone to join the chase.

"Everyone else, we're boosting hard and fast. We don't know their top speed, but I'm guessing it's at least as good as our own. We'll head directly for Belt Fourteen…" Wes glanced to the main screen, his Helm and Navigation Officer having put a star chart of the plotted course up on the display with transit time listed, "…so that's about three days direct. Cruising order will be *Cheetah*, *Generous*, *Lady Grace*, and you bringing up the rear with *Lion*, Kris. I doubt Cook will try to jump us, but if he does I want a frigate on either end."

A series of nods was the response, and Wes continued, "Alright. Follow my lead. Sharon, hold down the fort. We'll be back."

Sharon Stanton nodded and cut her connection, and then Katya Romanov bowed her head slightly, "Good hunting out there, Wes. I shall look after the fort while you're out."

With a smile, Wes bobbed his head, "Thanks Katya. Take care."

Romanov cut her connection, and Wes turned to his Helm and Navigation Officer, "Get the drives ready for a heavy burn."

While Wes was getting ready to leave Belt Two space, *Wolf* and *Honesty* were getting to within a day of Egesta space, and there we're going to see a turn in the narrative of the book. So far we've been watching Wes and Cook butt heads a lot; now we're going to change gears and spend a lot more time on Egesta.

And I wish I could say the days to come were going to be a fun and light, but who would I be fooling if I tried to say that? Take a deep breath, because we're about to get into it.

I'm going to break chapters here.

CHAPTER TEN
WELCOME TO EGESTA

"So while we're down there, you've got overall command, Jim," I looked to Jim Hannigan, and the Lieutenant Commander nodded evenly.

"We'll keep things up here under control, you just worry about fixing this," he replied evenly, and I had to smile. Jim Hannigan had been with me since *Friendly*, and his confidence was appreciated.

"We'll do our damnedest," Karen was beside me, and like me she was in 'landing' kit, with her sidearm and a set of extra power cells strapped to either leg.

With a final nod, she and I left *Wolf's* bridge for what felt like the last time — cryptic, I know, but we had a feeling that we'd never be back, or at the very least that it'd be a *long* time before we could return. Nothing like dread to add to such an occasion. Matt and Kyle Stranks fell into step with us as we exited the bridge, and in the corridor beyond Charlie Peters and his squad joined too.

Together we all marched towards the docking chute.

About an hour prior, Karen had supervised as Erica Martin gently sidled *Wolf* up to the second of five docking chutes protruding from the Egesta Government Dome's ore warehouse. We were thus parked next to *Friendly*, with *Honesty* locked onto the docking chute on *Friendly's* far side. Once the Hawke Guards and the last handful of volunteers came out of *Honesty*, the ship's XO, Lieutenant Commander Ashby, was going to break dock and take up a cruising orbit around Egesta, ready to be a rapid responder in case something unexpected showed up while we were tied up on the rock.

When I got to *Wolf's* lock I wasn't really thinking about that, though; I was steeling myself for what I was certain was going to be a horrible situation. Boy, when I'm right...

There were long files of SF guards and volunteer crew members carrying an assortment of mags and EP-5s along the corridors leading to the locks, all their faces as grim as mine must have been, all carrying small duffles with MREs, power cells and first aid kits. We weren't exactly a well-appointed ground combat force, but I was damned sure any miners with guns would think twice before trying to toy with us.

Well, they had better think twice...

As I came to a stop next to the lock hatch, I nodded to the Ensign running the door controls, and the hatch popped. Feeling surprisingly moved by the moment (sorry if that sounds overly sentimental), I turned back to the throng of armed crew and SF in the corridor, "Alright, we all know why we're here. The Independent Squadron started a mess; we're going to clean it up, as best we can. Stay safe and do *good* down there. You with me?"

That got a cheer, but I hardly heard it as I turned immediately and stepped through the open hatch. Karen was instantly beside me, her shoulder discreetly rubbing against mine for a few seconds. Charlie was on my other side, one hand on the handle of his MAG-90, the other swinging with that controlled sort of motion Special Branch officers bent on doing dirty work tend to walk with.

If nothing else, I was sure that Charlie and his team would do a hell of a lot of good. The rest of us would do our best, but Charlie and his Special Branchers would change the complexion of this whole affair.

Veronica Choctaw (who was about to be reunited with her troops), Matt and Kyle Stranks followed right behind us, barking orders to Ensigns and Lieutenants who'd been assigned command of the makeshift ground squads we'd assembled.

The volunteer force was on its way down.

Two ships over from us, Commander Mark Gunney was similarly standing outside his lock, and while most of his volunteers were already on Egesta, he had 150-odd Hawke Guards and a handful of crew ready to go down with him.

Looking to his XO and friend, Lieutenant Commander Ashby, he nodded, "Alright, I'll get this march of the damned started. See you on the flip side."

With a nod from Ashby, he looked up at the Guards, "We're walking into a mess, boys and girls. Let's find the bastards responsible for it and make sure they don't make it any worse."

The Hawke Guards didn't seem inclined to offer any verbal responses, but that didn't bother Mark. He turned and headed down the chute towards the ore warehouse.

As we got to the bottom of the chute and through the confusing reorientation chamber, we emerged into a huge open warehouse that had been segmented into 'rooms' by low walls built of crates. There was really no privacy — as we came through the reorientation chamber, we were able to see over those low walls — but there wasn't all that much here. About a hundred refugees were billeted (if such a generous term could be used) on one side of the warehouse, and a massive half-organized area of mixed supplies occupied another.

There were barely any green Defense Command uniforms around — maybe six were in sight as the massive throng of volunteers began to emerge into the chamber. I'd honestly expected to see a large command center, or at least a command post with a mobile comm and a small rapid response team of guards or Special Branch... optimistic, wasn't I?

As the docking chutes began ejecting over 350 volunteers into the warehouse, some of the refugees took notice, and as they perked up a surprised Ensign started jogging our way, his taught face brightening as he came to a stop before Karen and me.

"Sir, thank God. I wasn't told you were here already, but comms have been intermittent with Government House all day. Thank God you're here..." he was stammering and repeating himself, and as I studied his drawn, pale face, and noted the massive bags under his eyes, I realized the man probably hadn't slept for days.

I'd find out later that his fatigue was the reason he'd been posted back to the ore warehouse. This was the 'quiet' building, the place for rest. I had no concept of the horrors this young Ensign (who asked to remain anonymous) had witnessed.

"We're here, indeed. Where can I find Commander Kiley?" I asked quietly, and he nodded a couple of times.

"Of course, yes, Commander Kiley… you can just follow me over to our map, sir…"

As he turned and led the way, I bobbed my head to the officers who'd been with me at the briefing the day before, "Let's have a look."

While the junior officers started organizing their teams and nervously studied the gloomy warehouse, we headed for the map table — the nerve center of this building. It was a tippy alloy table with a creased and tattered city map on it, marked up with red and green pens, and with a portable comm and its docking station on one end. That was it.

Mark Gunney came to the table as soon as he realized that's where we were headed, and we all gathered around as the exhausted Ensign began explaining the situation.

"We're spread thin, sirs, ma'ams… I won't lie, a lot of our people are going to burn out I think. I mean, to be honest, I already have…"

It's not the sort of thing you expect to hear from an Ensign — usually an Ensign's unwritten job description is to be gallant and get noticed, in order to get an early promotion. But in a place like Egesta, career was the least of the concerns for the young professionals.

"That's alright," Karen's tone can be so soothing, almost motherly, when she needs it to be, and she quickly took over the impromptu briefing, very gently asking the questions to which we needed answers.

"So," she began, "we're the green lines?"

The Ensign nodded, "That's us. As you can see, ma'am, we're holding the six buildings we've held since Commander Gunney left. But we've now stripped down the guard forces to bare minimum. See, the Guild moved into town with everything they've got, now, and the government and the Boscawen mercs are holed up in the barracks on the other side of town…"

He pointed to a building on the opposite edge of the dome from the ore warehouse we were standing in, "Word is the government is planning a counterattack to retake the dome, but I don't know how they could be… there are so many Guild fighters in the dome now. Stalemate though, no proper fighting. Commander Kiley thinks the Governor is playing for time, waiting for you to show up, ma'am… then hoping peace can be arranged."

"The Governor knows we're not siding with anyone?" I asked too quickly, cutting off Karen's own question to the same effect.

"Yes, sir. Commander Kiley's been adamant, despite the Governor's objections."

Charlie was frowning, I realized, though I didn't know why… but Karen did.

"Ensign," she asked softly again (and in reality called him by name), "if there's no more fighting going on, why have you stripped your defenses?"

The Ensign nodded, and I don't think I can convey the unsettled vibration that seemed to run through him as he did. He didn't look entirely stable, and who could blame him?

"Well, ma'am, Guild control is not proving… benign, I think is the word. Ma'am. I mean. The Guild is a bunch of bitter miners, and it's wrong for me to say they're all really horrible people… but I think they only gave the guns to the horrible people. They're saying all civilians in the Government Dome are secret government fighters. It's turning into… uhm. We're seeing a lot of torture. A lot of… uhm…"

The way he couldn't actually finish that sentence sent a chill down my spine.

"It's alright," Karen said soothingly. "We understand."

We didn't. Well, no, I think we intellectually understood.

"Now, you and your guards here at the ore warehouse should go back to *Friendly* for some rest. Take the rest of the day and tomorrow off. We'll call you back if we need you, but it's time you sleep in your own beds and get some real meals. We'll take over."

The Ensign nodded gratefully to Karen, and then stepped away from the table, waving to the SF guards who were here with him. Those guards all seemed to be moving with a grim determination — most were older than the young Ensign, and it seemed evident they were probably the ones really in charge of the defense of the building, while the Ensign tried to regain his grip. That's not to take anything away from the Ensign; he'd volunteered to come down here, to help. He was young and he hadn't been ready for what he ran into.

I don't think anyone blamed him. If anyone did, they can come talk to me.

With a very deep sigh, I looked at Karen, "So reading between the lines, Andrea's using most of her volunteers as a mobile force, going out there to try to get civilians out of the way while the Guild troops roll in."

She nodded, and Charlie leaned forward, planting his hands on the table and letting his MAG-90 dangle by its harness over the map.

"We need to get out there," he said firmly.

Don't mistake that for a reactionary statement; Charlie's tactical mind was working double time.

"If our people are that worn down and they're witnessing atrocities, we need to pull them out before they snap and start intervening with firepower. If one of them opens up on a Guild unit the game's up — they'll overrun us before we can deploy our volunteers to stop them."

Definitely a concern — a serious one. You might be thinking 'well the cavalry's arrived, can't we just stop the Guild?'. Short answer: no, not yet. Not until there was a proper combat force on hand to fight back a horde of angry miners if we started a fight.

No, we were now in a better position than Andrea had been in, but we weren't ready to take on thousands of miners. Particularly not when so many civilians would get caught in the crossfire.

"Send my troops out to do that," Veronica Choctaw spoke for the first time. "This is the sort of thing we're trained for..."

"Yes, but I don't know how Andrea's people will react if non-Defense Command personnel try to relieve them. We'll have to put some SF with each of your squads," Matt Baxter inserted himself into the discussion, and Charlie nodded approvingly.

"Exactly. My squad will stay with you for now, Ken. Just in case someone tries to jump us. I think we better find Andrea..."

I nodded at Charlie's words, "Definitely. The only way we can stop all this is with a heart-to-heart with the leaders. I need Andrea's take on that, and then we're going to have some line-crossing to do."

There were a series of nods from around the table, eyes turning to me for final orders.

"Alright, Matt, you'll deploy our volunteers to these buildings to replace the existing security details. Send any of the volunteers who need a break back here. Kyle, coordinate with Veronica to get some of our volunteers with each squad she sends out. Charlie, you're with me. You too, Mark, I need your familiarity with the dome."

It went without saying that Karen and I were sticking together.

"Alright, let's move."

That's just what we did.

CHAPTER ELEVEN

TO THE STREETS

I had expected the streets of Egesta to be entirely abandoned, but they surprisingly weren't. Some families were moving from doorway to doorway when we found them, trying to get to the shelter of one of the Defense Command buildings. Their tearful relief at running into our long column of black, green and blue-clad troops was wrenching, so I tried to distance myself from it.

Others weren't as happy to see us. There was no line established here — Andrea had no way of fortifying the long main street that linked five of the six buildings she held, so the Guild fighters were wandering through in small gangs, trying to pick up the families that were running.

Pick them up on what charge, you ask? Come on, if the civilians are *running*, surely they have reason to flee from the Guild. Meaning they're obviously enemies of the Guild. Makes sense, doesn't it? Must have, because the four different Guild squads we saw on the walk from the ore warehouse down to the stadium seemed to believe it.

As we headed for that stadium, we passed the high school and the hospital, and I neglected to enter either. I didn't want to see what was in those shelters, which probably means I'm a coward. Sorry, I just wasn't ready to see people recovering from whatever had been done to them… not then.

The stadium was, as far as Mark could guess, the place to which most of the refugees were fleeing. It was about two-thirds of the way between the ore warehouse and the government buildings, nearer the center of the dome than the high school or the hospital, so it was easy for many families to reach.

Well, as easy as getting anywhere while being hunted could possibly be.

It also could hold many thousands of people, which made it a logical place to try to shelter large numbers of refugees.

I should point out, though, that moving on foot as we were, it took just about two hours to get there, and we weren't sauntering.

By the time we arrived, Matt had already split off almost eighty of our *Wolf* volunteers and SF to guard the hospital and high school, much to the relief of the junior *Friendly* and *Honesty* volunteers standing warily outside those buildings. Fresh troops, *food*, new energy… in countless ways, our arrival was helping the Defense Command personnel who'd courageously put themselves into the middle of this quagmire. That was gratifying.

When we entered the stadium parking lot, we found its outer reaches empty; closer to the stadium building, a few hover trucks were parked in what I think were bus drop-off lanes, and a crude checkpoint could be seen at the main entrance. There were, in fact, similar checkpoints on all sides of the building — and they were the only real defensive positions the building had.

And to give you a mental image, these checkpoints were simply aluminum sheds that I'm guessing came out of a raided hardware store, and they certainly weren't mag-shielded.

As our force poured into the parking lot, then, and the Hawke Guards in particular spread out on our west flank (the one facing the center of town), there was some confusion at the checkpoint (nearly 500 meters away). The exhausted Lieutenant at the post wasn't sure what she was seeing — she hadn't been informed we were coming, or that we'd even arrived. I suppose the communications between Government House and the stadium hadn't been working well either.

She sounded the alarm immediately, and prudently, and about fifteen SF and volunteers rushed out the main entrance with grim determination that I could somehow sense from even that long distance. Hopping into three of their trucks — one volunteer jumping into the cab and turning it on while the rest piled into the back and stood brandishing weapons — the guards came flying at us, only veering off when I (and I think all of the *Wolf* volunteers behind me) began to wave broadly.

Our green tunics finally gave us up as Defense Command personnel and the trucks turned back and landed, their guards leaping out and coming out to meet us.

It was another welcome greeting — they were so glad to see us I really didn't know how to react. I shook some hands, patted some backs, and found my way to the Lieutenant who'd been at the shed. She, too, has asked me to keep her identity secret, and so I will.

But as I shook her hand, she started shaking her head, "Peace and blessings be with you, sir. Peace and mercy be with you. We've hoped we'd have help…"

"And with you, Lieutenant," I nodded slowly. "This is your entire defense force?"

She replied with her own nod, "Apologies for calling it out, but we're particularly on edge. We think the Guild knows we have 4,000 refugees here. If they decide to take them we'll be unable to–"

"*Four* thousand?" My surprise shouldn't really have been so acute — this was, after all, the most logical place for a large number of refugees, but somehow I must have concluded that only fifteen defenders meant the stadium wasn't full.

"Yes sir, we have cots set up for them on the field… Commander Kiley had us take the beds from furniture and mattress stores. Defense Command will have to pay the damages after this is settled…" the Lieutenant was definitely more together than the Ensign we'd met at the ore warehouse, though her voice contained a layer of desperation that again chilled me.

Karen suddenly appeared at my shoulder, extending her hand and addressing the Lieutenant by name — evidently the Lieutenant and Karen had a history (that I won't get into here, because it might betray the Lieutenant's identity).

They chatted quickly, and as they did I excused myself and proceeded up the steps to the doors of the stadium, realizing as I did that there were dozens of faces pressed against the glass of the doors.

In the excitement of our arrival, no one had told the civilians inside that the guards rushing out weren't actually repelling an attack after all. Not quite thinking clearly, I stepped up to the nearest outer door, opened it, and then crossed the lobby, and opened the inner door.

There was an avalanche of people all of a sudden — many of them recognizing me from the media reports they'd seen over the past couple of years.

Somebody yelled, "It's Barron! Commodore Barron's here to save us!"

The noise that followed was overwhelming, and a crushing wave of people tried to get close to me to say something. All I seem to remember is the press of hands, hugs, tears and cheers… I'll admit openly that I think I've repressed a good deal of this, and I care not to recover too much of it.

What I do recall is Karen's arrival — drawing an even more positive reaction — and then Charlie forced his way in, along with Matt and about forty guards. I don't know how long it took, but the crowd was eventually calmed and returned to their cots on the football pitch in the center of the stadium, leaving Karen and I standing behind the top row of seats, hands on the railing, looking out over the contents of the building.

The scene looked bad to me at that moment, though soon I'd realize it was anything but. The stadium had been built to house as many as 20,000 fans, so the facilities here were coping well with 4,000 — washrooms were keeping up with the demand and so on. And it was generally clean.

But I felt entirely wrong for having been welcomed as I had been — these people thought I was going to fix their problems, and there's nothing like a press of desperate people who've been through horrors you can't imagine putting their faith in you to convince you that you're going to fail.

How the *hell* was I going to fix this? Surely I'd find a way — that's what our plan stated, after all…

Well, we all know how that plan turned out.

But I had to try, and Karen stepped in here to make sure I didn't collapse into a state of desperation. I simply couldn't — all the officers I was meeting had been here for so long and were still doing their jobs… what kind of leader would I be, exactly, if I showed up, took one look, and turned into a blathering fool when I saw the nicest part of town?

As you might suspect, I'm too arrogant and egotistical to let my pride suffer like that… and more importantly, Karen leaned right into me for a second, looked at me and asked soothingly, "What next?"

Now, I don't know why a simple question like that helped, but it did. Karen's brilliance when dealing with my beleaguered brain defied reason, and while after this she told me emphatically that she asked because she was herself desperately without direction, I know better.

I took a deep breath, straightened up off the rail, and turned to her, "I'll leave Kyle to take charge here with most of the remaining SF and volunteers. We'll head on up to Government House with the rest."

Karen nodded twice, then we both turned away from the stadium and headed back to the lobby where we'd been crushed by the crowd.

From the stadium it took another forty-five minutes to get up the road to Government House. The administrative building was off a side street near the house, and we weren't so worried about getting to it just yet.

As we kept moving on up the street we were traversing — this was Billings Avenue, by the way — the destruction of property became more and more dramatic. The Boscawen

Corp mercs and the Guild fighters had done some nasty street-to-street hammering in the area of Government House before the Governor had retreated to the Boscawen barracks, and it showed.

Most of the bodies had been collected, but we still came across at least half a dozen on the way.

We weren't seeing any families moving doorway-to-doorway any longer either. We weren't seeing anyone. Actually, these streets were the ones that were living up to my earlier expectations of abandoned roads.

Charlie and his squad were moving in a way I'd never really seen before; they appeared to be walking 'casually', but at the same time were aware of everything around them. This wasn't like a pirate boarding for them — they weren't searching everywhere around them down the barrel of their MAG-90s, but I had no doubt they'd shoot any threat before I even realized it was there.

When the single pack of Guild fighters tried to hide in an alley ahead of us, Charlie's squad was on them before the miners knew what was happening.

Led by a gruff fellow, this twenty-fighter squad had evidently been hunting for 'fresh meat', as they so quaintly put it, when they'd seen a *lot* of crisply-uniformed troops coming up the avenue, so they'd done what any scum would logically have done: they hid.

And as they crouched and shushed each other, a shadow appeared in the alleyway, looming huge. It was Charlie, backlit and with his hands on his hips, "Excuse me, but you're all going to stay right here until we pass, aren't you?"

The politely-worded question was offered with a tone that silently added "or I'll personally dismember all of you."

"We're not to pick a fight with no Defcoms," the gruff leader said rather meekly.

Charlie nodded, "Glad to hear it."

And then he went on his way.

No, we couldn't do anything about them. We surely could have arrested this whole squad, but their thousands of friends would've had something to say about it. And even with Stranks now at the stadium, there'd be no way to save the civilians we had under our charge...

As we walked on, and Charlie came forward again to walk alongside Karen and me, I found my hand was glued to the handle of my mag. I wasn't seeing anything in particular that appeared threatening, I just felt like we were surrounded by evil. Sounds melodramatic, perhaps, but that was the feeling — and having a mag in my grasp was about the only comfort I could find.

At least if that evil came forward, I could shoot at it. Simple comforts.

Government House eventually loomed ahead of us, and as it did Charlie held up a balled fist and halted the column. Veronica Choctaw — letting Charlie lead this expedition, I should mention, despite her technically higher rank — scattered her three companies of Guards across the street, taking up positions to deal with any unforeseen threat that might have presented itself. Matt's remaining SF scattered too, covering different angles.

Then, as Karen, Matt, Mark and I stood in the middle of the street, lone vertical targets in the broad avenue, Charlie took half his squad up one side, his second in command, Carly, leading the other half up the opposite side.

For some reason, the approach to this building was concerning him more than the others. Perhaps because communications had been spotty with Government House, or perhaps because we were close to the center of town and he was sensing extreme tension.

He was on the building's side of the street, so he was the first up the sidewalk to the checkpoint shed — just like the ones at the stadium — and there he scared the hell out of an Ensign who'd literally been looking the other way as Charlie approached. Special Branch moved with deathly silence, and the exhausted Ensign had no way to realize someone was behind her until Charlie's hand landed on her shoulder.

"We all clear here?" he asked with a steely tone, and she literally yelped and turned, trying to swing a clumsy fist at him.

This was Ensign Mei Zhang, of *Friendly*, who'd joined the ship just before I'd left and was due for her promotion to Lieutenant by this time. Charlie caught her fist and her mind changed gears instantly as she realized she was dealing with a Special Brancher.

"Sorry sir," she rasped, then nodded once, "we were hearing some commotion up the street. Commander Kiley was due back fifteen minutes ago, we were wondering if it as her."

Charlie nodded once, "We'll find out."

He turned and waved the rest of the column up, then did a bunch of tactical hand gestures to move his squad forward.

"When Commodore Barron gets up here, tell him to wait for us to come back. Tell him I say not to follow."

Charlie's well known in the Belt Squadron, so Mei Zhang recognized who he was and the significance of his message, and she nodded.

He then pressed on up the street, and when I arrived at the checkpoint and heard his relayed message, I decided to follow the orders.

This wasn't a pirate ship, I wasn't cut out to go first. Not at all.

Just as well, too, given what they ran into.

Chapter Twelve

Very Precarious

Andrea Kiley's driver had not turned off the truck, despite the barked demands of the fighters who were surrounding it. However, the overloaded pickup didn't have enough kick to climb over the thirty-odd Guild fighters — at least not quickly enough to avoid taking fire from the EP-5s they were carrying.

And a few EP-5 shots could probably disrupt the hover field long enough to knock the truck right out of the sky.

So Andrea was stuck in an argument with a Guild woman while, standing in the bed in the back, Gwen Jameson and Mikka Hong firmly held their MAG-90s, trying to dissuade the hungry-looking Guild fighters from reaching over the sides of the truck to grab any of the five civilians they'd picked up.

"No," Andrea was trying to keep her anger under control, "these are civilians and they're under my protection. You'll not be having them."

When she's starting to lose her temper, Andrea's accent grows more pronounced.

"I don't know, mechanical breakdowns to old trucks happen all the time out here, don't they?" the Guild woman said with a sneer.

For some reason I feel the need to point out the following again: yes, all the Guild fighters we were meeting in the Government Dome were this bad, this depraved. I know they may be coming off as some breed of cartoon bad-guy, always unthinkingly evil and whatnot, but the reality is that they were. Remember, the Guild had hundreds of thousands of active members and only hundreds of guns, so the leadership evidently entrusted those weapons only to the very worst, figuring they'd be the best fighters for that attack on the Government Dome.

That issue... well, you know how it plays out later. We can't paint all Guild members with the same brush, but I'll gladly condemn every bastard who took a gun, went into the Government Dome with it, and then started looking for 'fresh meat'.

Back to Andrea: her grip on her mag was tight. She told me later that she held it so tightly for so long that, when she finally got back to the relative safety of Government House, she had to spend time carefully unlocking her fingers, loosening the stiffened joints.

"Well, if this truck breaks down, we'll just have to walk them back to Government House," she was almost gritting her teeth.

"Three of you, five of them. That doesn't seem like good odds now does it? Come on, if you want to save the lives of yourself and those lovely Defcom girls in the back, you'll play ball. You don't want to end up in a room yourself, do you?"

The Guild folk were good at threats. Charlie Peters was good at his job.

None of the fighters realized exactly what was happening for several long seconds. By the time they did, their leader's face had been used to put another dent in the hood of the pickup, and a MAG-90 snout was being used to adjust the vertebra in her neck.

"So your squad is going to leave now, and stop trying to pick a fight with Defense Command, that's what I heard, isn't it?" Charlie leaned down and whispered into the gruff woman's ear, and she started to hiss something.

Pulling her off the hood, he drove his boot into her left knee from the wrong side, breaking her leg sideways and drawing a blood-curdling scream.

The fighters finally woke up to the reality that their leader had just gone from issuing threats to being beaten bloody, but as they tried to raise their own weapons, most of them found themselves looking down barrels of MAG-90s or sidearms — every one of Charlie's squad was holding a mag in one hand and a pistol in the other, covering two people.

"Now," Charlie bellowed, "I think your leader just took a fall! Don't you all agree that's what happened?"

The nervous fighters had been out looking for some 'fun', they weren't inclined to put lives and wellbeing on the line, particularly not against this many Special Branch officers who were so obviously displeased with the situation.

Charlie was counting on the 'easier prey elsewhere' instinct to dissuade them from making a fight.

And it worked.

One of the fighters grabbed his leader by the collar and, with many screams from her, dragged her indelicately down the street. The rest followed.

Letting out a short breath, Charlie reholstered his sidearm and turned to Andrea's window, "*Wolf* and *Honesty* pulled in three hours ago, we're deploying now, and we have 150 Hawke Guards with us."

Andrea barely managed to unclench her jaw, "Very good. Thanks Charlie."

He nodded once, "Any time. We'll walk you back to Government House."

The truck and its new escort moved on.

Matt Baxter was consulting with the officers in Government House 'Command and Control' and he wasn't liking what he was seeing. Officers from *Friendly* and *Honesty* who'd survived plenty of pirate fighting, boardings, and tense battles like Deep Black and Belt Two, were now on the verge of cracking. Here they were seeing a different sort of fighting — ship battles were, for the most part, clinical affairs. This place wasn't clinical. Unless you went with the 'insane' version of the word's meaning.

Pacing over to Karen and me with an anxious look, Matt kept his voice low, "Well, it seems they've got about fifty people out there in a variety of trucks. They never got the message forwarded from *Friendly* that said we were coming in, there's been interference or intermittent jamming on the comms for the past few days."

Karen and I both bent our heads slightly as our eyes turned to him — the way people do when they're talking quietly in the presence of those being spoken of.

"How's their state of mind?" I asked as softly as I could manage, and Matt's face tightened.

"They're not in any condition for this sort of work, or at least, I wouldn't send them out any more in the state they're in. I should say there are a few who are holding together alright, but mostly, I'd say we need to get them out of the field…"

Karen and I both nodded silently. We were seeing a lot of very good — *elite* — Belt Squadron officers near the end of their tethers. It was more than a little worrying, for any number of reasons. Would they be able to recover once aboard their ships? Was this what was to become of *us*?

It didn't bear thinking about, and the Briton heaved a deep sigh that revealed his own concern.

"I think we need to get this situation under control as soon as possible. If we want to have our crews back in any sort of state that makes them combat-effective…" his words reflected honest fear for *Wolf's* future combat ability, but the tone with which he spoke revealed greater concern for the humanity of his people.

Humanity, something none of us particularly wanted to have stolen from us…

The hum of a hover truck floating up to the curb outside Government House interrupted our conversion, and stepping quickly over to the window, Karen looked out and down and then back in, "That's Andrea and Charlie."

We immediately headed for the stairs, and ended up meeting Charlie and Andrea as they came in through the main doors. Behind them, Charlie's Special Branchers and two of Andrea's helped move five civilians towards a room full of refugees.

Charlie's grim expression alerted me to the sort of situation he'd seen out there, and then he followed that with words, "I did some leg-breaking. Nothing that'll start a war. I hope."

I nodded, "If you did it then you had to. Andrea…"

I really had no idea what to say to Commander Kiley.

She stopped and looked up at me, her gaunt face revealing none of the energy and enthusiasm with which she had for years approached her work.

"Let's have a chat, Andrea. I need to know exactly what the situation is around here. You have an office we can use?"

"Yes, of course," Andrea's tone seemed hurried, and she waved us back towards the stairs we'd just come down.

As Andrea stepped past us, Karen turned and followed closely, and I glanced quickly from Matt to Charlie, who shook his head. I managed a long blink, then nodded to acknowledge the silent assessment, and set off after Karen and Andrea.

I closed the door to what must have once been the Governor's office after I entered, and Andrea quietly walked over to one of the shelves and pulled a pitcher of clear liquid from it, pouring herself a glass.

For a second I chanced a worry that it was alcohol, but then she looked up at us, "Water?"

Karen had been thinking the same thing I had, but now she managed to sound as if she hadn't, "Please, that'd be good."

I nodded, "Yes, please."

Andrea filled two more glasses and brought them to us, a seemingly eerie calm floating around her. As she returned to the pitcher and took up her own glass, she let out a short breath, then began, "So the government's been in hiding since before Mark left, I'm sure he's told you about that. Is he here with you?"

Karen nodded, "He's downstairs talking to some of his people from *Honesty*."

"Ah. That'll do them some good, he's a very well liked CO," Andrea nodded. "We've been trying to get out into the city to keep the civilians protected… that hasn't been going as well as I'd have liked."

"Confrontations with the fighters?" Karen's voice remained low, and Andrea's eyes narrowed as she evidently remembered some of the run-ins she'd had. Like the one I described earlier.

"Confrontations, em… that's the right word, I suppose. We've not been taking any combative action, but we've been trying to put ourselves between the fighters and any civilians they're after. Seems their higher-ups have told them not to mess with us, so we've got a slight advantage there…"

Her voice trailed off for a moment, and I glanced at Karen before looking back to Andrea, "Alright, well, we've got 150 Hawke Guards. We're going to send them out to take over the patrols, and we've got some of our SF moving with each squad to make sure they're taken seriously."

Andrea was staring at her water as I spoke, and she was silent for a long moment. Karen and I exchanged uncertain glances, wondering whether she'd shut me out entirely… then she seemed to visibly shake herself and she nodded, "Good. My teams will be cycling back in on their own, so when they return the Guards can take their trucks back out. We've also left a number of trucks at the stadium and the admin building. They can use those as well."

Okay, she was thinking logically, rationally. That was a relief to me, as you can probably understand. I rather liked Andrea Kiley, and the last thing I wanted to see was her total self destruction. Well, perhaps not the last thing I wanted to see, but close-to-last.

"How've you been locating civilian pockets to go after?" Karen's prudent question drew Andrea's gaze.

"Sometimes we just cruise around listening for screams, sometimes we get comm calls, other times it's just based on rumor."

Karen managed to look unaffected, "I see. Alright, Andrea, I think you should go to bed, get at least a few hours sleep. We can get set up without you, and to be honest, I think you'll be much more effective with some rest."

The dark circles marring the pale, dirt-smeared skin under Andrea's eyes made it pretty clear she hadn't slept in a very long time.

She nodded slowly, and without another word walked past me and through a door into a side office. Leaning back and glancing through the doorway, I watched her lower herself onto a cot and close her eyes.

Neither Karen nor I really expected her to sleep.

CHAPTER THIRTEEN

A BREAK: TO BELT FOURTEEN

While all of this was going on, Captain Marshal Samuels was dealing with the rather panicked Governor of Belt Fourteen. When he'd arrived there the day before, he'd been made aware of the Egesta situation, and of the danger posed by Commodore Cook's lurking at Belt Two. He'd thus been torn: would he take *Alberta* to Egesta, another seventy hours beyond Belt Fourteen, or would he return to Belt Two to assist Wes with Cook?

Now, neither was an option.

"He's coming here, he's going to raid our base and if we try to stop him we'll be attacked and brutalized!" The Governor of Belt Fourteen was the somewhat paranoid Sherman Brstilo — a good politico, all round, but one who was inclined towards moments of blind panic now and then.

Indeed, one of those moments had brought Marshal out here in the first place; Brstilo had called Belt Two in a tizzy, saying he had seen a trio of sensor ghosts playing on the edge of his sensor grid, and feared the very worst. Well, I suppose that's not unwarranted panic (sorry, I sound like I'm being unkind to Sherman because his worries pale next to those we were seeing last chapter, but in fact I honestly can't blame him for his prudent call for help when his people were in danger).

Anyway, the sensor ghosts — not unlike those that had been haunting the Protectorate in *The Hawke Mission* — had vanished, but now Marshal was on site to deal with the anticipated arrival of the Independent Squadron in a few days. Sharon Stanton had sent word of their approach as soon as Wes and the majority of the Belt Squadron had moved out.

Now, Marshal had to admit a certain concern for himself — his venerable old *Alberta* was no slouch of a ship, and was only two years older than the oldest of the Independent Squadron vessels, but it featured none of the special upgrades the Independent Squadron had fitted.

And, perhaps more importantly, he was outnumbered eight to one until Wes arrived.

Those sorts of concerns, though, were his to deal with: Marshal had no intention of adding to the tension on Belt Fourteen. That sort of mood could lead to chaos, and that was the last thing that was needed under the circumstances.

"Governor, rest assured that we'll take care of this. Commodore Cook will have to deal with *Alberta*, and I can promise you that he won't have an easy time walking in here and taking your stores. That's my word, sir," Marshal's way of dealing with politicians is excellent: he's firm and earnest, and I'd always had a suspicion he'd end up in the senate some day.

The Governor was somewhat soothed by the tone, though his panic was still present, "Yes, but if he decides to use force..."

"There is no reason to expect that. I think he still intends to follow the strictures of regulations — at most to bend them. But I have orders from the Admiralty to hold all weapons here, and to release supplies to non-Belt Squadron ships on order from the First Lord, and the First Lord only. They won't be able to dispute those orders," Marshal was well aware that the orders were indisputable, but he also knew Cook mightn't bother with orders. However, he couldn't allow the Governor to believe things could spiral out of control.

Brstilo quieted for a moment, scratching his neck and leaning back in his desk chair. Marshal was standing in the Governor's office, I should have mentioned earlier.

"So... we'll be fine..." the Governor sounded anything but convinced, despite Marshal's best efforts.

"If you want to do something to enhance your security, you could always move your weapons stores out of your base. Hide them somewhere."

The Governor perked up, "Yes! Yes, that's a good idea... but where? We only have four domes, it would take him no time at all to find them. And then he might exact retribution on civilians for being forced to look..."

Cook's actions at Egesta had definitely unsettled the Governor — but again, that concern really wasn't unreasonable.

"I can take the weapons aboard *Alberta*, if it'd comfort you, Governor. No safer place for them than aboard a Defense Command frigate. Under the worst case scenario, I can run with them away from your colony, and draw the Independent Squadron after me," Marshal's tone was again certain and calm, and Brstilo just about went nuts. Not really a better way to put it.

"That would be incredibly good of you, Captain! Truly risking all for your duty. I shall see you commended from on high for this selflessness!"

Marshal's understated reaction wasn't quite what the Governor was looking for, but as the politico rushed around his desk and shook Marshal's hand, our esteemed Captain smiled politically, "Yes, glad to help, of course. I'll arrange the transfer then."

It took Marshal about five minutes to pry himself out of the Governor's grip, but once he got out of the man's office and headed back to *Alberta's* lock, he began to mull over what he'd just suggested and agreed to. Stuffing the seventy palettes of small arms that Belt Fourteen housed aboard *Alberta* was going to absorb just about all his cargo space... he'd have to coordinate that with the XO.

But there was more to it than just fitting the guns on board: what would he do, exactly, when the Independent Squadron arrived looking for these weapons? Of course he'd stand off with them, nose-to-nose, and deny them access. But would shooting ensue? If so, there was truly little chance of *Alberta's* survival — the ship was a Belt Squadron veteran with one of the very best crews in the service, but Cook had *six* frigates.

Well, Marshal would just have to do what he always did: pick his ground and stand it. He knew what was right, and by God he'd stand for it.

That's the sort of fellow Marshal Samuels is, and to be honest, that character makes me regret his inability to come to Egesta. Hell, I'd have loved the whole squadron to be there — we may well have been able to turn the tide had we all been present.

But Cook had to be dealt with, *and* there was a war on.

Marshal Samuels was doing his part for both.

CHAPTER FOURTEEN

IN COOK'S WAKE

Wes Pellew was sitting in his day cabin, and on his screen Captain Kris Jacobs was wearing a dark expression.

"I can't believe the speed they're managing," Kris' voice lacked its usual playfulness (I don't think there are many legitimately enthusiastic or playful voices in this book — not ones belonging to good people, anyway).

With a nod, Wes leaned back in his chair. Because they were cruising in close formation, realtime communication was quite possible between *Cheetah* and *Lion*, and the two Captains were using it to commiserate.

Cook had obviously gotten a head start on them as he headed out, but making maximum burn, the *Predators* and *Nobles* of the Belt Squadron should technically have been able to overtake, or at least get into sensor range of the *North Americas* of the Independent Squadron in the time they'd been cruising.

But no, no the modifications to the Independent Squadron ships were again proving significant. Cook's ships hadn't arrived on the edge of long-range sensors yet, and neither Wes nor Kris had any idea whether that meant the Belt Squadron ships were falling further behind, gaining slowly, or just keeping up with the Independent Squadron.

It was frustrating.

"What's really starting to bother me isn't that, though, Wes," Kris was frowning on the screen, and Wes tilted his head.

"So what's on your mind?" he asked simply, and Kris managed to snort a laugh.

"There's too much on my mind to bore you with, but what I'm worried about at the moment is what we're going to do if we catch them. We have orders to arrest Cook and his officers, don't we?"

Wes hadn't revealed to anyone the nature of his orders from John, though everyone who had been in the original briefing thought John had ordered Cook's arrest.

Well, there was no point hiding the truth from Kris, of all people, "Yes, I have orders direct from the First Lord to take him into custody… but there's also the matter of their ships. We're supposed to take them intact if we can, and we shouldn't unduly risk our own survival."

Kris' red eyebrow went up, "Well, I like the sentiment, but I'll tell you plainly, I have no bloody idea how we're supposed to pull that off."

"You and me both," Wes nodded. "If we can rendezvous with Marshal, we'll have five ships to Cook's eight, and that's enough, I think, to assume he won't actually attack us — he'd be taking too much of a risk. I mean, some of his ships would survive, but not all, and there'd be enough damage to keep them from making this blistering speed in future."

"Yeah, so he's going to choose 'run' over fight, because he knows he can keep us behind him…" Kris' words were again displeased. "But unless we can somehow board his ships and take their reactors offline, there's not much chance of us stopping him if he tries to run, is there?"

Wes shook his head, "No. No, I think that's something we'll have to work out when the time comes. If we get the chance, we may have to do some shooting, disable their pods perhaps… but carefully. I don't know if the range on their lasers was improved, but if it hasn't been, we've got an extra 3,800 km of range on him. That's… almost ten seconds extra shooting time, assuming we're charging straight at each other…"

That was the calculation Wes was being reduced to. *Cheetah* and *Lion* sported later-model lasers than the *North America*-class frigates… presuming the upgrades to Cook's ships hadn't extended their weapons range.

So perhaps an extra ten or twenty seconds of unanswered engagement time could be significant.

"We can hope for a lucky break, I suppose," Kris' tone was dejected, and Wes nodded. "Live with our fingers crossed…"

The intercom interrupted Wes, and he tapped the key on his desk, "Wes."

"You're going to love this. We just picked up *Yukon* at extreme range, still boosting at full speed!" That was Roslyn Young, *Cheetah's* XO (who I don't think I've mentioned up to this point, oddly enough).

Of course, what she was saying was quite significant: they'd picked up Captain Bahim's ship while it was still at full speed, meaning they *were* overtaking Cook's ships after all. Just slowly.

A smile flashed across Kris' face, "You and I need to chat more like this, Wes. Have I mentioned I'd love to win the lottery?"

With a grin, Wes stood up, "You'd just spend it on more guns for your ship."

"Something wrong with that?" Kris looked away quickly. "Alright, I'll see you on Battlelink in a minute?"

Wes nodded, "Yep."

The link died, and Wes headed out of his day cabin to the bridge.

As he arrived on the bridge, he headed straight to the front screens, coming to a stop next to Roslyn Young, who pointed at the main screen, "I guess the tune-ups Cook got weren't as fancy as he'd hoped."

Wes nodded, and just as he did Kris reappeared on screen three, Kate Levec having routed her feed there.

"Well, if we can see him I'm willing to bet he can see us," Kris' opening remark sounded almost hungry.

"I wonder what he'll do about us…" Wes' words were quiet. "Cook might have purposely ordered *Yukon* to drop back — maybe they're supposed to decoy us, lead us off on the wrong course…"

Right on cue, another Independent Squadron ship popped onto the screen next to *Yukon*; the frigate *British Columbia*. Both were still running at full speed, so evidently *Cheetah* was now living up to its animal namesake and catching up to the enemy… whoa, there's a Freudian slip… catching up to the *Independent Squadron*, not (technically) the 'enemy'. Martians were supposed to be the *enemy*.

"Sean Cook, look over your shoulder," Wes said under his breath. "Rozy, let's go to general quarters."

Roslyn Young nodded, and in seconds *Cheetah's* crew was flying to battle stations. Wes still didn't know quite what he was going to do.

CHAPTER FIFTEEN

ORGANIZING ON EGESTA

After about an hour of troubled sleep on her cot, Andrea Kiley woke in a cold sweat with a stifled yell, and Karen — somehow knowing precisely what to do — was immediately right there with her, gently pushing her back down to the cot and offering a few calming words. I have never been able to figure out how Karen knew what to do in that situation.

After a few minutes of gentle coaxing, Andrea settled back into a troubled sleep, and Karen stepped back out into the Governor's office, pulling the door to the sleep chamber halfway shut behind her. Standing in the office, Charlie, Matt, Mark and I simply went back to our business: we were standing over a map of the dome.

"So Veronica's troops have started moving out to relative north. By the look of things, the Guild's main force is coming through the tunnels from Dome Five," Charlie sounded like a man in the know, and he was — he was the only one of us, I think, who had a clear picture in his mind of what was going on here. "If it comes to a real fight between us and them, I think closing that tunnel will be essential. Dome Five is probably Guild loyal — that's why all their troops are coming in that way."

You're probably asking where Charlie had gotten this information. Andrea had been sending out observers and recording movements of Guild fighters for the entire week she'd been there, and while neither she, personally, nor her staff had had the time or the right state of mind to process what they were seeing, it instantly made sense to Charlie.

"To close it... you think we have the troops to close it *and* to fight the Guild bastards already in the government dome?" Mark Gunney's question was abrupt, but hardly inappropriate.

Charlie's eyes narrowed as he looked at the battered paper map printout, "I doubt it."

"But we could depressurize the tunnels with a laser shot from orbit," Karen picked up immediately on the thread of thoughts that was running through Charlie's mind — she was definitely on top of her intuitive game today.

And her suggestion made a lot of sense. Space was the only place in this situation that we had the real advantage: *Honesty's* lasers could cut through enough rock to punch holes into the large subterranean tunnels connecting the domes. As soon as pressure started to bleed, or more likely as soon as an explosive decompression took place, the automated safety systems built into the dome would shut hatches on either end of the tunnels to protect the integrity of the atmosphere in the domes.

Well, that's what'd happen in a Defense Command dome...

"Can we be sure their pressure-guard systems are online here, though?" Matt's question went right to the heart of that concern, and Karen pursed her lips, then shook her head.

"So that's not option one, then. If it comes down to it, we could try... but diplomacy first, definitely," Matt glanced between all of us.

I nodded in agreement, then found myself looking past Mark Gunney at the desk of the Governor, "Well we know where to find one of the leaders. Where's the other side's leadership?"

Mark shook his head, "Hell if I know. The Guild leadership committee is probably in Dome Five or Four... not around here, obviously. But let's think about this for a minute, what exactly do we have to bargain with? The Guild is obviously winning this fight, there's no reason for them to back down."

My eyes drifted back to the map, and I had to nod slowly — Mark had that right, certainly. Defense Command was here as a supposedly neutral third party, defending the civilians. If we started trying to throw our weight around when the government had just about collapsed, it'd look like we were moving in to take over.

And while taking over the situation at the moment didn't seem like that terrible an idea, we didn't have the means to.

But perhaps that means was coming... I hadn't checked in with John since getting here — I'd been too caught up with the problems we'd found to actually call Admiralty House.

"Alright, let's keep doing what we're doing for now. I'm going to talk to Admiralty House and see if I can get us some leverage. A transport with troops could be out here in a week, if John hasn't already sent one."

Nods came in reply, and I went in search of a working comm unit. With *Wolf's* powerful signal receivers so close, Guild jamming wasn't going to be a problem.

John Fiora was sitting at his desk, fighting another crippling pile of paperwork. This was a different pile than the one from the day before, but it was no less important. He'd been granted a huge avalanche of funding for ship construction and Fleet R&D had presented a number of construction package options that morning. This is a technical aside for those who like that sort of thing (and for my state of mind, because if I can find a legitimate excuse to take a brief break from talking about Egesta, I will).

Basically, the fleet was sitting at exactly 100 ships, including yachts, training ships, and the old comm ship escort frigates. That might sound like a large number, but it really wasn't even *close* to enough to look after the whole Empire during a crisis like this war. The four *Bonaventure*-class battleships were going to be a big addition in the coming months, but they weren't going to make up the defensive deficiencies John knew we were running into.

So ships needed to be recommissioned (yesterday's paperwork), but old ships were only going to be so useful — they weren't going to be proper front line units unless things got very desperate. That meant new construction was necessary... and interestingly (at least to me), new construction was going to mean a technological design step *backward*.

You see, the newest ships in the fleet — the *Predators* and the *Nobles* — were exceptional, but they were highly advanced and highly expensive to produce with the technologies we had available in 2231. At the same time, the *North America*- and *Canada*-class hulls were, by 2231, considered quite cheap and easy to produce, because the methods used in their construction were not as advanced and thus easier to reproduce at commercial contract yards.

Let me try to explain that a bit better: ships like *Wolf* were in 2231 so advanced that only Naval yards could produce them. However, technology across the board in ship production by 2231 was advanced enough to allow a ship like *Alberta* to be turned out of just about any civilian shipbuilder's yard — just with military-manufactured armor and weapons bolted in.

You can see where this is going.

What John was sorting out, then, was what he was going to build. He was holding the Naval yards at Luna for more battleships — he couldn't be sure he wouldn't need more, and while battleships took a long time to build (and generally, it was historical doctrine never to start building battleships in wartime because of this) the R&D folks were ready to shave corners off the production process for him. The battleships he was ordering — the eventual *Hokkaido*-class of four — would be about the size of the *Empire*-class (like *Warspite*), but were packing heavier weapons and improved speed. Not a bad tradeoff, that, and they'd be ready in two years. That's fast by battleship standards.

Then he was going back to the *North America*-class hull with a few improvements to drives and weapons, and ordering twenty-one ships, to be designated the *Asia*-class. Corvettes were a lesser concern at that stage; John figured (not wrongly) that older *North America*-class frigates could begin serving in many corvette roles once they were replaced by *Asias*. Nonetheless, fourteen *Australia*-class corvettes, virtually identical to the old *Canadas*, were to be ordered.

And the real plus to all of this: the construction of all these ships would take half the time of a comparable number of *Predators* or *Nobles*. Here was a case when quantity was definitely trumping quality, but it was for the best.

Anyway, that's what John was working on when my message got to him — my aside is now done. As he was searching through the list of recommended names for the *Asia*-class ships, he heard the priority message chime and looked up. My message was on his list, and he immediately laid down his pad and keyed it active.

I appeared after a short moment of buffering, and in his words, I looked like 'hell'. And that was after only a few hours on Egesta. Great.

"John, we're here and deploying. It's a real mess, and a lot of the officers who've been here for a week are near the end of their rope. I'm rotating them out as best I can, but aside from Special Branch and the Hawke Guards, I don't have any real specialists in urban fighting. I'm really hoping you were able to get some troops together for me right now. I want to negotiate, but the local government is holed up in a Boscawen Corp barracks and is in no position to come out… so I've got nothing to offer the Guild to stop the atrocities. If I could promise the wrath of a fully-kitted battalion, that'd be a different thing entirely… let me know as soon as you can. Thanks."

The picture froze as the message ended, and John immediately opened a reply window.

Jim Hannigan was still pacing behind the Sensors and Communications consoles on *Wolf's* bridge, despite actually being in overall command of the ship. With a number of his operators on Egesta as volunteers, he was helping make sure nothing slid through the cracks… and so he personally watched John's signal back to me hit *Wolf's* buffer, and keyed my comm.

"Ken here," my voice came over his headset.

"It's Jim, I have a reply for you from the First Lord. Where should I send it?"

I was in the Governor's office, and Karen and Charlie had just led everyone downstairs to check supplies and deploy fresh troops to areas where they were most needed.

"Down to the Governor's office. Have the code for it?"

"I do," Jim confirmed immediately. "And… sent."

I turned to the Governor's desk and found the remote for the wallscreen, then turned the display on. The buffering screen flashed up, then ended quickly as *Wolf's* strong signal raced through the building's comm rig.

John appeared, bracketed by almost comically tall piles of pads on either side of him, "Hi Ken, I'm glad to say I have *good* news for you. The Emperor was only too happy to dispatch troops to help us clean up this mess. They should reach you in another four days. I think he's going to use Cook against us sometime down the line, no matter what happens, and he wants to be the savior. Now I don't know the General commanding the force at all, but I'm told by some of my contacts that he's a good urban fighter… and by the sounds of it, the threat of getting crushed under a brigade… oh I should have mentioned that first, a *brigade*… of Imperial Army should get the Guild talking. Play it cool until they get there, though — if you get driven out of the Government Dome, the Imps aren't going to have any clue how to get in. Good luck, call me if you need *anything.*"

As the picture froze, I took a deep breath. I needed a lot of different things, but not many that I could, in good conscience, ask John for — not with the war on. I'd love to have saturated Egesta with Defense Command resources, but Imperial safety was already being put at risk enough because of Cook.

I dearly wanted to fix Egesta, but could I risk all of the Belt colonies to do it?

Some people, sitting in comfy armchairs and drinking fine liquors, have said rather matter-of-factly "why of course you could!" Funny how none of these critics, to my knowledge, lived in the Belt at that time. Most are from Earth, and have never known life without at least six battleships in orbit to make sure nothing untoward happens to them.

Anyway, help was coming — if you could ever, *ever* call Imperial Army *help*. Well at the time I thought I could.

Time to plan the next move.

Chapter Sixteen
Carrot and Stick

"Alright, so we have the stick, what's the carrot?"

Mark Gunney's question drew upon an old saying that I, too, was rather fond of — to get someone to do something, it was often said you needed the 'carrot and stick' approach. Basically, it means both an incentive (the carrot) and a punishment (the stick), and I think it originally related to donkeys or some such thing.

In this case, Mark was bang-on: we now had a stick — a brigade of the most blockheaded, unsympathetic killers around were coming to reestablish order on Egesta. If the Guild didn't play ball, they could look forward to a nasty, bloody, futile fight to the death.

So what could we offer them as a way out? If we didn't offer a way out, an ultimatum delivered to Guild headquarters might be answered by an instant invasion of the Government Dome — a bid to throw us out and to remove the possible foothold for the Imperial Army when it did turn up.

"Something compelling..." Matt glanced from Mark to Charlie and then to me. "Historian of the bunch, have any ideas?"

My eyebrows went up, "Well the usual desire in this sort of situation is free elections. The Guild has to believe it can come away from this with legitimate power that we recognize, and given the breadth of its membership, their victory at the polls would seem pretty much sewn up. So the promise of free elections monitored by Imperial troops might do it... if we can convince them it's not a bid by us to put in a puppet government."

"If they say no to free elections, we can do that anyway, can't we?" Karen asked quietly. "A brigade of Imperial Army on the ground, we could do whatever we liked."

Oh so painfully true, that statement.

"So we'll go in there and say we're giving them a last chance to do this peacefully and on their own terms. And if they don't go for it, we'll let the Imperial Army take a run at them, and see how they like no-holds-barred fighting with a bunch of blockheads whose weapons only have a kill setting," Mark's brusque words drew nods, and we all fell silent for a long stretch of seconds.

It was definitely a viable option — there was no doubting the gravity of the threat we were making; the reputation of the Imperial Army was known far and wide. Wherever they went off Earth, brutal death to the enemies of the Empire was a certainty.

I always like to think of Defense Command's operations as surgical and purposeful. The Imperial Army is more like an apothecary with a chainsaw.

"We'll go to the government folks first, tell them how it is. They'll be in no position to argue... at best, I think we might be able to get them off this rock alive. That should be incentive enough," I continued slowly.

Charlie, thus far not having said much, 'hmmed', drawing our attention. Looking up at us, he tilted his head, "What kind of government are we really going to get out of an election, though? Especially one that's so lopsided — the government won't have viable candidates… they'll all be dead or have fled…"

Another wrinkle — another of so many.

"The Guild will take it, and they'll have legitimacy, and their crimes in this dome could go unanswered," Mark agreed immediately. "We're going to let them walk?"

My jaw clenched. These guys were right, no question — a free election when the Guild held such a powerful intimidation card wouldn't be particularly free at all. What we needed, *really* needed, was a ceasefire, and a withdrawal of the Guild fighters from the Government Dome until the brigade arrived… then we could occupy the rock for as long as necessary to strip the Guild of its ability to intimidate, and *then* hold free elections.

"Yeah, we're not going to let any election happen in the near future," Karen was already answering the question when I opened my mouth. "Look, we just need to buy a ceasefire of five days — get the Guild to back out of this dome and believe that they're getting something out of it. Then we can let the Imps do their job and break them into small pieces for jailing."

"Given enough time under occupation, we can equalize the social situation here, get it leveled for free elections," I added, but Charlie's expression didn't seem to lighten at all.

Looking straight at me, he asked the hard question, "So we're doing exactly what Empire-haters say we do… we're going in with our own agenda and controlling the creation of a new government."

"One that suits our own sensibilities," Mark Gunney added helpfully. His tone was different — he sounded pleased. Charlie sounded troubled.

I nodded slowly, "This is the time for the guys in the big sandbox to stop the bullying in the little one."

It was probably an unnecessary metaphor, but it was all that came to mind at the time, and Charlie nodded slowly — he's never been a big-Empire advocate. On days like this one, though, I certainly was: I wanted to pour every scrap of firepower I physically could into Government Dome, and to start restoring order with zero tolerance. It would have solved the problem rather effectively, and it was something only the Empire had the resources to do.

It wasn't the sort of mission anyone could take lightly — and it wasn't the sort of mission that could be undertaken without good cause. It'd be far too easy to start expanding our mandate and to begin conquering free rocks on a whim because their local political situations supposedly 'warranted Imperial intervention'. No, not every situation demanded the Empire's military attention, but a choice one or two would… and Egesta was one of those that did.

It's unfortunate, as you know, that we didn't — weren't able to — do it right the first time.

I looked straight at Charlie. He and I occasionally differed on opinions, and I always — and I'm not just saying this — *always* respected his beliefs. Hell, I'd call him my conscience, except in many ways he's as twisted as I am. His concern here was painfully valid, but I still had to go forward with this plan.

And he knew I did.

"I don't like this option," he said plainly, "but I like doing nothing even less. Let's make it happen."

That's quintessential Charlie Peters, right there. He's sharp minded and has excellent political awareness, but when the chips are down, he cares most about protecting innocent lives. If the politics of saving those lives isn't ideal, he doesn't file an objection and back out of his job (as some people I know tend to): he puts his head down and goes into the fray, hell-bent on making the very best he can out of a horrible situation.

Guys like him are the reason why I wasn't worried about throwing the weight of the Empire at this problem — with people like him heading up this operation, we didn't have to worry about blind jingoism taking over. Our people on the ground wouldn't be wandering around believing the Empire was the panacea to all the solar system's problems, they'd be very aware of how heavily the Empire was treading, and would be mindful of minimizing any damaging footprints.

That's what leadership like Charlie's brought to messes like this.

Different leadership, well. You know.

Sorry, I've gotten way off track here. The decision had been made, we were basically going to buy time by promising free, impartially-supervised elections, but in reality we were going to control when the elections occurred and perhaps even how they played. And we'd take that control by force if necessary.

Leave a sour taste in your mouth too?

Welcome to Egesta.

We started getting ready to leave for the Boscawen barracks.

CHAPTER SEVENTEEN

GETTING TO THE BARRACKS

Our convoy to the Boscawen Corp mercenaries' barracks was made up of three hover trucks — the best three Andrea's command had left, which was to say two of them still had windshields. I was riding in the second one, at Charlie's insistence; he was in the first with three of his squad. Karen, Matt and Mark were with me, and the third truck, larger than the first two, held the balance of Charlie's squad.

I'd like to think our column made for an imposing sight as it hummed down Billings Avenue towards the other side of the dome and the Boscawen barracks, but I rather doubt we were intimidating. Perhaps this qualifies as black humor: the truck Charlie was riding had 'Your Floral Specialists!' emblazoned on both sides, and had a bouquet of flowers painted on the hood.

Desperate times, desperate measures.

A few Guild squads happened past us as we floated on down the avenue from the center of town, and then for a stretch of some kilometers we saw none. My best guess was there weren't too many civilians hiding in the vicinity — too much fighting going in that area to make it a safe hiding place.

Once we got closer to the barracks, though, we passed first a few, then many fighters, and they all began eyeing our convoy with an inappropriate hunger. We pointedly ignored them, until we came to their front line.

The Guild 'officer' commanding the barricade of the road heading on up to the Boscawen barracks seemed genuinely surprised to see us, and he marched up to the window of Charlie's truck and demanded to know what we were doing.

Charlie, with the polite diplomacy of a Special Brancher, explained that we were bringing terms of a ceasefire to the government, and that the Guild leadership was to be informed of those terms directly as soon as they were reported to the government.

The Guild officer didn't seem to buy this.

"You're going to reinforce them!" he bellowed. "Or you're going to take the Governor out of there!"

The yells drew the attention of all nearby Guild fighters, and they started to crowd around, brandishing their weapons and glaring at us.

I'm not sure what gripped me at this point — by now you well know the uncertain state of mind I was in. I can only assume that my subconscious recognized a chance for my now dormant cavalier attitude to resurface and do some good.

I opened my door, jumped out of my truck, and advanced on the Guild leader at an even clip, before Matt, Mark or even Karen could realize what I was doing.

Matt's mag was out instantly, but Karen got a hand on his shoulder before he jumped out after me, "No, Matt wait…"

She followed me, mag *not* in hand.

Mark then exited the truck, looking at Matt with a shrug, "She said *you* wait. I'll owe you a beer if you keep me from dying."

And by this time I was tapping the Guild officer on the shoulder, and becoming very aware of the number of EP-5s pointed at my head.

"You there, what's your name?" I asked as though I was merely upset about the hold up.

He whirled and brought his gun up, aiming it at my chin, but I reached out and pushed it aside, "*Excuse* me, you've got some bloody nerve, don't you. You do know who I am?"

The man's eyes narrowed and then he nodded, "Yes, of course I recognize you. I was just telling your man here that we weren't going to accept intervention. Now out of respect to you, I'll let you lot go on your way, but don't come back this way again."

I smiled thinly, "Well I do appreciate the respect… pardon us, Charlie."

Putting an arm around the Guild officer's shoulder, I turned him away from Charlie's floral truck, "Look, I just got here, and I think I know the basic situation. I may not, but that's not the problem right now. I just got orders from the First Lord of the Admiralty, I'm supposed to try to mediate this fight between your two sides… and if I can't manage it, a brigade of Imperial Army is going to be here in four days. And they're going to sort it out the way they sort out everything."

I was saying all this loud enough for everyone to hear. Rumor and hearsay can be a very powerful tool when properly harnessed, and I was hoping to cause enough of a stir to let word spread among the fighters on the ground: hell was coming.

"Now, the only way I can stop the Imps rushing in here with tanks and malice is to get a deal worked out between you and the government to hold free elections. I know the government will try to cheat you if they hold the elections, so I'll have the Imps oversee them to make sure they're fair, but I *need* a deal in place before they arrive. If their General shows up and I don't have a signed piece of paper, he's going to come through the main receiving lock and you're all going to die."

The Guild officer was speechless.

"*But*, if we get a deal worked out, he'll come in here, and become your best friend. He'll be the guy making sure the government can't tamper with the election results. The Guild speaks for the majority of people, right? With supervised elections, you'll get a legitimate government made up however you want it."

I was belaboring the free elections point, for obvious reasons.

After taking almost an entire minute to process what I was saying, the man looked at me and asked what, to my surprise, was an intelligent question, "Why are you telling me all this, sir?"

Sometimes celebrity did come in handy — I got a 'sir'.

And my cavalier tale-spinning mind was working, it seemed, "Well, first of all, I need to go in there and tell the government not to try to launch any sort of offensive. I can see you have them hemmed in, but if the Imps show up and you're in a firefight, they're just going to kill both sides. I don't want the government trying to take you out in a dying blaze of glory. Second thing, though, is I need a meeting with your Guild leadership. I need you to get word up the chain to them; they can comm my ship to set it up, wherever they like,

I'm not picky."

The man nodded slowly — to both his and my surprise. The crowd around, who'd 'overheard' everything, was beginning to buzz with quiet conversations featuring words like "Imps" and "shit" and "we're dead".

I took my arm from around the officer's shoulder, "Now, look, I need to get in there, but I know you can't let a convoy of trucks in, because we could be hiding stuff in them, or could be trying to smuggle people out. I know you have a job to do. So how about me and Karen and two of my other people go in, and the rest stay out here. You can search us before we walk in if you need to, and on the way out."

The Guild officer was still slightly wide-eyed, and now he was stammering, "Uh... no, no sir, I think we can trust you. You and Cap'n McMaster and two of your guys can go in. We'll trust that you aren't smuggling."

I smiled broadly and extended my hand, "Thank you sir, I really appreciate your trust. Let's get this sorted out so you can get to the polls, eh?"

The officer shook my hand, and then waved Karen, Mark, and myself through. Seeing our move, Matt hopped out of the truck and followed, determined to be the fourth guy. He nodded to Charlie as he trotted up behind us, and we passed through the front line and headed on up the road to the Boscawen barracks.

I felt very dirty.

I'm sure that sounds cliché, but I did. I needed a shower. Not just because that man had been filthy in terms of his personal hygiene, but because I'd been able, on no notice, to become his best buddy — to instantly bury my disgust with his position and his fighters, and to become the sincere-sounding friend of their cause.

Karen picked up on my personal disgust as we walked, and for just a second she leaned closer to me, her hand lacing with mine and giving it a squeeze.

We kept on walking.

CHAPTER EIGHTEEN

CONVINCING THE GOVERNOR

You'll notice I've started to abandon clever chapter titles again. Sorry, I'm sure they'll be back next book, but for now, well, it's hard to be clever.

The Boscawen mercs were as professional on this day as I'd ever seen them. I still don't know how Boscawen Corp finds these men and women — people who, when facing death for a cause not their own, can simply be cold combat machines. They're pricey, but somehow when you meet a Boscawen merc, you never get the sense they're in it for the money.

I don't understand it, but for the moment, it was what I'll call a 'refreshing change'. These weren't grimy rapists and murderers, they were pros, and as was their custom, they offered salutes to officers of Defense Command as we came up the carefully defended lane leading straight to their barracks.

Foxholes and alloy shield plates were everywhere, and when we got to the main 'gate', it swung open to reveal layers upon layers of firing positions. The Boscawen mercs, as I say, were top-notch pros.

An officer with a sidearm clipped to her hip approached us as we stepped into the barracks proper, and the gate closed behind us. She stopped smoothly as we entered, then snapped a crisp salute, "Major Scott, sirs, ma'am. Welcome to our barracks."

I blinked a couple of times as she remained in this crisp pose, and then realized she wanted me to salute back, so I did so rather blandly.

"Thanks for the greeting, it's good to be in some professional company after the conversation we had to have to get past the roadblock out there," Mark put in helpfully behind me.

Major Scott — Deanna Scott, I found out later — nodded, "We watched you from the tower, and had the parabolic microphones on you. Nicely performed, Commodore Barron, if I may say so."

I was having a tough time working up the same energy I'd had outside — perhaps my subconscious felt that, in professional company like this, I had no need to spin a tale.

"It wasn't all performance, Major. I need to see the Governor. The Imps are really on their way."

Without missing a beat, Major Scott nodded, "Very good, sir. We've already reported your statements about the Imperial Army to the Governor, she's expecting you."

"Splendid," I sounded thoroughly unimpressed.

Major Scott led us deeper into the barracks, and as we went we passed many Boscawen mercs — there had to be at least a hundred in here. No wonder the Guild hadn't been able to get in. As long as the power cells held out, there was no chance the rag-tag fighters could storm this carefully designed and well-defended position.

The Boscawens were ready for a siege — set to play the waiting game.

So would the Governor want to play ball, to promise free elections in return for safe passage off the rock?

The Major stopped before a door and waved us through it. Still leading our foursome, I edged past the merc and emerged into a dim room wafting with the scent of liquor. As Karen, Mark and Matt stepped in one by one, they all paused at the thick smell — not what we'd been hoping to encounter in the room holding the Governor, but perhaps not unexpected — and then the Major closed the door behind us.

A shadowy, rather melodramatic figure was seated behind a desk deep within the dark room, and as we stepped in the woman leaned forward, "I hear you want to take my rock away from me."

Now, as you've already no doubt noticed, I had no enthusiasm in this barracks, and evidently I had little tolerance to boot.

"I'm sorry, Governor... or wasn't it *Lieutenant* Governor a week ago... but *we* haven't taken your rock from you. The fighters surrounding this barracks have done that well enough on their own. I'll grant you, they did it with weapons one of my *very* misguided colleagues gave them, and that's why we're here, but the preconditions for this uprising are all of your own making."

By this time I wasn't being particularly charitable.

The Lieutenant Governor let out a deep sigh and collected a full tumbler of some strong variety of liquor, downing half of it, "I wish you were wrong."

The thought that went through my mind at that concession: well thank God.

"Look, I'll do anything for you to get me off this rock. I've got great mercs, but they're not going to hold out forever. You get me out of here, safe passage to a Belt colony, I'll do anything you want. Sign anything. Just get me the hell out of this."

The thought that went through my mind at that plea: oh shut up.

"Oh shut up," I blurted out. "You have no idea what's going on out there, do you? There are plenty of innocent people in a lot worse straits than you. I'll get you off this rock if you'll sign a ceasefire that gives me a chance to save them. That's it, that's why I'll do it."

Somewhat surprised, the Governor laid down her glass, "Excuse me? You make it sound like I'm at fault here."

Perhaps she'd drunk too much to realize she shouldn't argue with us.

"Didn't notice any civilians hiding in here," Mark Gunney chimed in helpfully. "Unless you're hiding them under your desk, I'm pretty sure you just locked them out."

The Governor bristled the way an intoxicated woman of her sort could, "Oh really. And how the fuck would I know who I could trust, hmm? Think you're so smart, so fuckin' humanitarian..."

With that abrupt outburst, she thrust herself to her feet and rounded her desk with a half-stagger, "You Imperial types think you're the shit. It's because of you that I'm in this position. We had them suppressed, we had the Guild on its knees and you brought them guns... why the fuck should I trust you, huh?"

She walked up to me and pounded a pointed finger against my chest, and as I opened my mouth to reply with a curt comment, I saw a blur, and then watched with no small measure of surprise as Karen took the Governor by the throat and rammed her against the desk, then laid her back on it.

"Listen to me carefully," Karen's tone was as quiet as the one she'd used with Andrea… but somehow it was now menacing. Context, I suppose. "You're a useless politician, you were dealing with a real problem in the Guild and you screwed it up. The guns would have come from somewhere else if Cook hadn't been here, but they did come from us. We acknowledge that and we're trying to *fix* things, something *you're* not trying to do. So here's what you're going to do now, you're going to sign a ceasefire that we draft, and we're going to haul you out of here and find you some bungalow on Belt Sixteen where you can waste away for the rest of your years. And if you object, I'm going to kill you. Right now, in fact."

So evidently the stress had gotten to Karen, too. I never needed to ask Karen about this moment — I knew precisely where she was mentally. The Governor was one of the causes of the problem, and while the Guild was another cause, and Cook was a third, this passive politico had done nothing but *hide* while her people died.

Perhaps I would have done the same in her position. Perhaps it would be the natural response and it was unfair of us to treat her this way. I didn't care about that, though — and neither did Karen.

The Governor was flailing now, trying to breath as her eyes bugged out of her head.

Karen pressed down a little harder on the woman's throat, and as I stepped around beside my Captain, I saw her expression — so cool, so reserved. This was 'killing Karen' — a version of Karen few people ever see.

Well, see and live to speak of, forgiving the cliché.

It's never a good idea to push Karen McMaster too far. Never.

Just as the flailing of the Governor began to subside, Karen drew her hand away, and panicked rasps for breath came next, with the Governor clutching her throat as if she could massage away the pain.

Karen straightened up and folded her arms, "You'll sign?"

The Governor's head lifted to look at Karen and I, looming large over her. I could almost see the calculation she was making in her eyes — if she called for the guards, could the mercs get in here to save her before Karen killed her? She decided not to risk it, which was wise indeed.

"I'll sign," she croaked.

We turned and left almost instantly, and I'm sure she went right back to drinking when we left.

That Governor, by the way, was Melinda Roux. You might recognize her name; her suicide a few years ago was headline news.

CHAPTER NINETEEN

THE WAY BACK

Getting out of the barracks was no trouble at all, which was probably just as well. I didn't want to have to turn back into the Guild's buddy again, no matter how good I seemed to be at taking on the role. As we filed back to our truck, Charlie watched us through the windshield of his vehicle with a concerned but steady gaze.

I nodded to him once, and I'm sure Matt gave him a more informative non-verbal report. The hover trucks hadn't been turned off during our visit to the barracks, so we simply climbed up over the crowd and turned around, then floated back down to street level and made our way back up Billings Avenue.

You might ask why we didn't fly high and get back more quickly. Well, we'd convinced one gaggle of Guild fighters that we were their friends, but there was no reason to assume all the fighters around would be so magnanimous. Flying high leaves a truck's hoverpad vulnerable, and if you take a hit in the pad, you're asking to go nose-first into the ground.

We were staying low.

And as it turned out, that was a good thing. Depending on who you asked.

The driver in our truck was one of Andrea's original SF volunteers, and was what I might term 'hypersensitive'. Another appropriate word might be wired. I'd elected not to try to change the drivers because these veterans knew the streets. If there was trouble, someone who knew the area would be a huge asset behind the wheel.

Now the driver slammed on the brakes, and the hover field reversed polarities and grabbed hold of the ground beneath us, bringing us to a jerky stop.

At first I had no idea why, and then I realized that ahead of us, Charlie and his officers were leaping from their truck. I was out my door before I was even thinking, with Karen, Mark and Matt all right behind me. Charlie must have commed Carly in the vehicle behind us, because instead of jumping out and chasing us, her Special Branchers hopped out and set up a quick perimeter around our convoy.

But why were we running?

Then I heard the screaming. So my mag came out of its holster.

Charlie's officers had sprinted down an alley so quickly I'd almost missed which one they'd taken. Coming to its entrance, I slowed down and brought my mag up to firing position, covering the left as I always did, Karen covering the right side next to me. Behind us, Matt was keeping an eye to the rear, and Mark, with a disapproving grunt, found his mag wouldn't charge. Cell burnout — it happens now and then, and always at bad time.

Another scream, and my eyes jerked forward. Way down the alley I could see Charlie's team kicking in a door, bursting in and opening a heinous fire with the MAG-90s. Had I been in a different mood, I might have thought it ironic: at the beginning of this, Charlie had been worried that Andrea's people would start shooting liberally. So far he'd broken one Guild leader's leg and rearranged her face, and now he was shooting.

I hastened my pace down the alley, but slowed as a ragged line of figures began spilling out of the doorway past the last of Charlie's officers. The Lieutenant was pointing each of the people towards Karen and me, and I finally realized precisely what this was: a rescue.

"Let's get them into the trucks, come on," I barked, and Matt instantly trotted back out of the alley and waved the florist truck closer.

Eleven figures ultimately emerged from the room, many of them in a desperate state, with tattered or in some cases *no* clothes, and with blood freely flowing. I didn't say a word as they started passing me, I just pointed towards Matt at the end of the alley. Mark and Karen waved them on too, and we all said nothing.

What exactly could you say?

Then there was a dull thud from the end of the alley, and I turned back, crouching and leveling my mag again.

It was nothing, or it looked like nothing, until I realized that Charlie and his officers were standing in the alley outside the door, tossing old-fashioned sonic grenades into the building...

Then they started running, and behind them the building began to collapse. He'd used sonic grenades at high intensity to help create a 'natural' looking implosion — after no doubt helping the process by shooting through the support beams.

The Special Branchers then ran back up that alley and passed us, except for Charlie who slowed next to me, "Those Guild fighters must have been arguing about whose turn it was. Started shooting each other, accidentally shot out the support beams. Funny what you happen across."

I nodded slowly, and met his eyes. I've never asked Charlie how many fighters were in that room, or what exactly they were doing when he found them. I did realize when I was researching this book, though, that we were in the same alley Andrea had visited days before with Gwen Jameson and Mikka Hong.

As I've said, Charlie doesn't give a damn about politics when it comes to saving people.

The rescued civilians piled into Charlie's truck, the driver handing them blankets to wrap up in... but there were too many for the florist vehicle, so the rest went in our truck. We sent them on their way, with Carly's truck for escort in case they ran across a checkpoint.

We'd walk back.

After half an hour of walking, we were in the center of the dome, not too far from Government House — nine Defense Command personnel filing slowly through what had been one of the biggest traffic nexuses on the rock before Cook had done his damage.

We were then sighted by a couple of Guild squads, and they decided to wander over towards us to have a look. As they approached, I tried to determine whether I had the energy left to play their friend — there were sixty or more of them, we'd have little chance on our own in a firefight.

But they slowed and kept their distance, perhaps knowing somehow about my talk with the Guild officer at the blockade, or maybe just remembering their orders not to pick fights with Defense Command personnel and realizing we had no refugees with us.

Whatever their reason, they stayed back, and we filed on right through the center of town, walking easily down Billings Avenue until we reached Government House.

Entering the building, we were greeted by Carly's half of Charlie's squad, and she reported evenly that the rescued people had been sent to the hospital under heavy Hawke Guard escort. She'd remained behind in case we didn't turn up — she and her half of Charlie's squad would be the first out to look for us in that case.

But there we were, all back together, so things were fine.

Right. Fine.

As you can probably tell by now, I wasn't fine. Karen wasn't fine. Matt wasn't fine. Mark wasn't fine. Charlie sure as hell wasn't fine.

But we *were* back.

So after nodding and delivering a few half-hearted comments, I proceeded up the stairs to the Governor's office. I holstered my mag (which I had unknowingly been holding tight since the alley) and stumbled into the bright room, making directly for the pitcher of water.

I didn't realize Andrea was awake until she asked me to pour her a glass too, and then I looked over my shoulder and nodded, "Of course."

I poured her glass and brought it to her, "How're you holding up?"

She sort of just stared at me, with eyes that were painful to look at.

I collected my water, drank some of it, and nodded, "Yeah. Yeah I can't even imagine what you've seen. What I've seen is enough for a lifetime, as far as I'm concerned."

Andrea Kiley nodded slowly, emptied her glass, and left the room.

I sat down silently on the edge of the Governor's desk and let out a long sigh.

Now we had to contact the leadership of the Guild…

CHAPTER TWENTY

CAUGHT UP

I'll gladly take the chance now to get off Egesta for a while, back to a place where some of the rules of war were happily still being observed. Sorry, 'rules of war' is a dated term, but put it this way: if Wes had incinerated the Independent Squadron in a gunfight, I'd have been alright with that.

But of course Wes wasn't incinerating anything — he was only just starting to get a look at the tail end of Cook's squadron.

Standing with folded arms on *Cheetah's* bridge, he stared at the main screen as range continued to tick down little bit by little bit. He was fairly certain that, by now, Cook had seen at least *Cheetah* on his squadron sensor scopes, but the illustrious Commodore wasn't changing course or trying to accelerate. His ships, we found out later, were usually capable of more, but their lack of recent yard time had left their performance less than optimum.

Gee, I guess that means starting a vicious and horrific civil war has its drawbacks.

Sorry. Sorry, that's bitterness seeping through. Though hopefully you can empathize.

"At this rate, we'll overtake them... hm... I'd say in about twenty hours," Kate Levec reported from behind her bank of consoles.

Wes blinked and turned to the Lieutenant Commander, "*Twenty?*"

She nodded, "I'm seeing increased drive emissions now, skipper. Looks to me like they see us coming and they're really starting to push the throttle."

Twenty hours still put intercept just under two days out of Belt Fourteen... that was fine... unless...

"They're hoping we're in overdrive and can't keep up..." he said quietly to himself, and standing nearby, Roslyn Young frowned.

"You thinking of showing them what they want to see?"

Wes smiled at his XO, "Why, yes!"

It was coming together in his head more clearly than I expect it ever would have in mine: Cook's ships were redlining their drives towards Belt Fourteen because they wanted to shake the Defense Command vessels in pursuit. But their engines were hurting, and they probably really wanted to cut their cruising speed to something less strenuous — a reasonable 180 kps or so (I should've mentioned this earlier, but they'd been toying with between 196 and 199 kps all this time). And if they did...

"We need to simulate a reactor failure," Wes said almost blithely. "If we can convince them we're not chasing any more, they might slow their cruising speed to spare their reactors, and then we could leapfrog them."

Sound dangerous and complicated? Well, I'd personally call it 'risky but innovative'.

But how were they going to simulate reactor failure...

"Give me Battlelink to all our ships, Kate," Wes turned slightly, then watched as Kris,

Isoruku Togo and Elise De Winter each popped up in their own screens.

"I'm going to fake reactor failure," Wes said evenly. "We think they're redlining their drives to stay away from us; if we look convincingly like we're falling off the pace, they might slow down just long enough to allow us to leapfrog them."

That got some wide-eyed looks of surprise — I've seen the recordings.

"Well… how exactly do you plan to pull *that* off?" Kris asked the most obvious (and pertinent) question, and Wes frowned.

A reactor cooking off would look like a big explosion on sensors, and would be followed by a slewing off course and probably the disintegration of the entire ship… obviously they wouldn't be *that* realistic in their gambit…

"I've read lately about the mine packs Admiral Stoll was using to delay the Martians on their approach to Earth," Isoruku Togo put in after a moment's silence. "Cluster together several crates of Starlight ordnance and push them out the flight bay, then detonate when they're alongside one of your wings. Combine that with a violent course correction and speed dropping off, and you may succeed in the illusion."

Wes' eyebrows went up, "No kidding. Alright, that's what we'll try. I doubt Cook's idiot enough to slow down as soon as we fall off their scopes, though… we'll have to stay off the back of his sensors for a day at least, then jump over him."

The COs on Battlelink nodded in turn; the plan Wes was putting forward was entirely unconventional, but the situation as a whole seemed to demand unusual approaches. I mean, Wes wasn't squaring off with an undisciplined pirate or a naïve Martian here: Cook was a bastard, but he was an experienced Defense Command bastard.

So doing something 'crazy' like purposely falling off the pace in a stern chase in order to hopefully convince the bad guys there was no reason to rush… that plan wouldn't be — *shouldn't be* — in Cook's playbook.

"Let's get it rigged," Wes turned and nodded to Roslyn Young, and orders were given. "Now, we just need to figure out what you three would be doing with your ships if you saw my reactor go."

Setting up the deception took Wes' crew only about forty minutes — not much time at all, considering the complexity of the plan. I can only imagine what it looked like to Cook himself, though I do know what it looked like to his sensors; we recovered *Nova Scotia's* logs after this whole mess was over.

I suppose it wouldn't be easy for you to picture if you've never seen a Version 6.4 sensor display board… the ones they use in the movies are almost always the later Version 7.1 models, because they're easier to find today and because they're what *Wolf* and the other *Predators* used.

Not that the software version of a sensor display really matters right now.

Cook, probably peering anxiously at his screen as he watched a number of elite ships slowly gain on him, saw a sudden blip — an explosion under *Cheetah's* starboard wing. The frigate slewed hard to port and began to go into an off-axis tumble, with the corvette right behind it just narrowly missing a collision. Then the frigate dropped off the edge of sensors. It was now moving quite slowly, and *Nova Scotia* and the Independent Squadron were racing away.

The lone corvette (the only other ship from Wes' force that Cook could actually see at the time) continued the pursuit for a couple of minutes, and then it finally reversed engines. It probably appeared to Cook that the Commander of the smaller ship hadn't known precisely what to do, but had ultimately elected to go back to scan the wreckage.

Not a bad play at all, then.

On *Cheetah's* bridge, Wes stood again with arms folded, keeping his balance by shifting his weight from foot to foot as the ship slowly tumbled. They were waiting for the last of Cook's ships to get off *Cheetah's* sensor display before they stopped the charade — it was doubtful that the sensors in Cook's squadron were better than those aboard a *Predator*-class ship. Once they were off Wes' screen, then, he expected that'd be a sufficient delay...

"And... they're gone," Kate Levec looked up at her skipper. "I think we're all clear now."

Wes nodded, "Alright, make speed 198 kps, get us back on course. Kate, the minute you see a hint of them on long-range scanners, we're going to have to slow down again. Keep a sharp eye."

His Sensors and Communications Officer nodded evenly, and Wes took a long breath. He had to hope this plan would work.

At his ultimate destination, Belt Fourteen, Captain Marshal Samuels was thinking much the same thing, albeit about an entirely different plan — *I hope this works.*

He was stuffing his frigate to the gills with palettes of small arms, and as he watched the heavy racks of weapons being floated up to his ship's cargo bays through zero-gee chutes, he had to ask himself the prudent questions again.

What would he do if Cook demanded to board and collect weapons? What would he do if Cook threatened the wellbeing of Belt Fourteen in order to get his hands on these guns? What if Cook picked a gunfight...?

There were plenty of unpleasant possibilities. Perhaps the only way he could remove some of the nastier ones from the list would be to leave Belt Fourteen... to go out and meet Cook in deep space, announce the fact that he was carrying all the guns Belt Fourteen had stocked, and then run... hoping to meet Wes' incoming ships somewhere out there.

The prospect of staying mobile did appeal to Marshal at this moment far more than the possibility of remaining tied to a single rock.

Yes. Yes, he'd have to leave, and draw Cook out after him.

Pulling his comm from his pocket, Marshal Samuels keyed in the bridge code and waited for a communications tech to answer, "Bridge here."

"Thomas, it's Sam. Have the XO prepare for departure. We're going to take these guns out of here, and try to lead Cook away."

There was a pause, then, "Aye sir. Orders passed on."

Closing his link, Marshal took another deep breath. He'd have to tell the Governor... what fun that'd be.

He turned and headed for the lock.

Cook was due for another surprise.

CHAPTER TWENTY-ONE

PASSING A NIGHT

I'd elected to sleep on the couch in the Governor's office, while Andrea ostensibly took another few hours rest on the cot in the side room. There was a second cot in there, which I left for Karen — her ability to deal with Andrea's troubles was far beyond anything I could have managed.

Of course, I didn't actually sleep. I tried to for about an hour, then I got up quietly and crept out of the office, trying not to wake anyone who actually might have been resting in the other room. By the time I got downstairs, I discovered that nobody really was.

Mark Gunney was in a reclining office chair, his still-inoperative mag in his lap, his eyes closed… mostly. He looked up when I came down the stairs, nodding, "Sorry I woke you."

I managed a weak smile, "Right."

Matt Baxter — despite his strained insistence that Karen and I get some sleep — was himself moving quickly from window to window on the ground floor, checking in with the sentries he'd set against any sort of attack.

"Ken," he reacted to my appearance without much surprise, "not sleeping?"

I shrugged, "Imagine that, I'm disobeying again."

He nodded, knowing that I wasn't being obstinate. None of us newcomers wanted to follow Andrea's downward spiral… or at the very least, we wanted to prolong our period of effectiveness as much as possible. Rest would be critical to that, you see, and we had enough officers around now to supposedly be able to sleep in shifts…

But, of course, the problem with that formula was the near-impossibility of sleep when one's brain simply wouldn't shut down. Horrified and shocked, my mind just wasn't willing to release control to my subconscious for the purposes of rest.

I can't even imagine how hard it must have been for someone who had seen and experienced much more than I had.

Matt left me to continue his endless patrol, and as he did I wandered towards the front of the building, where I realized Charlie was sitting on the step heading down to the street, MAG-90 sitting on his lap.

"Hey," I sat gingerly next to him, "how's it going out here? Can't sleep?"

Charlie's eyes were sweeping across the street, occasionally darting in the direction of the center of town while he listened carefully for any sounds of civilians in distress. As I asked my question he slowly shook his head.

"I probably could if I wanted to," he said quietly. "But you should go get some rest. No offense, but this isn't your specialty."

"Would if I could, my friend," I glanced towards city center as well, wondering what Charlie was seeing that I couldn't.

Those Special Branchers and their insanely-tuned senses… senses that made them indispensable on days like today.

Charlie was nodding in understanding, "Fair enough. Most of what we're seeing down here really isn't easy to digest."

I nodded, letting out a breath, "So, how've things been out here?"

"Quiet…" his voice tapered off for a moment as he edged forward to look past me before leaning back. "Carly, Jack and Freddie are set up in a first floor apartment across the street from us. Anyone comes for this door it'll be a nice crossfire. I replaced Ensign Zhang with Gloria and Joanne in the checkpoint box, and the rest of the squad's in the basement of this building… the windows down there actually lead up onto the street."

I blinked a couple of times as Charlie described the elaborate defensive arrangements, my eyes tracking back and forth across the seemingly abandoned street. There was no sign at all of the Special Branch squad being out here, Charlie himself excepted.

"High marks for stealth," I offered in a low tone. "Veronica's got people out looking for victims?"

"A whole company, with some of our SF. Word is they brought three people to the stadium, no more so far."

Didn't sound like many rescues at all… and hell, it wasn't.

But those three people's lives had been saved, and so you couldn't afford to sit on a step and brood about how much you weren't doing. That's one thing that bothers me about a lot of media coverage of these sorts of events: reporters these days have become so callous they start using words like 'only a few' or 'an inconsequential percentage' when talking about rescue efforts that aren't going extraordinarily well.

No question, some rescue efforts simply don't match the level of intensity for which they should be striving, but no one should forget that every life saved is incredibly significant to that person, her or his family, and so on.

So three wasn't as large a number as I'd like to have heard, but I'd certainly take three over none at all.

"How're you doing then?" I asked after a long pause, and Charlie's eyes continued to sweep over the black streets as if I'd said nothing at all.

Despite his roaming eyes, he managed a polite reply, "Been better, as I'm sure we've all been."

What Charlie must have seen in that room, I couldn't imagine. And you'll forgive me: under the circumstances I didn't try too hard.

We sat silently for the next few minutes, Charlie's eyes narrowing occasionally as he heard things that seemed out of place. After that slow-moving stretch of time I nodded in that way you nod when you're resigning yourself to something, "Alright, I'll leave you to it."

"Get some sleep," he said as I stood slowly. "Hopefully you'll be meeting the Guild leaders tomorrow."

My eyebrows went up slightly, "Yes. *Hopefully*. Right."

I didn't think too much about that possibility as I turned and headed back through the front door of Government House, passed Matt on another of his circuits of the perimeter, and then slowed to a stop next to the chair Mark Gunney was sitting in.

The Commander definitely wasn't asleep.

"So they've brought in three for the night," I informed him quietly, and he nodded somberly.

"Better than none. Worse than I'd like," his sentiments mirrored my own. "Charlie doing alright out there? Looks like he's on the edge, which probably means we'll have a pile of corpses if anything sets him off."

I frowned at the words — a prudent concern, certainly — and glanced back out the door, "You know what, I really wouldn't care. And since when have *you* worried about a pile of bodies?"

"As long as I don't have to clean them up, then hey, let the bastards get what's coming to them. Don't know if he's as gung-ho about that idea, though. He's got... what's it called... right, a *conscience*. And maybe one of those annoying *souls* too," Mark looked up at me. "I hear they sting."

The brusque half-humor masked a certain, honest concern. You've probably gathered from the series so far, and from Charlie's reaction to our initial plans on Egesta, that he indeed is one of the more... let's call it *considerate* people in the Belt Squadron. People like Mark and I have a tendency to be callous, or at least to appear so. Charlie's a combat machine, but he's also a fundamentally better person than me or Mark or any number of us.

So we had to worry just a little about whether this sort of scene was scarring him more than it was scarring the rest of us.

He would say it wasn't, and I'd actually be inclined to believe that claim, but on that first night, it seemed a prudent enough concern.

"Yeah, we should try to keep tabs on him, just in case," I nodded. "And each other for that matter. I doubt any of us are immune to what we're seeing. I'd rather we get this stabilized before we get to the stage Andrea's at... well, by the time that'd roll around for us, there'll be blockheads here to take over. But we need... we need to be wary of deterioration."

Mark nodded slowly, "Aye aye."

I stood silently next to Mark's chair for a couple of minutes more, then let out another long sigh and shook my head, "I'm going back up. You get some sleep."

"Yeah, as soon as you stop waking me up, I'm sure that'll happen. Probably try to fix my gun instead," Mark said dryly, and managing a thin smile I headed for the stairs.

I remember my feet feeling surprisingly heavy as I got to the second floor again, and as I turned for the Governor's office, I realized there was a slim figure standing outside the office door... or more precisely, standing with her back to the wall, head tipped back and eyes closed.

Karen looked like hell.

And since you all know how impossible I think it is for Karen to look anything but enchanting, that should be saying something.

Her head rolled sideways towards me as I approached with heavy footsteps, and I would have frowned at her, had I not been frowning already.

"What's going on in there?" I asked, managing a short bob of the head towards the cabin.

Karen tried to smile, and that was one of the few times I remember where that attempt didn't change my state of mind, "Andrea kicked me out. Guess I was snoring."

I made my own failed attempt at a smile as I stopped next to Karen and leaned back on the wall right next to her, "You *snore*? I think we know better."

"Yeah. No, I think she didn't want her insomnia to stop me from sleeping too."

With a long blink, I processed those words and nodded, "Yes. Yes that sounds more like it. So let's sleep out here."

Now you might say we weren't being good friends to Andrea, leaving her in there to fight her dreams alone, but... well... no, you're right. But I'm sorry, at that moment I couldn't focus on Andrea, horrible as that sounds. Karen was bloody good at everything, sure, but I didn't want her being eroded by horrid dreams. Not if there was a way to avoid it.

So instead of her having to try to sleep while a Commander in the cot next to her demonstrated what long-term exposure to the Egesta situation could do to her mental health, the hall would do.

I slid my back down the wall and pushed my feet out until I was sitting on the carpet, back still against the wall, legs stretching out in front of me. Reaching up and grabbing Karen's dangling hand, I pulled her down next to me, and then we leaned against each other and slept.

That was about as much normality as could be got on Egesta, and we'd take it.

We both slept for three hours.

Around here, one of my editors expressed a very valid concern: I hadn't really conveyed the scope of the tragedy. She's right — all I've described is what we saw in the single narrow corridor we were holding, not what was going on across the city.

Even in that corridor, I'll admit I've left out a lot of detail — the smell and taste of the air, some things no one should ever see... perhaps I've left those out because I couldn't stand to recount them. Whatever the reason, they're not here.

But I should provide more scope, so I will: the Government Dome (the colony's smallest) originally had a population of 119,000. By the time Andrea and Mark first arrived, we think 34,000 had been murdered. During Andrea's first week on the ground, our best guess is that another 18,000 were killed. In my first day on the ground, another 1,200.

All the bodies were thrown out the airlocks. Adrienne Thompson one day returned from her combat patrol fighting tears because she'd flown through a cloud of dead schoolchildren.

I'm only telling you a thin slice of what we saw. Words couldn't begin to describe the rest.

CHAPTER TWENTY-TWO
THE NEXT DAY

I woke up first, with the simulated sunlight that started coming in through the windows of the second floor. Despite all the chaos on Egesta, no one had messed with the settings of the Earthgreen dome covering the government city — we still had a regular day and night cycle. It didn't occur to me then, but changing that cycle could have proved useful in those early days.

What if we'd turned off 'night'? Could there be as much damage done by the Guild fighters without the cover of darkness?

Actually, for Earth readers of this, let me elaborate a tiny bit on how an Earthgreen dome works: essentially, during day hours the dome becomes opaque, with the projector panels lining it showing an Earth-like cloud pattern and a moving sun that fairly closely matches a twenty-four hour day. At night, the panels deactivate (after fading convincingly to black) and the dome goes transparent, revealing the real blackness surrounding the asteroid.

What if we'd left the lights on? I should have thought of that early on, but I didn't. It could have made a difference... but then again, many things could have made a difference in those early days.

Anyway, when I woke the House was relatively quiet — it was still early hours, really, and many of the people in the building had been out during the night and were patently exhausted. Gently pushing Karen's head off my shoulder and sliding her sideways to make sure she didn't fall over when I moved, I quietly stood and went back downstairs.

More movement down there, certainly, and as I picked up a morning kit from the kitchen — one with a mouth cleaning capsule and an MRE — I looked for Matt, Mark or Charlie. I found Mark as I popped the cleaner capsule, so I could only nod to him as I came to a stop at the front door, waiting for the fizzing of the wash to end.

"Charlie went out about an hour after you went up last night," Mark began helpfully, recognizing my inability to open my mouth. "He brought in fourteen people — they'd apparently been heading for the stadium unescorted and they got jumped. We just heard from Veronica, too: her total tally was six, including the three you knew about."

That was twenty people for the night. Like I said last chapter, that's nothing to shake a stick at... but I wanted more.

Finally the fizzing in my mouth ended, and I tore open my MRE breakfast, "Anything from the Guild yet?"

Mark shook his head, "They're unionized, remember. You'll be waiting for a while."

I bit off a piece of my MRE, not reacting at all to its lack of taste, "You know, I wish they were a proper union. I don't seem to recall any rapes and murders from even the noisiest wildcat strikes in the Empire."

"True enough," Mark grunted, then bobbed his head out the door. "Looks like

Charlie's coming back. He and his squad walked his rescues down to the stadium."

Leaning slightly to get a better view of the street heading towards the stadium, I caught sight of an exhausted-looking column of Special Branchers. Now, I say exhausted because I've learned what to look for when you have tired Special Branch personnel. I've been told by the uninitiated that they can't tell the difference between a Special Brancher on eight hours of sleep and one on none, but there are differences.

And you know what, I'm not going to elaborate. What good would it do for me to reveal the very subtle cues that allow you to tell if a Special Brancher is tired?

Suffice it to say that, as Charlie came up the steps to the front door, he looked more exhausted than I'd seen him in some time. And far graver than I'd ever seen him up to that point.

"Good morning," was the only offering I could muster, and he nodded to me in reply.

"Better for some than others."

I think he was referring to it being a better morning for those he and Veronica's people had managed to pull out than it had been for anyone who hadn't received Defense Command or Hawke Protection during the night.

Without another word, Charlie slid past Mark and me, heading for the rations. I didn't follow him — he needed some time to process, and I wasn't going to pressure him.

"I'm going to call Jim Hannigan and see if we've gotten any comms from the Guild. I want this thing settled today," my words were firm now, and Mark nodded. It was a great ambition, to be done with the situation by day's end, but it was an important one from my perspective.

Innocent people and my own personnel were all being victimized in their own ways by this situation — and while you might angrily demand to know how I dare compare the plight of my personnel to those innocents being killed and brutalized, I can only say it's my job to worry about them. Look, I was there at Egesta to try to help, but the people of the planet weren't my only priority. I had a duty to my crews, and I wanted this done. Today.

Turning away from Mark with a nod, I fumbled my comm out of my pocket, then turned on the unit and waited while it started up and found the nearest transmission grid. *Wolf* popped up on its frequency detectors a moment later, and I selected the ship grid and gave my thumbprint to access the higher levels of *Wolf*Net.

Pinging the bridge, I waited for one of Jim's techs to notice that my signal code was coming in, and then, after about thirty seconds, Jim appeared on my comm's small screen.

"Jim," my greeting was accompanied by a short nod.

"We're still hearing nothing but silence," he answered the question before I got to ask it. "I don't know if they're going to play ball."

Great, just what I wanted to hear.

How exactly was I going to get them to pay attention to my threats? Well, there was always the tried-and-true method: go big.

Go very, very big.

"Alright, thanks Jim. I'll have orders for the squadron in a few minutes, I'll call back."

He nodded slowly and then vanished.

Turning back to the doorway, I motioned to Mark Gunney. We went to collect the other officers.

Trying to choose an appropriate level of force for a compelling bit of gunboat diplomacy is never easy. I call it 'gunboat diplomacy' because that's what the Empires of old — with all their flaws — called it when they started shelling the locals to make them comply with Imperial policy.

Gunboat diplomacy is always something that our own Empire has tried to avoid — it's a great way to look like a bully if you use it too much. On this occasion, though, I wasn't worried about the optics of the situation. The practical concerns were damning enough as it was.

"We drill a hole in one of their domes, kill hundreds of thousands of their people," Mark Gunney relishes playing devil's advocate now and then, and his option was clearly the most grizzly of the ones under consideration.

I raised an eyebrow and thought about his words for a moment — giving the bastards a taste of their own medicine, albeit much more impersonally, had a certain appeal. But that was overstepping the acceptable parameters in so many ways.

"I'd prefer we start drilling out the tunnels — isolate the domes. Make them think we're cutting them off from each other for purposes of invasion. That'd get their attention," Charlie leaned forward over the map table we were surrounding, his weary eyes dancing from dome to dome and his finger sliding along the line of one of the tunnels he was referring to.

I believe I mentioned this option earlier in one context or another — basically, we *could* decide to cut through the rock between domes and slice apart the trans-dome tunnels, effectively isolating each dome from the others.

"Remember, though," Matt interrupted with his usual presence of mind, "anything we do that's perceived as hostile might bring down all the fighters in this dome right onto us. There could be a bloody field action here if we get their attention."

I met the Briton's eyes, then glanced at Charlie and he nodded, "No question. We start it up, they're going to come after us."

"But they've only got the EP-5s Cook left for them; we could probably handle them," Mark frowned.

"They likely captured more stocks of weapons — Boscawen field barracks, police stations... who knows. Bottom line, though, if we start a fight, it's going to end with us killing hundreds of them, and we may get driven out of here," Charlie's tone was as ragged as he seemed, and I let out a sigh.

We'd been able to get some traction the day before, but if we started shooting now...

"I don't think we can do this the way we want to," I said after a short pause, and the rest of my trusted officers and friends put on resigned looks.

There was no way we could fight our way through this, as much as I'd have liked to.

"So let's get two trucks out front. Charlie, pick six officers, sidearms only. Mark, Matt, you come with me and Karen, and let's go see if we can have a chat with the Guild leadership."

You'll be wondering if it was wise for all of the most senior officers to be heading out of the dome together — it was bad enough that we'd all gone together to the Boscawen barracks.

Matt was thinking the very same, and he cleared his throat, "Is it really wise that we all go?"

I looked up with a frown, then slowly shook my head, "No, of course it isn't. You and Mark stay here."

Both Matt and Mark opened their mouths simultaneously to protest, but Karen, who had come downstairs earlier and was not looking the most genial at the moment, shot them both glares that suggested their silence would be appreciated.

Karen has an infectious smile and an elegance that would shame many archangels, but when she's not in the mood to hear protests, she really can turn on the quieting menace.

"Look after things here. And make sure Lieutenant Commander Ashby's in position to open up whatever dome we end up in. Tell him I'll be on the comm to him if I need to make the threat," I looked immediately to Mark, and he nodded once.

With that, and a short glance at Charlie, I turned for the door. We all strode out of Government House together and waited for trucks to be brought to the bottom of the stairs. When they finally arrived, Karen and I climbed into one, and I tried to control my racing heart rate. Glancing twice at my dear Flag Captain, I drew some comfort from her stillness.

I was working my way through stages of unraveling, but after a few short hours of sleep she had things in hand.

After Charlie's picked officers piled into the truck behind us, I tapped the driver on the shoulder and quietly gave the order, "Get us to a Guild roadblock. A big one."

We hovered off.

Chapter Twenty-Three

After We Left

I'll get to what we found at the roadblock in a couple of pages: at Mark Gunney's request, I'm going to clear up right now exactly what happened about forty-five minutes after Karen, Charlie and I floated away. He never caught any flack for this in the service, or in the post-war tribunals, but that aborted smear campaign about six years ago tried to tarnish him with it.

So, being Mark, he's asked me to be completely candid about what happened when the Guild fighters chased a young couple into the park behind Government House. I don't believe I've described this side of Government House yet — you may be familiar with it from other sources, but let me be clear about it anyway.

You know that street side, Government House had steps climbing up to a main door — typical of colonial architecture, even in the free belt. Well, as is also typical, behind Government House was a large manicured garden of legitimate Earth-based vegetation, maintained at some cost to make the government look good and powerful.

By the time we got to Egesta, the lawn and bushes were dead and many were burned — these things need regular watering to grow, take it from an Earth-born — but the hedges still offered some cover, and the asteroid-stone-sided fountains, benches and daises all remained. Matt had three SFers posted on the back balcony, watching this park to make sure no fighters snuck up too close behind hedges, and some of the cover had been cleared nearer Government House to make sure we had a secure perimeter killing field.

About forty-five minutes after we pulled away, Mark was sitting at a table in the make-shift armory (formerly the office of the Communications Director) with a Hawke Guard Sergeant named Sprick.

"It's fused to the housing, sir, it melted bad. You're not going to be able to fix that," Sprick was saying darkly, and Mark looked up at him with a frown.

"I've actually fixed worse, just takes time."

He had his mag stripped on the table, and was prodding at it with some field tools (that always look like dentist's kit to me). Remember, the cell had overloaded back in that alley just the day prior, and with everything going on Mark hadn't yet been able to find time to fix the weapon.

A few minutes of prodding later, Matt stuck his head into the room, "Sentries on the terrace have something."

Looking up with a nod, Mark stood quickly, then nodded to Sprick, "Sidearm, Sergeant."

With a nod, Sprick reached behind him to a few mags he'd been tuning — mainly the old MAG-4 sidearms the Hawke Guards were carrying. Mark holstered the unfamiliar weapon and followed Matt out of the room.

Arriving on the terrace first, Matt later told me he first thought they were under some sort of mild attack; the EP-5s of the SFers were leveled down at the park. Seeing this, both he and Mark drew their weapons, and Mark led the way to the rail.

"They coming to sacrifice themselves?" the Commander asked brusquely, and the senior SFer shook her head and pointed.

Mark followed the finger down to the young couple in question, hiding behind a bench while a squad of rather bold fighters fanned out in the park behind them.

I suppose these fighters believed they could get away with a little chaos in the park behind our HQ — perhaps taunt us with it — but at the same time be safe because of our neutrality. Well, they were right about our neutrality.

"Matt, get some backup out here. Shirley, with me," Mark turned and headed down the stairs at the side of the terrace to the park below, one of the SFers — Shirley Falk, who he'd recognized from *Honesty* — following closely.

Matt turned back to the house and summoned the ready guards — the SFers who were the rapid response team for dealing with situations like this one. They started clomping out onto the terrace, bringing Defense Command numbers to eleven total, Mark and Shirley included.

Making no attempt to be subtle (because he never does), Mark walked straight up to the couple behind the park bench, drawing surprised stares from the fighters, who in turn began to drift together into a fourteen-person cluster a little ways beyond that bench.

With something of a glare of contempt, Mark bent down, grabbed the hiding civilians by the arms, forcibly pulled them to their feet, then turned and pushed them towards Shirley.

"They go inside," he said simply, then he turned back to the dozen fighters who were edging closer to him. "You all leave now, this park is part of the Defense Command safe zone and you're not welcome."

The words, he's since told me, were not easy to get out — the ones he wanted to say were 'Matt, open fire!' but he obviously couldn't use them.

The fighters began to back off slowly, and Mark turned back towards the House. What came next was a surprise to just about everybody. The woman from the young couple elbowed Shirley Falk in the nose, just like that, and pulled the SFer's EP-5 off her. Mark turned to this woman just in time to realize she was clamping down on the weapon's trigger, and he leapt sideways as a splash of electromagnetic energy lanced over the bench and just past the fighters, who now all turned with guns brandished.

While the man from the couple started manically screaming, the woman charged past Mark, spraying more energy at the fighters, who were now bristling and lining up shots on her, on Mark, and on the SFers on the terrace.

In that second, Mark assessed the possibilities he was facing — there was a very good chance this woman would start a firefight that would end messily, with some of the fighters getting away under cover of the hedges to report that Defense Command had started shooting at them. That could potentially spark a firefight... all while Karen, Charlie and I were with the Guild leadership.

That couldn't be allowed, so Mark made the tough call, raised his mag and fired.

But he hadn't checked the weapon's settings — there hadn't been time. He doesn't know to this day how he managed to go all the way out there with his weapon set to full... well he does: it was a MAG-4, it didn't have a display on the outer housing like our standard MAG-6s have to make power settings clear (that's one of the reasons we never adopted the MAG-4s).

But to Mark, that's no excuse. You have to understand, he's lived with guns around for most of his life, he knows well how to use them. And yet this one time, this worst possible time, he didn't remember to check the gun. It had been handed to him and he *hadn't checked it*. There really hadn't been time to open the cowl and review the settings on the cell, as one must do with a MAG-4... but Mark's never let himself off the hook.

He hit the woman in the back of the head with a shot he expected would knock her out. It blew out her forehead instead.

Mark didn't realize quite what he'd done at first — he saw a puff of red mist splash over the bench and spray the fighters, but he couldn't figure out where it came from. That lack of realization lasted for at least two or three seconds, and he started bellowing at the fighters, "Get out of this park before we *move you out!*"

Then, as Shirley quickly raced ahead of him to recover her weapon, she stopped and froze next to the fallen body, then looked up with a slack jaw.

Mark couldn't understand why she was so surprised, but then some nagging instinct drove him to look at weapon in his hand. He roughly keyed the release on the cowl cover and stripped off the cell cowl, then flipped open the indicator panel. After that he stopped thinking for a few seconds. The man from the couple jumped him while he was standing there — the screaming, raving man started swinging at him with telegraphed punches.

"You killed her! You killed her! Fucking Defcom! Fucking Defcom!"

Collecting her weapon and quickly checking the settings, Shirley Falk dropped this man with a shot, before a shocked Mark Gunney could react.

Mark holstered the weapon after that (without the cowl attached — he kept that in hand), and turned and returned to the terrace. Matt Baxter took two SFers down to collect the body and the unconscious man, and Mark Gunney went inside and stopped near the map table for a moment. He then looked up at the armory door and found himself moving through it in a flash.

Sprick looked up with a frown, "I can't see how you can fix your–"

Mark drew his mag and dropped it on the table in front of the Hawke Sergeant, "You provided me with a weapon that was set to *maximum.*"

Sprick's frown deepened as he looked down at the pistol, then looked back up at Mark, "Well. Sorry."

"*Sorry!*" Mark dropped the gun's cowl on the desk and then planted both hands on either side of it, leaning down close to the Sergeant. "If you were one of mine, you'd be confined to quarters for sixty days. This is a *peacekeeping mission,* no weapons should be set to lethal! Do you *realize* what could have happened out there? What if I'd tried to stun one of the Guilders? I could have sparked a war! As it was, I just blew away a civilian woman — *one of the people I went out there to protect!*"

Sprick swallowed at the thunderous tone, "But sir — I mean..."

"Are all the weapons you're tuning set to maximum?" Mark demanded without pause.

"It's... yes. It's better to be safe than sorry. The troops are more comfortable if their sidearms are a lethal option in this sort of–"

"You set *everything* to medium. *Now*. And I'm going to see about getting you busted to private. What the *hell* are you thinking, kill settings on a peacekeeping operation?" By this time Mark had straightened and was heading out the door, shaking his head as a shocked Sprick sat at the table in the armory.

Now, you might think that reaction harsh, or perhaps the anger Mark felt at his own oversight was being unfairly directed at the Hawke Sergeant. No doubt, there was some transferred rage there, but that doesn't make Mark's point any less correct. Hawke Guard policy of stunning with the rifle but keeping the sidearm at full power (to give the Guards the comfort of knowing that an instrument of lethal force was always at their hip if they needed it) was perhaps appropriate when storming a pirate base looking for prisoners, but in this situation, it could be catastrophic.

After that incident, the order went down for all Hawke sidearms to be turned down. We can only assume it happened, because thankfully, no Hawke Guard was forced to use her or his sidearm in the days that followed.

Whatever smear campaigns have tried to say later, this incident has been accepted openly as an accident in a combat zone, and has been so confirmed by all levels of adjudication, with both military and civilian tribunals having dismissed it. The setting on his weapon was too high, certainly, but no one in their right mind believed Mark Gunney had any intention of *killing* a civilian he'd just rescued.

And even if he had intended to kill her, under the Articles of Empire, in a combat situation, commanders are permitted to take whatever action necessary to protect the integrity of an Imperial position, within the strictures of 'reasonable judgment and application of force'. In other words, technically speaking, even had Mark intended to kill the woman, he would have been well justified in doing so under Imperial law, given the circumstances.

Delightful.

But while the law wouldn't fault Mark Gunney for protecting the integrity of the mission (and I should add, I very much doubt that Shirley, Matt Baxter or any of the SFers on that terrace would have 'seen anything' had there been a legal concern), Mark Gunney's been living a long time with this particular demon. It bothers him more regularly than most of the other demons in his life, though he doesn't reveal it much at all. He's 'over it', you see.

To you people out there who tried to smear Mark (those of you who survived the duels you challenged him to), you're scum, and back off. If you think anyone came out of Egesta with clean hands, you'd better smarten up. And really, that's the only blood I can think of on Mark's hands — why don't you come after me? When it comes down to it, I'm responsible for much, much worse.

CHAPTER TWENTY-FOUR

LEAPFROG

Once again, it's time for a pleasant diversion: let's see how Wes was doing against Sean Cook. As you'll remember, Wes had come up with the legitimately brilliant intent of faking a reactor collapse and dropping his squadron back out of sight. The plan was to give Cook breathing room, to allow him to ease off his blistering acceleration, and to thus create an opportunity to leap past the bastard.

By getting between Cook and Belt Fourteen, Wes was hoping he could preempt any possibility of there being a firefight over the colony... though he was still seriously outnumbered.

But being outnumbered didn't matter a damn to Wes Pellew. His first objective was to get between Cook and the Belt rock. He'd play the rest of the encounter from there.

"They're now making 182 kps, looks like they're resting their engines," Kate Levec reported on *Cheetah's* bridge. This was about the time of Mark's run-in in the park, so let's call it roughly ten hours after the simulated reactor failure.

Wes was standing on his bridge, his arms folded and his eyes locked on the main screen. He'd grabbed about two hours sleep in his day cabin during the night, but hadn't left the bridge deck at all during this cat-and-mouse shadowing affair.

Now it seemed Cook had decided he could safely decelerate, just about thirty hours out of Belt Fourteen at present speed.

It was time to change speeds then.

"Dropping back 175 kps. *British Columbia's* reducing velocity quicker than the rest. They may be touching up some reactor strain. Now 170 kps..." Kate Levec looked up over the shoulder of one of her techs at the Sensors and Communications consoles. "I think this is our chance, skipper."

Wes nodded, turning to the Lieutenant who had the morning shift at Helm and Navigation, "Mister Deng, prepare for combat acceleration. I want us to maximum combat velocity, 203 kps or better."

The Lieutenant nodded evenly, then began issuing orders to his staff. Wes turned back to Kate Levec, "Battlelink."

She nodded at the single word, then tapped a technician on the shoulder and issued the command.

Turning to the screens again, Wes waited as Kris Jacobs, Elise De Winter and Isoruku Togo appeared, and he nodded to them quickly, "Alright, we're getting our chance. I want full military burn, let's show them how fast new generation ships can move. Sound good?"

Kris smiled hungrily on the screen, "Been looking forward to this all night."

Wes nodded, "Let's go."

The link stayed active, though Wes walked out of the camera shot to stand near his

Helm and Navigation Officer.

"They're down to 165 kps, skipper. I'm thinking *British Columbia* must be cycling one of its reactors," Kate Levec put in quickly.

Looking up to his Helm and Navigation Officer, Wes took a breath, "Ready on my mark."

Lieutenant Deng nodded, and then Wes crossed back over to the screens displaying the faces of his fellow skippers, "Alright. We go... *now*."

No countdown, no fancy wording.

"Accelerate drives to full combat power, max burn, max output. Give it the throttle, Jimmy!" Lieutenant Deng barked the orders.

Despite the fact that she looked away from the mics, Kris' words came across the Battlelink because she essentially yelled them with charming Australian enthusiasm, "Let's pass these bastards, Jack. Pour it on!"

What came next must have been something of a shock to Cook. In the course of about a minute, he went from having clear sensor scopes to being *passed* by four Defense Command ships.

"We're cruising past them... now. They're re-accelerating... Jesus they're kicking quickly..." Kate Levec was narrating what she was seeing over the shoulders of her techs, and Wes nodded as he watched the icons of his ships and Cook's on the main screen.

The Belt Squadron elite were blowing past the Independent Squadron, but Cook's ships were indeed picking up speed to pursue much more quickly than Wes would have expected of them.

"They're not going to catch us, not at that accel," Kris said in a lower voice over the Battlelink. "Well played, Wes."

Both Togo and De Winter concurred with her comment, and Wes slowly nodded his thanks. His eyes were still locked on that main screen — they weren't getting much of a gap over the Independent Squadron...

"Reduce drives to 198 kps for cruising," he said evenly. "Kate, keep an eye on them. If they change course to go elsewhere, I want to know about it."

Kate Levec began giving orders to her technicians, and Wes did some math in his head. At their new pace, they'd probably hit Belt Fourteen in a day.

While Wes, Kris, Isoruku and Elise were leapfrogging Cook's ships, *Alberta* was about twelve hours out of Belt Fourteen, coming right for them. Marshal Samuels was sitting in his day cabin, reading a report from *Alberta's* engineering section. Apparently the extra load of small arms from Belt Fourteen's arsenal had reduced drive performance by two percent — a barely noticeable difference, even to a honed officer like Marshal, but a difference nonetheless.

That wasn't what he was really focusing on, though; no, his primary concern at the moment was much more practical: what was he going to do when he ran into the six frigates and two corvettes of the Independent Squadron?

He didn't know, of course, that Wes was coming straight for him — Wes hadn't signaled ahead because it was highly likely Cook would have detected the message as it passed him in space along the base course to Belt Fourteen. Wes was about to open contact with the station, now that he was in the lead, but that wouldn't help Marshall, because the comm laser would pass him in space.

So he thought he was heading out for an eight-to-one encounter, which certainly meant a different approach to dealing with Cook's squadron than he'd have liked.

He'd have to try to stop Cook with an announcement that he was carrying all the small arms from the Defense Command arsenal in his hold... then try to convince the Commodore to return to Belt Two to await further instructions.

And if that failed, and Cook came looking for the guns, that'd require escape; Marshal would have to run like the wind, and *Alberta's* engines would have to make that a possibility.

But how fast could the veteran frigate — a *North America*-class ship that hadn't been upgraded to the extent Cook's ships had — go in a marathon run from the Independent Squadron cruisers?

Turning back to his desk (sorry, I should have said earlier that he was standing as he read the report) Marshal keyed his intercom, then requested the engineering section. After a moment, Todd Novotny, the ship's Chief Engineer since Greg's days in command, arrived on the line, "Todd here, Cap'n. What can I do for you?"

"Hi Todd," Marshal moved to his chair and lowered himself into it as he began speaking, "I have a problem I'm hoping you might be able to help with. We might have to get away from the Independent Squadron in a day or so. We might have to *run*, and I'm reading this report you wrote for me... do you think we can outrun the Independent Squadron with the extra mass we're carrying?"

There was a pause at the other end of the line, and then some muffled voices as Novotny directed some questions to his staff of engineers.

"I can keep our cruising speed at 198 kps, Cap'n. That's all I can promise... more might blow the reactors, but I can hold 198 for a day, maybe two."

For your reference, *Alberta's* rated cruising speed was 192 kps, and its actual experience had been up to 196 kps. Marshal couldn't ask for more than 198 kps — that was a *Predator*-class ship's cruising speed, and it was no mean feat to manage it in a *North America*.

"That's excellent, Todd. Thank you. I'll let you know when we need it... if we need it, that is. I still am holding out hope that it won't be necessary."

"Understood, sir. That be all?"

"Certainly," Marshal nodded to himself, then tapped the intercom offline. He wasn't comfortable with the promise of fleeing from a monster like Cook, but he had to consider what was in the best interests of Belt Fourteen. That colony's best chance of remaining unaccosted was his diversion...

At least that was the situation as far as he knew it. For the moment, though, he was cruising on an essentially converging course, nose-to-nose with twelve incoming ships — four of ours, and eight of Cook's.

Had he known that, he might have worried even more...

CHAPTER TWENTY-FIVE
AT THE ROADBLOCK

Karen was first to hop out of our truck, and a hush seemed to fall over the crowd of Guild fighters that began to cluster around our mini-convoy of two vehicles as she stepped towards them. My guess is they were impressed by the fact that it was indeed the famous Karen McMaster who was visiting them. I got out behind her, and together we strode towards the crowd of fighters at the roadblock as if we were somehow their friends.

"Where's the commander of this barricade?" Karen managed to sound *not* hostile with the question, which was undoubtedly a good thing.

We were at a different blockade point than the one we'd visited on the way to the Boscawen barracks — this one was up Second Street towards the inter-dome tunnel to Dome Four. As she asked the question, a number of Guild fighters back in the crowd shot suspicious glances at each other, then started coming forward.

Seeing them, I bobbed my head in their direction, "This way, I think."

Trying not to look like we were staying abnormally close together out of certain fear, we walked into the crowd — and it parted before us as we headed for the self-identified leaders of the barricade force.

We met them in the middle of the group, and as we did, Karen and I stopped side by side, both of us consciously keeping our hands well away from our sidearms and our hips in general — we didn't want to appear as though we were scolding these people...

Yes, believe me, it was as disgusting a move of tolerance as I've ever had to make. By that I mean it made me feel *sick* to be pretending to accept these people.

The Guild commanders came to a stop opposite us, and the crowd huddled around as the leading man narrowed his eyes at Karen and me, "What do you two want, then?"

I tipped my head sideways, mustering all the false friendliness I could, "We talked to the commander of the barricades down by the Boscawen barracks yesterday, he said he was going to get us a meeting with the leadership."

"And why would he promise *you* that?" the commander here didn't sound impressed.

Karen was able to answer before I was, "Because we warned him about the imminent arrival of an armored brigade of Imperial Army troops. And we told him, and we're telling you, that if you haven't signed some sort of ceasefire with the government before they arrive, the Imps are going to pacify this whole rock."

The same wave of unsettled murmurs that we got back at the Boscawen barricade was repeated here. I guess communication between the various barricades wasn't that good — word of the impending arrival of the Imperials hadn't gotten as far as I'd hoped it would.

Oh well, that was the nature of this business. Sometimes the word spread, sometimes it didn't...

"Imperial *Army*…" the commander looked at the woman who I presume was his second in command, then turned back to Karen and me. "So you're coming to deliver an ultimatum."

It wasn't a question, it was a statement, near as I could tell. And as much as I really, *truly* wanted to say 'yes, an ultimatum — get out!', I couldn't. For one, I'd have been torn limb from limb by the crowd if I did something *that* brash…

"We're not particularly fond of the blockheads," I said dryly. "They show up here, they're going to start shooting everyone who resists, and they don't believe in non-lethal response. That looks bad on Karen and me if we let it happen. We were first responders, and people will wonder why we didn't fix it before the Imps arrived. So yesterday we got the Governor to agree to step down in favor of a free, supervised election, as long as your side backs off for the moment and a ceasefire is signed."

Tip my hand too far? No. No, by giving this obviously suspicious commander a glimpse of a plausible reason for our interest in brokering this ceasefire, I was hoping to cut through his skepticism. Why, he could have otherwise asked, would we not just wait for the Imps to arrive and then dictate the terms of peace?

Well, waiting and killing was my backup plan.

But the commander here bought my lines without too much reservation, "You want to parley, then?"

Karen and I nodded in tandem, and then the commander stared at us silently for a moment, "Alright. Hernando, you take over here. I'll ride with them, and Chuck, get the truck and follow us with your warwhores. Just in case this is some kind of trick."

'Warwhores' stopped me for a minute, until I followed this man's eyes to 'Chuck', one of the armed fighters, and he turned and waved to a gaggle of seven women who looked indeed as though they'd been workers in a brothel, each of them wielding an EP-5.

"You can join us in our truck, if you like," Karen managed again to sound non-hostile. "Your truck can lead, follow… whatever you think best."

"Chuck'll follow your Special Branchers," the commander said shortly, then stepped forward and waved for us to lead him back to our truck. We did.

Climbing into the floating vehicle, I got into the front seat and let Karen sit in back with the man. The driver gave me a nervous look but I steadied him with a short stare. The Guild commander got comfortable, then leaned forward, "Head for Dome Five tunnel. I'll get us through the checkpoints."

He definitely sounded like he knew what he was talking about — or at least like he wanted us to have confidence in his ability to get us around safely.

"Oh, I should introduce myself. Of course I recognize you both," he extended his hand towards Karen, and she took it without so much as flinching. "I'm Willard Smitt."

You probably recognize the name — from the tribunals, from the gallows. Sure enough, we were sitting in a truck with one of the chief architects of the slaughter, we just didn't know it at the time.

He reached forward and extended his hand to me, and I took it without too much hesitation. It was grubby and cold, appropriately enough.

Sitting back in his seat with a satisfied smile, he stroked the barrel of his EP-5 (yes, it looked as creepy as it sounds), "You two, shit. Definitely have to give you credit. Neither of you seems the least bit like you want to kill me right now. Good acting."

Ah yes, the sober assessment of our probable state of mind; I still don't know precisely whether he was trying to bait us or if this man actually had a grasp on reality. One thing Karen suggested afterwards was that he might have been hoping we'd talk him up as a big threat, and thus fluff up his ego.

I wasn't inclined to oblige. Karen certainly wasn't going to be helping him either.

We sat in silence as our convoy, now plus a single escort truck, floated on down the street towards the Dome Five tunnel.

CHAPTER TWENTY-SIX

CROSSING DOMES

While we were floating towards the tunnel to Dome Five, getting waved through various barricades as Smitt stuck his head out our window, the space above our heads was really quite active. Sitting in the truck, I had no evidence that we were getting top-cover, but since I'd ordered some, I was reasonably sure it was up there.

Lieutenant Commander Ashby had *Honesty* floating over Dome Five, the ship's bow laser zeroed in for a shot on the tunnel to the Government Dome if one was needed. That might sound crazy to you — shoot the tunnel we needed to use — but it was a good leverage move, something I could use if needed.

You know, the 'play ball or I kill you all' card.

Better than just that laser, though, Lieutenant Commander Adrienne Thompson, who I may not have mentioned at all in the last couple of books, had half her squadron of Starlights coasting in broad arcs over us, drifting back and forth over the Government Dome and Dome Five. More ordnance I could use to threaten the Guild leadership.

Sitting silently in the front of the truck, though, I wasn't thinking exclusively about the goings-on in the sky. I was also fighting the skin-crawling feeling that was creeping over me. I'm sure it sounds cliché, but then I imagine every cliché has an origin… and this must have been it.

It was terribly hard to avoid simply turning around and shooting this smug murderer in the face. I don't care if that sounds callous to you, that was the mental image that repeated in my head as he started *humming happy tunes*.

We rolled through blockades for the next twenty minutes, continuing to stay low to the streets to avoid misidentification and the trading of fire. I simply stared straight ahead as we floated on.

Our eventual arrival at the entrance to the tunnel was something of a non-event. Security at the mouth of the tunnel was lax, probably because the Guild fighters doubted any civilians would be fool enough to try to go to Dome Five — what I later would come to call 'Guild territory'. Some of the other domes were much more neutral, and might provide refuge, but Dome Five had long been the home to low-income miners' housing, and now it was the stronghold that was supporting this vicious force of fighters.

Not a good place to be if you didn't agree with the Guilders' agenda… unless you were us. Hopefully.

We cruised into the tunnel's hover vehicle shaft on the wrong side of the road, at Smitt's insistence, but there was no traffic at all, so it didn't much matter. On these free rocks, tunnels aren't like the ones we have in the Belt colonies — they don't have bright skies playing on vid panels lining their ceilings. Nope, this was a brown and rocky tunnel, harshly lit by yellow lamps, a number of which had been shot out or just weren't working.

The transit was thus appropriately gloomy.

It was also long. Dome Five was relatively far from the Government Dome, at least seventy kilometers. In an F-194 at full burn, that distance is literally the blink of an eye, but down in a dark tunnel doing a modest 179 kilometers per *hour*, it's about a twenty-minute haul.

Again, I just stared straight ahead. Karen did the same behind me, and Smitt probably kept looking pleased with himself — I didn't bother checking.

The driver was still anxious, but he'd managed to settle into a relatively steady rhythm, watching the lamps rush by as we poured on the speed.

After that long haul, we emerged into the bright simulated day of Dome Five, and the place looked pristine. I mean, it was clearly a low-income dome, and the streets weren't all shiny and gleaming, but compared to where we'd come from, they were untouched.

But there were people, *civilians*, in the streets, heading up and down the sidewalk, going about their daily business... they seemed to actually still have daily business here.

As we slowed down to transit through the residential streets, I noticed a park full of young children playing. *Playing.*

It struck me at that moment that this seemed like a movie — one of those where the main character sees all sorts of horrors and then goes somewhere else only to be shocked by normal, happy living. Now I can see why they write it into movies... because good grief, I was rendered entirely speechless by the carefree attitude of these people.

They had sent thousands of fighters into the Government Dome to rape, murder and otherwise terrorize, and yet they were playing and going about their daily business? It was good that I didn't need to say anything in those first moments in Dome Five, because I really wouldn't have been able to put together any civil words.

Of course, part of my mind recognized that this was in a way good for Karen and me: there would clearly be much to threaten in Dome Five. You're going to think what I say next is monstrous, and I'll concur that it is, but it's the simple truth — we had leverage here.

We could kill a lot of civilians if we cut this dome open. Children's faces swelling up and their little bodies getting sucked into space, people who were going about their business in the streets being eviscerated by shrapnel... these were things we saw in colonies that were abruptly hit by pirates. They're horrid scenes, some of the most gruesome I'd seen up to my arrival on Egesta, and the reason why I never stand for the romanticizing of pirates and rebels.

And yet I was sitting in that truck, picturing what a couple of well-placed laser shots from *Honesty* could do to this dome, and being satisfied with the *leverage* that'd provide *me*. I could massacre hundreds of thousands of people with a word into my comm. That gave me the bargaining advantage.

Yes, that's what I was thinking. And of all the things I experienced on Egesta, I'm pretty sure the sheer comfort that realization brought was the thing that took me the longest to come to terms with.

I shouldn't spend more time on my guilty conscience, though. I've been told by many people that I've nothing to fear from such thoughts... I don't know that I believe them. But I do know what my actions ultimately were...

Sorry. Moving on.

Smitt directed our driver down one of the main streets towards a community center, and then we turned into that building's parking lot. It was the 'Azure Horizon Community Center', later made famous for other reasons, and it was the headquarters of the Guild at this time.

Parking, the driver glanced at me with questioning eyes, and I nodded back, "Keep it running."

I hopped out of the truck, and Karen and Smitt jumped out behind me. Charlie's truck pulled up alongside ours and he and three of his officers piled out, each carrying only a sidearm. The warwhores and 'Chuck' pulled up in the next spot over, and then the women exited their vehicle and sized up Charlie's people with narrowed eyes.

Charlie and his officers tried not to stare at their unlikely counterparts — as he pointed out to me later, he didn't know in that moment what to be more insulted by, their poor fashion, their leering, or the fact that these prostitutes were evidently considered by Smitt to be sufficient security to contain his Special Branchers.

Those reservations were unimportant, though, and Charlie moved past the hood of his truck and joined Karen and me in front of ours.

"You're not all going in," Smitt stepped past us, heading for the front entrance of the Azure Horizon Center, then turning back with a lopsided grin. "We're not fuckin' simple. Three Special Branchers and we could all end up dead. I'll let you take one."

Charlie's response to that wasn't even directed at Smitt, he just threw a glance back over his shoulder to Carly and nodded, "You look after things out here."

She nodded in reply, then turned away with arms folded and began to stare down the leering warwhores.

"Well, this is a treat, the three of you. I think we might want autographs after you talk," Smitt sneered, then started up the walk to the front entrance.

I traded glances with Karen and Charlie, and then in near-lock step we all followed.

CHAPTER TWENTY-SEVEN
THE GUILD ELDERS

The Guild Elders, they called themselves. How did I find this out as I walked into the community center lobby? They had a sign up, a professionally printed but juvenile banner that in block print announced our arrival in the 'HEADQUARTERS OF THE GOVERNMENT OF THE GUILD ELDERS'. A couple of bored Guild fighters were standing guard just inside the door, and they looked somewhat surprised when we arrived in the lobby, but Smitt waved them down.

They went back to their conversation, which from the few lines I heard, was an argument over local sports teams.

This was a very surreal experience, overall — such a departure from the besieged barracks where we'd found the Governor. Didn't these people realize that they had an army out there committing the worst kinds of atrocities for *fun*? It seemed wrong for this dome to be so carefree.

We crossed the lobby and climbed some stairs. To our right as we went up those stairs was a busy day care, to our left a window looking out onto a bunch of teenagers playing ball on a low-budget but clearly cared for football pitch. As we arrived on the second floor, Smitt led us down the hallway to the right, then stopped at a doorway to the community center's office area and waved us in ahead of him.

Charlie had, through chance or intent, managed to get into the leading position of our group, so he led the way into the bright office section, all done in pastels. The area smelled of fresh paint, and as I stepped in I looked up at the wall to the left of the door and read, in the same block lettering, 'CHAMBERS OF THE GUILD ELDERS'.

I looked down, and had to mentally calm myself.

None of the elders were older than me. Alright, one of them might have been older than me. But mostly they were Smitt's age or younger, dressed like slobs, and the nine of them were sitting around a round table, arguing over wording.

Oh and by round table, I don't mean a round boardroom table, or the table of King Arthur. This was one of those low tables, meant for young children learning their colors and numbers. I sat at one in kindergarten.

All of these supposed elders were sitting on the floor around one. I'm not kidding. This was the leadership of the rebellion, these were the Guild leaders.

It made me wonder, in that moment, how these nefarious people managed to orchestrate a coup, even with Cook's guns. Of course it would be later, much later, that I found out who the real heads of the old Guild were, and where and why they'd put their heads down after I arrived.

Well, no point making you wait: the elders we were about to meet were all the popular leaders, the people to whom the workers looked for guidance because they were… well, *popular*. Half of them were somewhat capable of doing the job, but mostly these were popularity contest types. Smitt was a representative of the original hard-edge of the Guild, the only one who'd had the guts to remain in public when we showed up.

He was also probably the boldest and stupidest of that old Guild element, because he ended up on the gallows for his trouble. The other old Guild members had realized that, by unleashing a war against the government and then promptly winning it, they'd lost their foil — they'd lost their excuse for the crippling Guild fees that impoverished all Guild members. They couldn't become the next government because then their self-interest and shortcomings would become all too evident... so they handed the keys to this band of ambitious, popular youngsters, told them it was crucial that the Government Dome be pacified, and told them to write a constitution.

These elders were the scapegoats, and were either too naïve to know it, or too desperate to admit it to themselves. The real Guild leadership slipped off Egesta with a lot of hard currency sometime before Karen, Mark and I arrived.

"Fuck you, that's not what 'prevarication' means!"

That explosion came from the round table, and I couldn't bite back my retort in time, "Children, when last I sat at a table that size, I learned to share. I was six at the time."

Yeah, that didn't win me any friends. Eyes whipped around to glare at me, and I replied with a thin, sinister smile.

"What the hell are they doing here?" one of the elders got to her feet. "We've been hearing about your meddling in our private affairs. You have no right..."

"I'm sorry, I seem to think *that* makes it our affair," Karen interrupted instantly, pointing to the EP-5 hanging from Smitt's shoulder. "You wouldn't be in this tastelessly decorated playroom without our guns."

Probably a little too strong, that wording, but then can you blame Karen? I personally applauded the fact that she didn't go for the throat this time. Though I may have enjoyed watching the throttling of one of these fools.

The rest of the elders got to their feet, trying to generate some menace with their united stand.

"Look, in five sentences or less, here's the situation: you're about to have an armored brigade of the Imperial Army land in your laps, and if you're not promising free elections by the time they arrive, they're going to pacify you. I'm willing to bet you all would feel alright with elections, because you do seem to have popular support around here. If you resist or cause trouble, you'll be crushed. If you try to take me or anyone in my party hostage, this Dome will be opened up like a tin can by DCNS *Honesty*. Now's when you declare a ceasefire and pull your fighters out of the Government Dome."

Five sentences. Bang-bang-bang-bang-bang.

There were shocked expressions, dropped jaws, and so forth — of course I was coming in here with about as much subtlety as a brick through a window. Only marginally more subtlety than if I'd actually started the negotiation by shooting out their tunnels.

"And let's just add that your fighters in the Government Dome have been committing heinous atrocities, and there'll have to be people put on trial for that," Karen's cold tone earned her some icy stares.

Smitt — that bastard — cleared his throat, "I've been hearing some reports about that. I assure you, we'll be bringing those people to justice. Anyone who's partaken in such activity will be dealt with."

Since the evidence later revealed (with vid footage) that he locked himself and two of his buddies in a room with four young sisters, I'm not sure how I can even comment on that statement. Except to repeat that he ended up on the gallows.

"I, for one, think we should cooperate. A free election for a new Governor who has the support of both the people and the Empire would be a great statement of the stability of Egesta," he went on, turning to his elders.

It was around this time I think I started to understand his agenda. He was the last of the old Guild leadership left on the rock, and he'd been a 'glorious military leader' in this coup. He was probably more intelligent than any of the elders here... he thought he could win a free election and take over on his own.

Nope, he was going to be hung.

But he was working for us right now, and that was something at least.

Karen sensed the uncertainty in the elders, so she added some ominous words, "Have you ever seen what the Imperial Army does when it's let off the leash? The only words they reply to are 'we surrender'. You won't get terms from them. You can get terms for a free election with us."

Now, there wasn't going to be a free election for long years to come, as far as we three Defense Command personnel in the room were concerned. Charlie was stonily silent behind us because he knew we were lying through our teeth. Then again, he agreed with this move — remember that conversation of the day prior? Well he repeated it to me many times after: this was the right call.

"So... you'll call off the Army?" one of the elders asked hesitantly, and I shook my head — perhaps too enthusiastically, but I didn't care.

"No, they're coming. But if you go for an election, I can probably make sure their role here is one of supervising at the polls. You'll be disarmed to ensure a fair result, and the Imps will run security until your free state and government are set up and rearmed."

That much was true, actually. We just were going to have to wait a long time for the election, and do a lot of cleaning out of the leadership circles before then.

Of course, my definition of 'cleaning out' seems to have been much milder than what happened in the end...

Not a matter for the moment.

The elders started to exchange more nervous glances, and one of the more coherent ones dismissed us haughtily, "You will wait outside while we deliberate."

"Excuse me?"

I know, I should have been gracious and gone out into the corridor, but my tolerance was worn too thin. Remarkable, eh? One night on this rock and I was losing it. Delightful place.

The elder who'd spoken looked at me indignantly, "I said *get out*, before I order you removed."

I cracked a smile and laughed, literally laughed, "I'm sorry, removed by *who*? Those two stuffed shirts with guns at the door? The *warwhores* outside? Really, I've got six Special Branchers here. That's *Charlie Peters* behind me, not to mention Karen. You really think you've got enough guns within five clicks of here to stop us if we decided to put your heads on pikes?"

Yes, diplomacy — if you want to know how a be a good diplomat, take this as an example of what *not* to do.

The elders looked appalled — how dare we threaten to decapitate them? Smitt was standing aside, very quiet. He wanted us to get our way, he wanted an election he could win. He'd be hung instead, as I like to keep repeating.

Karen then added the next layer of pressure, drawing her comm from her belt and keying it to *Honesty's* signal network, then waiting for Lieutenant Commander Ashby to come online, "Ashby here."

"Captain McMaster, here, Commander Ashby. We're in gunboat negotiations with the elders right now. You have a fix on our position?"

"We do, ma'am."

That was a lie. He couldn't zero in on our precise position within the dome until he had about a minute of open comm to allow him to triangulate. He already knew what block we were on, though, so that was close enough.

"Excellent. If you don't hear contrary orders from me or Commodore Barron in ten minutes, I want you to open this dome like a tin can. Cut for maximum explosive decompression. Confirm that order as a 10-5-10."

You probably haven't heard '10-5-10' before in these books, because most Belt officers never need to use the crude expression. Basically it means 'bluffing', or more colloquially translated, 'bullshit'. Officers like me, Karen, Charlie, Matt and Mark never need to say it because we can convey the meaning to each other in more nuanced ways. Karen didn't know Lieutenant Commander Ashby well enough though, so she had to be sure he knew she wasn't actually ordering him to slice the dome open.

Fortunately, no one else in the room (except Charlie) knew what 10-5-10 referred to.

"You must be joking. You'd never wipe out a dome full of people just for your political causes, that's monstrous!"

Sorry, as if we were in court and I was having that read back by the stenographer, let me repeat that line, with some italics put in to emphasize certain statements: "You must be joking. You'd never *wipe out a dome full of people just for your political causes,* that's *monstrous!"*

So evidently that *wasn't* what they were doing in the Government Dome?

I honestly didn't know what I could possibly say to that. The word 'hypocrite' is so weak in some circumstances. Flying off the handle in a blustering fit of sputtering rage wouldn't really have conveyed my... my... rage, I suppose. I was about ready to cross the floor to start pulverizing the mouthy elder.

But I didn't have to.

There's been a lot of bone breaking in this book, and here's some more. Charlie put the speaker into traction for fifteen months with a few economical blows. The elder crumpled and started sobbing in shock, while the rest of the esteemed leaders backed away and gasped.

Smitt started chuckling softly to himself.

"You have no choice. Let's make that clear," Charlie said coolly, stepping back to

Karen's side.

Karen then managed to come up with some coherent words, because she's good with those, "Your fighters have been doing much worse than just wiping out a dome full of people. Torture and rape and murder, which will be answered for."

She stopped and took a very deep breath, that came out as a huff as she focused herself for what she *had* to say next. She didn't have a choice.

"After the election."

I managed a nod, "So you're declaring a ceasefire *right now*. Imperial forces will hold the Government Dome, you'll make arrangements with the Imperial Army Brigadier to turn in your arms for temporary storage. You'll *vote*."

The elders exchanged more panicked glances, and then a brave one managed to ask something I couldn't quite hear... I caught something like 'guarantees?' and guessed the rest.

"Your *guarantee*," I snarled, drawing my mag and crossing the floor to get hold of this woman's collar, "is that you will all *die* if you don't give me a reason to calm down."

My mag pressed against her temple as I slammed her back into the wall, and she swallowed and tried to nod.

The rest of the elders concurred, one of them managing to say what needed to be said: "Alright, alright. Smitt, withdraw our soldiers. We'll maintain our perimeter in Dome Five and Dome Two until your Imperial Army arrive. But if there's any government attack..."

"There won't be, or the Boscawen mercs will answer to us," Karen's level tone ended the discussion.

I stepped back and released the elder I'd pinned, and as I reholstered my mag she slid down to the floor, gasping for breath.

"We'll be going now," I said darkly, casting a glance at Smitt. He nodded, and then Karen, Charlie and I left quickly.

Before we killed someone.

CHAPTER TWENTY-EIGHT

CEASEFIRE

We came out of the community center at a fast walk, our determined strides keeping us well ahead of Smitt, who was forced to half-jog to keep up.

The Special Branchers waiting outside all noticed our hurried pace and Carly turned first, her hand drifting to her mag with some concern at our haste.

"Hands off it, bitch!" one of the warwhores hissed, raising her EP-5. I have to say, witnessing that exchange was like watching something out of a B movie — I mean seriously, why in God's name would the Guild arm hookers except for some sort of perverse shock value?

Well, actually, as Charlie pointed out to me, those were women who you could count on to be throat-cutters. They worked a brothel on a tough-as-nails mining rock, there wasn't much chance of them *not* shooting if they were told to.

Yes, I know it's a crude observation, but the situation rather warrants it. Believe me, I'm really looking forward to getting past this whole set of events and telling you about the mission to Jupiter — the next book. Indeed, at this moment I was growing ever more desperate to get off this rock and back to something… anything I enjoyed more.

Anyway, this hissed threat from the unlikely combatant drew cold stares from our venerable Special Branch team, and the whores bristled rather ridiculously (I'm shaking my head as I remember this).

"Smitt, tell your women to leave," Karen's words were sharp, and Smitt obeyed. He was obviously still pleased at the position he thought himself to be in — one where he'd gotten away with mass murder and was going to win a presidency in a coming election.

For those of you playing the home game, what was his fate to be?

Rhymes with dung, a word that might be used to describe his moral sensibilities.

Charlie waved his Special Branchers back to their truck with some of his tactical hand gestures, then nodded to Karen and me. We strode to our own truck and hopped back in, with Smitt joining us once again.

With a nod to the relieved driver, I waved towards the street that had carried us to the Azure Horizon building, "Get us out of here. We have our ceasefire."

Letting out a breath, the driver obeyed immediately, and we left the warwhores in our wake.

"That was impressive intimidation in there," Smitt again sounded too pleased with himself. "Seriously, I think you've done much good for our colony. I'll make sure all our fighters withdraw from that dome, and I trust you'll make certain the Governor doesn't exert any more control."

Karen took his EP-5 right out of his hands, turned it around, and pointed it at him, "You're going to have to forgive my rudeness, but I'm tired of listening to people I'd much rather shoot. So *shut up* until we get back to the Government Dome."

There was no disputing that, and Smitt was at least smart enough to realize he wasn't in a position to argue with Karen McMaster. Hell, even if he'd been armed and she hadn't been, he wouldn't have had a hope in hell.

We rushed back towards the tunnel.

About five minutes later, after my head had cooled sufficiently to allow me to speak in long sentences, *Honesty* got a signal that was forwarded immediately to *Wolf*.

Jim Hannigan was standing behind his consoles, helping a tech clear up the comm signal from a distress call somewhere in the Government Dome when the message popped up on a nearby screen.

Fuzzy as most camera transmissions from handheld comms tended to be in those days, it was a picture of my gaunt face (I looked like hell, I've seen the recording), but I nodded once and let out a relieved sigh, "Ceasefire is supposedly on. Let Mark and Veronica know that the fighters and the barricades should be withdrawing as soon as we get back. We've got a leader of some sort with us, he'll see to it. Once they pull out, I want sweeper teams all over the dome, make sure they're all gone. And I want the Boscawen mercs contained. Talk to you presently."

I disappeared, and Jim Hannigan smiled. This was good news — it was honestly good news.

"Send that to Government House."

Mark Gunney was standing on the terrace, staring at the park. In his holster was Andrea's mag — she'd been willing enough to lend him the weapon, since he wouldn't be trusting the Hawke spares anymore.

He didn't like what he was feeling. He did know, though, that he couldn't afford to dwell too long on it — not when that distraction could lead to the deaths of other innocent people. The shooting had been an accident, he was sure of that, and no one in Government House thought any less of him. He'd face whatever charges came later...

Matt Baxter was abruptly next to him, a smile on the black Briton's face, "Ken's secured a ceasefire. As soon as he gets back to this dome, the Guild should be pulling out."

Mark nodded once without really listening, then his mind kicked in properly and he glanced at Matt, "Good. Let's get teams ready to supervise that."

With a nod, Matt Baxter turned and headed back inside. After another moment spent staring at the red smears around the park bench, Mark Gunney followed him.

Andrea Kiley was coming down the stairs from the Governor's office when Mark stepped in. She'd been essentially sequestering herself up there that morning — now that relief had arrived, she'd elected to have her personal breakdown time away from prying eyes.

I won't get into the details, though I'm sure you can understand much of her mental strife. I certainly could.

She emerged seeming entirely impassive, though — and basically in control again. I have to say, of all of us on Egesta during those first days, she was by far the strongest. You've seen how little it took to unravel me, Karen and Charlie... part of the damage there, of course, was knowing what exposure to these circumstances had done to Andrea, but all in all I think she handled things much better than we did.

Perhaps out of sheer necessity.

Now, as she reached the ground floor and approached Mark Gunney, he nodded and offered a small smile, "Ken's scared them into a ceasefire. They're pulling out."

I'm sure in the movies this would have brought a smile to Andrea's face, she would have started to cry and fallen into Mark's arms or something equally melodramatic.

Andrea's eyes instead widened slightly, and she swallowed. As she later told me, the first thought that went through her head was 'why couldn't I have managed that a week ago?'

She then bowed her head slightly, "Good. We should make sure we have teams out there... they'll likely try to leave a wake of destruction when they go."

Mark panned his head slightly to one side and his eyes narrowed as he studied Andrea's reaction. It was clear to him that she wasn't alright — of *course* she wasn't. She wouldn't be for a very long time. But instead of making an issue of that now, he listened to her sound observation and nodded.

"Yes, they'll be looking for souvenirs. We'll send out every warm body we have... you'll need this," he pulled her mag from his holster and placed it in her hand.

With another nod, then, he stepped past her and began barking orders at nearby SFers, and Matt Baxter rapidly joined him.

Andrea Kiley walked over to the map table, pulled out one of the chairs near it, and sat down. Propping her elbow on her knee, she cradled her forehead in her hand for a few minutes. Then she got up and found Captain Jameson and Lieutenant Hong.

They went out to save lives.

CHAPTER TWENTY-NINE

WITHDRAWAL

As promised, once we dropped off Smitt he began recalling his fighters from all across the dome. That wasn't the end of our day, though — far from it. We know now that the ceasefire was in good faith and was destined to last, but at that moment, we had no way of being certain Smitt and the battered elders weren't going to just collect their army and, in a concentrated push, try to drive us out of the dome.

So we stayed out.

Within the first hour of the withdrawal, as Karen and I rode around the area of the tunnel to Dome Five in the back bed of the pickup so we could stand and yell as needed, reports began to come in of barricades being abandoned.

Then more reports, and eventually every team of Veronica Choctaw's Hawke Guards and the SFers we had on the ground began talking about the fighters pulling out. I wasn't relieved yet, or even when I saw squads of those bastards piling into trucks to float back to Dome Five.

Even as I watched the first of them leave from a distance, I was still worried.

Why? Well how about I tell you what Matt ran into in the first hour of the withdrawal. That's a good start.

Matt had six SFs with him, and he'd borrowed (with permission) one of Charlie's officers' MAG-90s, so he was walking with that weapon. They were in the area beyond the Administration Building, having moved fast on foot (as Matt can do, what with his discipline and fitness) out to territory that only a few sweep teams of Hawke Guards had been through the night before.

They'd come upon one group of fighters making its way out of town, had checked them out for loot or plunder, and then sent them on their way. Then they'd found another team of fighters holed up in a fairly expensive looking section of town, occupying the ground floor of a townhouse.

As Matt came upon the scene, the fighters were actually abandoning the position, but they were hauling with them four civilians, one of them bleeding significantly from the head, all of them very haphazardly dressed… or as Matt interpreted, these people had hurriedly been dressed for transport when orders to leave had come in.

Watching this Guild party come out of the townhouse from the middle of the street, Matt waved to his team to fan out and level weapons at the exit, then he crossed to the sidewalk and waited at the bottom of the stairs that led to the front door. The Guild fighters, themselves numbering only eight, took one look at Matt, then started pushing the four civilians at him. As he stared at them, they fled down a nearby alley.

Getting the civilians — none of them older than twenty — to sit on the steps, he called in an evac truck, but it took twenty minutes for one to arrive because so many other teams were finding similar scenes. The one that ultimately did arrive was already nearly full, and the four civilians were forced to cram in for the hop back to the stadium.

One died that night, from her injuries.

So, you see, the day was not done.

As Matt reported this despicable incident over the comm, other similar reports began to come in. Many of the fighters were trying to smuggle out trophy prisoners, for reasons I don't think I need to explain too explicitly for you. And there was no way we could put enough teams into the field to catch every one of these fighter units as it left its hideout… no, we'd need to check them all at the tunnel.

As Karen and I realized that, we were floating near that entrance with Charlie close behind. Karen got on her comm quickly, "Charlie, we're going to start inspecting the trucks on the way out, make sure no one's smuggling captives. You in?"

"All the way," Charlie replied instantly, and his truck — being driven by a Special Brancher — was suddenly past us. He beat us to the entrance of the tunnel, where the large open trucks that the Guild had requisitioned from this and other domes were being filled with fighters… and others.

By the time Charlie landed, a dozen trucks had already gone through, with at least sixty fighters and possibly their victims. There wasn't much we could do about that at the moment — with the Guild concentrating into a much smaller area, and with us spread to hell. When they'd been scattered all over the dome, it would have been a mistake to pick a fight with them. Now it would have been a disaster.

But since they seemed willing to give up their 'prizes' if caught, we could filter them as they left… and hope nothing violent came of it. Stopping them from taking people out was, I hoped, fundamentally less inflammatory than invading their dome looking for victims.

As our driver landed our truck near Charlie's, I hopped over the side behind Karen and stopped at his window, "You're going to start ferrying anybody we find back to the stadium."

The driver nodded. It was a very long day for him too… and to my shame, I don't remember the name of the rating who was behind the wheel. We didn't exactly keep close records for this mission, so I haven't been able to find out either. If you're reading, driver, get in touch with me, and accept my apologies. You did a hell of a job that day.

Anyway, Karen was well ahead of me, so I rushed to join her in the thickening crowd of fighters. Charlie was already sending one person back to his truck, and five of his six officers were hurriedly fanning out to make sure no line of fighters escaped attention. It was chaotic.

Karen took one line of fighters, and as she picked a spot on the ground and put one hand on the handle of her mag, she started waving people past her. I was somewhat surprised that the Guild fighters seemed to be cooperating — and as soon as she saw a pair of civilians who definitely didn't belong with the fighters, she pointed to them and waved them to our truck.

The Guild fighters who'd been holding them looked about as guilty as school vandals who'd been caught — you know, the 'aww nuts' level of guilt. Can you *imagine*? The cheapness with which they regarded the lives they were trying to take…

Alright, so I picked my own spot and started waving people through, and some aside. After a few minutes of this, when it was clear the Guild fighters weren't resisting our sifting, victims started waving subtly to identify themselves. That worked for at least five minutes, but thicker streams of fighters were arriving in the area at the same time.

Pulling out my comm as I continued to sift, I called for backup. There were, including drivers, only nine of us out there at the tunnel mouth. If one Guilder decided to fight for his prize, and his hundred-odd friends decided to help…

Well, with a lead in like that, you can guess what happened next.

Veronica Choctaw had sent us a squad to assist, and I distantly heard that report over the comm. Drawing most of my focus, though, was a series of yells from a few lines away. One of Charlie's Special Branchers was standing his ground while about a dozen fighters tried to intimidate him.

The safety of that Special Brancher was one concern that immediately leapt to mind… the other was that, inevitably, a brawl in which one of our Special Branchers killed several fighters before getting taken down would end with the rest of us dead.

Right on cue, the attitudes of the fighters around me started to grow a little less sporting. The mob mentality is a delightful thing. One stepped up rather close to me, "What the fuck are you Defcoms trying to pull?"

I moved in to close the last bit of distance with him, instantly drawing my mag, "What exactly do you think you're going to accomplish, small man?"

The top of his head was level with my brow, but his eyes were staring up with some indignance.

"You jump me and you die, fucker," he said lowly, in his 'tough' voice.

"Yeah, but I'll take you and at least two of your buddies with me. What good's that do for you?" I slid the power bar on my mag to maximum with my thumb, and I noticed his eyes dart to the weapon as I raised it to point skyward next to my head.

We didn't have to continue the conversation because, with timing that would have made Lia Hawke proud, a file of Hawke Guards in their blue tunics and wielding their MAG-65 rifles pushed into the crowd. Charlie got over to his besieged officer and managed to break up a potential brawl, and we went back to sifting.

But we didn't leave that loading zone until much later in the day — until well after the events you're about to read about…

CHAPTER THIRTY

REUNITED

Wes Pellew was on the couch in his day cabin, grabbing one of those rare naps prudence demanded of him. He was about forty minutes into it when there was a knock on the cabin door, waking him from the very light sleep. His eyes darted to the wall chrono: it had been about six hours since they'd leapfrogged Cook's ships... what could be happening...

He swung his legs off the couch and stood up, grabbing his tunic off the back of the nearby chair, "Come in."

Roslyn Young swung the hatch door open and leaned in, "*Alberta's* approaching fast. Marshal is on Battlelink and we'll be passing him in about forty seconds."

"*What?*" Wes was already pulling on his tunic and stepping past his XO as he asked the question. Emerging onto the bridge he found screen eight lit up with the image of Marshal Samuels.

Smiling, Wes nodded to his fellow Captain, "Marshal, Belt Fourteen alright?"

"Yes it is, though I didn't know I had help so close at hand. I'm turning and reversing drives now... I should be able to form up with you without too much lag. Do you know where Cook's ships are?"

The Independent Squadron was lit up like a tree on the main screen on *Cheetah's* bridge; Marshal's scans still couldn't detect Cook's ships because he was coming in from the opposite direction, and the Battlelink evidently hadn't been fully established.

"Ah, never mind. Just got your sensors up on my screen. It looks like our friend Commodore Cook wants the small arms of Belt Fourteen after all."

Wes nodded, "We're going to try to beat him there, dissuade him from making a fight over some MAG-90s."

Marshal smiled, "Well actually, I think I have that taken care of. Every small arm in the Belt Fourteen arsenal is sitting in my hold right now. There's nothing there for him to take."

That sent Wes' eyebrows right up, "Really?"

Nodding, Marshal's smile broadened, "Yes. I thought it might be good to come out here and draw him away from the base. His course wasn't hard to estimate, and meeting him in open space would negate the threat to Belt Fourteen itself."

"Good thinking..." Wes was quick to reply at first, but his mind began turning over options again, drawing silence.

Detecting Wes' thoughtfulness, Marshal busied himself for a moment with the turning of *Alberta* into line with *Cheetah, Lion, Generous* and *Lady Grace*. As he came into formation, the other skippers — all of whom had shut down their Battlelink to *Cheetah* because Wes was napping — reestablished fully integrated comms.

On screen four, Kris Jacobs beamed as she caught sight of Marshal for the first time,

"Riding in on the white charger again, Marshal?"

Alberta's skipper laughed, "You know that's the best way to get things done."

Kris nodded, then looked to Wes, "So Wes…"

Wes didn't reply, his eyes fixed on the main screen as his mind clocked through options. He was getting a bold idea… a bluff… something that could deflect any danger from Belt Fourteen. If he could drive the Independent Squadron away, perhaps that could buy enough time for reinforcements to arrive at Belt Two.

Perhaps they could do more than simply protect Belt Fourteen…

"Fearless leader, you there?" Kris' question was playful, and Wes looked up abruptly.

"Of course. And speaking of fearless, anyone in the mood to turn around and deliver an ultimatum to Cook?"

Ultimatum? Was that wise? Well, to be honest, I'm not sure if it was — I don't know if Wes' thought process was the best reasoned or most logical… but what position am I in to say a damned thing about whether Wes was being rational or not? While he was suggesting this, I was still recovering from the adrenalin high that came when I pinned a Guild elder to a wall and put a gun to her head.

Not planning on throwing any stones at the moment. No sir.

Wes' reasoning here, as he later revealed to me, had to do with his growing fatigue and his withering patience, combined with the arrival of Marshal's *Alberta*. The odds certainly had not been leveled, but now it was a five against eight contest, less than two-to-one odds for Cook's ships… and some of Cook's ships had obviously been experiencing reactor trouble.

Now might be the moment to drive him into flight, once and for all. That was all Wes could hope for under these circumstances — it wasn't a perfect option and it'd make the Independent Squadron someone else's problem in the near future — but it would protect Belt Fourteen, and hopefully all the Belt colonies.

If Wes could just convince Cook that prowling around the Belt colonies was more trouble than it was worth — that the integrity of his squadron, if not its survival, would be endangered by continuing this brusque course of action…

Might sound thin. Maybe it was.

But Wes was damned well done with running.

"Let's reverse burn and turn through 1-8-0. Battle stations. We'll tell Cook that if he wants to go to Belt Fourteen, he's going to have to fly around us, and he's going to have a running laser fight on his hands."

Wes' words drew surprised, but not *unpleasantly* surprised, looks from the skippers on his screens. They approved of the proposal; they were all for going after the Independent Squadron… so long as the moment was right.

And Wes had decided it was.

"Very good, rotating through 180 degrees and maintaining speed on a reverse burn," Kris' commentary lost its playfulness, and the other skippers repeated those orders in various wordings.

Nodding to his Helm and Navigation Officer, Wes ordered *Cheetah* around to do the very same, and then he looked to Roslyn Young, "Battle stations. Get me a laser plot on *Nova Scotia*."

Heading for the tactical consoles, she nodded evenly. Wes turned back to the main screen, watching as the orientation of the five icons of the Belt Squadron ships turned through 180 degrees without them losing much speed at all. The reverse drives then fired, and the ships maintained their 198 kps cruising speed.

"We'll have to decelerate slowly to bring them to action," Marshal was appraising the situation for the benefit of the other skippers. "If we slow down too much, they'll be able to leapfrog past us. I've never seen it done, but I'd guess it's possible."

Of course, Marshal hadn't been filled in on how Wes' ships had gotten ahead of Cook's so the other skippers just smiled to themselves and nodded in agreement.

"We send the signal and decelerate slowly, then maneuver laterally or vertically as needed to stop them getting round us," Wes concurred. "Let me know when you're all comfortably in position."

There were a few more seconds of adjustments as the five elite Belt Squadron ships settled into their cruising formation, and then they all went to battle stations and brought their weapons to full readiness.

"Laser plotting now," Roslyn Young reported from the tactical and operations consoles near the rear of the bridge.

"We're ready here," Kris reported over the Battlelink.

"Us as well," Marshal added immediately.

Togo and De Winter each concurred quickly, and Wes folded his arms and nodded.

"Alright, let's drop to 196 kps. Kate, I want realtime with *Nova Scotia* as soon as it's available. Everyone get a bead on one of their frigates, fire on my order."

There were nods on the Battlelink screens, and Wes took a deep breath.

"Buffering with *Nova Scotia* on screen nine," Kate Levec reported.

With another nod, Wes steadied himself. Time to play his hand…

And time for a chapter break.

CHAPTER THIRTY-ONE

STANDOFF

Cheetah, *Lion*, *Alberta*, *Generous* and *Lady Grace* began to reduce speed ever so slightly, the gap between the Belt Squadron and the Independent Squadron gently coming down.

Wes watched as the *Cheetah*Net loading display on screen nine slowly scrolled up to full, then he folded his arms and set his glare. Now was the time to be heavy-handed.

Sean Cook appeared on the screen, the Commodore's face a mix of mild shock and considerable displeasure, "Captain Pellew."

"Commodore Cook," Wes nodded at the introduction.

They stared at each other for a few moments, the Commodore clearly trying to size up Wes — was this Captain with inferior numbers really going to get in the Independent Squadron's way?

Yes. Yes, he was.

"I think you might want to get out of the Belt colonies, Commodore," Wes said flatly after a moment. "You're not going to have a pleasant stay at any of our asteroids, I can assure you."

"Excuse me, Captain? Last I checked, you didn't have any authority to fetter me. So unless you've been disobeying orders from Admiralty House and failing to take me into custody already, I'm sure you'll recognize the insubordination this constitutes."

Cook was, quite obviously, fishing for information — he had probably convinced himself over the hours of transit from Belt Two that, had he truly been in serious trouble, he'd have heard about it from Wes much earlier.

But now, facing a rather obvious showdown with the Belt Squadron, Cook was starting to wonder. Really, the man wasn't stupid, just thoroughly and criminally ruthless.

"My orders aren't your concern. I'm telling you again, Commodore, to get out of my patrol zone. I'm not going to stand for any ships menacing the Belt colonies, even if they happen to be under the black sun of the Empire," Wes was stalwartly standing his ground, as you'd expect him to do.

Cook's eyes narrowed slightly, "You need to get a clear head, Captain. We're eight ships..." the implied threat was pretty obvious, but to cover himself, Cook continued, "...and you could use our help covering the entire Belt sector. Who knows where the Martians and the pirates are — you can't be everywhere at once."

Ah, trying the bargaining approach — trying to sound reasonable.

Wes actually took a step forward, casting his eyes down to the deck plating in front of his feet and shaking his head before looking up with one of those 'I can't believe what you're saying' smiles of disbelief, "You're kidding, right?"

Cook's reply was a dark stare, and Wes seized upon the moment to deliver a verbal thrashing, "The reason we're spread so damned thin at the moment is because three of our ships are now trying to clean up a mess you made. And I think you're a liability to Belt security, actually. How could I trust any of your ships or your crews to behave properly in their conduct with Imperial citizens?"

Bristling slightly, Cook leaned forward, "We are *defending the Empire*, you just don't understand the sorts of distasteful things that have to be done to make sure the Empire is safe. You sit in the bright, shiny Belt colonies while we bust our asses out there, trying to keep the worst of the nightmares from showing up on your doorstep. And then *you* bastards take the credit for bringing down the Syndicate. You just don't understand the steel it takes out there — we've had to do things we hate many times, things you're too weak to do..."

Now, that's an argument you've probably heard many times before, in history or in fiction — the classic 'defense of the realm' argument. Complete tripe. I'm sorry, that has to have been the first time any of our Belt Squadron skippers was ever accused of playing by the rules too much. Do you remember how we started this Martian War series? Right, Karen and me storming a pirate hideout *by ourselves*.

Find that little operation in the rulebook somewhere, if you can.

See, Cook... well, Cook was an idiot. He was scum. He let himself get out of hand for no reason, and I say this fully aware that in the last fifty pages you've read about me threatening to kill thousands of people and putting a gun to one elder's head. I believe, under those circumstances, my actions were... understandable. I wouldn't *ever* recommend them to anyone else, I certainly never wanted to repeat them, but I came to terms with what drove me to that state.

Compare that with what had driven Sean Cook to start the insurrection on Egesta: he'd been on his way back from another unsuccessful cruise hunting for pirates, became bitter when he heard that the Belt Squadron had stolen the march on him again, and then had thrown a fit when a Governor had denied him 'privileges' which he had no right to demand.

So he starts a coup?

If I'm way off base here — if you think my actions and his are on the same level of *wrong* — that's your own concern. But seeing the recording of this exchange between Cook and Wes, I kept thinking things along the lines of 'that smug sonofabitch' and 'does he actually *believe* that?'.

You better believe Wes didn't let him get away with it, either, "What are you saying? We, the Belt Squadron, who've done all the serious pirate killing for the past, oh, ten years, *don't understand* how to fight pirates? You think we get this job because we look good on camera? Commodore Cook, your ignorance surprises me. Now I'll say it again, turn your ships away from Belt Fourteen and from the Belt colonies entirely, or I'm going to have to make this discussion a little more pointed."

Cook leaned back again, not quite sure what Wes was saying at first...

"Rozy, give me a shot across the bow," our determined Captain Pellew said quietly as he looked away.

Cook's eyes widened as the red beam from *Cheetah's* number one bow laser sliced silently through the void right in front of his flagship.

"Captain Pellew!" the Commodore's surprised words came with some panic. "You wouldn't *dare* engage us!"

Wes' eyes narrowed and he took another step forward, his face filling Cook's screen, "I just fired on you, Commodore Cook. Wouldn't you say that counts as engaging you?"

As I said earlier, Wes was playing a heavy hand here — all in and going for the supreme bluff. He had to scare Cook off course, send him running into the void.

And yet from Cook's perspective, there were problems with that option. He'd been out cruising for months, and *British Columbia* hadn't been into a dockyard for an overhaul in all of that time. He needed time to get his reactors serviced… wandering off into the void between Earth and the Belt would be bad for the health of his ships, and thus for his own prospects of salvaging this situation.

So Cook needed another option. Fight was one possibility, but he was at a disadvantage under the present circumstances — if he tried to return fire, *Cheetah* and *Lion*, with their larger lasers, could stand off just beyond his range and pummel his ships.

And then, on Cook's scope, something else suddenly appeared — something else to worry about.

"I'll surrender myself to you, Captain Pellew!"

Wes looked up in surprise as Cook blurted out the words. He couldn't see that new element on his scope, so he had no idea what had changed the Commodore's mind.

"Independent Squadron, come to all stop!" the Commodore persisted instantly. "Stand down weapons systems, prepare to follow Captain Pellew's orders."

Well, that seemed too easy, didn't it? Yep. Really easy.

"They're decelerating, skipper," Kate Levec reported quickly, looking up from her consoles.

Nodding, Wes looked over to the main screen and watched as the ships of the Independent Squadron began to disappear. Cook vanished from screen nine as *Nova Scotia* dropped out of realtime range.

"Squadron, reduce speed and reverse drives to negative motion. Stand by to accelerate after the fleeing enemy," Wes actually referred to the Independent Squadron as an *enemy* in that set of orders, appropriately enough.

Marshal, Kris, Isoruku and Elise all wore concerned frowns on the Battlelink, but they issued the appropriate orders. The Belt Squadron ships fired their drives to reverse their progress, killing their momentum and pushing them back into sensor range of the Independent Squadron.

"This looks to me like a trap to negate our range advantage…" Kris offered quietly over the link, and Wes nodded.

"Of course it is. He went way over the top with the surrender thing. *Cheetah* will target *Nova Scotia*, *Alberta* take *Nunavut*, *Lion* take *Prince Edward Island*, *Generous* try to fry *British Columbia's* reactors, and *Lady Grace* pound *Yukon*. Once we lay in the first shots, we'll close fast to mag range — we have them in a mag fight…"

Wes was ready for this, unwise though it might have been.

Of course, as you've doubtless recalled by now, things weren't going to work out as planned.

"Do we fire first, as soon as we have solutions?" Marshal asked the prudent question, as he's prone to do, and Wes frowned.

"Unless they're legitimately powered down, yes."
So that would be it then…
But of course it wouldn't be.

CHAPTER THIRTY-TWO

GREAT TIMING

The piece of the puzzle that Wes was missing as Cook panicked and offered his surrender was one he couldn't have possibly seen, and one which was ultimately erased from the logs of the ships of the Independent Squadron as they desperately tried to eliminate incriminating evidence.

Far off on the Earthward quarter of the Independent Squadron, an F-194 Starlight showed up on *Nova Scotia's* scope, making its maximum patrol velocity of 198 kps. Running towards the base course Cook's ships had been taking on a roughly perpendicular vector, this Starlight pretty much raced onto the sensor panels of Cook's ships, then fired its IFF laser — as was good protocol when a combat small craft happened upon warships of its fleet.

The IFF transponder identified it as the plane of Lieutenant Jorge Durham, one of the more junior pilots flying off of *Warspite* at that stage of the war.

Ah yes, *Warspite*. Remember that John had dispatched Greg not to Belt Two but to Belt Fourteen, because during that time of the season Belt Fourteen was substantially closer to Earth than Belt Two, and because trouble was obviously headed toward the former.

Now, as timing goes, I have to say this was pretty damned brilliant, but it's not as good as you might think — or at least it could have been a hell of a lot better. *Warspite* was actually nowhere nearby at all, the battleship was about seven hours away, still cruising at only 185 kps (its optimum cruising speed). Knowing that the Independent Squadron was out here *somewhere* though, Greg had decided to maximize his chances of running into it: he'd sent out a massive fighter scouting net.

What's actually remarkable to me looking back on that is the fact that more *Warspite* pilots hadn't seen Cook's ships, and that they hadn't found him sooner. The net Greg threw out was fairly broad, because the Starlight (configured for reconnaissance with missiles removed in favor of fuel tanks) has a maximum cruising time of a little over a day, and that meant the net patrol area was... well... huge.

But that doesn't matter: what does is that Lieutenant Durham had detected the radiation spike of a laser shot and had turned slightly off his designated patrol route to investigate.

Now, consider what Cook was seeing (I really do love it when things like this actually work out): Wes was playing a heavy hand, but he seemed to have only five ships to Cook's eight. And Wes wasn't being very open about what the Admiralty's orders had been. Cook was ready to give battle... or at least I believe he was.

Then the other shoe seemed to drop: a fighter from a battleship closed with him to let him know that he was about to have an Admiral and some nicely tuned-up battleships arrive on his Earthward side. He could outrun Greg's ships — *Warspite* and *Goliath* were both fine battleships, but they were by no means as fast as frigates. But could he escape Wes' wrath?

More to the point, if Cook turned and ran, Wes could fall on his rear and damage the ships of the Independent Squadron just enough to reduce their cruising speed, thus bringing the battleships back into play.

And let's go one better: Cook couldn't have known exactly what Greg had with him. A fighter from *Warspite* obviously suggested at least one battleship, but could that battleship have been escorted by frigates and corvettes that *could* have run down the Independent Squadron and leveled the odds in Wes' favor? It was a definite possibility.

Cook's decisions thus came from a place of some panic — I'd like to think he was suffering from a guilty conscience and seeing specters from all sides, but I suspect he was actually just a self-preserving weasel who realized that we weren't going to let him off the hook.

Even though he probably could have gotten away.

So when *Cheetah* reached sensor range of the Independent Squadron again, Cook's ships were clearly powering down.

Wes' eyebrows went right up, then his eyes leapt to the Battlelink screens, "Hold fire, they're cooling reactors!"

"Acknowledged," Marshal replied first, and the rest of our skippers followed quickly.

"Bring us in close, keep solutions on their ships — if they so much as blink I want them in pieces," Wes' tone revealed his suspicion.

Prudent suspicion — this was all rather convenient.

"Skipper, getting a read of an F-194 on my scope, coming in from an off vector towards Earth. Hang on a minute..." Kate Levec was frowning as she moved behind her technicians, getting to the board that revealed IFF. She smiled, "That's *Warspite's* marker, skipper."

Wes blinked.

Warspite? He hadn't expected help, but he deserved it, for the gutsy stand he'd made. Like I say, I love it when timing like this does work out. Doesn't happen all the time, but that just makes it sweeter when it does.

"Pilot's reporting he's on a broad sweep patrol out ahead of a two-battleship force under Admiral Noyce. *Warspite* is about seven hours away... pilot's going to head to the next appointed comm checkpoint to report this situation..." Kate passed on the message from the fighter as it came up on one of her tech's panel, then looked up. "That's seven hours to wait, skipper."

Wes nodded slowly, then turned back to the main screen. He now faced another dilemma: if Cook figured out he had breathing room, he might make a break for it... so heavy-handed pressing would have to continue.

"Alright..." Wes paused before looking up at the other Belt Squadron skippers, "Let's launch all fighters, I'm going to order Cook to deliver himself and every skipper and XO to us. We'll split them up between our ships to make sure they don't try some sort of fancy boarding, and if the ships try to get wild we'll have hostages and leaders."

There were nods from the Captains, and Kris smiled, "I want that Bahim fellow, if you don't have dibs."

Wes smiled, "He's all yours. He'll need to be able to stand for trial, though."

Kris laughed, and then Marshal Samuels inserted a useful bit of information, "That's a myth, in fact. Criminals don't have to be able to *stand unassisted* at trial, only be able to *hold themselves upright* with the assistance of a cane, walker, or another person. They have to be able to stand and *walk* to go to the gallows, though."

Marshal is one of the best-read officers I've ever known: he knows the important things. Even if he's honestly too much of a gentleman to have any fun with some of them.

Wes? Well of course he's a gentleman. But so am I, and look at what I've done.

Turning back to Kate Levec, he smiled hungrily, "Get me Cook on the line."

I really don't feel like transcribing the conversation between Wes and Cook that followed. It's in the fleet archives, you can look it up whenever you like. Suffice it to say the Commodore was trying his hardest to be very, very accommodating to our Captain Pellew, and he didn't even ask at first how far out the battleships were.

Wes ordered Cook and the skippers and XOs to leave their ships in unescorted small craft, and to board Belt Squadron ships. Cook agreed immediately, though just before he closed the transmission he started to wisen up: "Captain Pellew... how soon will I be able to present my case to Admiral Noyce. I still don't see *Warspite* on my panel..."

Wes' answer: "Rozy, fire across the bow again please."

Cheetah was sitting very close to *Nova Scotia* now — if you look at the shot on the cover of this book, it was taken by the camera mounted on one of *Cheetah's* Starlights about to start a patrol sweep around this time. That's how close they were, and the significance of that proximity was considerable. It would have taken even Cook's ships long minutes to get their reactors sufficiently back up to power for combat, and in the meantime, at point blank range, Wes' lasers could have done considerable damage.

Remember, lasers at long ranges are enough to essentially cut off drive pod wings. At point blank they're terrifyingly powerful.

Anyway, the warning shot was enough to silence Cook, and about five minutes after he cut his transmission, small craft began leaving the bays of the Independent Squadron's ships. Wes went down to the standby lounge next to *Cheetah's* number two launch bay and waited silently for Cook's pinnace to set down.

He'd of course summoned Major Marcus Atallah and the rest of the Special Branch squad to wait with him, but as he stood with folded arms and stared through lounge windows at the flight deck, he was only barely aware of their presence.

He was burning with anger about Cook — not just for the Egesta situation which he hadn't had to experience first hand, but for everything that came after the bastard had showed his face at Belt Two. I don't think Wes will mind me saying it: he very much looked forward to putting this man in the brig.

The *Nova Scotia* pinnace finally glided into the bay and landed, and the space doors closed behind it as deck crews in atmospheric suits hurriedly set about tying down the visiting ship. Once the deck lights flashed green to indicate positive atmosphere, Wes was first through the hatch to the flight deck, walking determinedly towards the *Nova Scotia* pinnace while Major Atallah's Special Branchers fanned out behind him. There was still some concern, of course, that this was a trap — there could be bombs in that pinnace, or some other funny business.

But no, the hatch of the small craft swung open, and Cook climbed out the side, then hopped down to the deck, trying to look dignified.

Turning to see Wes approaching him, he took two steps forward and puffed himself up, "Captain Pellew, I surrender myself into your custody."

Stopping just short of the man, Wes wasn't impressed by the introduction.

"Glad to hear it," was his dry reply.

"I now demand to see legal counsel, as I believe I am being persecuted for acts that are not unlawful under the articles of Empire…"

Scary thing about that is, by one or two interpretations of the articles, he was right. But interpretation of the articles (as Marshal had already helpfully pointed out) could be a double-edged sword.

Wes smiled and nodded, "Oh, of course."

Then, with a bit of theatre that became the talk of his ship's crew for the rest of his time in command of *Cheetah*, Wes waved over a flight deck officer who'd just pulled her helmet off. She approached and offered a simple nod, "Yessir?"

"Ensign, can you call the ship's lawyer for me? Tell her she'll have a client waiting in the infirmary. And can I borrow your number twelve wrench?"

Frowning curiously, the Ensign (now Captain Louise Sinclair) handed Wes the wrench from her tool belt, then activated her suit's comm. No one on the deck legally witnessed Wes backhanding the heavy wrench into Cook's mouth. No one on the deck would testify to the surprised look on Cook's face or the distinct crunch and wail of pain that followed, nor to the spitting out of all the teeth from the right side of his face. A work order was filed to clean blood off the flight deck, but that could have come from anywhere.

Cheetah's shipboard lawyer (one of the Lieutenants in engineering who'd taken the two-week course, and was thus rated to advise on legal matters, though was not a litigator herself) visited Cook in the infirmary later that day. According to the doctor on duty, the words "You're dead" were often repeated.

That lawyer obviously knew the law very well.

Now, before I sign off from this chapter, let me take a minute to answer a question that one of my editors asked quite legitimately after reading this. Said he: "Did *everyone* in your squadron make it a habit of physically breaking your enemies?"

If you're keeping score, in just the last several chapters, Wes wrenched a man in the mouth, Charlie Peters put an elder into traction for fifteen months, and I put a gun to someone's head. Go back further, and Charlie's done more, Karen's nearly throttled a Governor… I read the question from the editor and had to nod. During all these matters surrounding Egesta, we all seem to have subconsciously defaulted to a rather brutal setting.

I don't personally advise anyone reading to take this tack. Up until this period of events, and indeed, after things cooled off, I'd been a person who wielded words and theatrics as a weapon. Sure, I broke the odd pirate's nose, but I don't think I'd even used the word 'traction' in this series of Martian Wars books until Charlie put that elder into it.

So yes, the violence was getting rather... excessive. I'm sorry about that, but that's just the way we were responding to what we were seeing — to the sorts of monsters we were dealing with. It takes a hell of a lot to set off people like Karen, Charlie and Wes so badly that they physically harm people. I don't know if what we were seeing on Egesta and what Cook was doing in space qualify as excuses for beating the living daylights out of someone, but... well... it's how we responded. We're small people, I guess.

But then, unlike the people we harmed, we didn't murder, rape, pillage, or otherwise violate. We used some old-fashioned brute force, the oldest form of intimidation, and it worked.

I personally believe these people had it coming. They really, truly had it coming.

And they got it.

CHAPTER THIRTY-THREE

THE REST OF EGESTA

After we managed to get the fighters out of the Government Dome, things calmed down on Egesta. We kept strong forces at each of the entrances too, and ran intermittent patrols to other domes to make sure chaos hadn't settled in anywhere else.

We felt like we were in the clear — so much so that, approximately two days after the last chapter I wrote about Egesta, we were actually letting our refugees go back to their homes. That was a… well I hesitate to call it 'good', so let's go with *better* feeling than most we'd experienced over the first days there.

We stopped seeing atrocities, and I think that was critical. We were able to move through streets with our weapons slung, we didn't have to always listen closely for the sounds of screams, and we weren't playing games with the Guild fighters.

The dome was essentially secure.

On the fifth day *Wolf* was there, it was sufficiently calm for Karen and me to decide to send the *Friendly* volunteers back to their ship, and to have *Friendly* and *Honesty* switch places — *Friendly* would be the patrol ship, *Honesty* at the dock.

Andrea Kiley looked like a ghost when she left Government House. I'm not sure if there's a better way to describe it — I just remember quite vividly the pale, gaunt, vacant sort of stare she wore as she nodded in reply to her orders and collected her kit to return to *Friendly*.

Karen and I looked at each other as the young Irishwoman left with her officers. I can't in words describe the concern that came through Karen's stare at that moment, but suffice it to say neither of us were at all comfortable with Andrea's state of mind. I've been asked why we left her in command, if we were so worried… well, we weren't *certain* that she was in psychological trouble, and if we removed her from command, it could have ended her fighting career. We didn't want her good work at Egesta to be rewarded by her being moved to a desk for the rest of her life, so we gave her time away to recover.

I'm pretty sure it wasn't hard for anyone to detect Andrea's stress; most people, on the other hand, didn't see any signs of stress from Mark Gunney at all. His run-in in the park has stayed with him to this day, as I implied earlier, but he has the ability to get past things like that when he must.

That probably sounds cold. It's necessary.

Matt Baxter was his usual parental self, all through those last few days. He made sure Karen and I rested at regular intervals, and wouldn't hear of us over-extending ourselves. I don't believe he slept more than four hours over the five days we were in charge of the ground situation; we gave him forced off-duty time our first day back aboard *Wolf*, though that's getting a little ahead of the story here.

Let's go to the fifth day of *Wolf's* presence at Egesta, and actually that night, just as the simulated day was slowly fading into the blackness of true space. Karen and I were sitting in chairs on the terrace of Government House, which was now guarded by only one SF, and which did offer a spectacular view of the 'night' sky.

It's strange for me to think of the 'night' sky… for me the blackness of space has always been the ocean my navy plays in.

Karen had her eyes closed, though I don't think she was asleep, or at least she wasn't fully asleep. Her sidearm was lying in her lap, both hands were on it. That was perhaps an unnecessary habit by the fifth day, but somehow it didn't seem unwise.

I sat next to her, occasionally staring at her. She seemed peaceful, and so fundament- ally in control. Her eyes weren't flickering under her lids, there was no sign that her mind was racing, or that she was seeing horrible images in her mind's eye. I wasn't seeing horrible images myself — I was oh so very lucky that, unlike Charlie Peters and Andrea Kiley, I hadn't personally witnessed enough to have my consciousness completely dominated.

Ah, I haven't mentioned Charlie yet, so an aside there. He, like Mark Gunney, was appearing unflapped. He was doing his job, he was helping people. If there's a therapy for dealing with what Charlie had seen, helping people should be a large part of it. I think it worked for Charlie, though I know some of what he saw changed his perspectives on things, if only very subtly.

Anyway, that evening.

As I was staring at Karen, my comm chirped. Her eyes opened immediately at the soft noise, and she turned her head to look at me and the comm unit as I activated the screen.

Still holding watch from the bridge, Jim Hannigan nodded to me, "Sorry to bother you this late, but Commander Kiley's reporting a transport group on its way in now. They'll be in position to dock here next to us in about three hours. It's definitely the Army."

I was exhausted at this point, and none too concise or conversational, "Good news, Jim. Get them to dock and unload, we'll have the warehouse ready to have them in…"

Jim interpreted my slightly jumbled words and nodded, "Very good. They'll be there by the time you wake up."

I nodded, then closed the connection and looked back up at the night sky, wondering if I'd be able to see the transports as they cruised in. It was very good that they'd come… it meant we'd be able to leave soon.

"He's right, you know. You should get some sleep now," Karen's hand landed softly on mine, and I looked back at her. Smiling despite everything, she climbed out of her chair, "I'll check the perimeter and set things up with Matt. You sleep for a couple of hours."

I didn't quite manage to object, and despite myself I heeded her words. As she walked away, I dozed off.

A few hours later, Karen, Mark, Matt and I stood in the warehouse through which we'd entered the Government Dome, waiting near previously unused cargo loading chutes and listening to heavy clunking noises and other assorted sounds of arriving armor.

I have to admit, most of this night is a haze to me — I imagine it's fatigue, and quite possibly it's a result of me repressing things. I hope it's not the latter, but the possibility remains.

I do recall being somewhat impressed as the first of the hover tanks, a Mark III Serpent, floated out of the chute, then set down on the warehouse floor near us. The hatch on the vehicle swung open as it landed, and an Imperial Army Brigadier leapt out. It's a testament to how tired and frankly desperate I was that I was actually glad to see a red uniformed blockhead officer.

The Brigadier marched crisply over to us, and then saluted. We stared at him as he waited for us to salute back, and eventually he took the hint: we were exhausted, and well past saluting.

"Well, we're here to fix this mess," the Brigadier delivered his opening words. "What's the exact situation?"

We moved over to the map table — the very same map table I'd been briefed at when we arrived — and started pointing things out to him, revealing the nature of the situation and suggesting ways he could secure the area for the moment. All things you've heard before in this book — I'm going to spare you the repetition.

And then he wanted to talk to me privately.

Stepping away from the table and closing with his tank (the rest of his armor was idling in the egress bays of his transports), he stepped in close and lowered his voice, "So, Commodore, what have we promised them, and what're they getting?"

He was referring to the terms of the ceasefire, and he almost sounded hungry as he asked the question. Taking a breath, I met this Brigadier's eyes, "We said free elections, but there are too many patently dangerous people in their leadership to actually allow that. We need to hold back for a while, rebuild their infrastructure and try to find some moderates, then rig the election to make sure they get in."

That was pretty much the nature of the bold faced lie I'd used to coerce the elders into cooperating, wasn't it?

The Brigadier smiled, then clasped my shoulder, "Say no more, I understand. I like a man who does what he has to. I really do like you, Barron."

I suppose in that he was referring to the general dislike shared between blockheads and Defense Command personnel. You know, the dislike that leads us to refer to them as 'blockheads'.

I didn't even attempt to smile, "I'll turn it over to you, then. As soon as your armor gets deployed, I'm going to withdraw my people and get my ships to Belt Two. We still have the war on."

Word had, by the fourth day, reached us about Cook's capture, so we didn't have to worry anymore about that bastard coming back to this mess he'd created in an attempt to purge it by drastic means. The Martians and the pirates, however, could never be overlooked. Such was the nature of war.

"That's exactly what I was going to suggest," the Brigadier's smile broadened, and then he extended a hand to me, which I took. I had no reason not to at that moment.

With that he left me and climbed back into his tank, and within minutes a stream of armor ('armor' is a slang term referring to armored vehicles, by the way) was coming down the chute and through the warehouse. Karen, Mark, Matt and I began to plan for our withdrawal.

None of us realized then, nor could have truly known, what as going to happen when we left. We were all very relieved, but not in a satisfied sort of way. We didn't feel like we'd solved the problem, but we did believe we'd held out long enough to make certain the situation would remain stable, and then we'd handed it off to someone who could worry about it full time while we got back to our own jobs.

We thought, then, that we'd done reasonably well. No, that's too ambitious. We thought we could have done much, much worse. And now we believed we could move on, and get back to our old lives, our grander style and our ship fighting.

That's what we in fact did (with some silent reservations). We moved on.

Because none of us knew that Brigadier, none of us realized what he would do.

Who was that Brigadier? You probably already know: it was Howard Pedro Azuma.

And I shook his hand.

Chapter Thirty-Four

Getting Home

One of the test readers thought this was a 'rushed' ending, because I haven't detailed the day's worth of movement it took to get our people off Egesta, or the breaking of seals on the docks, or the plotting of the course to Belt Two, or the boosting away from Egesta. My editor disagrees, and so do I; to be honest, I couldn't stand to spend any more time talking about Egesta. Not now, and not then either.

To answer the question I'm often asked: no, while we were on the ground, Brigadier Azuma did nothing at all to suggest to any of us that he was going to turn the situation into what it became. And no, I won't talk about what it turned into right now; there'll be a later book on that, one that talks about our return.

I won't lie, I'm not looking forward to that book any more than I was looking forward to this one.

But let's catch up here: we left Egesta at full burn, with the ships' complements of *Wolf*, *Friendly* and *Honesty* all working at about half their normal efficiency. Veronica Choctaw's troops caught a ride back to Hawke One on one of the Army transports, carrying our copious thanks with her. I slept a lot, trying to recover from that five days of laborious peacekeeping, from the 'negotiations', and from guilty thoughts that I should have stayed and continued the operations there.

It took me days to finally accept that it wasn't my job anymore, that we'd done the best we could, and that I needed to put this whole affair behind me... for the time being.

How could I do that, you ask? Well, to begin, it wasn't really as simple as just 'putting it behind me'. The shadows of Egesta would loom for the rest of the war and beyond, but as you'll see next book, *The Jupiter Patrol*, my old bold humor and brighter style did slowly return. This was for a simple practical reason: that style is how I usually cope with times of stress, and how I get my job done.

And, of course, the war was still on. I didn't have the option of locking myself in my cabin for weeks on end, mulling over everything that happened. There was too much else happening — too many other lives at stake.

Besides, the situation had been cleaned up. As far as I knew, all would be well on Egesta.

The trip from Egesta to Belt Two took roughly six days. We weren't making our maximum cruising speed — we weren't in that sort of hurry. In that time, Cook and his crews were locked up for trial... I don't really care to get into that too much, but suffice it to say they got their just desserts: many ring leaders and senior officers ended up doing very hard time, or on the gallows. It took about eight months to sort out, and Cook was the last to hang — the symbol to everyone in the Empire and beyond of what Parliament and Defense Command thought of rape and murder.

So much for Cook's interpretation of the Articles of Empire.

When *Wolf* got back to Belt Two, it was quite a party. And you know what, after all the darkness, blood and death I've recounted over the last 56,000 words, I'm going to indulge, and tell you the happy tale of that return.

Arriving at Belt Two had been a relief unlike many others I've felt in my life. *Wolf* pulled into orbit over the base, slotting neatly into line with *Cheetah*, *Lion* and *Alberta*, while *Friendly* and *Honesty* rejoined *Generous*, *Lady Grace*, and *Sackville*. These were the nine ships that had defended Belt Two only a couple of months before, and it was a great feeling to see them all back together again, safely over the greatest base in the Belt.

The squadron had two new members, and what members they were! Of course, I refer here to *Warspite* and *Goliath*, the two fine battleships that Greg Noyce had brought out. Also present were the eight ships of the Independent Squadron, though they were nearly empty — remember, their entire crews had been interned for investigation.

So the space above Belt Two was impressively stocked with ships once *Wolf* arrived — a total of nineteen Defense Command vessels were within *eyesight* of each other, something you rarely get to see outside of Earth space.

No, the ships of the Independent Squadron didn't look menacing to me when I first saw them. They were great ships, as was to soon be proved; it was the women and men aboard them who had deserved all of our collective wrath. And who'd received it.

After arriving in Belt Two space, I briefly visited with Greg aboard *Warspite*. He informed me when I arrived, however, that Sharon Stanton had arranged a 'reunion' party for us on Belt Two, for the very night of our arrival, so the visit was cut short. I returned to *Wolf* to get into my dress uniform, having not been able to say much at all to Greg beyond 'Good to see you', and to report on the combat effectiveness of my three ships from Egesta.

Then it was off to the party.

CHAPTER THIRTY-FIVE

THE PARTY

Now, why a party? Well you must remember, we weren't just military figures by this time: our celebrity, particularly in the Belt colonies, was considerable — and it was essential. Morale and the support of the public at large is never a bad thing to maintain during a conflict, and during the fight against the Syndicate we'd done our share of social events (in front of the cameras) to make sure our cavalier personas were widely known.

Nothing inspired confidence in the Empire's military situation more than seeing your leading Defense Command heroes having a grand old time at a red-carpet event. It might sound ridiculous... but then it shouldn't. We still do these parties, more frequently than ever in fact, and they still work.

So this was a truly important and practical part of the job, and I won't deny, it was a distraction that I sorely wanted.

It was also less than a week before Empire Day, so it doubled as an actual holiday party.

When Karen and I arrived at the posh social club — the Beltminer's Club — in Belt Two's Capital Dome, and stepped out of our hover limo (yes, Sharon had pulled out all the stops and hired limos for us all), we were subject to deafening cheers, and many cameras. Apparently it had been big news at Belt Two — adopted 'local' heroes had not only fought the battle to save the colony, they'd gone back to Earth, saved the Empire, saved the free belt, and saved Egesta.

Sure we did.

Coming down the red carpet was an interesting experience — I wasn't in any sort of mood to be the showman Commodore, but that's what the job requires. I smiled and waved, pointed at a few people I vaguely recognized and stopped twice for interviews. Karen worked the opposite side of the rope line leading into the club, doing much the same, and I've seen the footage of us. Even I couldn't quite detect our exhaustion and the stress. We were putting on a brave face for the public, and frankly for ourselves.

Deception is something you get good at in our line of work.

Charlie had also been in our limo, but as had become his custom, he let us get a head start before he climbed out, thus giving the media the chance to cover Karen and me before turning back to focus on him. Charlie's never been as much of a showboat as the fleet officers of the Belt Squadron — he's developed a rapport with the media that essentially leaves him 'hands off'. I think the press likes to see him as the dashing, quiet, mysterious warrior, with crazy killing abilities. They don't ask too many questions; they just let the viewers' imaginations fill in the rest of his star status as a man of mystery.

He had that red carpet to himself until Wes' limo arrived. Wes has never liked doing press, though the press loves his self-effacing professionalism. Then came Isoruku Togo — surprisingly, a bit of a camera hog — and Elise De Winter after him. Then it was

Marshal Samuels, with his lovely wife Mel on his arm, followed by Katya Romanov.

Kris Jacobs arrived to much fanfare. As she puts it, she's one of the most 'lusted after' skippers in the fleet, and that's not a description she's ashamed of anymore. Imagine, the once-quiet young officer who Karen and I had so thoroughly corrupted, now mischievously playing to the cameras and positively flirting with some of the red carpet reporters. She never cared much for the press, of course, but damned if she didn't know how to work them.

Arriving then, in a limo Mark had insisted they share, were both Commander Gunney and Commander Kiley. You've had hints at Andrea's state of mind... well no, not hints, you've seen it. She didn't seem particularly ready to deal with a press onslaught, and Mark had decided he'd deflect some of the heat for her.

And yet, if you watch the footage from the red carpet, Andrea is smiling and waving, taking questions and bashfully deflecting a couple of marriage proposals (for some reason she *always* gets proposals). If you watch Mark's expression as he watches her, he's barely concealing his surprise — he'd been expecting to have to interdict with his usual good humor... but no. Andrea appeared quite alright.

Goes to show what kind of steel she possesses. She's told me I can put this in, so here goes: she'd put her mag to her temple and nearly pulled the trigger just five hours before this. I didn't find that out for some time, and you can see why if you watch the footage. She seemed like she was getting back to normal, no one would have had any reason to suspect.

We all survived the red carpet, and got into the club. Once inside, it was a different sort of melee. You've probably seen vids of these parties (or even of this one in particular). There's always a large dance floor, and surrounding it there's a mighty cocktail party with some tables, and two or three open bars. The press gets the gallery, so cameras can cover many details from above. Parabolic microphones are forbidden up there, but that's nothing a simple bribe can't fix, so we always watch what we say.

I won't bore you with everything that went on that night, just some of the highlights. And by highlights I mean the handful of things I can remember. These parties are always a blur (not for alcoholic reasons, but simple stress-related ones), and they usually involve me inconspicuously clinging to Karen, and vice versa. It's like having a wingman in a dogfight; if one of you gets tagged, the other one is there to interdict.

This party was apparently the hottest ticket in the Belt colonies — the 'Returning Heroes Gala' and all — so we were rubbing shoulders with the biggest names around. I met about a dozen CEOs in the course of an hour, but after that they all ended up drunk and occupied by their high-priced escorts. Celebrities — I mean *proper* ones — were also there in considerable numbers, including by chance a pair of actors who would go on to play Karen and me in one of the particularly bad movie renditions of *The Hawke Mission*.

The actress, wearing far too little clothing, seemed surprised by Karen's lack of... how do I put this... obscene bust size... when they met. This actress — and you probably know who I'm talking about so I'll not say her name and thus avoid the duel with her latest husband — was one who was quite proudly unable to fall on her face, as my father puts it. She has copious, surgically-installed bosom.

"Not very *tactical*," Karen muttered to me after the meeting.

I laughed at that — a genuine laugh, not the 'haha, your joke about cigars about which I know nothing has delighted me' laugh. That's why Karen and I hung together: it allowed us to survive these sorts of melees.

Greg — good grief, I forgot Greg — arrived with his Flag Captain, Val Rodriguez, and *Goliath's* Welsh skipper, Becky Afflighen. Those two Captains made it into the club safely, but being a long-time favorite hero of the Belt, Greg ended up stuck on the red carpet for almost an hour, recounting over and over again the story of the victory at the Battle Over Earth.

When he finally made it into the club, he joined a cluster of Belt Squadron officers who were only too happy to see him again, and they passed the evening chatting. I didn't really get to talk to him at all, owing to the number of rich people who thought it indispensable that I meet them.

That's not a dig against rich people, by the way. Only rich people who think that, because they're rich, I *must* get to know them.

Mark Gunney was pleasantly drunk by the later evening; I don't drink much at all, nor does Karen or Wes (we're all untrustworthy puritans according to Mark), but as the intrepid Commander Gunney pointed out to me once, when bad things happen it's his habit to get drunk, and to get over it. It may sound crude, but it was Mark's way, and I certainly don't judge him for it. Good grief, the number of indispensable combat contributions he's made, who in their right minds would criticize his habits?

The night wore on quickly — the only advantage to all the hustle and bustle — and thanks to the fact that a war was legitimately on, and that skippers could only leave their XOs running the orbiting ships for so long, officers began to escape early.

Greg vanished first, understandably. He was taking over the Belt Sector, the vast amount of paperwork he was facing could be expected to kill large draught animals. Val Rodriguez went too, though Becky Afflighen found herself in a shot-for-shot battle with Andrea Kiley, and our smiling Irish Commander knocked the Welsh Captain right out of the battle by midnight. I'd make some remark about Irish versus Welsh tolerance for alcohol, but we all know why Andrea was so readily able to drink beyond expectations. Charlie, having no one else to look after (as was the usual situation, since he and Lia Hawke were in a *secret* relationship) got her back to *Friendly*.

Mark Gunney disappeared sometime in the evening, probably having wowed the manager of the club sufficiently to get a nice waitress he'd been chatting with off work early. I have no idea when Wes left, but I know Isoruku Togo departed with an actress (he's always on camera, he's not easy to miss). Katya Romanov and Elise De Winter found their way out around midnight as well.

That was about all I managed to keep track of, and as I sat on a stool at the bar, hanging onto a glass of twenty-five year old scotch I'd been nursing for three hours (I told you I don't drink much), I watched the party descend into the usual ridiculous rave one expects of these things. Powerful people bring expensive companions, then pass out and the younger famous people start to collect the companions. Much bumping and grinding on dance floors, much flirting and sitting on laps and so forth.

Oh, and I better not forget to mention the painfully loud, droning music.

"The life of excess," Karen was sitting on the stool next to me, looking back over her shoulder. "I'm sure someone must love it."

I nodded slowly, deciding to drink the scotch in my hand.

"Water please," I nodded to the barkeep as I slid my empty glass at him, then I glanced at Karen. "Seems obscene, after everything that's happened this season all they want to do is throw a party..."

I'm glad no smuggled parabolic microphones were on me at that moment, actually. These parties were part of the job; it would hardly have been good for us to be overheard denouncing them.

Karen nodded, emptying her own drink (I don't know what she was drinking, honestly) and looking at me, "It's not our scene."

I cracked a smile, "You said to me a while ago that we were disappointments as celebrities. Right after we took Jones' house, I think." That's back in *The Rogue Commodore*, first chapter — I just checked.

Smiling too, Karen nodded, "We are."

The barkeep slid me a glass of water, and I drank it quickly, looking up at a chronometer to find it was already after 0100 hours. This wasn't unusual for Karen and I — part of our cavalier styling involved leaving late, because it adds to the impression that we're so irresponsible as Defense Command officers that we'd be crazy enough to do *anything* to pirates.

Of course, that effort to stay late inevitably leads to us sitting at the bar, drinking water and having the same 'culture of excess' conversation over and over... as if we haven't said it a dozen times before.

We tended to just sit there, then, until a bit later in the evening, and then we'd leave in a flourish, doing a few more interviews and deflecting the same old questions about whether we were spending the night together. That was always fun, people always seemed to want to know. There were actually two camps there for a while — those who were sure we were together, and those certain we weren't. It made us laugh.

But as I sat at that bar, and stared far too intently at a glass of ice water, I was finding myself without any tolerance for this scene. The loud music, the excess, the indulgence... I could tolerate it all before well enough, but not now. Not when I'd seen so much so recently. My job was to protect all these people from fates much like those of the people on Egesta, and yet if I stayed in this club much longer, I might well lose the will to defend them at all.

Sounds horrid, of course, but suffice it to say parties weren't for me, this sort especially.

"I think we might as well leave, I'm done with this place..." I glanced at Karen, and she frowned at me.

"Really?"

I nodded, "Come on, not our scene, and my tolerance for it is just not there right now..."

Karen's frown deepened and she shook her head, "No no, this is a morale job. We can't jump yet, people will talk about us leaving two hours early, and worry."

"There's a *war* on, they should worry," I protested damply, and Karen chuckled, emptying another clear glass of something.

"Yes, they should. But better that they don't," she laid the glass back down on the counter with a clunk, then hopped off her stool. "And if this isn't our scene, why don't we *change* it. We did just save the Empire and all."

With that she was gone out into a crowd of gyrating people (dancing, I should add, with none of the pleasant, sunny grace that Karen dances with in her cabin). I lost sight of her, and then I heard the music shut off.

Now I frowned, turning to look back at the barkeep, "What've you been giving her?"

He smiled and shrugged, "Not at liberty to say, sir."

"Bastard," I turned back to the crowd, now stopped in surprise at the silence (some of them could probably hear their own thoughts for a few shocking moments).

A murmur of discontent broke out, but it hushed as soon as Karen climbed up onto a table next to the DJ, holding the DJ's headset microphone in her hand, "You'll have to forgive us, but both Ken and I really would prefer a change of mood. This all is a little too intense for us, after the six weeks we've had. I know none of you will mind!"

She then hopped off the table and disappeared into the crowd again.

Real music started playing.

And I mean *real* music. I'm an old bastard, you know this by now, so by real music I mean not the music that was blaring, and not even the stuff Karen danced to in her cabin. This stuff was nice and slow, including the sounds of instruments made of wood and brass, with melody and rhythm.

Karen appeared at my side all of a sudden, had my hand in a flash, and was dragging me past stunned onlookers, right to the center of the dance floor.

"No..." I didn't really protest. I didn't really care to.

We stopped in the middle of the floor, and Karen smiled, "Here's the mountain, Commodore Mohammed."

I don't know what she'd been drinking, but then I don't think it mattered. It's Karen, *come on*, you know there was no resisting.

So I reached around her waist with my right hand, took her right hand with my left, she placed her left hand on my shoulder, and we danced. For two wonderfully long hours.

I am pleased (in a perverse way) to say that on no fewer than nineteen vid channels throughout the Belt, active broadcasts were within minutes interrupted with breaking news: live feeds of our dancing. Photos of us taken from the press gallery owned the headlines the following day.

Everyone wanted to know about us, and all I wanted to do was dance with Karen McMaster.

Go ahead, call me a sop.

CHAPTER THIRTY-SIX
A COMMODORE'S JOB DESCRIPTION

At a noon lunch-briefing the following day, as pictures of Karen and I beaming on the dance floor dominated the society pages and celebrity news vid shows, a number of Belt Squadron officers found themselves summoned to Greg's office on *Warspite*.

Karen and I were there first, giving more detailed impressions of what had happened on Egesta. Marshal Samuels arrived right on time at noon, with Wes Pellew on his heels. Mark Gunney then arrived five minutes late, which really was rather in character for him. We all stared as he came into the room, and Karen cracked a smile, "You do seem to be wearing different clothes than last night. Didn't have any luck?"

Mark shrugged, "I wasn't going to go back to her place when I could show off my ship's big lasers. Sure it costs me cab fare, but I get to freshen up in the morning."

That, if you don't know Mark, was a joke.

Probably.

Whether it was or wasn't, we all laughed, and we settled into the five chairs Greg had pulled into his office before our arrival.

"As you all know, I will be retaking command of the Belt Sector as of this evening. All I need to do is report a slate of promotions to John at Admiralty House, and he'll make it all official."

Promotions. Even to a group of elite and selfless officers like those in the room (myself and Mark excepted on the selfless part), that word had an almost electric impact. For myself, I rather hoped I was just going to be present to shake the hands as my old friends went on to bigger and better things — I'd barely been a Commodore for two months, I hardly expected to be getting an extra bar on the collar.

Well, actually I'd go from five bars to a single black sun if I made Rear Admiral.

Greg smiled knowingly at the tension in the room, "I've looked at all the reports you turned in since leaving Egesta, I've talked to Ken and Karen, and I already know all of you. We've fought together before, I don't need a great deal of extra information beyond that to know your quality."

We were all staring at Greg now. I'm sure it'd have been amusing to watch us all staring at him as though he were a wheeled car and we were moose on the highway.

Sorry, joke from Capital Island.

"Marshal, you first," Greg pulled a folder off the top of a pile that was camouflaged by all the other piles on his desk and handed it to Captain Samuels. "I know you'd like to stay near Belt Two if you can, because of your family situation. I'm promoting you to Commodore, and I'm going to put you in charge of a new Belt Squadron we'll be putting together. Part of the job will be to invent a way to secure our trade fleet against raiding; John and I have identified that as a major liability."

Marshal's eyes were slightly wider that usual, and he opened the folder and read the first few lines of the pages within, nodding to himself. Then, before Greg could go on, he did the gentlemanly thing, standing to lean forward and extend his hand to Greg. As the new Commodore shook the Admiral's hand, Marshal closed the folder, "Thank you very much, sir. I appreciate it."

Marshal Samuels, unflappable and a real gentleman no matter the circumstances. And soon enough destined to be the savior of Imperial commerce.

"Now, Wes," as Marshal sat back down, Greg pulled the next folder off the top of the pile and handed it to Wes, "we want you to fix the reputation of that Independent Squadron."

Wes' eyes widened slightly and he opened the folder in a hurry, "Commodore... of the Independent Squadron?"

Greg nodded, "Exactly. The Squadron needs a good leader now, and you'll have your choice of some of the best officers around to re-crew those ships. I'll brief you more on the mission we have in mind for you later, but in summary I'd just say that we know there's a pirate base somewhere out behind the Hawke Protectorate. Elsie McKinnon was after it, Commodore Cook was after it. I know *you* can find it, and get rid of it."

Wes looked up, nodding slowly before extending his hand, "Thank you, sir. I'll be shifting my flag to *Nova Scotia*, then?"

Greg nodded, "You will. Sorry to take you out of *Cheetah*, but Ken's going to need all the help he can get..."

As he was saying that, he pulled the next folder off the pile and tossed it to Mark, who was sitting alone in the 'second' row.

"Now you'll have bigger lasers to show off, Mark. Though I think you should probably settle down now that you're a respectable Captain," Greg smiled.

Mark caught the folder, flipped it open and snorted a laugh, "Yes sir, I'll reduce my quota to six women a week."

Another joke — he's a funny guy. And he was getting *Cheetah*.

"You'll be joining a new force when you command *Cheetah*," Greg looked from Mark to Karen and I as he said it, then extended the last two folders towards us. Karen took the one with her name on the cover, I took my own, and then we opened them almost simultaneously.

I then found myself staring at my name, and elsewhere on the page a new mission:'... will take command of the newly-constituted 'Jupiter Force', including *Wolf, Lion, Cheetah, Friendly, Lady Grace, Honesty*, communications ship *Wireless*, combat supply ship *Artemis Agrotera*... mission to investigate silence of Io base and reestablish communications presumed cut by Martian arms...'

I had a new job, that would take me all through 2232 to complete (and which I'll start describing next book, obviously).

And then I read a little further down.

"You were a Commodore for less than two months. I think that must be a record; it's as though you're promoting yourself," Greg's smile broadened, and then from the midst of the chaos on his desk he produced a small box and tossed it to me.

I didn't need to open it, the page I'd been reading said 'Rear Admiral', so the box had to contain my black suns.

"That's what you get for saving the Empire, more paperwork," Wes chuckled, and in something of a daze, I nodded, then realized I had a natural way to change the subject — it was highly awkward getting promoted in this company. I felt like the least capable officer in the room.

So I looked at Karen, "What'd you get?"

She had been reading a note on the top of the papers in her file, and she quickly shut her folder and looked up at me, "Uhm. Sorry, Commodore of the Jupiter Force. Keep you out of trouble."

I smiled broadly — everyone had gotten just desserts, it seemed.

But then I looked back at Greg, and his expression — while a happy smile — suggested more under the surface. I was suspicious for a moment, but then Greg started talking about deployments and timelines, the months we'd have to get our respective forces organized and what seasons were best for travel to various destinations.

It wasn't until years later, when for completely unrelated reasons I happened to be going through a stack of files left on Karen's desk, that I found Greg's note and the folder Karen had been handed. I never admitted finding it, but might as well be honest about it now.

In it were three different printouts of possible deployment options for her, and the note read as follows: 'Karen, we could use you wherever you choose to go. We leave it up to you, but we're sending Ken to command the new Jupiter Force heading out to Io. He'll be promoted to Rear Admiral. You can either take over the frigates of the Light Squadron of the Home Fleet, with the rank of Rear Admiral, or take over the new squadron of *Bonaventure*-class battleships as a Rear Admiral. Or you can join Ken on that mission, but there's no way we could push a Rear Admiral's rank through for you in that case, since Ken will already be there. Parliament is paying too close attention. It's your decision, just let me know — it doesn't have to be right now. Ken doesn't know. Regards, Greg."

I've never known what to say, or to think, when I read that.

She picked the lower rank and the obscure mission to the far reaches of the solar system. Because of me.

What could I say to that? It would have been better for her career, probably, to go with the *Bonaventures*, or even with the Light Squadron frigates. She'd have been a key to home defense, and she'd have been highly visible and rapidly promotable. She could have re-leveled our ranks after my lucky appointment...

I think that's what I'd have recommended to her. I'd gotten Commodore's bars because it had been *Wolf* that had happened upon the Syndicate flagship at the Battle of Deep Black; if *Lion* had been so lucky, Karen would have been the Commodore over the past six weeks, and everything would have been different.

So I would have strongly suggested she go to Earth and get her Rear Admiral's suns, skip those Commodore's bars altogether... and had she done that, I'd probably have been killed during the war.

But that doesn't matter, because it never was. She never told me that she had to pick anything, I never knew at all...

Anyway, that's all irrelevant right now. We had our new jobs, and after all our successes, the inevitable was happening — we were getting split up to fight in different parts of the Empire. In some ways it was bittersweet, but that evening *Wolf* hosted a celebratory dinner.

I was happy that Karen and I would stay together, and I had, for the moment, entirely forgotten Egesta.

The ordeal with the Independent Squadron was now behind us, and there was a new slate of adventures in store for 2232.

Stay tuned.

AFTERWORD

Well, you've made it through 60,000 words on one of the darkest affairs I ever found myself caught up in, and hopefully you'll be back for *The Jupiter Patrol*, the next book which I promise will be back to the lighter side, mostly. No, the shadows of Egesta would never stop looming over me, but most days they wouldn't loom large. Indeed, most of the time, I'd work hard not to notice them at all.

Such is the nature of surviving in this job.

When we get to 2232 with *The Jupiter Patrol*, we're heading out into the blackness of the solar system for a mission that has been celebrated in books and in one particularly awkward miniseries. It'll take a number of books to get us back to the Belt, I imagine — we spent a lot of time out at Io, dealing with a variety of challenges on the way out, while there, and on the way back. I'll rant more about all of that when we get there.

In the meantime, thanks for sticking through *The Independent Squadron*. There are more adventures to come!

THE
EQUATIONS NOVELS

The Earthers evolved after humans were driven from the Earth by an intelligent bio-weapon dubbed 'Omega'. They are faster, stronger, smarter, wiser, *better* than humans, and they are the only hope for the survivors of the human race as an interstellar war between two great alien powers absorbs the galaxy. But all is not as it seems, and the humans and the Earthers face challenges that overshadow the wars of alien empires and threaten to destroy their civilizations...

The Equations Novels by Kenneth Tam

Book One: THE HUMAN EQUATION (Oct 2003)

Book Two: THE ALIEN EQUATION (May 2004)

Book Three: THE RENEGADE EQUATION (Dec 2004)

Book Four: THE EARTHER EQUATION (July 2005)

Book Five: THE GENESIS EQUATION (July 2006)

Book Six: THE VENGEANCE EQUATION (July 2007)

Book Seven: THE NEMESIS EQUATION (July 2008)

Book Eight: THE DESTINY EQUATION (July 2009)

The Equations Novels are complete, but there are spinoff series and new stories in the Earther universe still to come!

For more information, please visit
www.earther.net

ABOUT THE AUTHOR

Born in 1984 in St. John's, Newfoundland, Canada, Kenneth Tam holds both a Bachelor's and Master's degree in history from Wilfrid Laurier University in Waterloo, Canada. His MA thesis examined the creation and operation of the Caribou Hut, a hostel for Allied servicemen in St. John's during the Second World War.

In 2006, Kenneth received a prestigious Canada Graduate Scholarship from the Social Sciences and Humanities Council of Canada. He was also awarded a Balsillie Fellowship at the Centre for International Governance Innovation during 2006-07. In that capacity, he worked for Mr. Paul Heinbecker, Canada's former ambassador and permanent representative to the United Nations. He presently serves as a Communications Consultant for Kitchener–Waterloo's federal Member of Parliament, Peter Braid.

Since releasing his first novel in 2003, Tam has promoted his books across Canada, speaking with junior and high school students, delivering writing workshops, and doing book signings at bookstores and Iceberg-organized events. He frequently appears as a guest author at science fiction events across the country.

Kenneth is a partner in Iceberg Publishing, the company he and his family started in 2002. He has authored many of the company's existing titles, and is also responsible for graphic design, including the company logo, website, banners, advertisements, and other marketing materials. He acts as a primary contact with printers and suppliers, and is also key in new author development and recruitment.

He remains very lazy about writing his author bios. When they told him to make this one longer, he mostly copied and pasted it together from the Iceberg website, www.icebergpublishing.com.

www.ingramcontent.com/pod-product-compliance
Lightning Source LLC
Chambersburg PA
CBHW030744030726
47497CB00001B/119